COME THE FIRST SNOWFALL

CHARLOTTE DAE

Come the First Snowfall
Eden's Green Book Two

Copyright © 2024 by Charlotte Dae

Cover Design: Cat Imbeaut (TRC Designs)
Interior Design & Formatting: Quirky Circe Book Design
Developmental Editing: Susan Doumont
Copy/Line Editing & Proofreading: Brooklyn Marie (Brazen Hearts)

FIRST EDITION

ISBN 979-8-9879428-2-6 (paperback)
ISBN 979-8-9879428-3-3 (ebook)

www.charlottedae.com

Author's Note

This book is a dark contemporary romance, meaning it contains sexually explicit scenes, graphic violence, and other mature situations. I understand that these themes may be triggering, so please feel free to email me at **charlottedaeauthor@gmail.com** or visit my website at **www.charlottedae.com** for a full list of content warnings.

Please note: *Come the First Snowfall* is a direct continuation of *Come Morning Light*. To minimize confusion regarding the characters and events in this story, I encourage all readers to begin with Book One of the Eden's Green Duet.

To the angels who crave a sinner's touch.
To the demons who dream of beauty.
And to the mere mortals who fall somewhere in between.

PROLOGUE
EVIE

THE RECEPTION — DAY 0

When I was a child, I often dreamed of dying. Not that I wished for it, mind you. At least not in the literal sense. But more times than I care to recall, I suffered through death's jagged, bony fingers reaching for me. They would wrap around my arm and pull me under into a vast, bottomless ocean of pitch, reducing my screams to nothing more than a cacophony of muted sounds.

Countless nights, I wished for the world to open its fist and free me from its wretched grip. The walls of my wooden tomb—that fucking wardrobe, to be precise—ceased to exist and instead fell away to darkness.

I had not experienced fear like that in a long time, except in my dreams, where I would pray in anguish for Papa to save me—the very man whose unintentional cruelty forced me into that tomb in the first place.

Now, with my back pressed against the frigid tile wall and my hand over my quivering lips, that ocean of crude oil and misery is rising dangerously high.

This must be a dream. It *has* to be a dream.

Or perhaps I really am crazy.

Just like Papa.

The faceless man on the opposite side of the metal stall door remains still. Slow, calculated breathing reverberates between the tile walls, sending a tremor through my body.

Papa, please.

A muffled cry pours from my lips when the door shakes in its frame, squeaking on its tortured hinges. The echo hits the stall like a tuning fork as he jerks the handle.

His hand slinks over the top and pulls on the door from above. Fear spikes low in my spine as the lock on my side rattles in its mount, barely hanging on.

Sliding to the floor, I crouch alongside the toilet before pulling my heels off, one at a time, in slow motion so as not to make a sound. If I have to make a run for it, I need speed on my side.

Thoughts of James jab at me, making me curse the distance between the country club and the reception tent at the bottom of the hill out back.

Armed with a heel in hand, I creep on my belly toward the adjacent stall.

James fades in a flash as I'm berated with memories of splintered wood, vibrating walls, and swaying coats. The stall door flings against the wall with a deafening crash, and my throat cinches in panic as I race to gather my legs into the other stall. Rough, angry hands grab my ankles and pull me along the floor, burning my skin as I'm dragged, on my stomach, across the tile. In an eternity that lasts merely a second, I'm right back where I started. My cries are shrill as I claw at the floor with all the strength I have, fighting to escape the clutches of the faceless man, who pulls me to him with such ease that I'm certain he's more beast than human.

The heel nearly slips from my grip, forcing adrenaline into my veins with every breath, every scream, as I'm dragged into the main part of the restroom.

I pray my screams are loud enough for James to hear.

I twist my body around, flipping onto my back despite his painful grip on my ankles.

That's when I see him. The man who has stalked the darkest recesses of my mind since I was a child—who proved to me that monsters are, in fact, real.

The man who I know killed Papa, despite the doubts of others.

He's bulkier than the mere sight of his shoes when I was a child implied. Older, stocky, with thick eyebrows and slick black hair. His face, distorted in fury, turns my blood to ice.

I kick and flail with every ounce of strength I have left, barely finding enough air to scream amid my panicked breaths.

He reaches for the shoe in my hand, but I twist my body away. In response, he lowers himself to a crouch on top of me, locking me in with his legs. I sit upright to meet him and bring the heel straight to his face. With one hard swing, I catch him along the cheek with the point of my stiletto, forming a pronounced gash where it lands. A loud, baritone cry billows from his lips as a trickle of blood seeps from his wound.

The blow he delivers across my cheek is sharp and quick, knocking me backward. The back of my head strikes the floor, and a ringing in my ears consumes all other sounds as my body goes slack.

He shifts above me, straddling me, wrapping a hand around my throat and squeezing hard. My head pounds as his eyes darken, almost black in their cruelty. But they glint with sadistic elation in the fluorescent lighting, as if filled with life.

The heel falls from my hand and lands with a soft *thud* right before his grip eases and air croaks back into my aching lungs.

But I find no comfort in its release, for another wave of panic ripples through me as I anticipate what comes next. All attempts to scream fail me, my throat and lips numb and hoarse. A sharp wheeze is all I can muster. Tears coat my temples as I peer at the monster watching me.

He's staring, and his weight is unbearable on my legs. What

little sensation they have left is fleeting. Fear sends a quick shiver racing up my spine as I realize my dress has hiked way up during the struggle, exposing me in a way I can't stomach.

Terrified, powerless, *trapped*.

With a grin of pure malevolence that makes my skin prickle, he reaches into his back pocket, pulls out a syringe, and snatches the cap in his teeth before spitting it onto the floor. Gripping me hard by my throat, he brings his face only inches from mine. His breath is warm and unwanted against my lips, like a kiss of death, incinerating me in my final moments of life.

I claw at the hand that holds my throat prisoner, then scratch at his face as he draws near. His grimace reveals his displeasure and pain, but he makes little effort to stop me. Instead, he grabs me by the hair, yanks my head to the side, and shoves the needle deep into my neck, right below my chin. I wince against the pinch mere seconds before numbness consumes me. My nails skim across his face as my wheezing devolves into moans. My vision tunnels, then fades to black as I unwillingly succumb to its fate.

A fate as cruel as the eyes of the monster who found me at long last.

Part I

CHAPTER 1
EVIE

MAY 28TH — DAY 1

A harmony of bird squawks penetrates the silence as my head throbs against a cushion. I can't see them—the seagulls, I presume. My eyelids fail me, anchored down with a drowsiness I've never experienced. The left side of my body aches, especially my hip and shoulder. Everything else is horrifyingly numb.

For a moment, I wonder if I'm home—if the man in the red shoes was all some alcohol-induced nightmare and nothing more. Perhaps I'm back at the Seaside Inn, by James's side, and this has all been another night terror. If only my eyelids would open. But the indisputable heaviness plaguing my body only pushes me deeper into the cushion on which I lie. I wait for James to shake me—to free me of my mental prison as he has before.

His touch never comes.

My eyelids crack a sliver, a hint of light forcing its way into my line of sight. But my uncooperative eyes refuse to open any further.

Maybe if I use my hands to pry them open...

Amid my searing headache, a panic brews heavy inside me as I realize my hands won't move.

They're bound behind my back.

Alarmed, I force my eyes open with a jolt.

They land first on a white stone fireplace directly across from me. Then a glass coffee table only a few feet away, then a white fur rug underneath.

I wriggle against my restraints, my movements minimal and inconsequential. The white leather sofa squeaks with each fruitless movement, and a wail forms in my chest. But it's absorbed into the gag secured around my mouth and comes out as nothing more than a muffled groan.

Feeling creeps back into my legs, and it's only a matter of minutes before I can feel that my ankles are bound too. My feet prickle awake as blood finds its way back down into my lower extremities.

A door opens somewhere near my head, and rapid footsteps enter the room. A pair of legs, covered in black slacks, rush past me. I crane my head to make out more, but the throbbing weighs me down to the leather couch like a ball and chain.

"Get these ties off her. Now," an unfamiliar voice roars nearby.

In an instant, there are multiple sets of hands on me, releasing my binds and freeing my mouth from its moistened gag. The air that fills my lungs is damn near euphoric.

A hand grabs my arm and pulls me to a sitting position, the leather protesting beneath me. Two men, dressed in black suits, make their way off to the side near a large three-paned mirror. Behind them are floor-to-ceiling windows that encompass the back half of the room, providing a panoramic view of nothing but ocean and azure skies.

Before me, now sitting on the coffee table and leaning in close, is a third man. He's also dressed in a black three-piece suit, with dark hair, a salt-and-peppered shadow of a beard to match, and fine lines creasing the sides of his eyes and across his forehead. A single antique key, brass and weathered, hangs from a string around his neck.

But it all fades in the presence of those scars.

Across the right side of his face, spanning from temple to chin and disrupting that trimmed beard, is mangled, burned flesh.

Almost as conspicuous as those scars are a set of piercing gray eyes, enhanced only by those aged peppering flecks in his hair.

"Are you all right?" he asks. "Can you stand?"

I massage my numb wrists, nurturing them back to life while ignoring his questions.

"Who are you?" My voice is hoarse and raw. "Where am I?"

"Are you all right?" he repeats, his tone stern.

My eyes narrow. "No, I'm not. Where the hell am I?" My cheek aches, a sensation I'm just beginning to realize, and I brush its torn flesh.

The man extends his hand, nearly grazing my battered cheek. But I jerk away from his touch, and my head pounds at the sudden movement. I wince and palm my forehead out of instinct.

He hands me a glass of water and three pills, retrieved from the coffee table beside him. "For your head," he murmurs.

I refuse with simply a stare.

"Take these," he insists. "They'll help with the pain."

"I don't want anything from you." I wince again. "Except to know where the hell I am."

He releases a frustrated sigh. "It's Ibuprofen. Nothing more. If I wanted to drug you, I would have done it already, and I certainly wouldn't need your cooperation to see it done."

"Drug me *again,* you mean," I sneer, cocking my head to the side. "Why don't you quit wasting my time and tell me why the hell you brought me here. Wherever *here* is." My focus darts around the stark white room.

He reaches for my hand, but I yank it away the instant his flesh touches mine. Still, he reaches for it again, gripping it harder this time.

He places the three pills in my palm, then holds out the water glass, waiting for me to take it. The sight of the water consumes me with a thirst that's eerily reminiscent of those long hours I spent locked in the wardrobe as a child, thrusting me into a battle between pride and unspeakable thirst. As I stare at the tablets, the latter wins. Imprinted on each tablet are the letters *IBU*.

I pop them into my mouth and swallow with a chug that depletes half the water. His lips twitch in approval.

"Finish the water, and we'll bring you more. You must be parched. The drug we used can have that unfortunate effect. It also doesn't last long, and it was a bit of a journey to get you here, so we needed multiple doses—"

My eyes widen in horror. "What in God's name did you inject me with?"

He tips his head toward the glass in my hand. "Drink, poca Neve. Then we'll talk."

His words are strange, and I can't place the language. Nonetheless, my brow furrows with irritation more so than confusion. This fucking prick drugs me, refuses to tell me a damn thing, then barks orders at me like I'm a child?

I stand on wobbly feet, the squeaking leather grating on my nerves. My bridesmaid dress is a wrinkled mess, one of the straps torn and dangling against my back.

The man stands from the coffee table, only an arm's length in front of me.

I don't owe him a goddamn thing.

Least of all my cooperation.

Meeting his gaze, I tilt the water glass, spilling its contents onto the floor at our feet. When it's empty, I let it fall, and it lands with a quiet *thud* on the fur rug.

"Fuck you," I say.

His stoicism holds firm. "Quite the defiant one, aren't we?"

"I think you mean pissed off."

"I never meant for you to get hurt. I realize you may find that hard to believe—"

"You're damn right," I cut in.

"But you're safe now, Neve. Safer here than anywhere else on Earth. Now tell me, who did this to you?" He gestures to my torn cheek.

I squint at him, confused. "Like you don't know."

"I don't. That's why I'm asking." His voice is slick with concern.

"You mean *commanding*," I correct him. He releases a long, exasperated sigh as he runs his hand through his kempt hair. Folding his arms across his chest, he merely waits for me to respond.

After several seconds of awkward silence, I comply with a whisper. "It was that ape of a man who I assume works for you. The one with the clicking red shoes." I look down at the floor, despising the mere mention of the monster.

"He struck you?" the man asks with a tight grimace.

"Please spare me the concern," I reply, exhausted.

The mangled flesh on the side of his face grows pink with agitation.

He looks past me and motions with his head to something or someone behind me. Less than a second later, my stomach lurches at that horrific yet familiar sound:

Click...

Click...

Click...

With only a few sickening clicks against the floor, the man in the red shoes emerges from behind me and into my field of view. Still clothed in a black shirt and slacks, the clicks silence as he stops near the end of the sofa, facing us.

"Come join her, please." The scarred man beckons, motioning next to me.

"W-Wait, what?" My mouth falls agape in horror. "Don't—"

"It's all right." He holds a hand up to silence me. "I told you you're safe here, and I meant it."

Bullshit.

"Come," he barks at the man in the red shoes.

He approaches, his steps silenced by the rug, of which I find no relief. His very presence is far worse than those fucking shoes torturing me with their clicks.

"Your piece," the scarred man commands, holding out his hand. The man in the red loafers reaches into the back of his waistband, retrieves a black handgun, and hands it over.

"On your knees," he orders.

The other man hesitates, his glance shooting in my direction, then back to the scarred man. After several tremulous moments, he sinks to his knees in silence.

The man flips the gun, holding it by the long part. His eyes glimmer as he bounces it in his hands. My stomach's ready to lurch as I look frantically around the room. Both men are between me and the door.

I debate the number of paces it would take to reach it. Are there more men outside? Would I be able to reach the front entrance before someone catches me? I don't even know where the front door is. All I know of my prison is this white room.

My thoughts are cut short when a loud *smack* fills the room: the sound of metal against flesh as the scarred man brings the grip of the pistol hard against the other man's face. A gash appears in his cheek, blood spilling from the open wound.

I scream into my palm as the scarred man raises the handgun again and brings it against the man's face with another blow. Blood spatters from his nose, striking my feet as he buckles from the blow.

The gun strikes a third time on the same spot as before, streaking his cheek with a deep crimson and covering it in spatter. He never protests. The scarred man releases a heavy breath and hands the bloody pistol back to its owner.

"You may stand," he commands, waving him up. My breath hitches as the other man reclaims his footing and wipes at the mess, further smearing it across his cheek.

"I told you she was not to be harmed, and I meant it," the scarred man growls, then nods toward the door, beckoning him to leave. The clicking of his shoes fades as he disappears down the hall.

"Why did you do that?" I ask, my eyes wide with shock.

"He disobeyed an order. He knew the consequences."

My heart's racing. "I don't understand. W-Who are you?"

Three sharp knocks thunder against the door.

"Come in."

A small-framed man with black hair tied back into a ponytail and a dark, trimmed beard hurries into the room. "Sir, we have a situation with our analyst," he says with a panic-stricken expression, ignoring me entirely.

"What do you mean?"

"I mean, we have enough DNA for him to pull up a full profile, and certainly enough to do a comparison, but he's now refusing to analyze the data unless we pay him more money."

"How much?" the scarred man scathes.

"Triple the arrangement."

"The man has a death wish, I take it?" His lips twitch but soon go placid.

"Unless he fancies himself invincible," the man in the ponytail replies.

Invincible.

"My father once told me that facing your fears was the closest you would ever get to being invincible."

My jaw slacks. I know his voice. I recognize his face.

"Wait," I say to the man in the ponytail. *"I know you."*

He gives me a side-eye, barely acknowledging that I've spoken. I step toward him, desperate to force his attention in my direction. But the scarred man steps between us.

"Careful. You've only just woken, and you're still not well."

"This man"—I point an eager finger at the man with the ponytail—"was at Krelborn Manor. He's the one who locked my cuffs and then left me in a locked closet. What's he doing here?" I growl.

"You must be mistaken, miss," the ponytailed man states dismissively. "I've never seen you before in my life."

"Bullshit. You think I would so easily forget the face of a man who locked me in some dark room, leading to one of the worst panic attacks I've ever had?" My body shakes all over again, this time from pure, unadulterated anger.

"Have a seat, Neve," the man with the scars orders.

"No. Fuck you. Get out of my way."

He stares down at me, his large frame dwarfing mine.

"Move," I demand. But he doesn't budge.

Rage boils inside me. My head throbs, my heart's pounding, and beneath it all, I'm fucking terrified.

Before I have the chance to rationalize a plan, driven by an uncontrollable need to be free of those dark eyes and this feeling of being trapped, I react. I spin my snowflake ring around, then bring my palm hard against the scarred man's face. But right before my hand makes impact, he catches my wrist and wrenches it hard. A sharp pain cuts straight through it, and I wince in agony. His gray eyes blaze like a plume of smoke billowing high above a forest fire. Fear supersedes my anger as I'm unable to anticipate his next move and desperate for him to release my hand.

And my gaze.

I await his wrath—a blow to my face, a shout in my ear. Something.

Instead, he remains quiet, his expression and demeanor calm. Too calm. His lack of movement makes my anxiety crest to an all-time high.

He lowers my striking hand and holds it in front of him. His gaze lowers to my ring, a single snowflake with a blue gem in the center, upside down on my middle finger. He runs his thumb over it, spinning it back around so it's properly seated.

"This would have done some damage if you'd managed to land that blow," he says. "Did you spin it around just for me? Or do you always wear your rings the wrong way?"

I wrench my hand back and leer at him.

His eyes bounce between mine, as if searching them for something beyond their edges. For what, I have no idea. Despite the pain in my head, my aching wrists, and the fact that I've been abducted by a man with grotesque scars, I cannot look away from his gaze. I'm locked in. It terrifies and mesmerizes me all at the same time.

"Forget the DNA analyst," the scarred man says, his eyes still peering into mine.

"What?" the man in the ponytail replies. "What the hell for? We need—"

"No. We don't. Not anymore." He looks at my ring once again, and the sudden vulnerability makes me cover it immediately. "It's her."

"But don't you want to be certain?" the other man asks, his brow furrowed with confusion.

"I am. I've never been more certain about anything." Fear tears through me as he repeats the words, "It's her."

I shake my head, goose bumps plaguing my flesh as a chill jolts my spine. He must be mistaken. Surely, he has the wrong person.

"Send Maria in here to escort her to her room," he commands.

"Wait, wha—" I begin, my eyes wide with horror.

"And send One Tap in here asap," he says, ignoring me.

"He's still on the Cape with your detail of men there. It'll be hours before he can get here."

"He was never supposed to remain on the Cape," he grumbles with frustration. "Send for him *now*."

"Right away." The man hurries from the room.

"Listen," I begin, my heart racing a mile a minute. "I have no idea what's going on, but I'm telling you, whoever you think I am, you have the wrong person." I'm desperate. I'd fall to my knees and beg if that's what it took.

"Is that so?" the scarred man asks, as if amused. "And what makes you so certain?"

A shocked exhale forces its way past my lips. "Because I have no idea who *any* of you are. Because I've never seen this place before in my life. Because..." I trail off. How do I convince him he has the wrong person when I don't know who I'm being mistaken for?

I avert my gaze. "Because I'm no one. I'm of no importance, and I never have been. If you're kidnapping me for some sort of ransom, you'll be hard-pressed to find anyone who would pay it. I'm nobody, don't you get it?" Tears of desperation pinch my throat.

The door opens and light footsteps approach. But my eyes are caught in his gray hurricane.

"You asked for me, sir?" a soft, feminine voice inquires.

"Yes. Please escort Miss Neve to her room."

"Certainly." The woman steps to his side and into my field of view. She's older, with stern eyes and graying hair tied back into a tight bun.

"*Neve*? Why do you keep calling me—"

"And please give her anything she requires," he continues. The woman motions for me to follow her.

"I'm telling you. You have the wrong person," I plead. But he continues to ignore me. Maria's gentle hand presses on my lower back as she guides me toward the door. Exhausted, confused, and defeated, I comply.

"Oh, Neve," he calls out as Maria and I reach the threshold, giving us pause. He takes several steps in our direction and locks eyes with mine. "Understand this. You've *never* been a nobody. Never." The storm in his gaze is far from subsiding. "It's precisely the reason I've brought you here." Beneath the weight of his stare, I shift with discomfort. "And I don't want to hear you refer to yourself in that way ever again. Capisce?"

Capisce.

Thoughts of Jenna come rushing in. She must be terrified, scrambling to make sense of my sudden disappearance. A coil of guilt takes root knowing that her big day was hijacked by the monster who's haunted me for so long.

It's all my fault.

But they must have the wrong person. This is a huge mistake.

Wait, did they hurt Jenna?

Fear strikes me broadside as I try to recall the last moments before everything went black. For the first time, I realize I have no idea if the man in the red shoes took or harmed anyone else last night.

Was James with her? Are they trying to find me? *Christ, Jenna. I'm so sorry.*

I have no words. Only a crippling concern for the only two people in my life who matter: Jenna and James.

Maria presses her hand against the small of my back once again, attempting to lead me from the room. But before I take a single step, the scarred man calls out to me once more.

"And one more thing."

I turn to face him, my eyelids heavy with exhaustion.

"Welcome home, Neve."

CHAPTER 2
EVIE

Her hair strikes a familiar chord first: the gray intermixed with more youthful black tones and tied back into that tight bun that rests low on her neck.

When I realize I've seen the woman before, it all rushes in like a windstorm of clarity and utter confusion.

"I've met you before," I say to her as she escorts me to "my" room.

"Right this way, miss," she replies, her breathing labored as we traverse yet another flight of stairs.

"You were at Krelborn Manor, too, weren't you? You and that man with the ponytail." I follow closely behind her. "You were the one who asked me to select a room—who told me my presence was requested downstairs at the start of the evening." Tightened lungs afford me only the shallowest of breaths. Whether it's from all the stairs or from the uncertainty of everything going on, I can't be sure.

She ignores me as we reach the top landing, opting instead to motion me forward with a quick wave of her hand. "Follow me."

I keep up as we make our way down a long corridor filled with sunlight from the span of windows on our left. The manor is vastly different from Krelborn. In place of mahogany wood and hallways lit only by flickering lantern light, this place is modern and bright, full of windows covered by sheer, billowing curtains. The white marble floors, interspersed with veins of silver and gray, chill my bare feet as I obey her commands to follow.

With each ocean breeze, the curtains flounce as we pass by.

"This here is your room, miss," the woman says after we make a right turn at the end of the corridor. My heart races, uncertain of what prison awaits me on the other side of the looming door.

It opens with creaking hinges, revealing a room of unquestionable beauty. A large bed against the wall to the right is adorned with white-and-blue linens, topped with a plethora of arranged pillows. The headboard appears to be a patchwork of reclaimed wood, giving the room a sophisticated yet quaint energy.

Against the opposite wall is a fireplace of jagged light-gray stone that spans all the way to the ceiling. A bank of windows along the far wall fills the room with daylight, illuminating the blue chaise that faces the balcony door.

"Through here," the woman begins, motioning toward a closed door near the bed, "is your closet. There isn't much inside, but you should find a few things that may fit until your things arrive."

My attention diverts to her. "Wait, what do you mean, *my things?*"

"There are several men who'll be gathering your belongings to have them shipped here," she proclaims. "They're probably there now."

"Hold on," I snap. "You're saying there are people in my apartment right now, as we speak? How do any of you people even know where I live?" I swallow a nervous gulp.

"I don't believe they're in your *home,* miss. They're in your room at the Seaside Inn on the Cape."

"My room?" I shake my head. "But...James will be there. Jenna. The whole damn wedding party. There are people who will be looking for me. At least, I sure as hell hope they are. If the men you speak of see them..." My voice trails off as I realize the danger

James and Jenna and everyone else may be in simply by being there.

"You need to rest, miss. You're visibly exhausted—"

"I need to get the hell out of here. Please. I need your help." I bite down on my bottom lip and wince at the sharp pain that follows.

She ignores my pleas and looks away.

"Well, if you aren't going to help me get out of here," my tone deepens, "will you at least convince the man of the house—I don't know his name—to forget about getting my things? I don't need them. Just please tell him to keep his people away from the Inn. Away from my friends. Can you do that, at least? Please."

She takes a step toward me, a sudden wave of what I perceive as concern crossing her face. "I'll see what I can do. On one condition."

"Name it. Anything," I choke.

"You remain in here until you've had some rest. You get yourself cleaned up. You dine with Mr. Moretti when he calls on you. You do as you're told. Understood?" The brashness of her voice catches me off guard.

I wrap my arms around myself, clutching at my elbows to ward off a chill that sends goose bumps skirting across my flesh. I give her a nod of compliance before she heads for the door.

She pauses at the threshold. "Your washroom is just through there," she says, motioning toward a door between the fireplace and the nearest corner. "In there, you'll find fresh towels and toiletries. Please, make yourself comfortable."

A simple nod is all she gives me before opening the bedroom door.

"And behave," she mutters as she disappears into the hall.

A GENTLE KNOCK ON THE DOOR FORCES MY SLEEPY EYES open. The padding of footsteps entering my room follows close behind. Panic hits me broadside at the sound of the unwanted stranger, and I roll over to see who has entered without invitation.

"Dinner will be served in the dining room in about thirty minutes," Maria says.

"I'm not hungry," I whisper.

"It wasn't a request."

My head is no longer pounding as I sit upright, but I'm groggy and yearn to lie back down all the same. "Do you intend to hold me down and force food into my mouth?" I ask, squinting at her.

"I reminded the boss that he was risking discretion by sending his men to the Inn," she boasts. "I upheld my end of the agreement. Now you must do the same and do as you're told."

I fling the covers aside in a silent forfeit and hop off the bed. Crossing over to the bathroom, I straighten my tattered bridesmaid dress, then pause. "Did he agree?"

"Agree?"

"To call off the search? Are my friends okay? James, Jenna...?"

"Perhaps you may ask him yourself when you join him downstairs. I'll be back to escort you in half an hour."

With only a few shuffles of her feet, she's gone.

The chill of the gray stone attacks my feet as I doff the bridesmaid dress and let it slip to the bathroom floor. My body aches, fear and tension causing every muscle to tighten in a vise grip as I wait impatiently for the water to become more temperate. The heat against my ragged skin once I step inside is, in a word, euphoric. With each passing second, I wash away the makeup that covers the bite mark on the back of my shoulder, as well as the other old bruises I bear, exposing James's lustful prowess across my body. But it does nothing to purge the new wounds. Despite it clearing away the gore on my torn cheek, the remnants of the red-shoe man's skin and blood under my fingernails, and the unwanted touch of the scarred man, the wounds are ever present. My wrists ache from my recent binds—bruises fresh on the horizon—and my throat and cheek sting from the monster's attempts to force me into submission.

The last of James's marks will soon be gone, trepidation turning my insides to ice as I fear their loss as if they were James himself. I don't have my phone. I don't have access to any photographs we took over the last week. I have nothing tangible left of him. Just a bite mark on my shoulder that's sure to leave some semblance of a scar, and bruises that will disappear completely in a matter of days.

I've never been so relieved to be scarred by another. I can't bear the thought that the deepest kiss I've ever received will possibly leave me someday.

Tears well, but I stave them off, bracing myself against the tile wall with outstretched arms and leaning into the stream.

Is James looking for me? Did he see what happened? Did he see who did this…?

Or does he think I left him?

Shit.

I swallow hard at the ravenous thoughts that pierce my mind. Oh God, please don't let James think I left him intentionally. The very idea grows like cancer until my knees buckle and I collapse to the shower floor.

I weep. Harder than ever before. And for the first time in my life, I refuse to be silent about it. My wails are animalistic, shattering me to pieces like a ship ravaged by a gale-force storm.

I want the oily pitch of my nightmares to seep out of the drain and rise until I'm drowning in my own darkness. I wish for it. I *beg* for it.

Papa, please.

"The monsters are here, baby bird. And they're coming for you. Now hide. And don't make a sound, no matter what. Don't let them find you."

I'm shaking like a brittle leaf, the water bouncing off the curve of my back as I hold my knees tight against my chest. They've found me, Papa. I'm so sorry. I don't know how. I don't know where I went wrong. I did everything you told me to. But somehow, I let the monsters get me.

Ragged breaths tumble from my throat as I clutch my soaked hair. Tears coalesce with the shower stream as I wait for the oily sludge to seep in and claim me once and for all.

As I anticipated, it finally calls for me, just as it did all those years ago. The darkness seduces me while it robs me of air and sanity as the hours tick by in my wooden tomb, making me more thirsty, more panicked.

More stark-raving mad.

Exactly as it is now.

The pounding of water against the tile silences as my vision narrows. Soon, the only sound is the beating of my heart against my eardrums. I can barely see the opposite shower wall, the steam is so thick. Closing in on me. Suffocating me. Just like those fucking wardrobe walls.

They don't know where I am, Papa. No one does. I'm sorry it was all for nothing. Your death. It was...all...for...

My eyes flutter closed, and everything goes black.

Black as pitch.

And the thumping of my heartbeat fades to an impenetrable silence.

❧

A FAINT KNOCKING SOUNDS IN THE DISTANCE. SO FAR away, in fact, I'm sure it's in my own head. Moments later, I'm enveloped in a soft warmth, the comfort undeniable. But it's taken from me all too soon, replaced with small slaps on my cheeks. Mild at first, then sharper, until my eyelids part and I'm greeted with the face of the woman with silver hair. Her voice emerges to the fore-front of my hearing. In an instant, it's all I can hear aside from the mild buzzing in my head.

"You've fainted, miss. Let's get you up off the floor." She reaches underneath me and pulls, and I grab on to her arms for support. My legs wobble as she escorts me from the shower stall and into the bedroom. I hold the towel closed around me with one hand as she guides my other arm and plops me down on the chaise.

"You mustn't turn the hot water up so high. Especially on an empty stomach. When's the last time you ate?" she scolds through pursed lips.

I'm exhausted in every sense of the word; my mind is a whirl-wind of confusion and fear, and every square inch of my body is suffering the brunt of it. But despite my compromised position, I can't ignore the audacity of her question—of what actually sounds more like an accusation.

"Well, let's see. I ate a meal and a few bites of cake at the recep-tion last night." I furrow my brow and glance toward the ceiling in a show of sardonicism. "Or, I guess, I'm assuming it was last night. I'm not sure what day it is, to be perfectly honest, because, well, oh yeah, that's right. I was drugged and kidnapped and taken to *this* fucking place." I gesture wildly with my hands. "So forgive me if I'm a bit malnourished, a bit exhausted, and a *lot* fucking confused."

Her shoulders straighten. "Dry yourself off. Get dressed. I'll be waiting for you in the hall." She marches for the door and disap-pears from the room.

The closet is a small walk-in, sparse save for a handful of slip dresses on hangers, plain T-shirts and simple drawstring shorts folded on a single shelf, and a drawer of panties underneath. No bras. No shoes. At least none that I can find. All the other closet drawers are empty.

I wasn't wearing a bra underneath the bridesmaid dress, and my stomach knots at the idea of having to be around *him* without one.

Thank God for my small chest.

I grab the navy-blue slip dress at random, drop the towel to the floor, and slip it over my head. It falls into place on its own, the fabric soft against my damp skin. My hair clings to my back and shoulders, wetting the dress's thin straps.

After dabbing my hair and donning a pair of fresh panties, I return the towel to the bathroom, where my disheveled bridesmaid dress lies in a ball on the floor. I scoop it up, carry it to the bed, and tuck it underneath the mattress. I can't bear the thought of anything happening to it. It's the last thing I have of James—of Jenna.

Of my life before today.

Once I'm confident it's out of sight, I make my way out into the hall, where the silver-haired woman waits for me with a pinched, impatient face.

"Follow me," she says, turning her back before receiving a response.

I oblige.

And follow her to where the scarred man waits.

Chapter 3
Evie

W hen I follow Maria through the parted French doors and into the dining room, he doesn't stir. He doesn't motion for me to enter. He doesn't greet me. He merely watches from the head of the table as I scan the room and take in my surroundings.

A coffee bar of whitewashed wood sits beneath a bank of large windows to my left, filling the space with evening light and emphasizing the collection of seaside paintings that encircle the room. Bursting with platters of food from one end to another, the long wooden table awaits far more guests than me alone—six, based on the number of chairs present. A cool, salty breeze fills the space, making the red centerpiece roses shift and the napkins squirm from alongside the two place settings.

"Sit," Maria instructs, gesturing toward the vacant setting across from the scarred man.

I make no effort to obey.

"We had an agreement," she reminds me with a pointed look. "I did as you asked. Now it's your turn to behave."

"And how do I know you actually said anything?" I ask her, my eyes narrowing with defiance. "How do I know any of my friends are okay?"

"Your friends have not been harmed," the man interjects,

making my heart skip a beat as his baritone voice cuts through the room. "Now, sit, Neve. Maria does not lie."

Rage rumbles inside my chest at the audacity of these fuckers. But before I can turn back around to Maria to remind her where she can take her next "behave" remark and shove it, she has already left the room with a silent swiftness that catches me off guard.

The scarred man stands and motions to the empty seat across from him. "Please. Have a seat. You must be famished." As if triggered by his very words, my stomach grumbles with hungry displeasure.

I sit despite my irritation. The small feast that spans the length of the table twists and tortures my stomach further. I avert my gaze anywhere other than the food, which I have no intention of eating.

"No need to await my permission to eat," he says, his eyes bouncing between me and the plate of food in front of me.

"I'm not hungry," I say, pushing it away and looking toward the open windows. I wonder how fast I could jump out of them. I'm slowly starting to learn the layout of this place, and I know we're currently on the ground floor. The edge of freedom seems so near. Perhaps it's all ocean on this side of the house and I would plummet into a watery abyss. Maybe he'll catch me right as I reach the windows, and who knows what awaits me after?

"I find that very hard to believe. It's been nearly a day since you've eaten anything."

My attention follows his stern voice. "So, you're saying today is Sunday the 28th? The day after the wedding?"

"Yes," he replies. "You've been here since very early this morning. When you first arrived, I figured sleep was the most important thing for you. But now I really wish you would eat something." He takes a quick bite of his food and dabs the corner of his mouth with the napkin pulled from his lap.

"Unless you have something wrapped and untouched, I have no

intention of eating anything you offer me. Just so we're clear," I snap.

His face remains static. "You seem so convinced that I've brought you here to merely drug you with every opportunity." He sips from his drinking glass.

"Can you honestly blame me?"

"I suppose not." The levelness of his tone fills me with suspicion. "Tell me what you need to feel more at home here, Neve. I want you to feel like you can trust me."

I chuckle at the brashness of his presumptions and begin drumming my fingers on the table alongside my cutlery. "Well, first off, you can start by telling me why you keep calling me *Neve*."

"Because it's your name," he responds without missing a beat.

"It's not my name. My name is *Evie*. I told you, you have the wrong—"

"That's not your name," he lashes, sending a shiver down my spine. "Evie is the name *he* gave you." He drops his fork to his plate with a loud *clank*.

My mind whirls with confusion. "What on earth are you talking about? Who's *he*?"

"The man who took you," he replies, pressing steepled fingers together on propped elbows.

"The man who took me? You mean *you*?" My tone is sharp with irritation as I point in his direction.

He taps his fingers together and looks away. "No, Neve, I don't mean me," he growls, his scars now flush with a pink hue. "I didn't steal you. You're not my prisoner. Don't you understand? I brought you home."

My stomach plummets into a darkness that rivals my night terrors. "No. I don't get it." I bring my hand to my forehead even though my headache is long gone. "I've never been here before in my life. I've never *seen you* before in my life. This isn't my home. I was born and raised in Seattle. Unless you've brought me back to

Seattle while I was drugged?" I look around, confused as ever. "I mean, honestly, I have absolutely no idea where I am." Shit. Another headache is brewing behind my temples.

"You're not in Seattle. And that's not where you were born."

My mind spins, the weightlessness of my body making me nauseous. "I don't understa—"

"One Tap is here to see you, sir. Just as you requested," the man with the ponytail says behind me, appearing near my right shoulder. What's his name? Jenna mentioned it once. Marco? I can't be sure.

"Please send him in," the scarred man instructs.

He disappears as silently as he arrived.

A flock of seagulls swoops low outside the window, casting a series of agile shadows across the dining table, temporarily blocking out the sun.

The footsteps that appear behind me are brisk and purposeful, growing louder as they enter. My vision narrows on the plate of unwanted food that sits in front of me, calling out to my voracious appetite with unnecessary cruelty.

"You asked for me, Boss?" a deep voice calls out, also painfully familiar.

"Yes. I have another job for you." The scarred man reaches for the dossier alongside his plate and holds it out.

As the man crosses into my line of sight, all the air rushes from my lungs with a crushing blow.

No.

"The DNA analyst has chosen to make an enemy of me," the scarred man continues. "All the information you need is here."

It can't be.

"I'll take care of it immediately," he replies, glancing at me out of the corner of his eye.

Ashton.

Wrath swells inside me and bursts open like a flooded dam, nausea following close behind at the memories of his unwanted touch on game night. The ringing in my ears dilutes all sounds into an indistinguishable mess, like muffled screams underwater. I no longer exist in my own body.

"You son of a bitch," I bite as Ashton passes me and heads for the door. I scoot my chair away with a deafening screech, my neck and ears aflame. "What have you done?"

"Neve," the scarred man calls out, but I ignore him and rush after Ashton as he heads down the foyer toward the front door.

"Answer me, you son of a bitch," I shout, hot on his heels. But he ignores me as he passes through the vestibule's double doors and makes his way to the front steps.

The early evening sun is blinding from its low position in the sky. I shield my eyes from the sudden attack of garish light, losing sight of him for a moment. My eyes refocus on a black Bentley that waits in the cobblestone driveway. Ashton reaches for the rear door handle.

"Ashton, goddammit. Stop." I yank him around to face me with a firm grip on his shoulder. Two sets of rapid footsteps approach from behind, but he holds up a hand and they fall silent.

I look over my shoulder and find two men, dressed all in black and armed with large guns, standing behind me. Racing to catch up to Ashton made me miss sight of them entirely. They back away and reclaim their posts alongside the front entrance at his subtle, silent nod.

He finally meets my gaze. "What do you want, Neve?"

A large pit envelops my stomach at the use of my false name.

"That's not my name, and you know it. What are you playing at? Do you think this is some sort of game? Did you do this? Did you tell that man where to find me?"

He shakes his head and holds up a hand to silence me. "That man?"

"The man with the red shoes? Are you the one who told him where to find me? At the wedding? Am I here because of you?"

His lips twitch into a sardonic smirk. "Oh, you mean *Click*?"

"Click?"

"Yeah, that's what we call him around here, on account of those clicking shoes he insists on wearing." He snickers, forcing my rage to reach atomic levels. "I didn't send him to you, if that's what you're asking." His eyes narrow on me. "Don't worry, sweetheart. You aren't here because of me. Not that I did much to stop it."

"You really are a piece of shit, you know that? Where's James? Did you do something to him too?"

"Hmm. Where could James be...?" He looks up at the sky, searching around in false wonderment.

"*Fuck you*." The words spew forth like venom on my tongue.

"Tsk, tsk, tsk...now, now, Neve. What on earth would that knuckle-dragging boyfriend of yours say if he knew you were saying such lewd things to me?"

My entire body shakes with anger.

"If you've hurt him, I swear to God, I'll—"

"You'll what? Your idle threats don't scare me, sweetheart. Just be thankful you're free of that prick once and for all." He flings the car door open but pauses before climbing inside. "Enjoy your new digs." He nods toward the lavish estate behind me and then disappears inside the Bentley. It peels off after he closes the door, leaving me behind in the driveway, enveloped in the golden rays of the setting sun.

My pulse has elevated to the point that my ears are screaming for mercy. More than once, I try to swallow back the lump lodged in my throat to no avail.

Before me stands a vast circular driveway of gray cobblestone. Just beyond are woods in all directions. Clearly, the ocean is to the back of the house. Who knows how far those woods go? Is there a fence along the perimeter? Could I scale it if there is one?

The armed guards behind me shift, and I can feel them approaching.

It's now or never.

"Neve, come back inside," a stern voice calls from the doorway.

Ignoring his command, I take a small step to the left, shielding my eyes from the sun as I examine the tree line. It seems so within reach, but I have no idea what lies beyond. Freedom? Hopefully. Death? Perhaps. All I know is, I can't stay here any longer. The scarred man has no intention of freeing me, that much is clear. And it's highly likely that no one knows where I am.

I'm lost all over again.

And this time, I may never be found.

With all forethought obliterated and my adrenaline stripping me of fear and consequence, I run as fast as my bare feet can carry me toward the tree line to my left. My dress dances around my thighs as I race along the perimeter of the driveway and into the woods. I don't hear footsteps behind me, but I also don't make a conscious effort to listen. All I can hear is the thrumming of my heartbeat blasting my ears and my labored breaths that tear my lungs to shreds.

The detritus is rough against my feet, and the woods are dense and filled with shadows in the fading light. Despite having endured similar conditions only a week ago as I fled from a man eager to indulge his most primal urges, running through these woods terrifies me in a way I can only equate to fighting for one final breath before I drown. I secretly wanted James to catch me then—to claim me in the pouring rain as the forest looked on. But now, being caught may very well cost me my life. The dread the notion bestows upon me makes me damn near weightless, and the ache in my lungs disappears as adrenaline gives me new life.

I dodge one tree after the other, left, then right, then right again, desperate for some reprieve in the form of a road, a house, a trail, or any signs of human life. But there's nothing.

No one.

Not a soul.

No one to save me.

A small animal scurries under a bush to my right just as a sharp twig digs into my heel. The warmth of the blood that seeps from my open wound gives little distraction amid the pain that follows. I stagger for several steps but quickly regain my momentum.

Several sharp snaps sound behind me as the foliage is crushed beneath pounding feet. Soon, I'm aware of panting breaths in the distance. Fallen leaves and dirt stick to my open wound as I race ahead, swatting at low-hanging branches. One catches me across the cheek, splitting the flesh open across my already-compromised cheekbone. I brush it with the back of my hand, leaving a small streak of blood in its wake.

My desperate, directionless escape lands me on my ass as the ground declines into a shallow ravine and my feet give way to the landslide of fallen leaves. They crunch beneath my bare bottom and cling to my dress as it twists around me and exposes far too much of my body.

With a muted *slap*, I slide into the ravine, which is nothing more than a pit of mud and water. My feet and legs are covered in filth, and the cut on my foot is screaming. After a string of muttered curse words, I manage to squirm onto my knees and crawl onto the opposite bank.

I right my dress and crane my neck to peer behind me for a second.

No one.

I listen for the sounds of snapping twigs and crunching leaves.

Nothing.

My lungs fill to capacity with the first deep breath I've given them since taking off from the driveway. A burst of energy courses through my veins, my vision narrowing in on every little forest detail as I run further into the green inferno. Moss on the trees, birds flitting on a nearby perch, the stillness of the air as the breeze fails to penetrate the forest walls. It all blends together into a blur of bark and foliage.

Until I see an opening in the trees up ahead. Not a meadow. Certainly not like the clearing in which I succumbed to visions of my father as we twirled together in the rain. This break in the trees is occluded by something looming. Something massive.

Something man made.

A wave of hope shocks me back to life as I force my legs to carry me a bit further. I pray for the presence of a person, just one person, who can be there—somewhere—to help me get to a phone, a car, anything.

The looming object draws near as I close the gap.

I can't make sense of it, even when I'm only feet away. Stopping dead in my tracks, I gaze high above me at the pruned hedge line. It spans into an indistinguishable distance in both directions, coming together at a ninety-degree angle right in front of me. My lungs burn with fatigue, and the stitch in my side lances me with an unforgiving blade. The arm I wrap around myself provides little comfort.

There don't appear to be any breaks in the hedge line. It's a solid behemoth of a trimmed brush that provides no escape as I desperately peer down both sides.

The woods are dense and foreboding and growing darker by the minute as the sun falls below the tree line. Just as the forest is enveloped in darkness, a spotlight off in the distance turns on, illuminating the entire area and forcing my gaze straight toward the garish light.

I fall to my knees, my heart thundering with torrential fervor.

Oh my God. A chill grabs hold of me as I realize exactly where I am.

Right as a pair of violent hands reach for me, yanking me to my feet.

Before me, clear as the spotlight that pierces the rising nightfall, stands the backside of a hedge maze.

The hedge maze.

It's Krelborn Manor.

A defeated cry escapes my lips as a man, panting and cursing under his breath, yanks me toward him by the crook of my elbow. My head swims as it catches up to the situation and registers that I've been recaptured—that I'm trapped on an island, and no one knows where I am.

Surrounded by the ocean.

Nowhere to run.

Nowhere to hide.

Once my paradise, now my prison.

I'm back on Eden's Green.

CHAPTER 4
EVIE

I tear my arm away from the man's grasp. He grunts with displeasure as he fights to maintain his hold on me and his firearm at the same time. For a split second, he loses me, and I nearly fall to the ground with the momentum of my struggle. In a dash, I turn my back to the hedge maze and run.

Within a handful of steps, just enough to become enveloped in the woods once more, I'm tackled face-first to the ground. The taste of dirt is bitter on my lips as I use all my strength to push against the man pinning me to the ground. My arms scream in agony as I fight against a force I can't overcome. I choke a cry into the mess of leaves as a pair of boots comes to a stomping halt mere inches from my face. They're polished black high-top boots that are now covered in muck thanks to the chase I put them through.

A commanding voice sounds above me. "Get her up."

The man pinning me to the ground shifts his weight, and my lungs fill with elation. With a rough grip on my arm, he climbs off me and flips me onto my back. His features are unremarkable, with brown hair in a military cut and a face easily lost in a crowd. His muted eyes rake across my body, landing on my bare legs, exposed by my disheveled dress. A shiver ripples through me as I yank the fabric down past my hips in horror.

Hovering above me, he's dressed all in black, with a rifle slung across his back, his stocky frame enhanced by his bulletproof vest. He leans in low and grabs my hand, stopping my attempts to pull down my dress. My throat pinches with fear at the sudden movement, and I press my legs together in a desperate, silent plea. Despite the darkness that has overtaken the woods and everything and everyone in it, a glint shines across his eyes as they trail down my body all over again.

A single fingertip traces along the outside of my thigh, raising the dress material up and back over my hips. I grab the hem and force it back down through gritted teeth, then bring my hand square across his face with a hard *slap*. He recoils for only a moment before grabbing me by the hair with brute force. A weighted scream escapes my throat from the pain.

"That's enough," the other man barks, his bald head as ruddy as his angered face. The man on top of me averts his gaze to the one standing behind me. His glowering stare creates an unspoken threat between the two, causing my pulse to skyrocket to the point of faintness.

"I'll be the judge of what's enough," he growls. "What the fuck do you care, anyway?"

"You want to sign your own death certificate, be my guest. She belongs to the bossman. You know what he'll do to you if he knows you touched what's his?"

His. My stomach drops.

"What difference does it make? She's spoiled goods. That means she's fair game before she's married off."

"Not if she's been claimed by the boss, you idiot. You really want to take that chance? You want to keep this up, I won't stop you. But I'm also not about to lie to the chief. Like I said, it's your funeral."

A low rumble resounds from deep in the hovering man's throat as he clambers back onto his own two feet.

"Smart man," the bald one mutters under his breath. A

euphoric wave of relief washes over me as my attacker joins the guard behind me. A chill sweeps my skin, forcing an awareness of just how crisp the night air has become and how ill-protected I am against it. I wrap my arms around myself after I gather my strength and climb back onto my feet. Within seconds, a bout of shivers takes hold.

As I straighten my wet mess of a dress and attempt to brush the leaves and dirt from its fabric, I hear one of the men say, "We have her. We're bringing her back."

I glance up. The bald guard is speaking into a cell phone.

"Wha—" he begins. "Are you certain?" He turns his back to me, as if fearful I may discover the nature of his conversation. "Of course. Consider it done." He lowers his phone and moves to my side. "Come with us."

He removes a flashlight from his vest, casts a beam of light into the darkness, and snatches me by the crook of my elbow. With a relentless grip, I'm pulled deeper into the woods before I can utter a single word in protest.

My muddy bare feet rake across the fallen pine needles and tufts of moss as I follow their lead.

"P-Please. W-Where are you t-taking me?" I ask through chattering teeth. Both men plod along in silence.

Now that I know I'm on the island of Eden's Green and have already seen the backside of the hedge maze at Krelborn Manor, I have a strong feeling I'm being led east. And all I know of that lies east of here, beyond the woods, is the ocean. My pulse accelerates, and despite the panic that traverses my veins like a live wire, it gives me a much-needed sense of warmth. My chattering teeth slow, and I'm now hyperaware of every sound, every scent. The smell of dirt, pine, and wet soil wafts around us as the low hoot of an owl echoes off in the distance. The breathing of my two unwanted companions falls in line with each step we take.

With a firm grip on my elbow, the bald man guides me over tree roots and under low-hanging branches and steadies me over unexpected dips in the terrain as the other one trudges alongside us.

"How much farther?" I ask, the cut on the bottom of my foot screaming with each step.

"It's just up ahead," the man guiding me by the elbow replies.

"Where are you taking me?" I ask again. But their silence only mimics their lack of response to my previous attempts at the question.

After one last duck under a low-hanging branch, the beam of light reflects off some sort of structure: a wall of cinder blocks covered by a metal roof. It glides over to a heavy metal door, rusted and ancient, as if no signs of life have been near this shed in decades.

The pit in my stomach expands until I'm choking on it. I stop dead in my tracks, frozen in place, praying this is all some horrible nightmare. This can't be real.

Papa, please.

"This way," my attacker says, pressing a firm hand into my back.

I dig my heels into the ground, fighting his touch.

The man holding my elbow pulls me forward as the other pushes against my back, and I catch myself as I nearly fall to my knees.

"Stop. You can't be serious. Please tell me you don't mean to lock me in there." A frisson of fear pinches my throat shut, creating a sharp pain as I wheeze my next breaths. The man pulls on my arm even harder, and my body is yanked in his direction. Stepping out from behind me, my attacker approaches the heavy door with his flashlight in tow. The bolt lock on the outside of the door protests with a loud *clank* as he pulls it toward him.

"Please. I beg you. I promise I won't run again. I swear it. Just don't lock me in there."

He slides a key into the bolt lock, and it clicks open. The sound of metal against metal grates at my teeth as he removes the lock from its hook and pulls it off the door. With a firm tug of the metal handle, the door creaks open, drowning out the chirping crickets and the low song of the nightly fowl.

Through the open shed door, I see absolutely nothing. Only total darkness.

"After you," the one with the crew cut says, standing in the doorway and motioning inside. His flashlight remains fixed on the ground near his feet, and I'm unable to see beyond it. What I do see, though, is a glint of light that bounces off his toothy, sardonic grin as he relishes in my plight.

The bald man, standing near the doorway and fixing his beam of light on me, nearly blinding me, says, "Don't make me carry you in there. Because I will if I have to."

Wake up. Now. This has to be a dream. It has to be. *Wake up.*

Papa, where are you? Papa? Papa, please.

Fear clutches my heart as all sense of logic escapes me. I could grab one of their flashlights and strike him with it. But what about the other? He'd be on me in a second. I could reach for one of their guns. But I've never fired one before. They'd stop me before I could raise it to my shoulder, let alone shoot it. And who knows what the *boss* would have in store for me if I failed? But I can't let them put me in there. Once I'm in there, I know it's all over.

With a soft crunch of leaves beneath my feet, and with all sense of terror, desperation, and forethought melding together into an amalgam of instinct to survive, I turn my back to the men in black.

And run like hell.

Chapter 5

Evie

The pounding of footsteps overtakes my rapid breathing, and I'm pinned to the forest floor in seconds. I flail my legs as I'm hoisted off the ground, reaching for anything within my grasp and screaming my lungs out. Forced to face the open shed door, I stare in horror as it warps, my vision playing nasty tricks, too mortified to comprehend what lies inside. And for a split second, I swear the shed growls like the belly of a beast.

The man holding me releases a series of grunts as he readjusts, pinning my arms to my side as he carries me toward the shed.

"N-No, no, no, no," I cry out at the top of my lungs. Beads of sweat creep along my hairline, and my feet scrape along the forest debris in agony.

That door. That looming entrance to my own personal hell grows larger as we draw near. Before I can croak out another no, I'm tossed to the ground at its threshold. The cold concrete floor bites at my palms as I struggle to sit upright.

Each breath echoes, hollow and quick, against the walls of this unidentifiable space. I can't see a thing. Or feel a thing, other than the freezing floor against my bare legs.

A flashlight clicks on at the entrance, where the two men in black stand, blocking my escape.

I shift onto my knees. "Please," I beg in a whisper. "You can't leave me in here."

An evil chuckle escapes one of the guards, and I jump to my feet in a bout of anger-fueled panic. They allow me to shove past them, and I collapse onto the forest floor, hyperventilating at the mere thought of being in that shed a second longer.

Their stifled laughter creeps low behind me before a flashlight catches me right in the eyes.

"Not so fast," a third person says with a menacing laugh, their voice tugging at my memory. "Wouldn't you care to stay a spell?" the man taunts in a jovial manner as he emerges from the shed.

"Please..." I beg, my lip quivering. The light expands as he approaches, filling more of my field of view.

"Aw, come on," the blithe rumble coerces. "A disobedient girl like you would do well to spend some time thinking about her behavior." A squeal of laughter slices through the woods as the man jerks about in his guffaw of amusement. Shielding my vision, I attempt to make out the man behind the voice. But all I see is a lanky silhouette.

A headache is brewing behind my eyes despite my best efforts to avoid the bright ray. As if reading my thoughts, the light flickers three times. The man smacks it to no avail.

"Enough of this," the bald man barks. "The boss wants her returned to the manor." He snatches me by the arm, and I make no attempt to fight him this time. Just get me the hell away from this horrible place.

"Until next time," the lanky man says, making kissing noises at me that make my blood curdle.

I DEMAND TO SPEAK WITH THE "BOSS" THE MINUTE WE

step into the foyer. The house is completely dark save for a single lamp in the front parlor.

The armed men guide me to him by my elbow, where he sits within the soft glow, tracing a finger in small circles on the sofa arm. "You disappoint me, Neve," he remarks in a cool, even tone. His scars are hidden in shadow, leaving only the normal half of his face exposed. Despite his stern demeanor, it softens him in a way I haven't seen yet. He appears regal, strong, and—dare I say it—even handsome.

With a wave of his hand, the men release me. For the first time tonight, I'm painfully aware of the soreness in my arms, sure to be bruised by morning.

"You've brought me to Eden's Green?" I ask with a sharp tongue, taking a step closer. "Why?"

"Go upstairs and get some sleep. We'll speak more candidly in the morning."

"No. *Now*," I demand.

He stops tracing and stands. "You're in no position to make demands." He motions toward the men in black. The handsy one unslings his rifle and hands it to his partner. He then grabs me by my wrist, bends low, and flings me over his shoulder like a sack of flour.

"What are you doing?" I cry out against his backside. "Put me down." I claw at him, but the bulletproof vest is far too thick. The radio fasteners on his shoulder dig into my stomach painfully. With one of his hands planted firmly on my ass, and my cries ignored all the while, we trek up three flights of stairs, down the long corridor of billowing curtains, and to "my room" around the corner.

I'm dropped onto the bed with a pitiful little bounce, my dress all twisted up and the caked dirt on my feet and legs flaking onto the bedding.

The guard promptly leaves the room. Much to my surprise, the boss stands in the doorway, staring at me. "Get some sleep," he repeats, reaching for the door handle.

"Please," I plead. "Don't lock me in here. I'm begging you." I leap from the bed. "I won't run again, I swear. Just please don't lock the door." I can barely choke out the last few words through the tightness in my throat.

"We'll work on trusting one another. For now, I don't trust you to stay put. Like I said, get some rest. You'll feel better after you sleep." He pulls the door shut before I can protest further.

"No, no, no—*wait*." I race for the door. But I'm too late. A key rattles inside the lock before it finally clicks, that horrible sound making my knees crumble. I sway on a wobbling floor, dizzy, frightened, and unable to focus on anything except for the doorknob. I twist it frantically, panting as the room warps, squeezing the life out of me like a cobra enveloping its prey. That dull ringing I know all too well deforms all other sounds as it crescendos in my eardrums.

I slide down the door, landing flat on my bottom, clinging to the handle. Squeezing my eyes tight, I lay my head in the crook of my elbow and await the panic attack that's fast approaching. My pulse thunders in my ears, competing with that incessant ringing that continues to build.

Papa, where are you? Don't leave me in here. Please.

Not again.

Papa...he's here. I can feel him. *See* him, in fact. He awaits me in the kitchen, wearing an apron covered in flour, and brings a spatula up to his forehead and salutes me with it. *"Morning, baby bird. I was wondering when you'd be getting up."* His grin is infectious and loveable, instantly making me forget that I spent the last six hours locked in that godforsaken wardrobe. He dabs a finger of flour onto the tip of my nose, and we laugh together until my sides hurt.

Papa, please.

Desperate for air, I cling to the last time I ever felt truly safe. Papa soon fades into a field of wildflowers, muted to a palette of stark grays. The electricity in the air is palpable as rain tickles my face. I stare up at the sky, feeling heavier by the second as my clothing soaks up each drop. I feel James is near, but I don't see him.

I also couldn't see him when he ran his hands all over my body during the blindfold game. I was enveloped in darkness then, too, but I wasn't afraid. In fact, I welcomed the absence of sight in lieu of the heightened sense of James's touch as he explored every inch of my body. The panic normally induced by the darkness somehow seemed manageable when James was near.

The taste of the plastic button on my tongue was pleasurable.

I can taste it even now.

The smoothness of it is sensual, in a way, and my tongue finds satisfaction as it glides over its four heart-shaped holes as it clicks against my teeth.

The sound is all too familiar, however, and my tortured mind can now only hear the clicking of malevolent footsteps.

Not just any footsteps; metal-plated shoes on hardwood flooring. I can't see the face or figure to whom they belong, only their scarlet hue.

Each *click* sends shockwaves through my flesh, maddening and relentless. And though I want—no, *need*—to scream for Papa, my cries fall silent into my hand. The blinding redness morphs into some sort of reptile—a monster not suitable for any fairy tale. I watch in horror as it grows long, spindly teeth and slithers along on a wide, scaled belly.

I'm trapped.

Again.

Papa, please.

I claw at my throat, desperate for air. A weight crushes my chest, but I can't register anything in my tunnel vision and hysteria.

Only the redness, the reptile skin, and that incessant clicking.

My heartbeat slows as my body surrenders to the lack of oxygen.

Eventually, my vision reduces to a pinpoint, a single speck of light, and then fades to utter blackness.

FOR THE FIRST TIME IN AGES, I'M WARM. MY EYES ARE heavy and insist on remaining closed, surrendering to the comfort that wraps me in its arms. It seems like months since I was overcome with such an unadulterated sense of calm and safety.

Traces of a beating heart thump lightly against my back, indicating I'm in the arms of another.

James.

I nuzzle against him as his arms envelop me even tighter. His chin finds the crown of my head, the rise and fall of his chest falling in synchronicity with mine. A soothing hand glides up and down my arm, and I inhale deeply, wanting to bathe in his scent.

But it's his scent that makes me pause. It's pleasant but foreign. Nowhere close to James's natural scent that consistently sends me into a tailspin of desire.

My eyes flicker open. Slowly, my surroundings come into focus, a flick of anguish pulling at me as I start to recognize them.

I'm on the floor in "my room," just as I was last night.

My prison.

And the man behind me is certainly *not* James.

I lurch forward in terror, but a gentle hand grabs me by the wrist to stop me. "It's all right, little one. You were having a nightmare of some sort. But you're okay now."

A half-scarred face comes into view, and my body tenses. "What happened?" My voice shakes as I brush an errant bit of hair off my face.

"I could hear you screaming all the way down the hall." He frees my hand and rests his arm on a bent knee. "When I came to your door, you were crying out for 'Papa,' and I could hear what sounded like scratching. When I came inside, you were making choking noises and clawing at the floor like you were trying to tear it open. I pulled you away, but then you started attacking your own throat. It's like you couldn't breathe." He surveys me as if waiting for me to speak. But I'm too shocked to respond. "You left these…" He motions to a series of linear marks on the wooden floor, and my mouth falls agape.

I drop my face into my hands. These night terrors are getting worse.

And I have no idea how to stop them.

"I was terrified," he whispers.

My eyes lock on him in an instant. Terrified?

"You don't strike me as someone who scares easily," I say. "Nor do I understand why you'd give a shit that I was about to claw out my own throat."

He rises to his feet and, with a stern voice, replies, "I guess that just goes to show how little you know about me." The storminess in his eyes is a bit subdued this morning despite his sudden shift in tone. "Care to shed some light?"

No. Not at all, actually. I don't know this guy from Adam, and I sure as hell have no interest in letting him into the most grisly moments of my past.

At the same time, I can't imagine how much harder this will all be if I'm locked in places at his whim. If my wings have already been clipped, I know I can't endure this if my cage is locked as well.

"The lock…" I tremble, nodding toward the door as I draw a knee to my chest and rest my chin on it. "I have this…thing…about being locked inside places."

His attention follows to the door as he quirks a curious brow.

"It gives me anxiety" is all I can bring myself to say about it.

I just hope it's enough.

"Understood," he says in a low, smooth rumble. He brushes a hand over his scars, then heads for the door, pausing at the threshold. "Get cleaned up and meet me in the kitchen. I can't imagine how hungry you must be."

He doesn't wait for a rebuttal.

The scratch marks on the floor command my attention. Four lines disrupting the wood, jagged but parallel, stretching several inches long. Glancing at my nails on instinct, I find that all the ones on my right hand, aside from my thumb, are torn and broken, with a small amount of blood caked underneath each one. Strangely enough, the pain has yet to set in.

Maybe the true pain is still on its way, to be endured long after the infliction.

Just like everything else in my life.

❧

I wish I could say that a hot shower washed away the fear for my fate right along with the mud and debris. But that would be far from the truth.

Pacing the room, I squeeze the towel along my hair, trying to tame my rapid breathing, when something on the bed catches my eye: a handwritten note resting on the pillow, with a slender silver key lying across the words. They stop me dead in my tracks. No one came and went since "the boss" left. At least not that I heard.

Overcome with the feeling of being watched, I scan the room, uncomfortably aware of each and every corner that's enveloped in shadow at this early morning hour.

Snatching the key and paper from the pillow, I examine them closely.

In beautiful penmanship, the note reads:

Your room key and a promise:
No more locked doors. Ever.

You have my word.

— Laz

Your room key and a promise:
No more locked doors. Ever.

You have my word.

CHAPTER 6

EVIE

MAY 29ᵀᴴ — DAY 2

It's the first semblance of calm I've felt since waking up in this wretched place. The boss—*Laz*, per his note—mentioned taking steps to build trust.

If what he wrote about no more locked doors is true, then it seems he not only heard me, he listened.

But being trapped in this unfamiliar place makes the idea of trust downright absurd, and his written promises mean nothing until I've seen them executed.

After freshening up and donning a fresh pair of panties and a slip dress—a light-green one that matches my eyes—I'm escorted to the ground floor by the same nameless bald guard who chased me through the woods last night. With swift steps, he maintains a significant distance ahead of me. I make no effort to keep his pace. If I'm left behind, so be it. Everything here is of ill consequence to me.

The main stairwell spills out into the foyer on a large S curve. A deep mahogany banister accents the lighter tones of the vast space, with ceilings that jut toward the heavens and neutral tones that remind me the ocean is just beyond the bluff.

A familiar, intoxicatingly delicious scent wafts into the foyer as we round out the last of the steps, growing stronger as I'm escorted to the back of the house.

The kitchen is filled with sunlight, a bank of windows overlooking the ocean filtering in the morning hue and enhancing the cabinetry's lighter earth tones. Maria stands at the stove with her back to me, her white button-up blouse covered with a black-and-white plaid apron. She flips a mass over in the frying pan, creating a medley of sizzles in their wake.

Crepes.

At the guard's behest, I follow him through the kitchen to a breakfast nook table by the windows, where the boss sits obscured by an open newspaper. That beautiful ocean beyond the glass appears placid this morning. Not a single whitecap in sight.

Maria dumps the crepe onto a stack by the stove and walks the plate over to me. In seconds, she and the guard are gone. Laz discards his newspaper and diverts his attention my way.

"I thought maybe this would be less formal." He gestures to the room with his fork before stabbing it into his crepe. "Please—" He takes a bite. "Eat."

"I already told you. I'm not eating anything that I didn't have to open or unwrap first."

He drops his fork to the plate and straightens his back. "We're doing this again, are we?"

"Oh, I'm sorry. Am I no longer your prisoner? Am I free to go, and you just failed to mention it?"

He exhales long and deep. "I told you. You aren't a prisoner here. You're *home*. And once you realize that, you're free to come and go as you please." He leans forward, propping his elbows on the table, and squares his gaze with mine. With a gentle hand, he reaches across the table for mine, studying my torn nails before I have the chance to recoil. "I meant what I said about you and me building trust. I told you no more locked doors, and I meant it."

I'm granted unspoken permission to take my hand back when he loosens his grip.

"Believe me," he continues, "I know there are a lot of things that are unclear to you. And I'm prepared to answer any questions you have. But make no mistake, Neve, you aren't the only one who's gone their whole life seeking answers to questions that have kept them up at night."

That last part tugs at my mind, but I brush it aside, adding it to the list of things I'm failing to understand. "What is it that you want?" I ask, the smell of food making my stomach grumble in agony. "Why have you brought me here? What do you mean when you say I'm *home*?"

With a passive wave of his hand, he halts my line of questions. "Let's try something." He rubs his palms together. "I want us to learn to trust each other. We both have questions that the other can hopefully answer. But I also want you to eat something. So we'll take turns asking the other a question. Except, each answer I give, you will take a bite of food before asking a question of your own. Capisce?"

Capisce. Memories of David and, inevitably, Jenna come rushing into my mind, and my hunger is replaced with painful knots. Do they have any idea where I am? Do they think I ran off without so much as a word to any of them? Are they even looking for me?

I nod. I can't deny myself food for much longer, and the cooling crepe in front of me has weakened my resolve.

And goddammit, I need answers.

"Only honest answers, got it? Otherwise, we can toss all hope of building trust out the window." He looks at me with a tilt, waiting for my nod of approval.

Which I give.

"Who are you?"

He leans back and moves his hands to his lap. "My name is Lazaro Moretti. *Laz* to you, *boss* to my men. *The Serpent* to my enemies. Born in Sicily, raised in Boston. Owner of Eden's Green. And the largest importer of illegal firearms on the eastern seaboard."

The air vacates the room on a dime. Despite the blunt and seemingly honest nature to his answer, I still have no idea who he is. "The owner of Eden's Green? As in, the entire island? What does that even mean? And you import illegal firearms? From where?" The questions are compounding on themselves, practically throwing me off balance.

"Sounds like more questions," he replies stoically. "And it's not your turn anymore. Eat."

I hesitate at first, glancing down at the cold, naked crepe in front of me. I debate adding toppings from the spread on the table. But the ravenous disposition of my hunger leaves me with little resolve, and I'm anxious to move on to the next question. I shovel in a bite of crepe and relish in the bland satisfaction it provides.

His grin widens in approval, and I swallow hard under his stare. "My turn." He leans forward, locking his eyes on mine. "What is your earliest memory?"

I crinkle my brow. "I have no idea," I reply, my hand suspended with the fork in tow. "Why on earth—"

"It's my turn to ask a question, remember?" he interrupts. "Don't answer so quickly. Really think." He bores into me with that piercing gaze, making me quiver like a leaf in a winter storm.

"I don't—" I begin, shaking my head.

"*Think*," he repeats.

He's relentless. I have to tell him something.

"I have early memories of my father reading me to sleep. Flashes of my childhood bedroom completely devoid of furniture, as if we'd just moved in. But that one may be wrong since my father said we lived in that house my entire life. I may be confusing it with a dream—"

"You aren't trying hard enough," he says on a frustrated exhale.

"What's it matter to you? Why would you even ask me—"

"Take another bite," he snaps, nodding toward my plate. "If you're going to keep cutting me off with questions of your own, then keep taking bites."

"But...I..." I inhale a second bite of food out of concession. It's even colder than before but oddly satisfying. "I answered your question and ate your food. My turn."

He crosses his arms over his chest and waits in silence. A million questions fly through my mind in a dizzying whirlwind. As if time is rapidly ticking by and I can only ask so many, panic settles in deep as I decide on which one to ask next. The man with the red shoes is never far from my mind—those clicking noises sent me headfirst into another night terror last night. But now I have a face. And it's as awful as I ever could've imagined. It eluded me my entire life. But that night, in the bathroom at the wedding reception, I came face-to-face with my monster. At the precipice of a woman's screams that chilled me to the bone only moments prior.

"The night I was taken," I say, straightening my posture and folding my arms to mirror his. "I heard a woman screaming. Twice. Who was she?"

He removes his phone from his back pocket, presses on the screen a few times, and says, "Theresa Lovejoy, age thirty-six, blond hair, blue eyes, co-owner of Cape Cod Caterers. Born August 8, 1986. Died May 27, 2023."

A pit forms in my stomach. "Wait. You say she died the same day as the reception? What are you talking about?" I grip my fork until my knuckles whiten.

He puts his phone back in his pocket, then takes a bite of his food. "You can stab me with that fork if it pleases you. But I promise you won't get very far before you're dragged right back here. And besides, it'll only set us back with this trust we're trying to build, wouldn't you say?" The corners of his mouth are threatening a grin, and it makes my blood boil more than ever.

"What did you do?" I whisper, my throat pinched.

"I didn't do a thing to that poor woman, Neve. But I did give the order. Let's just say, she saw too much. No one was supposed to see my men coming in or out of that country club. They had orders to move swiftly. But they got a bit sloppy, and she paid the price. Thankfully, I have enough of the Massachusetts State Police on my payroll to keep anyone from asking too many questions." He sighs, his eyes bouncing between mine. "For what it's worth, I really am sorry."

His attempts at showing sincerity have little effect on me.

"That's two bites you owe me," he says. "Eat."

I choke down two more bites of cold crepe, my hunger no longer satiated after the news of this poor woman's murder. At the hands of a weapons smuggler? None of this makes any sense.

"My turn," he starts. "What do you remember of your mother?"

I choke abruptly, erupting into a coughing fit that I stifle with my napkin. "I'm sorry, what?" My eyes widen with confusion. Papa spoke of her only once, when he told me how she died, but never again. And now she has resurfaced as a topic of conversation at the lips of a complete stranger.

I fidget with the ring on my finger while searching his eyes for some semblance of sanity behind all this crazy. "I-I don't feel comfortable—"

"You agreed to be honest with me. We both agreed. Now, answer my question—"

"Nothing," I bark. "Nothing, okay? I remember nothing." I slice the air to put an end to this. "Now, my turn—"

He raises a hand to stop me. "Not so fast. Again, don't answer so quickly. Take your time. I want you to really think about your answer. It's important."

"How is any of this—"

He points his index finger this time, silencing me.

Fearing this is only going to continue in circles, I sit back and settle in, poring over old memories with Papa in search of some elusive mention of my mother. After several long minutes that stretch like an eternity, I shake my head. "I don't remember anything about my mother. Honestly. She died giving birth to me, so why would I have any memories of her? Papa never spoke of her except to tell me precisely that. It was always too hard for him to talk about. So I never asked. He never even showed me a photo of her..." My heart is racing as frustration and guilt scorch my cheeks. "You can press this all you want, but like I said, I never—"

"The man lied to you, Neve."

Bile creeps high into my throat as I cock my head in disbelief. "What?"

"And deep down, you know it's true. Like I said, don't answer me so quickly. Really think. You feel his dishonesty in your gut, I know you do. Follow that instinct and *really think*."

I want to hit him. I want to leap over the table and tear his eyes out. Speaking ill of my father is a line I can never cross. He wasn't perfect. Far from it, in fact. But he was all I had. And now this deformed stranger is calling him a liar. My nerves fire with wicked abandon as I watch him from his smug, self-righteous perch across from me.

"You can strike me dead all you want to with that stare of yours. You aren't leaving until you've answered my questions," he mutters.

I prop my elbows on the table and let my face fall into my hands. *Think, Evie.* The grip on my scalp tightens as I peer into my lap. *Think.*

Something catches in my hair, and I pull my hands away at once. It's my snowflake ring, which is sitting askew. I reset it, losing myself in the blue gemstone.

A moment of tranquility transports me to a memory of snow-covered streets and rooftops. The sky is a sleet gray, not so unlike the eyes of the scarred man who sits across from me. But it's midday. I don't know how I know this, it's just cemented into the memory as clear as the winter chill. The world is as silent as the grave, save for one sound—a sound that, honestly, can't possibly be real. But there's no way I could've made it up. I've no frame of reference to do so.

It's my mother's voice.

I look away from my ring and meet Laz's gaze. His eyes bore into me as he runs his interlocked fingers against each other, his elbows propped on the table, seemingly eager to hear my thoughts aloud.

"There is one thing," I say, breaking the long silence. "But I can't be sure."

"Say it. No matter how little you remember. Even if you aren't sure. Say it."

"Sometimes I have this...dream. It's the same one every time. I don't remember much of it. It's more of a feeling rather than specific moments. But I can feel snowflakes on my cheeks." I gesture toward my face. "And the whole world is covered in snow— the trees, the rooftops, the streets. Fresh snow. No footprints or tracks. And it's as if the whole world has fallen silent, except..." I trail off.

"Go on," he presses, leaning in closer.

"I hear a woman's voice singing. Very close. Almost as if it's in my ear. At first, it's just her voice, and all I can see is falling snow. But then I see her face, and I realize I'm being held. I must be so young. A toddler, maybe. Resting against her hip as she sings to me in the falling snow. But it can't be her. I mean..."

"Why not?" he whispers.

"Because it's not her face I see when I look at her." I shift uncomfortably in my seat and push my plate away. "It's mine."

He sits back and smiles broadly—the first true smile I've seen him make. I've clearly given him the answer he wanted. Or, at least, one he's satisfied with. "What's she singing?"

I pause for several moments. The answer doesn't come easily as I struggle to recall the memory. Over and over, I replay it in my mind.

A fleeting few seconds and nothing more, but I play it on a loop until—

The song in my mother's voice worms its way into my consciousness, slowly at first. I hum the first few notes to myself before I can confirm that I have it correct. At merely a whisper, I sing aloud, "It's a marshmallow world—"

"In the winter," he sings softly, finishing the phrase. My mouth falls agape as he continues the next verse of the song that whirls in my head.

"Yes," I whisper in utter shock, my jaw falling slack. "How did you know that?"

He leans forward. "Because, Neve, I was there."

I shake my head as it spins beyond my control. But, despite my resistance, he continues. "Your mother didn't die in childbirth. That was a lie. And what you just described to me isn't a dream. It's a memory. The reason you've convinced yourself it's a dream is because, as you say, you were told she passed at your birth, and because she bears your face. But it's the other way around entirely. You bear hers. You look exactly like her, Neve. You are the spitting image of your mother. It's as if she's sitting here looking at me now. And this"—he claps his hands, just once, making me jump—"is exactly the answer to my question. *This* is your earliest memory. And I suspect it's the only memory you have of your mother."

I can't stop shaking my head. "I don't believe it," I mutter. "You knew her? How? What happened to her? Is she still alive? Where is she?" I push my chair away from the table as I lose composure.

"One question at a time, remember?"

"To hell with this 'one-at-a-time' bullshit. Please. You have to tell me. Why would my father lie about that? What's her name?"

He raises a hand to silence me. "Pick a question, and I'll answer it."

Questions upon questions tumble around in my head, buzzing

like a live wire. I land on the only question that I can't go another second without knowing: "Is she still alive?"

He averts his gaze out the window, where a flock of birds picks at the ground nearby. Turning his attention back to me, he shakes his head slowly.

No.

A pit engulfs my stomach. It's as if I lost her all over again. But how can I lose someone I never really had? All I have of her is a fleeting memory—a blip that was merely regarded as a dream and nothing more. Until him.

The man with the scars.

The man who now can't seem to look at me no matter how much I crane my neck in his direction. The man who'll beat someone with his own pistol one minute, then fall sullen for my late mother the next.

Who are you?

Who are you, really?

I have to know.

"My turn," he says, turning back to me, his demeanor back to business. "Where did you get that ring?" He looks at my snowflake ring, and I twist it under his stare.

Papa gave me this ring. When I started asking questions about my mother, he gave it to me as a way of putting a stop to the inquiries. It worked for a while. But as my father grew sick, bringing up my mother sent him spiraling into such fits of sadness and depression that I never brought her up again. The ring became my lifeline connecting her to me, and yet I knew nothing about it or where it came from. I worry that, if I tell him I don't know, he'll make me sit here and think about it until another long-lost memory pops into my head. And I simply don't have the patience for that right now.

So I tell him the first thing that pops into my head.

"Oh, this?" I hold my hand up, presenting the ring. "My friend Jenna gave it to me sophomore year—"

"Lies," he growls through gritted teeth, making my heart skip a beat. He pushes his chair back with a deafening squeal and approaches me. "You agreed to only speak the truth with me. And you've gone and lied right to my face. This conversation's over." He stomps through the kitchen, and I leap from my seat.

"Wait," I call out. "Don't go. There are so many things you haven't told me yet. About my mother. About why I'm here. I'm begging you, please don't leave."

His shoulders heave with a deep breath before he turns to face me. In a few paces, he's on me, reaching for my ring.

"I'll ask you again. And don't you dare lie to me a second time." His scars are flush as he hooks a finger in mine to raise my hand and display my ring. "Where did you get this?"

"Papa." I don't hesitate this time. "He gave it to me. He said it belonged to my mother. It's the only thing I have of her."

His face softens, and he takes a step back. "Thank you for your honesty," he replies.

My thundering heart evens out. "Why do you care so much about all of this? How did you even know I was lying?"

He leans against the kitchen island but maintains his grip on my hand, which I permit. His demeanor softens as he rotates the ring around my finger, stopping when the engraving on the band faces me: *Baciato dalla neve.*

"Wait." A new realization dawns on me. "Is this why you call me 'Neve'? Because of the engraving on my ring? *Baciato dalla neve*—"

"Kissed by snow," he whispers. The storminess in his eyes submits to a softer blue as they remain locked on the words.

I start to remove it, but he stops me. "Don't. Leave it on."

I pause.

"You're right," he begins in a delicate tone. My interest piques as his focus never wavers. "This did belong to your mother. And the reason I know that..." He peels away to meet my gaze. "Is because I gave it to her."

My mouth drops.

As he waits for me to speak, I sift through the jumbled mess of questions that threaten to challenge my sanity. "Who *are* you?" I whisper, uncertain of whether I mean it rhetorically.

His gaze flits between me and my ring. Eventually, his eyes lock on mine, and he responds with a single word: "Eat." He nods toward the breakfast table before exiting the room, leaving me behind with nothing more than a plate of cold crepes and an ocean of unanswered questions to keep me company.

CHAPTER 7
EVIE

MAY 30TH — DAY 3

Apowerful *crash* on the other side of his office door makes me pause as I raise my hand to knock. He's not expecting me. Why would he be? It's certainly evident by the raised voices that immediately follow the sound of broken glass.

"How did this happen?" a voice cries out on the other side of the door.

An indiscernible warble responds. I angle my ear closer to the door. I catch something about the lighthouse but can't decipher further.

"Send for men from the mainland if you have to. I want everyone on this. Bring that asshole back here *now*."

The sharp tone makes me want to turn and run. I shouldn't be here. But when the *clicks* against the hard floor grow louder, my shaky chest is the only part of me that moves.

A harsh gasp slices my lungs when the door whips open inches from my face. The man with the red shoes—*Click*, as they call him —leers at me from the doorway. His face tells a tale of a hard life, creased but not yet withered, with a prominent nose and a linear scar along his left sideburn. His slicked hair and bulbous features remind me of an old, worn-out Marlon Brando. But undoubtedly devoid of any of Brando's charm.

"Are you lost, baby bird?" he asks.

Baby bird. My stomach plummets into a bottomless void. No one has called me that. Ever.

Except Papa.

I regard him with a furrowed brow. "What did you just—"

"Let her in," Laz calls out from inside the room.

Click leans in, narrowing his gaze, bombarding my spine with a series of chills. "Can you fly, baby bird?" he whispers with a smirk.

My mouth falls slack. "What...?"

He leans in closer, the scent of cigars permeating the space between us and making my stomach lurch.

"Can you fly, baby bird?"

Confusion marbles with fear and grips me low in my belly.

"I don't—"

That fucking smirk stretches wider across his face, and he steps past me into the hallway.

My father's voice consumes me, the delicate use of his favorite pet name for me—baby bird—swimming around in my mind until I'm damn near drowning in it. How did he know that's what Papa used to call me? As much as Click haunts me, I'm overcome with the urge to follow him and demand he explain where he heard that nickname.

But I can't bring myself to chase after that agonizing clicking sound.

Laz is standing beyond a pair of leather sofas arranged in an L shape in front of a black stone fireplace. His hands rest on his hips as he examines the floor.

The mess is apparent in only a few steps: books in disarray, a shattered vase, a broken picture frame, and other random items that litter the space.

I wait for him to speak, but he barely regards me as I look around the room.

"I, um. I love what you've done with the place," I say. "It really gives it...character."

He finally meets my gaze, his eyebrow cocked. My heart skips a beat, thinking I may have overstepped. But much to my relief, he chuckles as he regards the mess.

"Yeah, well. That's what I was going for. So I guess it was a success."

My shoulders relax from the levity in his tone.

"Is everything all right? Did you need something?" He runs a hand over his shadow of a beard.

"Well, I...I suppose my timing sucks, but you left so suddenly yesterday, and I still have so many questions."

"About your mother," he states. It isn't a question. He knows exactly why I'm here.

"Yes," I say on an exhale.

He regards me briefly before stacking the mishmash of books on the floor. I kneel alongside him, scooping the mess of items in silence.

A broken picture frame near the sofa captures my attention. Behind the shards is an old photograph of a man alongside a young boy on a bed of ice, holding a fish at the end of a fishing line. I pull it from the frame to examine it further. The stacking of books ceases when Laz eyes me and moves in closer.

"Is this you?" I ask, angling the photo toward him.

He nods. "Yes. And my father. Ice fishing at Chauncy Lake." He takes the photo. "I couldn't have been more than about eight or so here." He hands it back, and I give it another look.

"Bass?"

He smiles. "You know your fish."

"I fished a lot with my father too. Before he..." I look away, but I can feel his eyes boring into me, and I force out an uncomfortable cough. "Here." I return it to him, and he places it on top of the stack of books.

I shouldn't be here. This was a mistake. He doesn't deserve to know a damn thing about Papa, especially considering that, deep down, I know this man and his men were somehow involved with his death. He knows far more than he's letting on, dangling that elusive carrot in order to force me into compliance. If stringing along answers to questions that have paralyzed me my entire life will keep me from running, then I must say, this man sure knows how to make me behave.

On one hand, all I can think about is James. Is he searching for me? How on earth do I escape this place and get back to him?

But on the other hand, Lazaro has everything I've ever wanted in my life before James. He has answers.

And I can't think of a more effective carrot to force me to cooperate.

Silence passes as a steady thrum of a heartbeat before Laz stands despite the mess. "Come with me." Not waiting for my permission, he grabs my hand and leads me from his office. The warmth of his firm grip melds with my clammy palms as I fear where this venture may lead.

I can't shake the feeling that I've upset him somehow. Despite his calm demeanor, the spontaneity of his actions frightens me. The old outbuilding in the woods races back into my mind, stabbing me with dread. It takes everything in me not to collapse as we traverse the stairs to the ground floor.

When we reach the front door, I pull hard against his grip, freeing my hand. He spins around.

"Don't," I plead, my heart hammering in my chest "D-Don't put me in there." I stiffen, ready to bolt for the stairs if necessary.

His eyes widen. "No. My God, Neve. I'm not taking you to the shed." His shoulders relax and his tone softens to velvet. "Please don't be frightened. There's something I want to show you. It has to do with your mother." He holds out his hand. "Trust. Remember?"

With my curiosity piqued, but terrified nonetheless that this may be a ruse, I take his outstretched hand and follow him out the door.

The garden paths at the north end of the estate grounds are truly magnificent. With whitewashed stone leading the way through a topiary of trimmed hedges and multicolored blooms, the world transforms before my eyes into a springtime utopia. Taking advantage of the pause in this morning's rain, a hummingbird flits off in the distance over a patch of crimson roses, taking flight as we pass by.

"*Can you fly, baby bird?*" Click's malevolent voice rattles me low in my core at the beautiful sight.

Dark clouds loom low on the horizon, teasing at a brief interlude of sunshine and nothing more.

The grounds remind me a bit of Krelborn Manor. They certainly have a similar aesthetic. But the gardens on this property are far more compartmentalized, with a maze of pathways that lead every which way, connected by a wider one that cuts down the middle.

At the far end of the gardens, we pass through the gap where the hedge walls part and give way to pebble paths. Except this time, in place of flower gardens, the hedges section off a series of grand stone statues, each one different from the last. Weeping angels and Greek gods in various stages of dress grace the garden. Their weathered, moss-covered charm truly a sight to behold. For a moment, I forget my purpose for being here in the first place.

I stop, my arm pulling against his as one statue after another catches my eye.

"What is it?" he asks, turning his massive frame toward me.

"What is all this?" I ask, craning my neck to find more. "It's absolutely incredible."

"I'm flattered," he replies, gentling his tone. "I developed a taste for the more extravagant aspects of the art world early on and never looked back. This collection has taken me decades to create, and I'm not sure I'll ever be finished with it, to be honest."

I break away from his grip and walk over to a nearby dead end in the hedges. Peering around the corner, I gasp. "Umm, are you kidding me? You have *Apollo and Daphne* here." My love of art is about to burst beyond my control.

He joins me by my side. "They're all replicas, I assure you. The real one is much larger."

The midday sun emerges from behind a cloud, casting wide rays upon us. I shield my eyes to admire it further.

"It's amazing," I say on an exhale to no one in particular.

"They're like having a small piece of the homeland here with me. Makes me feel a bit closer to my father, I suppose," he says.

I release a heavy sigh. "I understand. Believe me."

We bask in the silence and the heavy sun for a single beat before he takes my hand and leads me away from the statuary.

Beyond the hedge line, two rows of trees stretch off into the distance, creating a foliage alley. Each tree is consumed by beautiful white blossoms. The ones closest to us are the smallest, no more than saplings with blooms that could be easily quantified. But each tree beyond is progressively larger than the one before it, until the back half towers so high that their branches touch across the aisle. The result: a tunnel of trees creating a canopy alight with the spring blooms and a ground covering of ivory petals to match.

To call it exquisite would be the most egregious understatement of my life. It pulls me in like a siren's call as an ache in my lungs reminds me to breathe.

"I've never seen anything like this," I whisper, craning my neck toward the canopy as I venture deeper into the tunnel. I reach for a blossom and pull it close, inhaling its sweet scent. "From a distance,

I thought these were cherry blossoms. But they aren't. I've never seen these types of flowers before."

"These are Japanese snowbells." He joins me and brings a blossom to his nose. "I've been importing them here for a very long time."

Running a finger along its velvety petals, I ask, "How long?"

He releases the branch and faces me. "About thirty-one years." It's his unwavering gaze that makes me divert my attention to him. The storm in his eyes has long subsided, replaced with a gentleness that rattles me in a way I did not expect. I don't know whether to trust it or take it as a win. But if I can keep this going, I may be able to acquire the answers I crave, and maybe convince him to set me free. He just needs to feel like he can trust me. And as much as I hate to admit it, I need it from him as much as he needs it from me.

"I don't—"

"Your mother had a Japanese snowbell tree planted in her garden at the first sign of spring after you were born, as a way of welcoming you into the world. If she had it her way, it would've been done the same day as your birth. But she put me to the task, and I insisted that we needed to wait until the ground thawed."

My breath hitches at the casual way he speaks of her. Then again at my sudden confusion. "Ground thawed? But my birthday is April 18th. Why would the ground still be frozen?"

His anguished expression silences me. "Jesus. He really went to great lengths to keep you hidden, didn't he?"

Now it's my turn to look befuddled.

"You were born on January 9, 1992, Neve. It had been snowing for more than a day, and your mother was so worried that she wouldn't be able to make it to the hospital. Your father—your *real* father—wasn't home when she went into labor, so I drove her to the hospital myself. He arrived in time to see you come into this world, though." His eyes cloud over, and apprehension pinches my throat.

My real father. I can't bear the thought of anyone other than Papa being regarded in such a manner. And I'm not so sure I believe that I have a "real father" beyond him. How do I know this scarred man speaks the truth?

"Who is he?"

We walk several paces together, deeper into the tunnel, before he continues. "Have you ever heard of Diamondback Enterprises?"

I shake my head.

"No. I don't imagine you would. Nearly sixty years ago, it was the largest criminal organization in the nation, and it was owned and operated by your grandfather."

My gaze meets his.

"Your father, Frank, was poised from birth to take over his father's organization. These things are almost always a family business, after all, and your grandfather was never going to risk it falling into the wrong hands. After he passed, Frank took over permanently, and he's certainly made an enemy out of me."

"But you were in his good enough graces that you knew my mother. And were around to drive her to the hospital when she went into labor?" My nose crinkles with confusion.

"Make no mistake, Neve. Your father and I used to be very close. I've known him since we were boys, but everything changed the summer I turned seventeen." A warm breeze slices through the trees, sending petals cascading around us like a mid-spring snow. Instinctively, I catch several in my palm and admire them with a childlike grin.

I drop them to the ground as I ask, "What happened that summer?"

Muted sunlight filters in as we approach the opposite end of the tunnel. He sighs and leads me by my elbow to a bench that sits within the tunnel's shadow.

"I met your mother."

Shocked, I lock eyes on him. From my vantage point beside

him, all I see are his scars. But my need for him to continue super-sedes any repulsion, and I wait with bated breath for him to speak.

"My whole life, I knew of Diamondback Enterprises. Most poor kids did. I mean, many of them took menial jobs with the criminal underground to help put food on their families' tables. And I was no exception. Other kids ended up working for them without knowing it was being run illegally. The organization owned so many legitimate businesses in Boston, such as movie houses, bars, restaurants, laundromats...all of them fronts to launder their illegal income."

He drapes an arm along the back of the bench behind me, leaning in as he continues. "When I was a teenager, I took a job at a local movie house selling tickets. Frank, although only a couple of years older than me, was made assistant manager that same year. He was difficult to work for, despite our friendship, walking around like he owned the place. But I kept my head down, did my job, and never complained. Then one afternoon, your mother came to the ticket counter with a friend."

He looks away as if allowing the memory to take over completely. "At that moment, everything changed. She was sixteen then, vibrant and full of life. And the most beautiful creature I'd ever seen. She had the darkest hair against the fairest skin. The fairest Italian I'd ever laid eyes on, to be frank. And she had these light-green eyes that bore right through me."

His gaze locks on me with an impassioned intensity that forces me to break away in order to acquire breath. "I'd never seen anyone with eyes like hers in my life. And I haven't since." He shifts on the bench to face me better. "Until you."

The implications of his words are more than I can bear.

"She asked me to sneak them into the movie that afternoon, having arrived at the theater penniless. That laugh of hers was all I needed to concede. I snuck them in through the back alley, and she thanked me with an angelic smile that turned my little crush into a downright obsession. To be honest, it was the first time I ever broke the rules. And I did it for her without thinking twice."

I adjust to face him better, tucking a bent knee beneath me, and focus my attention on the unmarred side of his face as he continues.

"She waited for me until the end of my shift, her friend having left for the night. We walked the downtown streets and talked for so long that, before we knew it, we were enveloped in the early light of dawn. I received such a beating from my father that day, but it was well worth it. She came back a few nights later, and before long, Gabriella was coming by nightly."

Gabriella. A name I never would have guessed for my mother. But hearing it slide from his lips, I can't shake how bizarre any other name would sound now that I know the truth. It's perfect.

"Gabriella?" I ask, the word like sugar on my tongue.

"You never knew her name?"

I look away, my face flush with shame.

He presses his hand between my shoulder blades and leans in even closer. "It's okay. I didn't realize how little you knew." A small sigh escapes his lips. "Would you like me to stop?"

I shake my head before he gets all the words out, just as another cascade of white petals settles around us.

"I took as many shifts as Frank would give me so I could save up to buy her something special. He pestered me endlessly," Laz muses with a small laugh, "asking why all of a sudden I wanted to work so many extra hours. He was convinced my father would kill me if he found out since I was ditching school to take these extra shifts. But I never told Frank about her." His eyes narrow as if he's lost in thought. "By the end of the summer, I finally had enough to buy her something I'd had my eye on for ages."

I glance around to identify the source of his sudden pause, but I don't see anything. I urge him to continue, unable to mask the eagerness in my voice. "What was it?"

He looks at me for a beat, then trails his eyes to my lap and takes my hand in his.

"This," he says, twisting the snowflake ring around my finger. My pulse accelerates almost beyond my control.

"At one point, Gabriella had confided in me how self-conscious she was about her fair skin and pale eyes. She didn't look like the other Italian girls in the neighborhood, and what *she* regarded as flaws were precisely what locked me in. I told her once that it was as if she'd been *baciato dalla neve*—kissed by snow."

I rotate the ring to examine the band, despite having seen it a thousand times and knowing exactly what I'd find. As I run my thumb over the engraving, my mind races with a memory that isn't mine: my mother being gifted this ring as a girl by the man who now holds me captive.

"She kissed me when I gave it to her," he says, interrupting my thoughts. His lips upturn into a subtle smile.

"What happened, though? How did she end up with my father?"

He releases my hand and leans back into the bench, a heavy sigh coalescing with the intermittent breeze.

There's no reply. Instead, he admires the canopy of rippling leaves overhead, a handful of rogue petals dancing toward us as I wait.

When he says nothing, I break the silence. "I only ask because you two seemed so—"

"She was taken."

I choke on a gasp. "What do you mean *taken*?"

"Frank saw us sneaking out of the back of the theater while I was off shift one afternoon. It was a regular pastime for us, really—sneaking into movies, stealing kisses in the dark. He took one look at her, and I knew for the first time in my life, I was going to have to fight for my place in this world. Fight for her. Fight for *us*." He folds his arms over his chest.

"He turned on the ol' Frank charm, telling her that he would turn a blind eye to her not paying for a ticket if she agreed to go on a date with him." Laz shakes his head as if replaying Frank's audacity over in his mind. "She refused, and I hit him so hard that I'm lucky his father didn't send his cronies to kill me that same day. We tussled in the alley until we were battered and bloody, but I was a lot smaller than him, and I fared far worse."

Leaning forward, he rests his elbows on his knees. "She pleaded for him to stop, agreeing to go out with him only if he would leave me alone and let me keep my job. I begged her not to, but she said she couldn't bear seeing me hurt, and it was only one date." He runs his hand over his beard. "And that's the last time I saw her before they were wed two years later."

I shake my head, denying events I was never privy to before today. "What do you mean? You say it like she just disappeared?"

"She did," he replies, his tone as jagged as a rusty saw. "He took her. He saw what he wanted, and he took it."

"Are you saying he kidnapped her? Held her against her will for, what, two years? Then married her?"

"That's exactly what I'm saying," he gruffs. "In order to understand what that man did, you have to understand what it's like being part of such an empire. You see, these men in high places don't think the rules apply to them. And when you have most of the Boston Police Department on your payroll, it's easy to take what you want without consequence. Women are no exception. They're married off to men in power all the time. I lost Gabriella to your father that day. And to add insult to injury, after they were wed, he welcomed me back into their lives with open arms. Not because he wanted me to work for him again, not because he wanted to rekindle some sort of friendship. It was so he could parade her around in front of me and torture me with their union. He would kiss her as I watched from the sidelines, force me to bear witness as he announced she was pregnant with his children. It was the ulti-mate power move."

His tangent hits me like a ton of bricks. I lean forward, mirroring him, hoping to cradle my stomach from the blow it's been dealt. "Why did you stick around? How could you bear it?"

"I would rather be in her life, tortured every day by the fact that I lost her—despite her being right in front of me—than not have her in my life at all. And it was a way to keep her close while I worked out some way to get her back."

Leaning back against the bench and tucking both legs beneath me, I settle in for the rest of the story.

"I knew I needed money. Lots of it. I never had any interest in being part of the Diamondback Enterprises or any other criminal organization. My father earned simple wages, but it was an honest living, and I wanted to do right by him. But I would never be able to take on an organization like that one without the finances and manpower to match." He rubs his palms together as he speaks.

"It was a slow process in the beginning, earning notable wages by fixing horse races upstate. I soon discovered that what these assholes want is something they can't get anywhere else." He eyes me in his periphery before adding, "I didn't have money or scare tactics to coerce these jockeys into throwing the races. So I gave them information instead." He sits up and throws an arm on the back of the bench behind me.

"You see, Frank may have chosen to keep me close for his own cruel intentions, but in doing so, I overheard many conversations, befriended many of his henchmen, and learned all sorts of trade secrets to which I never should have been privy. I then sold that information to the highest bidder, made enough money to fix races, and before long, the money was flowing deep enough that I was able to build an army of my own. It's how I acquired all of this." He gestures to the space around us.

Questions flood into my mind faster than I can comprehend

them. There's so much I don't know, but for the first time, I doubt whether I even want to. According to Laz, my father took my mother by force. As much as I hope it's all a lie, I can't bear the thought of the truth evading me once again. I need to believe that what he's saying is true. For my own sanity. And for the trust he's so desperately trying to build.

He stands and walks over to a snowbell tree opposite the bench, then plucks a single blossom. As if in a daze, he says, "Your mother was so excited when she found out she was having a girl."

The change in topic gives me pause. But my desire to know more could not be more ravenous. I approach him, squaring my body with his.

"Please don't think that you were made from anything but love. She may not have loved Frank, and it wasn't the life she wanted. But she desired motherhood more than anything a traditional happily ever after would have given her. And she wanted you more than I could ever express."

A tightness grips my throat, but I swallow it back the best I can.

"The night you were born, your father let me in to see you. Gabriella had you cradled in her arms, and I'd never seen such elation. Do you want to know the first thing she said to me when I came into the room?"

My heart thunders in my chest as I fight the urge to sob. I nod as my vision clouds over.

"She looked at me with this beaming smile and said, 'Look, Laz. She's been kissed by snow. Just like me.'"

Regarding me with soft eyes, he wipes a runaway tear from beneath my lashes with a hooked finger. "She named you *Neve* right then and there." He reaches for my hand and places the snowbell blossom in my palm. "Like I said before. She planted a snowbell tree in honor of you. After your first birthday, she had a second one planted, and so the tradition continued each spring. Until the year you were taken. After that, she couldn't bear the sight of them. So I had them replanted here, and I continued the tradition of planting one every year in the hopes of surprising her with this one day."

A rogue tear is captured by the back of my hand as I brush it across my cheek. "Did she ever get to see it?"

His eyes darken, and he averts his gaze to the blossom in my hand. With a shake of his head, I have my answer.

"I'm so sorry," I whisper.

His eyes fix on mine, and yet, he doesn't seem to be looking at me. More like he's looking past me, his gaze distant and morose. Words fail me as I struggle with how to reply.

So I say nothing. I let his words seep into my mind, my skin, my soul, until they adhere to me like a missing limb.

As I replay his words, fighting off the barrage of questions that follow, he hooks a finger under my chin and forces me to look at him. "I made a promise to your mother long ago to keep you safe. And I'm going to do whatever it takes to keep that promise. Even if it means making sure you never set foot off this island again. You have no idea what dangers await you on the mainland, little one. You're safer here, with me, than anywhere else. And I intend to keep it that way."

My stomach twists at the implications of his words and his sudden shift in tone.

"Dangers? What are you talking about? What dangers?"

"Not what. Who."

"You're telling me there's someone who wishes me harm? Someone not in your employ?" The sound of clicking shoes rushes into my mind.

"No one in my employ will hurt you. Ever. You have my word. This is not someone who works for me. Quite the opposite, in fact. You were hidden away for a reason, Neve. So *he* would never find you. He came close, years ago. But you somehow evaded him and, much to our relief, he came home empty-handed."

"Who?" I snap, my voice tight with frustration.

"Your real father," he says, taking the blossom from my hand and letting it fall to the ground. "Frank Denardo."

I reel backward in shock. "*Denardo*? Wait, you don't mean...?" I can't even bring myself to say the words. I only know one Denardo in this world.

Just one.

David Denardo.

My best friend's new husband and the man who brought me to this island exactly one week before his wedding.

"I can only imagine what's running through your mind," he says in a manner too gentle for my taste, considering the bomb he's just dropped.

"David," I whisper on a pinched exhale. The tunnel of white blooms and rustling leaves is closing in on me, forcing a rush of panic into my belly. "Are you saying...?" The words catch, sharp in my throat.

"David..." Laz begins, filling in the gaps with information I can't bear to hear aloud. "He's your brother, Neve."

No.

The earth quivers beneath my feet.

I shake my head in disbelief. "N-No...No..."

"He'll be by later this week with your things," Laz says. "You can speak with him then. I'm sure you have many questions."

My senses are overloaded, and I can't make heads or tails of anything. "My things?" is all I can think to ask. I compare the likeness between David and me over and over in my mind. Besides our dark hair, we look nothing alike. His tan skin and dark eyes could not further set us apart. There's just no way...

"From your apartment," Laz says, interrupting the whirlwind that has overwhelmed my mental faculties. "And your room at the Inn."

My thoughts cut through the fog, focusing on the implications of his words.

"You said you wouldn't send your men there. I begged you. And you agreed," I cry out.

"Before you accuse me of lying." He points a finger in my direction. "Just know that your room was already cleared out by the time we had our conversation. So I did comply—"

"You're a fucking snake," I sneer, irritated by how blasé he regards my requests.

"Call me what you like," he replies, an angry slate overtaking his tepid eyes as he steps into me. "Your crass tongue won't get you off this island any more than your silence will."

CHAPTER 8
EVIE

Rolling from one side to the other, I stir restlessly in this gigantic bed. The balcony doors rattle as they're pelted with thrashing rain, and I fear they may blow wide open at any moment. The room's space and scents are painfully foreign, and the rain only adds to the ominous energy that's costing me sleep.

I rub my eyes and fling the covers off, scanning for options to brace the doors. Flickering disrupts my vision as lightning strikes in the distance. Mere seconds later, a rumble of thunder compromises my very heartbeat. It seems far enough away, but I don't abandon the idea of bracing the doors, just in case.

The chaise is heavy but manageable as I scoot it along the floor. Once it's butted against the glass doors, I watch the rain attack the trees at the perimeter of the circular driveway. They're barely visible at this late hour, and the streaks of rain forming deep Vs on the outside of the window panes aren't helping.

Lightning speckles the room for a split second before leaving me in darkness again. I trace the falling drops with my fingertip, watching them combine with others and become misshapen as new ones pelt the old.

Mesmerized, I listen for the sound of thunder off in the distance.

Muffled screams catch my attention instead.

Not like the screams I heard in the restroom on Jenna's wedding night. No, these are not screams that would make one's blood curdle. These are highly erotic cries, forceful and filled with pleasure only brought about by intimacy.

Without rhyme or reason, I follow the sounds, defying my instincts to stay out of trouble.

The room flickers again as I head for the hall. A guard sits outside my door, his head thrown back, mouth open as he snores in his chair. From here, the screams have grown so faint, I wonder if they've stopped.

Or if I imagined them amid the storm and my longing for James.

Back inside the room, however, they sound again, clearer than before. I chase them back by the balcony doors, where they only heighten in intensity. Following the noise with a craned neck, I wind up at the large painting of a lighthouse hanging on the wall adjacent to the balcony doors. It's as if the screams are coming from inside the walls, which makes no sense, but I press my ear to the painting all the same. Muffled but present, they resound from somewhere beyond.

Harder, I press my ear to the canvas, doubting my senses as the rain pummels the world around me. But it's there. Gasps of pleasure, screams of *more, harder,* and a series of *yeses* that downright make me blush. I lean into the sounds a bit further and nearly collapse as the painting swivels inward and drops me onto a cold concrete floor.

A harsh gasp escapes me as I squint into the darkness. Pitch black and eerily hollow, the chamber seems to stretch forever. Or it could be merely a foot deep. The dimensions are indistinguishable.

The screams are clear as day now, bouncing along the walls in a dramatic string of pleasure, making me shiver as I reach for the wall to brace myself. My hands land on rough stone, frigid to the touch and dry as a bone. But I don't see even a sliver of what may lie ahead. After a handful of cautious steps, I stop, too frightened to continue onward. The woman cries out her orgasm from somewhere unseen, and a twinge of arousal hits my peak.

James told me all about the secret passage in the library at Krelborn Manor. It fascinated me, and the discovery of this passage hits me with the same wonder. If only there were lights.

The woman has fallen silent, taking with it all my sense of bravery to follow it. With no light to guide my way, and an impenetrable silence that no longer leads me in a proper direction, I slink back the way I came and close the painting behind me.

A flash of light fills my room, but this time, it doesn't flicker. It brightens and then fades but lingers on. I follow it out to the balcony, warm summer rain soaking through me as I peer over the stone railing. A sleek black car stops in front of the manor, headlights on, engine running.

Waiting.

I debate waving my arms and screaming for the driver's attention. But without knowing who they are or their purpose here, I opt against taking such a risk.

After several grueling minutes of inactivity, my hair and sleep shirt sticking to my soaked figure, a woman emerges from the porch. She hurries for the car, her long dark hair trailing behind her. A short black mini dress hugs her form, and her stilettos are certain to be a hindrance in her race against the rain.

When she's secure in the back seat, the car speeds off, disappearing down the drive.

A lady caller, I presume. Who else could she be? Laz's twisted scars come to mind, and my stomach fills with repulsion.

I doff my soaked shirt, crawl into bed, and drift to sleep wondering what other unspoken secrets await within these foreign walls.

A ROUGH HAND SNAKES ITS WAY DOWN MY STOMACH, pressing me into the mattress as I writhe against it. As I moan into the darkness, my speech is impeded by the hand that squeezes my throat into a silent submission. I pinch my nipples erect as the hand that pins me slithers farther down my body, coming to its final resting place between my legs. The hand frees my neck and slaps my hand away from my breasts, gruff and menacing, taking them by the handful as teeth sink deep into their tender flesh. I choke on a scream as my pussy tightens around the fingers that thrust inside me with punishing intent.

I wrangle my fingers through his hair, silky and disheveled, pushing his lips further against my breast and forcing the mouth to bite harder. I crave the blood flow, the teeth marks, the bruises—the sharp pain that gives way to illustrious pleasure. Just like the bite mark James gifted me on my shoulder—the last mark of his I bear— I don't merely want evidence of him all over me.

I need it.

Or else it would be like he never existed.

I still cling to the hope that James will come for me. That he wasn't left thinking I abandoned him without a reason or a goodbye.

But after three excruciating days, I'm left with only a bridesmaid dress bearing his scent and memories of his possessive touch.

My nipples ache, tender and raw from his deep kisses, but they remain pointed and eager as his teeth rake across my abdomen. I buck my hips off the bed against James's teasing lips, waiting for him to take another bite. But he only laughs against my skin, his breath hot and tantalizing, as he settles between my legs. "Mmm, you've always been my good girl, Evie," he expresses against my clit, his words sending vibrations across my most sensitive parts.

I'm lying on my belly, grinding against the balled-up mess of a bridesmaid dress, thinking of James's lips finding every single inch of my body. In my mind, however, I'm arching my back in response to his touch, desperate for him to fuck me raw and claim my body all over again.

"*Uh*, James..." I moan as he takes my clit between his lips and suckles.

"That's it. Beg for me. Louder," he commands.

"James," I cry out, his head bobbing against my canting hips as he adds a second finger inside me.

"*James*," I scream after he pulls away from my clit, punishing me.

He laughs again. "That's better," he mumbles against me. No longer suckling, he takes my clit between his lips and tugs. With each pass, he releases it, rakes his tongue over it once, and then tugs with his lips again. He repeats this at a rapid pace until I'm tearing at my own hair and arching my back so high that I might break my neck. My screams penetrate the night as I climax hard against him. Trembles of pure, unadulterated pleasure immediately follow as he places a single kiss on my aching clit and stares at me from between my legs.

My orgasm, intense and unforgiving, soils the bridesmaid dress that I have pressed against me. I try to aim my moans into my pillow, but every sound rips through me without fair warning, and the echoing of my desire throughout the room only enhances every second of my fantasy.

With my heart racing a mile a minute and my breathing barely under control, I release the dress, bring the satin material to my nose, and inhale what's left of James's sweet scent on the fabric. My head swims with pleasure as I yearn to have his scent all over me.

I roll onto my back and rub the dress over my breasts, tight and pointed as they wait for the actual teeth my mind promised them. After teasing them with the satin, I drag the dress further down my torso. It doesn't feel like James, but his scent permeates my nose and, in an instant, the material transforms into his touch. With one end of the dress scrunched up in my fist, I part my legs wider and drag the other end of the material over my sensitive clit.

The satin has a cooling effect on my flesh, my clit singing at the sensation and teasing at the possibility of another orgasm. Each pass of the material soaks up more of me and coalesces James's euphoric scent with my own. As my body writhes to the new wave of sensations that are about to send me reeling, I press my fist and the balled-up material firmly against my peak. My breasts bounce in tandem with my working hand, and my moans transform into cries as another climax approaches. The satin is James's touch—his lips, his forceful hands, his lapping tongue. I slide against the bed in ecstasy, fucking my dress as if it were James himself.

So close. I'm so close, James. Don't stop.

Harder, I press the dress against me, my fist providing the friction I need to send me straight to the stars. I pinch my breast with my free hand, waiting for James to slap it away. But the slap never comes, so I pinch it hard enough that I convince myself I've been bitten.

The soiled satin glides over my sex for the umpteenth time, and I shudder with anticipation—

A series of knocks on the door makes my stomach tumble as I'm jolted from my fantasy. I sit upright in a flash, throw the comforter over me, and tuck the dress down into the bed, out of sight.

"Yes?" I say on a breathy exhale.

Laz pushes the door open and regards me with a little smirk as he props himself against the doorframe. "Did I come at a bad time?" he asks.

Umm, yes.

Shit. How long has he been standing out there?

"N-No," I stutter, trying to mask my sweaty brow and racing heart but knowing I'm likely not fooling anyone. Least of all him.

"Did you need something?" My tone is impatient, and my clit is upset from all the teasing and no second release.

"Get dressed," he commands. "I'll be back in ten minutes to come get you." He pushes off the doorframe and turns away.

My blood boils at his audacity.

"You know," I call out. "It wouldn't kill you to *ask* me to do something rather than just barking orders."

He turns and regards me with ardent eyes, unwavering as he runs a thumb over his scarred cheek. Such a subtle movement, but bile rises in my throat nonetheless at the threatening nature it may possess. My nakedness feels more apparent than ever, and I hug the comforter closer to my body.

"Would you kindly get dressed and be ready in ten minutes? Please?" He holds steady in the doorway.

A small sigh of relief escapes me.

"Make it twenty?" I ask, pushing my limits but knowing I need more than ten minutes alone to finish myself off again before getting dressed.

He responds with a single nod, then disappears down the hall.

I'll take it as a win.

CHAPTER 9

EVIE

MAY 31ST — DAY 4

The main hall in the south wing dead-ends at an arched door, apple red and nearly twice my height.

"What's inside?" I ask. "Should I be worried?" A tickle of apprehension targets my fingertips as I drum them against my thigh.

"Don't you think if I was going to do something to you, I would've done it by now?" he quips. My nerves ease up a bit when I catch sight of a subtle grin scrunching his scars and bringing light to his eyes.

The door rattles open with a distinct *clink,* and the hinges scream to life.

Daylight paints the room, courtesy of the French balcony doors and the wall of windows opposite the door. Similar to my bedroom, they overlook the forest's jagged tree line. It's a wide space, with skylights situated in a vaulted ceiling that filters in even more light, yet it's oddly equipped. A blank white canvas perched on an easel, accompanied by a stool, is situated near the balcony doors. Off to the right, a row of chestnut-colored wooden tables spans more than half the length of the room. They hold dozens of paintbrushes arranged in metal tins, tubes and bottles of acrylic and oil-based paints organized by color, charcoal and grease pencils, and wooden palettes of various sizes.

Off to the left, near a grand whitewashed stone fireplace, sits a large flat table, bare save for a shadow box on the far end. Propped against the walls on both sides of the room are an assortment of blank white canvases arranged in no particular order.

I'm at a complete loss for words. It's the most extravagant art space I've ever seen.

"David tells me you're a painter," Laz says.

My jaw slacks. "Yes, but—"

"I thought you could use the space. Have somewhere that's yours. That is, until you feel more settled into the rest of the house."

"So..." I crane my neck toward the skylights, admiring the room from all angles. "You're telling me this is mine?"

A light laugh escapes his lips. "Well, *I'm* certainly no painter. David tells me it's a passion of yours. In case you're feeling inspired, I wanted you to have a space to work. This room gets the best light in the house, if you ask me." He looks around as if it's his first time inside. "Is it to your liking? Does it have everything you need? If not, I want you to always let me know."

I run my hand over the tubes of paint, through the soft bristles of the brushes resting in their cans. It gives me life, making my heart sing in a way I haven't felt in weeks. The smell of the canvas, the perfection of an unused palette—like freshly fallen snow without a single shoe print. It's almost too beautiful to use.

Almost.

"It's incredible," I say on a deep exhale, punctuated with a delicate yet unintentional laugh.

"Do tell," he responds, as if mildly amused.

"Nothing. It's silly." I wave him off.

After a brief silence, he responds, "I'm flattered."

"Flattered?" I furrow my brow. "What do you mean?"

"You don't want to tell me something because you think it's

silly. That means you actually care what I think. My opinion matters to you. I'm flattered, considering you continue to revere me as nothing more than your captor." His hands remain in the pockets of his slacks as he casually closes the gap between us.

"But I don't care," I scoff.

He reaches me in only a few slow strides. "Then say it."

I let out a heavy sigh. "I was just thinking how the only thing that could possibly top this is to be gifted an entire library." My head swims at the attempts to transform my situation into a fairy tale, if only for a moment. "I don't know, I guess there's something about this that just feels so...familiar. It just, I don't know. Makes me laugh, I suppose..." I trail off and look away, my cheeks ablaze with embarrassment.

"I have a library. It's located in the north wing, with a rather spectacular view of the ocean. You want it, it's yours." He meanders past me toward the window. His eyes soften, glinting in the sunlight.

"I-I don't know what to say. Thank—"

"No need to thank me, princess."

My stomach twists at the notion that he understood my little reference. He turns his attention to me, his eyes transfixed with such intensity that I'm forced to look away, flames licking at my neck and ears. "Tell me what you're thinking," he demands in a low rumble.

"Nothing," I quip, my anxiety sky-high.

"Lies," he whispers hoarsely. "I always want the truth. You know that."

"It's just..." I trip over what to say to avoid upsetting him further. "It's a space I've always dreamed of having. But I never thought my life would have to take such drastic turns for me to get it."

His eyes narrow. "That you'd have to share it with a beast, you mean?"

I jerk away, stunned at his choice of words. "That's not what I said."

"But it's what you meant."

"No," I reply, shaking my head.

He heads for the door, throwing it open with an aggression that makes me choke on my breath. "Remember, princess," he says, his face flush as he tosses me a pained glance over his shoulder. "Library or no, there's no stately prince in this house."

CHAPTER 10
EVIE

JUNE 2ND — DAY 6

My hands are completely blue—cerulean blue, to be precise.

The last of the paint has been squeezed onto my palette, the tube jagged and warped. The woman's dress—the statement piece of the entire painting—is not quite complete, and now the last of the cerulean blue is gone.

I've been instructed by Laz to let him know if I need anything, and that includes additional supplies for my studio.

As I stare at my blue hands, my mind wanders to our last encounter. He seemed so angry. The irony of it all, though, is it wasn't his biting tongue that frightened me. It was the anguish lurking behind it.

And it's been waking me up at night ever since.

I know nothing of my mother's death, and I wonder constantly whether it's what drives the agony that cements itself across his face and embeds itself in his scars.

That crystalline glint of sadness in those eyes haunts my dreams as much as those horrible red shoes, shaking me awake with a surge of panic and...something more. Something far less hollow.

Loss.

But it's the sounds of his carnal pleasures that now *keep* me awake, and I'm not so sure I want to face him right now.

A shaky sigh of capitulation rushes from my lungs. Her dress is cerulean blue, dammit. I can't finish this piece without it.

Before I change my mind, I doff the apron covered in paint smears and head for his office.

The sheer curtains that line the connecting hallway between the north and south wings are stagnant today. Despite the row of open windows, I anticipate a billowing or two of the delicate fabric, but there's none. Summer is upon us, and I suspect today is going to be a hot one.

I pause to admire the ocean, absent from the view in my art studio, when I hear a series of rapid clicks down the hall.

Before I even lay eyes on him, I always know when Click is near. It's what I hate most about being a prisoner here. I can't escape the monster who has haunted my dreams, hunted me, and stolen me from the only life I knew, no matter how hard I try. In my mind, he lurks around every corner. I lie awake at night, waiting for the splintering of wood as he punches through my bedroom door, mimicking that sinister wardrobe when it all comes crashing apart. His grip on me is violent, a rough hand covering my mouth as he steals me in the night.

Click rounds the corner in my direction, yet I remain transfixed on the ocean's expanse, petrified and hoping he won't see me. His clicking footsteps draw near, and it takes everything in my power to quell the nerves that have ignited a pulse of its very own.

He's closer now; I can hear his heavy breathing.

Papa, please.

Just keep walking. Please, just keep walking.

With my back to him, my gaze fixed on a pair of seagulls darting toward the rooftop, the footsteps slow to a gut-wrenching stop.

Click mirrors my stance, staring out the window, our shoulders nearly touching.

"It's funny," he begins as the seagulls squawk across the sky in the direction from which they came. "They can fly anywhere they want." He points at them. "They just have to spread their wings and ride the wind until they end up somewhere they feel safe. That's the beauty of having wings. You're never really a prisoner if you can just...fly." He rasps a low laugh, and my stomach clenches, the wafting smell of tobacco making me want to retch.

I could walk away. I don't have to listen to this. But my feet won't move, and I can't shake the feeling that he still intends to steal me away, even though I've ended up in the very prison he intended for me all along.

The silence between us is excruciating. What does he want? Has he not tormented me enough?

A shudder takes over my body when he turns to face me. "What about you, baby bird? Can you fly?"

The floor drops and pulls me under, plummeting me into a sinking abyss. My father's soft voice—*baby bird*—echoes from all directions as I scramble to find footing in the dark void that surrounds me.

I look down, frightened that I may find a vacant space in place of the floor. But all I see are red reptile shoes. My throat pinches tight, and I caress it instinctively, desperate for a single drop of air.

I want to kill him. I want him to pay for what I fear he did to Papa—what I *know* he did to me. I want to turn a corner in this fucking house and not fear that I'll see his face. I want to wake up, just once, and not dread the sound of his awful shoes clicking in my direction.

A large gulp of air goes down like a knife blade as I ball my shaking hands into fists.

"Where did you hear—"

But he's gone. At some point during my desperate attempts to ward off yet another panic attack, he left.

My knees buckle from either panic or relief. Maybe both. I

steady myself against the window frame and listen to the fading squawks as the gulls fly toward the horizon, away from this island, and out of sight.

As I regain my composure, it's replaced with an anger that teeters on rage. How long does my captor insist on torturing me this way? How long must I endure the man with the reptile shoes, his wicked tongue, and that spine-tingling laugh?

Fueled entirely by anger, I run the rest of the way to Laz's office. I don't knock; I throw the door open as hard as my fury allows.

And come to a startling halt when I see Laz has company.

He stands casually alongside two men in front of a roaring fire, each of them dressed in suits, holding tumblers of amber liquid. They regard me with wide eyes, startled by the sudden interruption.

"Neve," Laz begins. "Is everything all right?"

Ignoring the stares of his guests, I reply, "No. As a matter of fact, I'm extremely fucking far from all right."

He turns his attention to the other men. "Gentlemen. Would you mind waiting down in the parlor? Bring your drinks. I'll be down in a moment." The two men silently excuse themselves, leaving us alone.

"How long is this supposed to go on for?" I bark as the door clicks shut behind the two strangers.

He opens his mouth to speak, but I don't let him. "You know, it's bad enough that you keep me prisoner here, taking me away from the man I love and the only life I knew in order to fulfill some obligation, but to keep me locked up with a bunch of men in your employ who insist on tormenting me—"

He holds up a hand to silence me, closing the space between us with only a few quick steps. "Who?" he asks with a sharp tongue. "Who's tormenting you?" His brow furrows and his eyes blaze. "Tell me," he commands. "Trust. Remember?"

I sigh. "Ashton, for starters."

He steps back in disbelief. "Ashton?"

"Yes, *Ashton*. The one you call One Tap. You have in your employ a man who sexually assaulted me at Krelborn Manor last month."

"What in the hell are you talking about?" he demands, angrier than ever.

"He groped me, kissed me, tried to force himself on me. I screamed for him to stop, but he only laughed. He's a fucking sadist. If it wasn't for James stepping in, I—"

"That's enough," he bites. "I won't stand for lies."

I step back, my eyes wide. "Lies?" Tears stab at my throat, and I berate my body for showcasing such vulnerabilities.

Several moments pass between us, my stomach churning at his temerity. "I may not have been completely honest about many things in my life with the people I care about the most. Whether it was from fear or doubt or this immeasurable desire to put all this shit behind me, I elected to keep many truths from the people I love. Even from myself. But this..." I shake my head, enraged that I even have to convince him of Ashton's deplorable behavior in the first place. "Is not a lie."

I wait for him to speak, but he only regards me with an unshakable, piercing gaze. One that is impossible for me to read.

"You talk about trust," I continue. "About always speaking the truth. But then you have the audacity to stand there and call me a fucking liar—"

"I believe you," he interrupts, his tone softening. "He was given a very specific mission, just as all my men were. He has always been one of my most loyal soldiers. But I do believe you, princess. Such actions are a betrayal of the most egregious kind, and I'll deal with him. You have my word. But you must make me a promise, right here and now."

"What more can I possibly give you, Laz?" I choke, my eyes heavy as my vision blurs.

"I want you to promise me that you'll never mention James again. Ever."

Squinting with rage, I say, "Are you serious? You want me to give you my word that I'll never mention the man I love—"

"Don't," he growls. "Don't you ever say that again. That life, which was entirely based on lies, is now behind you. He never knew the real you. He never even knew your real name. But I do. I know who you are, where you came from. And *this*"—he gestures to the room—"is your truth. This is where you belong. Not out there. Not with him. And the sooner you realize that, the sooner you can purge your thoughts of the life you once knew and begin anew...with me."

I recoil in horror. "You're insane. What are you thinking? That I'm just some skirt who you can order around like all the others that go racing out of here at all hours of the night, disheveled and used?"

In a calm, collected tone that grates my nerves, he asks, "You've seen them?" If I knew any better, I'd say he almost sounds pleased.

"Seen them? Hell, I can hear you. Sound carries in this house more than you seem to realize."

His eyes are molten, imprisoning me with a ferocity that sends chills radiating from my spine and into my fingertips. "Does it bother you?"

"Of course not." I force my gaze away, and it lands in the one place I know it shouldn't.

His scars.

I avert it, hoping he didn't notice. But when I catch sight of him, pulled in by his dominance, his face is flush with repressed anger.

"You're repulsed by me," he says. It's not a question. "You don't care that you can hear me fuck other women. It's that they're fucking a man who looks like *this* that you can't stomach." He brushes a hand over his scars.

After a painful gulp, I shake my head, bewildered.

"I don't pay women to warm my bed. I don't blackmail or coerce them. They give themselves to me freely. And it may come as a shock to you, princess, but they don't mind the scars. Do you want to know why?"

I can't choke out a single syllable.

"Because when I'm fucking a woman so hard that she forgets there are any other cocks in this world aside from mine, these"—he runs a hooked finger over the uneven skin—"seem to magically fade away." His face falls so stoic that a barrage of chills attacks my spine. "You don't believe me?" His eyes skim down my tall frame, and the crass presumptions twist me in knots.

Without breaking his gaze, he steps into my space, eliciting a fear I did not expect. "Women from all over beg for even a single night with me. You have no idea how many of them would kill for the life you have. For what I've given you. And yet you're still repulsed by me," he derides.

Because this isn't my home.

Because I'm your fucking prisoner.

Speak, Evie.

But I'm frozen, drawn into that flame in his stormy grays that calls me to it like a moth to firelight.

"Why did you even come here?" he asks.

I shake my head, defeated at my ill attempt to remember what brought me here in the first place.

Making a conscious effort to disguise my tremulations, I turn to leave. My need for James is stronger than ever.

If only he were here.

As I reach the door, he calls out to me. "Neve."

The use of my false name screams ill-regard for the life he took from me. I hate responding to it. But much to my dismay, I betray my self-worth and face him.

"One day, you'll see."

It sounds more like a warning, but I can't be sure. "What?" I ask as I swallow back a heavy sigh.

"They'll fade for you too."

With a blush that sets my neck ablaze, I hurry from the room. I can't bear to hear another word.

After rounding the corner at the junction of the south wing, past the corridor of windows and light, I pause to catch my breath. Peering down at my hands, I notice they're violently shaking.

And covered in cerulean blue.

CHAPTER 11
EVIE

JUNE 3RD — DAY 7

Knowing David is on his way reminds me of how ill-prepared I am for such a reunion. I barely ate anything at breakfast—and again at lunch, much to Laz's dismay. Every untouched bite of food was met with silent scorn, but with my stomach in knots, no amount of fervor could get me to swallow a single bite. The questions I have for David are enough to drive me mad, but they pale in comparison to the hatred that scours my insides at his betrayal against Jenna. The lies. The manipulation.

The danger.

All my life, I always thought the only prison I would endure would be my own mind. Only hearing my father's final moments forced me to fill in the blanks with my vivid imagination, and I've been trapped by the unanswered questions ever since. But now I know my father was right. The monsters are real, and they had been searching for me all this time.

And they've imprisoned me in a way that rivals my mental clutches.

I hated Papa in those moments—caged, thirsty, starving. Suffocating.

I despised him, in fact, and wished the first man I ever loved dead with such conviction that, upon my release from the wardrobe, I would throw myself in his arms and beg for *his* forgiveness out of sheer guilt and shame. The comfort of his arms was unparalleled, the only thing that ever truly felt like home. And so it went unmatched. That is, until a soldier with a possessive touch and an unyielding need to feel whole again sunk his teeth into me in the pouring rain. Cradled in his arms in the aftermath, lying against the warmth of his soaked and worn body, I found home again.

Cruelty rewarded with irrevocable affection.

I barely step away from the table in the breakfast nook when Laz peers at his vibrating cell phone and says, "David's here. He's waiting for you in the parlor."

Replaying every word of disdain in my head, I make my way into the main hall and down to the front of the house, where the parlor awaits.

Where David sits, elbows on his knees, peering into his phone.

He's dressed in a black suit, no tie, like he's just come from a meeting not so important that a tie would be critical. He doesn't see me as I breach the doorway, and for a moment, I'm rather relieved. Being watched in this place nonstop makes this little moment where I'm the one watching him, without his knowledge, feel as if I have a sliver of control back in my life.

Even if it's only for an instant.

He looks up at me and approaches with gentle apprehension. All the words of hatred and disgust I played on a loop in my mind while heading for the parlor have become so jumbled in my head that I find myself with no words at all. All that remains is this incessant tugging at my insides like a sickening freefall.

We eye each other for an eternity, the stillness becoming almost too much to bear. And much to my chagrin, I feel a brief moment of gratitude for the man I've come to loathe when he finally breaks the uncomfortable silence.

"It's good to see you," he says, his tone soft.

I hesitate for a moment. "I wish I could say the same."

"Look, Neve, I know you're confused—"

"Don't call me that," I say. "You know my real name."

He gives me a pointed look, which soon fades to one of placidity, as if surrendering to the fight before it has begun. With a quick nod, he concedes and continues, "I can't imagine the questions you must have—"

"I just want to know how you could do this to Jenna. How could you lie to her like this? Do you have any idea how much she loves—"

"I never meant to hurt her, Evie." He thrusts his phone into his pocket and takes several hurried steps toward me. "You have to believe me." His eyes are wide with a desperation I've seldom seen.

"Was it all a lie?" My throat is pinched, unprepared for the truth.

He releases a heavy sigh and looks at the floor. I can't stomach the delay any longer. But before I break the silence with venomous words, he says, "In the beginning, yes." He leans against the back of the sofa, crossing his arms in contemplation. "In the beginning, Jenna was merely a means to an end..." He trails off, brushing a hand over his beard and looking somewhere in the distance over my shoulder.

"For what?"

He surveys me before admitting, "For you." He goes oddly still. "When you walked into my nightclub the first time, I just..." He runs a gentle hand through his hair. "I had this feeling in my gut that you were my sister. We searched for you for so long. Twenty-eight years, if you can believe it." A heavy sigh passes through his parted lips. "We'd practically abandoned the search a long time ago, though, but then you fell right into our laps, and it turned everything upside down." He unfolds his arms and rests his grip on the back of the sofa. "You look exactly like her. You know that? Our mother was almost the same age as you when she died. I took one look at you and thought I saw a ghost."

A tremor of longing grips me low and deep.

"I called Laz immediately and told him that I thought my sister had just walked into Club Giada. And when I told him you were accompanied by some spitfire redhead beauty, I was ordered to cozy up to her no matter what to keep an eye on you. I took over as bartender that night solely to learn as much as I could about you. You confessed your closeness with Jenna that same night, and it was all we needed to put everything into place." A light sigh escapes his lip. "I wriggled my way into Jenna's life and, inadvertently, yours. Before long, Jenna became a regular at my club and was smitten, just as I planned."

He refolds his arms and shifts uncomfortably as I repress the urge to strangle him. "But that's where the lies stopped—at least as far as Jenna's concerned. I was supposed to court her until we could confirm your identity. We took your *one* drinking glass from the nightclub you'd been sipping on all night in order to perform DNA tests with a scientist on Laz's payroll. But there was some mix-up at the lab, and the sample was lost." He shakes his head, seemingly irritated.

"The fact that you lived in another state made it especially difficult to obtain something we could use for another test. Jenna had surprisingly little at her house that belonged to you, as far as she'd made me aware. So when I brought her to this island to propose, she fell so in love with Krelborn Manor and that ridiculous hedge maze that she begged me to do some sort of party with all of our friends before the wedding." He pauses as if waiting for me to cut in. But I wait with a silent fury and give him no retort.

"Laz refused at first. But when I told him your DNA would be all over that house before the weekend was through, he agreed. He offered me a handful of his men to serve as the staff and told me he'd front the bill for whatever we had planned as a wedding gift."

I survey him with a narrowed look and step toward him. "So the plan was to get my DNA from Krelborn Manor a week before your wedding. But I know something happened with the analyst because I heard Laz arguing about it on my first day here. The testing was canceled, wasn't it? You never did, in fact, confirm that I'm Neve Denardo. So you all can take your speculations about who you think I am and shove them up your asses." I cross my arms, mirroring him.

"The testing was canceled because we don't need it anymore." He stands upright, away from the back of the couch, as if emphasizing his point. "We can prove it by that ring on your finger. It was our mother's—"

"I know," I huff, pacing away and running an irritated hand through my hair.

"So you admit it's true?"

I look away, not knowing what to believe. An entire criminal empire seems to believe I'm Neve Denardo—the girl who was kissed by snow, the same as her mother. The girl with dark hair and pale-green eyes, the fairest of skin...

And a one-of-a-kind ring on her finger that once belonged to Gabriella.

He shifts in my periphery, reaching into his back pocket. At first, I think he's reaching for his phone, and I eye him intensely. Instead, he reaches for his wallet, removes something, and hands it to me. I hesitate, not wanting anything from him, but curiosity inevitably sways my hand. It's a photograph of a young boy with dark hair, roughly ten years of age, standing alongside a young woman holding a baby on her hip. I don't recognize anyone in the photograph, except for the woman, who bears my face and pierces my soul with merely a look. She's young—twenties, I would guess— her eyes soft and her smile delicate, the sun behind the photographer illuminating her porcelain skin in a warm glow. She seems so full of life despite the squinty look on the baby's face, her dark hair sweeping long against her back as she holds hands with the boy, who smiles wide for the camera. All the air seems to evacuate my lungs as I stifle the sadness that inches up my throat.

"I don't know what to say," I whisper, mesmerized. This is the first photograph I've ever seen of myself as an infant.

And the first time I've ever laid eyes on my mother.

After staring at the photograph for so long that the lines begin blurring together, I hand it back to him. He waves me off. "Keep it."

I don't refuse.

"I found that in an old box of your things in Dad's basement when we were looking for something of yours to compare for the DNA testing. The box was full of old toys, books, photographs..." He gestures to the image in my hand. "We really hit the jackpot when we found an old pacifier, though."

"Lucky you," I reply, peering back at the photograph.

"He'd kill me if he knew I took that. But fuck him."

In a flash, everything David said at dinner that night at Krelborn Manor comes racing back, about him losing his sister when she was only three. The sheer memory of that conversation suddenly transforms David into a man with softer lines and a pensive energy. So childlike that it stills my heart for several beats and forces me to peer straight at him and nowhere else.

That night, a pain I'd never before seen in his dark eyes came crashing down on me like a tidal wave, pulling me under so deep that it was impossible to breach its surface and come up for air. A youthful naivety and desire for acceptance consumed every feature of his handsome face as he spilled his soul at dinner.

"You lied to me." I squint, willing him to look at me. "At dinner that night. You lied. You said your sister died when she was three—"

He shakes his head before I have the chance to finish. "No, no, no. I never said she died. It was certainly implied, but I never specified, and you never asked. I said she was *taken* from us when she was three. Which is the truth. I did lie about her real name, though, changing it from the Italian word for snow—*Neve*—to frost—*Brina*—on a whim, but I was given strict orders not to say—"

"But after we left Krelborn, James told me that your father blamed you for her death."

"James doesn't know the truth. I was in charge of watching you that night. You were asleep in your room, and Gino Parisi—the man you call *Papa*—snuck in through your window and snatched you from your bed. I never heard a sound. No one knew you were missing until our parents arrived home that night and found you gone."

My knees quiver, and I reach for the back of the couch for balance.

"Our father beat me senseless that night," he says, unaware that his words are slowly killing me. "Despite our mother's protests. And I spent the rest of my childhood trying to prove to him that I wasn't a fuckup, the first half of my adulthood drowning my sorrows in booze and drugs, and the more recent years thinking of all the ways I could destroy him."

"You've been lying to James all this time?" I reply with a heaviness in my chest.

Wait. *James.*

My pulse skyrockets barely beyond my control.

"My God. James, he—" The words are like acid on my tongue. "He isn't part of all of this, is he? I mean, does he know what kind of work you're really in? Did he help bring me here?" The mere thought of such a betrayal impales me, and I can barely choke down a single breath. A ringing in my ears crescendos, pushing me to the brink of madness as I wait for David to either rid me of my misery or sentence me to death by it.

He shakes his head and squares his body with mine. "No. He doesn't know about any of this."

My lungs sing with elation as I inhale deeply and give them the air they so desperately crave.

"And it's going to stay that way," he commands with a pointed look. "He knows I own a chain of nightclubs in Boston. He knows I think my father's a prick. He thinks my sister's dead. And yes, that was a lie. I considered recruiting him, honestly. Hell, someone with piloting skills would be invaluable to our business. But he's too good for this life—too much of a boy scout. After feeling him out, I knew he would never concede to a life of crime, no matter how well it paid. He's a good man. And for his sake, lies were necessary here and there from the very beginning. But I don't want to lie to you, Evie. Because I need you to cooperate." His eyes bounce between mine. "For your own safety."

I want to believe him. For the sake of my sanity, I *need* to believe him. I just don't know if I can. Jenna never should have been dragged into this. And for that, my heart will never find forgiveness for the man who claims to be my brother.

His phone pings, interrupting my thoughts. He ignores it this time.

"I mean it when I say I fell for her fast," he says, staring at the floor as if in a daze.

I jerk my head at the sudden shift back to Jenna.

"Faster than I've ever fallen for anyone. It was her idea to get married, even though the thought had been on my mind for a while. We hardly knew each other, but she was unlike anyone I'd ever met, and I was—*am*—crazy about her. I need you to know that, Eves." He meets my gaze. "I would do anything for her."

"You've told so many lies since you came into our lives. How on earth am I supposed to believe you?"

"I suppose I'm asking you to trust me. As your brother."

Brother.

The notion is all too surreal, and hearing it aloud is even stranger. I still don't truly believe it.

"She was only ever supposed to be a temporary means to an end. A mission, really. Until we could bring you somewhere safe."

His phone pings again. This time, he removes it and reads the screen.

James? Even the thought of him on the other side of a mere phone call or text sends my heart tripping over itself with anxiety. How close he seems, yet, without knowing where he is or if he's looking for me, he couldn't be further away.

With a gruff sigh, he types a quick response and shoves the phone back into his pocket.

Right front pocket.

I've been eyeballing that phone since I walked into the room.

"But when it came time, I couldn't turn my back on her. Surely you can understand."

I could never turn my back on Jenna. In that, David and I share an undeniable common ground.

Feeling exhausted and tense all at once, I nod. But my response is interrupted when his phone rings from his pocket. The ringtone is "Only You" by Yazoo.

Jenna?

He removes the phone, eyes the screen, and hurries away from me to the opposite side of the room, staring out the bank of windows that face the front of the house as he whispers into the phone. "Babe, I told you. I'll be home this evening."

Jenna.

While he's preoccupied with the muffled voice on the opposite end of the phone call, I creep up behind him, praying that my reflection in the windows goes unnoticed.

Thanks to my bare feet, my footsteps fall on deaf ears. With as much stealth as I can manage, I step up behind him and yank the phone away from his ear. He releases a startled cry, his grip on the phone iron tight. But it's enough for me to yell "Jenna" at the top of my lungs before his eyes widen and he places an aggressive hand over my mouth.

"What the fuck?" he screams before pressing the button to end the phone call without so much as a goodbye.

She'll call back. She must've heard that.

"Goddammit, Evie," he screams, his eyes ablaze and his face flush with rage. I reach for his phone, ignoring the anger that drips from his bared teeth. He angles it away from me. But as he steps back, I grab his arm and sink my teeth into his hand below his thumb.

He releases a harsh cry, dropping the phone as the taste of copper slips between my lips. I swipe it from the floor and bolt for the main stairwell right outside the parlor, dodging his outstretched arms.

The phone rings in my hand, the song "Only You" ringing loud and clear as I scale the first three steps. The familiar sound makes me pause as I glance at the screen to connect the call. My ankle is pulled from behind, dropping me onto the stairs as my elbow bears the weight of my fall. There's no time to scream, no time to focus on the pain that shoots up my arm. David's heavy frame is on mine, pinning me down as he reaches for the phone I've tucked underneath me, the ringing tormenting me with the rescue that exists just beyond its blaring tones.

With a series of heavy grunts, I wriggle beneath him. He shifts to reach his arm under my frame, into the gap created by the step. But I fling my body sideways, which pushes him off me enough that I can regain my footing. He darts his hand toward the now-silent phone.

But I reach it first.

Gripping it with an iron-tight fist, I scale the steps two at a time as he mutters curse words close behind me. His footsteps are so close that I can't even take the split-second lead to look back lest he tackle me all over again.

"Evie, stop," he hollers. Rounding out the last of the stairs, I run as fast as my legs can carry me down the main hallway, ignoring his frantic cries.

I have no plan. None. The only room that comes to mind that I know I can lock behind me is the room Laz has assigned as mine. I hate thinking of it as *my room*. Nothing about this place feels like it belongs to me. Nor do I want it to. This place is a gilded cage, nothing more.

Clutching the phone, I pound against the hardwood floors of the vast hallway, running at full speed toward my room. David's footsteps echo behind me, nearly sending me into cardiac arrest.

I bank right at the hallway's junction, where the hardwood gives way to a strip of burgundy carpet down the center, deafening the sound of my feet and emphasizing the breaths that stab my lungs.

Reaching the door in less than a handful of strides, I throw it open and slam it closed behind me. I nearly drop the door key as I pull it from the nightstand drawer, my hands shaking as I shove it into the lock. David's body strikes the door right as the lock engages. The pounding of fists immediately follows, and I step away from the vibrating door with my stomach completely in knots.

"Open the door," David hollers with unadulterated rage. The banging only intensifies the longer I disobey, but I don't have time to focus on anything other than the elusive phone that now possesses more value than gold.

My lifeline.

I press the screen, awakening the phone to a home-screen picture of Jenna making a kissy face as she presses her cheek against David's. The sight of her gives me pause, flooding my insides with an ache that sends me into a tailspin of homesickness, yearning, and anger at the betrayal that has befallen her.

The home screen asks for a four-digit passcode. But I don't need it. Below the numerics, I find the "Emergency Call" button, and it takes me to a keypad.

I press the number nine.

Multiple sets of fists are pounding on the door now, accompanied by a cacophony of voices, each of which is screaming both versions of my name.

"Neve," Laz growls. "Open this door. *Now.*"

Fuck you.

All of you.

I select the number one. Twice.

"If you call anyone from that phone," David's panicked voice hollers from the other side of the thrumming door, "Jenna will be the one to pay for it."

The threat stills my hand.

With wide, perplexed eyes, I survey the door.

"Open the door, Evie. Please." David's voice is calmer now. "I'm begging you. Don't do anything stupid. Open the door."

Transfixed on the phone and the "911" that remains stamped on the screen, waiting for me to press the green call button, the cold chill of doubt creeps up on me and settles into my mind. I'm so close to a call for help, I can hear the operator's voice in my head. I can hear them asking me where I am. Hear their calm, collected tone as they tell me help is on the way. But just as the operator's voice loops in my head like a record at the end of its track, Jenna's voice inches its way in to match. Her beautiful, saccharine voice seducing me with its playful banter. I can feel her velvety touch as she holds my hand in hers, and the tremble that grips me low in my belly as she plants a kiss on my palm. The warmth of her lips has kept me company since she left my room that morning at Krelborn, momentarily lost only when James's touch was there to take its place.

"They will hurt her, Evie. Please, I beg you. Don't you dare call anyone." David's voice is riddled with panic, not at all the enraged voice that chased me down moments ago.

I'm not given even a second to respond—to ask what they would do to David's bride—before a sickening *bang* rattles the entire door. I drop the phone, startled by the sudden noise. Before I can fetch it, another bang quickly follows. Hinges rattle and wood splinters. Panicked, I grab the phone from the floor and stare desperately at those three powerful numbers on the screen. But if there's one thing more powerful than the possibility of being saved from my waking nightmare—my prison of scarred flesh, clicking shoes, and silent pleas—it's my unequivocal love for Jenna. The mere thought of her suffering because of my actions renders me immobile. That playfully sarcastic mouth, her loyalty, her ride-or-die nature, and the delicate touch of her lips on my skin; I need them more than the air I breathe. And I'll do anything in my power to protect them—to protect *her.* Even if it means sacrificing my own freedom.

I need time to think. To come up with a plan. In seconds, that door will be coming down in a smattering of splinters.

It's my only chance of escaping. I can't turn it over to them.

The banging noises are broken up now by the sound of wood shattering piece by piece. But it's all faded to a white noise as my mind thrums with urgency.

I need to hide the phone. Somewhere they won't find it.

Darting around the room, I consider every conceivable hiding place, time not at all on my side as the voices holler muffled words of anger.

All the places I tally up as potential hiding places are too obvious and would easily be found in a raid. The nightstand, the closet, underneath the bed. Hell, I even contemplate draining the toilet tank and hiding it in there. But they're certain to find it in all these places.

The balcony? No. Where would I hide it on the balcony?

Another bang.

If only I had discovered a loose tile in the bathroom, a loose floorboard...

Bang.

The large lighthouse painting on the wall eyes me in the

distance. Surely they wouldn't look in the secret passage? It would only give away its location as I watch them search the room.

After putting the phone on silent, I push open the hidden door and set the phone on the floor inside the entrance, where I can easily find it later. It's pitch black inside, lit only by the sliver of light from my bedroom. The dank, chilled air does little to quell my shakiness as another round of loud bangs and splintering wood pierces the room.

With folded arms, I wait by the balcony as what's left of the bedroom door bursts open and six men race into the room. Laz leads the charge, fury stretched across his face as he heads straight for me.

"Where is it?" he yells, the gap between us closing in an instant as he invades my space.

I plant my feet, reminding myself that these are the men who, only moments ago, threatened Jenna. It's shockingly all I need to find the strength to look the man straight in the eye and tame the shakiness in my voice.

"I don't have it," I reply, my voice stern.

"Where did you hide it?" he growls, his face flushing as my disobedience escalates. "Answer me." He wrenches my arm, and I fight the urge to wince at the pain. I'll never give him the satisfaction. I may be a prisoner here, but I'm no little mouse. Once you threaten Jenna, the claws come out, and it's your fucking funeral.

"I said—" I yank my arm from his grasp and squint in anger at his wretched face. "That I don't have it."

"Evie, please," David begs from across the room. For the first time since they entered, I'm aware of the mess they've made of everything. My bed has been stripped and overturned, the nightstands are on their sides, and the few contents of my closet are strewn about. The boxes of my things that arrived with David, stacked neatly by the door, remain sealed and untouched. I barely registered the chaos as I fell headfirst into the madness of Laz's stare.

But now, the reality and magnitude of my disobedience has truly sunk in, and there's no going back.

David is by Laz's side in an instant.

"I don't have it," I tell him, ignoring Laz entirely.

Suddenly, a sinking feeling hits me that they may elect to search *me.*

Think.

"I tossed it." I expel the words without another thought, nodding toward the balcony. They raise their gazes to the French doors behind me. "Over the railing."

Laz hurries through them and peers over the ledge. Below waits a series of full bushes. I know them well, having spent many hours staring at them, deciding whether they would break my fall or leave me with two broken legs.

He hurries back inside and snaps his fingers once, and his men stop what they're doing to give him their undivided attention. Two of them emerge from the closet, and another emerges from the bathroom.

"Two of you go outside and search the grounds below." He gestures toward the balcony. The two guardsmen near the closet hurry from the room. Without a single missed beat, he pulls his phone from his pocket and hands it to David. "Get that phone of yours deactivated *now.*"

"Laz," David begins on a slow exhale. "If Jenna calls again, and it says my phone is no longer in service, she—"

"This isn't up for discussion. We can't take the risk."

"But what do I tell her—"

"You have an entire boat ride back to the mainland to think of something, don't you? Now do as I say." His livid tone rattles my core as he storms over to a guardsman who is searching the mantel. "Don't let her out of your sight until we find that phone. Understand?" With that, Laz hurries from the room, mindless of the shattered pieces of wood, broken door, and overturned furniture at his feet.

After he disappears, David turns to me, his face pale, and barks, "This isn't a game. Don't you understand? He will order his men to kill her if they don't find that fucking phone. Is that what you want?"

"If something happens to Jenna, it won't be because of that phone. It'll be because *you* dragged her into your mess of lies and betrayal in the first place." I'm seething, teetering on the brink of a mania that may result in David's eyes being ripped out. "Don't you dare blame this on me. This is no one's fault but your own. *You* called Laz the moment I walked into your club. *You* told him you thought you found your sister. *You* agreed to cozy up to Jenna to get closer to me for reasons you all have yet to explain. And you're the one who refuses to get Jenna the hell away from this mess, despite proclaiming how much you actually love her."

His furrowed brow softens and his posture slacks.

In his weakened disposition, I consider making a reach for Laz's phone, which David still holds in his hand. But I don't. I can't repeat this whole mess again. And besides, they still haven't found the one I've hidden, and David's slumped composure—for a fleeting moment that thankfully doesn't take root—elicits a moment of empathy I wasn't expecting. There's no telling how much control David actually has in his life. He may be a puppet, strings pulled by the scarred man just as they're pulled for the rest of these assholes. But that doesn't change the fact that David put all of this in motion by calling Laz in the first place. I could've remained off the radar, living my life as it was, if he hadn't fucked it up with a single phone call.

My life as it was.

I release a painful sigh.

Before James.

I suppose I have David to thank for bringing James into my life.

Jenna partnered us up, but it's because of David that James ever came into my world in the first place. A pit forms in my stomach, pulling at my insides with an infinite length of chain as I imagine my life without him. It's difficult to truly recall how things were before he came along, despite having only known each other a short while. There are two dividing lines in my life I simply can't deny: my life after Papa died, and my life after James blazed his way in with no remorse, regrets, or apologies.

Both moments have imprisoned me, for better or worse. Since the moment James held me against him during the blindfold game, falling smitten amid our silent forfeit as his heart went wild against my ear, I've been dangling on a precipice. One in which I either dive headfirst into a spontaneous and albeit *insane* romance with a man I hardly know or cling to an orphaned life, devoid of family and a place to call home but keeps me tethered to memories of Papa's old-fashioned charm. I needed a place to feel safe. For years, that was in Papa's arms.

But on a dime, that all changed.

With James, the feeling of home called to me from the beginning, unspoken but louder than the explosive way with which he entered my life and stole my heart for his own.

A home I'd been without for so long.

"I can't protect her," David begins, cutting into my thoughts. "Not in the way you want me to."

"You can." I lower my voice and move in closer. He jerks the phone away in a protective maneuver. I pay it no mind. "Take her somewhere far away from here. Don't tell a soul where you're going. Change your names if you have to."

He shakes his head, poised to cut me off, but I don't allow it.

"She loves you so much. Sure, she'll have a ton of questions, and you can explain it to her when you get to wherever it is that's beyond the reach of this criminal empire. But you have to keep her safe. That's not a request. I'm telling you, you have—"

"I can't," he barks, slicing his hand through the space between us. "What you fail to understand is that there is nowhere in this world that Laz's empire doesn't reach. There *is* nowhere safe. Don't you see? His greatest enemy knows exactly where you are. The island of Eden's Green isn't exactly hidden. But Laz doesn't care, because he has enough power, money, resources, and people to ensure that you remain untouched by the man who wants you most, even if you're right under his nose. In fact, I almost think Laz gets off on it. You're so close yet so unreachable at the same time. It's the little cherry on top of Laz's mission to keep you safe."

"His greatest enemy? You mean Frank?"

"Our father, yes."

"Your father," I quip.

"*Our* father," he responds with an attitude that matches my own.

"Well, you'll have to forgive me for not jumping at the chance to refer to the man as 'my father.'"

"Or me as your brother?" His eyes droop into an almost child-like state of affection. It's enough to tear my heart into shreds. I avert my gaze, cursing the tears that attack the base of my throat.

"I—" I have no idea what to say. To think I had family out there all this time. How different my life may have been if I never had to navigate this world alone. Without Papa, I wouldn't have danced with the devil, my parched lips desperate for even a single drop of water as I wished for either the three knocks on the side of the wardrobe that meant freedom or for the world to swallow me whole and rid me of my soirees with death.

At the same time, a life without Papa meant a life without uncontrollable fits of laughter or slimy fish hooked on a line, cold toes wading through the waters of the Puget Sound, shared popcorn on movie nights, the failed attempts to braid my hair, cuddles during rip-roaring thunderstorms, and soaked skin as we spun in the falling rain. Brief though it was, my time with Papa created some of the best memories I'll ever have. Papa *is* my family. And since Jenna and James came into my life, I haven't needed anyone else.

"It just doesn't feel right—"

"David," Laz snaps as he bursts into the room. "Is it done?"

He steps away with a heavy sigh. "Yeah, I'm on it, Boss." He exits to the balcony and raises the phone to his ear.

"There was no phone outside," Laz sneers as he moves in closer. "I'll ask you again. Where is it?"

"I told you. I don't have it. I tossed it."

He opens his mouth to speak, but I interrupt. "Don't worry. I have no intention of doing anything to put Jenna in harm's way. And if it takes you nearly thirty years to find that phone, just as it took you to find *me,* then, well, the phone will be long dead by then, and there'll be nothing to worry about." I fight the urge to continue, but I'm pressing my luck as it is. It's apparent when his face flushes and his eyes cloud over with a torrential storm that threatens to destroy me.

I don't give him the opportunity to retort as I brush past him, step over the mess that consumes the room, and leave him without me as a witness to his oncoming rage.

CHAPTER 12
LAZARO

JUNE 4TH — DAY 8

Delicate yet refined, her features are as beautiful as they are deliberate, as if painted by an artist with perfect clarity of his vision and the precision to match. From the fullness of her lips to the contours of her nose and brow, the likeness to her mother is uncanny. Aside from this unusual fear of locked doors, she's a perfect replica of Gabriella.

Deep slumber has not yet claimed her, as evidenced by her shallow breathing. I fear she may wake at any moment. But I risk exposing my clandestine visit to reach for her hair. As dark as the shadows from whence I came, watching and waiting for sleep to finally consume her, that ebony hair tantalizes like the touch of satin. I long to be the pillow on which it drapes, or the sheets that snug her form.

Or the moonlight that bathes her angelic skin.

She stirs, twisting ever so slightly as she lies on her back, her face tilted toward the light. I free her hair from my loving touch and wait for her to settle again. But she sighs as if from discomfort, and I slink away preemptively, back into the shadowy recesses of the room.

She rolls onto her side, toward the moonlight, a spotlight on the face—the *obsession*—that has tortured me most of my life. I brace myself against the wall and wait for her breathing to slow, permitting my second approach.

Permitting another caress.

I need it more than she'll ever realize.

Gabriella was taken from me. But for the first time since that unmentionable day, I'm staring at the face of my second chance.

CHAPTER 13

EVIE

JUNE 10TH — DAY 14

The late-morning sun casts stout beams across the bed, forcing me awake from my dreamless sleep. I can't recall the last time I didn't dream, and I want nothing more than to close my eyes against the garish light and slip back into that blissful slumber.

But it's too damn hot beneath these covers.

The coolness hits my flushed skin all at once as I toss them aside and clamber to the edge of the bed. I bring my arms high above my head in a nearly orgasmic stretch before something on the night-stand catches my eye. I lean in.

A note.

Bringing it close, I see that it's handwritten, same as the last one.

Meet me in the atrium.
– L

Irritation rumbles low at his persistent brashness. Really, would it kill the man to ask? Pissed that such restful sleep has already been tainted with this shit first thing, I crumple it up, toss it aside, and ready myself for the day despite it all.

I've only seen the atrium once: when I snuck out of my room in the middle of the night my first week here and made a right down the hall instead of a left. It was barely visible in the darkness, the moon nothing more than a clipped fingernail in an inklike sky. In fact, the atrium appeared as nothing more than a giant void in the darkness, an empty space that suddenly dropped off on one side of the hallway. Bathed by minimal starlight, it took on the most rudimentary form. One I had no desire to revisit.

The expansive hall continues onward, splitting open into a rectangular loft that peers down onto the atrium's ground level. Filled with greenery and a floor of herringbone stone, the atrium reflects the sunlight with such intensity that the space seems almost holier than the rest of the estate.

Gripping the stone railing, I crane my neck upward. The ceiling, made entirely of glass like some elaborate greenhouse, casts angled beams of light onto the space below. For the first time, I have a true sense of the magnitude of this place. Identical wrought-iron spiral staircases stand in the two opposing corners, reaching up to the third floor and opening onto each level.

Trailing my hand along the cool stone as I approach the nearest one, I admire the grounds from above. Peppered with an assortment of shrubs and trees in addition to colors from flowers in full bloom, catching the light in an almost prismatic fashion, it's one of the most beautiful things I've ever seen.

In the center of the space, atop the stone floor, sits a round iron table with two chairs facing opposite one another. I gasp as I spot what sits nearby: almost amber in the striking glow, my cello waits in splendor, propped upright by its neck inside a metal stand.

My pace quickens, and I nearly tumble to the ground floor as my feet struggle to keep up. I reach my cello in a dash, pull it from the stand, and spin it, admiring it from all angles. The endpin crackles against the stone floor as it shows itself off to me.

It's mine. I recognize the linear scratch on the back that angles from the left waist toward the upper bout. Papa had rented the cello used for me when I was eight. When he bought it outright later that year, I loved it more than any gift I'd ever received. It was the scratch on the back—an imperfection on a perfect gift—that made me adore it all the more.

Hanging from one of its pegs is a small tag attached to a string, which had not been there before. There's handwriting on both sides.

On one side, it reads:

Play something for me.
— L

My brow furrows with confusion as I spin around, looking for the audience I'm certain lurks nearby. It takes only a quick scan of the room before I find Laz, arms folded across his chest, leaning against the frame of the other spiral staircase from the catwalk on the second floor.

His eyes lock on me, his stoic expression unyielding. Despite his unreadable face, his body language exudes an arrogance that picks at a nerve. It's as if he's emanating pride for returning what was rightfully mine in the first place.

A soft clanging vibration sounds from the stairs as he descends them and meets me on the ground level, his hands inside his pant pockets as he approaches. The smallest of wrinkles are visible across the front of his white V-neck T-shirt where his arms were folded, the outline of the antique key underneath barely visible. Other than that, he's looking especially crisp—and casual—this morning. It's nice to see him not wearing a full suit for once.

"What do you say?" he asks, nodding toward the cello cradled against me.

"About what?" I ask, a bit irritated by his second demand of the day.

And it isn't even noon.

"Did you read the note?" His aloofness holds firm.

"Yes."

"So...what do you say? Will you play something for me?" He steps closer. Too close for my comfort.

"Maybe I would if everything wasn't always a command."

He gives me a quizzical tilt of his head. "What command? I asked. You said you read the note."

I read the note dangling from a peg again.

Play something for me.
— L

Then I flip the tag over. On the back is one simple word—one Laz seems to think changes everything:

Please?

"Well, it seems you've developed a sliver of manners in the last few hours, at least since you left that note on my nightstand. Which, by the way, is creepy as hell. Why are you coming into my room—"

"Maybe if you'd flipped that note over as well..." He cuts me off with an arrogance that slices through his stoicism.

Sighing heavily, I concede to his sharpness. I'll bother him about coming into my room another time. Right now, I want to relish the fact that I have at least a small piece of my life from before back in my arms. My cello, in a way, is the first dose of freedom I've had since I awoke in this place. I run my finger along its scratch, reminding myself that it's really here.

In no time, Laz is carrying one of the chairs from the table and setting it beside me. He shifts the other so it's facing me and takes a seat, oddly anticipatory despite the fact that I never agreed to play.

I sit and cradle the cello between my legs. He hands me the bow from the table heel first.

With each drag of the bow across the strings, the entire atrium comes to life with a symphonic echo, mimicking the acoustics of an amphitheater. My fingers quiver with excitement, disguised perfectly by the vibrato of my wrist, as the sound emitted from its body quakes in tandem with each of my bow strokes. The C string is a bit out of tune, which I easily correct with a quick turn of its fine tuner and a few plucks of the string.

I have no particular song in mind. At the moment, I just want to hear it sing.

"It sounds beautiful," Laz says, breaking my moment of euphoria.

"Thanks." I look away, almost embarrassed. It's the first time I've ever felt bashful playing the cello, and the burning sensation in my cheeks makes me stop.

The atrium falls silent.

"Is something wrong?" he asks.

"I just..." Somehow, this feels wrong. I would play for Papa, Jenna, James, the whole goddamn world. But not for him. Not my captor, even though he seems to wait with almost untamable eagerness, his elbows on his knees and his index fingers steepled beneath his chin.

"Stage fright?" he asks.

"Not exactly."

"Not sure what to play?"

I exhale a soft sigh. "I suppose."

"Well," he begins, "just play the first thing that comes to mind." He sits back, crosses his legs, and rests a patient hand on his ankle.

Hoping for a spark of inspiration, I survey the atrium. Coming up short from my surroundings alone, I peek at Laz, who waits statuesque. His scars are on full display in the morning sunlight. I've become quite skilled at looking at them in my periphery, frightened to make my lurking gaze known.

For a moment, I wonder when those scars came to be, and whether my mother loved him even after he came to bear them. Such mystery within those twisted lines, I can hardly stand existing in the same space without knowing the answers that accompany them. But despite his deformities, I envy him. More than I ever thought possible.

He knew my mother, and he'll always have memories of which I can only dream.

With my trepidation ebbing, I glide the bow over the strings with purpose. Filling the atrium with a soft harmony of notes, I watch him out of the corner of my eye, past my quavering wrist. He shifts in his seat, uncrossing his legs and leaning forward as if engrossed in the song that emanates from my instrument. I reach the first chorus, played strictly a cappella—thankfully, he never asked me to sing—when he says in a deep rumble: "Excellent choice."

"You've heard it?"

"Of course. Live's 'Lightning Crashes.' Shit, that song is nearly thirty years old now, but it's a good one." He pauses for a moment. "What made you choose it?"

I avoid his scars and look down at my bow. "Honestly, I'm not sure. It's just the first song that came to mind."

"Will you play another?"

"Any requests?"

He shifts his weight and crosses his arms, his lips daring to twitch into a smirk but coming up short. "I rather enjoy guessing."

It takes only a moment for a second song to come to me. I skip the beginning this time and dive straight into the chorus. After several seconds of music filling the atrium, a low chuckle escapes him. "'Broken Wings'?" he asks. "God, that one's even older than the last one."

"You never specified that you wanted me to play current songs," I sass.

"I take no issue with your song selection," he replies. "I just wonder...has anyone ever told you that your taste in music is old enough to be your parent?"

Suppressing a laugh, I reply with a shrug. "I'm rather fond of the music Papa listened to when I was young." I straighten my back and realign my bow above the bridge, poised to play another song. "Something more current, then?"

"You play whatever your heart desires."

As a tease, I drag the bow over the D string for a split second before raising it off the strings. He cocks his head, seemingly confused.

Plucking along the fingerboard, I begin. Alternating between gripping the bow in my palm to pluck away at the strings and dragging it above the bridge with unparalleled fervor, I fall headlong into the rapid momentum of my song choice. I slide my fingers with familiar ease along the neck as they take on a life of their own. Before long, horse hairs from my bow have come loose and hang limp from their mount. I pay them no mind as I play well into the second verse, the song filling the atrium with a vivacity that reverberates straight to my core.

Despite his pensive look, I make it through the entire second chorus without so much as a peep from him.

I drag the bow for the final note with an ostentatious flair, my vibrato bringing my solo concert to a dramatic close.

The silence hangs heavy in the sudden absence of my cello's voice.

I wait for him to guess. But it seems I'm the first to speak. "Care to take a guess?"

"'She Talks to Angels,'" he states.

"Yes," I reply, my voice ripe with excitement. "It took a minute. Did I almost stump you?" Cockiness bubbles up inside me, yet I resist the urge to let it show on my face.

"No." His face is as stoic as ever, and my arrogance is as fleeting as a wave's stint on shore.

"Then why didn't you guess earlier, once you knew?"

The hardness in his face relaxes, devolving into softer lines. "Because I didn't want you to stop playing."

My belly blushes.

"You have a gift, you know that? I've honestly never seen anyone play with such ardor and skill. And I must say"—he nods toward my cello—"I'm even more impressed by the fact that you're able to play these songs without sheet music."

I inhale deeply, desperate to give my cheeks a moment of reprieve. "If I've heard the song before, I can usually play it by ear."

"You have a gift for audiation. That's impressive. Not many people, even musicians, have such a relationship with music."

"Audiation?"

"It's understanding music as if it were a language. Over time, if one trains their ears and understands the composure of sounds, they can master the art. Among other things, they can learn to recreate sounds with their instruments just as they would learn a foreign language."

"How do you know this?"

A light smile purses his lips. "Because you and I share the same gift."

My jaw slacks as my stomach pitters with the subtle flight of tiny butterflies. "You can recreate songs simply by ear?" I've never met anyone else who could. Personally, I never gave it much thought. Papa always insisted I use the sheet music my teacher sent home because I was instructed to do so. But after running through the song a few times, I would no longer need it. The notes, from that point forward, existed as permanent songs in my head.

He replies with a simple nod, then beckons me to play another with merely a look.

Shifting in my seat, I reposition my bow. "Shall I?"

"Please. But pick something really unusual this time."

Thinking for a moment, I wait. The song that comes to mind is a risky choice. But he's likely to be perplexed by it and rejoice in the game.

I drop my bow to the ground beside my feet and ignore his look of intrigue.

I won't be needing it for this one.

"I think I may have one that will stump you. But I'm going to need your help with it."

He scoots his chair closer, and it makes my breath hitch. His closeness is something to which I may never grow accustomed.

Now settled, he leans in as if to whisper something he does not wish the atrium to hear.

But he says nothing and merely waits for instruction, his eagerness palpable.

"This song follows a standard four-four count, like so." I snap my fingers to the tempo. "I need you to snap your fingers on the second and fourth beats, and don't stop until either you've guessed the song or I've stopped playing." If I didn't know any better, I would say his eyes came alive just now, ardent and untamable. Yet they elicit no fear, so I continue as if they didn't just pierce me with their restless flame.

"As you command."

I cock my head with confusion. Such an odd response. But he doesn't seem angry, so I push it to the back of my mind.

With a hooked finger poised on a string above the bridge and my others splayed across the neck, I wait for him to signal me that he's ready. He nods, and I begin right away, alternating between plucking the harmony and tapping my snowflake ring against the side of the cello's neck with every downbeat. It's a quick juggling of movements, but I've always loved creating different sounds with my cello aside from a bow to its strings. Plucking the strings is common, sure, but by integrating taps along the body or of my feet on the ground, I can mimic the sounds of multiple instruments with merely one.

Laz snaps his fingers on the second and fourth beats flawlessly. In seconds, we create a symphony of noises that can surely be heard from all corners of the estate.

Adrenaline captivates me as my heart races to the beat of our unusual duet. He leans back in his seat, legs crossed, his tempo maintained with each finger snap. For the first time since I've come here, he appears so...relaxed. Perhaps music is his weakness. Well, not weakness. His soft spot? It's unprecedented enough that I'm intrigued to explore the notion further.

The song comes to a close, and I await his guess.

"Well, you've done it," he begins, uncrossing his legs and leaning forward. "I can't even venture a guess."

My lips twitch in a gentle smile. "It's Laurel's 'Fire Breather.' One of my favorites."

"Fire Breather?" His scars blush with what I can only imagine is irritation. My nerves ignite as I recite a silent prayer that he doesn't take the song choice as a slight. The seconds that follow are torturous, my grip on the cello neck sliding amid my sweaty palms.

"I'll have to look that one up," he continues.

A heavy sigh of relief puts my lungs out of their misery.

"One more," he says. "I need to make up for my loss in that last round."

I take in the room around me. Shadows cast across our bodies as a flock of birds glide high above the glass ceiling, minimal silhouettes against the morning sky. The atrium, though modern in many ways, invokes a vibe of another era. With long, smooth Ionian columns of black-and-gold marble along the entire periphery, it's as if I've stepped back in time. Art Deco in many ways, with the green glass ceiling, the large plants, and the gray pavers in their angular pattern upon the floor. It's an oddly matched space compared to the rest of the house, which has a lighter, more coastal flavor. I imagine this space as if it were in a black-and-white film, and suddenly, it takes on a whole new life.

My next song comes to me in an instant.

Long, sensuous drags of the bow welcome the next song choice, filling the room with a beautiful, timeless melody that ripples from my instrument through my wrists and possesses my entire form. Swaying to the slow, delicate rhythm, I close my eyes as the lyrics fill my ears with their sweet sound. I could never do this song justice with my own voice, and I find myself thankful once again that I was not asked to sing my selections.

My hand glides along the fingerboard, pushing my cello into a sway that mirrors my body. The minutes pass in an instant.

As the song comes to a close, I open my eyes to await his guess. What I find, however, is a man still as death, piercing me with a look so fierce that I feel it physically penetrate my chest. Frightened and frozen in its wake, I nearly drop my bow.

"I—umm, I..." Speechless, I look away, bile rising high in my gut.

"The young lady has seen *Casablanca*," he states, stillness masking his emotions.

I nod, then chastise myself for my song selection. It's impossible for me to tell how it was received by my captor, so I second-guess the entire thing. "Can you name it?" I ask, daring to dabble further in the topic.

"'As Time Goes By.' A classic song from one of the greatest films in history." His expression softens, and I sit back with a sliver of relaxation. "I never would have pegged you for a fan," he states.

I open my mouth to speak, but he continues. "Although, considering how much older your taste in music is than you, it only makes sense that your taste in movies would follow suit."

My mouth quirks in a faint smile, relieved to have his approval.

"Well," he cuts, clapping his hands with such enthusiasm that I jump out of my skin. "That settles it. There is something I have to show you." Without waiting for my permission, he stands, reaches for my cello, and sets it back in its neck stand. Suddenly vulnerable in its absence, I reach around my abdomen in a subtle self-embrace. But it's short-lived. Laz sets my bow on the table, grabs my hand, and pulls me away in a hurry.

"Where are we going?" I ask, trying to keep up with his strides. In only a handful of steps, we exit the atrium and enter a long hallway of whitewashed parquet flooring that runs parallel to the back of the manor. Lined with picture windows along the left side, I catch a glimpse of the ocean beyond the cliff's edge. This hallway must fall directly beneath the one on the third floor with the billowing curtains. At the far end, we emerge in the kitchen, and now I'm really confused.

My bewilderment peaks when Laz pulls me toward the pantry at the far side of the kitchen, near the breakfast nook. He throws open the door, flips on the light switch, and pulls me inside.

The large space, roughly the size of a small bedroom, is lined with shelves along each wall, full of sustenance, bottles, jars, and canned items. Directly opposite the pantry door, Laz runs his hand along a vertical seam in the wall. I pause, intrigued, my breathing shallow with anticipation. A distinct *click* sounds from inside the wall as he pushes alongside the seam. The door pops inward, and he helps it along by pulling it toward him. A whoosh of cold air hits me broadside as the door opens completely, revealing a passage dark as midnight and wafting a musty, earthy scent of rain and moss. It echoes even the slightest of noises.

I'm convinced I can detect the thrumming of my racing heart within its walls.

Laz reaches behind a blush-pink decanter labeled "Rose Oil" on the shelf to the right of the door and removes a lighter tucked between it and the wall. With a single *clink* of the Zippo's lid and a flick of the spark wheel, the lighter comes to life.

He's the first to step inside.

For a moment, the darkness swallows him whole as he ducks into the corner near the door. But in seconds, the opening of the tunnel takes on an organic form as a plethora of candle flames fill the space with dancing light from the candelabra in his hand.

He waves for me to follow.

But after a few steps inside, my feet won't budge.

In the flickering light, my fears are confirmed when a spiral staircase appears, cut into the stone wall up ahead, leading downward into a vast unknown.

I shake my head. "No way. I'm not going down there. What on earth could you possibly want to show me that's *underground*?"

"Shall I have you guess?" he torments. "I think you'll love it."

"Why must the buildup of your surprises always be so... unnerving?"

His face, placid and unwavering, gives little hint of his emotions. If he's frustrated with me, I can't tell. "Because you're still frightened of me despite my best efforts. But as I've told you before, I've brought you here to protect you. If I wanted to harm you, it would be done, and there's nowhere you could go that would stop me."

My stomach plummets at the blasé way he utters such poignant threats.

"I didn't bring you here to hurt you, princess. Please, I'm asking you again to trust me." The candelabra remains steady in his grasp as he waits patiently for me to take his outstretched hand.

After a glance over my shoulder to the warmth—protection— of the golden spread of daylight behind me, I take the plunge and venture deeper inside the passage. In less than a few steps, I surrender myself to the stone walls, painted in darkness and elongated shadows, as a chill sends goose bumps cascading across my body. Laz's hand, however, is warm, a comforting sensation as he leads me down the staircase and further into the underbelly of the manor.

Each delicate shuffle of our feet sends a distinct echo in all directions, accompanied by the quiet mimicking of our breaths within the hallowed walls.

The staircase spills into a grand tunnel that stretches far beyond my line of sight. We continue onward despite the protestation of my trembling limbs. The candlelight illuminates Laz's face with a warm hue, casting fearsome shadows that enhance the presence of his scars. Much to my relief, he doesn't catch me eyeing him.

He releases my hand and reaches for a large metal lever set horizontally along the stone wall. After a forceful upturn, it creeks to life as it settles into its upright position, opening another door.

The room that waits beyond is even darker than the tunnel itself.

"Wait here," he instructs without so much as a glance over his shoulder.

I obey.

Minutes tick by, the frigidity more apparent in my stationary state. I run my hands over my arms and bounce the chill away. Through the ajar door, I can't make out what transpires within, and it's killing me not knowing what he's up to.

Suddenly, Laz appears in the entrance, and I've never been so happy to see his apathetic face. "Come." He pulls the door open and guides me inside.

I'm transported to another world. The room stands aglow from the flickering flames of countless candles set throughout the wide space. Candelabras that stand taller than me and single candles supported in candlesticks of all shapes and sizes adorn the space in a blaze of magical twilight.

The room is vastly empty save for a horseshoe-shaped bar in the center, a few round tables off to the left, most tipped on their sides, a stage at the far end to the right, with an old piano sitting catty-corner, and a dozen chandeliers, long extinguished, dotting the high ceiling overhead. Cobwebs stretching between them catch the light of the flames, adding to the ambiance that has long been lost in time.

Despite the decay, it stirs my imagination to the point of near breathlessness. Not a single surface doesn't bear firelight, and it's a beauty I never surmised outside of a fairy tale.

Spinning in all directions, I ask, "What is this place?"

"It's an old speakeasy," he replies. I find him, propped against the bar counter in his typical stance, hands in his pockets, watching me. There's a glint of pleasure in his eyes.

"An old speakeasy?" This is incredible. "Why on earth is there a speakeasy underneath your house?"

He pushes away from the bar and saunters toward me. "Because this island used to be a hub for smuggling alcohol to the mainland during the prohibition. It was owned by a man named Lawrence Krelborn, and he was one of the largest importers of alcohol in the early nineteen thirties."

"Krelborn?" I ask, already knowing the answer to my question.

He nods. "Krelborn Manor was built just before the turn of the twentieth century. It was his home for many years. This estate, and the other on the west side of the island, were also owned by him. But during his heyday in the thirties, he leased them to his two business associates until the time came when he had a family of his own and could pass them down to his future sons. The three men created an empire and lived quite lavishly during their reign here. Large, garish parties—very Gatsby, if you will—with men, women, musicians, magicians, artists, and aristocracy from all over the world. This was one of the many spaces that permitted them to celebrate their imports in secret. Some of the finest people alive at that time danced the night away, drank to their fullest merriment, fell in love, and perhaps even broke hearts right here between these walls."

Taking my hand, he guides me past the bar, toward the stage. I imagine a flashy curtain, the deep color of their imported wine, consuming the wall behind it as a jazz band takes control of the night with its lively music.

As we approach the stage, my feet feel the change in the floor. The existing carpet or tile has long since been stripped away to the blanket of concrete underneath. But encompassing the entire back half of the room is a square of smooth, dusty hardwood.

A dance floor.

Men and women, dressed to the nines in their fringe, bow ties, and feathers affixed in their headbands, dance around me in a soiree of drunken laughter. Quick flicks of heels catch my eye as they kick up in a Charleston dance, and dresses fly as women are flipped to the beat of a jazzy tune. Couples sneak kisses in the darker recesses of the room while waitresses refill drinks. Smoke hangs heavy among the patrons, fists slam on tables from rapacious gamblers losing their hands in poker, and beads of sweat trickle from the singer's forehead as he transitions into another song that keeps the night alive.

I can see it all. And I long to be among them. "This is absolutely incredible," I whisper.

The wild candlelight nearly makes my fantasies of the rowdy nightlife a reality—the shadows dancing across every surface and stirring all forms of imagination.

My breath hitches as a gentle song catches me off guard. Laz, now sitting at the piano next to the dance floor, adds the final, perfect touch to the ambiance. Such breathtaking sounds emanate from the aged instrument, transporting me in mind and spirit to a period I've never witnessed. I feel it—in every cell, every vein. I'm consumed by the music he creates in this lair of rhythm and fire-light. Perfect, melodic, and pushing me to the brink of tears knowing it cannot last forever, he performs a sweet seduction of notes that fills the room and pulls me from within until I find myself standing by his side.

Without a single break in the song, he nods at the piano bench, motioning me to join. I settle onto it beside him, staring with reverence as his fingers glide across the keys in a flawless dance of their own. When the song comes to a close, I pray for the courage to beg him to play again. I've never experienced such beauty from the fingertips of another, and I long to claim it for my own and never allow my soul to exist in dreadful silence again.

Much to my heart's relief, only a single beat passes before Laz pumps life back into the instrument all over again. With a rapid, ostentatious glide of his fingers across the full splay of white keys, the room resonates from the glissando that sends my adrenaline straight to the stars. He transitions directly into Stevie Ray Vaughn's "If the House is a Rockin'," which excites my entire being. Bouncing in place as his hands play with such speed and fervor that they nearly disappear altogether, he transforms into a man I never expected to find. Musically gifted and finding lightness in its creation, he frees himself, his energy changing entirely under the influence of song.

Under any other circumstances, such passion, flair, and talents that, in my eyes, are unmatched, may have been enough to push me over the edge and make me fall in love.

Instead, I sing. Lord, help me. With the room filled with the echoes of bombastic music that makes my spirit soar, I sing every word. But after only a handful of lyrics, he's singing right along with me.

Without pause, he segues into "Great Balls of Fire," and our even stranger duet continues.

I laugh. Harder than I've laughed in weeks, and certainly harder than I ever expected to in his company. Clapping along to the beat that penetrates even the darkest crannies of the old speakeasy, I capitulate to the tenderness in my heart, the warmth in my belly, and the gift of song Laz has bestowed upon me.

As it comes to a close, his fingers fall still upon the keys. My heart rate has skyrocketed and my cheeks are sore from laughter. I no longer fear the silence that hangs between us. But I do wish he would play another.

He regards me with the softest eyes I've seen from him yet. "It looks good on you," he tells me, towering over me as he straightens his posture.

I cock a confused brow. "What does?"

"Laughter."

Try as I may, I can't fight the impending grin that stretches from ear to ear. "You too," I reply. And I mean every word. "Will you play another?" I ask, adrenaline giving me the courage to speak freely.

"Yes. But on one condition."

I release a skeptical sigh. "Which is?"

"Whichever song I choose, I want you to sing it as I play."

My stomach twists on a dime. "Laz, no." I shake my head. "Y-You don't want to hear me sing. Trust me."

"I must disagree. You were just singing a moment ago. It was beau—"

"We were singing together." Oh God. "And the piano was so loud, you could barely hear. That doesn't count."

"Then I won't play."

I sigh more heavily this time. *Fuck.* "Okay. But what if I don't know the song?"

"Then I'll select another until we come upon one you know."

"What's to stop me from pretending I don't know any of the songs you select so I don't have to sing?" I wince at the notion that I just exposed my hand. But goddamn, that adrenaline is like liquid courage.

When he gives me a slight tilt of his head, I can't help but lock eyes on him and question whether I've screwed up somehow. His face, as if etched in stone, conveys no hints of what he may say next.

"Trust," he finally speaks. "That's what will stop you. And it's how I'll know you aren't lying to me."

I acquiesce with a gentle nod. "I'll sing. You pick the song, and I'll sing if I know it. You have my word."

"Very good," he replies, bumping my chin with a hooked finger before turning back to the piano. He caresses the keys in a sly display of fortitude as I wait with nervous anticipation of which song I'm doomed to sing.

The song is slow, a tender cadence that ripples through his fingertips and flows into our little sliver of the world.

I recognize it instantly. It would never be my first choice to showcase what little singing abilities I possess. But a promise is a promise.

With nervousness far exceeding my comfort, I sing. My voice is nothing like Stevie Nicks, the woman who originally brought the song "Rhiannon" to life. And I don't try to make it so. Instead, I sing of a woman of true independence, incapable of keeping both feet on the ground, with my own voice on full display. Avoiding Laz in my periphery and instead diverting my attention to the candles atop the piano, I sing about a woman who takes to the sky, drifts with the wind in body and spirit, and emulates the darkness both physically and in dreams. I make special efforts to showcase the vibrato in my voice, an extra touch that always made Papa beam with pride.

My nerves subside after the first verse. With confidence reached only with the realization that I'm completely alone, underground, with no one to hear me but Laz, I sing with utmost poise. Composure ignites me with newfound grace as I bring the song to its coda, a light vibrato resonating at the base of my throat with the final note.

Rapid breaths assault my lungs as I await his critique.

His eyes are on me; I can feel it.

"You sing beautifully." His voice is so soft that it rings like a silver bell in my ear, and his face is devoid of all signs of judgment. I can't help but believe him.

It doesn't stop me from shaking my head, though.

"Don't do that," he berates. "Don't dismiss or minimize your gifts. Your voice is beautiful, and I don't make such statements lightly."

My stomach performs a dizzying flip.

"Did she also have a beautiful singing voice?" I ask, alluding to my mother.

He nods. "But yours is different. Did Gino teach you how to control your voice?"

I pause, reminding myself that the name *Gino* is referring to Papa. "No. We sang often. He would pluck away at his guitar, and I would play my cello. Or we would sing along with the radio whenever the mood struck. It was a surefire way to get me to laugh, so we often sang during harder times. Especially after he grew sick..."

A rigid pause cuts my unintentional confession short.

He's the first to break it wide open. "It sounds like I've discovered another talent. You, young lady, are full of surprises." He bumps my shoulder with his, a playful gesture. I take it as a win, and any remnants of trepidation that simmered deep within me subside.

"Of all the songs you could have picked, why 'Rhiannon'?"

"Because she reminds me of you," he answers with pointed certainty.

"Who? Stevie Nicks?"

His lips twitch with a smile. "No. Rhiannon. The Welsh goddess of a great many things, including the moon, femininity... and forgiveness." Candlelight dances within his gaze as he pauses. "She's a woman of strong character and great strength, prevailing in a world that was cruel to her despite their wrongful accusations. She rides a horse as pale as the moonlight and is accompanied by three birds with song so powerful, it can awaken the dead and lull the living to a slumber that lasts years."

Despite my piqued curiosity, and a sliver of intrigue as to how he knows all this, confusion trumps all. "I'm failing to see the connection," I jest.

"Some translations refer to her as the Night Queen. Ruling the darkness with courage and a willful spirit, she transformed her fears into a source of power. Rather than run from the world's cruelties, she learned to rule them. You can too. Don't be a slave to your nightmares, princess. Become their *queen*. I see her strength in you. You're a headstrong little sprite who can take what haunts you and force it straight to its knees. Perhaps in time, you'll learn to rule the night, just as she has."

Heat rises from my abdomen and up into my neck, cheeks, and ears. All the while, fear tugs at my insides at the notion that he's alluding to the nightmares that torture me without warning or remorse. He's seen them once before, and it led to a promise of no more locked doors. But he speaks as if he's heard me—*seen* me— struggle with the demons that tease my mind and make me wish for death beyond that one encounter. My stomach drops when I recall that he's been in my room without me knowing, leaving notes on my nightstand, and...what else? If I was once again crying, scream- ing, or lifeless with paralytic fear, and he bore witness, he never said a word.

It tears me up inside. Hitting me with an unforgiving stroke, the desire to be held during my darkest moments plagues me. Just as James held me. I *need* it. Goddamn, how I need it.

If this is recurring, it's only a matter of time before he insists on knowing the entire truth. The question is, do I tell him? I let James in because I wanted—no, *needed* to trust him with my secrets to surrender my heart. Laz, well, I need to trust him too. But for a very different reason. To conquer the darkness that resides within these walls, within my flesh and mind, and take back the night—to *rule* it, as its queen? Yes.

A thousand times, yes.

If only I could find the courage to take such bold steps with my captor.

"I'm flattered" is all I can squeak out, my mind racing a mile a minute.

"I mean every word," he whispers. Before I can mutter a retort, he runs his fingers over the keys, poised to begin again.

With a dramatic glissando that rouses the entire room, the song "Saturday Night" fills my ears with its lively attitude. As his fingers dance across the keys and I clap to the rowdy beat, we sing in perfect harmony—with great difficulty, however, as our duets are frequently spliced with bouts of laughter.

We laugh until my sides split, begging for respite, and my lungs grow tight with a pleasurable ache.

Even as the sun slips below the horizon and Rhiannon's moon rises high in the velvet sky...

We laugh.

CHAPTER 14
LAZARO

JUNE 12TH — DAY 16

It's been nearly eight minutes since she last muttered the word *Papa*. Her breathing has mellowed, and her fingers now rest delicately amid the short hairs on my chest. I resist the urge to tilt her face toward me and kiss her lips. I've certainly dreamed of doing so nearly every night since she arrived. But I don't wish to wake her—to disturb her long-awaited peaceful rest. And lying still in my arms as she releases steady, warm breaths upon my skin is second only to that elusive kiss itself.

For now, holding her against me is everything I need.

I trail a lazy finger over her bare shoulder as she falls deeper into her slumber.

I discovered a whole new hell tonight, one far worse than any I've experienced before despite the countless times I've looked the devil straight in the eye in my lifetime.

Having been stricken by yet another night terror, Evie's cries for *Papa* echoed through the corridors and forced me to bolt upright in my bed. But the sound of her screams was not the worst moment. Nor was the sight of her wide, horrified eyes as she lay frozen in bed, or the choking sounds that pushed from her throat between cries. It was the fact that I was forced to wait it out until her night terror passed.

I frighten her. It's as clear as the scars that mar my face and condemn me to a life of averted glances. As a result, I couldn't risk the poor girl seeing me in her darkest moments. If I raced to her side to hold her as her paralysis rooted deep within her, I feared my presence would only make matters worse. Waiting in the shadows for her affliction to pass, I cursed God or the devil or the entire fucking universe itself for terrorizing her so.

Again.

This is the fifth night since I brought her here that she has awoken me with her cries.

And this is the first night I've worked up the courage to hold her after.

Once a deep sleep overpowered her terrors, I crept from the dark recesses of the room and slid in alongside her, clutching her against me. She fell so seamlessly into my arms, never stirring, with only a gentle murmur of tranquility as I cradled her.

Soon, I alone will be enough to overwhelm her demons. If only she would surrender herself to me, allow me to protect her in all the ways I'm destined, she would never know true fear again.

Her mother used to let me hold her like this. Without a spoken word, I knew Gabriella felt safe in my arms. The way she released delicate sighs against my chest as she rested her head on it, purring as I ran my fingers through her hair...

❧

THE NIGHT WAS AS STILL AS THE STATUES THAT NOW litter my garden. Beneath a velvet sky dotted with stars, she and I lay in the grass behind the shoebox of a house I called home. Silent, we reveled in the serenity of the stillness, our togetherness, and the fluttering of our smitten hearts. I discovered true love that night, at least as much as my silly adolescent heart could fathom love in its most intimate form.

"Look," Gabriella cries, sitting bolt upright and leaving me chilled in her sudden absence. She points upward, the shimmering remnants of a meteor trail streaking across the sky. "We must make a wish," she beams as I sit upright to meet her.

She doesn't wait for permission as she shuts her eyes and moves her lips in a silent prayer. Despite my ingratiating pull to know what those lips are saying, I don't dare ask. I want her wish to come true, whatever it may be.

"Did you wish for something, Laz?" she asks, her dark hair catching the moonlight as it sways across her back.

"Y-Yes," I murmur. My heart is in my throat, and I berate myself for not wishing for a better poker face or a more controlled heart.

Perhaps a tongue that isn't in knots.

Wordless, she awaits my confession with eager eyes.

But my insides are too twisted up to admit my wish. Despite the way her pale-green eyes seem to illuminate the night all on their own, pulling me in with a vivacity my young heart is too weak to deny, I remain silent.

"I'll tell you my wish if you tell me yours," she says, breaking the silence with a warm plea.

"No." I reach for her, placing a gentle palm against her cheek and my thumb over her lips to silence her. A bashful smile splits them apart.

"Why not?" she teases.

"Because if you say it out loud, it won't come true," I whisper. I lean in close, our noses nearly touching. Despite the heat of her breath against my thumb, a nervous shiver courses down my back.

I've never been kissed before. For many long nights, I dreamed about all the sensations that come with it: the taste, the caress of a tongue against mine, the racing of my ravenous heart, the twitch down below that follows. My God, how I want Gabriella to be my first. The girl hasn't left my mind since I laid eyes on her nearly three weeks ago. Since then, I've run my hands through her hair and relished the way she trembled as I held her and traced delicate fingers up and down her arms. Yet countless hours have been spent imagining her taste. Those beautiful lips, pouty to perfection. Untouched—unkissed—same as mine. It's a tragedy, really. Lips like hers need to be kissed. I just don't know if my timid little heart can work up the courage to—

"Then don't say it," she replies, knocking me back into reality. "I want yours to come true too."

Despite the smile she bears, a subtle yet distinct sadness rests within her eyes.

"Are you all right?" I ask.

"Show me," she commands, her voice soft yet surprisingly stern.

I tilt my head. "Show you what?"

"If you can't tell me your wish, then show me."

My mind whirls like a sandstorm, pelting me with all the reasons I should abort the entire night. When all attempts to speak result in only a weird series of stuttering noises, I wait as soft laughter escapes her lips.

"I-I don't know," I begin. My mind is racing so fast, I'm not sure my words are sensical in the slightest.

Or even in English.

She reaches for me, cupping my face in her delicate hands, just as I dreamed of doing to her a thousand times. Leaning in with the grace of a queen, she presses her beautiful lips to mine. The storm falls away to delicate wisps of snow as my mind shifts to focus on one thing.

The only thing that matters.

Her.

And the way her lips fit against mine, with a taste befitting Venus herself. Unlike anything I could've ever imagined, I waste away in them. Each passing second, my mouth begs her to never free me from its entangled love affair with her own.

"You're beautiful," I say, the kiss she bestows upon me giving me the courage to speak my mind.

"You must be seeing your own reflection in my eyes," she replies with a youthful innocence that matches my own. I kiss her again, emboldened with passion and a desperation to hold on to that perfect taste.

CLINGING TO WHAT FELT LIKE A LIFETIME MUDDLED down into a single moment of meteor trails and viridescent eyes, I was so in love after that kiss that I knew there would be no going back after that night.

NEVE'S FINGERS TWITCH, FOLLOWED BY A SMALL SIGH against my chest. The memory of Gabriella fades as I wrap a tighter arm around her daughter and intertwine my fingers in her hair.

I kept my promise, against the odds of never finding Neve after she was taken all those years ago. She's a fighter like her mother, and I ache for the day she realizes that I've brought her here to be her protector, just as Gabriella would have wanted.

But I frighten her. The scars I bear because of her may very well be what makes her elusive heart impossible to capture. If only she could see the man behind the monster. The man who, despite his hair-trigger temper, dreams endlessly of heaven.

Not hell.

And would move mountains for her despite how her eyes linger on the repulsive half of my face.

Gabriella saw me for who I was. Loved me, laughed with me, set her eyes and heart aflame for me.

I couldn't save her after she was taken from me. But I can save Neve. And I will stop at nothing until I know the men who hunt her are vanquished and their world turned to ash, even if I have to strike the match myself.

For now, I'll keep Neve safe by conquering her demons one night terror at a time. And until she stirs from her sleep, alerting me that she is soon to wake, I'll remain right here, keeping her safely enveloped in my arms.

In her mother's place.

CHAPTER 15

EVIE

JUNE 16TH — DAY 20

Bathed in light by the swell of the full moon, I sit upon the terraced grass, legs outstretched and crossed at the ankle, merely existing beneath its elegance. A cone of silver reflects upon the ocean's expanse, illuminating a horizon that leads to a world far beyond my reach. The air is still tonight, but it doesn't hinder the chill that nips at my skin nor the hypnotic roaring tide at the base of the bluff.

Beneath the last full moon, I navigated my way through a twisted hedge maze in search of a man I couldn't bear to lose. In a strange way, the night James and I met seems so long ago. If I allowed it, my mind would be driven mad by everything I wish I'd said if I knew things would end up like this.

Like a restless spirit, Laz's shadow passes by the window that towers behind me. He's watching me. I can feel it.

Running from this place certainly crossed my mind when I slipped past the sleeping guard at the rear terrace doors. But I have no plan, and, to be perfectly honest, I long to enjoy the company of the moon and nothing more tonight.

As I strive to put thoughts of James aside for the sake of a single day without tears shed, I reach for memories that precede him. Last summer, to be exact, brought forth by that celestial beauty above. Before long, the gentle sway of a catamaran overtakes the grass beneath me, and I find myself lying on my back on the boat's trampoline, gazing at that illustrious moon. Jenna lies beside me, a small beam separating us as we embrace the night in a comfortable silence.

Dozens of boats sitting at anchor speckle the waters beyond the Boston Harbor, existing as nothing more than a sliver of dotted lights in the distance from our spot against the dock.

"He called me again," Jenna says out of the blue, interrupting the peaceful silence. "This morning."

I've been staring at the moon for so long, I fear I may go blind. If that's even something the moon can do.

"Who? The guy from the club?" I ask nonchalantly, knowing Jenna will get to the meat of her story whether I press her or not.

"Yeah. David," she reminds me.

"And?" I ask with a little smirk I'm sure will be disguised by the late hour. "Are you going to put this one up to the chase?"

An unusual stillness captures her; Jenna's usually very decisive and not at a loss for words. It's enough to peel my attention away from the stars and turn my head toward her.

"I'm not sure."

But Jenna always makes men chase her. Something isn't right.

"This one scares me, Eves."

Her words knock the wind out of me. "What do you mean?"

Fixated on the sky, her hands behind her head, she replies, "He's very...eager. Assertive..."

"He knows what he wants," I reply with a shrug. "You love that in a man."

"Yes. I do." She locks eyes on me. Despite their ferocity, there's a sadness in them that I hope I'm misreading in the darkness.

She releases a labored sigh. "I'm afraid I might fall in love with him."

I scrunch my face at the notion. We only met the guy a few

weeks ago. To be fair, though, Jenna has certainly made crazier statements and even crazier decisions in the past. In a way, I'm not surprised to hear this. But the trembles coating her words have me waiting in quiet misery.

Water laps against the side of the boat as the sway carries the seconds along. All the while, she remains fixated on me.

"Would that be so terrible?" I ask, concerned by the trepidation in her voice.

She doesn't answer as she looks away, a pensiveness pulling her from the present.

"There's no sense in running away from love, Jen. If it's meant to be," I tell her, hoping to bring that sparkle back into her eyes, "love always has a way of catching up to you eventually."

The grass pricks at my bare legs, bringing me back to the sea of stars that keep a watchful eye over Eden's Green. It's the first time I've really thought about that placid night on the boat with Jen. Her kiss came later that summer—a warm, passionate kiss that withstood many beats of my confused heart. The sweetness of her lips lingered for so long that I'm certain I can still taste it.

But that night on the boat, in hindsight, was seemingly one of many attempts she made these past years to gauge my feelings for her—of how I might react if she fell in love with another. Jenna isn't one to fall in love easily, so I never feared losing our friendship to a man who might sweep her off her feet.

She's been a part of me since the day we met. When she thrusted herself upon my life, there was no turning back. And deep down, I knew nothing could ever tear us apart.

A surprise kiss—though tender and rife with affection—was no exception.

I certainly never dreamed that she would be snatched from my life under circumstances as outrageous as these. For the first time, I'm truly frightened that I may never see that sly smile or beautiful hair, or hear her snort with laughter again.

"She's magnificent, isn't she?" Laz says in his quiet approach, his face angled toward the moon.

With Jenna the only thing on my mind, I whisper, "Yes."

He makes no move to sit beside me, but his closeness is felt all the same as I crane my neck from below.

"It's late," he says, meeting my gaze.

I huff a laugh as I lie back on my elbows. "Do I have a curfew now?"

"Not exactly," he replies, his tone soft but his face as placid as that starry sky. I'm learning to embrace the little victories, regardless of how small they may be.

Lightheartedness seems to soften his stance, his hands tucked in his pockets.

"Can I ask you for a favor?" I ask, watching him stare at the sea. His attention follows my voice to the grass at his feet.

"Ask me anything, little one, and it will be done. Within reason, of course."

I hesitate, searching for the right approach to such a request as I sit upright. In the end, I come up with nothing, so I just blurt it out. "Would you permit me to call Jenna?" I ask in my most dulcet tone.

He shifts to square his body with mine. "Absolutely not—"

"Please, Laz." I climb to my feet. "I wouldn't say a word about you or where I am. You would be there to listen, to know that I'm not saying anything out of turn—"

He holds up a hand to silence me. "Do you take me for a fool?"

"Of course not," I reply out of sheer panic. "She needs to know that I'm okay—"

"No."

"Then permit David to tell her that I'm all right. Please. She must be worried sick, and I can't stomach the thought—"

"It's out of the question," he barks. Fear forces me to take a step back.

"At least let me write her a letter—"

"This conversation's over," he states with a grimace that makes my blood turn to ice.

"What conversation?" I sneer. "You screaming at me for asking for a simple favor?" I cross my arms over my chest, willing him to challenge me. I debate calling him a fucking coward. But who knows what that would lead to next.

"There's nothing simple about that favor, and you know it." He turns away and heads back toward the house. My cheeks and ears are aflame as all the curse words befitting such a man run rampant in my mind.

He reaches the terrace doors right as I holler, "Then, can I at least get a new goddamn door for my room?"

Without a quip or glance, he slips into the house, leaving me alone with that cursed moon and all the longing that comes with it.

CHAPTER 16
EVIE

JUNE 17TH — DAY 21

Amends must be made. Finding my way back to his good side and staying there is my only hope of ever being granted permission to contact Jenna. It's a notion I made peace with at the expense of a decent night's rest last night.

As a result, Laz's absence weighs heavy on my mind. I await him at breakfast, yearning for a glimpse of that warmth in his eyes despite the cruelty that lurks somewhere in their cast shadows.

And the chance to set things right.

But the breakfast table is graced with my presence alone, and I eat in bitter silence, wondering where the lord of the manor has scampered off to. Not a peep through his office door, not a single ruffled paper or heavy sigh—sounds I've grown accustomed to as I pass by with featherlight footsteps.

Also absent from the hallowed halls is the sound of clicking shoes. Not that I miss it. In fact, it's the only peace the silence provides.

I peer into each open room as I pass, searching for him—or any signs of life other than the guards, who sit bored at each entrance.

A sudden realization peals through my mind that this unusually empty house may be my only chance to find a flashlight somewhere.

The battery life of David's phone sits at only 8 percent as of this morning, the drop of each percent taking with it another sliver of hope of freedom. Using the flashlight function to explore what little of the passageway I was brave enough to venture has drained it faster than I expected. I made it as far as a stone spiral staircase at the end of the tunnel and lost the courage to see where it led.

Or, if not a flashlight...

A lighter.

Crossing the house with hurried steps, I race back into the kitchen. I throw open the pantry doors, flip the light switch on, and step inside. The full shelves obscure the lighter's hiding place. But I remember precisely where it was.

The oil decanter's dusty-pink hue is prominent among the unremarkable items in the pantry. As I push it aside, a wave of disappointment attacks my insides when I find nothing there. I move the surrounding items, making a concerted effort to put them back in their place before moving on to the next. I shuffle around the entire pantry, even searching the same areas over again, convinced I may have simply missed it.

Unless...

It might be in Laz's pocket.

Shit.

With hands on my hips, I take in a deep breath and try to refocus. The pantry's a bust, but surely there's another lighter or flashlight around here somewhere.

I turn to leave, reaching to pull the doors closed behind me. But my mind shifts focus to a beautiful, sultry sound resonating from somewhere unseen. I fall still, tilting an ear in all directions. Though faint, it's a delicate, sweet sound that makes all others fade in its presence. Suspecting where it may be coming from, and why it's so distant, I reenter the pantry and press my ear to the passageway door.

Mimicking Laz's actions, I press alongside the seam in the wall until I hear the telling *click*. The door pops ajar, and I pull it inward with mild difficulty. It's much heavier than I imagined.

The passage is pitch black, as expected. Yet those delicate musical notes resound louder than before. Reveling in their rhythm, I hesitate, lost in the reverie and the way they pulsate up the stone staircase ahead.

My eyes slowly adjust to the darkness as I inch inside, following nothing but the music. With outstretched fingers, I guide myself along the rough wall as the light from the pantry dissipates, and I descend the stairs with slow, intentional steps. I pray for my eyes to adjust, but my wishes prove fruitless, each step pulling me into thicker darkness than the last. When I reach the bottom with precarious footing, I exhale with relief.

The music has grown loud enough that I can no longer hear the rapping of my racing heart. Down the tunnel, a speck of golden light appears off to the left, peeking from the speakeasy door that sits partially open.

I creep down the hall and peek inside.

Laz sits with his back to me from his seat at the piano. His body gently sways as his fingers bear the brunt of the rhythm, so graceful with their intent as they saunter across the piano keys, filling the room and the passageway with a seamless melody.

I know this song.

Pressing my forehead against the doorframe, I watch him as the song tugs at my memory.

Then it hits me.

Without anyone singing the lyrics, it was a bit more difficult to place. But in a flash, the notes bring to mind an ethereal Juliet, adorned in angel wings as she meets the onlooking gaze of her precious Romeo. Her knight in shining armor in more ways than one, as he's dressed as an actual knight while the rest of the crowd masquerades about under the roof of House Capulet.

Laz's body moves with a more dramatic spirit as he reaches the crescendo of "I'm Kissing You" by Des'ree.

Before long, I realize I'm not breathing. Standing captivated in the doorway, my presence unknown, I watch him make beautiful music in the heavy gleam of the candlelight. Dozens of lit candles decorate the room once again, spilling more wax upon their respective surfaces in ivory spears.

Transported by song to fair Verona, I relish the romance between Shakespeare's most infamous lovers. Two children of opposing houses, both naive and woefully stubborn, making the ultimate sacrifice without permission or regret.

All for the sake of love.

I close my eyes, surrendering myself to the dreams the music elicits. The room's golden tones pierce through my eyelids, and in its warmth, I see hair of wildfire red, fair skin, and a smile that lances my soul.

Jenna.

With her every exhale, her hair wisps about, dancing across her face as she locks eyes with mine. She calls to me with merely a look, and I obey with a racing heart and a kaleidoscope of butterflies in my gut. My heart aches for her. I miss her more than I could ever tell her—more than she would ever believe.

The candlelight bounces across my eyelids, intertwining with her hair aflame. Frozen in an unmistakable calm, I wait for her to say something—to ease my suffering as I pine for James to find me again, just as he swore he always would. Jenna always knows what to say in my worst moments, or when my tongue betrays me and my mind goes blank. But she says nothing. She merely smiles with that wicked little grin of hers, like she knows everyone's secrets better than they do, and reaches for my hand. Her touch is so gentle, I barely feel it at all. But when she raises my palm to her sensuous lips, I feel everything—*everywhere*—in a single instant.

The tingle that takes root down below, and the way my stomach flips from her kiss, is unexpected but certain. My pulse, once an indicator of fear and betrayal in the past, has now forced my eyes wide open. Just as it did with James, it's bringing forth something altogether new, and I can't seem to make sense of it.

As the song ends, I feel oddly vulnerable in the sudden absence of its notes—like a lullaby cut short as a child reaches the brink of sleep. Jenna fades from sight along with the music, and I ache for her with leaden lungs.

Laz trails his fingers across the keys, playing another song with a soft, hypnotic sound. I don't recognize it, but it's beautiful all the same.

This newfound sense of longing for Jenna—matched only by that which I feel for James—dances across my flesh like Laz's fingertips on the piano. Perhaps it's sheer longing for the woman I've adored for so long, and fear that we may never see each other again, that prickles my skin in such a manner.

Perhaps it's loneliness.

All I know is, one thing is certain: I care about Jenna and James more than my tortured heart can bear.

With the certainty of tomorrow's dawn, I make an unspoken surrender to Laz. I won't argue with or disobey him anymore.

Because Jenna's safety depends on my cooperation.

And I cherish her enough to finally obey.

With a deep exhale, I breach the entrance of the old speakeasy, the flames casting vivacious shadows that create a false audience to Laz's concert. Almost trancelike, he carries on, and I debate making a noise so as not to startle him.

As if reading my mind, he looks over his shoulder.

I stop.

My heart skips a beat as I await his wrath. But he merely regards me with soft eyes and, without missing a single note, spins back around and returns his attention to the piano. My presence is clearly of no consequence, as he neither scolds me nor motions me to come closer.

With silent steps, I continue, still uncertain as to why I'm even here. Swept up in the wistful sound of his talents, my spirit filled with vigor coupled with apprehension, I don't plan my next move. I simply make it.

I reach him, the warmth of the candles doing my flushed cheeks no favors. He doesn't stop playing, despite how he must sense my closeness.

Bending low, I brush my hands down his chest, embracing him in a hug from behind. The music halts as my cheek presses against his handsome one. He doesn't say a word, but he also doesn't push me away. His surprise is palpable as his chest heaves under my touch.

He turns to face me, his nose bumping my cheek and his breathing ragged. I ignore it and continue sliding my hands over his chest, past that mysterious key that hangs around his neck, down...

With as much subtlety as I can muster, I run a hand toward his pant pockets in search of the lighter. But just as my touch glides over his muscular abdomen, I fall motionless when his lips press against my throat in a soft kiss. My legs are unsteady. Several beats pass before he removes his lips, his breath hot against the skin he just took for his own. I swallow deeply, frozen in place, my mind tussling with whether I'm more caught off guard by the kiss itself or the unexpected softness of his lips. It's a gentleness I certainly never expected, and my stomach betrays me with a drunken twirl of excitement.

Withdrawing my touch, I move to the side to catch his eye. But with a quick movement that I did not anticipate, he pulls me onto his lap with a firm arm around my waist. I land with less grace than I would have liked, my hip catching a handful of piano keys and filling the hollow room with an echo of dead notes.

An unintentional laugh escapes me as I land right where he wants me, and I wrap my arms around his neck for balance. He smiles at our closeness, and I return it for the sake of my unspoken promise to Jenna.

In an attempt to disguise my shaky nerves, I lock eyes on him. What I find there is enough to calm my rapid heart, even if only for a moment. For the first time, I'm close enough—and *still* enough—to appreciate his smokey eyes. A vivid combination of blue and gray, like a crystalline bay beneath a bank of nimbus clouds. They pull me in in a way my inner pluviophile craves. With the silly thought of knowing I'm a weirdo who's more enticed by rainstorms than sunny days, I exhale a gentle laugh.

"What is it?" he asks with a light smile as he tucks my hair behind my ear.

"It's nothing. I—" I hesitate, still unclear about the lines I've drawn for myself when it comes to Laz. He traces a finger along the crown of my bare shoulder, then down my back and across my shoulder blade. Goose bumps plague my flesh with his tantalizing touch. I both hate and adore the way my body responds to him.

He begs me to continue with an unwavering look.

"Your eyes always seemed so gray before. I just never noticed how much blue there is in them."

"You really are an artist," he replies.

I squint in confusion.

"To be able to distinguish such colors, especially in this poor lighting." He bumps his chin toward the rest of the room.

"Or maybe I'm finally allowing myself to really look…"

The creases along the outside of his eyes are enhanced in the room's soft glow, riddled with wisdom I imagine dwells within. I search them for answers to my plethora of questions. But they're nowhere to be found in that piercing gaze.

So I reach for them.

Without thinking, I raise a hand to his cheek. Shocked, he recoils and grabs my hand before it lands on his face. I flinch at the sudden movement and regard him with horror as I realize how close

I came to touching his scars. They had eluded me since I arrived inside the speakeasy, even after I was pulled onto his lap.

The flickering light casts eerie shadows across the disfigurement; shadows I'm now seeing for the first time. His furrowed brow gives him a menacing look despite the hurt that lies in his downturned eyes.

"I-I'm sorry," I stammer.

"Why did you come here?" he asks in a low growl.

"I—" Jenna's red hair flashes before me. "I came here to make peace with you."

He regards me with a look of intrigue. "You did?"

"I don't want to fight with you anymore, Laz. I can't." A shallow sigh teases past my lips. "If this is my future, being here with you, I can't continue swimming against your current. I just needed to tell you..." Unable to meet whatever victorious smirk may grace his face, I look away.

Catching the light from atop the piano, the Zippo lighter sits amid the fingers of candle wax that have spread across its surface.

I ignore it.

For now.

He forces me to face him with a hooked finger under my chin. Much to my surprise, I see neither victory nor smugness on his face. Instead, I'm met with softened features and an endearment reborn.

"You have no idea how long I've waited to hear you say that," he says so softly that it's nearly a whisper. He doesn't wait for a response. Leaning in, he plants a kiss on my naked shoulder as he pulls me close.

And I let him.

In a way I can't fathom, let alone explain, his light kiss recharges me with a newfound sense of confidence. Perhaps it's because he could have gloated in my most vulnerable moment of surrender? Maybe it's because he could have exploded when I reached for his scars, but he maintained composure and nearly succumbed to timidness?

As he pulls away, I reach for his face again. He jerks from my touch a second time, but I continue reaching for him nonetheless.

"It's okay," I coo. "I'm not going to hurt you."

He seems uncertain, but he doesn't recoil a third time. His eyes remain fixed on mine as I bring my palm to his mess of scars and cup his face in my hand. He twitches ever so lightly under my initial touch. But his eyes close, and he captures my hand with his, securing it against his face. A tremble shakes him, and the longer I keep my hand pressed to his scars, the more his harsh demeanor crumbles and is replaced by one of almost childlike innocence.

I wish I knew what was going through his mind. He seems so frightened, with so little control over his faculties. Yet, at the same time, he seems so at peace. A dueling juxtaposition of emotions I can only imagine is completely foreign to him.

I want him to open his eyes and look at me, to see that my expression bears no judgment or ill-intent. But, as if ashamed, they remain closed. I seize the opportunity to fetch the lighter with my free hand and slip it into my pocket.

"Laz," I whisper. His eyes open then, slowly, uncertain. They are watery, glistening as the candlelight revitalizes them with new life.

In the darkness, with my hand covering the majority of his scars, I can imagine his face as if it bore none at all. He's a handsome man, a lady-killer who has undoubtedly broken more than a few hearts over the years. But his mangled face has hardened him, turning his heart as leaden as his livid eyes. It's nearly impossible for me to imagine him otherwise—softer, gentler...worthy of my mother's love. But in this moment of unspeakable vulnerability, I catch a glimpse of that younger soul for the first time.

"Can I ask you something?" I begin, cutting through the pensive silence.

"As I said. You can ask me anything, little one." He uncages my hand and circles my wrist instead.

I raise a cocky eyebrow as I lower my hand from his face. "Oh really?" I ask. "No quid pro quo?"

"Are you trying to tempt me?" he asks.

I smile and respond with a shrug.

"What is it that you want to know?" He tightens his grip around my waist, pulling me closer, and runs a gentle thumb across my back.

I pause. I know exactly what I want to ask. I just have no idea how to ask it. I choose my next words—and my tone—with caution.

"I want to know..."

His inquisitive look cuts straight through me, and my breath catches.

"H-How did it happen?" I nod toward his scars, my heart hammering so hard that I fear it may break loose and leave me lifeless in his lap. I can sense his discomfort, his suppressed rage, and it scares me to death.

"Please." The dancing flames make his eyes come to life with the vivacity of a shipwreck ablaze in a raging storm. The only thing that has kept me from leaping from his arms and fleeing from the room is the need for his answer.

When he finally inhales and runs a hand over the good side of his chin, I take questionable comfort in how he hasn't raised his voice.

He exhales a soft growl. "It was your father," he admits with a heavy tone. He tightens his grip around my waist. Now that I've opened this floodgate, I'm certain it's a subtle move to ensure I'm not going anywhere.

"Father? You mean Frank?" My jaw falls slack, and I make no move to mask my surprise.

"Yes," he says, his face like stone.

"Why would he do this—"

"To punish me," he interrupts. "He thought I was the one who took you."

"When I was little?"

He nods, his eyes plagued with a sadness that rips my heart wide open. But the anger that simmers just beneath stalls me. I question whether it's safe to nudge the conversation forward.

Much to my relief, he breaks the silence and says, "After you went missing that night, your father went on a rampage. No one was safe from his endless interrogations and torturous blades. Some men didn't make it. They genuinely had no idea where you were. But Frank didn't believe them, and he slit their throats all the same."

I gasp and shift uncomfortably, and he loosens his grip until I'm settled.

"I can't believe it," I whisper.

"What can't you believe? Frank is a criminal. A *monster*. Are you still so surprised that he's capable of murder? After everything he's done? To you? To your mother—" He stops himself, and I lock eyes on him in a flash.

"What about my mother?" I ask in a panic. "What happened to her?" My throat pinches as I look upon him in horror.

"Which answers would you like first?" He runs an irritated hand through his hair.

I almost apologize but stop myself. I'm not sorry for asking so many questions, and I'm certainly unapologetic for inquiring about what happened to my mother. He'll have to suck it up and deal with it.

At the same time, I realize how overwhelming this must be for him. He clearly doesn't want to talk about any of this but is willing to do so for me. I shouldn't count my blessings. So I don't press the issue.

For now, at least.

"I didn't mean to change course," I tell him with the utmost delicacy. I urge him to continue by running my fingers along the nape of his neck.

He sighs against my shoulder, gives it another gentle kiss, and continues.

"It was only a matter of time before Frank and his men came around to me. I still worked for him at that time, and I never gave him reason to suspect I was up to any foul play, even though I had imagined killing him more than a thousand times, in a thousand different ways. But after so many people were held to the knife, victim to answers they didn't have, we all knew no one was safe. He was so hell-bent on finding you, in a way that seemed to exceed the frantic concern of a loving father. He was out of his mind. And everyone, even those who worked for him, was terrified of him.

"He showed up unannounced at my house one night with seven of his men. He invited himself in, had me surrounded in seconds, and demanded that I tell him where you were. By then, I knew Gino had you, and I knew what danger you were in if Frank ever found you. I intended to do everything in my power to make sure you weren't found. It was a secret I swore to take to my grave."

"What danger? What secret?" I ask with an exasperated breath.

He runs his fingers through my hair like a father coddling a frightened child, and I instantly think of Papa. Despite the golden hue in our little slice of the speakeasy, the conversation has me so scared that I'm now painfully aware of how dark the rest of the room is. Shadows loom all around us, quaking in the flames, sending chills straight up the back of my neck.

He continues, "I refused to answer his questions. Reminded him how long we've known each other and how I've never given him any reason not to trust me. But, as I said, he'd completely lost his mind by that point and resorted to torturing even his most faithful subjects." He looks away, lost in another moment in time, and I fear what awaits him there. "He rejected my reasoning, my attempts at civility, and..." His fingers come to rest in my hair behind my ear, his touch unexpectedly warm.

"You don't have to tell me," I begin, despite my unyielding need for answers. The sadness in his eyes is enough to make me want to put an end to this. If he'll comply.

"They grabbed me, dragged me into my kitchen, removed the stove grates, and set it alight."

"Laz, you don't—" My stomach churns, suspecting where this story is heading and regretting that I ever asked the question at all.

"They held my face to the flame, demanding a confession. I fought so hard, but there were too many of them, and my screams went unacknowledged. It was useless. There was no reasoning with him, no convincing him I had nothing to do with your disappearance. He was on a mission—frenzied beyond even the most questionable levels of sanity—and he would stop at nothing until he found you."

"But you knew who took me," I reply, suppressing tears that tease at my throat. "You could've told him that much, at least. He never would've hurt you like this—"

"I was never going to give you up," he barks, making my heart skip. I search his eyes for clarification. As if suspecting my intentions, he averts his gaze, and I'm faced with his scars.

"I was never going to give him anything as it pertained to you." His voice softens. "That's all I meant."

I can't withhold my tears any longer.

"This is all my fault," I whisper, shifting off his lap. He tightens his grip around my waist, but I break free and slide over onto the bench beside him, facing away from the piano.

"Don't ever think such things, let alone speak them," he warns as he spins away from the piano and reaches for me. I slink away, but with a quick tug at my elbow, he pulls me back to him. I refuse his gesture of closeness and sink to the floor at his feet instead, suddenly exhausted.

"How can I not?" I say, weary with regret from a decision I never made. "If it wasn't for me, they never would have done this to you." I glance at the right side of his face. "It's deplorable. Unspeakable. I—" I shake my head, failing to find the proper words to convey how awestruck I am. "How could you not kill him?" I whisper.

He tilts his head toward me as if seeing if he heard me correctly. I don't wait for him to retort. "How could you not kill the man who did this to you?" I reach for his scarred cheek, but he stops me by taking my hand in his.

His eyes bounce between mine, as if searching them for his own answers—answers to questions I may never understand. As my mind reels with the possibilities, he says, "I've thought about killing your father every day since I was seventeen. But I can't seem to come up with a way that's befitting of what he truly deserves."

"Please don't call him my father," I beg. He rests our coupled hands on his knee, and I prop myself against him. "I have only one father. Papa was—"

Papa.

"Hold on." I stop. "You said you knew who took me when I was little. How did you know that Eugene—er, I mean Gino—had taken me? I didn't think anyone knew?"

He squeezes my hand as he exhales a cumbersome sigh. Now it's my turn to search his face for answers.

"Your mother..."

I perk up at the mention of her, straightening my back as I crane my neck to lock eyes with him.

"She came across some egregious information your father— sorry, *Frank*—had hidden in his office. She told me everything. You were in serious danger, and it was critical that you be taken as far away from Boston as possible."

"Wait." My heart is stampeding out of control. "*My mother* orchestrated this? She's the reason I was taken? How on earth—"

He nods, his eyes glazing over with a haze that both frightens me and piques my curiosity. "Remember, princess, your mother was taken against her will when she was a girl. She was a prisoner and, therefore, was rarely ever left alone. Plotting a way to have her only daughter sent away, unnoticed, and have it look like she knew nothing about it was no easy feat when always under someone's watchful eye. Your papa was the only person she was frequently left with unattended."

"Why's that?"

"Because he was her seamster."

I lean away in surprise. "He was her tailor?" Papa was always quick to stitch up holes in the knees of my jeans, to let the hem out as I began outgrowing my clothes until we could afford new ones. But I never knew him to possess the skills of an actual seamster. Certainly not one who would be tasked with making the clothing of the wife of one of the most powerful men on the East Coast.

"Semantics," he replies. "She was often escorted to her private seamster's shop, which, over time, only serviced Gabriella due to the fat wads of cash Frank would give him for his full-time services. He never wanted his wife to wear the same thing twice. Such travesties would only show the world that his finances had limits. And the boss found that completely unacceptable.

"Gabriella confided in me one evening, not long after you disappeared, that she had arranged for Gino to take you all along. But she had to make it look like a random kidnapping so he would at least have a head start to get you as far away from Boston as possible. She hoped Frank would suspect his enemies, another crime syndicate known as the Sabbie Mobili, a nasty Sicilian gang that stuck around just long enough to intercept Frank's imports that were en route to the mainland before taking their pillages back to Italy without a trace."

I shake my head in disbelief. "Did it work? Did he suspect them?"

"Not really. At least not as long as she hoped."

Although I already know this story ends with me right here on Eden's Green, in the hands of Lazaro Moretti, the story still manages to draw suspense.

"Once she told me, I offered her money to send to Gino," he continues. "Everything I had was hers if she wanted it, to ensure you wanted for nothing. But she refused. She had squirreled away money for months to give to Gino when the time came. And she insisted she kept me in the dark so Frank wouldn't harm me if his questioning came around to me."

"But she told you about Gino. She put you in danger just by letting you know her plan. Why would she do something like that?" My words eke out at a higher pitch than I intended.

"Because she needed someone to talk to, and she knew she could trust me." Laz smiles, and even though I don't understand what could possibly make him smile at a time like this, it comforts my frayed nerves. "She knew I would never tell Frank who took you. Even if it cost me my life."

Draping my arm over his knee, I rest my cheek upon it and sigh heavily. I can't remember the last time I was this exhausted. Everything about my life feels like a lie. To discover that I knew so little about who I am, where I came from, and who my real parents are is enough to drive me mad. On top of that, the only constants in my life, Jenna and James, are ones I may never see again.

He runs his fingers through my hair, petting me as I beg the candlelight to spell out the answers I need within the shadows they cast. Skirting across the floor within arm's reach, they call to me, and I fall, almost trancelike, into the reflected flames.

"You seem to hate Papa," I mutter, unmoving as I stare off into the distance. "You speak of him so vehemently. If he was only trying to fulfill my mother's wishes and help get me away from Frank, why do you hate him so?"

He continues gliding his gentle fingers through my hair. In an instant, his breath is warm against my ear. "Because I wanted you."

I pop my head up, meeting his gaze, shocked.

"After you disappeared, and she finally told me what she had done, I demanded she explain why him. Why did she never think to entrust you with me instead? I reassured her that I would have done everything in my power to keep you safe. That I would've taken you to the other side of the world if necessary. But she held firm with her decision. No one would suspect him. At least not right away. A seamster bears witness to so many things but is rarely *seen*. And Gino had apparently always wanted children. He was kind and gentle, and she knew you would be in good hands with him. According to your mother, Gino obliged easily when she laid out her plan, regardless of the danger it put him in. He adored you. But honestly, I think that was only part of it.

"No matter what I said, she never seemed to regret her decision to give you to him. And, over time, I grew angry out of spite. Out of guilt..." He trails off.

"Guilt?"

He inhales deeply. "When I pleaded with her to justify her decision, she said she wanted a better life for you than the one I could give. A safer life. One far beyond the reaches of Frank's empire, of which I was a part. Even if she knew she would never recover from the pain of sending you away, giving you to Gino was the safest choice.

"I told her I would've left it all behind. But I don't think she saw a path forward that would've worked if she gave you to me. And I hated that, in immersing myself in Frank's crime syndicate to keep an eye on her and one day get her back, I inevitably lost you in the process." He looks away, and I follow his gaze to nothing more than a myriad of shadows.

"You loved her," I say. It isn't a question, and I'm not sure why I said it aloud.

"Yes." He regards me with a sullen face. "I couldn't save her. And for that, I'll never forgive myself. I promised her that I would take her secret to my grave. That I would do everything in my power to keep Frank off your trail and keep you safe for as long as I could. I couldn't save her, Neve. But I could still save you."

I look away, a slow irritation building at his incessant use of the name *Neve*. And it's undoubtedly showing on my face.

Cutting in before I have the chance to speak, he says, "Why do you take such an issue with the name your mother gave you?" His face twists with frustration, and it's unfriendly at best in this wicked light.

I shake my head, but this time, it's out of confusion and a need to stall as I find the proper words that won't upset him. "It feels wrong. I don't know. It's not the name I was raised with. It's not the name Papa gave me. It just feels so dismissive of him and the sacrifices he made to keep me safe."

"And what of the sacrifices your mother made?" he sneers. I've upset him.

"I would never dismiss my mother. Never. Hell, I would give anything to have known her. To speak with her, even if only for a moment. I want more than anything to know her scent or the sound of her voice. But I never will, Laz. My mother holds no memories for me. But Papa, he was my best friend, my companion, the only one who mattered to me for so long. And Evelyn is the name he gave me. Everything else feels like it belongs to someone else. I don't know this Neve person. I don't know her family or her life. Certainly not in the ways you do."

He looks away. "I won't disrespect your mother by calling you by a name she didn't give you. I know part of her plan was making arrangements for Gino to have both of your names changed. But it feels wrong, now that we've found you and have you somewhere safe, to maintain this charade and continue calling you by a false name."

"Well, I won't disrespect Papa by answering to a name he didn't give me when putting everything on the line to give me a new life."

His face softens, and for a moment, it seems as if he may laugh. But he suppresses it, much to my dismay. "It seems we're at an impasse," he replies.

I nod.

"I suppose we need a nickname for you, then, princess."

A light laugh escapes me. "Just not *princess*. Please."

"Okay." He hooks a finger under my chin. "Any suggestions?"

I mull it over but come up with nothing. I shake my head, defeated. "You pick one."

"Stubborn?" He smiles, pleased with himself. "It's befitting, no?"

Laughing at his ridiculousness, I reply, "I told you, Laz. I don't want to fight you anymore. I'm going to make an effort to be more...amicable."

"Obedient?"

"Amicable," I reiterate, proving his point entirely.

He nods in compliance, his mouth stretched in a handsome grin. "Well, then. You have my word that I will never ask anything of you that would take advantage of your newfound obedience."

"*Amicability.*"

"Whatever."

"There's a difference."

He sighs heavily as he concedes. "Is this your way of convincing me there's a better nickname for you other than 'stubborn'?"

"You're right." I look away in playful shame, fidgeting with my snowflake ring as I twist it around my finger.

A heavy silence lingers, the energy shifting as the playfulness fades in lieu of more somber tones. I search his face for understanding, desperate to know what he's thinking and why the sudden change in his expression.

"Is everything all right?" I ask, suppressing the fear that lurks in the expanding pit in my gut. For a while, I forgot how Laz's moods can shift on a dime. I was relishing his openness, his vulnerability, his willingness to let me into the darkest recesses of his soul. It made me feel as if I may be able to return the favor one day. Now, my mind is screaming for me to leave while we still exist in the calm that precedes the storm. But my heart, always without a compass and consistently lost, aches to hold him as he risks devolving into nothing more than a blubbering mess in my arms.

He reaches for my hand and runs his thumb over the snowflake. "She gave this to Gino the night she said goodbye to you for the last time." His eyes glisten in the soft glow. "To give to you one day."

His mouth moves to speak again, but he's wordless.

I can hardly bear it.

"Papa said he wanted me to have it when I was old enough," I say, hoping to reignite the light in his eyes. "He said he destroyed all photographs of her out of grief when she died. Wouldn't even tell me her name because it hurt so much to remember her. I understand now that we didn't have these things because she couldn't risk giving Papa anything of hers. No photographs, no letters. She severed all ties. Giving me this ring was a big enough risk already."

Pausing to give my thundering heart a moment of reprieve, I pray for the strength to forgive her for leaving me alone in this world, in this way. I wished for her so many nights, dreamed of a faceless figure who would scoop me up into her arms and hold me against her bosom. Papa told me she died giving birth to me, and I despised myself for it for far too long. I didn't feel worthy of such a sacrifice.

But it didn't happen that way. The truth has been right in front of me this entire time. I just never knew it. As I gaze down at my ring—*her ring*—I doubt that I'm worthy of this sacrifice either.

"This ring symbolizes so much more than you realize," I tell him. "You gave this to her as a sign of your love for her. And she gave it to me. I'd like to think that, in some way, she was transferring that love to me with this ring. A tangible way for me to always keep her close."

His head falls into his hands, and I chastise myself for the pain I've inflicted despite my best intentions. My throat tightens as I imagine my mother—young, vibrant, with my same reflection—handing her baby to a man who will take her away forever. She made the ultimate sacrifice to keep me safe.

For love.

Laz was ready in an instant to leave behind the only life he knew in order to protect me. Suffering permanent disfiguration as a result and creating a plethora of enemies in his wake.

Also for love.

I only wish I knew whether it was for *my* love.

Or for my mother's.

"I-I'm sorry," I stammer.

"Go," he says, his voice sharp but muffled behind his hands.

"What?"

"Go now. Leave me."

His voice breaks, and I shy away at his demands.

"I'm not leaving you like this—"

"I said *go*," he shouts, standing bolt upright with a rage that rattles me to the core. The bench wobbles and comes to a loud crash against the piano.

I scramble to my feet and race for the door.

Once inside the dark corridor, I freeze outside the speakeasy. It feels wrong to leave him like this.

Shuffling noises echo inside, and after several minutes, a gentle sound comes from the piano once again. Speaking of my mother is one hell of a dangerous trigger. But there are some things I have to know. There will be more questions. There will be more rage. And I will come prepared for it.

As I slide along the wall and come to a halt against the floor, serenaded by song, I imagine love in all its forms. But they fade away to a disfigured face marred by flame—a man bittered by loss and grief, replete with anger, who seems to ache for my tender touch and the promise of a better tomorrow.

CHAPTER 17
EVIE

JUNE 18TH — DAY 22

With three quick flicks of my thumb over the spark wheel, the lighter springs to life with a single flame. I'm weary of its usefulness solely based on the minimal glow it generates in the dark tunnel. It's only a matter of time before Laz realizes it's gone and that it's me who took it. So I need to see how far these tunnels go—and discover a way out—as quickly as possible.

I traverse the corridor with caution, running my fingers along the stone wall for extra guidance and support. A series of iron lanterns devoid of candles line the walls, generating bizarre shadows cast by my lighter.

A cool breeze strikes, riddling my flesh with goose bumps and fluttering my shift dress. I recognize it, though, which makes it easier to follow the raking chill. My breathing takes on a more distinct echo as I come face-to-face with the stone spiral staircase that juts downward into the unknown.

My pulse skyrockets at the sight of such a descent. Who knows how far down it goes?

Or what waits at the bottom.

This is what I came here to do, and goddammit, I'm going to do it.

On the main corridor's wall, opposite the top of the stairs, I draw an arrow pointing in the direction of my bedroom with a yellow grease pencil I snatched from my art room. In order to map out these tunnels, I need to know where I've already been.

And how to get back if I've run out of time.

With one hesitant step at a time, I make my way down the stone steps. They wind downward in a tight spiral, barely wide enough to slink down yet allowing a greater illumination from the licking flame. With every few turns, I draw a yellow arrow on the wall, pointing up the stairs toward my room, then resume tracing my fingers along the wall for balance.

The further I go, the harder it is to proceed past a single step. I hate every second of being down here. If it wasn't for my ring, which I have been rubbing frantically between my fingers, as James taught me, I would likely be a catatonic mess on the floor.

The stairs spill into another hallway, despite their continued descent. I enter the passage, stopping dead in my tracks when my fingers brush against something hard, metal, and freezing cold against the wall. I hover the lighter over it to examine it further.

An iron handle.

But there are no apparent seams in the wall.

The handle turns with ease, and a groan echoes down the passage as the door breaks away from the seams hidden in the stone lines. Shoving it hard with my shoulder, I manage to overpower the door's weight and push it open.

I emerge in a sunlit room, close the lighter with a soft *clink*, and tuck it into my bra.

It's a bedroom, neat and pristine, with a large bed made up of dark linens, a single chaise facing the fireplace opposite the bed, a dresser, and a row of sheer navy curtains drawn back, allowing the room to fill with light.

The secret door swings closed with no help from me, and I turn in a panic to catch it.

But I'm too late. It disappears into a wall with nothing but a giant framed mirror standing in its place alongside the fireplace. I scramble to find a way to open it, to no avail, and realize my only way out is through the bedroom door.

I hurry over and press my ear to it, listening for footsteps, voices, *anything*.

But I hear nothing.

A large photograph on the mantel catches my eye, forcing a lump high into my throat.

As if beyond my control, I step closer to it, wanting—no, *needing*—a closer look.

It's a massive black-and-white photograph, serving as an elegant statement piece. In it stands a young woman, arms outstretched, seemingly mid-spin on the shore of a vast beach. Her hair is windswept behind her, and her dress billows into the surf. She has the darkest hair, the lightest skin...

And my face.

It isn't me. Which means only one thing.

It's my mother.

This must be Lazaro's room.

Without giving it a moment's thought, I race to the dresser and fling open the drawers. I'm not quite sure what I'm looking for. A key to the front door, a cell phone...

After pushing aside stacks of folded clothes in one drawer after the other, I close them with irritation.

I peer at the nightstand next, bare on top save for a single bedside lamp, complete with three simple drawers.

Flinging the top one open, I halt my search as my breath catches. Lying on top is a firearm, silver and polished so clean that I can practically see my reflection in it. Its heft far supersedes what I imagined as I remove it with shaky hands.

It's no key, no cell phone. But it may be the ticket I need to get the hell out of here.

If only I was certain I could pull the trigger.

My head swims with adrenaline and fear as I balance it across both hands, the words *TAURUS* and *.357 MAGNUM* etching themselves into my brain just as they are etched into the gun itself. I brush my thumb along the cylinder. It's locked in place and doesn't spin like I've seen in the movies.

"It's much heavier than it looks, isn't it?" a voice says behind me.

A sharp gasp escapes me, and I nearly drop the gun onto the bed.

Laz is propped against the doorframe, watching me impassively with his hands in his pockets. "Go ahead. Aim it at me."

I falter as my breaths become labored. I've never held a gun in my life, and I have no plan. Yet I raise it all the same. Fear has dead-locked my whirring mind and forced my hand into thinking all other options have abandoned me.

Now's your chance to escape, Evie. You may not get another opportunity.

Shoot him.

"That's it. Make sure to use both hands. You want your grip tight and controlled," he taunts, calling my bluff and playing me for the fool that I am.

Because, despite my desire to kill this man and run like fucking hell, I can't move. Not under that gaze that pierces me, forcing me to list all the ways in which this plan could fail.

I could miss. It's a logical assumption.

He could survive the gunshot, and then who knows what he'll do with me after.

I could kill him and hardly make it to the front door before his men are upon me.

I could make it out the door and end up never finding a way off the island.

"One thing you should know about firearms," he says, stepping into the room. "Is never put your finger on the trigger unless you intend to shoot it." He steps toward me in a slow, calculated manner, his hands remaining in his pockets and those stony eyes unwavering.

I'm gripping the gun with two hands, just as he instructed, but it does little for the way my nerves explode like a goddamn fireworks show.

"Stop," I choke out as he approaches.

"Or what?" he asks. "You're going to kill me? Run out of this house victorious and back to the life that you fear has since forgotten you?"

Forgotten me. The mere idea pricks at me with a thousand needles.

As my mind is berated with a mirage of images—Jenna running her fingers through her fiery hair, James's teeth sinking into my flesh, the thunderous applause that erupts as my bow comes to a final rest across my cello strings, the sound of rain pelting the wet earth—the gun is ripped from my hand, and I'm pushed onto the bed.

"You think you're pretty clever, don't you?" he sneers. "Would you mind telling me how you even got in here?"

I lock eyes on him and fold my arms across my chest in a protective move. "Through the door. How else?"

"Did I give you permission to do so?" he growls. "*Answer me.*"

I shake my head. "No. But I didn't exactly ask, now, did I?"

"You were snooping." He remains stiff as he towers over me. "Care to enlighten me?"

"I was...just..." I glance at the gun in his hand. "Looking for a flashlight."

"A flashlight?" he asks with a cocked brow.

I nod. "Sometimes..." The lie inches its way in. "I like to visit my art studio at night. When I can't sleep. But...the shadows in this house are...not so easily managed."

He sighs and takes a seat beside me on the bed. "You pick an odd time to ask for favors."

"Not favors. Favor. Just one."

"Are we arguing semantics again?" he huffs.

With a shrug, I ignore his need to always have the final word.

The gun lays flat in his hand as he holds it out to me. "Have you ever fired one of these before?" His tone levels out a bit. "Have you ever even held one before today?"

"No," I mumble.

"Well, the first lesson with firearms is to always treat them like they're loaded."

"Oh, believe me, I was," I reply with a sardonic squint.

He regards me with blazing eyes. "Smart-ass. Next time you want to point a gun at me, you may want to make sure the damn thing is loaded rather than just assuming it is." He pops the cylinder open and angles it toward me, and I see straight through all six holes. With a flick of his wrist, the cylinder pops back into place.

"It seems you've found yourself in quite a predicament," he says, followed by a series of *tsks*, sending chills straight into the back of my neck.

"I've tried to give you a home here. I've been doing everything in my power to make sure that your father doesn't find you. To keep you safe. You even expressed that you wouldn't fight me anymore. That you'd be obedient. I'm at my wits end trying to figure out what more I can do."

A pinkish hue overtakes his scars. "You still don't trust me. That's obvious. I just don't..." He trails off, peering at the gun in his lap.

My heart hammers with abandon from the uncertainty of what awaits me.

Finally, he looks at me. "You say you've never fired one of these before. Perhaps we should remedy that. I can teach you how to shoot."

My face scrunches with confusion. "What? Why would you teach me how to handle a gun?"

"Because we're learning to trust each other, remember? What happened here"—he glances around the room—"hasn't changed that. It's a setback, sure, for which I fully intend on punishing you. But it hasn't changed what I'm trying to build here, with you." He traces a finger along the long part of the gun. "You're obviously acting out like this because there's something about being here that still scares you. Maybe I've done a piss-poor job of making you feel like you have the freedoms you need. So if I teach you how to shoot, maybe you'll feel more in control of your own life again."

I have yet to understand how learning how to shoot a gun will make me feel more in control if I'm not then given a gun to keep as my own. But there's a sincerity to his words that makes me consider his offer.

"Okay," I whisper.

The rosy hue of his scars slowly fades, and he continues with a softened tone. "Okay. First, never assume a firearm is unloaded just because someone says it is." He pops the cylinder back out and hands the gun to me. "Examine it. Make sure there is nothing in the cylinder." He thrums his finger over it, forcing it to spin with a series of monotonous clicks. "Hold it," he continues. "Familiarize yourself with its shape, its weight, its...contours."

My cheeks are ablaze under the weight of his gaze and the salacious way he says the word *contours*. The rubber grip does little to disguise the sweat on my palms as I point the firearm toward the floor, just as his grip on my arm commands.

"Never put your finger on the trigger unless you intend to shoot it," he repeats as my index finger lazily wanders toward the trigger. I readjust it as instructed.

He takes the gun from me with gentle hands and snaps the cylinder back into place with another flick of his wrist.

A storm slowly rolls back into his eyes. "Now that you've seen for yourself that it's unloaded..." He straightens his back. "You can receive your punishment."

My stomach plummets to the floor. "What? I—"

"Lie back," he demands.

Blood pounds mercilessly against my eardrums. "Why? Please, I won't—"

"You ask too many questions," he snaps, forcing a startled gasp from my lungs as he grabs me hard by the throat. He pushes me onto my back with a tight grip, then shifts to kneel between my parted legs.

He sets the gun on the bed and runs his free hand under my dress. I draw my knees up instinctively to shy away from his wandering hand, but he's too quick, and my panties are pulled to my ankles in a flash. I try to scream as I claw at the hand that grips my throat, pushing at his arm and wriggling in any way that will put distance between my naked parts and the heat of his body as he hovers over me.

I shove at his massive shoulders and dig my nails into his fore-arms. But it does nothing to make him recoil. If anything, it only makes that fucking smirk appear and those scars take on an even more grotesque, menacing facade.

Cold metal grazes the inside of my thigh. Bucking my hips against the foreign sensation, I fight with what little movement I have left despite his heavy frame pinning me down.

Further and further up my thigh, he snakes his gun until it bumps my peak.

"Don't move," he warns with a cruelty that's better suited for the pits of hell. "The more still you are, the less likely you are to hurt yourself."

I heed his warning despite my unrelenting desire to fight him until my last breath.

"And who knows, you may actually like it..." The tip of the gun penetrates my pink flesh as his words prickle my ears. Deeper and deeper, he forces it inside me, the cold metal pressing against the walls of my most intimate space.

Terrified it may do some real damage if I struggle, just as he warned, I remain frozen in place.

"That's it," he hisses like the fucking snake he is, thrusting it in and out with long, lascivious motions. He leans in closer and releases my neck, trailing his free hand down my body.

Avoiding his gaze, I turn away, and he further cages me in by pressing his forehead to my temple. Hot breath rakes my cheek as he pumps the gun faster inside me, and I wait for tears to fall freely at any moment. But the tears that have been teasing at my throat never find release.

I shut my eyes and imagine a place far from here. James's glasses have drifted down his nose, and I bring a delicate finger to the bridge to push them back into place. His hands are busy, after all, parting my ivory legs and shoving my panties to the side. Those incredible fingers drive into me hard, his lips running in tandem with his tongue over my cheek, down my jawline, and onto the eager flesh of my neck.

A hand reaches low and touches my sex. Two fingers form a V on either side of my clit and caress up and down—a new move for James—mirroring the rhythm of each thrust inside me. My clit aches for direct contact, fuming with anger as it's teased but never touched. It fills to the max regardless, and in an instant, the little bitch is begging for that V to pick up speed.

I cant my hips, bucking them wildly as James rams his cold fingers inside me. A deep, raw moan erupts from my lungs as he plants a firm kiss on my neck.

"Don't stop," I exhale, my body on the verge of exploding all around his invasive fingers.

"Oh fuck, don't stop," I cry out this time, my eyes squeezed tight and my muscles clenching.

Pleasure and unadulterated rage explode from within me, a

sharp scream following close behind. I jerk uncontrollably as my orgasm unfurls through every square inch of my body.

Panting in the aftermath, I wait for James to turn my face toward his and plant a deep, passionate kiss on my lips. But his touch is absent.

I reach for him, slowly opening my eyes, waiting to feel the frame of his glasses or the softness of his cheek.

Instead, my fingers graze over rippled flesh.

My eyes jolt open, and a sharp gasp expels from my parted lips when I see nothing but a mess of scars.

And a pair of thunderous eyes staring down at me.

"*No,*" I whimper, crawling backward on my elbows in horror.

He sits back and tosses his soiled gun onto the nightstand.

"I'm glad you enjoyed your punishment," he torments. "I told you there was a chance you might like it." He stands, peering down at my bare legs and hiked dress. "I'd be lying if I said I didn't also enjoy it."

His laugh shakes me to my core.

"Get yourself together, put some shoes on, and meet me downstairs in ten minutes. I'm going to teach you how to shoot, Neve. How else will you truly appreciate the power of what just fucked you senseless and made a mess of my bedding?"

He disappears from the room without so much as a retort from me.

I want to scream. I want to cry. I want to run so far away from this place that this will all fade to nothing more than a horrible memory.

But as much as I want to slap that smug face and flee from my gilded cage, curiosity has bested me, and I can't trust my own desires anymore.

Perhaps it isn't the gun that's so powerful, but the one who wields it.

And I want to be that powerful. I not only need it to survive, but I *want* it.

To feel alive.

So I grab a pair of shoes as instructed, meet him downstairs, and follow him out the door.

CHAPTER 18
EVIE

The clearing in the woods is filled with afternoon sun, exposing the paper target affixed to a nearby tree.

Apprehension pokes at me with a sharp finger.

"Are you ready to learn how to shoot?" he asks.

Well. Yes and no.

I answer with a single nod, then run a hand over my flitting stomach.

He removes a black handgun from the back of his waistband. It doesn't look like the one from before. This one is blockier, solid black, and lacks the slender part that, well, took me by surprise less than an hour ago.

Laz runs through the basic safety measures and anatomy of the gun—a Glock 21, so I've been informed—pops the magazine out, shows it to me, and then slaps it back in. With a loud *click*, he racks a round into the chamber—so many things I'm learning today—then raises an eyebrow at me before handing it over.

"Widen your stance," he instructs as he moves behind me and presses his frame against mine. "And never put your finger on the trigger unless you intend to shoot." His cheek grazes mine as he leans in and places my hands in the proper positions—one hand on the grip, the other cradling the base. The gun is heavier than I expected, but not quite as heavy as the revolver.

"Keep your elbows bent." His voice rumbles low in my ear. A tremble shakes me when he traces a single finger through my hair, brushing it across the light perspiration that dots my upper back, exposed to his touch courtesy of my dress's scoop neck. It takes several seconds before I realize he was moving my hair out of his way, and I fight the twinge of foolishness that makes me blush.

"This is the front sight," he explains, pointing to the nubbin at the front end of the gun. "You want to use it to aim." He grabs my arms from behind. "Line it up with your target," he tells me softly. "When you're ready—" He drops his hands to my hips, making my clit twinge. "Fire."

I'm nervous as shit. My palms are sweating. What if it blows my hand off? I'm not the right person to be shooting guns. I'm not tough enough—or brave enough. Maybe this wasn't such a good idea...

I close my eyes as I bring the trigger back, and the firearm explodes through the clearing like a fucking bomb went off. A screech billows from my lungs as I damn near drop the thing. Laz is quick to take possession of it, nearly rolling with laughter.

"What the hell?" I cry out, the sound of my voice muffled as my hearing struggles to regain focus.

"The first shot is the hardest, I assure you." A flick of his hand directs me to retake my stance in front of the target.

"I don't think—"

"I insist," he says, his demeanor shifting to more serious notes. "You'll never get it unless you practice."

Squinting, I examine the target from afar, waiting for him to take up his spot behind me. "I didn't hit it," I say, pretending to be disappointed.

"No." He purses his lips as if to suppress laughter. "But you will before we're through here. I promise you."

I PULL MY ARM TAUT AGAINST HIS, HALTING AS WE approach the overgrown end of the snowbell tunnel. A blanket rests upon the array of fallen petals, complete with a basket, two wine glasses, and a bottle of wine inside an ice bucket.

"What is this?" I ask, already knowing the answer but apprehensive at the implication.

"I had lunch laid out for us." He pulls me along with a firm grip. "Come. Join me."

"Hold on a second." I dig in my heels and give him a sideways glance. "Is that a request or a command?"

He sighs heavily. "Neve. Would you please join me for lunch?"

"If you're giving me the choice, I'm going to have to respectfully decline," I reply.

He scrunches his brow. "You decline?"

"That's right. I do." I drop his hand and step away. "What you did to me today was unthinkable. You do realize that?"

He squares his body with mine and folds his arms, piercing me with those torrential eyes. Breaking the silence, he huffs, "I'm waiting."

"For what?" I scoff.

"For you to paint me as some villain in this bullshit tale, inferring I attacked you when you were snooping around in places you shouldn't have been in the first place." A red hue creeps into his face as he clicks his jaw.

"Are you implying that I deserved what you did simply because I was in your room without your permission?"

"You're actually going to stand there and attempt to convince me you didn't enjoy it? You came all over my gun, for fuck's sake," he sneers.

"That's completely unfair. You forced me down and assaulted me on your bed. Do you think I asked for any of that?"

"You writhing beneath me and moaning 'don't stop' sure as hell made it seem like you did."

My shoulders slump in defeat. "Listen. I have no idea what you want from me. You say you brought me here to keep me safe, but then you regard me with salacious looks, touch me in ways I never asked for, and use your lustful prowess as a way to punish me. One minute, you're sweet and kind, generous in a way I never would have expected, and the next, you're downright cruel. You snap at me, storm out of rooms, then lecture *me* about building trust. This back-and-forth is making me insane. And I just want to know, at the end of everything, what is it that you actually want from me?"

He steps away, rubbing the back of his neck, his moans barely audible despite the growing silence between us.

The trees shiver overhead and send a wave of petals dancing to our feet, transforming the space into a snow globe of midsummer blooms.

With an open palm, I catch them as if they are actual snowflakes, my periphery alerting me to Laz moving toward me with a sudden urgency that makes me gasp.

He's on me in a second.

My heart skips as he removes the Glock from the back of his waistband, pops out the loaded magazine, shows it to me, and then shoves it back in place.

A shudder attacks my spine when he slaps the gun into my hand and falls to his knees before me. His grip around my hand is tight, trapping it on the firearm, pressing the muzzle to his forehead.

"What are you doing?" I cry, my voice tortured by the tightening in my chest.

"I've just shown you it's loaded, so now you know that I'm trusting you with my life. You keep that gun pointed right where it is and listen to me closely. Understand?"

I fight the trembling that paralyzes me, his eyes planted on mine. His tone and demeanor are so calm that a wave of confusion and fear amalgamates, ripping me in half.

"I knew nothing of the woman you were before I brought you

here. Only your name, your face, and a promise I made to your late mother. But over the last few weeks, I've come to know you in ways I could've only dreamed. You're a woman who managed to evade the largest crime syndicate in the eastern seaboard during a home invasion when you were only a child. Afterward, you picked up the pieces of your life despite being orphaned by it and forced to navigate this world alone. You are so much stronger than you give yourself credit for.

"You have the power to save yourself, just as you have since you were a child. Now's your chance," he continues. "I'm on my knees, begging you to embrace that fire within and take what you want from me. Even if it costs me my life."

Tears cloud my vision as I watch my captor looking up at me in complete submission.

He isn't asking me to spare his life.

He's begging me to value mine.

I lower the firearm, my hands slowly regaining composure. "I'm not going to shoot you, Laz." I toss the gun onto the picnic blanket, and he hesitates before rising to his feet.

"You ask me what I want?" he says, his voice softening to a silken tone as he reaches for me. "What I want is for you to realize that you aren't the damsel here. You're the goddamn *queen*. Some men base their worth on whether they can swoop in and save the girl. Other men thrive on knowing they've chosen a woman who's powerful enough to save herself in the first place. And you *are* that powerful, Neve. You decide your own destiny, no one else, and I want to help you unleash the queen I know you have inside you. Just give me your heart, your loyalty, your compassion, and I swear to you, I will be your slave."

My heart races as I absorb his declaration, the word *slave* tossing around in my mind like a ship in a raging sea. His scars begin to fade as tears smear them into a blurred uniformity.

"I'd be lying if I said my intentions haven't evolved since you've been here. I brought you here to keep you safe. But over time, I came to realize that you don't need me for that. And it scares me to death. I don't want to lose you, Neve. I made a promise to your mother, but it's so much more than that for me now. I *see* you. In some ways, better than you see yourself."

I brush the back of my hand across my eye, a coolness hitting the wet streak that's left behind.

"I know darkness plagues you," he says. "I have my own that I failed to escape long ago. But you don't have to be its victim. You can be its ruler. Let me show you, and I promise, when you've taken your power back, you will come to find that this"—he looks around the garden tunnel—"is not your prison...it's your *kingdom*."

He pulls me down to the blanket, leans in, and whispers his next words against my ear. "Will you surrender to the darkness and rule with me?"

It's a request.

Not a command.

He examines me closely, waiting for a response. I shy away from his grasp, finding it unbearable to stare into those torrential eyes a second longer.

"What are you asking of me, Laz?" I wrap an arm around my waist despite the warm breeze that ruffles my pale dress. "You wax poetic as if you have feelings for me—"

"Maybe I do," he says.

I turn to him, my brow furrowed and my throat so tight that even breathing hurts.

"That's insane," I reply.

"Why is it so crazy? You fell for a man in less than a *day*. Imagine what your heart can do when given a lifetime."

A lifetime.

This can't be happening.

But despite the fear that makes my feet go numb, there's something about his words, his belief in me—his *submission*—that makes my spirit soar and ignites my darkness with a torch of warmth and devotion.

Even though his words lull me into a tremulous state of affection and acceptance, at the end of it all, I can't shake the real reason he has chosen *me*.

"Because you wouldn't be saying any of this if I didn't have my mother's face." I run my fingers through my hair with a weighted sigh and climb to my feet.

He's quick to follow.

"And I don't wish to be cherished for my mother," I continue.

He closes the gap between us in an instant, his hands coming to rest on my cheeks as he fixates on me. We exchange the same air as he leans in close and regards me with pleading eyes that no longer threaten.

Only adore.

"Listen to me. I won't deny that you possess your mother's ethereal face. You're breathtaking, just as she was. But I swear to you, that's where the resemblance stops. There are so many things that are uniquely you. The way you drum your fingers against your leg when you're nervous, the way you hum the song 'Tiny Dancer' while you paint, how you fidget with the prongs of your snowflake ring when you're deep in conversation, or how you sink into the rhythm of your cello and ignite my entire core with the euphonious music you create. These things are undeniably *yours*, Neve. Not hers. Not anyone's. Only yours. And I adore them."

His eyes bounce between mine for as long as it takes for me to catch my breath. Not waiting for a response—thank God—he sinks back to the blanket, pulls me down into his lap, and cradles me around my waist. With a soft caress of his thumb over my cheekbone, he trails his gaze down to my mouth. When he leans in for a kiss, a torrent of alarm and desire singes my core. I turn away just before our lips touch, and his kiss lands below my ear.

"I'm sorry," I say, choking back the shame of the embarrassment I may have caused.

"A queen never apologizes," he breathes against my cheek, his words like satin against my skin. "Please..." he coos. "Tell me what you need." He rubs his thumb on my back with tender affection.

I know now that I was never his prisoner, at least not in his mind. Quite the opposite, in fact. He yearns to have his power challenged; that much is evident. But he doesn't want it challenged by just anyone. He wants to submit to a companion who is worthy of such trust. Someone who, despite the transfer of power, will always be his true equal.

And he has chosen me as that companion.

Now I understand his adamancy about building such trust in the first place. It isn't to stop me from running. At least, not entirely. It's because it would be impossible for him to submit to me without it. He doesn't just want a promise of companionship and loyalty from me, he *needs* it.

And after living a life in which everyone bends to his whim with a snap of a finger, I can only imagine what an aphrodisiac it must be to find a woman who challenges such power.

Which may be the Achilles heel I need to survive.

But I've never made commands of anyone, always opting to be submissive instead.

I caress his undamaged cheek, not sure what to say.

"Shall I feed you?" he purrs, breaking the silence.

I nod, and his lips stretch wide in a devilish grin as he reaches behind him for the basket. Still holding me firmly in his lap with one arm, he flicks a lid off a container with his thumb. He removes a raspberry and brings it to my lips, and I take it in with a slow curl of my tongue.

"Delicious," I murmur against his ear, running my fingers along the nape of his neck.

He shivers against me as the canopy of blossoms rustles, and a snowfall of petals cascades around us.

With his fingers intertwined in my hair, he pulls me to look at him. I avoid his scars the best I can, my attention fixated on the chiseled jawline and beautifully aging features on the pristine side of his face.

He presses a kiss on the dip of my neck, and my body agrees with a pleasurable ache.

"I'm begging you," he exhales into my neck. "Let me kiss you."

My fingers trail through his black hair, and I release a small moan as he places a second kiss on my neck.

"You just did," I reply, touching the dip where he planted his kisses.

"No, I mean *here*." He runs his thumb over my bottom lip, forcing it open.

"Is that a request or a command?" I torment before kissing his thumb.

He shakes his head slyly but smiles, enjoying this little game.

"May I place a kiss upon your lips?" he asks. His eyes are on fire, searing into me with a desire I've never seen.

"Maybe." I hold his gaze. "If you're good."

He straightens suddenly, a sharp gasp expelling past my lips as he pulls me closer with a rough grip around my waist. His eyes are feral, and a low growl emanates from his chest as he presses me down with what feels like every ounce of his strength. Tension shoots through my legs as his boner digs into my panty-covered apex.

Shit. This has gone too far.

I want to win his trust, but now I'm unsure how to do that and not end up fucking the man.

Based on the way his hard cock makes me throb with violent abandon, at this moment, I'm not too sure I want to find a way out of fucking him.

And it scares me to death.

Thoughts of James spin my mind nearly to the point of nausea, a tumultuous merry-go-round of the man I love and the dwindling hope that he's still out there waiting for me.

Laz fights to bring my lips to his as I jerk away from his attempts. It's a game to him, evident by that little chuckle he emits with each failed attempt.

As far as I'm concerned, I'm willing to break a lot of rules to win my freedom and find my way back to James. But not this one. Laz doesn't get to have my lips. Simply put, they don't belong to him. Hell, none of my body belongs to him. It belongs to the man who claimed it in the pelting rain. But there's something about a kiss on the lips that's far too intimate and makes this feel painfully real.

And he sure as hell doesn't get to fuck me. I would never do that to James. Except now I'm in a delicate position where I have to make Laz *think* he'll have the opportunity at some point.

It's a dance I've never performed.

And it may very well cost me my life.

I have to stop this.

He pulls down the top of my dress, bunching the material as he gropes my breast.

But fuck, it's hard.

Several snowbell petals brush my cheek as I arch my neck, opening it to Laz as he destroys it with a voracious appetite. They fall down the neckline of my dress, tickling my breasts.

"I want you," he groans, his breath hot and his voice animalistic. "I'm your slave. Command me. Tell me what you need..." He gropes at the same breast, harder this time, and I wince slightly.

"Tell me, Gabriella. Please..."

My entire body stiffens, and the air is sucked from my lungs. For a moment, I'm completely frozen, hoping to God my ears betrayed me.

I push against him, stopping his carnal tongue and forcing our eyes to meet. He recoils as he realizes what he's done.

"Shit, Neve. I'm—"

I'm back on my feet in no time, despite his outstretched arms.

It's the exact faux pas I needed to stop this passion play and avoid fucking the man.

But the pain that claws at my insides is something I never expected. He called me by my mother's name. Despite the fact that it's beyond weird, hearing another woman's name on his lips creates a sinking feeling in my stomach that I pray isn't showing on my face.

"I'm so sorry. I..." He's the most crestfallen I've ever seen.

I don't understand the anger that festers inside me. It hurts so much to even look at him. "I need to go." I turn away, but he's back on his feet and stops me with a firm grip on my elbow.

"Don't go. Please. What can I do? Tell me, and I'll make it right. Trust me—"

"There you go with the *trusts* again." I wrench my arm away.

He looks at me with heavy eyes, forcing me to confront their turbulence.

"I suppose it shouldn't surprise me. You've been calling me by the wrong name since I got here." Turning away, I cross my arms, my shoulders slumped with a jealousy I can't shake. His touch on my shoulder is tender, making it impossible to repress the tears that brew in my chest.

"But this one hurt the most," I say. My voice cracks, and I berate myself for not hiding my emotions better.

I rush out of the tunnel before he can respond, away from those pleading eyes, putting as much distance as I can between me and the echoing of my mother's name as it rustles through the ivory trees.

CHAPTER 19

EVIE

JUNE 19ᵀᴴ — DAY 23

I think I might be lost.

The first junction was ages ago, and I've encountered two additional forks in the tunnel system since then. They've yet to lead me to any sort of way out.

At each fork, I went right, leaving an arrow on the wall in grease chalk to help me find my way back. The dampness has increased drastically, evident by the way my clothing is clinging to my wet skin. The lighter flame dances seductively, swaying to its own beat as my shoes slap the small puddles on the floor. Sharp, inverted points of moisture drip along the stone walls, and the only sounds that accompany my heavy breaths are the plink of drops hitting those puddles from above.

Baciato dalla neve—kissed by snow. I feel kissed by snow right now. It's absolutely freezing down here.

The tunnel descends deeper, the air frigid and almost unbearable. But no matter how much I try to stave off the cold, wrapping my arm around my torso or rubbing my arms to ward off the goose bumps, nothing helps.

Just a few more steps. I urge myself to continue despite seeing nothing up ahead. This tunnel has stretched longer than I expected, with no turns, junctions, or exits.

I stop dead in my tracks when a light flashes up ahead, briefly illuminating a metal ladder. With my heart in my throat, I wait. For what, I'm not entirely sure—

Another flash.

With timid steps, I approach. Above the ladder sits a metal grate, its rungs wide. A third flash of light pops from above.

I place the ring back on my finger, shove the chalk into my pocket, and scale the ladder.

Once I reach the top, I position the lighter through the rungs, but the minuscule ring of light pales in comparison to the vast, open space above. I expect to see trees, hear the whispering of leaves, feel the damp chill of the coastal breeze. But all I see is darkness, and there's a stillness on the other side of that grate that sends chills racing down my spine.

Again, that light appears for a split second, then disappears.

I tuck the lighter into my pocket and, through gritted teeth, use all my strength to push hard against the grate. It doesn't budge. It does, however, leave a decent coat of rust on my hands, which I wipe on the ladder rungs.

The lighter is useless, so with each bright flash above, I watch. The brief moments of illumination reveal bits of stone wall and nothing more.

"Who-o-o." My echo reverberates into the darkness above, disappearing high above my head.

And then it dawns on me. This must be the lighthouse on the east bluff. I've seen it a hundred times from the library windows. Laz said it was decommissioned years ago, but it still has a functioning light that's serviced weekly. Feeling a sense of relief that I now know where I am, I descend the ladder and head back the way I came, marking the tunnel walls with arrows and a large *L* for *Lighthouse* as I go.

With a low growl, my stomach reminds me of how long I've lingered down here, tracing and retracing my steps for hours. I slink back to the spiral steps, realizing I've likely been away for too long as it is.

⚜

One of these days, I'll actually count the number of steps in this creepy stairwell that bring me back to a more comfortable temperature as I approach my room from the secret passageway. Because I'm winded as hell.

As I reach the backside of the secret-passageway door leading to my room, a soft clinking noise catches my attention from the other side.

There's someone in my room.

I tuck the lighter in my pocket and press my ear to the cold stone. The clinking has ceased, but there are definitely footsteps. After a few seconds, something closes with a soft *click*. Confusion taints my anxiety at the subtle sound. The last time I was in my room, I still didn't have a door. When I demanded a new one last month out on the terrace grass, I conceded to the forfeit and opted not to bring it up again.

With little certainty that the coast is clear as I doubt the silence beyond, I wait for several noiseless minutes to pass before entering my room.

It's exactly as I left it. Except for my new door and a large bouquet of exquisite red roses sitting in a clear vase on the night-stand. Beside it sits a black flashlight that I've also never seen.

In true Laz fashion, there's a note tucked between the stems:

Please accept my sincerest apologies.
You have every right to be upset.
I just hope you can find it in your
heart to forgive me.
— L

PS A new door for your room,
and a flashlight, per your request.
I never want you to fear the shadows here.

It's certainly a thoughtful gesture, and it warms my heart a bit. Overwhelmed and in need of some release from the anxiety that always comes from exploring the tunnels, I freshen up and head to my art studio.

My painting waits on its easel where I left it, beckoning me to finish. The turret windows bring a plethora of afternoon light into the space, a welcome change from the tunnels that are as dark as my nightmares.

I grab my charcoal pencil from the table of supplies and resharpen its point before taking a seat on the stool.

A knock sounds at the door.

"Come in."

Laz enters but waits by the door after closing it behind him, as if waiting for me to beckon him forth.

So I do.

"I came by your room. But you weren't there."

"Is that right?" I make a concerted effort not to let on that I know about the flowers.

"I was just coming by to apologize..." he begins, walking toward me.

"It's water under the bridge," I lie, dragging my pencil over the canvas to complete my outline. The use of my mother's name still stings, but until I come to terms with why it hurt as much as it did, I can't keep discussing it with him. I need it to be behind us.

My response seems to be enough because he turns his attention to the fireplace, against which all of my completed works are leaning.

He kneels and flips through them—three in total. "These are all of the same woman?"

I kneel beside him as he picks one from the group and holds it up. It's a painting of a woman in a long pink dress, standing on a terrace adorned with flowers while overlooking the ocean. Her back is to us, her fair skin aglow against her long black hair that flutters in the breeze.

"Who is it?" he asks, his eyes alive with avid interest.

I shake my head with uncertainty. "It's..." It's tricky to explain. "As you know, I never knew my mother, and I've spent my life wondering what she looked like. So whenever I paint, it always ends up being of a woman I imagine bearing her likeness."

He returns his attention to the painting. "But she isn't facing us in any of these."

"Yeah," I whisper, blushing with unexpected shame. "I never knew what she looked like." I never told Laz about the photograph David gave me. And I don't think I ever will. Keeping it to myself is like having a piece of her that's only mine.

He sets it back down with the others and stands. "Sure you do. Every time you look in the mirror, Neve, you see her face." Now it's my belly that's blushing as he holds my gaze. Straightening his vest, he makes his way over to the charcoal outline on the easel. "This is your chance." He gestures to the canvas. "To make one where you can see her face."

I smile at the thought and certainly consider it. "You're right." As I stand, the lighter shifts in my pocket, and a chill shoots up my spine. I completely forgot it was in there, and I never know when Laz is going to get handsy these days. He can't know that I have it.

I walk over to the supply table and set my charcoal pencil down. Looking over my shoulder, I note that Laz has meandered over by the windows. I remove the lighter and slip it into the canister of paintbrushes right as he turns back around to face me. My heart stops, unsure if he saw me.

He pulls another stool over and sets it beside mine. "Do you mind if I watch for a bit?"

I breathe a heavy sigh of relief.

With my charcoal pencil in tow, I join him. The art springs to life with each stroke, the face, gown, and flowing hair all coming into view. She stands on a grand staircase that spills wide at the bottom, with curves that match her own. A magnificent chandelier hangs overhead, with angular, gothic windows in the background.

His scars are on full display as he gawks at my artwork. "This is exquisite," he says before pushing his stool back to admire it from a distance. "Truly. Not a speck of paint, and already, it looks just like you both."

My heart flutters with appreciation.

"Why don't you keep it?" I say without a moment's thought. "When it's finished, of course."

He eyes me for a long time. "Do you mean it?" There's an almost childlike innocence in his question I've never seen from him.

I nod and give him my warmest smile. "Consider it yours."

He leans over and kisses me on the cheek. Something metal brushes my shoulder, and I lean back to discover the source. The antique key has slipped out from under his shirt and brushed against me with his kiss. I can't take my eyes off it. It's so rare that it makes an appearance.

"That key." I jerk my head in its direction. "Is it some master key that opens every room in the house or something? If I were to lock my bedroom door, would you use it to get in?"

He withdraws as if surprised by my sudden change in topic. But he doesn't shy away, and he doesn't seem angry, so my heart is unruffled.

"I know you would never lock your door," he replies, avoiding my question as his stoicism returns.

"But would you use it if I did?" I'm not quite sure why I'm pressing the issue, but the fact that he's using my phobia as a chance to one-up me is a challenge I'm willing to accept.

The silence hastily thickens as he averts his gaze to the floor. With a softened voice, he asks, "Would you want me to?"

There's something about the sincerity of his question that makes the butterflies in my stomach take flight. In a flash, I recall the moment I awoke in his arms, a night terror ripping me to pieces my first night here. The next one may not be far off, and I can't stomach the thought of enduring another without a soothing voice to guide me through. "Yes," I whisper.

His grin is slight but powerful all the same. "Then my answer is yes." He reaches for my hand and brings it to his lips. "Do you forgive me?" His breath is hot against my knuckles, and my heart races with smitten vitality as he presses my palm to the handsome side of his face. Pain-stricken, his downturned eyes await my response.

"When I finish the painting, will you let me help you decide where to hang it?"

His expression relaxes with a twitch of a smile. "Of course."

"Then my answer is yes," I say, stealing his words. He moves my hand from his cheek and presses his lips to the sensitive flesh on the inside of my palm, sealing our deal with a gentle kiss.

Chapter 20
Evie

JULY 1ST — DAY 35

With each step, the plinking of drops intensifies, growing louder by the second. I proceed with such caution, I'm barely moving at all, releasing a sharp exhale when freezing water soaks through my shoes and clings to my feet and ankles. Startled, I jump back, realizing I've come to a dead end in the tunnel and have stepped into the sizable pool collected at the bottom of the decline.

The flashlight bounces all around as I take in the space, landing on an iron ladder partially submerged in standing water. A cascade of rainfall pelts the pool through the holes in the maintenance-hole cover above.

The first few steps toward the ladder are the hardest. The water is freezing, and it pricks my skin with such intensity that I'm forced to move with slow, calculated steps as it rises higher on my bare legs.

As slick as ice and nearly as cold, the ladder is difficult to grip at best. Only two rungs up, and my sneakers slip out from under me. With the flashlight captured in my teeth, my scream is muffled as I catch myself in a panic. The closer I get to the metal cover above, the harder the soil and water pelt my face. Blinking furiously, I reach the top and push the cover as hard as I can.

It won't budge.

Pushing, pulling, shaking...none of it makes a difference. The fucking thing won't move. I climb up another rung and, bending at the waist, I press my shoulder against it. Filthy rainwater soaks me to the bone, and I grit my teeth against the flashlight as I press with all my might. It shifts ever so slightly but does not open.

The flashlight pops out of my mouth amid my efforts and lands in the pool below. Frustrated, I stare idiotically, as if waiting for my eyes to admit they've deceived me. Thick strands of hair stick to my face, obscuring my vision as I weigh my options. The longer I wait here, the deeper that pool of water will grow.

In one last ditch effort, I push my shoulder against the metal cover one last time, screaming all the way. It bucks, shifting in its mount. It's all the hope I need. Water glides over my neck and shoulders as the cover rises, washing away all the doubt I ever had in my endeavor. My muscles ache as I push it aside and stare at the drab night sky beyond.

Scaling the final rungs, I emerge from the hole and survey my surroundings. Despite the heavy rain, the houses across the street are plain as day.

As are the handful of boats that rock wildly in their moorings along the docks.

Sporadic lights dot the edge of the street and illuminate a few straggler windows at this late hour.

People.

This has to be the north end of the island.

And God willing, this will be my way off the island.

Now that I have the tunnel route mapped out, all I need is someone willing to smuggle me ashore on their boat.

It takes everything in me not to race to one of the houses and bang on the door. But I only have one shot.

Best-laid plans are never rushed, and I need to be smart about this.

Finding my way to the north end is a victory, but my pride is short-lived as I scurry back to retrieve my flashlight.

With great difficulty, I replace the metal cover and drop into the tunnel, a loud splash kicking up around me as I bottom out. The water has deepened even in the last few minutes, but I can't worry about that now.

Bending low, I feel around the pool in search of the flashlight. My fingers grow numb as the frigid water compromises my dexterity, rain pattering heavily and soaking me to the bone.

So it makes no difference when I fall to my knees, purse my lips to avoid getting any of the mucky water in my mouth, and begin frantically feeling along the tunnel floor. My hand brushes against something solid, and encouragement warms my frozen skin.

The flashlight fits snuggly in my grip as I hightail it out of there and race back toward the manor lest I freeze to death.

It isn't until I'm back in my room, with the flashlight replaced on the mantel in its usual spot, that I realize the grease chalk is nowhere to be found. It must have fallen from my pocket while I was searching for the flashlight.

Which means the route to the north end of the island remains unmarked.

CHAPTER 21
LAZARO

The last time David was this inebriated in my presence, he was barely eighteen years old. He had rushed to my home, alcohol ripe on his breath, desperate for a safe haven away from his father. "Worthless piece of shit" were the words Frank used to describe his son that night. It was all David would tell me about what happened, and I never pried. I gave him a place to stay, and it was more than a month before he returned home.

Now, his eyes are red-rimmed and glazed over as he leans against the mantel, staring into the fire as if searching it for answers. His suit is disheveled, his hair a mess, and he drunkenly knocks over a framed photograph of his mother as he teeters senselessly.

It's me he hates this time.

"It's done," he says in a warbled slur. "She's gone." He pinches his eyes shut and inhales a shaky breath. "She hasn't returned my calls since she left. My marriage is over before it even began."

Reaching for his shoulder, I struggle to find the proper words of comfort. He knew the mission, and he agreed to partake. Everything else was up to him.

He shrugs my hand away and reels on me. "What was it all for?" he cries. "This is all your fault. I lost everything because of you. D'you have any idea what you've done to me?" His eyes glisten as he slings slurred words laced with mistrust and hate.

I can't disguise the irritation in my voice as I point a finger in his face. "I told you to get to know her as a way of keeping an eye on Neve until we could come up with a plan to bring her here. I never told you to fall in love with that girl. And I sure as hell never coerced you to propose. That's on you, David. Understand?"

He was never one to take being lectured lightly. So I'm not entirely surprised when he shoves away from the mantel with the photograph of his mother in hand. Before I can protest, the frame flies across the room and crashes into the closed office door, shattering to pieces on the ground. "You son of a bitch," he seethes.

I approach him, but he slinks to the couch and buries his head in his hands. "I lost her." Sobs echo low in his throat, muffled in his palms—the slow decay of a man's heart as it clings to the hope of love. "It's all over."

It's a torment with which I'm far too familiar.

I sit beside him and reach for his shoulder again. He does not shrug me away this time. "David, listen to me."

He remains unmoving. I need him to look at me, to understand the sincerity of what I'm about to say. With my soft squeeze of his shoulder, he unburies his sloven, downtrodden face and regards me with heavy eyes.

"If you love this woman—I mean *truly* love her—then you stop at nothing until she's back in your arms." I jerk him firmly, forcing him to keep his eyes on me, hoping to shake some sense into him and get his mind right. He's weak. Once, it was only his father who made him cower like this. Now it seems Jenna has the same power over him. He'll never fix this if he doesn't get his shit together. He should've been mine, and the love I bear for him will always be equivalent to that of a real father's. But I can't watch him spiral again, not after he's come so far. Knowing this mission to keep Jenna close has made him so distraught cuts me with a blade I cannot bear. And there's no one to blame but myself.

"How can I get her back when I've given her so many reasons

not to trust me?" He shies away before climbing to his feet, then folds his arms and paces toward the roaring fire.

"She wants answers," I reply. "If you ever hope to gain her trust, you must give her the answers she needs." I join him by the mantel. "Look at me."

With a slight twist of his neck, he eyes me out of his periphery.

"I said '*look at me.*'" I repeat my command with more bite than before. The boy is stubborn. Some things never change. I stuff my hands in my pockets and wait for him to give me his full attention, growing more agitated by the second. Finally, he squares his shoulders with mine and runs the back of his hand over his mouth, clearly parched for another drink. But I'll be damned if my son consumes even one more drop tonight.

"Do whatever it takes to get her back. If it's answers she wants, then she shall have them. Tell her who I am..."

David's eyes widen, and a deep crease forms between his brows. "Are you serious—"

"Tell her what the mission was," I say before I can stop myself. Advising David to reveal everything I've worked so hard to keep secret is about as easy as swallowing glass. But, aside from Neve, there's no one else in this world I care for more than David. He was never supposed to fall in love with that woman. Never. That was a risk I would've never permitted. But who am I to dictate the affairs of a man's heart when I have so little control over my own? I would turn this world to ash for David without thinking twice about it. And that's the only truth I need to properly advise him in his fragile state.

So I continue. "Tell her who Neve really is, and why we worked so hard to find her and bring her back here."

He exhales sharply. "How can I do that when *I* don't even know the real reason?"

Cocking my head, I ask, "You jest?" I'm in no mood for games.

"No," he replies slowly, as if reconsidering the word as it's said.

"You know as well as I that we brought her here to keep her safe. Why else—"

"Safe from what?" His glazed eyes come alive with staunch combativeness. "All this time, I've followed your orders...without question. You say it's to...keep my sister...away from my father. Bu'why?" His drunken shouts fill the room, and I make no effort to tame them. "He's a piece of shit, sure. But...how long is this going to"—*hiccup*—"go on for?" David teeters a bit, and I reach for him.

He steps away.

"D'you want to...know...what I think?" he slurs. "I think you... and my father...have been in a race for nearly thirty years to see who...can catch her first. Like she's some goddamn prize. Well, congratulations, Boss. You've won." He opens his arms wide in a sloppy gesture of victory. "At the expense of my marriage and Neve's freedom and my happiness..." A small burp escapes him, forcing a pause in his sling of ridicule. His legs buckle, and I catch him this time. A murmur catches in the fabric of my blazer as he leans into me and settles on the couch.

To engage this further would be irresponsible and meaningless. He's not thinking clearly, and there's no reasoning with him in such an intoxicated state. "Lie down, David. You need to rest—"

He shoves me away.

Heat rises in my neck, prickling my ears as irritation washes over me all over again.

"You won. She's here...with you. The last remaining piece of my late mother..." With a slow drag of his tongue over his lower lip, he locks eyes on me, their subtle twitches more apparent in his static state. "Who happens to look *exactly* like her," he sneers.

Chills punish my spine as David holds me captive with his gaze. If there's one thing he's always excelled at, it's reading people. It has certainly come in handy in my employ more than once. His narrowed eyes bore holes into my soul, and I fear the time has finally come that he's seeing more than I'm prepared to reveal.

"I made a promise to your mother to keep you two safe. The plan to bring Neve home was simply to fulfill her wishes—"

"And not for atonement?"

I flinch away and crinkle my face in shock. "Beg your pardon?"

"Please tell me...that you didn't bring my sister here, against her wishes...as some way of using her to atone for my mother's sins." He collapses onto the couch and averts his gaze.

The heat in my neck has spread to my fingertips, and my breathing grows erratic.

"Sins?" My fists curl into a ball.

"For what she did to herself."

I pace away from David, unable to stand the sight of him. Festering like an open wound, rage courses through my veins. "You'd be a damned fool to speak again," I warn.

"She was Catholic, and she took her own life—"

"What are you saying to me, David?" I reel around to face him. "*You believe your mother is in hell*?" I grab him by the collar of his blazer and bring my wrathful face to his. I want him to see the anger inside me—to understand the risk he's taking by going down this road. But his inebriation keeps him stoic, if not a bumbling fool, robbing me of my upper hand.

"Believe me," he whispers, staring me down and making no move to shrug me off. "I pray every single day that she isn't."

I release his collar with a violent shove, sick of his words and his putrid breath and his inability to say such things to me when lucid.

Coward.

"Take one of the spare rooms and sleep it off. Just get the hell out of my sight," I growl, on the verge of burning this whole fucking place to the ground.

"Perhaps she's your last chance at salvation?" he mumbles, as if his words bear no weight to them at all. He stumbles against the coffee table as he clambers to his feet, knocking it askew. I watch him bumble back upright, wiping his mouth with the back of his hand before continuing. "Maybe my baby sister is your last chance" —*hiccup*—"to make things right with God." His eyelids droop as his speech is interrupted with more hiccups.

I fear he may collapse at any moment, but irritation stays my concern. "What are you prattling on about?"

His knees buckle, and I catch him. "The promise..." he mumbles against me. "To my...my mother." A humming echoes from his chest, almost childlike as his eyelids drift shut. "I made a promise too."

"Look at me." I shake him, fueled by anger that's eclipsed only by concern for my boy.

"I promised to love her..." he babbles incoherently. I set him down in the lounge chair, the fireplace crackling in loud bursts as it inches toward nothing but ash.

"Jenna," he croaks, on the verge of passing out.

Propping him upright with an arm around his shoulder, I lightly smack his cheek to keep him awake. His eyes flutter open for a moment, and he wobbles his head upright.

"You'll get her back," I whisper to him as his gaze meets mine. A gossamer sheen coats his eyes, no longer booze-induced, but rather the product of a broken heart.

"Fulfill your promise...to Mother," he mutters as his head falls against my shoulder. "Make things right with God..." His breathing evens out as he goes slack.

The state of Gabriella's soul is never to be questioned. Were it not for his drunken stupor, I would chastise him for disturbing the peace of his mother's eternal rest with such an egregious statement. But despite their periodic incoherency, David's words strike me with a fear I cannot subdue. Never before have I questioned Neve's true purpose here. Never.

Until now.

She's more than Gabriella's daughter, and certainly more than merely a woman who wanders these halls. She's the song, the wind, the blustery winter snow that bites at my flesh, reminding me I'm alive and making my soul take flight.

Heavy and raw, like the last gasp of a dying man, the truth of David's words penetrate every fiber of my being: is Neve my last chance at salvation?

My heart wants her. There's no sense in denying it any longer.

But could it be that my soul needs her?

Regardless of whether my heart or soul wins this lonely battle, she has set my heart aflame just the same. And David is in no condition to know the truth.

"Your mother's with the angels where she belongs," I whisper. "And your sister is no more my salvation than she is yours. I've survived beyond the point of redemption for as long as you've been alive." I peek down at him. With deep, throaty breaths, David has fallen asleep against me.

"If anyone has a seat in hell," I murmur, knowing I'm the only one to receive it. "It's me."

CHAPTER 22

EVIE

JULY 31ST — DAY 65

With a quick step forward, which should have been backward, I crush his foot with mine for the third time. "I'm never going to get this," I say, pulling away with a heavy sigh.

He releases his grip from around my waist and steps away to pause the music. "Just keep the count going in your head. Ballroom dancing can be tricky, but you've got this. Come, we'll try it again." He presses play on his phone, and the lively music kicks up again. He finds the small of my back and holds my hand in his. "On the count of three."

"It's so dark in here," I protest, looking around the old speakeasy. It's easy to lose track of time down here, no windows or daylight to show the passage of time. But shadows from the candlelight provide a comforting company, making it easy to find peace in its darkness. "Perhaps if there was more light, I could see what I was doing a bit better—"

"You should be able to dance blindfolded. It has nothing to do with being able to see. You need to let me lead. Feel the pressure of my grip here—" He pulls me against him with a quick tug at the back of my waist, and my breath catches at the sudden jolt. "And *here*." His hand squeezes mine as he tugs on my arm, outstretched to my right. "Go where my steps tell you. Everything else is just flourishing."

He counts up to three, then steps forward with his right foot, his hip checking mine and forcing me into a backward step that mirrors his. The rhythm is familiar at this point. As I keep time in my head, I grip his hand tightly and succumb to the pressure points in which our bodies are joined. The music is quick—almost *too* quick—as I fumble and nearly step on his foot a fourth time. But he catches my misstep and steps forward with the foot opposite my fumbling one, pushing me back in balance. In a split second, I'm back in the rhythm of the dance. He doesn't spin me this time. So far, that has only led to me stepping back into the rhythm with the wrong foot and losing the timing of the beat.

I find my groove as the song fades to an end, and I can't disguise my prideful smile. I've finally made it through an entire song without stepping on his toes.

"You did well," he says, his curved lips matching mine. "But if you're ever going to master the spins, you need to learn to follow my lead. It isn't the timing or the rhythm that's the problem. You're a musician. You know how to keep a proper count in your head. It's that you don't fully submit to me. It causes stiffness that leads to missteps, and it only takes a fraction of a second to lose the tempo."

My smile fades with defeat.

"Here. We're going to try a different dance. One that will really help you learn to follow but at a much slower pace." He scrolls through his playlist, his face illuminated in the screen's harsh glow. For a split second, I'm enticed by the phone, an elusive connection to the outside world. But I promised to obey, so it will stay right where he puts it.

A gentle plucking of a guitar, accompanied by the clacking of drumsticks, echoes through the room as the song begins. A beautiful, feminine voice fills the space soon after, and I pause as Laz positions himself in front of me.

"What is this?" I ask, motioning toward his phone.

"'Knockin'" by the Carolina Chocolate Drops. It's the perfect beat for blues dancing."

"Blues dancing?"

"Yes," he replies with a velvety rumble. "It's a partner dance that should help you learn to follow. I'm going to teach you the basic steps, and we'll go from there."

Holding my hand outstretched to the side, he places the other firmly at the small of my back.

"The steps are different from before. Much simpler, in a way. We're going to glide to the side—" He shifts his weight sideways, and his grips force me to follow. "Then touch your feet together."

I oblige.

"Then glide the other way."

Our bodies find a natural rhythm, bouncing from one side to the next as we mirror each other in a seamless glide. With my gripped hand, he pushes me back, and I naturally step backward with my right foot. "Keep the side-to-side rhythm going no matter what," he tells me as I nearly pause. I slide back into the foundational motion as he pulls my right foot forward with a gentle tug on my waist.

"If I pull you in close," he begins, closing the gap between us. The heat radiating off his body is a pleasant contrast to the dank space's chill. "The connecting points become even more apparent." He presses his hips to mine, pinning me against him, and my lips accidentally graze his shoulder. My face flushes with a deep, crippling blush, and I pray he doesn't see it.

"If I arch you away from me—" He leans into me, forcing my back to bend away in an upper body dip. My pulse soars as he lowers himself into my neck, the song slowly disappearing and leaving me with only my frenetic heartbeat. "See how your body responds by matching mine?"

Chills rake through my entire being when his exhale finds my neck.

He brings me upright, and I take in a quick but deep breath to regain my bearings. "If I push you away with a tightened palm—" His grip tightens on my hand and pushes me away, opening our partnered stance. "See how I can force us to open the space between us? Now we can walk." As he steps forward, I step to match with my opposite foot. After several strides, he spins back the way we came, and the pressure on my hand and lower back forces me to follow.

"Very good," he says, looking genuinely pleased. "You're starting to take direction quite well."

I raise a cocky eyebrow at him.

"When it comes to dancing, that is." He corrects himself with his typical stoicism. "Next time, we'll try micro blues."

I tilt my head.

"It follows the same basic steps, but the follow and lead are *very* close." He presses his palm to my lower back and pulls me flush against him. A sharp gasp escapes my lips, grazing his chin, and he chuckles.

"Every..." He runs his hand along my back and finds the low hem of my shirt. His thumb skims my bare skin underneath, forcing my legs to quiver. "Single..." Leaning in low, he brushes his lips against my jawline. "Movement..." He presses his hand against my bare back, my camisole resting at my midriff with a small knot tied in the front, exposing a sliver of skin to the cool air. Without thinking, I wrap my arms around the back of his neck for stability, a motion that only brings him closer. "Connects us."

I anticipate his kiss as he breathes against my jaw, unsure how I should react once it happens. I don't want it. At least I think I don't. But for every second his breath dances across the surface of my skin and makes me shake, I find my willpower tossed to the evening wind.

He pulls away, kissless, and regards me with soft eyes. "Next time."

I merely blink in compliance, an odd foray of butterflies in my gut catching me off guard.

The music cuts off with a single tap to the screen, which then goes black. The dance floor in the old speakeasy turns opaque, and I drift closer to the piano, where the majority of the lit candles await.

"Will you play something for me?" I ask, looking over my shoulder at him with a coquettish flair. He follows me at a casual pace, his hands in his pockets.

"No," he replies pointedly.

I stop mid-stride, and he laughs at my agape mouth. "But I will play something *with* you." He gestures to my cello, which has inadvertently found a new home alongside his piano down in the old speakeasy. Playing duets has become our new pastime, and Laz rarely plays without my cello accompaniment anymore.

Taking a seat behind my instrument and resting it between my legs, I wait, ready for him to join me at the piano.

"Your pick this time. I'll see if I know it," I tell him. He runs his fingers over the keys. I'm poised with my bow hovering low above my strings. In only a few chords, I recognize his selection—Fleetwood Mac's "Landslide"—as it emanates from the piano.

A sultry sound reverberates from within my cello as it does its best to provide the bass notes of the song. Following along with ease, my wrist falling into a comfortable vibrato with each pass of my bow, I watch Laz fall into the rhythm. But just as my eyes begin to close, moving to the song I know so well, the piano comes to an abrupt halt.

My eyes fly open.

I stop playing.

"Are you all right?" I ask. He's staring at his fingers as they rest on the keys. My mind clambers to determine why the sudden pause, my apprehension growing with each passing second.

His fingers come back to life with the opening notes of a song I no longer recognize, the beautiful notes resounding through the vast, open space. Shifting my weight, I lower my bow, unable to join our duet. Suddenly, an altogether new sound stills my hand.

Laz is singing.

His beautiful voice is powerful yet sultry with controlled vibrato and emitted as if no one else is around to hear him. Words of two lovers retreating inside themselves—their own hearts—spill from his lips. A song of wishful childlike affection coupled with ageless adoration and romance. A love that must withstand the test of time or, tragically, fall by the wayside.

I can't help but think he's singing about my mother.

The lyrics flow effortlessly, and I fall—mesmerized—into their melody. By the second chorus, I've left my cello and joined him on the piano bench, watching him sway to the music he creates. The instrument is now alive with sound, each note played to perfection, and I can't take my eyes off his fingers as they dance across the keys.

The final note is somber, my palpitating heartbeat replaced with an urge to cry in the following silence.

Laz gazes at the keys, frozen.

I wait for him to speak.

He's shaken; that much is abundantly clear. If only I could climb inside that head of his for even a minute. Perhaps, one day, I'll come to understand my captor a bit better. But the man is, unfortunately, as much of a mystery to me now as he was the day I awoke in this house. I tread lightly out of habit.

"You have a beautiful voice," I say.

His gaze remains transfixed on the piano.

I need him to face me—to tell me what he's thinking. His broad shoulders slouch with a tiresome defeat I've not yet seen, and I resist the urge to throw a cradling arm around them.

"Can I ask you something?" His voice is far too serious for my comfort.

"Of course," I reply.

He looks at me then, squinting with wordless judgment. "Have you ever loved someone with such conviction that you would be willing to die for them?"

My eyes widen, but he doesn't see it, for he returns his attention to the piano as soon as the words pass his lips. Almost absentmindedly, he presses the A key lightly, and a quick, high-pitched note fills the room.

Caught completely off guard, my psyche is pierced with a barrage of questions.

"I—" I have no idea where this is coming from. My mind plummets into a maelstrom of memories; insignificant to anyone else, but to me, they're the moments that made my life worth living. Jenna cradling me in her arms after I told Connor I couldn't do this anymore. Her soft caress of my hair as she told me that, as long as I remained steadfast on my own two feet, I was unstoppable. Strong, courageous, empathetic, and kind were the words she used to describe me. Qualities most only dream of finding in a partner, and she made me swear I would wait to share them with someone who was truly worthy.

I remember caricatures bearing our faces at the state fair, dancing around the house like idiots while we sang shitty boy band songs, getting drunk off wine coolers while we lay side by side, staring at the ceiling and dreaming of life after college.

And the kiss that rattled my entire world. The one in which I made a silent vow never to bring up again—a vow I broke the morning after game night. But in true Jenna fashion, she made everything better with a gentle touch and, once again, a kiss. Just as powerful as the last, but one I did not shy away from a second time.

My palm tingles every time Jenna enters my mind now. Like a shadowy effigy that haunts my skin and tugs at my mind, torturing me with the reality that I may never see her again. Or ever feel her lips on my skin.

James dashes into my memory as I flex and unflex my left hand, trying everything in my power to subdue the tingle that has left Jenna permanently embedded in my skin. But it's no use. Despite the way I recall James's breath against my ear, his youthful insecurity toward his glasses that fills me with warmth, the sound of his laughter, the frigid waves crashing against our ankles as we tackled each other in the surf, and the powerful embrace of his arms, that tingle never leaves my palm.

Would I die for James? I imagine where he is at this very moment. Back in New York, explaining to his friends how he met someone at the bachelor party and then making up some excuse as to why things didn't continue beyond the wedding. I picture his sister, Sara, sitting beside him on a couch in some apartment, trying to help him make sense of it all. "I just don't understand. She told me she loved me. We had the most amazing week together, and she just up and vanished. It doesn't make any sense."

It's been two long, arduous months since I last saw him, holding sway in his arms and entangled in those piercing eyes. By now, I can only imagine the dates Sara has set him up with to help him move on. It's as far as I allow my thoughts of James to go anymore. Any further is much too painful.

But would I die for him? The question seems simple but couldn't be further from it. He was a beacon of light in my darkened, troubled mind, and made it so easy for me to open myself up to him, which I certainly never expected. We were strangers when we began our week together, and he turned my world upside down over the span of one unprecedented night. I felt like I was in love. Was it lust, passion, quelled fear, and requited romance that I mistook for love? Possibly. Will I ever know for sure? Unlikely. Because it sure as hell felt like love at the time. Does it still feel like love? To be honest, it feels more like heartache. I have no idea how long James will wait for me, if at all. And if I never get off this island, a part of me hopes he didn't wait. He deserves so much more than that. The whole world, in fact.

I just thought I would be the one to give it to him.

He should move on. It's what's best. But I'll be damned if I torture my mind for a single second imagining him with someone else.

The tingle in my palm—and Jenna's precious kiss—brings me back to the question at hand. *Have you ever loved someone with such conviction that you would be willing to die for them?*

I meet Laz's gaze and flush as it dawns on me that he's been watching me this entire time. His eyes bounce between mine as he awaits my answer.

"Yes," I whisper.

He sighs, as if relieved. "You're very lucky. Most people go their entire lives and never feel such love."

Lucky? I fixate on his scars, dismissive of the potential consequences of my wandering eyes. The tingle in my palm grows electric as my heart aches for the woman I'll never see again. "I'm not so sure *lucky* is the word I'd choose."

"Give it time," he tells me with a soothing voice. "You'll come to understand how lucky you are one day."

I press lightly on a random key. "I hope so," I whisper, mostly to myself. With mindless abandon, I strike slow, random notes on the piano, one after the other. He doesn't ask who I would die for, for which I'm grateful. I'm sure he has made his own assumptions, but I don't speak a word to the contrary.

Tears tug at my throat knowing the danger Jenna has been roped into, whether she knows it or not, all because of David's betrayal. Deep down, I know I'll always be held captive by the thought that there's nothing I can do to help her.

Transfixed by the piano keys, I make a solemn plea to Laz and whisper, "Please don't hurt her." I'm nearly strangled by my words. "You can do whatever you want to me, just please leave her alone."

His shoulders stiffen as he regards me with troubled eyes. I can't bear to look at them. But he cups my face in his hands, forcing me to meet his downtrodden expression.

"I won't," he replies. "I would never do that to you."

A whip of relief fills my lungs.

Just as a heavy sigh rushes past my lips, tears threatening to spill, Laz leans in for a kiss. Taken aback, I turn my head before his lips touch mine, and it lands on my cheek, the déjà vu of the moment making my skin flush with guilt.

The rush of elation knowing Jenna is safe ignites my entire core. His kiss makes my heated skin tingle, and despite my surprise, I welcome it. This is the first time I've felt true happiness in ages, and I want to hold on to it for as long as I can. When I don't pull away, it becomes an unspoken invitation for him. He turns to me, pulls me in close with a firm grip around my waist, and trails his lips down my cheek toward my neck. Sighing between kisses as he goes, he pulls me against him with each erotic exhale.

James is fading. As much as it makes my stomach twist in knots, it's a truth I can't deny. I miss him more than I ever thought possible, but I'm losing him all the same. I want to cry, to scream at the top of my lungs until my life resets itself, but I also want to fall into Laz's arms and kiss him for his reassurance of Jenna's safety. This whole time, it's what I needed to feel alive again. Just knowing she's okay is like shocking my dying heart back to life.

And I'm certain Laz knew it all along.

He's straddling the piano bench now, his body pressing against mine. His lips eager as they claim the front of my neck, which I've arched to meet them. I'm lowered onto the bench with a purposeful grip on my back. In an instant, he's on top of me, pushing my shirt up and trailing kisses between my breasts.

Jenna is safe. The notion is a newfound euphoria that stimulates every square inch of my being. As his lips consume what they please, my mind grasps at the possibilities of what Jenna and I would be doing at this very moment if we were together.

Would she kiss me again? Doubtful. The next move would be mine to make. Would she recoil if *I* kissed *her*? Possibly. She wouldn't understand it. She's never known me to feel such attraction. But Jenna isn't just a woman. She's *the* woman. The one who turns everything on its head and makes me rethink everything I thought I once knew about myself.

If only I had realized it before it was too late.

Laz brings his kisses down my torso, and my thighs part as he approaches the top hem of my flowy skirt, my peak throbbing with want.

What does Jenna taste like? And I don't mean the lips that have already pressed against mine with trepidation and desire. I mean *there.*

I know what James tastes like. A metallic sweetness that drives me wild and sets my core on fire. Plain as day, his taste emerges on my tongue. *I remember.* He commands me to look at him from down on my knees. The eye contact as I take him in my mouth is very important. One of his favorite parts, in fact, as he delicately explained to me one afternoon on the Cape. In a secluded section of beach in P-town, I rode him until I screamed his name, and he had to clamp a hand over my mouth lest we be discovered by beach stragglers. I took him in my mouth afterward, just as a good girl would when commanded. And I looked him square in the eye as my tongue swirled his tip. It pleased me to please him, and I was a very good girl that day. The memory sends the flavors of my own "butterscotch" as James called it—and his own "pineapple sweetness" dancing on my tongue.

I remember.

In a flash, I open my eyes and see nothing but elongated

shadows and firelight. Laz kisses my hip bone, the sensation pulling me back into the present.

"Wait," I say in a panic. He regards me from below, his eyes wide with concern. "I can't do this. It isn't right. James, he—" I stop myself, but the damage of speaking his name has already been done, evident by how Laz's face twists with irritation.

I sit upright and clamp my legs together, my heart racing. His back stiffens as he waits for an explanation. I don't give him one. My reasons are my own, and he would certainly never understand.

"You're awfully faithful to a man you're certain to never see again," he sneers. It cuts deeper than I deserve.

"I don't expect you to understand—"

"You think I don't know what it means to wait for someone?" He stands in a huff. I watch in complete shock as he starts to walk away. But before I can say anything, he pivots and closes the gap between us, poised yet irate. "Day in and day out, you close yourself off to me, to everything I'm trying to build with you, assuming I can't possibly understand what you're feeling. How naive can you possibly be to think that I don't know what it's like to want someone you can't be with? To wish for things to be different? To have people stand in the way of the one thing you want most? If you spent even a sliver of time thinking about someone besides yourself, you may find we have a hell of a lot more in common than you realize."

His words knock the wind out of me. "What would you have me do, Laz?" I stand from the bench, inches from him, accepting his unspoken pissing match. "I can't give you what you want. My *mother's* love. I'm not her. But it's clearly what you expect—"

"I don't want Gabriella's love. I want *yours*. And I won't stop until—"

"You say you want mine only because she's no longer around to give it to you."

"Bullshit," he states, his voice ripe with irritation.

"Can you honestly blame me for thinking that?"

A labored sigh escapes his lips, and he runs a hand through his hair. "Tell me what you want, then. Call the shots."

I recoil, confused. "Huh?"

"Set your boundaries," he says pointedly, as if he's been repeating himself.

"I don't know what you—"

With a quick, forceful grip, he tosses the bench aside with a loud crash and hoists me onto the piano keys. A startled gasp shakes me as the dead notes rattle the room and he plants himself between my parted legs.

He doesn't wait for permission.

Pushing me back against the piano, he dives into the flesh of my neck, sucking the life out of it and exciting the lonely and forever greedy pink down below.

"Command me," he exhales into the crook of my neck.

"W-What?" My voice quivers.

"Command me. Tell me to taste your lips." He shifts, poised to press his lips against mine, but I dodge his attempt once again.

"No," I moan, secretly hating my own refusal.

He pauses, confusion intermixed with the scowl that contorts his face. Jenna once kissed them in an attempt to claim them. But I didn't know how to make sense of it then. James followed behind her and claimed them while we were locked in an escape room. I don't know to whom they belong anymore. All I know is my lips haven't felt like mine since Krelborn, and it isn't my place to give them to anyone else. But I can't deny the way his strong hands make my skin vibrate.

I don't want him to stop.

He replies with a rough, punishing kiss in the dip at the base of my neck. "Do you command me to touch you, little one?"

My body hardens, frightened by the fact that I don't know the right answer.

"Command me to touch you."

If anyone is making the commands, it's him. I can't tell him to touch me. I don't want to be the one who makes the decision. Not while his hands are creeping up my skirt, toward the apex of my legs, where my body craves them most.

"Then command me to stop." His hand finds the edge of my panties, now soaked as my clit pulsates with a white-hot heat. I choke on my own thoughts, same as the words that dissipate in my throat before they're uttered. I don't want him to stop. Those fucking hands are everything right now. But to surrender myself to Laz would only cement his control over me from this point forward. He's lonely, same as me. And being lonely is such a powerful thing for two people to have in common.

"You can't, can you?" he teases, locking his eyes on mine as his fingers slip beneath my panties. I don't revere his gaze for long. Just as his fingers make contact with my clit, my eyes roll back and I collapse against the piano. The enharmonic notes of random keys struck beneath my weight combine with my heavy sighs, echoing in a rhythm that mimics my racing heart.

His body contours against mine, his boner tenting his slacks and pressing into my pelvis. Two fingers slide alongside my clit in that infamous V formation, teasing either side but never coming into direct contact, a tortuously erotic sensation that makes me feral with desire. Faster, his fingers pump against my delicate flesh, forcing me to arch further into the piano, which digs into my upper back.

Entirely lost in the overwhelming sensations that have taken me hostage, I sweep my arm behind my head, reaching to entwine my fingers in my hair as Laz keeps me pinned against him. But the back of my wrist knocks a candlestick over from its spot atop the piano, spilling wax in its wake. My eyes fly open in horror as a small flame catches upon the piano. Laz sneaks a peek at the potential disaster, his V never letting up for a second lest my impending orgasm ebb. With one swift motion, he slaps the flame with his bare hand, snuffing it out without so much as a wince. I cringe at the pain he must have endured, but I detect no signs of it on his face in the golden hue of our wicked tomb. I'm not given much time to ponder it. With a frightening, animalistic aggression, he grabs the front of my camisole with both hands and tears it straight down the middle. I gasp so loudly that it nearly comes out as a scream.

My breasts are revealed by his untamed urgency. He grips one angrily, leaving a warm coating of wax across its naked flesh. It tightens on my skin as it solidifies, but the warmth in such a sensitive place sends my body reeling. Dragging his hand over my chest, he pulls the warm wax with it, spreading it over my nipple, the curve of my breast, and across my abdomen, until it dissipates against the fabric of my disheveled skirt.

The V resumes, attacking the edges of my clit with a newfound sense of purpose—as if irritated by the interruption and making up for it with pure hostility. Paraffin smoke fills my nostrils in the wake of the snuffed flame, igniting my core far beyond that of the candle from whence it came.

My orgasm approaches as he thrusts himself against me, his muscles corded and flexed to the max as he works my body with one hand and grips the piano top with the other. As I release my cries into the darkness, my pussy aches for the aggressive thrust only emulated with penetration, flexing irritably as my body tightens with desire. I hold on for dear life, clawing at my hair and tightening my legs around his waist.

"Sing for me," he growls low in my ear.

My eyes fly open, confused. Nearly on the brink of orgasm, I can barely focus on anything else, and I'm certain I misheard.

"Sing for me," he repeats, his tone commanding in a way that rattles me to the core.

I release my erotic cries toward the heavens, abandoning all defenses and self-control as I sit on the precipice of falling apart in his arms.

"That's it. Louder. *Sing for me.*"

The piano shakes as Laz nips at my neck, and my entire body seizes against him. I scream my orgasm until I'm certain my lungs will give out. The shadows quake as the candles teeter, and the keys beneath me compete with my *singing* with their own consonant cries.

With my heart flitting beyond my control and my breathing erratic, I wait for him to say something. "That's my girl," he breathes against my neck, arousing my pink all over again. He abandons my tender flesh and locks his eyes on mine, firelight reflecting from within. "You really do have a beautiful voice," he rasps.

My cheeks and ears burn in a deep blush, and I give thanks to the dim light for disguising it so beautifully.

"Come. Let's get you to bed. It's late." With his face as placid as stone, I can't read what he's thinking. But I don't get the chance to focus on it for long before he scoops me up in his arms and carries me to the door.

As I hang on to his neck and cradle my head against him, we make our way to my room in silence. When he lays me in my bed, it's with the utmost tenderness, and I dabble with the notion of asking him to stay. Such a request may be misconstrued as an invitation for sex. But I'm certainly not ready to leave his strong embrace.

"Rest easy, little one," he coos, brushing an errant strand of hair away from my face before cutting out the bedside light. His silhouette leaves my bedside as I succumb to the postcoital exhaustion with a subtle flick of a smile.

CHAPTER 23
LAZARO

I shut her bedroom door, making certain she'll hear it.

But I don't leave.

The shadows in the far corner of her room hide me well, a veil in which I've become all too familiar. Any second now, she'll turn onto her right side. After only a handful of breaths, she'll release a delicate, nearly inaudible sigh—heard only if you know to listen for it. Once she sighs, the clock begins. Fifteen minutes; that's the amount of time I need to err on the side of caution and ensure she's fallen into a deep sleep before I make my move. Any minute now, she—

There it is. That beautiful sigh, like a whispering zephyr between her parted lips.

So I wait, counting down the minutes as she falls into her slumber. Bathed in moonlight from beyond the sheer curtains that cover the balcony doors, she has never looked more beautiful. Enhanced by how I can feel—with every inch of my soul—that she is finally surrendering herself to me. Slowly but inevitably, she will be mine in all the ways I covet.

Like the statues that decorate the grounds, I wait, motionless, until her body succumbs to nightmares. They happen almost nightly now, for which I secretly rejoice. Her moments of terror have become my new playtime, and if I can't prevent them, then I can sure as hell soothe her in their wake. An intimacy I never thought possible, but one that has become a genuine addiction.

I just have to wait.

The beam of moonlight has scarcely shifted. By now, however, I'm certain of the passage of fifteen minutes.

Shirtless, I slip into the bed alongside her, toss the covers aside, slip her ragged camisole off her shoulders, pull her skirt past her hips, and toss them to the floor. Her panties immediately follow.

She doesn't stir. My darling Neve is a deep sleeper, which is likely to her dismay.

Yet much to my delight.

The wax on her left breast has hardened in the cool air, but her other breast rests soft and supple in my hand as I envelop her in my arms.

She won't know I'm here. Come morning light, when a nightmare takes her and makes her go rigid, I will hold her close, calm her with a gentle touch, and wait for those fingers to glide across my chest, scrabbling for safety.

And when her paralysis subsides, she will stir against me with a long, languid exhale. My cue to slip out of her bed unnoticed before she comes around.

I just have to wait.

❦

No different from her previous night terrors, her body suddenly jerks against mine. It may not seem like it, but she's still asleep, overpowered by what haunts her. Eyes shut despite her cries, with a thin bead of perspiration dotting her brow. I debate dragging my tongue over it, the mystery of its taste toying with me.

She cries out, yet her mumblings remain indiscernible. The only word I can make out is *Papa*. And after all these moonlit visits, I remain uncertain whether these cries are for Papa to save her...

Or for someone to save her from him.

Her stirring makes our spooning difficult, but I hold her against me all the same. Cupping her breast, I give it a tighter squeeze with each sob she emits. My mind whirrs with the notion that they are for me—a feral pleasure that prevents restful sleep in my presence. The more she shakes, the louder her cries grow, and the harder my cock stiffens against her.

There isn't a single inch of her body I haven't touched at this point, but I have yet to find a way to abate her suffering when she needs it most.

Choking noises—low at first—curdle deep in her throat. This is the worst part for her—the struggle for breath. It's also the hardest part for me to hear. Her suffering in these moments was once unbearable, but I know well enough now that the worst of it always passes. So many nights, I've pondered what runs through her mind when she's frozen in panic beneath the sheets. I may never know.

She gasps for air as she clings to the blanket, but I yank it from her grasp and toss it aside. It won't help her.

Spooning against her backside, I kiss the back of her bare shoulder, admiring her naked form as it's painted in moonlight.

I caress her bare bottom, rubbing my erection over the swell of her buttocks. The choking noises have only worsened as she fights for breath.

Rolling her onto her back alleviates the sharp gasps, but her breaths become more pinched as a result. Hovering above her, I skim my tongue over her waxless nipple, relishing in the way it points for me. Her chest heaves as she wheezes, providing a bit of a challenge as I take her nipple into my mouth and suckle it deeply.

Parting her legs is easy, and I settle between them. The line of my body presses against hers as I plant hard kisses against her neck, her chest, her breasts.

Snaking my way down her form until I'm between her legs.

Her wheezing intensifies and her legs stiffen unnaturally. With difficulty, I hook my arms around them and pull myself closer. Her paralysis fights me every step of the way. But that's also part of the fun.

With long, unhurried strokes, I lap my tongue over her exposed lips. They've parted for me far more easily than her legs did, and for that, I'm forever grateful. Wetness coats my chin—a perfect sweetness that never lies—as I stab my tongue inside her rapidly, then drag it out and over her clit.

My darling Neve does not writhe for me, nor grip my hair or throw her head back in throws of passion. It's the only part of my secret visits that tortures me. I long for her screams of pleasure, to feel my cock bottom out inside her as she wraps her legs around me.

My cock is bombarded with blood, aching as I imagine such moments of carnal pleasure. I pin her down with a sturdy hand upon her abdomen as if it's necessary, feeding the fantasy that's come alive in my mind.

Allowing my tongue to give her clit its undivided attention, I remove my fingers from it and penetrate her with them instead. I capture her clit between pursed lips, flick my tongue over its swollen tip, and drag my fingers through her lips and back inside with a roughness that makes me moan.

When her pussy clamps down hard around it for several seconds, and a new wave of wetness coats my hand, I know my Neve has come. She's likely unaware; there are certainly no cries of orgasm emanating from her other lips or sultry movements of her body against mine.

But I know it.

And my cock is begging for the same release.

Rising back onto my knees, I hover above her. The choking noises have lessened, but they're still present. I watch her face pinch with fear, her brow furrowed and her lips tight with silent screams.

Gripping my swollen cock, I drag it between her lower saturated lips, coating the tip in her wetness.

God, I want to fuck her. Take her in all the ways I'm certain she'll learn to love. I lean in low, grazing my nose against her cheek, and dip my cock between her lips again.

Such *warmth.*

My cock pulsates angrily.

Such *pleasure.*

Fuck, I want her.

I rub her wetness all over it, lubricating my length as I stroke it hard.

Such *need.*

I drag it over her parted lips again. *Fuck, I could come from this alone.*

Her wetness is everything.

I *want* her.

My breath assaults her cheek.

I *need* her.

Touch me, my darling.

Precum spills into my palm.

Please.

Beg me to fuck you.

Beg me to fuck you so hard, you'll be forever ruined for other men. James will vanish for good as you relinquish yourself to me in a whirlwind of passion we'd create together. You're mine. Now and always. Your fate was sealed the moment you were carried into my home—our home—and someday, you will realize that I'm the only one who matters.

Someday, your fear will turn to love.

My pelvis swells with my rapidly approaching orgasm.

Fuck. *Yes.*

Just touching my tip to her wetness sends coils of blistering heat through my core.

She's everything.

God, her entrance is so close.

I pant against her cheek.

Neve—

My orgasm rises just as her eyes flicker open.

In a flash of panic, I freeze, cock still in hand. *Fuck, fuck, fuck.*

I search her eyes frantically, but her gaze does not meet mine, despite how close our faces are. Even in the darkness, I can detect the distance that lies within. She's still enduring her nightmare, and paralysis still possesses her.

I release a hearty sigh of relief as I bathe in the creamy jade of her eyes.

This is nothing new, and for a moment, I criticize myself for panicking in the first place. She often opens her eyes, even when still engrossed in her nightmare.

But it also means I don't have much time left before she awakens.

Now that her beautiful eyes are on full display, my arousal heightens. Somehow, it makes her more present, and I crave her mutual affection as a drowning man pleads for air.

Her gaze remains fixed on the ceiling as she releases rapid, troubled breaths. Soon, this will all be over for her. As relieved as I am by the notion, I must act now.

Lacking any sense of gentleness in my rushed efforts, I bring her hand down to her pussy and run it through her own wetness. Her fingers are pliable, which means her paralysis is subsiding.

Shit.

I cup her hand over my cock, trapping it with my own, and run it over my length with tight, rapid strokes. Burying my face in her neck, I moan against her flesh as my body resumes its rush to orgasm.

How soft her fingers are against my most intimate parts. So effusive and eager to please.

"Neve," I groan. "That's it."

I kiss her neck. Nip at her. Sing praises of her perfect touch, longing for those parted lips that begged to be kissed.

"My darling girl."

I force her hand to stroke me faster.

"You belong to *me*," I seethe between nips as I writhe upon her.

Her wetness on my cock guides her purposeful strokes beautifully.

"My beautiful Neve."

Cum seeps from my cock, slowly at first, as the explosion rapidly approaches.

"Mine." The word inches out in a low growl as I ejaculate all over her stomach. I cry out, push myself up, and shoot the last of it onto her chest, painting her body with the cum she forced from me.

I can barely breathe. In the luminescence of the night, covered in my cum, those soft eyes searching for sleep, she has never looked more perfect.

I wipe her off with a towel from the bathroom, but not before dragging my finger through the ejaculate that's speckled on her wax-covered breast. Raising the soiled finger to her mouth, I rub it over her lower lip.

If she will not allow me to taste those lips, then we will just have to taste each other in a different way. I only wish I could be there to watch as she flicks her tongue over it and her face twists with confusion.

Replacing her skirt and panties, then bringing the sheet back over her body, are the final touches before I exit the room. With my clothing in hand, I slink away unnoticed.

Without a sound.

CHAPTER 24

EVIE

AUGUST 1ST — DAY 66

The wax on my left breast is a hardened shell, as if perfectly encapsulating our intimacy in the speakeasy. Nearly the color of my skin, it makes my breast seem artificial. Fortunately, it peels off with relative ease. The entire front of my torso seems tacky to the touch, which I speculate may be from the wax he dragged over my torso, and there's a wetness between my legs that I'm honestly shocked is still left over from Laz's feral commands upon the piano.

But there's a saltiness on my lips I cannot place. No matter how hard I try to replay last night's events, I cannot make sense of it.

A gentle sigh sets my mind right when the pattering of rain strikes my balcony doors. After recharging my inner pluviophile with its earthy scent, I head to the shower to erase the evidence of yesterday's weakness off my body for good.

A HEAT WAVE HAS OVERTAKEN NEW ENGLAND THIS PAST week. As a result, it's been pouring rain since dawn. So I retreat to the library, the best place to be during a good rainstorm.

The selection is overwhelming, to say the least. Reaching all three stories of the manor, stopping short of the cathedral ceilings beyond, the dark wood bookshelves hold more titles than I've seen in my life. I could spend ten lifetimes perusing the selection and still come up with nothing to read. I'm terribly indecisive in that regard.

So I head back to my room, rummage through my unpacked boxes, and wrangle my old MP3 player, a small portable speaker, and a copy of a book I've cherished reading on rainy days since I was little.

Flipping through the playlist, I chuckle at the heartwarming yet somewhat bizarre selection of songs Jenna and I came up with last year. She had found the player in an old shoebox in my closet, mixed in with other little keepsakes, and asked if I still had the charger for it. Before I could answer, she called out "Bingo" as she shuffled through the contents and removed it from the bottom of the box. We hooked it up to my Bluetooth speaker and reveled in the somewhat awesome—perhaps a tad lame—but completely nostalgic playlist.

We decided to wipe it clean and leave only the songs that could potentially be used for her wedding reception. I renamed the playlist *Jenna's Big Day*, and together, we went through the entire library of songs. We danced around like imbeciles, deleting the songs that didn't pass the wedding muster afterward. I'd never laughed so hard in my entire life.

Before long, we had a lengthy list remaining for Jenna to use later on. But she left the player at my apartment the following afternoon, telling me to hold on to it and add songs as they came to me.

"You can surprise me with the full list later." By the time Jenna had all the audio files she needed for her big day, the player ended up right back in my apartment where I wanted it, a keepsake in its own right, as it makes me think of Jenna every time I turn it on.

I'm grateful it ended up with my things. I couldn't bear the thought of it being lost or left behind.

I land on the song "Fine By Me" by Andy Grammar, and my heart pitters with affection. I recall the way James and I sang it to each other in the most ridiculous fashion, dancing around his—*our*—room at the Seaside Inn, jumping into his arms and spinning around like lunatics.

To see my fiercely protective nerd of a boyfriend hang loose and act silly was the highlight of the week we spent on Cape Cod preceding the wedding. We collapsed on the bed together, filled with exhaustive laughter and raw throats.

"Let's never leave," he whispered in my ear as the laughter quelled and I sank into his arms as the little spoon. I bit my lower lip with a smile. He didn't wait for a reply. Honestly, he didn't need one. I'm sure he knew I didn't want to leave the Cape any more than he did—that we both yearned to press pause on the passage of time and fall into the dream that had engulfed us both.

In a flash, the memory strikes me with a sharp blow. I curl in on myself at the sudden attack, my arm over my stomach. But the pain is masked by smittenness as James continues to invade my mind. His face appears clear as day, his voice sultry in my ear.

And those hands.

It takes everything in my power not to caress myself to thoughts of those hands between my thighs, tight around my neck, inter-twined in my hair...I often fear that he will fade beyond return, but here he is, so clear in my head that he may as well be right next to me. I can taste his lips, feel his warmth, and hear the gentle laughter that makes my heart sing.

I shuffle through the remaining boxes that are stacked near the bedroom door, searching for the book, needing to satiate James's pull on my mind. For a moment, I fear it didn't make it in with my things. The lump in my throat grows as I toss other books onto the floor in a hectic search.

Ah-ha.

At the bottom of the box, there it is: *The Princess Bride* in all its hardcover glory.

I gather my items and head back to the library.

Lying on my back on one of the large corded area rugs, I dive into the story I've read a thousand times. Despite its familiarity, it now makes me think of James, and I need it to keep him alive. The stuffed animal I'm using for a pillow is lumpy but serviceable.

The lashing of rain teases at making me drowsy as I struggle to hold the book up. The words on the page blur as my eyelids droop, Inigo and Westley's sword fight coming to a sudden halt.

"You know," Laz's voice sounds from the doorway. My eyes pop back into a full state of wakefulness. "This room you're lying in...it's full of books."

I lower mine to my stomach and wait for him to finish his sardonic lecture.

"It's called a *library*, and I told you, it's yours." He stands at my feet and studies me from above. "There's no reason for you to have to read the same book over and over."

"I'm aware. And I appreciate your concern over my repetitive reading habits. But honestly, there's something to be said about the comfort of a story you've read a thousand times. It almost becomes a part of you." Much to my surprise, he lowers himself to the floor and lies beside me on the rug.

I remove the stuffed animal from behind my head and offer it to him. He takes it from me and eyes it with an air of suspicion. "This doesn't look like a very comfortable pillow," he teases. "I mean, it's a giraffe. The complete opposite of fluffy." He spins it around in his hands.

"Jenna won it for me at the state fair the summer before sophomore year. There were other animals to choose from, but she insisted on this one."

Analyzing it in his hands, he asks, "Why's that?"

My attention returns to the ceiling. "She demanded the giraffe from the attendant, handed it to me, and said, 'For the girl who has legs for days.'" I smile at the memory.

"She's not wrong." He hands it back, and I lay it on top of my book beside me.

For several minutes, we lie in silence, peering up at the exposed wood beams in the ceiling. But I find the silence between us oddly comforting. Much like within the pages of William Goldman's classic tale, I could reside in this state of contentment a hundred times over. But as the beams begin to double the longer I stare at them, a slight pulling sensation tugs at me from the inside. A feeling far too familiar, akin to falling from a great height. Last night's dream comes racing back to my consciousness without mercy.

"I had the strangest dream last night," I say, hoping to find some resolution to the images that still keep me tethered. He shifts to look at me in my periphery.

"Is that right?"

I nod. "I was falling endlessly. Just plummeting forever without any bottom. I've never had a dream like that before."

"It's not such an uncommon experience," he replies. "Were you alone?"

I ponder my response for a moment. "I...I guess, technically, I was alone, but..." I roll onto my side, prop myself on an elbow, and address him directly. "It *felt* like someone else was there."

"In what way?"

"It's hard to explain. Even though I was falling, I wasn't afraid. Almost as if...as if I knew there was someone waiting at the bottom to catch me."

"Your papa?"

I hesitate, mulling it over. "Perhaps. I'm not sure." I roll onto my back again, feeling oddly defeated. But Laz reaches for my arm and pulls me close. With my cheek resting on his chest, lying nestled in the crook of his arm, I settle against him, his T-shirt soft against my skin. He runs featherlight fingers up and down the back of my hand, propped lovingly on his chest. In seconds, his heartbeat has drowned out the rain entirely, and my attention can no longer focus anywhere else.

Déjà vu strikes me as I lie in his arms. All of this is too familiar, an unmistakable contentment akin to Papa's embrace. So many nights, I slept in Papa's arms. There was nowhere else I wanted to be, for nothing compared to the sense of security I felt when he held me close.

"You came into my room last night, didn't you?" I whisper, unable to contain my speculations as I trace a finger over the antique key that's tucked beneath his shirt. My heart races to match my words as they spew forth before I can stop them. But I don't fear his wrath. Not anymore. Not while his fingers drift so gently across my skin. Not when he leans in to smell my hair, thinking I'm none the wiser.

Not when I have so little left that's mine.

He stiffens against me, his discomfort palpable. I half expect him to lie. To say he came into my room in the middle of the night and held me while I slept would be one hell of an admission. But it wasn't a dream. It couldn't have been. He felt as real against me then as he does now.

Ever so slightly, his grip around me tightens, as if fearful I may leave. "You...seemed so frightened. I could hear your cries all the way in my room." Noise travels with ease through that passageway, no doubt. "At first, I came to check on you, but..." He trails off. I wait patiently for him to continue, but the silence hangs heavy around us, thickening by the second.

His honesty speaks volumes, and it's all I need at this moment. I don't mind that he crawled into my bed and held me while I slept. Hell, I can't deny the way my nimble little heart pitters at the notion. I wish I knew what I looked like in those moments. What do my cries even sound like? Jenna told me that she once heard me cry out for Papa in my sleep. The nightmares themselves are always so fresh in my mind. But my reactions are completely foreign to me. Even the paralysis makes it nearly impossible to focus and retain what's happening. Only those sounds, those images, that sensation of being unable to breathe...the thirst, the hunger, the unshakable fear—it's all I know in those moments. Everything else is a complete blur.

I fear I may lose myself in the rabbit hole of my broken memories. Forever is nowhere near long enough to figure out why, after all these years, Papa's memory and the unknowns of that night still wage war on my subconsciousness. Laz's arms—much like James's—are the only peace I know anymore.

"I'll stop," Laz whispers, cutting through the wistful silence. Such simple words, and yet they pack such a punch that they nearly knock the wind right out of me.

Trying my darndest not to sound too eager, I reply, "Please don't."

Hooking a finger under my chin, he guides my gaze upward to meet his. Placidity has taken over that raging storm that normally torments his eyes. He doesn't respond. Instead, he leans in and plants a kiss on my forehead.

Becalmed in each other's arms, we lie together long after the pattering rain eases its attack on the picture windows.

Laz is the first to speak. "Did someone catch you?" he asks.

Confused, I lock eyes on him. "Catch me?"

"In your dream. Did someone catch you from your fall?"

I nuzzle closer to him and inhale deeply. "Yes."

He sighs so softly that I almost miss it.

Almost.

"What did it feel like?" he asks.

To be free of my seemingly endless fall? To finally be static and embraced in a pair of protective arms? To feel Papa's warmth against my skin again? Laz's natural scent makes my head swim euphorically as I ponder his question, and I consume it one deep breath at a time.

"It felt like this," I reply.

He locks his fingers in my hair, holding me against him in the tightest embrace, and I fold to his whim like a paper doll in his arms. The warmth of his breath penetrates every pore of my being, igniting me from within as he presses his lips into my hair.

Running a delicate hand over his abdomen, I acknowledge his intentional clutch with a silent motion of my own. His sighs are no longer discreet, spilling from his lips with each pass of my hand over his chest, the rigid outline of the key beneath his shirt, his solid core.

Within seconds, his slacks have tented out of the corner of my eye, and I debate whether to simply ignore it.

But a plan hits me, so I go for it.

I slink my hand down his abdomen toward his erection. He arches beneath me and releases a low moan as I caress it. When it's completely engorged, I slip my hand into his pants and grasp it, skin against skin. His size is a pleasant surprise, nearly giving me pause as he writhes in my hand. Now in the full rhythm of his sexual euphoria, I notice his eyes are shut, his neck arched. Now he's the paper doll in my hands.

I can't tell if he's close, despite his deep, guttural groans and the way his grip around my shoulders leaves no chance for escape. There's no precum, so it's difficult to gauge. Squeezing, I tease at his tip, then run my hand down his shaft with long, intentional tugs. He jerks beneath me, and I can sense he may soon come undone.

Looking up at him, I ask, "Will you do something for me?"

His moaning stops as he regards me with ardent eyes. "Anything."

I stop stroking, poised to strike a deal.

His demeanor changes in an instant, riddled with irritation. In a quick move that strikes me with complete fear, he grabs my wrist, yanks my hand out from his slacks, and flings my hand away.

"It isn't a bargaining chip," he growls, sitting upright in a flash. I back away, terrified.

"Well, go on. Out with it," he urges vehemently, that storm once again raging in his eyes.

I shake my head. "Forget it," I whisper.

"No. It was important enough for you to put your hand on me, despite my sneaking suspicions that you had no desire to do so. So out with it—"

"That's not true," I press, finding my voice again. "I wanted to. I just—" With a heavy sigh, I brush my hair away from my face. "I'm sorry. It was wrong of me..." I examine my hands in my lap, suddenly ashamed.

"What is it?" His voice is calmer now.

"Really, I shouldn't have—"

"Enough. You want something from me. *Ask*." His tone delivers a sharp bite. Refusing at this point would be impossible.

"The man with the red shoes..." I pause, the mere mention of him making bile attack my throat. "The ones that look like reptile skin."

"Click?"

"Yes."

Laz's eyes are locked on mine, waiting with fragile impatience for me to continue.

"I...I don't want him coming around here anymore."

His forehead creases from concern. "Listen, I know he was rough with you when he brought you here, and I detest that you were handled in such a way. But I've made damn sure that he'll never lay a hand on you again. You're safe here—"

"It isn't about that, Laz," I nearly scream. I can't believe how fucking naive he's being. "It has nothing to do with the way he manhandled me in the bathroom at the goddamn country club. This is about that night. The night my father died."

He holds his hand up to stop me from speaking another word. "What are you talking about?"

I leap to my feet, addled and frustrated beyond measure. "What do you mean what am I talking about? I'm talking about the fact that he was there—*in my house*—the night my father died. One of *your* men. And probably more, according to all the voices I heard that night. And now I'm forced to remain here, sharing a roof with a man who has tormented me for most of my life."

He stands, squaring his body with mine. "I told you already, my men were never there. Ever. I've worked like hell to keep Frank and his men off your trail. When they came back to Boston empty-handed, I was hopeful he'd give up his search for good. There were no more leads. But now you're saying you heard voices, *saw* someone in your house. Click of all people? I don't understand. What did you see? What noises?"

The rabbit hole tears wide open, beckoning me to tumble inside. "I heard the awful clicking of his shoes and saw the red reptile pattern. I could hear his breathing. He was so close, I was certain he'd see me…" I pause, realizing how dangerously close I am to revealing things that would only sully Papa's memory. I let my ex-boyfriend Connor in a long time ago, and I shouldn't have. On a complete leap of faith, I trusted James with the information I swore I would never speak of again. But, for reasons still unclear to me, my feelings for James demanded it. I have no regrets.

With Laz, I can't be sure.

"The man in the red shoes…You obviously saw him, but he couldn't see you. Where were you, Neve? If you were in the house that night, how did you evade capture?" The sternness of his tone locks me in place.

"What does it matter? I—"

"It matters immensely," he cuts in with a fierce tongue. "It's important that you tell me exactly what you saw that night." He straightens his back and reaches for me, but I step away from him, eyeing the door.

"You have no idea what you're implying," he continues, his tempestuous eyes revealing a fury I yearn to never see again. "Don't you understand? Click has been working for me for over twenty years. The man was a bouncer at a local bar whom I hired as a driver. He's only ever worked for *me*." He takes a step toward me as if challenging my truths against his own. "So you see, if he was, in fact, there that night, then that means I have a goddamn rat in my ranks. And rats suffer far worse than anyone else. They beg for death before their end. Understand?"

I nod, a ripple of fear turning my bones to ice as I imagine Laz torturing a man to the point that he's pleading for death.

"I was...hiding. In the standing wardrobe in my room." I'm so sorry, Papa. "He was in my room. I could hear his shoes clicking across the hardwood floor. I could see the reptile pattern through the crack under the wardrobe door." My cheeks scorch with shame.

"Could you see his face?"

I shake my head.

"His outfit? Jewelry or tattoos?"

"It was so dark in the room, I couldn't see much else."

He tilts his head in confusion. "It was so dark, you couldn't see if he had tattoos, jewelry, or even make out his outfit. But you're certain you saw that his shoes were red and bore a reptile pattern?"

My stomach drops. That hideous look of doubt clouds his eyes, filling my insides with complete disdain. But I stand my ground.

Fuck him.

"I don't give a shit if you believe me," I seethe. "I know what I saw. I'll never forget the sound of those horrible fucking shoes. The way he shook the hell out of that wardrobe, trying to break it open. I knew in my heart he was there to kill me. And because of him, that night, I lost the only person in my life whom I loved. I was locked inside that wardrobe for days while my father was hanging, lifeless, from his own belt. And now I'm trapped all over again. Except this time, I'm stuck in a house with my father's killer coming and going as he pleases." I cross my arms in front of my chest in hopes of quelling the tears that prick at my eyes. "So I'm telling you to please keep that man as far away from me as possible. Do you think you can do that?" My tone is sharper than his.

He steps toward me, but I make no effort to move away this time. I refuse to be intimidated by him. Much to my surprise, however, he releases a gentle sigh and, with a softened voice, asks, "You were locked inside?"

Shit. I shift uncomfortably. *Please forgive me, Papa.* "Yes," I reply, my tone as soft as his.

"It was Gino who locked you in?"

The admission sears my tongue like acid. I can't say it. Not again. And not to him.

I nod, my gaze trailing toward the floor, ashamed. Waiting with bated breath for crass words about my papa to begin spilling from his lips, I berate myself for using the word *locked* moments ago. It was wrong of me to say. Hell, now I feel like I never should have opened this can of worms to begin with. If Click wanted me harmed or worse, he would have done so by now. And there's no way Laz would allow it. At this point, the only torture Click has bestowed upon me is the terrorizing memories of that night, and the taunting way he keeps calling me *baby bird.*

"That was good thinking on his part," Laz says, cutting my thoughts short.

"Wait, what?" Never did I expect him to take Papa's side. It was only seconds ago that he didn't believe me in the first place.

"There were people in your home, as you said. Locking you in that wardrobe was him thinking on his feet with what little time he had. It sounds like he saved your life that night."

My mouth falls agape. How can he speak so matter-of-factly about Papa's intentions? How can he be so blasé about the days I spent trapped inside that wooden box? Papa saved my life that night? Are you kidding me? I almost died that night because of him.

"Yeah" is all I can muster, slipping out in a whisper.

I hurry for the door.

"Neve," Laz calls out.

"I need some air," I reply before disappearing into the hallway. With frantic steps, I traverse the stairs down to the main foyer. I pivot at the bottom landing, away from the front door, and head toward the back of the house. Ignoring the guard who waits at the rear terrace entrance, I race past and throw the French doors open.

"Hey. You can't go out there without permi—"

"Fuck off," I bark. Fortunately, I don't hear footsteps behind me as I cross the stone terrace and head for the gardens beyond.

Once my feet have touched grass, I break into a sprint. Racing past the garden walls covered in ivy and a sea of roses in full bloom, I stumble onto the stone path as it weaves through the statuary. I follow its turns, past the solitary statues, mossy and worn, to the opening on the opposite end. The snowbell tunnel awaits just beyond, and I don't stop until I've reached the far end, where the trees are massive and covered with blossoms as white as winter.

I collapse to the ground, greeted by a blanket of damp grass, crisp leaves, and fallen petals. Tears flow freely down my cheeks as I cradle my head in the crook of my elbow. How I long to hear Papa's voice again, to hear his laughter tear through the space around us, turning a heavy heart as light as a feather and making even the darkest dreams feel worlds away. His tender embrace and words of wisdom, so purposefully diligent, always soothed me into a delicate repose that now leaves me with an endless longing in its absence.

But for all the ways I ache for him, the fear he elicited in me in his worst moments slices me with shame, regret, and—dare I even think it—hatred. If only I could tell him how my moments of weakness in which hate slinks its way into my heart could never overshadow the love and affection I cherish in his memory.

"Please, Papa," I say, tracing my finger through the snowbell petals on the tunnel floor. "If you're here, show me." I blink through the tears. "Show me a sign, Papa. Please. I have to know if you're here. There's so much I want to say..."

Curling up into a ball, I weep harder than I ever have before. He isn't here. He isn't listening. And the moments of hate I felt for the first man I ever loved will continue to consume me with guilt-ridden shame until it corrodes my insides and I perish along with him. Wrapping a comforting arm around my stomach, knowing the corrosion has already begun, I sob until I'm certain my lungs will give out.

As if trying to silence me, a harsh wind cuts through the tunnel, whipping the trees into a frenzy that scatters a myriad of petals upon me. Pausing mid-sob, I watch as the blossoms continue to fall, a rip-roaring blizzard daring to leave their trees as bare as they were on the first day of winter. They land in my hair, tickle my eyelashes, stick to my tear-stricken face, and land in my open palm. In seconds, I'm completely covered, and the tightness in my chest has lessened.

"He's listening," Laz says from somewhere behind me. I didn't hear him approach. But I'm not startled.

He kneels beside me and brushes the petals from my wet cheeks. "And so am I." With a single pass of his thumb, he wipes the tears from beneath one eye. "Whatever it is you want to tell him, say it to me. I'm listening. And I'm certain he is too." His voice is as soft as satin.

With each passing year, the list of things I've wished I could tell Papa has only grown beyond my control. I wouldn't possibly know where to begin. But Laz's touch—so warm and gentle—makes his facade of Papa even more believable. Before long, my heart takes me exactly where I need to go.

Where it all began.

Looking Laz dead in the eye and nowhere else, I say, "Papa, you used to speak of angels. Beautiful, ethereal creatures who would watch over me and keep me safe..." I pause to fight the blush that threatens to silence me. "My mother." I look down at my hands, watching as I rub a snowbell petal between two fingers. "But overnight, your angels turned into demons—*monsters*—something that frightened you in ways that made you transform into someone else entirely. I never understood any of it." I meet Laz's piercing gaze. "I wish you had explained it to me. Told me what you saw. More than anything, I needed to understand why they wanted me. But my questions were always met with silence."

Laz runs a finger across my palm, where a stray petal rests. "You know," he begins. "My mother used to speak of angels too. Arc angels, guardian angels...even the ones who had fallen. But to her, they weren't ethereal. And some of them may not have been considered beautiful. To her, they looked just like everyone else. The embodiments of the ones we love who have passed on. Everywhere; all around us. Many people believe in angels, Neve. It isn't so unusual—"

"But what about demons? Monsters who stalk you in the night? Threaten the ones you love? Elicit such fear in you that you lock your own child inside a wardrobe bolted to the wall, all for her own safety?" The words race out of me before I can stop them. "Papa became ill. It was all so sudden. Overnight, really. It kills me that I never understood what was going on with him in his final years. But it's nothing compared to the hatred I felt for him in those moments. Or the unspeakable guilt that followed..." I swallow the painful lump in my throat.

"I don't understand," Laz replies. "I didn't know Gino very well —your mother certainly knew him better than I—but I never knew him to be ill, to see things that weren't there. If you're implying he was delusional, there was never any indication he was suffering from such an illness when I knew him. And I know that your mother never would have left you in his care if she had any idea he endured such visions."

"The visions seemed to come on overnight. I doubt she had any idea he suffered from them. I'm not sure *he* even knew or saw it coming." I brush the petals off the front of my shirt as another breeze kicks them up around us.

"When was the first occurrence? Did something trigger it?" He runs a gentle thumb across the back of my hand as he holds it.

It doesn't take me long to recall the first time Papa grabbed me by the arm, violently shoved aside the contents of my wardrobe, and threw me inside. The click of the lock didn't send me into the panic-filled tailspin that it does now.

I hadn't come to fear it yet.

An avalanche of memories bombards my senses as I recall the events of that Saturday afternoon. The window panes wept with a drizzle that had been without pause the last three days. It was late-winter Seattle weather that inconspicuously infringed upon our spring. Johnny Cash spilled his baritone voice at a low volume from the stereo in the corner of the living room, where I lay upon the rug, reading a worn copy of *Alice's Adventure in Wonderland*.

"It was shortly before my ninth birthday," I begin. "I remember because Papa brought it up during breakfast that morning. He asked me if I had any ideas of what I wanted to do to celebrate. It was such a serene and peaceful day. But then it all changed in an instant..." I shift uncomfortably.

"Papa came into the kitchen through the back door," I continue, not giving much thought to coherency as my mind flits with memories I'd much rather forget. "The slam of the screen door made me jump. I remember that. I remember losing my place in the book I was reading."

Laz's stare is unwavering.

"I remember how soaked he was from the rain. The way the drops fell from his hair and onto his face. The smell of wet earth hung so heavily on him. But the worst part was how scared he looked..." I glance away.

"He grabbed me by the arm and pulled me to my bedroom. It wasn't anger that seemed to drive him, but fear. I'd never seen him behave remotely like it before. And it terrified the hell out of me. I didn't fight it, though. He flung open the doors to my wardrobe and pushed me inside. All he said to me was *'Don't make a sound, baby bird. Not. One. Sound.'* Then he pressed his finger to his lips, closed the doors, and locked me in." Little rivulets of terror pierce my belly at the memory.

"The minutes dragged by like hours. It couldn't have been more than half an hour before he came for me that first time. But it felt like an eternity. For the first several minutes, I tried to convince myself that Papa was playing a game. But it wasn't long before I realized Papa's terror was as real as that wardrobe itself, and that maybe there *was* something out there to truly fear."

"How long did this go on for?" he asks.

"Until he died." I'm honestly surprised the question even needed to be asked. "Less than three years later."

"You were eleven when he passed, correct? Frank's men returned from Seattle in the fall of 2003." His hardened tone catches me off guard.

"Yeah. What does it mean—"

"Nothing," he interrupts. "It's—"

"Don't say it's nothing," I protest, straightening my back. "If you know something, I need you to tell me." The bile has risen so high in my throat that I fear I may choke on it.

He places a gentle palm on my cheek. "I don't know anything yet. Just give me some time to look into things. If I find anything, I swear to you, I'll tell you everything."

I fall into his embrace, and he holds me in his lap tighter than ever. The breeze has kicked up into a full-blown wind, the rustling of leaves and snowbell blossoms singing across the tunnel of trees. But I don't care. For the first time in my life, someone has given me the hope of answers. And I'll cling to that euphoria for as long as I can.

"What did he say about the angels he saw?" Laz asks, likely with the intention of taking the conversation back to more pleasant memories. "Did he ever tell you what they looked like?"

I shift slightly to meet his gaze. "No. He never described them." Just like the monsters. "All I remember is him telling me there are angels all around us, watching over us and keeping us safe. Guardians who always protect us." My shoulders relax as I release a long exhale. "Every night, when he would tuck me into bed, he would plant a kiss upon my cheek and say, '*Rest easy, child. Your fears lie with your angels tonight.*'"

"He wasn't wrong," Laz replies. "The fact that your mother entrusted you to him over me has certainly influenced my feelings for the man. But I also knew him to be very smart. If he says there are guardian angels all around us, I believe him."

The kindness Laz is showing Papa comforts me in a way that makes me slink against him without effort and nestle my forehead into the crook of his neck. It's a relief to hear a sliver of respect for the man who raised me, despite the animosity he bears from my mother's decision.

"I believe him too," I reply.

A worrisome thought suddenly hits me, and I sit upright with concern. "But Laz," I begin, turning to face him. "What if your mother's right? What if they simply look like everyone else? Papa was always so protective. I'm certain he would've sent me an angel if he could. But how would I know? What would it even look like?"

With a firm grip, he cups my cheek in his palm and pulls me close, his breath warm against my lips. He's so close, my vision fills with those gray eyes—cloudy yet far from a weathered storm. My stomach flips as I realize why those enigmatic eyes feel so familiar; they look just like Papa's.

"I know he sent you someone, Neve. A creature who will

protect you at all costs. You want to know what your angel looks like?" His breath teases my parted lips. "Look upon *me*, child." He kisses my tear-stricken cheek as I throw my arms around his neck in a passionate embrace. In an instant, Papa's natural scent floods my senses as his memory sets my heart aflutter, and his voice, spilling from Laz's lips, fills me with a reborn sense of safety and affection. Papa's presence permeates the space around me—the blossoms planted in my mother's name dancing in the summer wind—as I fall steadfastly into the warm embrace of my guardian angel.

Part II

CHAPTER 25
JENNA

MAY 28TH — DAY 1

The police station is alive with the monotonous tone of phones ringing, the gentle din of voices in the lobby, and photocopiers humming in the distance. Together, they generate a combination of white noise, making my pulse ratchet up a notch and pushing me even closer to insanity.

"What can I do for you, ma'am?" the young police officer asks from behind the bulletproof partition at the front counter.

I lean into the metal speaker to address her. "I need to file two missing persons reports." I check my phone again with trembling hands. Still no word from David. He was supposed to meet me here fifteen minutes ago.

"Don't worry, he'll be here," Steph says, placing a hand on my shoulder. It does little to quell my nerves, but it means the world to me that she and Keith are here. Concern weighs heavy in their eyes, wrestling with their well-maintained composure.

The officer cocks an inquisitive eyebrow. "You said *two* reports?"

"That's right. Two." I sigh.

"Can I have their names, please?"

"Evelyn Foster." I inhale deeply, fighting for the strength to continue. "She was at my wedding reception last night, and no one has seen her since. Her boyfriend, James Pierce, is also missing."

The front lobby doors swing wide open, and a warm breeze filters into the air-conditioned lobby. *David?*

No. It's my mother, looking hurried as usual. I'm sure there was some big meeting she missed to be here. She adjusts her large purse over her shoulder as she rushes over to me. "Honey, you look so pale. Have you eaten anything today?"

"No. I've been busy with other things, in case you haven't noticed." I turn my attention back to the partition and the officer who's drumming her fingernails on the counter.

"You said they've both been missing since last night?" the officer asks.

"Yes, that's right."

"What time last night?"

I glance at the ceiling, recalling last night's events. I'd been drinking, same as everyone else, so the timeline is fuzzy at best. I rake my fingers through my hair, look back at my phone—still no word from David—and shake my head. "I-I don't..."

"I last saw James when the reception was starting to wrap up and he said he was going to grab Evie. She was up in the restroom, I believe. I don't think it was much later than one a.m. or so," Keith cuts in.

The restroom. *Yes.* "Yes, you're right. I last saw Evie in the restroom last night. David spilled champagne on my dress, and I asked Evie to come with me to help me clean it up. Steph was in there too." We exchange glances. "She also saw Evelyn." Would Evie even be missing right now if I'd never asked her to come with me? My face scorches like a motherfucker as fear and guilt tug at my insides.

"I'm sorry to tell you this, as I can see you're all quite concerned. But your friends have only been missing for just over twelve hours.

They need to be missing for at least twenty-four hours before we can file a missing person's report."

"No, no, no." I put my palms together in a desperate plea. "You don't understand. This is so unlike Evelyn to just go MIA like this. She left her purse *and* her phone at her seat in the reception tent. No one has heard a peep from either of them. They aren't in their rooms at the Inn. I'm telling you, something is very wrong here."

"You need to give it a little more time—"

"What I need is for you or someone around here to start taking me seriously." Multiple heads turn in my direction, and Keith's warm hand finds my back in a comforting move.

"I'd be more than happy to make a phone call to the mayor and get his take on why no one is willing to take a formal report here," my mother threatens. "And to see if perhaps there's someone better suited for your job—"

"Mom, stop. Don't we have enough going on without you threatening to have people fired every time someone gives—"

"Maddie?" A portly middle-aged man emerges from a side door behind the partition, dressed in business-casual attire. "Madelyn Murphy? I thought that was you." His grin stretches from ear to ear.

As if Massachusetts wasn't small enough already. It always feels minuscule when my mother parades around the fact that she knows absolutely everyone due to her successful real estate business. In fact, it's downright suffocating at times.

Like right now.

"Bill. How wonderful to see you," she replies. He enters the lobby and greets my mother with a friendly handshake. He looks at the rest of us before returning his attention to her. "What brings you down here?"

"Two friends of mine are missing," I cut in. "Since last night. But no one here seems to care."

His smile fades. "I'm so sorry to hear that. Please, follow me."

He waves us on and escorts us through the lobby, down a long tiled corridor, around the corner, and past a wide open room of cubicles to an office beyond. "Please. Have a seat." He motions in front of his desk, where only two chairs are present. Keith and Steph take a seat on the sofa situated beneath the lone office window off to the right.

The man scoots his chair closer to his desk, flips open his pocket-size notepad to a fresh page, clicks his pen, and says, "For those of you I'm meeting for the first time, my name is Detective Gambrils, and I'm going to ask you a series of questions. Please take your time answering them if you need. And if you can't remember all the little details, that's okay. You can always reach out to me if they come to you later on. For now, we'll start with the basics. What are the names of the missing persons?"

"Evelyn Foster. She's my best friend and was the maid of honor at my wedding last night."

"Congratulations," he mutters as he scribbles Evelyn's name.

I ignore him, too anxious to regurgitate answers so we can get this fucking show on the road. "The other missing person is her boyfriend, James Pierce. He was the best man."

"And that is spelled...?"

"P-I-E-R-C-E," I reply.

"And when was the last time you saw each of them?"

"Toward the end of the reception, David spilled champagne on my dress and—"

"And David is?" he interrupts.

"H-He's my husband." The word feels so foreign on my tongue.

I reach into the outer pocket of my purse for my phone, but my mother's firm hand on my arm stops me. "I found Evie—er, *Evelyn*—on the dance floor with James. I asked her to come with me to the restroom to help me clean my dress. We were all drinking, so the time is a bit fuzzy."

"I'm not much of a drinker," Keith chimes in, leaning forward.

"I remember waiting for Steph to come back from the bathroom. The DJ called *last song* shortly after Jen and Evelyn left. I remember it only because I was disappointed that Steph wasn't around for the start of the last dance of the night. It was around one a.m."

"You're certain of the time?" Detective Gambrils asks.

"I returned before the last song ended," Steph explains. "Keith and I danced the remainder of it. Once it ended, the DJ started packing up, and the remaining guests were starting to disperse. I checked the time then. It was just after one a.m."

The detective nods in approval, jots a few notes, and returns his attention to me. "You said you went up into the restroom with Evelyn?"

"That's right," I begin, resisting the urge to chew on a fingernail. "Inside the country club. When we got there, Steph was inside washing her hands." I nod in her direction.

"Was there anyone else in the restroom with you?"

"No," we both reply.

"You're certain?" His gaze lances through me, and I swallow deep.

"I'm pretty sure. Like I said, I had a lot to drink. I certainly didn't see or hear anyone else."

"There was no one else," Steph insists.

"Once you were inside, what happened?" the detective continues.

"She and Steph helped me clean up some champagne that spilled on my dress. And then...I left while the two of them stayed behind." My throat tightens as I choke back tears.

"You mean your friend didn't leave the restroom with you?" He raises a curious eyebrow.

"No. I left them there." My voice drops, and I can't bring myself to look at him. I'm so ashamed. Perhaps none of this would've happened if I'd stayed with her. I capture my thumbnail in my teeth, gnawing nervously.

Where the fuck is David? I ignore my mother's side-eye glance and check my phone. Still no word from him.

"So, the last person to see Evelyn was you?" Detective Gambrils says, turning his direct attention to Steph. She blanches, her eyes falling wide.

"Y-Yes," she replies. "I suppose I was." She inhales deeply, her shaky breath emitting a small rattle upon its release.

Keith takes her hand in his, but it doesn't seem to relax her.

"What do you remember about the last time you saw Ms. Foster?"

"I..." She shakes her head, and I wait with bated breath for her to fill us in. I sense her memories may be as fuzzy as mine. "She congratulated me on catching the bouquet. I told her how happy I was for her and James. They seemed to really hit it off." Her gulp is audible. "She told me she felt the same about Keith and me." Steph studies the floor as if racking her brain for clarity.

"She hugged me," Steph continues before meeting the detective's gaze. Tears have welled in her eyes, and I ache to alleviate any pang of guilt she must be feeling. "I told her I'd see her back at the reception, and then I left the restroom."

Keith pulls her against him, and her head finds his shoulder.

"Did you see anyone coming or going from the country club? Anyone you didn't recognize? Did you see or hear anything unusual?" the detective asks.

She pulls away from Keith's embrace and shakes her head. "No. I didn't see anyone. But..." Her sudden silence pricks me bloody. "As I was making my way down the garden path toward the reception tent at the bottom of the hill, I thought I...heard...something."

My stomach lurches.

"Could you please be more specific about what you heard?" Detective Gambrils presses.

"It wasn't clear, and I really didn't think anything of it...until just now."

I shoot her a pained look. "What are you saying, Steph?" I can't bear another second of this.

"It could have been a scream," Steph continues. "But I honestly can't be sure. I'd already made it out the back entrance of the country club, toward the garden, and was halfway down the path when I heard it. There was music and laughter coming from the tent. It could just as easily have been a fox or something." She drops her face into her hands, her yellow hair falling lazily over her shoulder, and I fight the urge to shake her until she alleviates this new wave of panic she's bestowed upon me.

"You said you heard a scream?" the detective asks.

"Y-Yes. Well, no. Not exactly." She releases a heavy sigh. "I don't know."

Keith and I exchange glances, uncertain of what to do with this information.

"I really don't know what I heard. It could have been a scream. It could have been a sharp laugh...or an animal...or something else entirely." Her flustered gaze meets mine, as if seeking reassurance from me that I'm not upset with her.

I push my chair back and make my way over to her, squeezing onto the couch beside her. "It's okay," I tell her, pulling her in for a hug.

"I'm so sorry, Jen," she says, her voice weepy and strained. "I didn't think anything of it, or else I would have said something to you that night. I don't know what I heard." Her body trembles against mine. "I never should have left her in there alone."

I pull away to lock eyes on her. "This is not your fault. Don't you dare beat yourself up over this. We have no idea what happened last night." I look over at the detective. "But we're going to find out, aren't we?" I didn't mean it to sound as threatening as it did.

The detective doesn't seem to take any offense and simply replies, "We'll certainly do our best." He flips to a new note page, scans the room, and says, "Can any of you tell me the last time you saw James?"

I pause briefly, clawing at last night's events in my head. "Honestly, I don't recall seeing him once I came back from the restroom."

Keith shifts in his seat. "I saw him on the dance floor—"

"I saw him too," Steph cuts in, a wave of pep seeming to overshadow her tears.

"Just as the DJ was starting to pack up," Keith continues. "He told me he was going to go get Evie and let her know that the reception was over. I figured they left straight from there, since the parking lot was on the opposite side of the club from the reception. I didn't give it much thought until Jenna called me this morning and said that Evie's purse was still in her seat at the wedding party table and that no one was answering when she stopped by their hotel rooms."

The detective takes several moments to scribble his notes. "What time did you find her purse?" He looks at me.

I sigh. Fuck. I have no idea. "I found her purse probably about half an hour after the guests had left. I was gathering up my things from my seat when I saw it on the seat next to mine. Her phone was inside. I figured she'd forgotten it. I mean, she'd been drinking quite a bit too. I took it to her hotel room before heading home, but no one answered."

"Did you tell anyone else you had her purse? That you found it unattended?"

"I told Dav—my *husband*—David. He tried calling James to let him know we had Evie's purse, but James didn't answer. David inevitably told me not to worry about it and we would bring it to her in the morning."

"And did you? Try to take it to her this morning, I mean?" the detective asks.

I peer at my hands, my face flush. "I didn't wait until this morning. I couldn't sleep. Something just didn't feel right. I can't explain it. It was just a gut feeling, you could say. I snuck out and tried to take it to her room then." I stare at his name plaque at the front of his desk—*Detective B. Gambrils*.

"I knocked on her door. Room 311. But no one answered."

He takes copious notes as I explain.

"But I wasn't surprised. I figured she was probably staying in James's room—room 312. But no one answered there either. And the front desk wouldn't let me in—"

"And this was at what time?"

I release a frustrated sigh and grip my hair at the roots. "I don't know." My hair tumbles over my shoulders as I drop my hands back into my lap. "It was the middle of the night. It was still dark out..."

"Hey, it's okay." His tone is soft and soothes my racing heart a bit. "How did James and Evelyn get to the reception? Did they take their own car?"

"No. David and I had two limousines arranged to take the wedding party from the Seaside Inn to the West Cove Country Club."

"So James would not have a personal vehicle still in the parking lot at the country club, then? Did everyone leave together after the reception ended?"

"No." Keith stands and paces. "Everyone ended up scattering at the end of the night. A few of us went to grab a bite at a local bar and called an Uber. I figured James and Evelyn did the same and went off on their own."

"It's certainly a possibility," the detective agrees.

"But that doesn't explain where they are *now*. Or the scream Steph heard—"

"We don't know for certain that there was a scream," the detective interrupts, holding a hand up to further cut me off. "We don't know much of anything yet."

Irritation pinches me from the inside out, and my calm tone falls by the wayside. "Evie must have noticed that her purse is missing by now," I cry out. "I would be the first person she'd contact to try and find it. If there was a way to check their rooms..." I take a deep breath, but it doesn't subdue the anxiety.

Ignoring my mother's horrified look at my raised voice, I ask, more calmly than before, "What if there's a note or something? I just need to see..."

The detective clicks his pen shut and leans back in his chair. "Well, that just leaves one final question: are you all up for a little road trip?"

Chapter 26
Jenna

The front desk clerk at the Seaside Inn looks at me like I'm a complete moron. "I'm sorry," he says, "but both occupants have checked out already. Their keys were returned this morning."

I must be losing my fucking mind.

My mother opted not to join us, prattling off all the appointments she "just couldn't miss" this afternoon. Shocker. I wasn't sorry to leave her behind. But now, with this weasely little prick and his thinning hair and small shoulders drowning in that bland suit, I wish my mother was here to throw her weight around as "Mrs. Madeline Murphy."

"What are you talking about?" I bark. "I came by their rooms last night and no one answered." My heart's about to give out. "I told the front desk clerk that I hadn't heard from either of them and to hold the rooms until we could sort this all out. I even paid for an extra day. Did you see them when they checked out?"

"I'm so sorry for the confusion, ma'am. No. Your husband came by this morning and told me your friends had been located and there was no need to secure the rooms any longer." All the air seems to vacate the room as an enormous pressure pulverizes my lungs.

"What the hell?" I ask as Keith and I exchange glances. "Why would he do that?"

The detective raises a gentle hand to silence me. "Are you the manager here?"

"Yes, sir."

"Wonderful. My name is Detective Gambrils." He extends a hand to the hotel manager across the counter. "And this young lady here has two friends who have been missing since last night. Would it be all right with you if I have a look around the rooms they were staying in? We'll be out of your hair in no time."

His kindness grates on my nerves. I want nothing more than to bulldoze the entire place until someone starts giving me some answers.

"Of course. Right this way."

The elevator opens on the third floor with a soft *ding*. Just down the hall, Evie's and James's rooms stand opposite each other.

We begin with Evie's, room 311.

Detective Gambrils removes a small flashlight from his pocket and shines it on the outside door handle. The manager inserts the key card into the slot and pushes it open as the beep sounds.

My stomach drops the moment I enter the room.

It's completely made up to receive new guests. The beds are perfect, fresh towels are rolled, and everything is irritatingly neat and tidy. Not a single article of clothing, not a single coffee cup, not a single piece of trash present.

No note.

The detective walks through the room, shining his light on every surface, looking in the trash cans—which are empty— checking around the beds, inside the nightstand drawers. Nothing.

Steph and I check his work behind him for good measure.

"I don't understand. It's like she was never here," I say on a heavy exhale.

"The room has been turned over to receive new guests," the manager replies. "But when housekeeping came up here, the rooms were empty of belongings. It would have been reported otherwise."

"This isn't right. What kind of game are you playing here?" I race to the door in a huff, making Keith sidestep lest I plow right through him.

"Open this door. *Now*," I holler from the hall.

The scrawny man shuffles across the hall to room 312, with the detective hot on his heels.

But inside, it's exactly the same as Evie's room. Everything has been cleaned, washed, and changed out for the next guests.

No matter how hard I press on my temples, I can't make the incessant pounding of my pulse stop. I rip my phone out of my purse and call David again. No answer. "Call me. *Now*. It's an emergency. Just like the last eight times I called," I snap at his voicemail. I turn my attention to the others. "Do you guys see anything out of the ordinary? Anything at all?" I plead.

The hotel manager speaks up. "Obviously, there has been some sort of misunderstanding—"

"Did you see anyone come and go from these rooms at all today?" I ask him.

He shakes his head.

"Jesus, you're about as useful as tits on a boar, you know that?" I snarl.

"Okay, let's just calm down." Keith reaches for me, but I shrug him off.

"I will *not* calm down. Something is very wrong here. Don't any of you see that? Am I going fucking nuts here?"

Steph races to my side and throws an arm around my shoulders.

The manager regards me meekly. "Perhaps you should try asking your husba—"

"*What do you think I've been doing this whole time?*"

"All right, Jen. Come with me. Please." Keith gently grabs me by the arm, and I let him this time. I can't be in that room for another second anyway. It feels like a vacuum devoid of air, and I can't fucking breathe.

Steph, Keith, and I are silent all the way back down to the lobby. When the elevator doors part, he catches me by the elbow before I disembark, and I pause to meet his gaze.

Three little words spill from his lips, short, simple, and insignificant to anyone else, really, but they breathe a new life into me all the same: "I believe you."

※

"GODDAMN YOU, *BOIL*." I GLARE AT THE POT FULL OF stagnant water, flames gently licking along the bottom on the gas stove burner. I've concluded this fucking watched pot is never going to do as I ask. *Yeah, yeah, I know the phrase exists for a reason.* But shit, it's either stare at this pot of placid water or stare at my phone and be reminded of each passing moment that David's not responding. I'd almost be inclined to think something may have happened to him, too, if I wasn't so upset.

I tap the screen on my cell phone and check the time: half past seven at night.

Still no word.

I curse him under my breath for a multitude of reasons. First, his best friend is missing and he doesn't seem to give a shit. And second, because he can't even be bothered to return my texts when he knows I'm worried sick.

As if he's reading my thoughts, a key inserts into the front door. A wave of adrenaline courses through me and spikes right at the base of my spine. It's a bizarre combination of relief that he's all right and absolute fury at, well, everything else. The door swings wide, then closes with a soft *click*, and in seconds, feet are shuffling down the hall toward the kitchen. David emerges near the dining table, dressed in a black suit and looking so dapper and unfazed that I want to kill him.

I turn my attention back to that fucking pot. I can't even look at him.

"You're not going to believe the day I had," David begins, and his audacity is all I need to lose my goddamn mind.

"I don't want to hear it," I bark as I turn to face him and lean against the counter. "All I want to hear from you is why in the hell you didn't show up today, and why you didn't return any of my calls or texts?"

"Babe. I told you there was an emergency at the club. They needed me down there. It couldn't wait."

"Yes, and you also said you would meet me at the police station after. That it 'shouldn't take longer than an hour.' That's why I waited to go to the station in the first place. So you could come with me."

"You're right." He puts his hands up as a subtle surrender. "I'm sorry."

"Why don't I believe you?" I fold my arms tight across my chest. It oddly gives me strength for what I'm about to say next. "How do I know your apology isn't just some bullshit lie like all the others you've told me today?"

He straightens and takes several steps forward. "You're calling me a liar?" His eyes are ablaze, but his forehead wrinkles in a sadness I did not expect. It makes me want to burst into tears. But I've been suppressing that urge all day, and I'll continue to do so here and now.

"Maybe I am. Explain something to me. The hotel manager gave me a rather interesting tidbit of information today. He said that *you* were the one to return their room keys to the front desk."

David scans the room before returning his attention to me.

"So tell me something. How did you get their hotel key cards, huh? If they've been missing since one a.m., how in the hell did you get their key cards? Oh, and I love how you made time for that but couldn't be bothered to take two seconds out of your day to call me." I jab an angry finger in his direction. "And while we're at it, why don't you tell me where all their stuff went. What did you do with it?"

He takes another step toward me, and my heart skips at the realization that I'm slowly being cornered.

"I really think it's best that you lie down and get some sleep. You're talking nonsense right now."

"Don't do that. Don't you fucking do that. Just answer my questions." Tears are brimming, turning my vision cloudy. I choke them back, but it grows harder with each passing second.

He puts his hands up again, taking cautious steps as if he's approaching some wild animal. "Babe. I didn't have their key cards. I never did. I simply told the hotel manager that we found them and their rooms didn't need to be held after all. This all feels like it's being blown way out of proportion. And I don't have their stuff. Hell, I never even went into their rooms, okay? But if it was all gone when you went, maybe they came back for it?"

I shove past him and rush over to the dining table. Evie's purse sits on one of the chairs, and I hold it up to him ostentatiously before dropping it back down onto the seat. "I still have her *purse*, David. Her phone, her money...everything is *here*. Don't you think there's some chance she may want this back? You really think she would come back to the hotel for her things and not notice that she didn't have her purse?"

"I..." He releases a deep sigh and turns away from me. A silence weighs heavy between us, and I feel beholden to end it.

But he's the one to speak first. "I think you know as well as I do that they likely ran off together. And it kills you that she didn't ask your permission first," he sneers with a cruelty I've never witnessed before.

"Fuck you," I choke out, dumbfounded.

"Fuck *me*?" His eyes go wide, and he takes another step closer. "Maybe it hurts because you know it's true. You just hate that

Evelyn has found someone who took her away from you." He jabs a finger in my direction as his voice raises even higher. "That you can't be so involved in her decisions, in her *life*, anymore. That's it, isn't it? She can't possibly be sailing off into the sunset with James as we speak, because that would be too damned inconvenient for you. She has to be *missing*, right? That's the only explanation you can possibly wrap your head around, because there's no way she would possibly leave you."

I shake my head, desperate for his shouts to fall away and leave me unaffected. But the opposite happens, and my throat aches as I fight the urge to bawl my fucking eyes out. "It just doesn't make sense," I say, pressing my hands to my cheeks. They're on fire. "It's just so unlike her to leave unannounced like that. She doesn't do things like—"

"Like what? Be spontaneous? Fall madly in love with a guy she's only known for a *day*?" David's mocking tone is aggravating, but at least he's no longer yelling. He approaches me and reaches for my hand. It's sweaty but gentle, and I welcome his tenderness.

He continues barely above a whisper. "Ten days ago, you would have thought I was crazy if I suggested Evie would meet someone and fall in love in less than a day. But now, here we are. Maybe she's not the person you always pegged her to be, Jen. Maybe she's more spontaneous than you think. Or better yet, maybe James brings it out of her, and this is a new side you're just now seeing. People change when they fall in love, babe." His brow relaxes. "You know I'm right."

He pulls me against him in a warm embrace, and I let the tears fall freely against his shoulder. Maybe he's right. Maybe this is a new side of Evie I haven't seen before. Hell, it's probably even new to her. I should be happy for her. I should give her my blessing and move on with my own life. It's my first day as a married woman, and it's been an absolute day from hell. It's high time I sail off into my own sunset.

But it still doesn't all connect. I can't shake her sudden silence, the fact that David lied to the hotel staff, or the fact that her purse is still here.

I pull away from David and swipe at my cheeks. "Why did you tell the hotel staff they'd been found if they hadn't been?"

He steps back several paces and sighs, frustrated.

"Why in the hell would you do that?" I say. "Do you have any idea how crazy I sounded when I went back there today? In front of the detective, no less?"

He tilts his head and squints. "You brought a detective back to their rooms?" His angry tone stabs with intent.

"Of course I did," I mutter. "Have you not read any of the texts I sent you?"

"I've been busy—"

"Doing what, again, exactly?"

"*Working.* Jesus Christ, how many times do I have to say it?" Our tender moment is clearly over, replaced with shouting and imminent mistrust. "I mean, do you want to go down there and ask my associates what I've been doing all day since you obviously think I'm fucking lying? I told you this morning there was a problem with the latest liquor shipment. As it stands right now, we have enough to get us by the next seven to ten days. And that's it. Supply lines are still backed up because of COVID, and I'm trying to bring my bottom line back up from when we had to close all the nightclubs during the mandatory shutdowns. This is how I make my money, Jen. This is how I pay for all of this." He gestures wildly around the room. "And if you think I'm taking any sort of handout from your parents, think again. It'll be a cold day in hell, you got it?"

I don't have the energy to argue about my parents and their money, so I don't even refute. Sheer exhaustion hits me all at once, and suddenly I don't have it in me to continue any of this anymore. "I can't do this right now."

He closes the gap between us, pinning me against the dining

table, and reaches for my cheek. "Listen to me. I know you're worried about Evie. I'm worried too. James is my best friend, and I pray he's all right. But it's too soon to tell if anything is wrong, and I choose to believe they're okay until we have every reason to think otherwise."

My mouth falls open. "You never told me you were concerned. Why wouldn't you tell me that? This whole time, I've felt so alone—"

"We all handle shit in our own way, babe. I like to bury myself in work and pretend everything is okay. You, on the other hand, can't help but meddle."

My sigh of concession is a heavy one. He's right.

He presses his lips against mine in a firm, passionate kiss. He's done talking.

And so am I.

My lips part for him easily. His taste makes me quiver as I rake my fingers through his dark locks, his beard tickling as he traces rough kisses along my throat. I throw my head back and release a series of moans toward the ceiling as he yanks the straps of my sundress past my shoulders and exposes my breasts to the cool air.

My entire body responds to his touch, aching in all the ways that make me bend to his will. I'd do anything for him. *Anything.* So long as he relieves that desperate pulsation between my legs. So long as he keeps tracing circles around my erect nipples with his eager tongue. So long as he keeps rubbing his hand over my panties with unforgiving fervor, hitting all the right places.

"Take him out," he whispers against my neck, his breath scorching the flesh he just nipped. I don't move out of fear he'll pull his hand away from my panties.

Leaning away from me to lock his eyes on mine, he repeats, "Take him out." Grabbing my hair by the root, he gives it a hard pull, and I wince from both pain and pleasure. I nod and reach for his belt buckle. I fumble at first—I can't see what I'm doing—but I unbuckle it quickly enough, unzip his pants, and let them fall around his ankles. "Keep going," he growls, keeping my hair captive in his grip. I hook my thumbs into his boxer briefs and pull them down far enough that gravity takes over for me.

He frees my hair, hooks his arms under my legs, and pulls me closer to the edge of the table in one swift motion, taking the breath right out of my lungs. Pulling my panties to the side, he reaches for his cock and thrusts it inside me. My panties dig into the inside of my leg with each violent thrust, but I'm unfazed by it. David fills me with each cant of his hips, my walls parting as he bottoms out inside me.

Dishes rattle on the table, and wine glasses tip over and shatter.

Faster, he fucks me.

Louder, I scream.

I wish he'd lean forward more—push me further onto the table. Then his pelvis would find my sweet spot, and I could come undone in seconds. But when I try to pull him down, he fights me and remains upright. In fact, he hooks his arms around my legs again and pulls me even closer until my ass is no longer on the table at all. I'm held up merely by David's cock and his arms around me, the edge of the table making contact with a sliver of my lower back.

He won't kiss me. I try bringing my lips to his, but he dodges my attempt and buries his face in my neck.

We aren't making love; that much is clear. He's fucking me. And I don't think he'll let me come this time.

His breath scorches my neck as he grunts his way to orgasm. After a few more rapid thrusts, he releases an animalistic groan and spills himself inside me.

We stay connected only in flesh for several breaths before he pulls out, lowers my feet to the ground, tucks everything back into his pants, and steps away.

"What about me?" I ask willfully, disheveled, fully aroused, and ready for my own orgasm.

He meets my gaze with conflagrant eyes, sending a tremor down my spine. "Don't ever call me a liar. Ever."

Without another word, he leaves me unsatisfied and heads upstairs. His office door slams overhead, hitting me with a jolt.

Tears spill all over again, but I make no attempt to wipe them away this time. My chest aches with displeasure, and my body is reeling from a *need* for pleasure.

Broken glass litters the table, the settings now in complete disarray. I reach for the larger shards, hugging them to my chest as tears flow uncontrollably.

The sound of a sharp sizzle catches my attention, and I drop them back to the table. Then another sizzle...one after the other in rapid succession.

Shit.

I rush back into the kitchen and watch as the water boils over, making a complete mess of absolutely everything.

CHAPTER 27
JAMES

MAY 28TH — DAY 1

Blinking through the disorientation and the piercing headache does nothing, for my sight does not return. My glasses are gone. I can't recall at what point I lost them. But it makes no difference considering the darkness that surrounds me. Material, damp with the moisture from my breath, sticks to my lips with each inhale.

Cotton.

The floor digging into my shoulder is cold, like concrete. I'm unable to reach for the material that obscures my vision. My arms are weighted, and my wrists sting as if cut and raw beneath heavy metal. Hefty chains dragging across the floor groan with each movement I make, and a wave of panic takes root.

Relax. *Focus.*

I crane my neck, listening for the slightest clue as to my whereabouts, but there's nothing. And all I'm awarded for my efforts is a shooting pain in my kinked neck.

"Only focus on what you can control. The rest is of no importance." My lieutenant's voice rings loud in my mind, as if he's here now, scolding me in my ear.

My legs have little feeling in them, either fallen asleep or pinned beneath something that has robbed me of circulation; I can't be sure which. I can move my toes and feet—*barely*—but it grants me a momentary sigh of relief nonetheless. At least I'm not paralyzed. That's something.

Falling still, I force my other senses to take over as I remain sightless. The air is dank and musty. Trees rustle in the distance, accompanied by a baritone owl hoot. At first, I was convinced I was in some sort of basement. But now I'm wondering if it's some sort of shed. My mind reels with the possibilities but doesn't land on one because, in the end, I truly don't know.

A shuffling noise catches my attention nearby, small scrapes along the concrete, and I flinch with surprise.

Footsteps.

"Who's there?" I ask, my voice so gravelly I barely recognize it.

Silence.

But the shuffling continues, closer this time. Fear brings my legs back from the dead, one nerve at a time. Nowhere near quick enough, I come to find.

A rough hand hooks me by the arm and wrenches me into a sitting position. Based on the position of his thumb on my arm, I can tell he's right-handed. I try to memorize his scent, but my attempts are cut short when my hood is removed and the cool air hits my damp skin.

The room is dark, and for a second, I wonder if the hood was something I imagined. Everything is just as dark without it.

A Zippo lid clicks open, and the lighter comes to life with a spit of the spark wheel. It illuminates the wall in front of me, where a man, middle-aged and rotund, raises it to a cigarette held in his pursed lips. Before he clicks the lid shut, I catch a glimpse of a second man leaning against the same wall, arms crossed, studying me from behind his heavy brow. The man who yanked me off the floor stands in my periphery, his dark boots the only thing visible.

The room falls to darkness along with the extinguished flame, but it's short-lived when a flashlight beam cuts on and shines right in my face. I shield my eyes, the chains hooked to my wrists rattling from my efforts.

As my eyes adjust to the light, I find two guards, dressed all in black tactical gear, each armed with AR-15 assault rifles, standing on either side of a heavy steel door.

This is some sort of shed or above-ground bunker. It's completely empty, appears to be made of concrete, and is likely abandoned. My wrists and ankles bear their own length of chain, each one affixed to a shared steel loop mounted in the floor.

"You must have a lot of questions," a man says behind the blinding light. "But I have a few of my own." The beam bounces as he shuffles closer. "Permit me to go first?"

I don't say a word. It's critical that I listen to this guy divulge as much as he's willing before I say anything in return. Information is powerful and may be the only upper hand I receive.

"You have nothing to worry about, as long as you cooperate. Nod if you understand."

I nod. A tackiness on the back of my head becomes apparent, with my hair matted in a way that makes me think I've been bleeding. It would certainly explain the screaming headache.

"The woman you were with—the one in the light blue dress..."

Evie. My mind spins in a panic, racing to recall the last time I saw her. How did I get here? I think back to David's wedding reception, which is nothing but a blur of sounds and colors. But Evie's face—alight with laughter beneath a canopy of false stars—rings true in my mind. But when was the last time I saw her? Is she all right? Where is she?

My heart races like the stampede of a thousand stallions. I can't bring myself to think about what they may have done to her. If I do, my rage may keep me from making it out of here alive.

I won't say her name. The less they know about Evie, the better.

"Do you know the woman I speak of?" the gruff voice asks.

I don't answer. If they want to volunteer information about Evie without me saying a word, then that's the best-case scenario. There's no way in hell I'm giving them anything that might lead them to her.

But after a brief silence, something metal presses against my temple.

"I won't ask again."

The click of a hammer cocking back sounds by my ear, engaging the handgun.

"Yes," I say, averting my eyes from that fucking flashlight beam.

"Her name is Neve Denardo, and I've been told you're quite fond of her."

I cock my head, confused. The throbbing in the back of my head is more prominent than ever. "Denardo? Wait. Do you mean David? David Denardo?"

"No. Not David." The voice is irritated. "I'm talking about his sister, Neve."

"His sister? Brina?" I shake my head and squint against that horrible light. "She died a long time ago. What the fuck is going on here?"

"She isn't dead," the man states, taking another step closer. "And her name isn't Brina. Neve Denardo is very much alive. And she bears a mark on her shoulder she claims *you* gave her. Explain."

Wait, what? I try to look past the beam of light in hopes of seeing the man's face. All I can see is a sliver of his hair. The rest is obscured in shadow. "Who in the hell are you? What's going on here?"

"Just answer the question."

This is all wrong. Either Evie has been mistaken for someone else, or she's been lying to me this whole time about who she really is. A boulder stacks itself upon my chest, suffocating me with the notion. It can't be true. I refuse to believe she's been lying to me.

But considering where I am now, I realize I can't be certain.

"I don't know Neve Denardo," I say with as much conviction as I gather. "If David has a living sister, I've never met her."

The man crouches, mere inches from me. For the first time, I can see the major features of his face. His peppered hair, his trimmed, dark beard, and the burn scars covering the entire right side of his face. "You would know her by a different name. A false name, but one she swears by. Evelyn Foster."

Hearing her name aloud knocks the wind right out of me. On top of it all, my worst fears have been realized: he knows Evie, and if he's seen the mark on her shoulder, then he has her, *somewhere*, and God knows what awaits her.

Rage churns my insides. If I even *think* about what they'll do, or may have already done to her, there's nothing in this world that would stop me from killing them. As long as I'm locked in these fucking chains, she isn't safe.

My body comes to life with a new sense of purpose and urgency. Completely enraged, I pull at my chains, my training going straight out the window as I reveal my weakness to my enemy with the mere mention of my girlfriend's name.

"Settle down," the scarred man warns. "She's safe."

Pulling on my chains proves fruitless, accomplishing nothing except exhausting me through sheer defeat. "Bullshit, she's safe," I sneer.

"Safer with me, here, than anywhere else on earth."

Panting, and with my face contorted in anger, I ask, "What do you mean she's David's sister? She never said—"

"She didn't know," he interjects. "She still doesn't, as a matter of fact. But I'll certainly fill her in when the time is right."

All this time, David never said anything to me about Evie. That entire weekend on Eden's Green, while Jenna was playing matchmaker with the two of us...how could David not tell me that was his sister? Unless...

"Does David know?" I ask

The stoicism of the man with the scars makes me want to explode.

But the fucking prick doesn't answer, forcing the uncertainty of it to weigh me down more than these fucking chains. He backs up to the wall, his eyes fixed on me.

"What do you want with us?" I ask, terrified of what the answer may be.

"Miss Evelyn Foster is finally home, where she belongs." He kicks away from the wall. "And *you* are an insurance policy."

He approaches, arms folded over his chest. "You marked her, didn't you? That mark on her shoulder? She bears permanent scars on her body because of you." His voice has gone colder than before, sending a chill racing up my torso and into the base of my neck. The silence seems almost punishing as the armed men advance on me. "A woman of such beauty should be cherished, no? But you've damaged her flesh beyond repair."

The guards reach me in only a handful of steps. My pulse accelerates. "I never did anything to Evie that she didn't want me to. I would never hurt her—" The buttstock of a rifle is the last thing I see before it comes crashing down on my face, breaking the bridge of my nose with a sickening *crack* and knocking me back into complete darkness.

CHAPTER 28

JAMES

MAY 30TH — DAY 3

The sun slips toward the plane of the rooftop, casting a narrow beam of light through the open slit in the concrete—the *only* slit—set high on the wall opposite the door. The way the sunbeam shifts across the room tells me the slit is in the east wall of the bunker, same as the entrance. Based on the muted nature of the light, I'd say it's barely dawn, ushered in by the twitter of morning birds not so long ago.

The walls are composed of painted cinder blocks, chipped and timeworn, spanning the length of ten blocks along each wall. It's a perfect square. These cinder blocks appear to be standard size, which means this room is roughly thirteen by thirteen feet. I count fifteen cinder blocks to the ceiling, making it ten feet high.

To keep me focused, I rely on the details. *Focus on the things you can control.* So I take in my surroundings until they've been committed to memory. The rectangular slit, for example, is open to the elements. A glorified airhole, if nothing else. I doubted it initially, but then a bluejay flew in at the first sign of morning, proving me wrong. The open space serves as an echo chamber for the constant chirping of birds. Which means, between the chorus of fowl and the quick scratching noises of critters scurrying along the roof, I know there must be trees nearby.

There are exactly sixty-two links in each of my main chains, one for my wrists and one for my ankles. Using the distance between my thumb's joints, I measure the approximate length of each link. Each one is roughly one inch, making each length of chain about five feet long. It's not enough length for me to reach the door, but it fortunately allows me enough length to minimally pace as I weigh my options.

Made of welded steel and appearing to be slightly less than half an inch thick, the chain is heavy as hell, making pacing a cumbersome task. But the worst are the metal cuffs affixed to my wrists and ankles. My flesh is raw and torn where the metal shackles rest, with blood caked at each contact point.

The only thing that matters is coming up with a plan.

I have no idea when my visitors will return. The sun has risen and fallen since their first visit, and my chapped lips only serve as a torturous reminder of how parched I've grown. To top it off, my nose is broken, the metallic taste of the blood in my sinus cavities still assaulting my tongue. The floor is speckled with it, spat out in fits while fighting for air once I awoke to a mouthful of blood.

My stomach rumbles, desperate for food. But I push it aside. Food is of little consequence. Water is far more crucial.

The man with the scars told me I'm his insurance policy. For what, I'm not entirely sure. But it tells me that he needs me and, therefore, likely won't leave me out here to die. That means someone should be returning soon, with water at the very least.

I must act fast.

From what I remember, the guards were armed with at least one assault rifle each. But men adorned in so much gear are rarely without backup ammunition and weaponry. The other men in the room, I couldn't quite tell, for the shadows were far too heavy to make out anything beyond that blinding light. I err on the side of caution and assume all of them are armed. Which means I need to somehow gain the upper hand, without so much as a penny to throw at them.

I search my pockets again, sincerely hoping I overlooked something the first time. All I come up with is the red plastic button in the right front pocket of my pants. Just the feel of it in my palm makes me think of Evie—the way it looked on her tongue as she held it out for me to snatch. The way her breath hitched as I ran my hands all over her in search of it. Her pulse was off the charts, and it told me everything I needed to know about the woman who would come to steal my heart before the night was through.

The last time I saw this button, she was kissing it *for luck*. How silly it seems now, all things considered.

I wonder where she is at this very moment. She's nearby, I can feel it—as if tethered to me with her own chains. In a temporary lapse of faith, I had nearly felt hatred for her. She's David's sister. How is this possible? And am I now imprisoned because of this long-kept secret?

But, whether intentional or not, the man with the scars lifted the weight of my loathing with three little words: *she doesn't know.* Guilt scours my insides, more rapacious than ever, for ever doubting my dear Watson.

It'll take a hell of a lot more than cinder block walls and shackles to dissever us from one another.

She's okay. She *has* to be. For my own sanity, I need to trust that she's all right.

I kiss the button and return it to my pocket.

For luck.

Frustrated, I remove my bow tie, which is so loose and askew that it practically removes itself. Racking my brain, I come up with no use for it. As long as I'm chained to this concrete floor, it makes no difference whether I can reach the door handle, with or without the aid of a flung bow tie.

Searching my clothing further, I pat along the breast pocket of my tuxedo jacket. Nothing. But amid the bustle of my search, my hand grazes the boutonniere on the left lapel. A wave of adrenaline shoots through me, the chains rattling as I run my fingers over the backside of the jacket. Secured in the shape of an X, two needles remain affixed to the inside flap, holding the boutonniere in place.

I remove the pins with all the patience I can manage. *Slow and steady. Don't fuck this up.* They're so thin, I can't help but wonder if they'll even work.

"Don't count your blessings." My mother's words resound in my mind, the sentiment echoed in my sister's voice, as she was always one to repeat the wisdom of our mother, especially when I never asked for it.

Holding one needle through pursed lips, I attempt to bend the other. It slices my finger bloody, the slickness further compromising my dexterity with the narrow item. With great pains, it finally bends into an L.

I insert both needles into the lock on my left hand, but I can barely reach it with the one that's trapped by that shackle. My wrist screams in agony as I twist it beyond its limits, manipulating the needle in conjunction with the other.

The needle slips from the lock and lands with a gentle *plink* on the floor. This fucking blood is making it impossible to grip the damned thing. I wipe my hand on my pants and wait for the bleeding to stop, holding both needles between my lips with impatience.

A wild breeze sweeps past the outside walls, filling the room with an airy rumble. Tree branches scrape the roof overhead as the sun suddenly disappears.

If I lose any more light, I won't be able to get this done. And these needles may be my only hope for escape. I can't risk them falling into the wrong hands.

My finger is still bleeding, but I work around it, holding the needle with an even tighter grip and working the lock until I'm certain my hands will give out.

A branch snaps somewhere outside the door right as the lock on my wrist shackle clicks open.

Shit.

The rusted metal handle on the outside door squeaks loudly, poised to tear wide open. Frantic, I slide the needles into my pant pocket and close the shackle loosely around my freed wrist. Diluted daylight fills the room, and the smell of rain is heavy in the air. A storm is coming.

In the doorway stands a man silhouetted against the light. With unhurried steps, he enters, his face inching into view. Long dark hair is drawn back into a low ponytail, complementing his full dark beard.

I've seen him before.

I rarely forget a face.

He drops a jug of water onto the ground near the door, then slides a large plastic bucket in my direction. Its scrapes are unpleasant as it comes to a stop a few feet away.

"Enjoy," he says with a malicious smirk before turning to leave.

"What, no dinner?" I ask, pushing the limits of the situation but curious as to whether these fuckers plan on providing any semblance of sustenance.

He swivels around and heads straight for me, his back as straight as a soldier in formation, then stops and hunches low. He's so close that I can detect every nuance of his clothes, his hair, his face.

"You hungry, comrade?" he mocks, then reaches into his pocket and removes a knife with a long, slender blade. Taunting me, he drags the blade across my cheek, leaning in closer. But I don't flinch, and I dare not look him in the eye.

I let him have his moment, trusting my gut and what it's telling me: this man did not come here to kill me. And he's definitely not the one in charge. That's the man with the scars, and if the leader gave the order to hurt me or worse, this man never would have turned to leave.

"Starving," I respond, calling his bluff.

He picks his teeth with the blade, his nonchalance a desperate attempt to showcase his vigor. I've known men like him. Low on the totem pole and desperate to stake their claim on what little freedoms they have. "Perhaps I shove this blade under your fingernails..." He waves it in front of me, his eyes dancing with delight. "Peel them off, one at a time, then feed them to you? Would you like that?"

"It's not exactly what I had in mind." And then it hits me. *Marco.* That son of a bitch who locked Evie in that closet under the stairs. The man who messed with her handcuffs and left her a trembling mess when I found her. "But I appreciate the offer." I swallow hard. "Marco."

He stands and surveys me with a pinched face as if he can't believe my own gall. "You remember me?" His expression morphs into one of odd amusement.

"I hardly forget a face," I say. "You're the one who locked Evie's cuffs on game night at Krelborn. You locked her in the room when there were to be no locked doors. You're a ripe piece of shit, you know that?"

He laughs, and it grates my nerves to the point that I fear lashing out at him and spoiling the fact that I have freed one of my hands. "I can get carried away sometimes," he jests, finding far more humor in the situation than I ever will. "What can I say, it's my job." He flashes the knife again, and it's all I need to understand his role in all of this. "Although, I didn't lock her in the room. Someone else did. But I did pass the key along..."

Thoughts of killing him tug at my mind as rage boils inside me. But I have to remain calm, or I'll never make it out of here.

And I have to find Evie.

It takes a great deal of effort to ignore the fact that this man ever caused Evie duress.

"You're the guy who tortures people for information," I state as I narrow my gaze. "I'm right, aren't I? Who the hell are you people? Some sort of gang? The goddamn mafia?"

With a flash of a smile, he turns to leave. "Take care of yourself, comrade. We'll see each other again soon." He looks at me over his shoulder. "And enjoy those fingers while you still have 'em."

With an obnoxiously high-pitched laugh, he slams the door shut and disappears from sight.

I wait for the sound of his footsteps crunching in the foliage to disappear completely before fetching the needles from my pocket.

It seems darker in the room than minutes before, which I can venture a guess is from the impending storm. I have to work fast.

Blood is caked on my fingers, creating a sticky film that honestly works to my advantage. It aids my grip on the bent needle, which I work in the lock in conjunction with the other. I grunt in frustration, finding little torque in the flimsiness of both needles. I bite my lip. The needles are in the correct spot, they just won't—

Click.

Fuck yes.

The second wrist shackle unlocks, and I release a heavy, victorious sigh. My wrists are torn and ache with abandon, and my arms and shoulders scream in agony. But it's cushioned by the taste of freedom.

Two more to go. Excitement sends my blood pumping to new levels.

But I'm not free yet.

Cramping fingers threaten to slow me down, but I don't let them. Nor do I appease their desire to shake. I pause to take several deep breaths, reminding myself that only a level head will get me out of this.

And this is my only chance.

Focus on what you can control.

Okay, here's what I know: the locks in the ankle shackles have the same configuration as the ones on my wrists. Requiring the same amount of tension with the bent needle and equal pressure scrubbing the pins within, the ankle shackles should unlock the same as the others.

But these locks are deeper, the shackles thicker, and the scrubbing needle barely reaches the other end of the lock. I grunt and groan, refusing to stop despite defeat rearing its ugly head. I can barely feel my fingers anymore, except when I slice them again and again on the flat pinhead.

I nearly give up. Consumed with exhaustion and utter frustration, I want to throw the fucking things across the room. Curse words flow freely from my lips. Everything hurts.

This is an absolute nightmare.

Click.

Holy shit. Frozen, I stare, dumbfounded, as the shackle around my right ankle loosens.

In an instant, all the pain in my body disappears. Adrenaline soars to new heights, and I practically perform a victory dance right here in this hellhole.

The bent needle falls to the floor as I pull them from the lock. It's so dark now that I'm forced to search for it by touch alone. With oppressed concern, I run my hand over the cold concrete and find it near my left foot.

The pattering of rain hits the roof, and the smell of damp soil invades my senses. With only minimal light, I race to see this endeavor through to the end. Both pins are inserted into the final lock. But the scrubbing needle has bent from my struggles, so I pop it out, hold it between my teeth, and try to straighten it back out.

It looks like shit, but it's straighter than it was a second ago.

The rain is thrashing now, pelting the roof as if inflicting a barrage of gunfire. I can no longer see what I'm doing, and I pray I don't lose the needles again. My finger grazes the lock, and I follow its outline to insert the needles blindly.

Muffled by the downpour, a noise, like something smacking the outside of the door, laces me with panic. The outer door handle clinks with a rusty groan that fills the dank space. I gasp in horror and race to loosely enclose my wrists and freed ankle in the shackles.

A hooded figure steps through the door as I shove the needles back into my pocket. Hiding my hands between my bent legs, it's all I can do to hopefully disguise my transgression. My chest and shoulders heave with my rapid breaths.

Dripping wet, the person enters, leaving a smattering of water on the floor. A flashlight shines in my eyes, forcing me to squint.

"What have you been doing in here?" the voice asks.

It's Marco.

He removes his hood and eyes me skeptically. I fight to steady my breathing, but something tells me it's too late.

"I told you I would come back," he continues, strutting in my direction. "I've been given strict orders to see that you're kept alive." He snickers, sending a wave of goose bumps across my skin. "Poor old man. Perhaps one day he'll get it right."

"Get what right?" I ask, swallowing the bile back down where it belongs.

He kneels before me, his dark eyes illuminated by the garish beam of his Streamlight. "That he really ought to be more specific. See, he only told me to keep you alive." Marco brandishes the knife and teases it in front of my face. "He never said in what condition."

He lays the flashlight near his feet, freeing both hands. With the light no longer in my eyes, I scan the room—and him—with abandon. He's armed. There's a handgun in his waistband—no holster. That would only slow him down.

It appears to be a Glock 9mm, but I can't be sure in this poor lighting.

The loose shackle falls past my wrist when he suddenly grabs my hand, nearly giving me away. With a powerful tug, he wrenches my arm and pins it against his side, captured by his armpit and a firm grip on my wrist. "What the—" I cry out, but he ignores me and digs his elbow into my arm to keep me still.

He laughs as I fight to free myself. But the more I struggle, the more my unlocked shackles jostle, and I fear they may fall open. I can't let him know that I've unlocked them. It could mean the difference between life or death.

All of that falls away, however, when he shoves the knife blade under one of my fingernails. I scream in agony, a sharp pain shooting through my entire hand as blood trickles down my finger and into my palm.

The gun tucked in the back of his waistband is so close.

Forfeiting all attempts to conceal my unlocked binds, I yank free of his grip. He spins to face me, and with an angry roar, I bring my right knee square with his nose. The knife drops to the ground as he covers his face in anguish, falling back on his ass.

I shake the shackles from my wrist and reach for his gun. He lunges at me, an awful grimace on his face, just as I make contact with the grip. Several excruciating blows land on my already-broken nose, sending a fresh pool of blood over my lips, past my chin, and onto my shirt. But I feel such indifference to all of it. Pain is temporary. All that matters is getting out of here alive.

He reaches behind him, and I know exactly why.

Before I can think about my next move, I simply make it and dig both of my thumbs into his eyes. His wailings are guttural and raw, but I don't stop until there's blood. Even then, I press further. Flailing in my grasp, he falls off me and lands square on his back.

Now's my turn to lunge.

Much to my dismay, I fall short of landing on him. My left ankle shackle is still locked.

The chains that once restricted my arms lie on the floor like dead snakes. I grab one and pull it close, taking control of the only item within reach I may use to defend myself. When I look back, however, I'm greeted with the muzzle end of a pistol.

And it's aimed right at my face.

I don't pause. Not for a second. I simply react.

The gunshot blasts just as I jerk the gun up and away, striking the ceiling. I barely hear the ejected casing *tink* upon the ground, for our combined grunts as we tussle over the gun echo almost as loudly as the gunshot itself.

He puts up a hell of a fight. My torn, battered skin is screaming almost as much as my muscles as I fight to keep that gun away from my face.

Out of breath, he pants heavily, and I anticipate his surrender. But he maintains his strength the best he can, leering at me from below with his bloodshot eyes. When I jerk the gun from his relentless grip one last time, he releases it, and it flies into the far corner, disappearing in the darkness.

Shit, shit, shit, shit.

I'm still tethered.

Which means I'm as good as dead.

I can't let him get up. If he does, it's game over.

He twists beneath me, trying to crawl toward the gun. Scratching at the floor, he fights with what seems like everything he has while I keep him pinned beneath me. I yank his head back with a full grip on his forehead, from which he screams his fucking lungs out.

Leaning in, I press my forearm against the back of his neck, pinning his head to the floor. His struggling reaches an all-time high as he kicks and claws and releases frustrated cries.

Growing exhausted with each passing second, I fear how this all may end. If I let up for even a second, and he wriggles free, he'll go for the gun that's beyond my grasp and shoot me down.

I don't look away this time. Feeling around on the floor for the nearest chain, I happen upon the heavy burden in seconds. I drag it close, the sound alerting Marco as he jerks beneath me, freeing his head from its pinned spot on the ground.

But he'd be sad to learn it's just the move I needed him to make, for he has unknowingly exposed his neck for me.

Quick as a snake striking its prey, I pull the chain in, wrap it tight around his neck—using my elbow to keep the excess tight—and pull with all the strength I have left.

Until the thrashing stops.

Until his limbs are no longer twitching and that gurgling sound has long since passed from his lips.

Until my lungs are the only ones that still draw breath.

Gracelessly, I roll off him and onto my back, exhausted and struggling for air.

The rain is pounding harder than ever. Either that, or the ringing in my ears is enhancing nature's wrath. What I wouldn't give to fall asleep right here. But I have to move fast. It's only a matter of time before they realize their torturer is missing.

I sit upright, fish in my pockets for the needles, fetch the flashlight, and go to work on the final shackle. With the Streamlight pinned between my neck and chin, this lock is the easiest of all with the aid of so much light. It clicks open in only a handful of scrubbing motions, the sound of my freedom a mere clank of a final shackle upon the floor.

My ankles ache, and each step I take leads to a different leg cramp. But I can't let it slow me down. I remove Marco's raincoat and slide it on before scooping up his gun and securing it in my waistband.

The jug of water is full, and I drink my fill before deciding to leave the rest behind. With the flashlight in hand, I head for the door.

Pulling the hood up, I peer out at the dense forest that surrounds me. From the doorway, I look for a trail—some sort of path that would lead to *something*. But there's nothing.

I step out into the rain and turn to eye the structure that held me captive. A large concrete building fills my field of view.

Good riddance.

Confident in the cardinal directions I decided earlier, I put my back to the doorway and face east. I have no idea which way to go. One way is just as good as another when everything looks the same.

The forest, consumed by the haziness of the rain, tells me nothing.

So, randomly, I select north.

With Marco's dead body now replacing mine in that frigid tomb, I take a deep breath and run steadfast into the woods beyond.

CHAPTER 29
JAMES

The heavy rainfall obscures my vision as the woods grow increasingly dense. Completely soaked, my best man attire weighs me down, making each step a laborious one. My lungs ache and my throat is raw. But none of it compares to the stitch in my side as I hightail it over the uneven terrain as fast as my tired feet can carry me.

Every few dozen yards, I pause to listen for the sound of footsteps, snapping twigs, or hell, howling dogs. Who knows what these people have at their disposal. The rain, however, is thrumming so loudly that someone could likely be right behind me and I wouldn't hear it.

And that makes me paranoid as hell.

Now I'm looking over my shoulder constantly and cannot keep my footing as a result. I trip and fall to my hands and knees, a sharp pain shooting through the wrist that bears the brunt. My palms are scraped and indented with pebble marks that hurt like a son of a bitch.

Covered in mud and soiled leaves, I crawl back onto my feet, check for the gun in my waistband, and continue to run.

I stop short as the ground ahead inclines steeply, and I debate whether to find another way around. With the ground turned to mush and these fucking loafers having zero traction, I doubt I can make it up and over this hill. I look all around, weighing my alternatives, of which there are none. Not unless I turn around and go back the way I came in hopes of a steadier incline either to the east or west.

The only way to go is forward. I can't go back.

I plan out my path of least resistance along the hillside, taking note of the large boulders I can use for footing from the base to the peak. It's so dotted with trees, however, it's difficult to see all the way up. And the rain certainly doesn't help. But I trudge ahead, hoping endurance will make up for the loss in stability.

Within seconds, I question this entire plan. My footing is lost so frequently that I resort to scaling the muddy hillside strictly on my hands and knees. Rocks and twisted branches dig into my flesh, snap under my weight, and tear gaping holes into the knees of my slacks. Tattered and bloody, my palms leave behind blood swipes everywhere I grip, which are then washed away as if I was never there.

Clawing at the mucky earth, I gain so little ground that I fear my strength may give out before I reach the top. But with one foot surpassing the other, and bit by bit putting one more inch of hillside behind me, I traverse with scorching lungs and unwaning efforts.

My knees slip out from under me, and I faceplant into the sopping foliage and waterlogged soil. The pain that shoots through my broken nose is nearly debilitating, forcing me to cup it in agony and scream through gritted teeth. Blood pours over the contours of my face, the taste of copper rolling into the back of my throat.

Fueled with a newfound sense of anger that can only be compared to madness, I clamber up the remainder of the hillside. Torn, beaten, and broken in more ways than one, I fall onto my back at the crest of the hill, desperate for sleep but empowered by my victory.

The ground levels off and transitions into a slight decline as it spills into a clearing off in the distance. Despite the dense woods in the immediate vicinity, a sliver of the horizon peeks through the clearing. Relief recharges me as I head closer, where the trees part and the ocean beyond becomes evident. It's a beautiful sight despite the gunmetal-gray water, toneless and covered in white caps from the raging storm.

As I inch my way to the tree line, I catch sight of a lighthouse on the bluff. Weathered yet statuesque, it's beige with white trim and a black metal dome, sitting with majestic flavor at the edge of the headland. Its light comes incrementally, but I see no signs of life.

At least I know I'm on some sort of coastline. Attached to the side is a small square outbuilding with a flat roof and identical coloring to the lighthouse itself.

Soaked to the bone and covered in blood and muck, I head for it with little hope that it's accessible. Being away from the tree cover makes me nervous as hell, but I don't see anyone as I haul ass to the outbuilding.

It's locked. A rusted chain encircles the handlebar, which is held together with a single padlock. I reach for the pins in my pocket, which, much to my surprise, are still there. But my hands are so slick with blood and mud, and the rain is so unforgiving, that they slip from my fingers and tumble to the ground. I fall to my knees in a panic, pushing the water that cascades around my feet away, my ripped fingernail screaming all the while.

The pins are nowhere to be found.

My mind reels a mile a minute, trying to come up with an alternative plan.

I happen upon an irregularly shaped rock the size of a softball several feet from the lighthouse door. I have no plan. So I opt for the option when all other plans fail: smash it until it breaks.

I bring the rock down hard onto the padlock, smashing it with all my might. Grunting, panting, and slinging curse words at the fucking thing, I bang it against the lock with such anger that I'm certain the entire coastline can hear. But it's all worth it when it finally busts open. I drop the rock, my hand jammed, sore, and bloody as ever, and rip the chain away.

After multiple slams of my shoulder, the door flies open with a solemn creak.

A small bedroom awaits, with a twin cot along the far wall, a single dresser next to it, a wooden desk beneath a pair of windows facing west, and a louvered closet in the adjacent wall. To the left is a large wooden door, likely connected to the lighthouse itself. Much to my surprise, it opens with relative ease.|

A metal staircase, as white and aged as the exterior trim, spirals upward and out of sight.

The stitch in my side increases tenfold as I steadily make my ascent.

About midway up, the staircase cuts through a room containing a line of wooden tables affixed to the stone wall. A multitude of papers are spread about haphazardly, but one particular sheet among the mess catches my eye.

A topographical map, revealing the hills and valleys of an entire island. On it, an *X* marks my location—labeled *Siren's Point Lighthouse*—situated on the eastern shore just north of someplace called "Moretti Estate."

The other papers on the table are ledgers with rows and columns of numbers and dates, as if torn from some sort of log book, which I find nearby. Its binding is worn, and many of the pages fall loose as I pull the book close. The entries catalog the maintenance dates and times of the lighthouse, with the latest entry less than one week ago. On the front, in faded black ink that's barely legible, are the words *Siren's Point Lighthouse*

My stomach lodges high in my throat when my eyes skim the map and land on the south end of the island. There, written plainly in cursive handwriting, are the words *Krelborn Manor*. Dread hits me with a powerful blow, buckling my achy knees. At the top of the map, next to the cardinal compass, in small block letters, are the words *EDEN'S GREEN*.

I turn away from the table and hold my head to stop the spinning.

I'm back on Eden's Green.

But *why?*

None of it makes sense. And Evie's here, too, somewhere. She has to be.

Reexamining the map, I force myself to concentrate. *Focus on what you can control.* I debate taking it with me and examining it later but opt to commit it to memory here and now. *Never rely on things that can be lost.*

On the southwest side of the island is a third residence—McCarthy Manor. Two main roads form a crooked plus sign through the middle of the island, and one curves along the west perimeter, ending at Krelborn Manor. A handful of smaller roads lead into each property, and some sort of village sits at the north end. There's a dock at the west side, just south of McCarthy Manor, which must have been where our ferry docked on game night.

I fold the map up in a rush, tuck it into the soaked breast pocket of my jacket, and continue up the stairs.

The rain seems to be letting up, for the echoes of the thrashing storm have faded into a more subdued pelting noise.

The door to the lantern room at the top of the stairs is locked, so I head to the windows from the chamber just below it. The entire space consists of more windows than it does stone, giving me the chance to take in the entire island as far as I can see. Bouncing from window to window, I examine the view. Despite the fact that they're covered in trails of rain, I can make out the peaks of rooftops beyond the tree line to the north. The center of the island has a rise in elevation, its hills preventing me from seeing the west side.

But to the south, situated inward from the bluff near the edge of the tree line, is a sprawling manor of aged brick and stone. Turrets sit on the western corners of the estate, which is shaped like a curved *H*, with two vast wings connected by a central point. Between the manor and the lighthouse is a crescent-shaped beach, and on the other side of Siren's Point is a long, ragged coastline of cliffs, with a sliver of beach situated at the base of the headlands.

I head back down the stairs, trying to come up with some sort of plan, desperate for rest.

The cot in the outbuilding calls to me, but I can't risk—

The slam of a car door stops me dead in my tracks. I'm nearly at the bottom of the stairs, but I can't see anything. Treading lightly, I tiptoe to the open wooden door that connects to the outbuilding and peer through the windows on the opposite side of the room.

A black sedan, distorted through the rivulets of rain, sits idling outside. Footsteps resound upon the cliff stone.

Panicked, I scan the room for a place to hide. The lighthouse door faces the same direction as the one to the outbuilding—I would never make it out unseen. Unless I time it just right, but I can't see where the person is through these smeared windows, and—

The door handle creaks as it twists. I race to the louvered closet, throwing the doors closed behind me in breathless trepidation.

Peeking through the slats in the door, I wait with bated breath as the person steps into the outbuilding, shakes off the rain, and looks around the room, his pistol drawn.

I draw mine as well.

Click.

Click.

Click.

With each step the husky man takes, his shoes click on the floor. Expecting to find cowboy boots or the like, I'm instead greeted with red loafers.

Made of reptile skin.

My stomach plummets as I stare in disbelief. Evie's story about her papa and the night he died comes racing to the forefront of my memory.

It's him.

It *has* to be.

I hold in a shaky breath.

He's finally found her.

Each of his strides makes my insides tumble as my heart rate spikes. Beads of sweat form along my rain-soaked hairline.

There are eight rounds left in the magazine of Marco's Glock.

Just make them count.

For a second, I grasp at the hope that he may turn and leave or head into the lighthouse to continue his search. Once he scales the steps, it would give me the head start I need to escape. But then I remember the lock on the outside door. I broke it to gain entry, and there's no way it went unseen.

Fuck.

He has Evie. Somehow, I know it in my gut. The man who tried to take her when she was a child has finally found her. He...and some asshole with a burned face. Rage courses through every vein as I think about what they want with her. Her safety is the beginning and end of everything—the only thing that matters. And I know myself well enough to know that I cannot abandon the search when someone like Evie is at the other end of it all.

I can't leave without her.

Each breath is hollow in this cramped closet, each one growing more rapid than the last.

Especially when he disappears out of sight.

There's a small bathroom near the connecting door, which I pray is where he ventured. Because I don't hear those horrific shoes clicking up the metal spiral staircase.

I lean in closer to the doors, peeking through the slats. I can rarely recall a time I've felt this physically vulnerable. Trapped. The clicks have completely disappeared. But at the same time, there have been no sounds at all. No doors opening, nothing dropped. No toilet flushing.

Where in the hell is he?

Three loud clicks from his shoes suddenly attack the floor just as he appears before the louvered doors. I gasp, his face only inches from mine. As I aim my pistol toward the door, he steps back and aims his. I won't make the shot in time. I react rather than think, falling to my knees on the closet floor before five gunshots tear through the doors and strike the wall behind me. Splintered wood and shards of stone rain down upon me as I cradle my head in a fetal crouch.

He's certain to throw the doors open to admire his work.

So I wait.

The doors fling open wide, and I lunge at him, knocking him to the ground with a grating yell. His gun goes flying as I land on top of him. I consider throwing punches but think better of it and clamber to my feet to aim my pistol at his face.

"Where is she?" I demand.

He only laughs. The venom in my veins turns me rabid.

"Where is she?" I yell. "What do you want with her?"

His cheeks and bulbous nose are as red as his shoes as he huffs for breath. "When you're my age, boy, you'll come to find that secrets are worth more than gold. And when it comes to secrets, I'm a very wealthy man. I would take a bullet for each and every one of them."

His words are laced with mocking ambiguity, and I debate beating the answers out of him out of desperation.

"You won't talk?" I say. "Fine. Then you'll take me to her." I don't wait for him to refute before leaning down and pressing the pistol next to his nose. "*Get up.*"

He obeys and holds his hands up in an act of surrender.

"Move." I motion with my gun toward the door, forcing him to exit first. The gun is aimed square at his back as we approach the car. "Where are the keys?"

He turns and points to the breast pocket of his blazer, then moves to grab them. "Hey," I bark. "Don't move." I approach him cautiously, keeping the pistol aimed at his face, and pat him down. Aside from the keys, I don't feel anything. I remove them from his coat pocket and then toss them to him. "You drive."

I never lose aim as I make my way to the front passenger door.

"Keep your hands up."

He does as instructed, lowering himself into the driver's seat with some difficulty, his hands still raised. Holding the gun with my right hand, I open the front passenger door with the other. As it flings open, several shots are fired from the driver's seat. They ricochet off the open passenger door, whizzing past me as I duck in horror.

I stumble backward and fire off several shots of my own through the front windshield. There's a sudden pause in the gunfire.

So I run like hell.

The car sits between me and the tree line, so I take off toward the lighthouse. But several more shots zoom past me, striking the stone wall and nearly knocking me onto my ass.

I pivot and run for the edge of the bluffs, with absolutely no plan other than to get the hell away. A pathway cutting into the cliff face becomes apparent as I reach the edge. I don't pause for a single breath.

The ocean crashes in a fury that matches my own, the tide making its way in as the rain heads out. The wet sand coating the hill gives me more traction than I had on the hillside, but it's not enough to keep me from falling to the ground more than once. And with every switchback, I fear the hail of gunfire. Surrounded by sand and dune grass and not much else, there's zero cover on this path.

I can't afford to stop to see if he's following me; I don't take a second to listen for the sound of footsteps. My heavy breathing, the roaring waves, and the thick scent of brine in the air are all that fill my senses.

The bottom of the path comes into view. It dead-ends at a cut-out in a jetty at the base of the cliff. Just beyond is the beach I saw from the lighthouse, sandwiched between here and the Moretti Estate.

The sea smashes the rock wall, smothering the rocks embedded in the sand as it reaches for the outcrop at the end of the beach. A gurgling noise echoes low and deep as I approach the entrance to the cave within. Faint hints of daylight filter inside from somewhere at the opposite end, as well as through a large pit in the ground filled with seawater. Crashing against the wall of the pit, then sucking back out with the tide's pull, the ocean growls like the belly of a hungry beast.

The rock is slick. I tuck the gun into my waistband and brace myself along the wall, following its curvature as I take cautious steps deeper into the cave. Before long, it has curved to the point where I have lost the pinpoint of daylight from whence I came, and my only hope is the light that waits deeper in the pass-through.

There should be a small beach on the other side of all this. I recall seeing it from the lighthouse. But there's no place more vulnerable than a beach. No cover, nowhere to hide. I need a plan. Fast.

The large hole in the cavern floor becomes more precarious the more light I lose. With a racing heart and frayed nerves, I inch along the wall. Looking ahead, I notice the floor growing slimmer as the hole overtakes the rock path beyond.

For the first time, I pause to think of a plan.

Water sprays onto my feet with each crashing wave. One wrong step, and there'd be no reason for the man in red shoes to give chase any longer.

A gunshot rings through the cave, the sound piercing my

eardrums and making me lose my footing as it ricochets off the rock. I scramble for the wall and catch my grip on its jagged surface. My muscles ache, and my palms are screaming from everything they've endured, but I hold on. I retrieve the gun from my waistband and hold it up, peering into the darkness in search of Evie's monster.

A single spark of light flicks in the chasm as a second bullet strikes near my left hand.

I turn my back to the wall and take aim, but I can't see him anywhere. A third bullet pierces the darkness, but I don't see where it hits. I fire three aimless shots in return, but it only causes a hail of gunfire upon me.

I empty my clip in seconds, ducking behind the bend, desperate for a pause in which I can make my escape. But it's no use.

"Give it up, Pierce," the man taunts, his voice booming through the tight space. "You've nowhere to go."

Another splash of frigid water douses my shoes. Frantic, I look all around, my eyes landing on the watery tomb at my feet. The ocean level has risen, splashing higher and with greater cruelty than I care to witness.

"Toss your weapon," he demands, creeping into view around the bend. His pistol is aimed at my chest.

I toss it to the ground, teetering on a forfeit. Using the darkness to my advantage, I search my pockets in a last grasp of desperation. The pins are long gone; the map in my breast pocket is useless.

I have nothing.

Save for the red button in my pants pocket.

I pinch it between my fingers, running my thumb along its curves. *For luck.* It's as if Evie's voice is bridled to the plastic piece, just as her lips were on game night. Her words sing in my mind, filling me with an ardor I fear this man will steal from me at long last.

Holding on to a sliver of hope that he means to bring me in

alive, I step away from the wall to square my body with his. My eyes have adjusted enough that I can see his face, twisted with anger for making him work this hard to stop me. I hold my hands away from me in an act of surrender, the button pinched between my fingers.

It seems to please him, for his lips curve into a wicked smile. "Any last words?"

And just like that, I know it's all over. He doesn't mean to bring me in; he means to kill me. My courageous sister, my spunky niece, my incredibly supportive parents—everyone I hold dear flashes before me in an instant, reminding me of all the things I'm about to leave behind.

Evelyn.

Those incredible seafoam eyes. Like a siren luring me toward a rocky shore, they flicker seductively, then disappear. The way she whispers my name in my ear, honeyed yet lustful, as if it's the only name that's ever graced her lips. How she falls apart in my arms, entrusting me with all the pieces, making me fall head over heels over and over again.

"Yes," I reply, imbuing my tone with defeat.

He shifts his weight from one foot to the other. "And what's that?"

After a final pass of my thumb over the red plastic button, "For luck" grazes my lips in a whisper as I teeter it on the edge of my thumb and forefinger.

"Catch."

I flick the button at his face, and it catches him below his left eye.

He recoils in shock.

Without thinking about anything other than the carnal need to survive, I lunge at him. But a shot rings out, booming through the hollow cavern before I hit my target. An unbearable pain tears through flesh and bone, the momentum of the bullet ripping through me and stealing my footing as it knocks me into the open hole in the cave floor.

Straight to the turbulent waves below.

CHAPTER 30
JENNA

MAY 31ST — DAY 4

David's side of the bed is untouched. The coffee maker is unbrewed.

I don't think he stayed here last night.

After he stormed into his office three nights ago, I cut the stove off and left the kitchen and dining table in complete disarray. It was never my intention to wait up for him, but with each passing minute upon crawling into bed, I brain-fucked to death why he was still in there. The pondering led to tears shed, and I wound up crying myself to sleep.

This isn't how I imagined married life; especially not the first few days. On a dime, David has become so cold and distant that I don't recognize him anymore.

Now he's away, to God knows where. Probably at work, trying to further prove the point he made so poignantly before. Maybe he's also avoiding me.

I debate calling him, but I don't want to give him the satisfaction. The asshole can call *me*.

I walk from room to room, like a ghost ambling for some semblance of purpose. The quiet is ripe with vexation, and I can't help but shudder at the stillness. I can't simply do nothing. Evie is out there, somewhere, and every second she's gone, a part of me withers away to dust. But more than anything, all I can think about is the way David lied to the hotel clerk about James and Evie having been found and returning their room keys to solidify the falsity.

He's up to something. It's a feeling I can't shake.

I make my way across the second-floor catwalk to the opposite side of the house.

David's office is locked, increasing my suspicions tenfold. We have no housekeeper, no "staff" of any kind. Which basically means he wants to keep *me* out.

Well then, *deary*. Challenge accepted.

I run my hand over the top of the doorframe, thinking there may be a spare key up there. Nothing.

James picking the lock at Krelborn Manor comes racing back into my head. He used two bobby pins, bent one into the shape of an L, shoved them in the lock, and then...what? I have no clue.

But I do have bobby pins and YouTube. I'll just have to figure it out.

I race to the bathroom and remove two bobby pins from my vanity drawer. I bend one, just as James had, then grab my phone off the nightstand and dive right into lock-picking videos, one after the other.

After what feels like an eternity, I think I have a solid handle on the concept.

Now to execute.

The bobby pins pop out more than once as a result of my sweaty palms. I wipe my hands on my pants, which helps, then resume raking the top bobby pin inside the lock in some method the internet calls *scrubbing*.

Yeah, okay.

Call it what you want, I just need this to work.

But like the little cocksucker that it is, the lock won't open. I've reset the pins at least a dozen times at this point, referring back to the videos each time. I have no idea what I'm doing wrong. James made this look so easy.

My arms are tired, and defeat is looming as I sink to the floor and rest. Maybe I can break the door down? Take it off its hinges?

As defeat shakes its weary finger at me, Evie's face flits into my memory. Not just any memory—*the* memory: our kiss. Leading up to it, I'd never felt more terrified. But I knew she was worth the risk.

She always has been.

I'll never forget her taste, the softness of her lips, or the way she didn't recoil. She was surprised, sure, but she never became upset. And I've wondered every day since if the surprise in her eyes was less about the fact that I'd kissed her at all, and more about the way in which she was learning I was bisexual. I never told anyone, but she's always made it so damn easy for me to be, well, *me.* I just knew she had to be the first to know. God, in hindsight, I can't believe how long it took me to tell her. Keeping it a secret from Evie, of all people, felt almost like a betrayal. After the kiss, she told me she didn't think she could give me what I was looking for. But she held me in her arms all the same and planted kisses in my hair as I came to terms with her unrequited love.

Her affection and support only made me love her all the more. And it's been slowly destroying me ever since.

I have to find her.

With a fresh wave of vigor, I attempt this bobby pin bullshit yet again. I've lost count of the number of attempts at this point, but I refuse to give up. A battle with this lock is a battle for Evie, and I will never stop—

Click.

Holy Jesus fucking shit.

It worked.

I throw the door open with a wave of adrenaline.

The very air in the room reminds me I'm not welcome. An analog clock ticks from somewhere inside, adding fuel to the fire of my trepidation. I head for his desk, positioned in front of a built-in bookshelf that encompasses the entire back wall. The bookshelf is a complete statement piece, deep blue in color, adding to the space's masculine vibes in conjunction with the wooden accents throughout. It would be a rather beautiful room if it didn't feel so uninviting.

Every file cabinet drawer attached to his desk is locked. I scour the bookshelf, the desktop, and the end table alongside the leather lounger by the window, but everything is miraculously clean, as if his office leaped from the pages of a magazine. The only drawer that opens is the under-desk drawer. Inside are very few items: pens, paperclips, and other unnoteworthy items.

But something toward the back of the drawer catches my eye. I remove it and examine it closely. It looks like a remote control, but it consists only of a numbered keypad 0-9, #, *, and a green circular button at the bottom. Smaller than a credit card, the little thing is certainly peculiar. I point it at the TV on the opposite wall, but nothing happens. Not much of a surprise there: I already saw the remote on the end table. I flip it over, examining the thing like it's some ancient relic. Pushing buttons aimlessly makes fuck all happen.

With a frustrated huff, I collapse into the desk chair.

I press the green button again, but this time, a single faint beep sounds somewhere nearby.

I perk up and press the button again. The sound leads me to a small receiver tucked beneath the front lip of the desk. Bending over awkwardly to study it, I find a small rectangle resembling a digital clock face but without any numbers displayed. And it's flashing a little red light in the top right corner.

I shuffle down to the floor and reexamine the remote, puzzled. Surely this thing requires some sort of code. But what in the heck could it be? I don't even know how many digits. This could take forever, and I have no idea if there's a restricted number of attempts allowed. Knowing David, there's probably some alarm that will go off on his phone if there are too many incorrect entries.

Well, you have to start somewhere. I enter David's birthday: 10-02...

As I type, red numbers fill the rectangle, and I realize the receiver holds up to six digits. I include the two-digit year, then press the green button. Three rapid beeps sound. I try the top file cabinet drawer, but it's still locked. Okay, three beeps means a wrong entry.

I rack my brain for more six-digit codes. Our wedding date is a bust. So is my birthday and the date he graduated from college. Heck, I even tried the opening date of his first nightclub, our address—1023 18th Street—our first date. Nothing. I'm terrified that I'm running out of tries, so I take time to really think. What other dates would be significant enough to use as a code? Maybe it isn't a date at all. I try the last six digits of each of his bank accounts, but I'm only rewarded with three rapid beeps.

I draw my knees to my chest and grip my hair with irritation. I don't know his social security number by heart. There are so many things it could be that I would never be able to guess. The date of his mother's death. His baby sister's? Maybe his baby sister's birthday? I don't know any of these.

One last date comes to mind: the day we first met. I remember it was Evie's birthday. We went to Club Giada for a night out. He was working behind the bar and had his charm turned up to the max, and I was hooked within minutes. Several weeks and many dates later, he confessed that he owned the place and was merely "playing bartender" to work his way into a conversation with me.

Such a charmer.

I type in the date: 041822

A single drawn out beep sounds in conjunction with a soft *click*. The sentimentality of the cracked code thaws my irritation with him ever so slightly as I fling the file drawers open and scour them with eager eyes.

The files are all labeled, just as neat and organized as David himself. Documents for his different nightclubs: sales receipts, tax documents, employee forms. Nothing of interest. I slide the folders frantically, pulling each one open and peeking at the contents within. But there's nothing here that gives me even a hint as to why he's been acting so strangely. Perhaps he really is telling the truth? Maybe he's hurting as badly as I am but doesn't know how to deal with it other than push it aside and pretend everything is all right? This may have been how his parents dealt with his sister's death, solidifying his passivity toward truly terrible situations.

I give up. Either I hear the truth from David's lips or accept defeat and hope the police can find Evie. I shove the file drawers closed, but the top drawer stops short with a low groan.

It won't shut.

Peeking inside, I notice a file folder misaligned on its rung. Reaching to the very back of the drawer, I pull all the files forward in search of the culprit. But something captures my attention at the back. It's a file with a tab labeled *Project Winter*.

Curious, I remove it and plop it on the desk. When I begin flipping through its contents, the whole world around me drops away in an instant.

Along with all the air in the room.

Oh my God.

I cover my gaping mouth, stifling the cry that's trapped in my throat as my stomach plummets to the floor, rendering me paralyzed by what awaits inside.

CHAPTER 31
JAMES

JUNE 1ST — DAY 5

An abyss of salt and death. That's my new prison.

All sense of direction is lost, all hope for survival diminished.

It's where I meet my end.

Thick, unpalatable brine coats my lips and lungs. The thirst. That godforsaken, unquenchable thirst.

And numbness. Everything, everywhere.

There's nothing left.

Except for a single word that echoes in my ear, low yet angelic, in a voice I'm certain is Evie's: "Wake."

But it's overtaken by the roaring waves as they destroy everything in their path, including me.

"Wake," Evie repeats.

I can't see her, and I'm convinced her voice is merely a taunt as I stumble down my road to perdition.

I'm in hell. I'm certain of it.

Salt. So much repulsive salt polluting the waves that strike me with such force that my bones can barely withstand it.

"*Wake*." She unleashes another command, more adamant than before.

The roaring fades as a pinpoint of white light emerges from behind my eyelids. It grows exponentially until it's all I see. I can't squint. My eyes are already closed. But the increase in brightness does not waver, and I'm filled with horror as it singes my eyes.

I can't scream.

I can't breathe.

Saltwater has filled my lungs, and I now belong to that awful light. It claims me with a bite I cannot escape. But I refuse to submit to this devil in the white light. I claw, spit, and tear at the garish glow, fighting for my soul.

The sound of the ocean raging in my ear suddenly vanishes, the silence deafening in its own right. My eyes flicker open, yet all I see is that bright light. But this time, it's surrounded by blue sky and billowy clouds. A flock of birds call upon the sea as they glide across my field of view.

"Well, what d'you know? It lives," a stoic voice says somewhere off to the left. I tilt my head away from the light, toward the sound. A man sits in a chair nearby with his elbows resting on his knees. His wavy brown hair is tucked behind his ears. He could be my age, but it's difficult to say. The creases along his forehead and at the corners of his eyes may age him beyond his years. And the five-o'clock shadow doesn't help.

He hustles over to the window and draws the shades. Little specks of light obscure my vision. "Sorry about that," he says before making his way back to his seat alongside the bed. "That afternoon sun can be brutal."

"Where am I?" I ask with a raspy voice. My throat feels like sandpaper.

"My house," he answers.

"How...?" I swallow hard, but my mouth is so dry that it accomplishes nothing. "How did I get here?"

The man stands and holds a cup and straw to my lips. The water goes down with some difficulty, but it's the best thing I've ever tasted.

"The boss put out orders to the entire island. He had everyone out looking for you. Still does. Those of us with boats"—he nods in some arbitrary direction beyond the edge of the house—"were ordered to patrol the shoreline, looking for someone who matches your description." He sets the cup down on the nightstand and eyes me questioningly.

My entire body aches. Even the smallest movement sends a sharp pain through my entire left arm, which I now see is secured inside a makeshift sling of what I think may be a T-shirt.

"The boss?" I ask, not entirely sure what answer I'm looking to receive. "The man with the scars?"

He cocks an eyebrow as if impressed. "So you two have met?"

I nod, and a dull ache hits me in the back of the neck.

"What does he want with you?" He reclaims his seat and leans back into his original position, his elbows propped on his knees, eager for information I'm not sure I want to divulge.

I remain silent.

He straightens his back. "Well, whatever it is, it must be pretty good. He has the whole island whipped into a frenzy trying to bring you in alive."

I tilt my head, confused. "Alive? Why?"

"You tell me." After several moments, he concedes to my silence and stands with a heavy sigh.

"Is your plan to heal me up and then turn me in?" I look him square in the eye, trying to mask my trepidation. "Why am I here?"

The man stalks back over to the bed and rolls his sleeves to his elbows. "You're a serviceman, yes? Air Force?"

My brow furrows with confusion. "Yes. How—"

"Your tattoo. The eagle on your back. The banner in its talons says 'USAF,' with a date range I can only assume are the dates you served." He sits back down in the chair. "Which unit?"

"Twenty-sixth STS," I reply, surveying the room.

He holds his forearm out to me, and I return my attention to him. Beyond the edge of the rolled sleeve, on the inside of his right forearm, is a fallen soldier tattoo.

"You also served?" I ask, the palpitations of my racing heart beginning to subside.

"Army. I was a desert medic for almost eighteen years."

Finding comfort in this stranger the longer he speaks, I reply, "Same." I sigh. "Not the medic part, just the overseas part."

"Iraq?"

"Afghanistan."

He nods, a small but powerful gesture of understanding.

After a minute that stretches far too long, he says with a stern voice, "Listen." He rubs the back of his neck. "You've been here at my house for the last day and a half. I found you lying face down on a rock near the shoreline while I was patrolling the waters, as instructed. You're lucky it was the middle of the night."

He stops pacing and squares his stance with the bed, his hands on his hips. "You looked dead. But when I went to pull you into my boat, you still had a pulse, and it was apparent you had suffered a gunshot wound to your left shoulder. When I removed your shirt to better examine you, I saw your tattoo..." He runs a hand over his scruff and shakes his head. "I just couldn't call it in."

"But you have no idea who I am," I retort, finding strength again despite my croaky voice. "That's a hell of a risk you're taking for a complete stranger."

"You and I both played in the same sandbox," he says, casually holding on to the metal foot railing. "There are some loyalties that outweigh their risks."

He makes his way back to the bedside. "But this house is no substitute for a hospital. And if you don't get to one soon, that wound is likely to become infected. I was able to stitch it, but I have limited supplies, and you really should have it checked out. You're lucky it was a through-and-through." He sits back down. "So, in three nights from now, I'm going to smuggle you off this island."

I jerk my head back in his direction. "No." I use my good arm to push myself into a sitting position, but my ribs hurt so badly that I'm convinced they're fractured, and I collapse with a wince.

"Don't move," he asserts, reaching for me.

"I can't leave." I grimace as I run a protective hand over my ribs. "I can't leave this island."

"You don't have a choice." He adjusts the pillow behind my head, but it does little to stifle the blow he's dealt. "When you don't turn up, dead or alive, it's only a matter of time before the boss orders house-to-house searches. It isn't safe for either one of us if you stay here—"

"I'm not leaving without her," I interject, more forcefully than I intended.

His brow furrows. "Her? Who are you talking about?"

"He took Evelyn." I lock eyes on him. This isn't a game, and I need him to know it. "And I'm not leaving this island without her."

Images too real to ignore come racing back into my mind. The bathroom at the country club, completely empty in my desperate search for Evie. The cargo van at the far end of the parking lot, with a handful of men gathered at the open back doors. The sight of Evie's motionless body in the back...

I tried to stop them. God, how I tried. I landed many blows, the sensation of bones cracking beneath my vengeful fists propelling the madness I needed to keep me standing.

To save my Watson.

But there were too many of them, and when a pair of hefty arms pinned mine from behind, that's when I lost the upper hand.

Despite the blows I dealt, they weren't enough.

And the blow they dealt was worse. Much worse.

Goddamn, how I tried to save her. But I failed. The twisting in my gut is likely to be my death sentence. Yet I deserve far worse.

I failed.

Never again.

Never.

Yes. I remember it now. Still in pieces, but the picture is coming back to me nonetheless.

One minute, we were dancing to her favorite song, and I fell headfirst into those pale eyes, and the next...

The man's eyes seem heavy as he sits back in his chair. "Evelyn?" he asks, as if trying to understand my meaning through her name alone. A languid sigh passes his lips before he says in a soft voice, "She's your girl." It doesn't sound like a question, more like an affirmation of understanding.

I nod.

He leans forward and rubs his intertwined fingers together, staring at the floor in what seems like disbelief. "Jesus, it all makes sense now," he whispers.

"What?"

"It's a small island. And it's an even smaller village." He looks toward the window as if in a daze. "People talk. We hear things we often aren't meant to." He turns his attention to me. "There were rumors that he brought a woman back from the mainland. We didn't know who she was, and no one had seen her. It all started three days ago, when the boss gave us a direct order that anyone we don't recognize, man or woman, is to be returned to his estate immediately, no questions asked. Sounds to me like he's afraid she may escape."

My stomach twists in agony. I should be there, with her, protecting her at all costs. Taunted by my failures, I swallow deeply as I'm reminded that not only is my Wats in complete danger, but I have absolutely no idea how to get her back.

With all the conviction I possess, I regard him with desperate eyes. "Help me get her back. Please."

He stares at me for a long time, and I'm hopeful he's considering my plea. But his heavy sigh tells me otherwise before he even speaks. "I'm sorry, but I can't do that."

My heart drops.

"Sunday night, I'll sneak you off this island in my boat. I'll drop you off, we will part ways, and you'll never see me again. At that time, my duty toward a fellow soldier in need will have been met. After that, you can do what you want. If you want to risk everything and find a way back to this island to save your girl, you'll have to figure that out on your own. I told myself I wouldn't let you die, but that obligation ends the moment we dock on the mainland. Got it?"

He's saved my life and put himself on the line in more ways than I deserve. I can't ask anything more of him. I acquiesce with a gentle nod, racked with guilt and fear. He hands me the cup, and I gulp the rest of the water down, desperate to rid myself of the saltiness that lingers on my tongue.

"Why Sunday?" It seems so random.

He straightens his back and crosses his arms. "All of the fishermen in this village make an honest living, but we live here during the fishing season with very strict permissions." He pauses, and I fear he feels he's said too much. Much to my relief, he continues. "We can only come and go from the island on designated days of the week, and we must receive permission from the boss to do so. He pays us for our silence with his dealings, and in exchange for the hefty sum, we have to perform certain deliveries of our own."

I cock my head. "He's a smuggler?"

The man exhales a quick laugh. "Built an empire on it."

"Drugs?"

"No."

He doesn't offer the correct answer, and I don't press him for it.

"Why do you stay? I mean, if he's forcing you to work for him—"

"When he bought the island, we were given an ultimatum: work for him or leave. Some of us have had homes here for generations, and this is a prime fishing spot, available only to us due to the strict security on and around the island. Leaving was a lot to ask."

I get it. In some odd way, it makes sense.

"You should get some rest," he tells me, stretching his back as he stands.

I call after him as he heads for the door. "What happens now?"

He turns back to me. "We wait for Sunday. And keep our fingers crossed that they don't do any house-to-house searches before then. If so, your ass is going under my floorboards." He flashes a smile, and I breathe a sigh of relief.

Just as he breaches the doorway, I call out one last time. "Hey." He looks over his shoulder at me. "What's your name?" I ask.

He reaches into his pocket, removes a toothpick, and wipes the pocket fuzz off. "Emerson Shaw," he says before plopping the toothpick into his mouth with a grin. "You?"

"James," I reply, breathing heavily from the pain that rips through my shoulder. "James Pierce."

"Good to meet you, James." He slaps the doorframe, his ring clacking against the wood. "Let me get you something to eat, and some more pain meds. Now that you're awake, you may be in for a long night."

CHAPTER 32
JENNA

JUNE 3RD — DAY 7

That voice.

It's all I can hear anymore. It called my name, frantic and shrill.

Evie's voice.

It has to be.

Like a dagger piercing what little of my heart remains, that voice is killing me, one cut at a time, playing on a loop that manages to drown out my rapid heartbeat.

David knows where she is, and the fucking lies *will* stop. Here and now.

He still isn't home. For the past five nights, he's been gone, with nothing more than a periodic phone call to fill me in on the latest lies of the crises at work. Last-minute trips to meet with business associates...it's all bullshit, I know it. And the longer I go with that fucking file and its contents staring back at me, the more infuriated I become.

Minutes fade to hours as I wait in the front room, staring out the window. I called David earlier today, demanding he finally bring his ass home. He insisted he'd be home tonight.

I refuse to leave until I see him.

I want my face to be the first thing he sees before I demand an explanation of the voice I heard during our phone call.

And the contents of this file, which I've tucked behind the couch cushion as I lie in wait.

Sitting on the window bench seat, twisting my wedding band around my finger, I watch as the clouds envelop the house in shadow, obliterating the sunlight and making me pray for rain. It's unpleasantly humid today. A storm would do everyone some good.

My heavy eyelids flitter back open from my unexpected slumber as headlights come up the driveway. Much to my surprise, it's completely dark outside and pouring rain, disorienting me with the loss of time. According to my phone, it's a quarter past nine.

I bolt from my seat and hurry to the front door as a key jimmies in the lock.

David looks alarmed to see me as he walks inside. "Jen?" He tosses his keys on the table in the foyer and runs a hand through his soaked hair. "Everything okay?"

Ignoring him, I walk over to the sitting area in the front room and prop myself on the arm of one of the couches, arms crossed over my chest. "Where is she?" I demand.

He follows me with a mystified look. "What are you talking about?"

"Where is she?" I scream, cutting through the bullshit. "I know you know where she is. And I want you to tell me. *Now.*"

His huff grates on my nerves, but not nearly as much as the way he dismisses me by dropping his head back with exasperation. "Not this again." He peels his blazer off with an attitude and tosses it over the back of the opposite couch. "What in the hell is going on with you?"

"What's going on with *me*?" I pop to my feet and remove the file from behind the cushion. I hold it up with a flamboyant flair. "I found this in your office."

David's eyes widen before his face contorts into an infuriated scowl. "You broke into my office?" he sneers. "You went through my things—my *private* things?"

"You bet your ass I did," I retort. "And I can't wait to hear you explain why in God's name you have a file with Evie all throughout the fucking thing." I open the folder, but I'm not really looking at the contents. I'm more focused on screaming my piece.

"There are photographs of her—walking out of her apartment building, putting gas in her car...This one here..." I hold up a black-and-white photograph of Evie walking into the art museum where she works. "Going to work." I fling it onto the floor. "It's as if you've been *stalking* her. There are sketches of her face all over the place here, birth certificates with her name on it, as well as for someone by the name of 'Neve Denardo.'" I'm flipping through the contents so quickly, I nearly drop the whole thing. "Photocopies of checks made out to her dad, Eugene Foster. Documents bearing the name 'Rose Parisi.'" I toss it all onto the coffee table, and the papers scatter in disarray. I can't look at them another second.

I've never been this angry. My heart is racing so fast, it takes everything in my power not to sit down to catch my breath. But I can't waver. If ever there was a time for me to stand my ground, it's now.

"Jen." David holds his hands up and approaches me an inch at a time, as if waiting for me to pounce. "This isn't what it looks like—"

"Which is what, exactly?" Tears fill my eyes, but I refuse to let them spill. "I heard her. I heard her call for me." I choke back a sob. "You saw her today, didn't you? What have you done?"

"Babe." His voice is so calm that I barely recognize it. "You're scared. I get it. And I worry it's getting the better of you. I don't know where Evie is." He's speaking so slowly, I wonder if he truly believes I've gone mad. "I haven't seen her—"

"Cut the shit," I cry out. "I heard her. And you can try to excuse your way out of it all you want, make me out to be a lunatic all over again. I don't give a shit. Just stop wasting my fucking time and tell me why you've been stalking her."

He eyes me intensely before taking a seat on the opposite couch and lowering his head into his hands. It's several grueling moments before he speaks. "I haven't been stalking her, Jen." He sighs heavily. "I can see how this looks...I'm just...I need..." He runs his hand over his beard and looks out the window before looking back at me. "I just need you to trust me."

I shake my head. He must be completely out of his fucking mind. "Tell me where she is." Obstructed by my tears, he stands as a blurry mess, but it does nothing to mask the bite in my demand.

"Jen—"

"Tell me where she is," I scream at the top of my lungs. "If you want me to trust you, then at least start there." Sobs pierce my throat, but I force them back the best I can.

"I don't know where she is," he murmurs.

"Bullshit."

"You asked for the truth—"

"And yet you're still lying to me." Swallowing hard, I plan a different line of attack. "Who's Neve Denardo?" I'm desperate for any answers at this point.

He retracts, taken aback.

"You have her birth certificate in there. Why? Who is she?"

But he only sits there, stone cold. I want to shake him, pummel him, just to get him to do—or say—something. He stands and braces his hands on his hips. Looking down at the smattering of Evie's face across the coffee table, he finally says in a soothing tone, "There's so much I wish I could tell you, babe." His shoulders slump as he turns crestfallen. "But I just can't. I'm sorry."

As if from the powerful blow of a sledgehammer, I'm bowled over by the only truth that seems to exist between us anymore: it's all over.

"Fine," I say, storming toward the front door. "Keep your secrets."

I grab my car keys and rush to the Benz in the driveway. He calls after me, but I don't stop as I climb in the car and throw it in drive. Putting this nightmare behind me is the only thing I have control over anymore.

Not even the tears that spill freely down my cheeks as David watches me from the driveway before he fades away in the rearview mirror.

CHAPTER 33
JAMES

The bilge pump compartment of Emerson's tuna boat is cramped, uncomfortably humid despite the freezing ankle-deep water, and reeks of briny fish and mildew. But it was the only safe place to stow me away, according to him, in case his commercial fishing vessel was stopped and searched at one of the boss's water-based security checkpoints.

It's been about fifteen minutes into the journey, and I'm struggling to find the confidence that we're in the clear. Emerson assured me he received clearance from the boss to leave tonight, but with an ongoing island-wide manhunt, I don't share in his optimism.

So when the raucous engine suddenly cuts to a gentle hum, indicating that we're now idling, it strikes fear in me all the same. My shoulder hurts like a motherfucker, worsened by the rocky sway of the boat. I crane my neck to examine the trap door located above a four-rung ladder, listening for sounds that may determine my fate. Footsteps overhead are faint, and the accompanying voices are muffled. But there are multiple, which scares the shit out of me. I put all my trust in Emerson, a complete stranger who felt beholden to a fellow soldier. I have no choice at this point but to have faith that he'll come through for me one last time.

More footsteps.

But the voices are gone.

Any second now, that trap door is going to open, and I'll be staring down the barrel of a gun. I inch toward the ladder and listen intently.

Nothing. Only the blood that bombards my eardrums.

Sweat beads and spills down my temples. The air is so dense in here that I wonder if this is what it feels like to be buried alive.

This is it. Any second, it's all over…

The force of the boat's acceleration pushes me back from the ladder, and I land on my ass on the bilge deck. The engine's hum resumes, and my knotted stomach sighs with relief.

By the time the hour-long journey ends, the engine's roar has diluted itself to a white nose that damn near soothes me to sleep.

The vessel knocks against the dock, the reverberations stunted and loud from my spot inside the hull. With the engine cut off, it's the first time I've noticed the pattering of rain.

Emerson rips the trap door open and peers down at me, hooded and drenched. I take his proffered hand, and he pulls me up the ladder and onto the deck.

The dock is slick beneath my bare feet and shimmering from the marina lights. The button-up flannel shirt he gave me rests lazily over my left shoulder and sling, soaking up the rain as I wait on the dock.

"Harwich Port. This is where I leave you," he says. "Straight through there"—he points beyond the parking lot, vacant and as still as the dead at this late hour—"is Route 28. It's your best bet at finding a phone this late."

I take in my surroundings. The town is asleep, alight only by amber street lights. "I can't thank you enough." I brush the soaked hair away from my forehead. "Honestly, I wish there was something—"

"Just take care of yourself, Pierce," he replies, extending his hand out to me.

I shake it, filled with gratitude and a bit of guilt for my inability to repay him. "You too."

Emerson hops aboard his vessel and disappears into the wheelhouse. With no money, cell phone, or plan, I watch him depart, swallowed by the thrashing rain.

Troubled by thoughts of where to go from here, I turn away from the docks and head for the main road.

The street is lined with homes of gray shaker shingles with white trim. Splashing through puddles, I amble around, looking for a business that may still be open. I need a phone.

A ripping current along the perimeter of the street washes away everything in its path as it pounds the gutters. Nothing is stirring tonight—not a single car passes by, not a single dog barks, not a single silhouette occupies a window.

My shoulder screams in agony, and I'm so parched that I debate collecting the rain in my cupped hands and drinking from it what I can.

A sign bearing the name Harbor Road comes into view, and I follow it aimlessly. After several blocks, I finally escape the stretches of houses and emerge onto a street lined with shops and boutiques. The street is as silent as the grave, almost apocalyptic, the shop windows blacked out and not a single sign of life in any direction.

After a grueling walk that transforms minutes into hours, a cluster of lights up ahead reinvigorates my sore muscles and torn feet. My T-shirt sling is practically rags at this point, soaked to the point of near uselessness. But I ignore my current state and hurry toward the lights.

A convenience store lies up ahead, just past Bank Street. Inside, it's completely empty of people save for the portly bald man behind the counter. With glasses and a trimmed white beard and mustache, he has a kind face that quells my nerves. That is, until he surveys me from over the top of his glasses and says, "Sir, you can't come in here without shoes."

With a pained look, I beg the man to have mercy on me. "I've been in an accident," I lie. "I don't have my phone. I just need to make a call." I pause, waiting for him to either take pity or throw my ass out.

He eyes me up and down again, his gaze landing on what's left of my sling. "I suppose that'd be all right." He grabs the landline off the receiver and holds it to his ear. "What's the number?"

I rattle off David's number, and he dials it, then hands me the phone. The seconds tick by as I wait for him to answer. Instead, I'm met with an operator telling me the phone is out of service.

There's no one else local who can come get me. Other than David, who's likely in Boston right now with Jenna.

Jenna.

I don't know her number.

The man behind the counter—Carl, according to his name tag—eyes me suspiciously. "No answer," I tell him. "Can I try another?" It's as if I'm in prison, and I'm only allowed one phone call.

He sighs, presses the receiver, then says, "Go ahead with the number."

"Well, I..." I laugh, trying to lighten the mood. "I don't exactly know the number, but..."

Think.

"Do you by any chance have a cell phone on you?" I ask him.

Carl squints at me but answers my question. "Yes."

"Can you look up something for me? I just need the phone number for a realty company. Umm..." What in the heck is the name of the realty company Jenna's parents own? If I can get in touch with them, maybe they can help me find David. "Murphy... something."

"Murphy One?"

"Yes," I exclaim.

He scrolls on his phone, and I wait patiently as water drips from my hair and onto my face. I wipe at it with the back of my hand, but it makes little difference.

The bell over the door rings, and two teenagers walk in. They glance my way before heading for the back toward the coolers of drinks.

"Ah. Here it is," Carl says. He punches the phone number into the landline and hands it back to me. It rings so many times that I'm convinced there's no voicemail set up. Finally, a groggy female voice picks up. "Can I help you?"

A rush of elation kicks my heart rate into high gear. "*Yes*. Mrs. Murphy? Is this Jenna's mother?"

At the mention of Jenna's name, she seems to wake up a bit. "Yes. Who is this?"

"This is James Pierce. I was the best man at her wedding. Listen, I'm in a bit of a bind, and I need to get in touch with David. But I don't have my phone or wallet, and I'm—"

"James Pierce?" she asks, as if in disbelief.

"That's right. I called David, but it says his number is out of service. Is there any way you can—"

"James?" A high-pitched, flustered voice cuts into the phone from the background, startling the hell out of me. "James," the voice continues, now directly into the receiver. "It's Jenna. Where are you?"

"Jenna," I say, filled with relief. "I've been trying to get ahold of David, but his phone—"

"Don't call David," she exclaims. I fall silent, riddled with confusion.

"What do you mean? Why—"

"Just tell me where you are, and I'll come get you."

"I'm at a gas station near Route 28 and Bank Street," I reply. "In Harwich Port."

"Stay right there." The urgency in her voice makes my heart

skip. "I'm on my way." As I reach to give the phone back to Carl, I catch Jenna saying something through the speaker. I bring it back to my ear. "What was that?"

"It's extremely important that you listen to me."

"I'm listening, Jen," I reply, seeds of apprehension taking root in my gut.

"Whatever you do, you can't call David," she says. "It isn't safe."

CHAPTER 34
JENNA

As I speed down Route 3 toward Harwich Port like a fucking madwoman, the rain bombards my windshield as my wipers struggle to keep up. At this time of night, I should be able to make it in an hour. I just hope that James doesn't grow impatient and wander off. Or, worse yet, try calling David again.

Panicked, perplexed, but also feeling unusually amped, I cling to the hope that Evie is safe. Even if she isn't with James, he must know where she is. I'm one step closer to bringing her home.

I honk at cars that delay too long when stop lights turn green and shout obscenities at slow drivers taking up the passing lane. If I'm not careful, my adrenaline may be the death of me. But I don't care. Getting to James is the only thing that matters right now.

I turn onto Route 6, and with less than half the journey to go, my head is abuzz with how I'm going to break this to James. David isn't who I thought he was, and there's no telling how much of this James is privy to. It certainly crossed my mind that James may have had a part to play in all this. But without David, I have no one else to turn to. I'm taking a chance on James—counting on him as someone I can trust—and I hope I'm not wrong.

After for-fucking-ever, the Cumberland Farms gas station finally comes into view. My arrival is announced with the manic squealing of tires as I barrel into the parking lot. An indiscernible figure standing beneath the overhang near the entrance becomes engulfed in my headlights. He's hunched over, soaked, and... barefoot?

With the engine still running, I jump out of the car and run to him.

"James?" The mess of a man hurries over to me, and I throw my arms around him in a tight embrace. "Are you all right?" I cry, pulling away to get a better look at him. He's holding an empty bottle of water, and the sight of his sling makes a lump form in my throat. He only nods before heading to the car.

We sit idly in silence. It pains me to look at him—his face is swollen and battered, a wheezing sound emanates from his nose every time he breathes...

And that sling.

What in God's name happened to him?

"I should get you to a hospital," I say.

He shakes his head. "No. I'm okay. Hospitals are required to inform the police of all gunshot victims, and I can't have—"

"You've been *shot*?" I cry. "My God, James. W-What happened? Where have you been? And where's Evie?"

He slumps against the headrest and peers out the window, his silence making my blood curdle as I soak in his demeanor. He seems so weak, so fragile—so unlike James—and it scares me to death.

I pull away from the gas station, the squeak of the windshield wipers and the pattering of rain filling the silence between us.

We're back on Route 6 when, out of the blue, he whispers, "She's on Eden's Green."

The shock of it nearly makes me veer off the road.

"Beyond that," he continues, "I have no idea."

Focusing on the road has become impossible. Thank God there's hardly anyone out and about on the Cape right now. "Did she go there of her own accord?" I ask, fearing the answer before it's given. "Or was she taken?" That last part physically hurts to say, and I swallow it back as if that may absolve its impact. But it doesn't work.

James is silent for far too long. I can't take it anymore. With a quick veering of the steering wheel, I jerk the car over to the shoulder and throw it in park. James finally looks at me then.

"I need you to talk to me." Tears are brewing, but I stave them off. "What in the hell is happening?"

His piercing gaze makes me squeamish. Much to my relief, he finally speaks in a soft, almost trancelike voice. "She was taken, Jen." He looks away, his attention aimed out the windshield. "I saw her... in a van. Tied up..." He trails off. "But I haven't seen her since the wedding..." It's as if he's fallen under some spell cast by the streaks of rain that paint my windshield. "I awoke in some bunker or something." He brushes his soaked hair away from his eyes. "There's a man. I don't know his name. But he has burn scars all over one side of his face."

"What?" I gasp.

James turns to me then and cuts through me with eyes like razors. "He has her."

My insides fall to the floor. This can't be real.

In an instant, the sound of the windshield wipers is driving me batshit crazy. James's silence has me seeing red, and all I can think about is stealing a boat to head back to Eden's Green. I can't stop the barrage of questions, the endless guilt that tears me in half, or the helplessness that comes with not having any semblance of a plan.

"What do you think he wants?" is all I can manage to say.

He shakes his head, his shoulders slumped in defeat. "I have no idea."

"James," I whisper, waiting for him to look at me. "I need you to be strong here, okay? I need your help. I can't do this alone. Evie needs us, and I don't have David anymore, so you're all I have to get her back."

He furrows his brow. "What do you mean, you don't have David?"

I shift in my seat and rest my arm on the steering wheel, perplexed. "I..." Now it's James's turn to stare at me. I can't ignore his plight as his widened eyes beg me to continue. "I found a file in his office." I shake my head at the memory. "It was full of photographs, sketches..." I look at him. I need him to see that I'm telling the truth. "James. They were all of Evie."

His chest buckles from a sharp exhale.

"There was a birth certificate in there for someone named Neve Denardo. There were photocopies of checks, a copy of her work schedule at the museum...It's like he had been stalking her."

James falls back against his seat and holds his forehead. I fear he may faint.

"James, I have to ask..."

"Don't," he warns.

"Did you know about any of this?"

The pained look on his face is one I won't soon forget. "*No*, Jen. And I hate that you felt you even had to ask."

"You and David have been best friends for so long. You can't blame me for wondering." My voice has become shrill. "Has he ever mentioned the name Neve Denardo to you?"

His eyes pinch shut, and I fear I've given him a headache.

"What do you think it could mean? Why is this happening?" Tears sting my eyes. Any hope I had that James may be able to shed some light on where in the hell Evie has gone is falling by the wayside.

"I don't know," he whispers.

Defeated, drained, and sick of this fucking rain, I pull away from the shoulder and drive the rest of the way to Chatham in silence.

I PARK IN THE DRIVEWAY OF MY PARENTS' CAPE house and help James out of the car and up the front steps. The rain has not let up, and by the time we enter the foyer, we're both completely drenched. After a brief tour of the house, I escort him upstairs to the guest room.

"Your bathroom is here," I say, heading over to the opposite side of the room. "There are fresh towels on the counter."

James sits on the edge of the bed, visibly exhausted.

"The sheets on the bed are clean. I'll get you a new toothbrush and things in the morning so you have them. Oh, and let me grab you some dry clothes." I hurry from the room and race down the hall to the master bedroom. My mother always brings her clothes back to the Boston house when they're done vacationing in this one. My dad, however, likes to leave what he can here. Thank God for the simplicity of my adorable father.

There are a few flannel shirts hanging in their closet and some pajama pants in the dresser. I scoop them all up and bring them to James.

I find him sitting on the bed with the phone receiver to his ear. "Sara, please don't cry," he says. "I'm all right. I promise, I'll explain everything soon." He pauses. Frozen near the old-fashioned writing desk under the window, I wait to move or speak until his phone call is over. "Please give Maya a big hug for me. I'll call you soon." A voice sounds through the receiver just before James hangs up the phone.

His breathing is heavy, his skin blanched and pale, and he's clearly too exhausted to change into something dry.

With a gentle touch, I brush the hair away from his closed eyes, towel off what I can, adjust the sling around his arm, drape a throw blanket over him, and watch as his breathing evens out into a deep slumber. It's only then that I realize it's okay for me to breathe.

I never thought James could appear so weak—so frail. It terrifies me more than I care to admit.

I can't lose him. He's all I have left of Evie, and I need his help.

In so many ways, I feel responsible for him now, and I sure as hell can't leave him.

Desperate for a swift recovery, I watch him sleep for way too long. A twinge shoots through my back, forcing me to leave James behind and crawl into a bed of my own.

I cut the lights, leave the door open a crack, and head into the hall. But that's as far as my willpower allows. I can't go back to Boston. Leaving the Cape while Evie is still out there, and leaving James while he's in such poor condition, is something I'll never do.

Next to the bedroom door, I slide down the hallway wall and listen to James's steady breathing. In time, my eyes flutter shut, my own exhaustion taking over and lulling me into a dreamless sleep.

❦

STIFF AND ACHY, I TRY TO MOVE, BUT MY ENTIRE BODY protests. Falling asleep sitting upright was the worst effing idea. Now my ass is completely numb, my legs tingle—not in a good way—and my back feels like I aged forty years overnight.

And something is digging into the nape of my neck.

As my eyes flit open, I see James sitting next to me, propped against the wall, with his good arm around my shoulders. There's a blanket draped over the two of us, and a gentle snore emanates from his open mouth. I shift to see him better, and to make a mental note of his ridiculous snore face. But my movement shakes him, and I kick myself for ruining the Kodak moment.

He snorts awake and looks around, disoriented.

"'Morning, sunshine," I say, my voice groggier than ever.

"Hey," he croaks. He licks his dry lips as his eyes threaten to shut again.

"James," I begin softly. He meets my gaze. "What are you doing out here?"

After a long, dramatic yawn, he shrugs. "I woke up in the middle of the night. Was going to grab some water from the kitchen, but then I found you out here sleeping. I didn't want to wake you, but I also wasn't sure if you'd want to be alone..." With sleepy creases embedded in his face, there's an innocence to him that I find truly endearing. "I figured you'd be going back home to Boston." The last part of what he says is strained as he removes his arm from around my shoulders and stretches it outward.

"I was going to..." I wipe the drowsiness from my eyes. "But I just...couldn't." Wrapping my arms around myself, I struggle to find a way to explain it. "I just can't leave the Cape. Not yet. Not without..."

His frame stiffens as his head settles against the wall. "Evie."

Silence is all I can give him.

"I know what you mean," he says at the tail end of a heavy sigh. After a long pause, he asks, "So what's the plan?"

I gawk at him, confused. "*You're* asking *me*?" Defeat rears its ugly head. Much to my surprise, he says nothing in response. Only stares, waiting for me to continue. "First and foremost, we need to get you healed up. And then..." I blink about a thousand times, not knowing what to say.

"And then?" he asks with weary affection.

I lean away from the wall to face him dead on. "We get her back."

CHAPTER 35
JENNA

JUNE 7TH — DAY 11

James shifts uncomfortably on the couch, a small wince twisting his face as he babies his makeshift sling. It's a T-shirt, newer than the one he arrived with, and still completely insufficient in my opinion. But James insists it's fine.

"Here." I snatch a throw pillow from the lazy chair and tuck it underneath his arm.

He holds out a hand to stop me. "It's all right—" He sucks in a sharp inhale as his slinged arm settles onto the cushion.

"I really wish you would let me help you," I protest, settling on the coffee table across from him.

"You've done plenty, Jen." His face relaxes, but his brow is dotted with perspiration. His pain is tangible, never gone from my mind. Yet he still refuses to let me take him to a hospital. Knowing that I'm his only hope for getting him on the mend scares the absolute shit out of me. I know nothing about tending to wounds, and I sure as hell can't diagnose a damn thing.

I've been changing the dressing on his wounds multiple times daily, following his guidance. But as of this morning, the stitches on the back of his shoulder don't look well. They're inflamed, and he seems to be in more pain than when I first brought him here.

"James..." I begin, preparing for him to continue with this charade that he doesn't need help like the stubborn shit that he is. "Your stitches are inflamed, especially the ones in the back. I'm no doctor, but..."

He settles against the back of the couch and exhales deeply.

"You're pale," I say. "You don't look so good."

"Like shit, you mean," he teases.

"Well, I was trying to be polite." I bump his knee with the back of my hand. "But if we're being honest..." I wait for him to look at me. "You stink."

His lips curve in a little half smile. "Gee, thanks."

"I'm serious. If you would just let me help you—"

"I don't need your help bathing."

"My nose says otherwise." I cock my head, waiting for him to continue being a pain in my ass. "You can't properly wash yourself in your condition."

"I'm able to clean what matters just fine on my own."

"I beg to differ. Your hair is a greasy mess. I can see it from here—"

"What does my hair have to do with my stitches?"

"*Everything*." I don't mean to raise my voice, but the redness of his stitches scares me to death, and I wish he'd put his pride aside for one second and admit he needs help. "It's hygiene. It's..." Frustrated, I shake my head and run upstairs to draw him a bath. I'll throw him over my damn shoulder and toss him in if I have to.

The only bathroom with a tub is the one in the master. I get the water nice and warm, then pull a handful of bath beads from the cabinet and toss them in. The water turns sudsy before my eyes.

Now to fetch that walking mule of a man—

I jump out of my skin when I turn to see James standing in the bathroom doorway. "Jen, what are you doing?" His eyes are so heavy, I fear he may topple over. I know he's in a lot of pain, and I doubt he's been able to sleep well because of it. There are so few ways I can think of to help him. If he'd only let me start somewhere...

"I drew you a bath, and I'm not taking no for an answer."

"I don't need you to give me a sponge bath."

"I'm not giving you an option," I refute. "Now, come on." I reach for the buttons on his shirt, but he steps away.

"I don't think it's appropriate," he says.

Now it's my turn to sigh heavily. "Jesus, James. Give me a little bit of credit, all right? I'm just trying to help."

His shoulders slump in a silent forfeit as I slip his shirt off and let it fall to the floor. The sling is harder; as soon as I untie it and gravity takes over, he sucks in a harsh breath. I set it on the counter, take him by his good hand, and guide him to the bathtub. I cut the water off and reach for the button on his pants, but he stops me.

"I got it."

I nod as a wave of uncertainty washes over me. The line is unclear, and I have no idea if I'm about to cross it—or if I've crossed it already. He's Evie's...and I'm married. But none of this means anything to me beyond doing whatever it takes to make sure he's on the mend. The guilt that has taken up residence in my stomach, constantly repressed for the sake of my sanity but never gone, is powerful enough that it would cripple me if I let it. James, in a very roundabout way, is in this situation because of me. I brought him to Krelborn Manor before my wedding, successfully set him up with Evie, and got him involved in whatever *this* is that has taken her captive and nearly sent him to his grave. He's one of the kindest and bravest men I've ever known.

He's been shot because of me.

I have to fix this.

"Okay. I'll close my eyes, and when you're in the tub, just say so."

I cover my eyes and await the sound of splashing water. When it doesn't come after several moments, I peek through my fingers to see what's taking so long.

What I find is James, one foot in the bathtub, poised to step in fully...

In all his naked glory.

Eek. I never meant to see it. But holy shit, even flaccid, he's, well, a *big boy.* A salacious flame ignites in my belly at my impromptu peep show, laced with equal parts shame and inappropriate curiosity.

Before he catches me looking, I close the gap between my parted fingers.

"Are you in?" I ask, trying to disguise my shaky voice.

"Yeah," he mumbles.

His knees are drawn to his chest, his injured arm hangs limply at his side, and he's covered from the waist down by the sea of bubbles dancing across the water's surface. In a way, there's an innocence to him I've not seen before—a vulnerability that he's finally allowing to peek through. Hopefully, this means he's more willing to accept my help.

Because I'll always give it.

I kneel beside the tub, scoop water into a small pitcher, and tilt his head back. He doesn't protest as the water pours over his hair and onto his back, nor does he say a word as I massage shampoo into his chestnut locks. Based on the small moan that emanates from his pursed lips, I'd even say he likes it.

I massage soap into a loofa and brush it over his back, careful to avoid his stitches as he rests his head on his knees. I then hand it to him with the instruction that he clean himself while I rinse the shampoo from his hair. He does as he's told but stops short as I run my fingers through his hair to work the shampoo out of his locks. With each pour of warm water over his head, it's as if he's forgotten where he is. His eyes never open, and he never speaks a word, but the lowest of moans—one after the other—rumble in his chest, and it makes me giddy. I almost laugh, suppressing the urge to tell him, "See. This is what happens when you *let me help.* It feels good, right? I freaking told you so…"

When the shampoo is gone and his hair is slicked back and clean, I sit back and admire my work.

And that's when he finally opens his eyes. His grin is slight but riddled with humility.

It's all the "I told you so" that I need.

"Finish scrubbing," I instruct, nodding toward the loofa in his hand. "Or I'll do it for you."

He reaches below the bubbles and cleans himself as I lather my hands in a fresh batch of lavender-scented soap.

His eyebrow raises.

"For your face," I explain. "Close your eyes."

I massage the soap over the rough stubble on his cheeks and chin, in the contours of his nose, and over his forehead. He has beautiful skin, even with the age lines that extend past the outer corners of his eyes. It's worn, sure, akin to a weathered soldier, but it's taut and refined, stretched across that chiseled jaw that I'm sure drives the ladies wild.

The water pours gently over his face from the pitcher, starting at the hairline and cascading in a cleansing waterfall. I brush the excess away from his lashes and notify him when it's safe to open them.

"Better?" I ask.

He nods with a crooked smile.

I fetch a clean towel from its hook, then turn away so he can stand from the tub privately. A few breaths that sound as if they're sucked between clenched teeth escape him, and I fight the urge to spin around and offer assistance.

"S'all right," he mumbles, and I take that as my cue. He's done a poor job of drying himself off. Wrapped around his waist, the towel is held closed with his good hand.

"Here." I reach for the point where the two ends of the towel meet, just below his navel. His abs twitch from my touch as I remove it from his grasp. Making a show of it, I crane my neck up to face him and close my eyes. "Relax. I'm not looking. Just let me secure it, and I'll grab a robe." I tuck one corner of the towel behind the other before opening my eyes.

The robe I fetched from a nearby hook slides on with ease. We leave his bad arm out, hanging by his side, waiting for the area to properly dry. I tie it closed, then give him the go-ahead to drop his towel.

"One more thing," I begin, pushing him onto the bathtub ledge. The look of intrigue on his face is almost comical as he follows where my hands guide him. "That scruff on your face." I grip his chin and run a finger over his coarse stubble. "I think it's time for it to go."

He scrunches his face at me. "I can shave with one hand, Jen. I don't need you to—"

"You don't trust me?" I feign playful sadness as I cross my arms.

He runs his hand over his cheek with a heavy sigh. "You know I do."

His raw honesty gives me pause, and I damn near lean in and hug the man. "But I don't know. Maybe I should keep the beard?" He caresses it again. "What do you think? Does Evie like beards?"

The mere mention of her name hits me with a sharp slap of longing. I cling to her, devote my entire heart and soul to her, and become weak with each passing day that she isn't beside me. Hearing her name has not grown any easier.

I'm certain my face is as crestfallen as I feel, evident by the downturn in James's eyes as he regards me apologetically. He doesn't say it aloud, but I receive it all the same. Not that he has anything to be sorry for. There may never be a time in which Evie's absence doesn't sit heavily between us.

"Go for it," he says, rubbing his knuckles over his scruff and straightening his back from his perch on the bathtub ledge. "I trust you."

A lightness overwhelms the heartsick energy as I squeeze a dollop of my father's shaving cream into my palm and apply it to James's face. With steady, confident hands, I glide the razor over his stubble, a slight crackle piercing the silence with each pass. His eyes are closed, but he seems relaxed.

He really does trust me.

I wipe away the remnants of the shaving cream, his freshly shaven face looking as dapper as it did at my wedding. With a little pinch of his chin, I say, "There. Good as new."

Back in his bedroom, I tend to his wounds with disinfectant from the medicine cabinet, adhere fresh bandages to his stitches, and reapply the sling.

Now the hard part.

Standing with my back to him, I listen to the low grunts of frustration as he tries to don a fresh pair of boxers with one hand. I know better than to offer to help, and it pains me to hear him struggle. But if letting me take a razor to the guy's neck doesn't show him that I'm willing to lend a hand with anything, then nothing will. If he needs me, he'll ask.

Maybe.

He's still one of the most stubborn people I've ever met. A bath-time compromise won't change that.

The sound of crinkling sheets cues me that it's okay to turn around. He's climbed into bed, upright against the mountain of pillows I've created for him. Exhaustion overwhelms his face, and I urge him to get some sleep with a gentle tuck of his covers.

As I turn to leave, he grabs my hand. "Thanks, Jen."

Flattery flits across my skin in a gentle wave. "Don't mention it." I throw him a glance as I breach the doorway. "Besides, there wasn't much you could do to stop me." A wisp of a grin graces my lips.

"People always see things my way...eventually." I wink before closing the door behind me.

He returned my smile, which I suppose is a good sign. But his stitches are redder than ever, having become more inflamed since this morning.

Everything is far from fine. He needs help I'm not equipped to give.

For his sake, I simply can't play by his rules anymore.

Chapter 36

James

JUNE 12TH — DAY 16

Improvised explosive devices detonate with lethal force somewhere in the distance. Going against all instincts to run like hell from such man-made brutality, I follow the sounds in a frantic race. Terrified for the safety of my comrades, I turn every which way through the twists and dead ends of the looming hedge maze. It's dark. *Too* dark—a starless, moonless night, shocked to life by intermittent explosions and muffled cries beyond my line of sight. It's a battlefield absent of desert sand or jagged rocks dotting the barren Afghani landscape. Only hedgerows that stretch miles overhead and continuously change before my eyes.

And that earsplitting scream.

Where once was an opening, the hedgerows grow rapidly and fill the gap. A new split appears in front of me, the branches bending upon themselves and slinking away to create a new opening. It's impossible to know where I've already been.

Like a banshee in the night, that blood-curdling scream fills my ears, louder than before, forcing me to my knees. The earth shakes beneath my feet, and the hedges rustle erratically. Exhausted and terrified, I struggle to find my footing, determined to find where it's coming from.

Because in my heart, I know it's Evie.

The explosions boom at a deafening decibel as they draw near, my legs growing heavier by the second. Hedges twist into foul faces covered in scars. The ground gives way to deep pools of mud, hotter than the stifling air, sucking me past my ankles and rising rapidly.

Another scream emanates from Evie's lips right as the mud reaches my knees.

I can't move.

Evie. I try to scream her name, to tell her that I'm here. I'm so close. She's safe...

But not a single sound escapes me beneath the weight of the mud, which creeps up my torso toward my chest.

A shrill, sinister laugh echoes from the hedges, mocking my demise as I fail to save her.

Flailing only sinks me deeper, and in seconds, the boiling mud has crept past my chest and overtaken my nose and mouth.

My skin is aflame, bitter from the scent of sulfur and smoke as my flesh sloughs into the muddy grave. There are no screams anymore, only the shrill thumping of a frantic heartbeat, one I'm uncertain is my own, but I'm driven mad by it nonetheless.

As if a boulder is pressing on my chest, I ache for breath.

That telltale heartbeat slows as the screams fade.

I'm sorry, Eves. I'm so sorry...

⁂

A WISP OF RED HAIR, CROWNED IN A HALO OF LIGHT, draws my attention away from Evie's diminishing cries.

"Jenna?" My voice is so hoarse, I don't recognize it. Severely parched, I can barely move my tongue. It creeps over my lower lip, which is chapped and grotesque.

"He's awake," Jenna exclaims, her voice laced with relief.

The halo dims as the room comes into focus.

A woman approaches my bedside.

I've never seen her before. Brunette hair is swept back into a low bun, and her scrub top bears a wild assortment of daisies on a green background. She has round, pleasant cheeks, a reassuring smile, and a gentle touch as she presses her palm to my forehead. Subtle wrinkles line her forehead, with one vertical wrinkle sitting prominently between her brows. It doesn't hinder the kindness in her eyes, however.

There's something about her that reminds me of my mother.

She removes a stethoscope from around her neck and presses it to my chest.

"What...?" I'm too exhausted to speak, and so weak that I fear I may be dying.

"Ssshhh," she replies softly. "Save your strength." She replaces the stethoscope.

Jenna appears beside her. "This is Susan Wilkes. She's a nurse at Cape Cod Hospital. Your stitches were badly infected," Jenna says. She wraps her arms around herself, as if worried how I may react. "She's here to help you."

Susan looks at me. "You were having a very restless sleep, no doubt from the pain. I've given you a shot of antibiotics which should help with the infection. Unfortunately, you'll have to stick with Tylenol until I can find a way to get some pain medications for you."

She stands from my bedside and addresses Jenna. "Make sure he stays hydrated and gets lots of sleep. He'll be uncomfortable for a few days until the infection goes down. Until then, keep a close eye on him." Jenna follows her to the door. "Change his bandages every few hours, make sure the area remains clean and dry. The best thing you can do for him is keep him comfortable. He needs to sleep."

"I can't thank you enough," Jenna replies, chewing her lower lip.

"I'll be back tomorrow to check on him." She places a loving hand on Jenna's arm. "He's going to be okay." She meets my heavy gaze. "I'll see myself out. Rest easy, Adam."

Adam?

Jenna joins me at my bedside as Susan disappears out the door. The cold towel she presses to my forehead is heavenly, but I'm beyond parched.

"Water," I cough.

"Oh." She fumbles for a glass on the nightstand. It's making me tense to see her so discombobulated.

I manage three full gulps before I lose breath and release the straw. Instantly, I feel my voice returning as the liquid coats my throat.

"Do you think it's such a good idea?" I ask, silently impressed with how many words I managed to string together before my voice cracked.

She sets the glass back on the nightstand. "I had to do something," she replies defensively. "And before you say anything, she's assured me she won't say a word to anyone."

"You promised me—"

"I know what I promised." She stands in a huff and paces away. "You had a terrible fever. Chills. And your stitches looked terrible. What else was I supposed to do?" She crosses her arms over her chest, standing her ground.

"Nothing." I look away. Based on the amount of sunlight that filters into the room, I'd say it's roughly midafternoon. A soft breeze rustles the tree outside the window, and a sense of calm comes over me. The pain in my shoulder is damn near debilitating, but I'm filled with nothing but relief knowing that nightmare is behind me.

I'm not upset with Jenna. If anything, her tenacity and stubbornness almost force me to smile. Fatigue, however, overpowers such inclinations.

"It's not like I didn't think it through," she says, still on the warpath to convince me I'm in the wrong. "I called Doctor Brumbaugh, a hospital CEO here on the Cape who's a friend of my parents. I asked him to send me someone who wouldn't ask any questions, and he swore he'd keep my parents out of it."

I bring my attention back to her. "Why would he promise such a thing?"

She slumps down onto the bed beside me, shoulders slouched. "My parents set me up with his son years ago." A heavy sigh spills from her lips. "Over the brief time we dated, let's just say he...wasn't very good to me. Dr. Brumbaugh owes me one."

A ping of hatred pokes me raw as my mind guesses at the man's deplorable behavior. It's the only time I've been thankful for the fatigue that rules me. I'm certain my rabid concern is not showing on my face.

I tuck my index finger underneath hers where it rests in her lap. She squeezes it gently, a subtle gesture of reassurance that everything will be okay.

"So, why Adam?" I ask, trying to change the subject.

A smile graces her face as her eyes dart from mine to my neck and back again. "Well..." She tucks her hair behind her ear, playing at timidness. "Evie told me about her..." She points to my Adam's apple. "Playtime."

I'm almost too tired to be embarrassed.

Almost.

"I thought it was important to give you a false name. You know, just in case she ended up telling someone. Adam was the first name that came to mind."

I avert my gaze, a rare timidness rearing its ugly head. She shifts on the bed, leaning in, begging for me to look at her. "No need to feel embarrassed," she says, seeing right through me. "I'm not easily shocked. And you have a great neck for it." She laughs, and I wish I had the energy to laugh along with her. "Honestly, I'm just sorry I didn't think of it first. David has a great Adam's apple."

Needless to say, it's not exactly the type of thing I want to think about when it comes to David. Ever. But I suppose that's cemented in my brain now.

I appreciate her attempts to make me feel better, but I've never felt weaker in my life. Not even when a piece of shrapnel nearly took my leg off a decade ago. Without proper medical care, this is the most frightened I've been regarding my recovery. But I could never let Jenna know that. Worry rests heavily in her eyes, clear as day, no matter how hard she tries to hide it by making me smile.

And it breaks my fucking heart.

"You did the right thing, Jen. Thank you," I say. "Everything's going to be fine. In fact"—I stretch back against the pillows—"I think I'm feeling better already." I swallow hard as a bead of perspiration trickles down my temple.

Utter piss-poor timing.

She straightens her shoulders before climbing off the bed, her expression rife with irritation.

"Please don't ever lie to me, James," she says, regarding me crossly from the foot of the bed. "I'm not Evie. I don't need you to be strong for me. And I sure as hell don't need you to chase away my apprehensions, especially if it means you have to lie in order to do it."

Her folded arms silence my retort.

I inhale deeply and wait for my heart to calm itself. She's right; she's not Evie. Both warriors in their own right, but with vastly different strengths. Jenna is blunt—almost *too* blunt—without a worry or concern about the opinions of others.

Except for those who matter, I suppose.

Spontaneous, confident, assertive...these are the qualities that draw people to Jenna.

Evie, however, is a gentle soul; she's more bashful than most, finding comfort and solace in the talents that naturally flow through her.

But she's a goddamn fighter when she needs to be.

It's a juxtaposition that keeps me intrigued by the mystery that is Evelyn Foster.

"You're right," I reply, my eyes locked on hers as thoughts of Evie skim across my mind. "I shouldn't have lied to you." I swallow again, this one more painful than the last, as my throat has returned to cotton. My gulp catches her attention, and she hurries back over to the glass of water on the nightstand.

After I take a drink, she waits by my side, peering at me from above.

"The truth is, my shoulder is killing me, and I'm exhausted. I feel like absolute shit."

I never thought such words would make her lips curl into a small grin, but they do.

"Thank you for telling me the truth," she replies as she pats my leg. "I'll grab you some Tylenol and something to help you sleep."

My feisty caretaker heads out the door, and her absence is almost as painful as the bullet hole in my shoulder. Jenna provides a sense of comfort that fuels me with the strength I need to press on and distracts me from fever dreams of shrill screams and wartime terror.

I can't do this alone. Despite everything I thought I knew about myself, this is a situation I simply don't know how to navigate without her.

I need her.

And I'd sacrifice all the painkillers in the world if it meant she would stay put, right here.

By my side.

CHAPTER 37

JENNA

JUNE 26ᵀᴴ — DAY 30

James discards his sling to the floor while Susan removes the last of his stitches from the back of his shoulder. I sit beside him at the dining table, my mind wandering in a thousand directions.

Not a single sign of pain or discomfort graces his face.

I wish I could say the same for myself.

Rubbing the sleep from my eyes, I struggle to find any semblance of energy. My eyes are chronically puffy these days, tears spilling without provocation or obvious reason. I've hibernated in my room, away from James, during my toughest moments, unwilling to add to his stress during these times of healing.

I debate telling him about the phone call from my mother this morning. David has apparently been calling her nonstop, begging her to reach out to me since I haven't been taking his calls. But I think better of it. James is taking a huge step toward his recovery today. The blackness under his eyes has already faded to a dull yellow, and his nose seems back to normal after having been set by the nurse. In time, I'm certain he'll be as good as new. He's a quick healer, according to Susan, for which I secretly envy.

I'm certain my heart will never heal from this.

It's only been three weeks since I brought him to the Cape house, and he's already breaking free of his sling, like some caged animal freeing itself from its tethers. In some strange way, it's as if his body knows what a time crunch we're in and is just as stubborn as he is.

A text message from Steph last night gave me a moment of respite. After she checked in on any updates regarding Evie—a truth I couldn't bear to tell—I chose to divert the conversation to a more pleasant topic: she and Keith are on their way to Barbados, the two lovebirds about to embark on their first prize as winners of the tournament. Together.

Last night, the distraction of her texts warmed my dying heart.

Today, it's merely a reminder of everything I've lost since game night.

"You'll have some decent scars," the nurse says as she pulls out the last stitch. "Fortunately, there are over-the-counter creams that can help."

James dismisses her with a light laugh. "Nah. It's fine. Besides, Evie likes scars."

I squint with irritation but relax my face before he catches sight of it. How can he do that? How can he talk about Evie as if she's merely gone into town and will be back any minute? It's such preposterous bullshit.

Clearly, we're dealing with this in dramatically different ways. His constant hope is as refreshing as it is annoying.

But to be perfectly honest...without it, I'd be truly lost.

He shoots me a glance, and I twitch a weak smile. That's all I can manage right now. Anything more would be a lie.

"Are you okay?" He mouths the words in silence, as if afraid of the nurse overhearing as she applies an ointment to his damaged flesh.

A single nod is my response as I spin my wedding ring in a daze. It slips over the knuckle easily; I never had the chance to get it fitted.

I let it fall onto the table and stare as if it were suddenly a million miles from my grasp. The nurse's voice fades to a gentle hum as she explains something about keeping the area clean and dry.

I see the nurse out, expressing utmost gratitude, then make my way up the stairs and to my room. Tears are rearing their ugly head again, and I don't want James to see me cry.

Not again.

I close the bedroom door and sink onto my bed, brain-fucking the day I kissed Evie and wondering what exactly went through her mind at that moment. If only she were here to ask. Oh, how I thought there would always be more time to discuss the things that mattered. And now she's gone, and I may never know what thoughts ran rampant through her mind when I pressed my lips to hers.

A soft scraping noise sounds against the door, and I flick a look in its direction. Puzzled, I follow it. When I open the door, a small piece of paper tucked into the jamb falls to the floor.

In James's chicken-scratch handwriting, the paper reads:

You don't have to be strong for me either

I look up and find him leaning with his good shoulder against the doorframe of his bedroom, watching me from down the hall.

Before I can utter a word, he cauterizes my impending tears with a handsome grin, then slinks back into his bedroom.

I should go talk to him. I want to. In time, I know I'll lose the strength to keep all of this inside and will spill everything to him.

For now, I'll give myself one final day to grieve alone.

I press the paper to my chest, absorbing the power of his words and covering where they're needed most: the shattered pieces of my heart that Evie and my failed marriage left behind.

CHAPTER 38
JAMES

JUNE 29TH — DAY 33

Jenna's mother has been blowing up her phone with probative questions regarding the state of her marriage and wanting to know when she'll be returning to Boston. As a result, Jenna's been absent frequently as she runs interference, appeasing her mother with lunches out and telling her only enough to keep her at bay.

The house is always eerily still in her absence. Though I worry about her constantly, it's the only opportunity I have to get the hell out of this house for a while.

She would kill me if she knew, and I feel partly guilty for lying that I'd stay put. But these walls are starting to close in on me, and I need some air.

The pale-blue button-up shirt and jeans she bought me fit like a glove. With the sling off, I can finally wear clothes that fit, and it helps me feel some semblance of normalcy. Jenna has been spoiling the hell out of me since she brought me to her parents' Cape house, despite my insistence that she do otherwise. But she seems to need it, honestly. I think it helps keep her mind preoccupied. So after a while, I came to accept her doting with grace.

The heat is unforgiving this afternoon, the humidity ripe with the summer sun. I don't make it far from the house before beads of sweat form along my back and brow line. Thank God for that coastal breeze. Trees rustle accordingly as tourists pass by, hitting up all the bodegas Chatham is known for, and kids scream with delight in a prim, grassy yard. One might say it's a perfect day.

In all ways but one: Evie is still missing.

It's been one month since my Watson was taken, and I'm no closer to forgiving myself for leaving that island without her than I was the day Jenna came to my rescue in the pouring rain. Walking briskly does little to quell my nerves as my mind reels with thoughts of Evie. The man with the scars torments me, filling my head with hatred when I think of what she may be enduring. To say I want him dead would be a brash understatement. He has taken what's mine, and I'll stop at nothing until she's back in my arms where she belongs.

I need a plan.

Frustration makes my heart rate rise, and I can't think straight. This humidity is unreal, making me regret this little outing entirely. On a split decision, I duck into a tavern on Main Street.

Only two patrons occupy the bar off to the right, their attention engrossed on the sportscasts playing on the various televisions. They remain transfixed on the games despite the ringing of the bell as I enter. Other than them, the tavern appears vacant.

The air conditioning settles my nerves as I take a seat at the bar. The bartender, a scrawny middle-aged man with a receding hairline and a green polo shirt, approaches me. Before he even opens his mouth, I order two fingers of scotch on the rocks.

"Coming right up," he replies with a light slap on the bar top.

The Boston Red Sox are playing the Chicago Cubs on the nearest television. And the Red Sox are getting their asses kicked. I nearly laugh at the things that used to matter. David and I would hit up Red Sox games all the time. If they lost, we would drink our sorrows away at some nearby bar and place bets on how they'd fare in the next game. Now, how the fucking Red Sox play is the furthest thing from my mind.

The bartender sets my drink down, and I sip on it. It doesn't relax me like I expected, but for the first time in a while, I feel free.

The bell over the door rings behind me, but I pay it no mind. Even as footsteps shuffle toward the bar, coming to a stop when the individual takes a seat on the stool beside me.

"Whiskey double," he tells the bartender. "Neat." He sighs as he settles in.

I bring the glass to my lips, focused on the game.

There's an awkwardness to the silence. Why he didn't choose one of the dozen or so available stools that are not next to someone is beyond me.

When the bartender hands him his drink, I watch the man bring it to his lips in my periphery.

"I'll tell ya," he begins before he sips. "This is certainly a shitty day to be a Red Sox fan."

I actually hear him gulp his drink and can't help but roll my eyes internally. The game is of such little importance that I can't even mutter a response.

"You a fan?" he asks.

I sip my drink. "No." It doesn't feel like a lie.

"That's a shame."

His presence is oddly irritating. I really want to be left alone.

"Are you waiting for someone?" he asks.

I set my drink down, harder than I intended, and finally look at him. His face is so familiar that my stomach clenches. I study his full head of wispy dark-gray hair, his ebony eyes, and his aged features... I'm almost certain I've met him before.

"A woman, perhaps?" he continues with an inquisitive attitude.

His audacity is more than I can stand, and I'm sure it's showing on my face. I make no effort to hide it.

"Look. I don't know you, and I'm not interested in conversation, all right?" I toss a twenty on the counter and head for the door.

"Evelyn Foster," he says.

My heart skips a beat, mortified. I reel back around to face him, ready to pounce. "What did you say?"

"You're looking for her." He brings the glass to his lips in a blasé manner.

My tongue is so swollen with rage, I can't speak.

"If I'm wrong," the man continues, "by all means, leave. But if I'm right..." He stands and straightens his blazer. "Then let's talk." With his drink in hand, he motions toward the back of the tavern.

Torn between the urge to pummel him to a bloody pulp but also find out how in the hell he knows Evie, I watch him make his way to a booth in the back corner.

I follow.

Sliding in across from him, I wait impatiently for him to speak. He squints at me from over the top of his whiskey glass, as if studying me as he sips.

"Who in the hell are you?" I ask, my restlessness getting the better of me. "How do you know Evelyn?"

"Let's just say she and I go way back."

I cock my head with confusion.

"You're a friend of hers, no?"

I run my hand over the nape of my neck, desperate for a break from this asshole's cryptic bullshit. "You could say that."

"Did she ever tell you it's a false name?"

My eyes widen. This is all too familiar. The man with the scars asked me the same thing.

"You'll have to excuse me," I say. "I'm having a serious case of déjà vu. Someone else asked me something similar not that long ago."

"And this person was…?"

"I don't know." I release an exasperated sigh. "He never told me his name."

"Did you get a look at him?"

I nod. "Well, somewhat. It was dark. But there was no mistaking the—"

"Scars on the right side of his face?"

I slump against the back of the booth as the wind is knocked out of me. "How did you know that?"

He takes another sip of his whiskey. "The man's name is Lazaro Moretti. And he's the one who has Evelyn."

I shake my head, confused. "How do you know this? Who is he? What does he want with her—"

He holds a hand up, imploring me to pause. "Moretti and I go way back. Since we were kids, in fact. He worked for me for many years, until he started wanting what wasn't rightfully his and ended up my greatest rival." He fidgets with the cocktail napkin beneath his glass as he speaks. "You see, a man in my profession is bound to acquire enemies over the years. It comes with the territory. And he's at the very top of my list."

He shows the bartender his glass, asking for another round.

"You want another?" he asks.

Nothing sounds better than another drink right now—or four. To drown all of this out would be nothing short of divine. But there's no way I'm going to lose myself in this. Not when there are so many questions that have yet to be answered.

I wave off his offer.

He sets his glass down and continues. "I've been searching for Evelyn her entire life. Unfortunately, Moretti found her first. But she doesn't belong to him, James. She never has. So I'm coming to you asking for your help."

"What do you want with her? How do I know what intentions you may have?"

He sighs. "She's my daughter."

Twisting in on itself, my stomach bears the brunt of this unexpected blow. "I'm sorry. What?" Without thinking, I elect to call his bluff. This Moretti guy already confessed that Evie is David's sister. But I can't let this guy know that. Not when I have no idea who he is or what he wants.

Denying his claim with a shake of my head, I reply, "Her father died when she was little. Hanged himself, or so they say. She told me all about it—"

"The man who hanged himself is the man who took her from me." His eyes narrow, and it rattles me more than I expected. "Snuck in through her bedroom window when she was only three years old. Snatched her right from her bed. I haven't seen her since." He gulps the last of his drink and slams the glass down.

"Does she know?" I mumble under my breath from behind my hands, terrified of the answer either way.

He shakes his head. "Not that I know of."

Sitting idle in a complete state of consternation, I gesture widely and ask, "Who are you, anyway? And how do you know my name?"

He palms his empty glass. "We've met before."

"I beg your pardon?"

"At my mother's funeral." He waits as the wheels spin, eyeing me the entire time. I search his face for answers but find none in those age lines.

Then suddenly, it hits me why he seems so familiar. "You've got to be kidding," I whisper, mostly to myself. "You're David's father." The memories befall more abruptly than I anticipated, and I realize the man is speaking the truth. "Frank, right?"

"That's right." He smiles, seemingly pleased.

I'm not sure it's entirely sunk in yet that David knew all this time and never told me. It's mind-numbing to try and think of how far back the lies go. But a part of me doesn't want to know. None of this even feels real.

"I know she's David's sister," I say. "The man with the scars dropped that bomb on me while I was his prisoner." My chest tightens at the memory. "She was taken during David's wedding reception." I hate to ask, knowing full well the terrible response that may be coming. "Was he part of all of this? Does he know where she is?"

The bartender appears on my right and sets Frank's drink down in front of him. He takes a sip before answering. "I would imagine so, yes. David hasn't spoken to me in years, as I'm sure you know. In fact, my mother's funeral was one of the last times we spoke. He's taken quite a liking to Moretti. Over the years, they became extremely close. *Too* close. It wasn't safe for me or my business to keep David in the fold. Especially after things went missing..." He trails off and shakes his head. "I'm sure Moretti loves knowing he stole my son—and now my daughter—right out from under me."

This was David's doing. He orchestrated it with this Moretti guy, and he used his wedding as the moment to strike. It's a painful truth that can't be taken back—nor forgiven.

My gut is rolling with hampered aggression. How could I have not seen any of this coming? How was he able to keep all of this from me? It certainly explains the file Jenna found. All those photographs of Evie, all those documents. He's been working for the man with the scars, watching Evie's every move. My head is spinning, and my initial instinct is to blame the alcohol.

But that's not it.

I'm losing track of all the lies, and I hate that Evie is caught in the middle of it all. More than ever, I'm overcome with the urge to steal a goddamn boat and rescue her from Eden's Green once and for all. I want nothing more than to put it all behind us. This tangled web of lies and betrayal will only grow with each question I ask.

I can't stand it anymore.

"Why are you here?" I ask. "What on earth do you need my help for?"

"You've been to the island. You know where she's being held—"

"No." I shake my head. "I never saw her while I was there. I don't know where she is. Trust me, there isn't much help I can give—"

"But she knows you. I know you two are seeing each other—"

I hold up my hand to stop him. "How on earth do you know that?"

He raises his glass but thinks better of it and sets it back down without taking another sip. "I have eyes and ears all over the place, son. Including the Cape. You spent a whole week here together in May. The reports that came back to me were, well, informative."

It takes everything in my power not to lunge across the table and strangle him. To think Evie and I had our privacy invaded this entire time...

His tone softens as if he's aware that his safety is in question. "She doesn't know me. But she knows you. You're a familiar face. If I send my men to that island to bring her back, I can't be sure she'd come willingly. Not even with me. But you, on the other hand..."

What a slick son of a bitch. I have to give it to him—he's good. Using me as bait to bring Evie home.

"You want me to join your rescue mission for the sole purpose of having a friendly face that Evie trusts to ensure she doesn't run for the hills when you arrive?" I ask, trying my best to disguise my mocking tone.

"Something like that."

"Well, I suppose there's only one thing left to do."

His eyes widen with satisfaction, and he extends a hand out to shake on the arrangement.

"Go to hell." I slide out from the booth, infuriated.

"James, stop." He follows me from the table. "You and I both want the same thing."

I'm fearful we've attracted attention from patrons. But my back is to the main part of the tavern, and I can't see anyone other than Frank.

"We both want to get her back." His calm demeanor enhances his potential sincerity. But my trust in him is nonexistent.

Standing in the middle of a chaotic maze of lies is the woman I love, needing me to find her. From the night we met, I told her I would always find her. *Don't ever doubt me.* But after all this time, I'm no closer to devising a plan than I was the day I awoke in the bunker. I will find her. There's no force on earth that can stop me. But, as much as it kills me to admit, I can't do it alone this time. The island is surrounded by armed guards—so unreachable it may as well be on the moon.

I never should have left without her. Sickened with guilt, I succumb to the only option I have left.

And that's Frank Denardo.

"If I do this," I begin. "I want you to promise me, here and now, that when she's rescued, she comes with me. She's *mine*, got it? And I'll be dead before I allow anyone else to take her from me again."

A smile stretches wide across his face. "Son. You have a deal." He reaches into the breast pocket of his blazer and reveals a business card. "Call me if you need anything. I'll be in touch." He slaps my bad arm as he passes by me, and I suck in a painful breath through my teeth.

He tosses money on the bar and slinks out the door with the gentle ring of a bell.

As I head back to the house, three damaging thoughts bombard my consciousness: David is Evie's brother, David works for the scarred man, and David helped him kidnap her.

David.

Amid all the lies and uncertainties, one thing is crystal clear: David is the common thread through all of this.

And I fear what it may do to Jenna if she ever finds out.

I've withheld the fact that David is Evie's brother all this time, opting to keep her in the dark for her own sanity. Someone needs to be strong for her right now, and it sure as hell should be me.

Despite the promises we made to never lie to one another, I know, deep down, this is yet one more thing I simply cannot tell her.

CHAPTER 39

JENNA

JULY 15TH — DAY 49

The bag of popcorn tears open with ease, and I spill its contents into a large bowl. The scent wafts through the kitchen, a pleasant, familiar smell that makes me salivate. With the bowl in hand, I turn to head for the living room but halt when I see James leaning against the wall of the pass-through from the kitchen.

I gasp. "Christ, Pierce. Make some noise when you walk, would you?"

"Sorry," he murmurs, then takes a step toward me. I hand him the bowl, which he takes from me with a raised brow. "What the heck is this?"

I pause. "It's popcorn, genius."

"It's so white. Where's the butter?"

"There isn't any."

"You expect me to eat popcorn with no butter on it?" He looks so positively butthurt by the notion that I stifle a giggle.

"It's better for you this way. Less calor—"

"Don't you dare say it," he teases. "I don't eat popcorn for its health benefits."

"Well..." I snatch the bowl and flash him an obnoxious smile.

"More for me, then." I pop a piece into my mouth and make a loud *mmm* sound just to annoy him. But before I head for the living room, I can't help but make one more jab: "And can I just say…" I motion toward his attire, specifically his unbuttoned shirt. "We get it. We *all* get it. You have abs. You don't have to always leave your shirt open to show them off as a reminder." I roll my eyes as I brush past him.

He feigns confusion—poorly—before following behind me.

We take a seat on the couch, and I set the bowl on the cushion between us. As I scroll with the remote, looking for something to watch, I catch him fidgeting with his shirt out of the corner of my eye. "It's summertime, Jen. It's hot. What can I say—"

"It's air-conditioned in this house." I give him my most sarcastic eyebrow raise. "Nice try."

"Yeah, but this shirt is long-sleeved and flannel. It's hot—"

"Your new stuff's in the dryer as we speak. That's all that was left in my dad's closet for now."

"Doesn't make it any less, you know, *hot*." He pops a piece of popcorn in his mouth for emphasis, and I can't help but laugh.

"Fine, fine, leave your shirt open. I'm just thankful that your chest is as bald as a newborn baby's ass and I don't have to worry about any nasty chest hairs falling into the popcorn."

He goes in for a small handful, and I finally land on something on the television that piques my interest. But my attention on it is short-lived when a piece of the butter-free snack pelts me square in the face.

"What the—" I look over at him, but he's eating popcorn out of his palm, pretending he's none the wiser.

I snatch a piece and chuck it at him. He acts surprised, looks at me like I just slapped him, then throws another piece at me. It catches me right between the eyes.

Okay, this means war. Erupting with laughter, I scoop a huge handful from the bowl and throw it at him, piece by piece. He does the same, and in seconds, it's an all-out battle.

I spring from my seat and duck for cover behind the lounge chair near the kitchen pass-through. But he's on me in a second, pelting me with popcorn as I try to crouch out of the way. He's a much better aim than I am, but I still get him in the face more times than he's likely to admit when this is all over.

My sides ache from laughter.

Scanning the room, I look for better cover. But there isn't any. James stands between me and the foyer. So I choose to make a run for the kitchen.

Just as I pop out from behind the chair, James is on me, armed with the entire bowl of popcorn. He wraps his good arm around me and tackles me to the floor. I scream between laughing fits, playfully begging him to free me, which he does, but not before dumping what's left of the bowl directly into my lap. I play at being shocked, then call him a dick for good measure as I brush the popcorn onto the floor.

"Just look on the bright side," he begins as he pulls me onto my feet with an extended hand. "It's butterless. So at least it won't ruin your clothes." His face is a cheerful shade of pink.

"You are *so* dead," I jest before leaping straight at him. But my attempt to tackle him to the ground is thwarted when a series of aggressive knocks sound at the front door. The lighthearted mood immediately shifts as we exchange looks of concern.

"Is it Susan?" he asks.

The knocks sound again.

Shaking my head, I wave James up the stairs and hurry to the peephole. The floor gives way when I see David standing on the other side of the door.

Another series of rigid knocks makes me gasp.

I race up the stairs and find James around the corner, hidden from the foyer's line of sight.

"Just wait," he says, gripping me by my shoulders from behind as I peek around the corner. "They'll leave in a minute."

The doubt in his voice matches my own.

"Jenna," David hollers from the porch before knocking again. The door rattles violently, and I shiver in James's grip. He pulls me in close.

"Jenna."

Silence follows the incessant pounding, but my breaths are stilted nonetheless.

"Is he gone?" I whisper, fighting the brewing tears.

A key inserts into the lock, and a wave of nausea hits me hard.

"Oh...my God," I cry out in a sharp whisper. "The key." I reel around to face James. "The key from the planter outside." My hands shake as they cover my gaping mouth while the front door creaks wide open.

"Jenna," David yells from the foyer. "Your car's in the driveway. I know you're here."

Shit.

"*Jenna.*"

"I have to go down there," I whisper to James, who responds with a furrowed look of disapproval.

"No way. I can't let you—"

"If he searches this place for me, he may find you here. I'm not going to risk that. No one can know you're alive. Not until we get her back."

Before I can change my mind, I rip myself free from James's grasp and hurry for the stairs, ignoring his whispered pleas.

I stop on the top landing. David locks eyes on me from below. "Jenna," he says on a relieved exhale, gripping the railing.

"What are you doing here?" I ask, fighting back the tears that poke at my eyes from the mere sight of him. I love and hate this man all at once, and I have no idea which will prevail when all is said and done. I never wanted to see him again. Truly. But, seeing him now, I'm overwhelmed with how much I still miss him.

He scales the steps two at a time.

I meet him halfway.

Without missing a beat, he presses his lips to mine in a kiss that nearly knocks me off my feet. His beard tickles, filling my belly with nostalgic warmth. But I return the kiss only for a second before coming to my senses and pushing him away.

"I don't want you here," I proclaim. "You need to leave."

"Not without you."

"I'm not going anywhere with you. Now go," I snap before turning away. He reaches for my hand to stop me.

"You're my wife, Jen. You belong with me, all right? Enough of all this. Come home. We can talk about—"

"Talk about what, David?" I reel on him. "The fact that you've been lying to me this entire time? I have nothing to say to you—"

"If you'd just come home, I'd explain everything."

"Tell me here." I square my body with his but take another step up the stairs so I'm towering over him. I want him to look *up* at me when he explains why in the hell he's been lying to me.

"I'll tell you at home—"

"You can tell me here." I cross my arms and wait. "Why don't you start by telling me where Evie is."

He sighs and runs his hand through his black hair. "I..." He shakes his head, the lie already making its presence known.

"Leave. Now." I turn away and head up the stairs.

"Jen, wait."

"Go to hell—"

"Evelyn Foster isn't her real name."

I stand, frozen mid-step, doubting my own ears. "What are you talking about?" The absurdity of it all almost makes me laugh.

He races up the steps to meet me, and I don't shy away. "I love you too much to let you just walk away like this. And you deserve to know the truth..." He trails off as his eyes bounce between mine. If he's waiting for me to speak—to interrupt his explanation of the truth—he's in for a long wait.

"Her name isn't Evelyn," he finally continues, repeating the words that keep me stilted. "It's Neve. I know you saw that name in the file."

I study him, riddled with confusion. "I saw a birth certificate for someone by the name of Neve Denardo—"

"That's right. *Denardo.*" He shifts his weight and leans against the banister, discomfort stretched all over his face. "She's my sister, Jen."

A sickening flip of my stomach makes me want to wretch. "Your sister?" This has to be some sort of twisted joke. "Your sister died when she was little—"

"That's not exactly true." He cuts in. "She didn't die. She was taken."

My legs can no longer withstand me, and I slump to the stairs, gripping the handrail as if I'm clinging to life itself. David reaches for me, but I refuse his gesture.

James was right. It *is* hot in here.

"She's been missing since she was three years old. We've spent so many years looking for her. Over time, we gave up hope that we'd ever find her. But that all changed."

I cradle my head in my hands, wishing I'd wake up from this nightmare. "How long have you known?" I ask. Speaking has become laborious, as there's suddenly no fucking air in here.

He sits beside me on the step. I can't help but take it as a bad sign.

"Since you two came into my nightclub last year."

I jerk my head up in absolute shock. "Since the day we met, you mean?" Acid reflux attacks my insides. I want to pummel him, push him down the stairs, scream until there's nothing left of me.

But then I think of Evie, and a whole new bout of sickness hits me with a sharp blow. "Did Evie know...?" My words catch as tears jab at my throat. "This whole time?" This can't be happening. If only this was some sick ploy for David to get me back. It wouldn't work, but at least I could retract every sliver of doubt regarding Evie and her intentions.

Much to my relief, he shakes his head. "She knows the truth now, but she's only just learned it. She never lied to you." Despite his words slicing through me with near-fatal intent, I take comfort in the fact that he seems to speak each one of them with care. The blows are dealt, but I sense his attempts to keep them as minimal as possible.

"That's your job, apparently," I sneer. "So, what was your plan, exactly? You meet me and Evie and then...what? Use me to get closer to her?" Tears spill out of sheer hatred, and I climb to my feet. I can't stand the sight of him. "How could you do this to me?"

David grabs my hand to stop me. "It isn't what you think."

I rip my hand away, and he holds his up in an act of surrender. "Just listen to me. Please," he begs. "I'll tell you everything I can."

I fold my arms again, waiting for the bullshit to spew from his lips.

"When the two of you walked into my nightclub that night, I saw you on the security monitors. The sight of Evie shocked the hell out of me. So I went to the front of the house to tend the bar to see it with my own eyes..."

He runs a hand over his beard. I wait impatiently for him to continue.

"I had this feeling it was her from the moment I saw her. She looks exactly like our mother. Not that she would know that. There's no way she even remembers her."

I can't stop the venom that infects my words and tone. "So... what? You found your sister, and I was just the consolation prize?"

He cowers at my insult, and it pinches me with guilt for a brief second.

"I was following orders—"

"*Whose* orders?" I holler.

His silence is as deafening as my racing heart.

I huff, but he grabs my arm before I can turn away this time. Pulling me close, he locks eyes on me before he continues. "In the beginning, I was given explicit instructions to get to know you. To date you. Anything to keep Evie close until we could get to the bottom of all this. Just because she looked like my mother didn't exactly mean it was her. There were experts brought in, scientists to analyze DNA samples—"

My eyes widen in horror. "You're crazy, you know that?"

"But I was never ordered to fall in love with you, Jen." He ignores my insults as he stands to lock eyes on me. "But I did. Yes, I asked you out because the boss ordered it. But everything that came after was completely real. I mean, how could I not fall in love with you?" He cups my cheek, and I lose all ability to turn away. "Marrying you was my choice. It was never an order. I wanted to spend the rest of my life with you. I still do. You're my whole world, babe. I'm begging you to give me the chance to fix this."

Tears spill as I search my heart for forgiveness. But everything just feels wrong. He's a different person to me now, and all I can think about is what's happened to Evie.

"*She's only just learned it.*" David's words come spilling back into my mind. He knows where she is. He's spoken with her, or at least received updates regarding Evie and *what she's learned.* How can he continue keeping this from me?

"Where is she?" I ask again, a fresh batch of tears turning my throat raw. "What have you done with her?"

He sighs. "I haven't done anything with her—"

"But you know where she is," I scream, reduced to a blubbering mess. "How can you ask me to give you a chance to fix this when you won't tell me what happened to her?" I white-knuckle the handrail, my quivering legs about to send me plummeting.

"She's on Eden's Green, isn't she?" I blurt out without thinking. I'm so desperate to hear him admit the truth of her whereabouts that the words spill without a moment's thought. And I instantly regret them.

David retracts, his brow creased with skepticism. *Shit.* What have I done? I can almost see James banging his head against the wall at my slipup.

I scramble to course-correct. "This man—the one you call *the boss*—is he the one who took her?"

David hesitates, staring at me so intently that it's as if he's begging me to let it go. But he doesn't.

For me.

He nods, his expression crestfallen.

"Did you know he was going to take her during our wedding?"

He nods again, shame glazing over his eyes.

A violent anger rumbles inside me, drying my tears one question at a time. "Why our wedding? How could you do something so—"

"We needed a time and place where we knew, without question, that Evie would be there. The hardest part was getting her alone."

I shake my head, dumbfounded. "How could you possibly orchestrate something like that?" My voice is more shrill than I intended, but I don't really give a shit anymore. "Wouldn't you expect her to be attached to James the entire night?"

"Jen," he whispers, as if begging me to drop it.

"Answer the question."

"I..." He looks away, and for the first time, he looks older than his age. Exhaustion peeks through his downturned eyes, the fine lines of his brow more pronounced than ever. "I spilled the champagne on your dress on purpose." He finally looks at me, but I'm too upset to notice the way his eyes have begun to glisten. "I suggested you grab Evie to help you. Remember?"

All at once, the entire facade comes crumbling down. The promises we made, our future together, and the love I felt for a man

I no longer recognize…it all creeps through my fingers like making a fist around a handful of sand. I couldn't hold on to any of it even if I wanted to. My entire life has been knocked on its ass in some ill-begotten attempt at a future with a man full of nefarious intentions.

"What if I was still in the bathroom with her?" I ask, my voice so pallid that I'm not sure I spoke at all.

David takes me by the hand, and my buzzing skin doesn't afford me the faculties to ward it off. "The boss was adamant that no one was to be harmed."

My chest heaves with incoming tears.

There it is. By his own admission, had I not gone ahead of Evie that night, a decision I regret with every fiber of my being, I may have ended up right where she is.

There's no need to speculate over which fate is worse. This one is. Because, had I been scooped up that night as well, at least I would be with her. Being imprisoned with Evie by my side is heaven compared to a world of freedom without her.

"I need you to leave," I say. I want to collapse into a pool of tears, but I can't while he's still here.

"Jenna, please. I'm begging you. We can fix this—"

"David, leave."

"I'm not leaving without you. I love you—"

"I said get out," I scream, tears streaming down my face. I race up the steps and bound for my room. But James catches me as I round the corner and pulls me against him. We sink to the floor, and he holds me tight as I sob into his chest.

David doesn't follow me. Through my cries, I hear the front door click shut, and I know in my heart that he won't be coming back.

Despite the lies, the deceit, and the trust that I can never get back, my tears aren't just for Evie now.

They're for David—for the hate I bear for him.

And for how much I already miss him.

Part III

Chapter 40
Lazaro

AUGUST 5TH — DAY 70

David fidgets with the orb from my desk, spinning it between his palms, waiting for me to speak first. In my wingback chair, I survey him with steepled fingers. "I'm going to ask you a question, and I want you to answer me with complete transparency, understand?"

The orb pauses mid-spin as he nods.

"The week your father sent his men to Seattle in search of your sister, I went to New York for business and asked Click to keep an eye on you while I was gone. I need to know if he ever came by to check on you."

A moment of pondering passes before he answers. "I'm not sure. To be perfectly honest, I don't remember much about those few months."

"You didn't see him at all? He claims he went by your campus every day. Surely you must remember if he came by at least once?"

He shakes his head. "What's going on?"

A surge of irritation takes root. "I need you to think. Is there anyone who can vouch for him being present? Someone who may have seen him?"

David replaces the orb back on its pedestal, a sardonic smirk splitting his lips. "Well, I can think of one person. The man who truly never let me out of his sight in those days." He sits back and crosses a leg. "James Pierce."

Fucking terrific. "So the only person who may be able to confirm whether I have a rat in my ranks is now floating somewhere in the Atlantic?" I run an irate hand through my hair.

"I wouldn't be so sure..." David trails off, uncrossing his legs and leaning forward.

"Elaborate," I bark, more harshly than I intended.

"Well...I paid Jenna a visit a few weeks ago, just as you suggested. Needless to say, she wasn't pleased to see me." He averts his gaze as a pained look pinches his features. "She's staying at her parents' house on the Cape."

"Okay," I urge, anxious to know where in the hell this is going.

"I didn't make it too far inside, but when I walked in, there was popcorn all over the floor in the living room..."

My eyebrow quirks facetiously. None of this seems relevant.

"And medical supplies on the kitchen island."

"Maybe she hurt herself?" I ask

"She wasn't hurt," David protests. "I saw her." He sighs heavily. "Besides..."

I gesture wide, emphasizing my impatience. "Besides *what*?"

"Jenna never makes popcorn only for herself."

"You're saying she isn't alone in that house."

"That's right. And I'm saying I think James may be alive...and staying with her."

"That's a hell of a leap, don't you think? Just because you saw popcorn and medical supplies—"

"I also ran into Raymond the other day. He made a comment about how it did him good to hear that I've reconciled with my father. I asked what he was talking about. Apparently, he saw me with Frank at a tavern in Chatham a few weeks back." Leaning in even closer, he grabs the edge of my desk, as if to whisper the next part as a secret. "The kicker? I haven't been in the same room as my father in over a year."

"So, what you're saying is—"

"That my father's loan shark saw him with someone he mistook for me."

"And you think it's James?"

David nods. "I think he's alive. From a distance, it would be easy to mistake us."

"And now he's working with your father to get Neve back, no doubt." I sit upright, poised as if a plan has already come to me. "I have to bring him in."

"Why?"

"Well, for one thing, he can still be used as leverage to ensure Neve behaves. Plus, if she catches even a whiff of him attempting to rescue her, there will be no taming her." And most importantly, she's mine.

"Why not put him to use?" David asks. "Bring him here. Let Neve and James be together."

I nearly choke at the notion.

"But in exchange, make him work for you," David continues as if none the wiser.

I tilt my head, confused. "You tried to bring him into the fold years ago, and you said it didn't work."

"No, I said it *wouldn't* work because he's too much of a boy scout to do your bidding. But things are different now. He has a lot more to lose. The man is a pilot." David slaps the arms of his chair excitedly. "Do you know how useful he would be? Maybe Neve can be used as leverage against him too. He'll behave for her. And you can keep her here, safe and sound, with James joining your ranks."

Such an arrangement would never work. To see Neve in the arms of another would only make me tear the man's limbs off, and then he'd really be useless to me.

"I'll take your suggestion under advisement," I lie. "But tell me this. You've known for weeks now that James may be alive. It perturbs me to think you kept it from me for so long."

David snickers. "I almost didn't tell you at all."

A roiling boil of rage eats away at my insides. "I don't believe I heard you right."

"He's my best friend, Laz. Or, at least, he was. I'm not quite sure where our friendship stands these days. If he's still alive, it certainly wasn't for a lack of trying on your part. Do you have any idea what he's done for me? I owe him my life. If you think I'm going to just hand him over to you, you're crazy."

"Then why tell me at all?" I huff, heat rising in my neck.

"Because the only thing worse than seeing him killed by you is the very notion that he's in cahoots with my father. If that asshole has sunk his teeth into James, I'd rather see him dead." He runs a hand over his beard and crosses his arms. "But I implore you not to kill him. Put him to work. His loyalty is one of his biggest attributes, and Neve's safety would cement it."

A gravelly exhale emanates from my chest. The boy makes a good point. It would certainly ensure that Neve stays put. But the thought of the two of them sharing these halls, sneaking glances or more, sickens me with hate. James needs to be brought back here. But Neve can never know unless it's absolutely necessary. I won't stand for him taking what's mine.

David can keep his friend. Neve will learn to love me, without interference. And James will be in my back pocket in case I need it.

"I need to find a way to draw him back in," I say, appeasing David's request with reasons that are solely my own.

"It needs to be something he can't possibly turn away from," he replies before pressing his palms firmly on the arms of the chair. "You just need to ask yourself..." He leans in with a poignant head tilt. "How far are you willing to go to see that it's done?"

CHAPTER 41
EVIE

AUGUST 9TH — DAY 74

I press the note to my chest, still enamored by the words that awaited me when I crawled into bed last night:

Rest easy, child.
Your fears lie with me tonight.
— L

Bewitched by Papa's words written in Laz's handwriting, I race from my room in search of him, adoration ignited within me.

This late in the morning, the kitchen is usually as quiet as the rest of the house at midnight. But the clanking noises of pans and dishes rattle through the wide corridor, stretching far beyond the kitchen.

Peeking around the corner, I find the source of the noise. Laz frivolously whisks in a metal bowl held in the crook of his arm. Dressed again in a white V-neck T-shirt and black slacks—this must be his idea of dressing down—the cords of his biceps flex in beats as he whips the life out of whatever dwells in that bowl.

The kitchen island is an absolute mess, and the smell of half-cooked batter hangs heavy in the air. He seems to be completely enmeshed in his own world, evident by how he doesn't see me until I'm nearly beside him.

"I never pegged you as a cook."

He pops his attention toward me, startled. "I have my moments," he says with a laugh.

I regard the mess of ingredients, soiled utensils, and random bowls and plates that litter the island. "Are you sure about that?" I tease.

"Only one way to find out." He turns his back to me as he tends to the pan on the stove.

"Let me guess..." I scan the sprawl of items. "Flour, eggs, salt, milk, pads of butter...Pancakes?"

"Close. But no dice."

"I give up, then."

"So easily?" he mocks.

"Well, my other guess would have been crepes. But based on the way you're making them, there's no way that's the answer."

He stops the pan mid-tilt, the batter running in a funky shape, and turns to me. "What makes you say that?"

I smile to soften his look of disappointment. "Because the batter is nowhere near runny enough. This is more like pancake batter. Here, let me show you."

I run the bowl underneath the faucet and add a dash more water. After a quick whisk, I add a fresh dollop to the pan.

"The key is to get the pan piping hot. That way, you get those amazing crisp edges." The batter spreads as I tilt the pan, and in moments, the sizzling pop of the cooking batter sings in my ears.

"I didn't realize you were a crepe expert, among your other many talents," he jests.

"I'm not, trust me. This is how Papa used to make them. I've watched him do it a thousand times."

When it's time to flip, I reach for the spatula. But Laz goes for the pan's handle instead. "Step aside, you." He bumps my hip with his, and I comply with a gentle laugh. "This part I can handle." With a flick of his arm, the crepe slides from the pan, flips, and is caught with ease.

"Very impressive," I say, clapping. His lips creep into a little smirk.

After we've made a small stack on the plate beside the stove, Laz says, "You were probably expecting Maria when you walked in here."

"Actually, no. I come in here around this time every morning and fix myself something to eat." I wipe my hands on a gray dish towel. "And again in the evening."

His face pinches. "What do you mean? She hasn't been making your meals for you?" His tone warps into a low rumble.

"It's not a big deal. Really. On my second day here, I told her I wouldn't eat anything I didn't make myself. You know, since the whole needle-in-the-neck incident." I gesture toward my neck with a cocked eyebrow, hell-bent on making sure he knows I'm being facetious. "She didn't put up much of a fight. Instead, she gave me the times of day the kitchen would be free for my use."

Leaning against the counter, he regards me and folds his arms in front of his chest. "Can't say I'm entirely pleased to hear that."

I pause, my heart rate escalating.

"But I understand," he finishes, his expression plagued with defeat. "Shall we toss these so you can start a fresh batch yourself? We can use new ingredients..."

The sincerity in his tone ripples through each word, nearly knocking me off balance with a sensation I never expected. Guilt? Trepidation?

No.

Trust.

The fear that took root inside me the moment I awoke in this place has dissipated into nothing more than a memory. For the first time, I'm acknowledging my sense of trust and compassion for Laz.

"No. It's all right," I reply earnestly. "I trust you."

Without missing a beat, he reaches for me and envelops me in a warm embrace. As he holds me against his chest, his heartbeat thrums wildly in my ear. When I'm released, he gives my chin a quick squeeze between his thumb and forefinger and regards me with a soft smile.

I take a seat in the breakfast nook as he places the plate of crepes on the table. He barely has the chance to slide in across from me before his phone pings in his pocket. With a small grumble, he removes it.

"Fuck," he mutters as he furiously types a response into his phone.

I hesitate to ask. But I'm riding high from his embrace, so I ask if something's wrong.

He scoots his chair back in a huff and puts his phone back in his pocket. "I have to go."

Disappointment hits me, a bitter shock to my system. "Are you sure?"

When his eyes meet mine, his face relaxes, and he releases a small sigh. "I'm so sorry, little one. There's an urgent matter I have to attend to, and it can't wait." A sudden sense of loneliness hits me broadside.

Bracing himself against the table with one hand and gripping my chin with the other, he leans in close. Butterflies flit furiously in my stomach in anticipation of a kiss—our first—but also from uncertainty as to whether I'm ready to accept such a move.

His lips never reach me. Instead, they graze my ear as he whispers, "Have dinner with me." The goose bumps originate right where his words touch my skin, then cascade across my entire body.

The desire to have him stay right here pulls at me with such ferocity that I fear I may drown in it. But a sense of ease presents itself with the newfound knowledge that he'll be back in time for dinner.

And he wants me to join him.

"Apologies." He chuckles. "*Will* you have dinner with me tonight?" he asks with a lilt so subtle that it nearly masks the playful, hubristic nature of his rephrase. His scars have blurred beyond recognition with his closeness, teasing at a face that once was.

"Of course," I whisper.

Bringing my hand to his lips, he places a soft kiss on my knuckles. "It's a date."

It takes everything in my power not to stop him as he crosses the kitchen toward the door—not to beg him to stay. Why is it that every time my heart welcomes another into its own embrace, surrendering itself to the affection it craves, I lose them?

Papa was the first.

Not so long ago, James was the last.

But now that's changed, indisputable by how Laz somehow ended up in the agonizing lineup.

He makes it as far as the island before turning back to me. "This afternoon, a seamstress will be by for your measurements for your fitting. If you'd be so kind as to meet her in the white room at two o'clock?"

My longing is replaced with confusion. "Fitting?"

"For the masque."

"Masque?"

"Did I not tell you?"

I shake my head and stand from the table.

"The midsummer ball." He approaches. "I host it every year in the ballroom in the north wing."

"You definitely failed to mention it." I cross my arms, bewildered.

"Well, this is going to be the biggest party yet. We have something quite extraordinary to celebrate this year, after all." He locks eyes on mine and runs his hands along my arms, as if trying to warm me up to the idea.

"Don't worry about your costume. It's all taken care of. Just be in the white room at two o'clock to meet with Elizabeth. Please don't be late. Her time is precious. And expensive."

He plants a kiss on my forehead and leaves the kitchen promptly, perhaps expecting me to protest. I certainly considered it. If he intends to parade me around an entire party of people, showing off his *prize,* I want no part of it. Although my heart is laxing, it's upsetting that he's still unwilling to admit his role in all of this, the effect he's had on my life, all the things—*people*—he's taken from me. Some responsibility on his part is perhaps all I would need to surrender myself to this fate completely.

But I can't.

Not yet.

Not while I'm still a pawn in a game I don't understand.

I slip my shirt back over my head as Elizabeth reaches for a garment bag draped over the back of the couch. The white room is flooded with sunlight, and I bask in its welcomed glow. She's an incredibly polished woman, with dark curls that highlight her olive skin, possessing a matronly beauty that exudes warmth and confidence.

The entire time she had me propped like a statue in front of the tri-view mirror, measuring what felt like every single square inch of my body for this dress fitting, I debated whether she was someone I could trust. If only I could give her a message for Jenna, just to let her know I'm okay.

When I asked her how she knew Laz, her only response was "*No inglese.*"

I spent the rest of the fitting in awkward silence as she tugged and pinned the muslin around my figure, wondering if this was Laz's plan all along: to keep in his employ only seasoned militant men, young men who do his bidding in the hopes of power *someday,* or women who are either distant or don't speak a lick of English. If his plan is to make me feel the most isolated I've ever felt in my life, it's working.

She hands me the garment bag with an inviting smile, and I resist the strange yet undeniable urge to hug her. *"E un regalo di Lazaro,"* she says before gathering her things. I have no idea what she's saying, but the beautiful Italian drips from her lips like honey, and I ache for her to speak again.

"Wait," I tell her just as she reaches the doorway. She stops and turns to me, her sewing bag slung over her shoulder. I don't want her to leave. I know nothing about her, but she's a friendly face in this faceless world I'm now living in. And knowing that she has the luxury of walking onto a boat and leaving this island behind, no questions asked, makes me want to keep her here even more.

But who am I to keep this stranger here a minute longer than she's scheduled? I shift the garment bag to my other arm, trying my best to disguise my discomfort. My head reels with all the messages I want her to deliver back to the mainland.

With a heavy sigh and a gentle nod, I mutter, "Thank you. No, wait—*Grazie,*" I correct myself. I know at least that much Italian. Her smile beams as she turns away and disappears out the door.

The garment bag crinkles in my lap as I take a seat on one of the sofas—the very same one on which I awoke when I was first brought here. Aside from the low ticking of the large gear-laden clock on the mantel, the silence envelops me—*suffocates* me. I can still remember the first time I laid eyes on Lazaro Moretti. The way he looked at me as he sat on that same coffee table, so presumptuous, so certain. And there I was, not understanding any of it. I suppose that part hasn't changed much. Suddenly, the garish daylight feels too much, as if shining a spotlight directly on my plight.

I make my way back to my bedroom and lay the garment bag on my bed. When I open it, the dress within takes my breath away. A beautiful silver satin dress, pearlescent in its sheen, with small, delicate straps and a cowl front. Affixed to the hook within is a handwritten note, in typical Laz fashion:

With all the sincerity, devotion,
and humility
I have to proffer my goddess
of art and song,
I ask that you please meet me on the
terrace at eight o'clock.
— GA

My core ignites with a smitten glow as I read the note over and over, pausing on the *GA* with bashful approval, solidifying the final surrender of my heart.

Guardian angel.

❦

I ADMIRE MYSELF WITH ONE LAST LOOK IN THE bathroom mirror before giving my appearance the final stamp of approval. My makeup is on point, and the dress looks positively breathtaking, hugging my form from breasts to hips. I can't help but commend Laz for his accurate guess at my dress size. The ensemble, however, is screaming for jewelry: a necklace, earrings, the works. None of which I have here with me, despite a rather cumbersome search of my boxes. So I try to hide it by sweeping my freshly curled hair over one shoulder and pinning it in place.

A knock on the door pulls me away from my desire to incessantly fuss with my hair, making sure each curl is in the exact proper place.

I'm nervous. And fidgety. I have no idea why. Laz has seen me in my roughest form, without makeup or a single care given to my general appearance for the past two months. Even after my things were brought over, and I found a small assortment of my makeup among my other toiletries, I never bothered. Who was I making myself up for? Well, tonight, it's for him. And the thought has my cheeks scorching and my stomach flipping on an endless loop.

Because—dare I say it—this is a *date*.

A laborious sigh escapes me as I give myself one last pass before heading for the door. *A date.* So much of this feels completely absurd. But I can't deny the way I've watched the clock these last few hours, waiting for the sun to set and the night to truly begin. How I've peeked my head into the hallway to hear if he'd returned more times than I care to admit. I haven't seen hide nor hair since he left this morning, and the way I wait for my guardian angel's return is the only certainty I seem to know anymore.

When I open my bedroom door, one of the guards—the bald one with the stoic face—awaits me. Can't say I'm all too pleased to see him instead of Laz standing there.

"I've been asked to escort you, miss. If you're ready?" He holds an elbow in my direction. I pull the door shut behind me and grab the crook of his arm. In a peaceful silence, we make our way to the main hall, down to the first floor, and toward the rear terrace doors.

The guard stationed at the back opens the French doors for us, and I'm escorted onto the top tier of the stone terrace. Laz is standing by a round table, dressed to the nines in a black tuxedo. This is the first time I've seen the terrace all made up, and it takes all the air from my lungs in one fell swoop. Thousands of twinkle lights strung across the pergola's wooden beams create an incredible faux night sky. A white tablecloth covers the two-person table, which is adorned with a gorgeous arrangement of crimson roses, crystal glasses, full place settings, and champagne chilling in an ice bucket. Laz waits for me with a single red rose in his hand.

My heels click along the stone, and my heart races as I approach him. Despite the way his eyes seem to drink up every square inch of me with an ardent stare, I'm suddenly self-conscious about my appearance. I wish I'd been given more time to primp, tease, obsess over my hair and makeup a bit longer. I feel so...incomplete. My nerves have been dialed up to a thousand, and I pray my neck and chest aren't blushing, despite the heat I feel from within.

He hands me the rose, his grin widening. I accept it and hold it to my nose, the world falling to darkness as I close my eyes against its beautiful scent.

"You look absolutely breathtaking," he says, leaning in close, the words skimming my cheek. He reaches around my waist and pulls me closer. The rose petals graze my bosom as he plants a kiss on my neck, directly below my ear. He holds it there much longer than I anticipated, and with each passing second, my heart thumps maniacally, and I fear he may feel my rapid pulse through his kiss.

Once we're both seated, I can fully appreciate tonight's arrangement. Beyond the edge of the pergola, the night sky is crystal clear and radiant with stars. Off in the distance, the sound of waves crashing against the cliffside, now masked in darkness, adds to the mystical ambiance, and I sink right into it.

I barely notice the server filling our glasses with champagne as I stare at Laz. I can't take my eyes off him. I've seen him dressed up before. He's in a suit more often than not. But there's something about him that's just...different tonight. Unable to put my finger on it, I scan every inch of him, just as he did to me moments ago. Perhaps it's the all-black tux that has the butterflies flitting about in a frenzy? It certainly is a dashing look. But I've seen him in all black before. The handsome side of his face is aglow, and I fall into those ashen eyes as I realize it isn't his handsome appearance that has me captivated; it's his confidence.

"You're looking very dapper tonight," I tell him as I place the cloth napkin in my lap.

He releases a gentle laugh. "You jest. But thank you."

"I'm serious," I argue with a smile. "You clean up nicely." Not that I've ever seen him unclean.

He reaches for his filled champagne glass, and I follow suit. "Shall we toast?" he asks.

I nod. "What shall we toast to?"

There's a brief pause, during which Laz's eyes lock on mine. My heart quivers with anticipation. "To new beginnings," he says.

"To new beginnings," I parrot. We clink glasses.

The champagne is smooth, and the bubbles tickle my tongue with a finesse that makes me dive right in for a second sip.

Conversation flows from our lips with an ease I never would have expected. Between bites of food across multiple courses, we talk as if the arrangement between us is entirely different. Tonight, he's no longer my captor, and I'm no longer his prisoner. With the comfort of a long-standing friendship, we regale each other with stories from long ago.

I tell him stories about Papa, the songs he would sing as he plucked away on his guitar; I fill the night with tales of growing up in Seattle, inform him of how I fell in love with the cello and begged Papa for lessons. How I discovered my love for painting while I attended St. Jermaine, finding refuge in it as a way of avoiding the other kids, who were often cruel about my orphaned status.

I tell Laz about my aunt Rose, whom he says he never met, and how she left me in the front office of St. Jermaine one afternoon, and I never saw her again. He hears about my job at the art museum, my love of books, how I once used to teach English Literature in Boston. As I approach more current times, I avoid stories about Jenna for the sake of maintaining the genial nature of the conversation. He laughs at my jokes, asks me questions about my life, and relates my stories to his own when suitable. Every question he asks, I answer with utmost honesty.

In return, he rounds out the final dinner courses with his own stories. He tells me about his baby sister, who died from illness when she was an infant. How it should have torn his family apart, but instead, only made them closer than ever amid their grief. I hear stories about how he grew up terribly poor and all the odd jobs he took when he was just a boy. The lessons his father would teach him about hard work and sacrifice—*a man is only as good as his word.* Beautiful tales spill from his lips about his late mother's hometown of Kardamyli. How the sapphire water stretches as far as the eye can see, and the terracotta rooftops dot the hillsides like a work of art. He even promises to take me there someday. "Where the Ionian Sea meets the Aegean Sea...a place so exquisite should never be left to mere stories alone. It must be seen to be believed."

He regales me with tales about how he came to own all of *this,* gesturing to our surroundings as he speaks. Not once does he mention my mother, to which I'm just as grateful as I am heartbroken. Every piece of information he gives me makes my time here worth it, and in many ways, it's all I have anymore. I never would have known anything about her if I'd never been brought here.

Time passes in a blink of an eye. Our final plates have been cleared away, and a slight chill from the night air has gripped my bare arms, yet our conversation is still flowing with ease. Running my fingers along the stem of my champagne flute, I remain mesmerized by Laz's voice. Deep, sultry, and full of more stories than I could ever contribute on my own.

The golden hue from the twinkle lights bathes him in a warm glow. His face is alight with laughter as he runs his hand across his chin in playful amusement. Thanks to the champagne, my heart has slowed to a reasonable pace, and I pay no mind to the passage of time.

My eyes land on the subtle lines in the outside corners of his eyes, made prominent with each smile. I follow them down, along the edge of his chiseled jawline, covered in a short, well-maintained shadow of a beard. Dark, just like his eyes, but peppered with white flecks throughout. His beard shows more signs of his age than the hair on his head, which is still predominantly black with little recession. His hand rests easily against his chin as he speaks, and I realize he has not once looked anywhere else but at me since I sat down. Captivated, I fall headfirst into those nimbus eyes, my inner pluviophile desperate to chase whatever lies within.

"What is it?" he asks, looking oddly amused as he cuts himself off.

That smile. *Jesus.*

"Oh, it's nothing." I wave the moment away. "I'm sorry, I didn't mean for you to stop." I reach for my champagne flute. "Continue—"

He leans back in his seat and pierces me with a look. "Something tells me whatever is on your mind is far more intriguing. Please." He gestures with open hands. "Enlighten me."

I swallow the last of my champagne, then trace my finger along the glass rim as I mull the words over in my mind. "It was just a thought. Really, it's no big thing."

But his gaze would suggest otherwise.

There's no backing out of this now, no changing the subject. His persistence is apparent without uttering a single word.

He crosses his arms and leans forward, resting his elbows on the table, settling in for what's coming next. Fortunately, the kindness in his eyes is unwavering, which becalms my otherwise restless heart.

"I was just thinking how..." I take a deep breath as I study him. That face—weathered yet handsome, wrought with wisdom, talent, warmth, and incomparable devotion akin to Papa himself—challenges my mind, my senses, and whatever forms of love my silly little heart deems possible.

"Your scars," I blurt out before I can stop myself. He shifts in his seat but does not break his eye contact.

"What about them?" His face falls somber, and it makes me ache.

"It's just..." *Ache.* I sigh. *Such a small word to describe my torment.* How I wish to right the wrongs he's endured, to give him the strength that Frank took from him, to climb inside his heart and mend the pain, the losses, the lessons, and the tortures that have shaped the angel who now sits before me.

"I don't see them anymore," I say. The realization hits me hard, and judging by the way he slinks back into his seat and regards me with glistening eyes, I think it did so for him too. I expect him to acknowledge his scars in some way—to brush a hand over them or even turn to look toward the blackened cliffs beyond, pointing the handsome side of his face in my direction and obscuring the other. But he does nothing of the sort. Instead, he scoots his chair away, comes around to my side of the table, and extends his hand. Still as the statues that adorn his garden, I wait, allowing several beats of my frantic heart to pass before I accept it.

Without a word, he walks me to the edge of the terrace and down a set of stone steps to the lowest tier of grass. The last of the summer's fireflies flicker in the gardens below and in the trees at the edge of the property, as if mimicking the starry sky. The air is comfortable despite the slight chill nipping my bare skin as the humidity depletes with each passing hour.

"Will you dance with me?" he asks softly. I peel my attention away from the stars and lock eyes on him, smiling as he pulls me in close, hardly waiting for my answer. Resting my arm around the back of his neck, I realize the only sounds we have to dance to are the crashing waves that tear at the shoreline and the chirping chorus of crickets in the distance.

"There isn't any music," I whisper before biting my lip with a playful smile.

He pulls me even closer with a firm grip around my waist, causing my breath to hitch. "We're musicians," he says. "We make our own music."

We sway in silence for only a moment before I ask him to sing something.

"What would you like me to sing?"

"Whatever your heart desires," I flirt. "I'd listen to you sing anything, you know that."

As I rest my cheek upon his shoulder, the warmth of his closeness is all I need to send my stomach into an erotic tumble. In only a moment's time, he begins to sing in alluring, dulcet tones as the lyrics—blithely romantic and originally brought to life by Peter Frampton—spill from his lips. I know the song well, but I let him sing it on his own. It's the most beautiful rendition I've ever heard, his voice whispering across every pore of my being. I don't dare interfere with my own voice. But, as if reading my mind, he asks me to sing it with him.

I oblige.

Without the aid of our beloved instruments, and with nothing to hide behind except, perhaps, the veil of darkness on this midsummer night, we sing to our hearts' content. By the time the song ends, I realize that, without protestation or regret, I've fallen headfirst under my guardian angel's spell.

❧

THE SINGLE SPHERE OF ICE CLINKS AGAINST THE SIDE OF the tumbler as Laz hands me my glass of freshly poured scotch. "You'll never taste a scotch as fine or as smooth as this one," he beams, taking a seat beside me on the black leather sofa. It's not my drink of choice, but I'm willing to give this fine scotch its fair chance.

I've been in his office before, but never by firelight alone. It gives the room an eerie feel, casting shadows in every corner and disguising the copper accents and finer details. But there's comfort in the warmth of the roaring fire, which is why I selected the seat that was closest.

He tinks his glass with mine. "Cheers," he says, then brings it to his lips. I follow suit. The scotch, though smooth just as Laz proclaimed, leaves a bitter bite at the back of my throat. But, as it makes its way down, it leaves a trail of warmth through my entire core, which is downright pleasurable in its own unique way. So pleasurable, in fact, that I follow it immediately with a second sip. And then a third.

I set the glass on the coffee table before I lose myself in it entirely. Laz sets his down as well and leans in close. "I always enjoy the pleasure of your company," he moans as he pulls me in close, kisses my cheek, and grazes my nipple with his thumb. His kiss is slow at first, as if waiting for me to stop him. When I make no such move, he trails his lips to my jaw, then lower, onto my neck. My body comes alive, thousands of electric volts raking through me with each touch of his flesh against mine. It's a sensation so foreign to me that it frightens me as much as it sends me reeling with pleasure.

And confusion.

I've been drunk before.

This isn't it.

His kisses grow harder as my skin tingles with abandon. The way his tongue caresses the curvature of my neck, the way his lips press hard against my collarbone, my shoulder, my cheek, is ripe with what feels like a desperate desire to claim even a sliver of my body for his own, just as James did.

"Command me," he roars in my ear between kisses, his breathing heavy. He runs his thumb over my parted lips. "Command me to taste these lips."

Shaking my head proves fruitless, for I'm doubtful he even sees the motion with his face buried in the crook of my neck. I want him as much as I don't. But my head is buzzing in a way I can't make sense of, and the helplessness of it all terrifies me.

"I want you, my queen." Salacious words hum against the flesh of my bare shoulder, sending a tingle straight to my core. "I want you..." He caresses the swell of my hip and kisses the dip at the base of my neck. "Command me to take you." His kisses fall to my breasts, which are still protected behind my dress. But I can't say for how long.

"What are you?" I manage in a whisper, my head pulled by dizziness. The temptations, the seduction, the heat of that roaring fireplace—it's as if I'm being lured into my very own hell. "You're no angel..." I trail off as the room moves around me. "With your serpent tongue..." My eyes grow heavy, but I fight to force them open. "I fear you may actually be the devil."

The room twists on itself as I fall back onto the couch, the fire commanding my full attention. Flames appear to break free from the confines of the fireplace, reaching with sweeping arms into the room. It frightens me for only a moment, but the beauty of its crimson heat has me mesmerized.

He yanks my dress down, exposing my breasts to the warmth before cupping them with an angry grip. "Even the devil was an angel once," he replies in my ear, hovering over me and leaning in low. "Now. Command me to taste your lips." His tone is harder than ever as he presses his body against me.

"No," I whisper, pulling my attention away from the flames. The walls are vibrating, and my breath hitches with fear as my gaze flits around the room. Despite my attempts to convince myself that it must be the erratic shadows, a chill rakes my spine and plants itself in my tailbone.

"No matter," Laz says, sounding so far away that I'm not entirely sure he spoke at all. "Those aren't the lips I'm interested in right now." The room continues to move as he slips away, out of sight.

The exposed wooden beams in the ceiling are shaking now. They're difficult to see in the darkest recesses of the room, but they're shaking. I'm certain. The leather sofa is cool against my bare skin, but my exposed breasts are scorching from the fire's heat.

With a slight tilt of my head, I focus on our scotch glasses on the table. Where they stand, there are now four instead of two. My attention finds Laz, whose head bobs between my parted legs, of which there are now four, my dress bunched up to my waist. Everything in the room has doubled. I can't seem to remember how or when Laz ended up between my legs. Or recall when my dress was hiked up in the first place.

Bile rises high in my throat as my heart thunders with apprehension, adrenaline, and the odd pleasure from the electricity radiating through my skin, making me feel alive in ways I never could have dreamed. But despite the unprecedented effects my body is experiencing, I want it to be over. The lack of control and understanding of what is happening makes me want to run from the room and never look back.

But I can't move.

The pleasurable tingle that once coursed through my body now pricks with fear. Pure, unadulterated fear. Dizziness has consumed all my faculties, for the room is no longer vibrating, it's spinning. Nausea attacks my insides as my eyelids grow heavier. My vision tunnels to a pinpoint, and my parted legs slack. With a buzzing noise resounding somewhere deep inside my head, my leaden eyelids shut, and the room goes black.

Chapter 42

Lazaro

The satin dress slips off with ease, and I drape it over the back of the neighboring sofa to keep it pristine. I unfasten her heels and slip them off one at a time, dropping them onto the floor alongside her panties.

Her feminine taste is still ripe on my tongue, a flavor I've come to crave more than the scotch that allowed me to taste it in the first place. I want more. And I could easily have more if I wanted. She's unmoving now, unconscious on the sofa, and as naked as I've ever seen her in the firelight. Standing over her, I take several moments to admire her beauty: the perfection of her curves, the smoothness of her delicate skin, the way her dark hair cascades over the edge of the sofa, and how her parted lips are practically begging for mine. For a moment, I consider kissing them. Why not? She's denied me their taste ever since she came here. I could easily take them for myself right this second, and she'd never know.

But it isn't just their taste or the softness of their supple flesh that I desire. It's the insurmountable pleasure that comes from kissing a woman who *wants* to be kissed, who returns the passion with such intensity that it makes your flesh ache with need. It's the caressing of one tongue against another, the soft moans that intertwine so tightly that you can't be sure if they came from her throat or your own. It's the mutual exclusivity of her love and desire that I need above all else.

I turn away from her sleeping form. *I can't do this.* It's undeniably wrong. And it's likely to destroy everything I've worked so hard to build with her. The friendship I'm convinced we've established, the hope of something more. The trust.

I'm about to destroy it all.

But it's necessary. If I'm going to keep her safe, I need to keep her here. With me. And as long as there are people out there who pose a risk of taking her from me, I must do whatever is necessary to ensure she remains mine.

Even if it means this.

In preparation for my next move, I remove my blazer and drape it next to her dress before rolling up my sleeves to my elbows. She doesn't move even the slightest. If it wasn't for the gentle rise and fall of her chest, her vitality would certainly be of concern. But the drugs I put in her drink were measured with utmost precision. Neve is the most precious thing in the world to me. I would never be so careless with her wellbeing.

Straddling her motionless, naked body, I lean in low, grazing her jaw with the tip of my nose, breathing in her scent. Her breaths are shallow but calm. *A good sign.* I place a gentle kiss on her cheek. "I'm so sorry," I whisper before sitting upright and admiring her perfect body one last time.

Before I completely ruin it.

CHAPTER 43

EVIE

AUGUST 10TH — DAY 75

A powerful *thud* against my balcony door wakes me from my vivid nightmares. My head throbs so severely that it makes even the worst hangover feel like a picnic. Through tired, squinty eyes, I peer over at the door. Something flits on the other side, creating a ruckus. A soreness plagues my entire body as I cast the covers aside.

I ache. Everywhere. And I can't for the life of me understand why. I ponder every detail of last night but am interrupted by another loud *thump* outside. Climbing to my feet, I detect the distraught shadow of some sort of bird fluttering with agitation through the sheer curtains.

Shielding my eyes, I take great care not to let the distraught creature inside. It's a bluebird, flapping its wings but not taking flight. It takes several hops backward, flaps its wings again, and eyes me suspiciously.

"It's all right, little fella," I say, approaching with featherlight footsteps. "Did you hurt yourself?" I take another step forward, but it flaps its wings, and I back away. The poor thing is terrified. But I don't see anything wrong with it. It likely flew into a window and is stunned.

I have no plan of action, but I take another step toward the bird anyway, thinking it may allow me to be of help this time. But that bird is as smart as I am foolish, and it hops away with an erratic flap of its wings. A multitude of feathers cover the balcony, evidence of its struggles.

Kneeling, I extend a hand for it. This time, it remains still, and a wave of hope washes over me.

That's when I see it.

In the crystalline midday sky, there's no denying my own eyes, which are now wide awake and ripe with horror. Upon my wrist is a circular bruise, deep purple and pitted with the indentations of what I can only assume are teeth marks. Shaking, I bring my arm closer and find more bruises that creep up my arm. They're nearly identical to the one on my wrist and are painfully sore to the touch.

Forgetting about the bird, I race into the bathroom and doff my clothing, choking back the sickness that rises. Terrified, I stand before the mirror and force myself to look. Deep purple bruises cover my entire body: up and down my arms and legs, and across my torso, each one paired with a ring of teeth indentations.

It's the ones that paint my breasts that command my full attention.

I pore over every single thing that happened last night. I remember dinner out on the terrace. Most of the topics of conversation have escaped me, though. There was dancing—I think. So much of it is a complete blur, with the most important parts absent entirely.

The tile is freezing on my bare bottom when I sink to the floor, but it falls out of mind as I draw my knees up, cradle my head in my hands, and allow the tears to spill. Through blurred vision, I regard the bruises on my breasts over and over. I can't stop looking. And each blemish makes me more enraged than the last. Especially the rings of teeth marks that encircle each nipple.

As I weep in desolate silence, soreness in other areas of my body becomes more apparent—places where I'm certain more bite marks must exist; I just can't see them well. My bottom, for instance, aches similarly to my arms and legs. But the longer I keep my knees drawn to my chest, the more I detect soreness in an area that turns my insides putrid. Shaking violently, I stretch my legs out in front of me and let them fall open. I lean in low and peer down at my vulva, terrified at what I suspect to find. And there it is. On the outside of my labia, encompassing the tender space between my vaginal lips and my upper thigh, is a deep, contused bite mark.

I weep. I scream. I kick at the sink cabinets and wail into my drawn-up knees. Rocking back and forth with an anger I can't even begin to control, I grip my hair so tightly that I fear I may rip it clean out. But I doubt I would even feel it. I don't feel anything anymore. Only disgust, hatred, betrayal...and faithlessness. How could I be so stupid to think Papa sent Laz to protect me? A guardian angel tasked with only one purpose: to keep me safe when Papa no longer could. Foolishness—pure and unadulterated—crashes over me with a strength far superior to repulsion and anger. My cheeks and neck scorch with shame, and I chastise my ridiculous heart for betraying me once again.

Fueled by the myriad of emotions that risk leaving me a paralyzed mess on the bathroom floor, I scoop up my pajamas, don them as quickly as I can manage, and head straight for Laz.

THE OFFICE DOOR CRASHES INTO THE WALL BEHIND IT AS I throw it open and storm inside. He's at the far end of the room, standing behind his desk, facing Click. My mind doesn't seem to register that Click is here despite Laz's promise to keep him away, because all I'm seeing is red. Laz pushes away from his desk as I approach.

"Are you all ri—"

I slap him. I slap him so hard that my palm throbs from the blow. He reels slightly, runs a hand over his compromised cheek, and regards me with a hardened expression.

"*What did you do*?" I wail, tears spilling freely as I thrash my arms against him. "What did you do? What did you do?" I repeat this senseless mantra as I slam my fists against his chest, the entire world devolving into a blurry mess amid my tears.

"Neve, stop," he barks, grabbing both of my arms to still me. But I pull hard, desperate to wrench them free.

I'm unsuccessful.

"What in the hell's the matter with you?" he shouts, his face hideous and flush with anger.

"You did this to me." I hold my bruised arm in front of his face. He looks away as if too ashamed to face the truth. "Did you think I wouldn't notice?" Tears fall past my chin and onto my shirt.

"Listen," he begins, his tone level and his expression returning to stone. "Just let me explain—"

"Fuck you," I scream, then slam my fists against him in a barrage of anger all over again. I shove him, putting every ounce of strength I have behind each blow, but he barely moves an inch. His grip on my arms is tight, digging into the bruises he already left for me. I scream, not from the pain, but from the agony he created—from the sight of his wicked, distorted face and his calm demeanor on one of the worst days of my life, and from the fucking sound of Click's shoes as he shifts his weight somewhere behind me.

Wrenching my arms with all my might, I manage to free myself from his grasp. My stomach leaps into my throat as I fall backward and collide with his desk. A cacophony of noises follows, and I turn my attention to the smattering of items that now litter the floor. His desk had little on it to begin with, always devoid of clutter. But what little once sat atop his desk is now strewn across the floor.

Desperate to flee the room, I step away from Laz. But my foot catches the base of the lamp that lies broken against the hardwood, and I collapse onto my hands and knees. Something soft warps beneath the weight of my palm. It's a cigar; one of many that are now scattered all over the floor. The metal cigar box from whence they came lies upside down, teetered on its open lid.

Firm hands grip my shoulders from behind, attempting to pull me up. But I keep myself planted right where I am. Something has caught my eye, and I refuse to move until I've had a closer look. With a chill so deep that it nearly cuts me in two, I reach for the object that's partially obscured beneath one of the cigars.

The room is eerily quiet. Or maybe it's because my heartbeat is deafening, leaving no room for any other sounds. The item settles in my palm, which is ripe with sweat and shaking so hard I nearly drop the damn thing. It's a round plastic button, as red as a rose.

With button holes in the shape of hearts.

I've only ever seen a button like it once in my life: during the blindfold game at Krelborn Manor. Its shape, weight, and dimensions are as familiar to me as James himself, who plucked it from my mouth with a victorious smirk and kept it with him ever since.

For luck.

I suck in a tremulous gasp, a small cry eking from the back of my throat. The last time I saw this button was at the wedding reception. James flipped it in the air like a coin, held it out for me to plant a teasing kiss, and then placed it back in his pocket. *"For luck,"* he had said to me that night.

It was the last night I ever saw him.

"Where did you get this?" I demand, seething with rage and locking focus on the button.

Silence.

"Where did you get this?" I reel around, screaming at Laz to answer me. Heat rises high in my neck and ears, and I can't fight the trembling that has consumed my entire body. His calm demeanor is enough to make me want to rip my own eyes out just so I don't have to look at him anymore.

He takes a step toward me, his hands held out as if to calm a wild animal. I stand and take a step backward to match.

"Where did you get this?" I repeat, a new batch of tears streaming down my face.

Laz shakes his head ever so slightly and releases a heavy sigh, as if defeated.

"We found it," he begins, glancing over at Click before returning his attention to me. "In the caves near the lighthouse." He runs a contrite hand over his stubble.

"In the caves?" I ask, blinking feverishly through the tears that compromise my vision. None of this makes any sense. "This button belongs to James. He had it on him the last time I saw him. But you're telling me it somehow ended up in the sea caves..."

Laz slowly closes the gap between us. My legs feel so heavy that any effort to move away seems impossible. "Listen," he says. "I know you're confused, frightened. And I accept all the blame and want nothing more than to make it right. I will tell you everything. The bite marks, the button...I'll answer anything you want to know. If you'll have a seat—" He gestures toward the couches, but for reasons I can't confirm, the sight of them makes my stomach rumble with nausea.

"How did this get here?" I ask through gritted teeth, refusing to take his bait.

"Neve, please—"

"Fuck you." I hurry for the door, squeezing the button, desperate to keep it close.

"James had it on him," Laz calls out.

I stop dead in my tracks.

"It was left behind in the sea caves, which is where we last saw him."

Despite every fiber in my being warning me not to, I turn to face him. "What exactly are you saying?" My voice is pinched. He towers over me, close enough that I could slap him again if need be. But I don't back away this time. I need answers, and there's no way in hell I'm leaving now.

"James was here." Laz sighs again, the truth emblematic of his defeat. I place an apprehensive hand over my abdomen, protecting it from the blows I know are coming.

"I brought him here with you. He was a guest in the outbuilding at the south end of the property. But he escaped." The pit in my stomach is lessened by the word *escaped*. Maybe James is here, somewhere on this island, at this very moment. Hope warms me from the inside out. He must know I'm here, and he would never leave me behind.

"We caught up to him, though," Laz continues, robbing me of what little hope I desperately cling to. "In the sea caves."

I break away from his penetrating gaze and turn it to the button in my palm.

"He's dead."

His voice sounds so far away. So faint, in fact, that I question if it was even real. But I don't ask him to repeat it. Once is more than I can bear. All the air in the room vanishes instantaneously, my lungs now as deflated as the sliver of hope I once bore for my life and freedom.

My future. *Our* future.

I can't bear to hear another word. This can't be all that's left of James. It can't be. This isn't right. He's lying. Once again, Laz is spinning tales to get me to surrender to him. This is a game. It's all a fucking game, and I refuse to believe any of this is real.

Enraged and out for blood, I hold steady and muster a response. "You're a goddamn liar."

I flee from the room with nothing on my mind other than getting to those sea caves. If any of this is true, and James was killed in that cave, then there would be something to prove it. There would be blood, right? Unless he drowned. Or was strangled. *Shit*. Wait, maybe he fell? Maybe he got away? I rarely see a gun in Laz's waistband anymore. But how long ago did this happen? My God, has James been dead all this time? My thoughts form a dense, impenetrable fog as I race into the hallway toward the main staircase.

"Neve, stop," Laz calls out as I breach the top steps. I descend as quickly as my legs can carry me, clinging to the banister for dear life when I nearly tumble in the process.

"I told you not to fucking call me that," I shout without a single look back.

I round out the bottom steps.

"Rhiannon."

I pause dead in my tracks, only a few steps shy of the foyer. The guard at the front door looks on, his eyes wide. Laz's steps are quick behind me.

In mere seconds, he has me enveloped in his arms in a tender embrace.

Why, though? None of this makes sense, and my confusion only further enhances my anger. I'm not Neve Denardo. That girl died at the innocent age of three and has tormented a slew of people in her absence. If he doesn't understand that by now, he never will. To call me Rhiannon, though? A queen—a *goddess*—a figure of feminine power and beauty, conquering the darkness that would otherwise hold less capable individuals captive? It's a power move. It has to be. Only in this case, he's giving power rather than taking it. And he's giving it to me. It's only a name, sure. But from him, it's practically a forfeit. He's exposed his queen, ripe for the taking, stepping aside and allowing me to checkmate. It shook me enough to make me pause, and I pray I've made proper sense of it all.

"I need to see them." I weep against him. "I need to see the caves."

He studies me briefly before responding. "Come with me."

The Bentley still has a new-car smell and is so impeccably clean that it appears as if it was just driven off the lot today. But my admiration is nonexistent as I push everything in my mind aside and focus only on James. He can't be gone. There's no way. He's a soldier—a *fighter*—and I never should have doubted his loyalty. All this time, he's been here, a captive, same as me. Not back in New York, not going mad with questions, pondering all the reasons why I abandoned him that night. I need the caves to give me some semblance of hope that he may have made it off this island alive.

The car ride is dead silent but quick. We reach the cliffside near the lighthouse in minutes. I notice the path etched into the face of the cliff before I even exit the car.

I don't wait for an invitation or permission before shoving out of the vehicle and heading for the pathway.

Laz is hot on my tail, urging me to slow down, to let him lead the way.

No way in hell.

The path, overlooking a beautiful crescent of beach down below, is full of switchbacks as it descends the rocky cliffside. The sand and loose dirt make the journey far too precarious for comfort. More than once, my bare footing gets away from me, but only once do I land straight on my ass. The sand provides little cushion, and the bruises already present on my derriere make it all the more painful.

"I should have had you put on shoes before we came out here," Laz says with a low grumble as he grabs me by the arm to help me up.

Honestly, shoes are the least of my worries. What an absurd thing to say.

I press on, ignoring him.

The path switches back toward the jetty wall for the last time, the large opening in the cave's side finally visible. It's more lit than I anticipated, with an opening at the far end providing a guiding light. The cave is wider than it is deep. In fact, it isn't very deep at all. It hugs the cliff's edge and runs the width of the jetty. At this end, the waves that crash against the beach have no doubt eaten away at this cliff over countless years, creating the hole that now serves as its only accessible entrance.

The rock at my feet is slick with moisture, and the salty air coats my lungs as I enter the cave. As I creep in deeper, keeping one hand on the cliffside wall, I approach the center of the jetty's belly. The ceiling follows the edge line toward the ocean beyond, creating a dome of rock on all sides. But, where the rock wall hits the water line, it has been eaten away from years of erosion. As a result, a deep, cavernous pit has formed in the floor, flooded with ocean water that enters freely from beneath the cliff's overhang. A sliver of daylight penetrates the water in the pit from the outside, creating a stunning turquoise color.

Each wave obeys the tide's rhythm. When it sucks back out into the open ocean, there's an iota of relief—a sense of safety—that quells my nerves. But then a wave comes crashing back in again, spilling water onto my feet with more ferocity than the last, and it sickens me with fear.

"The tide is coming in," Laz says somewhere behind me. Despite the booming of his voice as it bounces across the cave walls, it's nothing compared to the roar of each incoming wave that torments the rocky pit. "We shouldn't stay here."

I look frantically all around me. For what, I have no idea. Something—*anything*—that indicates James may have made it. So far, the only ways in and out that I can see are the way we came, or through the pit in the floor that spills out into the open ocean on the other side of the wall.

"What happened here?" I ask, mesmerized by the crashing waves.

Laz appears at my side.

"He escaped. My men searched for him everywhere. Click found him here. There was a struggle of some kind—"

"Wait, it was Click who found him? You said *you* were the one down here in the caves."

Laz pauses. "No. I never saw James that day. Click found him here."

"But, if you weren't here, how do you know James didn't get away? What if Click was lying—"

"He wasn't lying, Neve." And just like that, whatever power he had bestowed upon me has vanished in the blink of an eye. "Click shot him, all right? He shot James, who then fell into the ocean. Right here." He gestures toward the pit below. "That's the last any of us saw of him. The man is dead. Understand? Now, there's nothing to find down here, and the longer we stay, the more dangerous it becomes." He pulls me away from the pit with a firm grip, but I yank it away, rabid with rage.

"He was shot?" I scream, the words slashing my tongue. I know Click is a liar. He was there the night Papa died, despite Laz's denial. I know it. And now he claims to have been the one to put an end to James. I don't trust a fucking thing out of that man's mouth.

The waves ebb and flow in a symphony of splashes that have rendered me soaked from the knees down.

"He could have made it," I say aloud, mostly to myself.

"He didn't." Laz's frustration is palpable.

"How do you know that? How can you be certain?"

"Because he was shot in the chest," Laz growls. "Because he fell into the goddamn ocean. And because of *this*." Laz yanks my wrist toward him, forcing my hand open, exposing the red button. "He had this in his hand when he was shot. He dropped it right here before he fell into the water. Click said that he asked James if he had any last words before putting a bullet in him, and James whispered what sounded like 'For luck.'"

My stomach drops under the weight of a thousand boulders. *For luck.*

Click isn't lying.

Which can only mean one devastating truth:

James is dead.

My lungs collapse, desperate for air, and I sink to the cavern floor in a daze. With each spray of the crashing waves, the salt stings my eyes and tattered flesh with a newfound sense of hostility.

The seconds fly by as the ocean rises higher in the pit, encroaching on our dampened space, threatening to submerge the entire cave floor.

"We need to leave," Laz barks, his voice hollow and distant.

How easy it would be to end it all. To simply push off from the top of the pit and let the ocean carry me away. The island seems to be growing smaller by the minute, pieces of it eroding away with each incoming tide. But mentally, the island has never been bigger than that wretched house anyway.

My throat tightens with the onslaught of tears as the cavernous walls close in around me. A cloud shifts in the sky, obscuring what little daylight we had, enveloping me in momentary darkness. The waves crash higher, spraying my face as I creep closer to the edge.

Propped on my toes and bracing myself with both hands, I wait for the tide to drive itself back into the cave. The air rumbles louder, as if I'm sitting poised within the belly of some oceanic beast.

The water swirls inside the pit, a fresh wave only seconds away.

Sunlight enters the cave again. As I teeter on the edge, the ground a slick mess, my soaked palms struggle to maintain their grip on the rocky floor. A wave rushes in and bombards the pit, crashing with a feral anger that certainly matches my own. My feet slip out from under me, and my palms scrape the jagged rock as the wave soaks my entire body. The water is freezing, but the adrenaline coursing through me shoves it out of my mind in a flash. As the tide flows back into the open ocean, I slip toward the pit, the current a force of nature I can't withstand.

With my breath catching in my throat, I claw at the rocky floor as my legs slide out from under me and into the violent water below. In a flash, I recant it all. This isn't what I want. It can't end like this. All my fears, each and every regret, flood my mind. Everything I wish I could have done, all the things I never got to say. This can't be it.

Rushing into the cavernous pit with a bombastic roar, another wave hits me broadside, attacking my dangling legs. My grip wavers as I squeeze my eyes shut. The salt has made it nearly impossible to keep my eyes open, and they sting more than I can bear.

A tight grip encloses my arm, pulling me up.

I open my eyes.

Laz is on his knees, his arms now secured around my waist as he wrenches me away from the edge of the pit. He's soaked too. The entire cave is now moistened by the spray of the incoming tide.

"What the fuck were you thinking?" he shouts, kneeling beside me. He yanks me to my feet, not waiting for a response, and ushers me to the cave entrance. The sunlight pierces me blind, an unwelcome addition to the salt that already torments.

"Now, you listen to me," he growls, leaning low to square his face with mine. "I made a promise to your mother that I would keep you safe, no matter what. And there is nothing—and I mean *nothing*—that you can do to keep me from my word. Understand?"

I damn near choke on the audacity that spews from his lips. "Your word?" Sardonic laughter brews low in my gut, but I dare not release it. "*Your word?*" I hiss again. "You mean this?" I shove my bruised arm in his face.

He recoils, irritated.

"Is this the *word* you speak so vehemently about? To keep me safe? Does this look like protection to you?" I shove past him and beeline for the beach to the right of the cave. Where the jetty meets the sand, the waves roll in with broad strokes. As luck would have it, the tide rolls back just as I make my move. Forever grateful for my long legs, I leap down off the jetty's base and into the wet sand below. My feet bury deep with an indelicate *splat*, but I press on.

Laz hollers something behind me, but the waves pounding the surf drown him out to a mere mumble.

As fast as my legs can carry me, I run the length of the beach. The wind tussles my hair as the salty air fills my nose and mouth with its briny redolence. My feet slap the wet sand as I stick to the shoreline, occasionally ending up in ankle-deep water as it creeps inward.

The other end of the beach is fast approaching. I scramble to come up with some sort of plan as the cliff on the opposite end draws near.

A set of arms envelops me from behind and tackles me to the sand, forcing a guttural scream from my aching lungs. Laz is on me, his face contorted in anger as he pins my arms over my head. I gasp as a wave rolls in and soaks my backside, leaving wet sand in its wake.

"You're a real piece of work, you know that?" Laz says, seething with anger. "Get up." He stands and yanks me to my feet.

"You said I wasn't a prisoner here. That the house, this *island,* is as much mine as it is yours. I'm not going back to that house. Not with you. Not ever. *Leave me here.*" I turn away from him, but I don't make it a single step before he whips me back around to face him.

"You're coming back with me. And I don't want to hear another word about it." He jerks me by the arm, pulling me back toward the direction from whence we came.

Like a child berated by her father, I feel minuscule. Dismissed. Unheard.

I wrench myself free once again, ready for the fight that I'm certain is coming. "Go fuck yourself."

He doesn't move. Instead, he merely regards me with a hardened expression and a stillness that drives me mad. It's as if he's patiently waiting for me to come to my senses.

Prick.

Water pools around my ankles, causing me to sink with each outward pull. There's nowhere to run. This beach is surrounded by cliffs, Laz is standing two feet away, and, as if I even need reminding, I'm on an island. Exhausted, defeated, and utterly devoid of hope, I blink against the tears welling in my eyes. My achy chest makes what I'm about to ask even more painful, but I refuse to take one more step toward that fucking car without knowing the truth.

"Why did you do it?" My voice barely escapes my constricted throat. I hold my arms out, the contusions on full display in the high sun. He hangs his head low, avoiding my gaze, before he breaks the silence.

"I had to." He rubs the back of his neck and releases a sigh.

"Bullshit," I bite.

"I don't expect you to underst—"

"Try me."

A wave cuts into our shins. His shoes and slacks may be ruined at this point. But I certainly don't give a shit.

"It's Jenna," Laz says.

"Jenna?" Just saying her name makes my blood curdle for ever thinking I had nothing more to live for. I press again. "What does Jenna have to do with *this*?" I eye the battered flesh of my arm.

"I needed something to keep her in line. David's no longer welcome in her life, so I can't use him to keep an eye on her. At least not to the extent I prefer."

"Keep her in line?" My eyes widen with shock and utter confusion.

"She's been talking to the police, Neve. She's a liability. And I can't have that. So I took some compromising photographs of you and sent them—"

"You *photographed* me?" I leap forward, shoving him hard with both hands. He makes no move to stop me. I'm honestly not sure which is worse. "You did this to me, and then you took pictures?" I shove him again, but he barely budges. "What the fuck is wrong with you?" I'm screaming so loud, my lungs burn.

He lets me take out all my anger and aggression on him, taking every blow I deliver with a coolness that only makes me strike harder. It seems to make little difference to him. His massive frame is no match for me. In time, the pain, fear, sheer heartache, and bitter loss of trust has me defeated.

I collapse to my knees, exhausted. Waves encircle us both, but I no longer have the energy to stand. In a way, I secretly welcome them. Maybe they'll wash away everything that tears me apart, everything that haunts my dreams, every broken promise, and every memory that tortures me with its tether to my old life.

"Just answer me one thing," I plea, my head throbbing from all the tears shed as my soaked hair sticks to my face. I crane my neck to look at him from below. I want to see his eyes when he answers. "Did you rape me last night?"

Deep furrows cut through his brow and his eyes widen, horrified. "Jesus Christ. No." He sinks to his knees in the incoming wave and reaches for me. I back away.

My mind whirls, desperate for the fortitude to exclaim everything I want to say. But pained silence is all I can manage. Based on the way his eyes soften despite his agonized expression, I'm convinced that my silence has spoken louder than the words that tug at my mind. With little effort, I pull my feet from their sunken state in the wet sand and step past him. I have nothing more to say.

The car ride back to the house is deathly quiet, rousing my restless nerves. When he finally parks in the circular drive, his guards approach, ready to transport the car to its proper place. Laz holds up his hand to stop them.

"What I did..." He shifts in his seat, facing me. "There's no excuse for it. But I swear to you, even if it takes the rest of my life, I'm going to make things right. You have my word."

I meet his gaze with puffy eyes and cheeks that itch from dried-up tears and seawater. He seems sullen. Perhaps even repentant. But it does nothing to stir my deadened heart.

"Your word means nothing to me."

Turning away from that horrid, disfigured face, I throw open the door and hurry into the house without so much as a backward glance.

Chapter 44
James

"Jaaaames."

A sharp, anguished scream cuts through the house, filling the space around me from somewhere upstairs. I drop the pan in the sink mid-wash and race from the kitchen to the foyer, frantically wiping my wet hands on my jeans.

"*Jaaaames*." Jenna's voice pierces through me a second time as she bounds for the stairs. Her face is tear-stricken, her cries bursting from her as if beyond her control.

"What is it?" I ask, my insides tortured by what could have possibly transformed her into a dithering, shaky mess.

"It's Evie," she says, shoving her phone into my hands.

My stomach drops at the mention of her name.

"Look," she urges, gesturing toward the phone.

I don't want to. There are very few things that would devolve Jenna into a series of untamable sobs like this. And since Evie's safety is the only thing that keeps me going anymore, I fear I may not be brave enough to face what awaits me on that phone.

"Someone hurt her," Jenna weeps.

Three simple words.

Nothing more.

But they're a death sentence all the same.

The phone trembles in my hand as I force myself to look—to be brave for my Watson, just as she deserves—at the series of picture texts that sit idle on the screen.

A punch to the gut would be far more forgiving, as I'm nearly doubled over, desperate for air. It can't be real. None of it. There's no fucking way in hell this is real.

As if having lost a deal with the devil himself, who bartered for my very soul, I lose all sense of mercy in an instant. My understanding of all things good and evil, right and wrong...all of it vanishes from sight, memory, and intuition, and is overtaken by one solitary thought:

Vengeance.

There are seven photographs on Jenna's phone, each one more gut-wrenching than the last. The first is a close-up of Evie's face. She appears to be sleeping, but it's impossible to know for sure. The next five are a series of close-ups of different parts of her naked body and all the ways they've been marked: one of her neck, one of each of her breasts, one of her abdomen, and one of her overall naked figure as she lies unconscious on a black sofa.

As I scroll to the last photograph, however, the phone nearly drops to the floor as fury grips me with an iron fist and turns my entire world ruddy. The photo is of her private area, and front and center is a full-bite contusion. The teeth indentations are prominent on her skin, deep red with hints of purple. And it's located on the inside of her thigh, right up against her labia.

Her body is covered in bite marks. Aside from her face, her entire figure has been abused. My face is aflame with rage, heat licking up my neck and into my cheeks and hairline. I swipe at the perspiration on my forehead with the back of my hand, looking about the room as if it may pity me with answers as to how to fucking process this.

"What do we do?" Jenna asks between sobs.

I stare over her head in a daze. Numbness combats the anger

inside me, pulling me apart as visions of Watson's battered body destroy me with a mercilessness of their very own.

Stumbling backward on compromised footing, I collide with the front door and drop my head into my hands, desperate for the pounding to stop; a pounding that, despite my mortal need for mollification, does nothing to drown out the words Jenna speaks on merely a broken whisper: "Do you think...he...raped her?"

The cry that emanates from my throat is so feral, so animalistic, and so unfamiliar to my own ears that I cover them to muffle it. I've never heard anything like it, but I can't seem to make it stop. Breaking down walls and tearing limbs from the person who did this to the woman I love is the only sanity I can pull together anymore.

Unleashing a maelstrom of anger, I trounce the front door with both fists, unleashing barbaric cries as I thrash against it. My wounded shoulder screams in agony, but its pain is laughable compared to the one that imprisons me with such unspeakable misery.

"James," Jenna says, touching my shoulders to assuage my outburst. I stop flailing and cover my face with both hands. I refuse to remove them, for I never allow anyone to see me cry.

Never.

But in true Jenna fashion, she ignores my unspoken dismissal, evident by how her body bumps mine as she shimmies into the small gap between me and the door.

"James," she pleads, pulling on my wrists. But I refuse to let go, surrendering to the sobs that make my body quake.

I catch sight of her tearful face as she ducks beneath my arms and throws hers around my waist in a tight embrace. Clenching my eyes shut, I scramble for ways in which to pacify the thoughts that I'm certain will haunt me for good as the last of my tears spill.

Saving Evie is the only thing that matters, and it needs to happen *now.*

Ignoring Jenna's sudden look of confusion, I step away and dash into the living room, ripping the landline phone from its receiver.

"It's James," I tell Frank after he finally picks up. "Listen—" I pause. "Something's happened. We can't wait anymore. We have to go *now*."

Frank replies, saying he's come up with a plan, but he needs more time to organize all the moving parts.

"No, you don't understand," I bark, outraged at his lack of urgency. "She's in serious danger. We have to act now—"

He cuts me off, his subtle reminder of who's in charge, and demands my immediate attendance at his location.

"Okay. I'm on my way." I hang up the phone and hurry for the door.

"Who was that?" Jenna asks.

"I have to go."

Fearing that my terror will reflect at me from her eyes, robbing me of the strength to keep a level head and see this mission through, I avoid her gaze as I reach for the door.

"*Stop.*" She shoves the door closed just as I open it, then blocks it with her body, her arms folded. "Talk to me."

"You're wasting time—" I try to push past her, the trails of blood left on the door in the wake of my torn fists catching my eye for the first time.

"Just stop. Just stop all of this and talk to me." She's screaming so loudly that I can't avoid her any longer. Her face is beet red despite her tears seeming to have stopped.

And I was right. My terror rests with unease right there in her emerald eyes. But I'm not frightened by it, as I thought. Instead, I'm wounded with guilt as I witness all the ways these photographs are clearly killing her too. What a prick I've been not to take even a second to understand Jenna's position in all of this.

"I'm nothing if not stubborn, James. And you're not leaving this fucking house until you talk to me."

Running a hand through my hair, I release a heavy sigh. Frank is waiting on me, and I can't bear another minute spent not making my way back to Evie. But I never told Jenna about Frank, for her own sake, and now I have no idea how I'm supposed to slip out of here without a barrage of questions from the woman whose gaze is ripping me apart.

"Look, I..." I begin, my shoulders relaxing as my tone lowers to levels of civility.

She cocks her head and gives me a narrow side-eye, urging me to continue with an irritability that matches my own.

"You have to promise not to kill me," I tell her.

She takes a step back and looks at me in horror. "Jesus, Pierce. What did you do?"

"I met with someone a few weeks ago who said he wanted to help me get Evie back."

Her jaw drops. "I'm sorry. *What*?"

"We've been communicating frequently, trying to come up with a plan. We came up with some ideas, but it can't wait any longer. We need to act now—"

She holds her hand up to stop me. "Wait. Hold on a sec. You're supposed to be lying low, remember? Have you forgotten what would happen if the wrong people find out you're alive? What were you thinking—"

"I was thinking that I don't have a fucking *plan*, Jen," I shout right back. "What am I supposed to do? You think I can just rent a fucking boat, sail over to the island, and waltz into some heavily guarded fortress and ask him to hand her over? I'm one person. *One.* I'm not a goddamn army."

"Your solution, then, was to put your trust in a complete stranger and tell him about our situation?" Sadness seems to have been stripped away by the anger that reddens her skin all over again.

I back away, hating that I have no choice but to tell her the truth. "It isn't a stranger." My voice drops to reaffirm the truth. "It's David's father, Frank."

She gasps. "Are you insane? Do you have any idea what would happen if David, of all people, found out you're still alive? And here, with me?"

"David and his father haven't spoken in years. You know that."

"Honestly"—she crosses her arms again—"I don't know what to believe anymore." An attitude coats her words in a way that cuts deep.

My shoulders slump as I surrender to her accusation. She's right. I kept this from her.

She has every right not to trust me.

"Why wouldn't you just tell me?" she finally asks.

"I didn't want to worry you," I reply, meaning every word. "You've been through enough already."

"James..." She slowly closes the gap between us. "We're never going to make it through this if we start keeping things from each other. You don't understand. I *need* to get her back as much as you do." She looks away. "Let me help you." She takes my hands in hers, her eyes finding mine with a softness that makes me wonder if she's searching them for my surrender.

A laborious sigh emanates past my lips. "You're right. I suppose this means I ought to start by telling you that I think those pictures were meant for me."

She drops my hands and takes a step back. "How do you know that?"

I hold her gaze. "The bite marks." Saying it out loud makes my blood curdle all over again. "He asked me about the bite mark on Evie's shoulder when I was held captive on the island. He seemed highly displeased. I don't think it's a coincidence that he chose to mark her body in such a way."

Her face blanches at the context of my words, as if on the verge of making her ill.

"He must have sent them to you knowing I no longer have a phone. Which also means he knows I'm still alive...and that you and I are together. Why else would he risk it?"

She pauses. "Maybe he doesn't know, but he's using these photos to find out. Maybe he's baiting you? And if he sends them to my phone, and you're still alive, he likely knows that you'd be the last person I'd keep them from. Whoever this person is, he obviously knows us pretty well."

I ignore the sickening drop in my stomach, choosing instead to admire Jenna's cleverness to make such deductions. It was wrong of me to exclude her from Frank's plan. She would be an asset, if Frank permits her partnership.

"I told Frank I'd meet him," I say before I can second-guess the decision. "You're welcome to come, if you'd like."

Apathy can seem so appealing when you've been plagued with sorrow for so long, which is made clear by the way she accepts my invitation with downtrodden eyes and a simple nod, and follows me out the door.

CHAPTER 45
JENNA

Grady's Tavern on Main has always been a sleepy little hub for as long as I've known. With rarely anyone coming in or out unless the Red Sox happen to make it to the World Series, it's easily overlooked among the endless stretch of coastal boutiques, souvenir shops, ice cream parlors, and seafood restaurants. Only the locals know of it, visiting, I'm sure, out of pure nostalgia.

Sam, the owner, is a respected man in this town. A simple, humble man, working long hours to keep the place afloat. My parents always had nothing but nice things to say about him. And it's because his tavern is as simple as the man who owns it that I could not be more confused when James parks my Benz in front and ushers me inside.

The place is completely vacant, including wait staff and bartenders. All the televisions are on, tuned to various sports events —namely golf—but the volume is so low that the closed captions have taken over.

James takes my hand and escorts me to the back, down a flight of steps covered in dank merlot carpet. At the bottom of the stairs is a heavy barn-style sliding door complete with a metal latch. He knocks and announces himself, and within seconds, the door slides open, revealing a large, dimly lit storage room. Boxes are stacked high in multiple corners, shelving units cover the back wall, and small horizontal windows line the opposite walls near the ceiling.

What's odd is the large table in the center, spotlit by an old hanging lamp, covered in an assortment of papers, and a man, dressed in an all-black suit, standing behind it. Beside him stands a slender woman in a black leather skirt and white blouse, with long blond hair that falls down her back in loose waves, with lips of cherry red.

Two men, also dressed in suits and armed with guns, stand on either side of the door, making my heart accelerate to dangerous levels.

"James," I whisper, pulling at his arm. "We shouldn't be here." My Spidey sense is tingling from the crown of my head to the balls of my feet. What was he thinking coming here? He gives my hand a gentle squeeze of reassurance, but it does little to quell my nerves.

"James," the man in the black suit says, gesturing for him to come closer. The seriousness of his tone makes me want to hightail it the hell out of here. But James's firm grip keeps me trudging forward. For some reason, I trust it.

"You have me worried to death, son," the man in black states, ushering us over to the table.

As if noticing me for the first time, he says with a scowl, "And who's this?"

James squeezes my hand again. "This is—"

"Jenna," I interrupt. "I'd say it's nice to meet you, but that would be a lie. And let's be honest, it doesn't matter who I am, does it? James says you have a vested interest in getting Evie back, and I want to know why. I want to know who in the hell you are, and I want to know what the plan is." My neck, cheeks, and ears are scorching with irritation, and I'm so sick of being the last to know every freaking thing.

The man in black smiles. "I like this one." He gestures toward me but looks at James.

James gives me a cautionary side-eye, then squeezes my hand. No more gentle reassurances this time; this one is a warning. "Well, you should," he says. "She's your daughter-in-law."

The man in black scrunches his face with confusion.

"This is Frank?" I motion toward the man I've already deemed a pain in my ass. James only nods.

Frank chuckles, and it makes my skin crawl. "It's nice to finally meet you, Jenna. I'm sure we would have met at the wedding had David thought of inviting me." He looks me up and down, and my insides squirm. "You're quite a beaut, aren't you? David always knew how to pick 'em." He claps his hands together just once, as if ready to get down to business, then caresses the svelte blond woman's ass, which she acknowledges with a flick of a grin.

Every ounce of judgment I have for this douchebag is stretched tightly across my face. "How are you even here? This is Sam's place—"

"Was Sam's place," Frank responds with a smirk. "I bought it from him a few weeks ago."

"What do you mean? Sam has owned this place forever," I reply.

"Everyone has a price, Jen. May I call you 'Jen'?"

I can't even bring myself to respond. This man is grating my last nerve. Even though I understand why James felt it necessary to bring him into the fold, I hate it all the same. Accepting his help seems like making a deal with the devil.

"James. Why don't you tell this assclown about the texts I received this morning before I go postal," I say through gritted teeth.

Frank only laughs.

He hands him my unlocked phone and tells him, "There are seven total. They came in from a restricted number."

As Frank skims the phone, I scan the table, desperate for anything that will keep my mind from imagining those horrible photos. Fearing they will forever be etched in my brain, I curse the man who inflicted them under my breath. If I had it my way, I'd batter his own body tenfold and leave him with a pulse only if I'm feeling generous.

Before me lies an assortment of maps, documents, and what look like blueprints. Frank returns the phone to James without so much as a twitch of concern. It bothers me more than his smug laugh.

"We need to come up with a plan. Now. This can't wait any longer. You've seen what he's already done to her—"

Frank holds up his hand to stop James's rant. "Son, what do you think I've been doing?" He motions to the papers on the table. "Come. Let me show you." He pulls a large map out from underneath a pile of papers and places it on top. "I had this made up based on how you described Eden's Green to me. From the map you said you tried to commit to memory while you were on the island, as well as what you saw from the lighthouse. Here, take a look..." He hands it to James, who turns it to face him, studying it intently. It's several minutes before anyone speaks.

Map? Lighthouse? I don't understand any of this.

"See this dock here?" Frank points to the southwest shore. "This is the largest dock on the island. This must have been where your ferry docked on what you call 'game night.' This is the point of entry for the plan I've devised. But first, I have to know: does it seem like an accurate representation of what you saw on the map you found?"

James nods. "Yes. And the topography seems to be what I remember. This is incredible." He reaches for other papers, but the large blueprint seems to really grab his attention. He releases a small huff as if in awe. "Is this what I think it is?" James asks, his eyes wide with intrigue.

"A blueprint of Moretti's estate? Yes."

"How did you get this?"

"Everyone has a price, son. I paid the county clerk a hefty sum for it. But at least now we know the layout and can plan accordingly."

Together, they go over the plan. And not once does it involve me. My blood boils the longer they discuss, and I'm slowly losing the battle of suppressing my screams of frustration. If I lash out, however, I know I'll never be allowed back here. I try to find satisfaction in the fact that I'm at least privy to the discussion.

James should know me well enough by now to know that will never be sufficient.

Once we've left this horrible basement, I'll be happy to remind him.

"So what do you think?" Frank asks, peering at James, both mirroring each other with arms braced on the table. "Do you think it's a workable plan?"

James's eyes seem glazed over, as if he's drunk on hope and a newfound strength to slay the damn dragon. "Workable?" He scoffs. "Hell. It's absolutely *genius.*"

CHAPTER 46
EVIE

AUGUST 16TH — DAY 81

I pray for thunder. I pray for rain. I pray for all the powers of the universe to smite the garish full moon and spare me its piercing light. Its celestial sister lit the sky the night James and I first met. A tranquil beauty as I fell headfirst for the man who was yesterday's stranger.

Now I can't bear the sight.

For the past six nights, a stern knock on my bedroom door has interrupted the haziness in my mind. At seven o'clock on the dot.

And for the past six nights, I've ignored it.

Long after the knocks had vanished, I would sink back into my bed, hold my wrinkled mess of a bridesmaid dress against my chest as if it were James himself, and dream of better days. Like clockwork, the tears would come, further soiling the gown as they spilled past my cheeks and into the powder blue satin. It's the last tangible piece I have of James, for I haven't seen the button since the caves.

Tonight—the seventh night—the knocks do not come per their usual schedule. As the clock on my nightstand ticks away, its metronomic rhythm driving me mad, seven o'clock passes to five after in the blink of an eye. Seven ten soon gives way to seven thirty, and I'm certain these nightly visits have ceased for good.

But just as the clock reads 7:33, a slight scraping noise sounds behind me. I roll over to eye the door but see nothing out of the ordinary.

Sitting upright takes more energy than I could've expected, grief and heartache turning my body to lead.

On the floor just inside the door is a folded note. With great pain, I slink to the floor and open it.

Dinner tonight in the dining room.
Eight o'clock sharp.
— L

I toss it aside and crawl back in bed. *Like hell.* My eyes barely drift closed when a rigid rap sounds at the door.

"Go away," I holler, then cover my head with a pillow.

Three hard knocks sound again.

"I said go away," I shout at the door, my head throbbing from all the tear shed.

A masculine, steely voice on the other side of the door answers. "I've been instructed to escort you, miss."

I throw the pillow in a huff. "Fuck off."

"I've explicit instructions not to leave here without your accompaniment. It's best if you open the door and come with me."

"The note says eight. Get lost."

"Ma'am, it's five 'til."

What? I sit upright and cradle my aching forehead. I must have drifted back to sleep. "You know what? Fine," I mutter and hop off the bed in a fit of irritation.

When I fling the door open, the same ol' guard who's always given the unfortunate task of being my escort stands before me. His eyes widen, likely because I look as shitty as I feel.

"Would you like to freshen up? I can stall the boss for a bit if you need—"

"That won't be necessary," I retort, passively running my fingers through my tousled hair as I brush past him and into the hallway. My white T-shirt, blank except for my art museum's logo near my left breast, and these simple blue pajama shorts will do just fine.

The dining table is rife with candlelight and a feast suitable for a dozen. Ablaze with a dancing glow, it's a stunning display, to be certain. It takes everything in me not to compare it to the old speakeasy—memories of better days I'd just as soon forget. If this is an attempt to impress me, though, I want nothing to do with it.

Laz stands at the far end of the table and gestures for me to take a seat opposite him. Begrudgingly, I sit where I'm instructed.

The plate before me is piled with food, sending my voracious appetite spiraling with greed.

"You haven't been eating," Laz states, regarding me with a disapproving look as he takes his seat. "You refuse my nightly invitations to dinner. You leave your proffered meals untouched. I can see from here the weight you've lost. It isn't healthy, and I won't stand for it."

He pushes the food on his plate around with his fork, irritated. But he pauses for a moment before he speaks. "No one understands how taxing grief can be better than me. Trust me. But this refusal to eat..." He takes a bite of food before continuing, chewing with an angered flair. "It ends now."

Trust me? Go fuck yourself. "Like hell, it does," I murmur.

"Like hell?" He slams his fist on the table, making the dishes and silverware clink as I jump out of my skin. But I don't cower. My life has, in an instant, become devoid of all potential losses or gains. I can't feel anything anymore. No one is coming for me. James is gone. And I'm forced to merely exist by the whims of a man who'd rather clip my wings and keep me as his pet forever.

"You heard me," I reply, finding fearlessness in both exhaustion and indifference. "How many times do you think you can drug me and still expect me to consume whatever's put in front of me?"

He drops his fork and straightens his back. "If I wanted to drug you tonight, there'd be nothing you could do to stop me."

"So you've said," I taunt. "You should get that printed on a T-shirt."

"You're behaving like a child. Eat."

I shove the plate away, looking nowhere else but him. "No."

He crosses his arms and sits as still as the dead. It's unnerving, but I refuse to let it show.

"I will shove every last bite down your throat if I have to." His voice rumbles low and deep.

It's interesting, I'm coming to find...the confidence that awakens from impassivity. It's all that fuels me anymore. "I'm not eating your goddamn food. Ever. If you want to drug me again, then do it." I lean forward, driving the point home. "But I'll be damned if I make it so easy for you."

"It's useless trying to get a rise out of me. You can bait me all you want, but it won't work. I won't bite."

I nearly laugh, stopping short with a quick, sardonic exhale. "That would be a first for you, wouldn't it? We both know you're nothing but a monster who just *loves* to bite."

His eyes narrow, fury twisting his face into one of sheer malice. But before he can respond, I continue my string of cruelty, which seems to have fallen beyond my control. "So why don't you take your idle threats, your machismo bullshit, and your sick, unnatural obsession with my mother, and shove it up your ass."

I await his wrath. I'm certain it's imminent, for his scars flush with a crimson hue.

He pushes his own plate away with an aggressive shove. "Now, you listen to me." He stands and leans in, both arms propped on the table. "If you *ever* disrespect your mother's name again, I'll—"

"You'll what? Huh? You'll take my freedom from me?" I gesture to the room. "Hold me captive? Kill the man who meant the world to me? James is dead because of you. Don't you get it? I have nothing left to give you, Laz. Your threats mean nothing."

"I told you to stop—"

"Or what?" I repeat my idol threat, hoping this time it'll stick.

He kicks his chair back with sheer violence and storms toward me. For the first time since I entered the room, I'm completely terrified. But again, I don't cower. I would never give him the satisfaction.

With a sharp tug on my arm, he yanks me from my seat and drags me further down the dining table. "What the—" is all I manage before he sweeps the platters of food aside and they crash to the floor in a smattering of chaos. I open my mouth to protest again, but the words don't make it out before Laz slams me face down on the table in the void he's created. It knocks the wind right out of me, and I shudder at the hostility that has befallen me.

"If you insist on behaving like a child, then I will be forced to treat you like one," he growls before slapping my rear end with his full palm. My shorts stifle the blow, but the area stings nonetheless, and I exclaim an agonizing cry. In a state of utter panic, I claw at the table, trying to push myself up. But he keeps me pinned with a firm grip on the back of my neck.

"Laz, stop," I beg. But another blow lands square on my ass. The tenderness of the area—still compromised from the healing bite marks—elicits an even louder scream from me this time.

By the third blow, tears are pricking at my eyes.

"James is dead," he taunts as he lands a fourth blow. "Say it."

"Go fuck yourself," I shriek.

"James is dead. *Say it.*" His screams are louder than before.

Tears spill down my cheeks as I beg for it all to end. My bottom aches, each blow sharper than the last. But despite the hatred that flows through my heart for Lazaro Moretti—a monster both inside and out—it's the first time since I learned about James's death that I've felt, well, *something*. It's painful, and I want nothing more than for it to be over, but at least the fear in my heart reminds me that it's still beating.

He lands several more blows on my raw, aching behind. But I no longer scream. Instead, I wince and weep uncontrollably. Before long, I've lost count of the strikes, and my searing throat won't allow me to scream anymore.

"James is dead," I rasp, forfeiting the fight. Tears tickle my nose as they traverse the bridge and spill onto the table.

The blows stop.

My whimpers fill the room before he finally pulls me from the table and envelops me in his arms. My cheeks are as tender and inflamed as my behind, but my tears are silent now, soaking into the front of his button-up shirt as he kisses the crown of my head. "Shhh…" he coddles. "It's all right." He plants another kiss. "You're mine, Neve. And you know that now. Everything is going to be all right."

Petting my hair as one would a child in hysterics, he continues. "I'm so sorry for everything. More than I could ever express. My only hope is that one day, you'll learn to see me for who I really am: the man behind the *monster*, as you've called me. And that you can find it in your heart to forgive me." He releases a frustrated sigh and tightens his embrace. "If you would just give me a chance—"

I pull away from him and square my gaze with his. "James is dead." I reiterate the painful truth he beat from my lips. "What chance could I give you that you would possibly deserve?"

I don't wait for a response, and I certainly don't ask for permission before slipping from the room, wiping away the tears that cloud my vision as he calls after me.

His pleas fade as I disappear up the main stairs. I don't go back to my room; I can't spend another minute in there. So I hurry down the hall, past the dimly lit paintings that haunt the shadows, until I've reached the red door.

My art studio's ambiance is so devoid of passion that it nearly fills me with tears all over again. Once a space of colorful visions coming to life, the scent of fine oil and acrylic paints transporting me back to the art museum I will never see again, it's now a drab, lifeless tomb just like everywhere else in this godforsaken house.

Still propped alongside the fireplace are each of my paintings. My completed masterpiece of a woman who bears my face, sitting on a terrace overlooking the ocean, rests front and center. It's arguably my best work. Certainly my bravest, for it's the first that features a full face—a skill I've always been self-conscious about. I was waiting for the perfect time to give the finished piece to Laz. He seemed to love it so much and checked in on its progress often. But now I despise every brushstroke. It's hideous, just as he is, and I can't bear the sight of it.

Emboldened by rage for my captor and contempt for the artwork birthed from my soul, I grab each one and toss them into a pile in the middle of the room. Frantically, I spill the contents of the paintbrush holder on the table, ignoring their clacking as they roll onto the floor. The lighter I stowed away lands among the scattered brushes, and I reach for it without hesitation.

The pungent smell of paint thinner singes my nose as I douse the pile of art with the entire can, then toss it in with everything else.

The flick of the spark wheel is quick.

The eruption of the ball of fire is quicker.

Thick plumes of smoke fill the space in seconds as flames lick high toward the ceiling. The heat wafts onto the balcony, where I watch the chaos through its parted French doors. From here, I can still see the paint as it bubbles off the canvas and turns as black as the smoke around it. The images have gone, replaced instead with char and mostly reduced to mere flecks of ash.

On the opposite side of the roaring flames, Laz bursts through the door. Click and a handful of guards follow close behind. He doesn't seem to see me at first. Instead, his full attention falls to the fire that rages on. With frantic gestures, he shouts at his men, but I can't make out the words. The guards disappear out the door as Laz shields his face from the towering flames.

That's when he sees me.

For many seconds, he holds my gaze, but he makes no move for the balcony. When his guards return, fire extinguisher in tow, his attention diverts once again to the crisis at hand.

White puffs of carbon dioxide replace the flames with as much speed as they first appeared. The smoke dissipates from the blast of the extinguisher, driven outside onto the balcony, filling my lungs with its cruel heat.

My coughing fit doubles me over, turning my chest into a scratchy mess. Once it passes, I catch Laz out of the corner of my eye. He's kneeling before the pile of ash and remains, shoulders slumped.

Completely alone.

He picks at the pile, holding up various pieces of char as if in disbelief that it's all destroyed.

I sink to the balcony floor and watch him, bile rising high in my throat, not knowing where in the hell to go from here.

With his hands and arms covered in soot, he looks over at me one last time. Anger, malice, disdain...none of them are present in his downturned eyes. Only despair.

I open my mouth to speak, having no idea what to possibly say. But Laz exits the room without so much as a glance over his shoulder, leaving me alone with nothing to keep me company but the lingering smoke, a pile of embers and ash, and my caustic guilt.

THE SETTING SUN NO LONGER LINGERS, BEAUTIFUL streaks of ocher in the dusky sky having been replaced by an inky sea of stars. Laz sits on the terrace steps, his head in his hands, silhouetted by the last inch of pale hue that lines the horizon.

Awarded only a few steps forward before my courage fails me, I pause. I have no plan; no clue what to say. I debate turning back and returning to my room. Perhaps he'll make the first move at some point? But watching him there, sullen and without any fight left in him, I can't bring myself to walk away.

"I know you're there," he murmurs, looking out toward the evening sky. "Either come and sit or leave me be."

The calmness in his tone is nearly as unnerving as his temper. I take a seat alongside him with great pain, courtesy of the tenderness of my rear end. But the effort truly lies in my attempts to avoid the glisten in his eyes lest I turn into a blubbering mess right here and now.

"I'm not going to ask you why you did it," he says, breaking the plodding silence. There's a sincerity in his voice I haven't heard in ages.

It doesn't make any of this easier.

A low, hefty sigh escapes his lips, as if created by an unspoken forfeit. He doesn't wait for a response. "I never should've hit you."

I peer at him, my interest—and hope—piqued. Whatever corrosion my insides suffered in the name of regret from this fretful night is slowly mended by his words.

"Why did you?" I ask, my voice barely above a whisper.

As if searching for the right words, he shakes his head. "I just... couldn't seem to get through to you. I feel like I've tried everything. I was desperate for something that might finally..." He runs a hand over his beard and exhales deeply. "Make you listen."

I lock on his gaze without intention of turning away this time.

Whatever sadness transpires, I'll bear it with him. "I know what you mean," I reply, the smell of smoke from my tarnished paintings still permeating my hair and skin.

His face relaxes, all furrows fading as if from a new understanding. "I cherished those paintings," he says, making me go cold all over despite the softness of his voice. "The one you gifted me...I'd never loved a piece of art more. And no, it wasn't because it bore your mother's face." He stares at me, as if ready to pounce in case I retort. "It's because it bore yours."

My throat pinches as tears resurface. A million thoughts fill my head all at once, and yet, words fail me despite them all. The only thing I can come up with to quell the aching in my chest is "I'm sorry." I drum my fingers against my leg nervously before stealing his words in a whisper. "I suppose I was desperate...for something that would finally make you listen."

He looks at me and grabs my hand to stall my anxious fingers. The gesture brings warmth into my tortured belly, and I sigh with uncertain relief. "I suppose you and I are more alike than we care to admit," he says, then kisses the back of my hand and gives it a gentle pat.

The last of the sun's rays disappear for good when Laz turns to me and whispers, "I never should've done what I did that night. It's inexcusable." His face rests in his palm, his arm propped on a bent knee. "Can you ever forgive me?"

Forgiveness seems like an impossible feat, so I don't know how to respond. But I know this feeling of guilt all too well. All the times I cursed Papa, hated him with every fiber of my being while I was trapped by his doing, then fell into his arms, riddled with apology and shame for my cruel thoughts of contempt.

I can't say I will. But I also don't say no. My silence as I turn my attention to the stars is all the answer I can give right now. He's just going to have to understand that.

We sit together, eyes averted toward the sky, until our necks are kinked and all semblance of tears have faded.

When I crawl into bed, remembering the nights in which he would hold me in this very spot, I conciliate tonight's transgressions and submit to how alike we really are.

I drift to sleep knowing it's a notion I will carry with me for the rest of my days.

Chapter 47
James

Frank's trust in me seems more apparent with each passing day. What began as a solo invitation to his home to further discuss "the plan," over time, evolved into a formidable partnership that strengthened my faith that we would soon have Evie back. He gifted me an entire wardrobe of black suits so I would "seamlessly blend in with the rest of his men," as well as a cell phone so he could "reach me at all times."

Last night, after a long night of brainstorming at Frank's home, I stayed at a local hotel on his dime.

Jenna was not pleased.

Not that she came right out and said it. I always check in with her every few hours via text whenever I'm with Denardo. Normally, her responses have been consistently prompt. But when I texted her last night to let her know I wouldn't be coming back to the Cape until morning, it took her over an hour to respond. And when she did, her text consisted of only two simple words:

JENNA

Be safe.

She's obviously irritated with me. But not so upset that my wellbeing is no longer a concern of hers, which I suppose is a win in a way.

Regardless, I vowed to leave first thing in the morning and return to her.

◈

I CREEP INSIDE THE CAPE HOUSE, EXPECTING JENNA TO still be upstairs, asleep. Instead, I find her in the living room reading a book on the couch. She does not look up when I approach.

"Hey," I say timidly.

"Hey," she replies, not once glancing up from the page.

I come around to the front of the couch, lift her outstretched legs, and plant myself beneath them. She doesn't even flinch.

"How's the book?" I ask, testing the waters.

"Fine."

I sigh and rest my hand on her foot. "Jen, look. I'm really sorry—"

"You can leave your key on the table in the entryway," she says as she nonchalantly turns a page.

"What?" I ask, taken aback.

"That's why you're here, isn't it? To return your key? Frank has given you someplace better to stay?"

"No." I snatch the book and toss it onto the coffee table.

Her jaw plummets. "*James.*" She balks. "You could have at least let me put my bookmark in."

"Sorry," I say with utmost sincerity. "I just...I need you to listen to me—"

"No, *you* listen," she barks, pushing herself against the cushion to sit more upright. "You want to know what prompted me to go snooping around David's office that night I found all that stuff on Evie? It was because he *stopped coming home.* Don't you get it yet?"

"It isn't like that—"

"Frank is sinking his hooks into you," she replies as she slaps the back cushion of the couch. "And after all the stories David told me about him…" She trails off. "It scares me to death." Her voice is strained. "But nothing scares me as much as knowing that I've already lost Evie…and David. And now I feel like I'm losing you too." Her eyes glisten as she folds her arms and looks away.

"You aren't going to lose me." I pat her ankle. "I have no loyalty to Frank, and beyond the fact that we both share a common goal, he means nothing to me. We need his help. I hate that we do, but we have little options. When all is said and done, I don't care if I ever see that man again."

She tucks her fiery hair behind her ear, the redness that dotted her neck from her frustration slowly fading. "Swear it," she insists.

"I swear."

After she brushes her eyes with the back of her hand, they land on my attire. As if seeing me for the first time, she squints with confusion. "Who died?"

Looking down, I chuckle at my solid-black suit.

"You look like you're going to a funeral," she continues.

I brush off her sarcasm. "Denardo bought it for me. I didn't pick it."

"I don't like it," she states. Her disapproval of this entire situation has been duly noted.

Prince Harry stares at me from the cover of his book on the coffee table before I hand it back to her. "Any good?" I ask, not really interested, but I'm desperate to make her feel better.

"It's all right," she responds, taking the book back and flipping through its pages in a blasé manner. "Royalty gossip is one of my guilty pleasures." She closes the book and fidgets with the corner of its dust jacket. "It's no desert island book, though." She looks at me through her eyelashes as her lips twitch in a smirk.

My sigh is ripe with levity. "Evie told you about that, too, did she?"

"Ohhh yeah." Jenna's eyes widen playfully as her lips spread to the fullest grin.

A part of me fears what else Evie may have told her. But despite how hard I dig, I can't seem to find a sliver of bashfulness regarding our time together anymore. There are so many more important things to worry about. Jenna seems to get me, and any fear of judgment she may have falls by the wayside.

She licks her lips and says, "Oh, and James. Swear to me one more thing."

"Name it." I'd swear the entire world to her if it meant having her trust.

"I want to rescue Evie as much as you do." She withdraws her legs from my lap and sits up taller. "So don't ever leave me behind again. Ever."

With a smile and softened brow, I reassure her with a simple "I won't."

"Swear it," she insists.

I take her by the hand and look her square in the eye. "I'll never leave you behind, Jen. You have my word."

CHAPTER 48
JAMES

AUGUST 26TH — DAY 91

One morning, I'm escorted into Frank's personal arsenal located off his home office. It's roughly the size of a bedroom, and each wall is covered from floor to ceiling with gun racks and locked metal cabinets containing heavy artillery —some military grade. With a wide, sweeping gesture, he insists that I "pick one of my choosing, so long as it could be discreetly hidden in my waistband." I select the Glock 22 .40 caliber pistol and tuck it into the back of my new black slacks.

I'm often ordered to stand guard at the door while he meets with associates from all over the eastern seaboard. They gather around the boardroom table tucked away in a room at the back of his home. Ordinarily, the oval table's glass top would be covered with the maps and blueprints that were once stored in the basement room of Grady's Tavern. Not anymore. He moved the meeting spots to his home outside Boston, and I can't help but wonder if it was to make it harder for me to return to the Cape each day. He even offered me a spare bedroom, insisting that I stay with him to put an end to the "senseless commute," and guarantee my availability whenever he needs me.

The meetings venture later and later into the night, and the commutes become more laborious when performed with tired eyes. Jenna's tongue lashings are frequent, insisting that I stop bending to Frank's whim.

Left with little options, I ignore Jenna's pleas and attend to Frank's requests without pushback. I need his help, and I'm willing to do whatever it takes to get Evie back.

Over time, I've come to stand guard at every meeting, pretend not to hear the warbling of his associates as they gather around the conference table, and accompany him on every outing at his insistence. He pays me handsomely for my time and efforts. At first, such offerings were disguised as a "helping hand." But the payments only grew with each errand, and before I knew it, I'd found myself slipping into Frank's ranks.

If I didn't know any better, I would say I slipped in incredibly high, for no one else who served beneath him was allowed to enter his office, let alone his boardroom. I, on the other hand, went everywhere with him.

❧

Frank's office is quite the sight to behold, yet it provides little distraction from the incessant pull to check my phone for replies from Jenna.

Her faith in me is waning. I can feel it. My texts to her grow more frequent, while hers only become more curt the longer I'm away from the Cape house. One-word answers are all I receive anymore: "Good," "Okay," "Sure." The guilt of ostracizing her from the plan to rescue Evie is tearing me apart, especially after swearing to never leave her behind.

This house feels like a lodge plucked right out of a Rocky Mountain ski-resort town. Cathedral ceilings of exposed chestnut beams, mocha leather sofas, and deerskin rugs. His office blends right in with the aesthetic, with an earth-tone stone fireplace, antlers nailed to the chimney above, and large picture windows overlooking the Atlantic that peak at the top to fall in line with the point of the ceiling.

I wait next to the fireplace, arms crossed in front of my hip, waiting as he continues his heated conversation on the phone about some meeting that's supposed to happen later today. I'm fidgety, but I try my best to hide it. I can't stand all this waiting. He has a plan, and it's brilliant. But it's killing me how long we have to wait for the right time to strike. It takes every bit of strength to keep those photographs of Evie out of my mind.

Evie is mine.

Mine to protect.

Mine to keep.

With her permission, I claimed her, just as she wanted. I marked her body, ravaged her, and swore to keep her safe as I cradled her in my arms.

We left that island as one.

Now her body has been abused in a way I can never forgive, and I'll do whatever it takes to right the wrongs that have been inflicted upon her.

Even if it means standing here and twiddling my fucking thumbs while Frank deals with "business."

I decide to pull my phone out and text Jenna. But just before I make my move, Frank hangs up his call and shoves his cell phone into his pocket in a huff. "Come on," he barks, pushing the chair back in a quick burst. "We're leaving."

We head to the garage and hop into his black Maserati, per usual. I've learned to stop asking where we're going. If he wants me to know, he'll tell me.

"I received a call this morning confirming a recent arrangement I made," he begins as we peel out of the driveway, tires squealing on the main road. "Moretti is heading to the Cape as we speak to negotiate a trade for Evie."

I jerk my head toward him in shock. "And you're just telling me this now?"

"I tell you what you need to know, when you need to know it. Don't question me, son." The use of the word *son* always grates on my nerves, solidifying all the ways in which he treats me like an employee or worse.

"So what are you willing to give to get her back?" I ask. It's a bold move, asking such a question, but this news is paramount, and I can't stomach being left in the dark any longer. Suddenly, I feel akin to Jenna more than ever before, and my insides rumble with remorse all over again.

He shoots me a look of warning, and I don't press the issue further.

The trip to the Cape is a silent one, but my mind is anything but. Evie's seafoam eyes and the sound of her voice whispering in my ear consume me, making it nearly impossible to maintain my composure. I imagine her frightful tears transforming into ones of joy as she runs into my arms. I scoop her up, hold her tight, and swear to never let her go. I steady her racing heart with words of reassurance that she's safe at last, and she kisses me so hard that my lips bleed with unyielding passion.

This is it. If Denardo can make this happen, then "the plan" will be null and void, and Evie and I will be reunited sooner than I expected.

We arrive at the tavern quicker than we legally should have.

In the basement, Frank's men are already inside. They must have parked in the alley out back; their cars weren't out front. Frank points me to the far corner, hidden in shadow along the back wall. Two men, dressed in suits identical to mine, stand guard on either side of the back door leading to the alley, waiting for our visitor.

The time on my new Rolex shows 1415 hours, and my Glock is safe and secure in my waistband. But I don't know when Moretti is expected to arrive.

Five minutes give way to ten, then fifteen. It's so fucking quiet in here that I may go insane. Frank sits in the chair behind the empty round table, texting God knows whom.

My need for Evie's trade cripples me, and I don't know how much longer I can stand here just waiting.

A car pulls up in the alley behind the tavern, the gravel crunching under its weight and pulling my attention to the present. Car doors slam, footsteps follow, and before long, three figures appear on the concrete steps leading from the alley to the backdoor.

The men enter, two of them guiding a third by the arms—*Moretti*.

Moretti bears a hood over his head, the sight of which floods me with memories of my similar circumstances, and they're unpleasant at best. His wrists are also bound, which only adds to my torture. Once the door has been locked behind them, they wait for Frank's orders.

He merely waves his fingers, and the men rip the hood off. The bound man squints against the lamplight.

My stomach drops.

"What is this horseshit?" Frank hollers, motioning to the man. "Moretti arranges to meet with me and then sends his goddamn lackey instead?"

The man coughs nervously as a strand of brown hair falls into his eyes. "I've been asked to come here and negotiate a price to keep Neve right where she is."

Wait.

"The agreement was to arrange a trade so I could get her back. And now, not only does Moretti insult me by not showing up to conduct his own negotiations, he's now asking to *buy* my daughter out from under me, is that it?" Frank's nose is practically touching the bound man as he shouts in his face, blocking my view of him.

The man does not seem to flinch. He merely replies, "Name your price."

Frank paces away, rubbing the back of his neck.

I finally have a full view of the man.

And suddenly, I can't breathe.

I know that face.

Ashton.

I reach for my gun, my face scorching as rage rips through my entire body. But with great pains, I stop myself. The prick works for Moretti. That, by itself, is enough to send me over the edge. And now he's negotiating to keep Neve captive on that island. Unable to steady my breathing, I doubt I can maintain my composure much longer.

Frank stops pacing to close the space between him and Ashton. "You dare put a price on my daughter?"

Ashton remains stoic and unmoving. "Per the boss, I've been permitted to offer you a sum of thirty-one million. One million dollars for every year you kept her from him, the man to whom she truly belongs."

"You son of a bitch," I lash out, rushing at him until my gun is mere inches from his face.

"That's enough," Frank scolds. He snaps his fingers and holds his hand out for my gun. But I ignore him. My hands are steady, certain of their target, and ready to pull the trigger.

Ashton only smirks, making every muscle in my body tense. "Well, well, well. If it isn't Mr. Pretty Boy himself. Never expected to see you here, working for Big Man Denardo." He chuckles, and my index finger twitches on the trigger.

"Your weapon," Frank demands, his hand still out. "Now."

For a second, I consider killing him. He's working for the man who has Evie, which means he's potentially had access to her all this time. The thought alone nearly pulls the trigger.

Shaking, I unwillingly lower the gun and hand it to Frank, never taking my eyes off Ashton.

"We do this my way," Frank warns. He nods his head toward the back corner, where he insists I wait.

I oblige with only one thing on my mind: Ashton's fucking smirk.

He tsks. "Careful with him," he says to Frank despite looking at me. "While the two of you big boss men are playing tug-o'-war over Neve, *this* one"—he points at me—"will undoubtedly swoop in and take her for his own. I mean, he seems to think he staked his claim on game night and will come for anyone who tries to take her from him. Or anyone who even touches her, for that matter." He snickers. "I should know, right?" He flashes me a conniving grin, and all sense of control disappears.

I lunge at him with every ounce of energy and hatred I can use to fuel my strength, knocking him onto his back. Wasting no time, I swing, landing blow after blow on that smug fucking face. I hate him. More with each passing second.

He tries to block my blows with his bound hands, but it serves him little aid. Bones crack beneath my knuckles, and there's so much blood, I can't tell the source. My hands ache, their flesh torn, but his face is faring far worse. Evie's screams from the hedge maze echo in my head, drowning out the gurgling cries that escape his throat.

When the red slowly fades, I slump to the floor, exhausted, left with only burning lungs and a ringing noise that overwhelms my other senses. A pair of hands grip me by the front of my shirt and yank me to my feet.

"Don't you dare start something you aren't prepared to finish," Frank sneers, his face twisted in anger and mere inches from mine.

"What?" I ask, sickened by the suggestion.

"That man insults me. Sends a goddamn lackey to do his job, someone who put his hands on my daughter, no less."

I'm released with a hard shove before he slaps my pistol in my hand. "You finish this, Pierce," he fumes. "You finish it *now.*"

Ashton rolls onto his side, agonizing groans emanating from his lips.

This isn't a game.

In an instant, the reality of it all comes crashing down.

I shake my head in refusal.

"I'm sorry. What was that?" he asks through gritted teeth, eyeing me crossly.

"I said no. I'm not killing him. I never agreed to this—"

"You agreed to help me get Evie back. This asshole is standing in my way—"

"You're out of your mind."

"You're disobeying my orders?"

"I've seen enough death for one lifetime," I shout, outraged and out for a different kind of blood. Dusty Afghani desert air filling my lungs makes me breathless by the sheer memory. "I never agreed to this." I toss the pistol onto the floor, and it slides out of sight into the shadow from whence I came. "You do your own dirty work, Denardo. I'm only interested in one thing, and that's getting Evie back. Everything else is your show."

I disappear up the stairs into the tavern despite the shouts bearing my name that follow.

When the asshole is ready to get Evie, he knows where to find me.

I've been gone too long as it is.

And Jenna is waiting for me.

CHAPTER 49
LAZARO

AUGUST 27TH — DAY 92

Click's waiting for me to speak first, and I can't for the life of me speculate as to what he's thinking. He never fidgets or displays any of the other telltale signs of uneasiness, making him a difficult man to read. Ordinarily, I like that in my soldiers. It's an asset to have in men who do the hands-on part of the job. Now, however, I'm at a loss for knowing whether he's as trustworthy as I always deemed him to be.

He sits in front of my desk, a leg crossed over a knee, putting those tacky red shoes on full display. I've always hated those things, insisting over the years that wearing shoes that make so much noise is the exact opposite effect of what I need in an ambush of my enemies—who can hear him coming from a mile off. His response was always the same: anyone worth fearing never needs to sneak up on his enemies to get the job done.

Neve swears she heard them the night Gino was killed and Frank's men stormed her home. They returned to Boston empty-handed, and Frank was more stirred up than ever in the wake of their failure. Several of them never lived to see another dawn; Frank does not take kindly to incomplete assignments.

She also swears she saw them. Those horrid, distinct shoes that he's had replicated over the decades and created as a signature look. I hate to believe it, wanting nothing more than to chalk it up to the darkness playing tricks on a frightened child. And I'd like to think she knows better than to lie to me by now. Our trust is in dire straits, at my doing, but that doesn't mean I wouldn't turn the whole fucking world to ash for her in the blink of an eye if it came down to it. A rat in my ranks is one thing; a man who terrorizes Neve Denardo is another. And that person has only one thing coming for them.

Death.

"September of '03, Frank sent men to Seattle in search of Neve. I had business to attend to in New York and asked you to keep an eye on David while I was away. Do you remember this?"

Click responds with a purposeful nod. "Yes."

"And did you?"

"Yes," he responds, without even a hint of fluctuation.

I lean back in my wingback chair and examine him. His eye contact never breaks from mine.

"Are you going to ask me why I'm inquiring as to your whereabouts at that time?"

"No," he replies.

I wait for him to elaborate, but the silence only grows.

"I have reason to suspect that you went with Frank's men to the west coast."

Click's composure holds firm.

"I have an eyewitness who claims she saw you there."

Still, he remains unmoving.

"Would you care to explain yourself?" I lean forward and plant my elbows on my desk.

A hint of a squint is all I detect before he finally speaks. "I was in Boston, as you instructed. Surely David can attest to that?"

"David doesn't remember much from that time. You know what he was going through." I wave a hand as if brushing it aside.

David's downward spiral is a thing of the past I'd just as soon forget.

"And this eyewitness of yours…is who, exactly?" he asks with a sharp squint.

"You know I never reveal my sources."

Click places a casual hand on his crossed ankle. "Well, I suppose that puts us at a crossroads where it's my word against hers. So, now, you must ask yourself, who do you believe?"

I won't shy away from his sly challenge, but he's right. It's his word against Neve's, and I don't know—

My phone vibrates on the desk, interrupting my thoughts. I unlock it and find an unread picture message coming in from an unknown number.

Ashton's wide, lifeless eyes stare up at me, blood pooling into the divot in his neck, coating his teeth and lips and matting his hair in a grotesque fashion. The gunshot wound in his temple is apparent, but it doesn't stir me as much as that desolate stare. I reassure myself that it was necessary lest shame rear its ugly head and make me doubt the real reason I sent Ashton on that errand.

He hurt Neve, and that was never part of the mission.

"What is it, Boss?"

Swept away in thought, I stare at the photo until the screen goes black.

"It's One Tap," I whisper, not entirely sure I believe the words flowing from my own lips. "He didn't make it." I bounce the phone between my fingers before tossing it onto the desk, wondering if Click's stoicism will break in the wake of such news.

Aside from uncrossing his legs, he doesn't stir. "May I speak freely?"

"Will I regret it?"

"Perhaps."

Always such a blunt asshole, that one.

"Speak as freely as your heart desires, Click," I reply with a heavy sigh, Ashton's lifeless eyes still etched in my mind.

"Was it worth it?"

My scars burn from the boldness of his question. "Would you care to elaborate?"

"Ashton was a good man. Always loyal and obedient. There was no way Denardo was going to accept any sort of bargain for Neve. You sent that boy to his death, and you know it."

"Are you questioning my orders?" I square my shoulders, and he leans back.

"No, sir. But you said I could speak freely—"

"And by all means." I gesture widely with my arms. "Continue."

"Are you sure you sent that boy to his death for the right reasons? Ever since you brought that woman here, things have become..." He eyes me up and down. "Compromised."

I sit back, my fingers steepled, silently urging him to continue.

Click leans forward and points his index finger on the desktop as if scolding me. "The mission was to bring Neve here to fulfill a promise you made to her mother before she died. You've done that. But since she's been here, things have started falling apart. Marco is dead. Ashton is dead. You suspect *me* of foul play. Your stronghold is now compromised all because you couldn't stick to your own mission—"

"And how exactly have I strayed from my own mission? Please, enlighten—"

"It was never part of the mission for you to fall in love with her," he shouts, catching me off guard as his gravelly voice cuts through the space between us like a guillotine.

Irritation pricks at my scalp. "You're out of line—"

"You know it as well as I do," he sneers as he stands, his voice laced with malice as a tendril of hair falls from its slick and into his eyes. "Shortly before she died, Gabriella professed her love for you, scars and all, and now you're convinced that this woman will do the same. How many more of your men have to die before you realize she's not Gabriella, and you'll never be able to have with Neve what you had with—"

"That's enough," I cut in with a sharp tongue, jumping to my feet to address him head-on.

"Unless this is about revenge." Click refuses to let up, as if some floodgate of truth has been unleashed from his lips. "Is that what it is? Denardo took Gabriella from you in more ways than one. Was all of this really just to keep some promise to her, or were you meaning to avenge—"

"I'm not using Neve as a fucking power play." I lean on the desk with locked arms as I stare him down. The goddamn balls on this guy are one for the ages. If I didn't need him so badly, especially now that Ashton is dead, I'd shove his face into that roaring fire just as mine was—

"So I was right from the start? You had one of your own men killed because you've fallen in love with a woman who wants nothing more than to run from this place...and from you." He squints at me, fearless.

A fucking death wish.

That girl *will* love me.

I lower my head with frustration.

"Leave," I bark, pushing away from the desk. "Now."

Neve is mine. She always has been.

Despite the words Frank spat to the contrary the night she was snatched from her bed.

But goddammit, none of it matters anymore. I have Neve, whether he likes it or not. And I'll stop at nothing to keep her safe and away from his reach.

Even if it meant having to mark her body in a way that tears me apart. If only she knew the fear in my heart the night I learned she was gone—knew how a piece of me was lost right along with her, only to be reclaimed once she awoke in a disheveled bridesmaid dress right here in my house. Someday, she will forgive me. I'm certain. She just needs time to heal, and to learn how much that night changed absolutely everything...

If it had been any other family, this place would've been swarming with cops. But not the Denardos, and not their estate, where police would ask too many questions and pry too deep into Frank's affairs.

I arrived shortly after being summoned—along with the rest of Frank's men—via a violent outrage over the phone: no questions, just get here.

Men are scattered throughout the living room, dressed sharply for an occasion that didn't warrant it, putting forth their best efforts to appease the boss. Me, well, I was at home in bed when my phone rang off the hook, so my ass is here in jeans and a T-shirt. That's the best he's going to get out of me at this late hour.

"What in the hell's going on?" I ask Demitri, Frank's accountant, a weaselly little man with glasses and a receding hairline despite his round, youthful face.

"I don't know," he replies. "Boss said it was urgent. I didn't ask any questions."

The suits throughout the room bear mournful expressions as if someone has just died. I know the look all too well. Frank's business is a dangerous one, and there have been more funerals over the years than I care to recall. But this time, it's different. Something's not right. A thick, somber energy permeates the room, and I can't shake the trepidation that lingers in the air.

Amid the silence, faint, muffled cries resonate from upstairs, pulling my attention upward toward the exposed wooden beams of his chalet-style home.

Frank races down the stairs, emerging in our field of view. Those who were sitting about rise to their feet, ready for instruction. His face is red with rage, and his bow tie hangs loose around his neck.

"Neve's gone," he says, addressing the room.

A confused murmur resounds through the gathering. Confusion hits me first before I'm smacked with trepidation. The only word I hear as the room warps around me is the only one that matters: gone.

His words fade as my mind races. The sobs upstairs pound in my head as the room rustles with concerned and angered chatter.

None of it matters. Only the cries.

I slink past the crowd and bolt for the stairs, traversing them two at a time. In an instant, I recognize the source of the wailing.

David.

My heart thrums louder than my shoes as they pound against the dark hardwood.

His screams pierce the room before I even enter.

Gabriella is on the floor, cradling him in her arms, rocking him as he sobs against her chest. The strength to fight her own tears wears heavy on her face.

"Laz," she says, her voice breaking as she chokes back a sob.

"Is he all right? What happened?" I ask, falling to my knees and reaching for David. He recoils from my touch, and it strikes me with a painful bite. She tightens her embrace around the boy, patting his leg and giving him gentle whispers of reassurance. I resist the urge to reach for her, to take her in my embrace and whisper my own words of comfort. Instead, I wait for her to tell me what on Earth is going on.

"He hit him," she says, her eyes glistening with early tears. "He's never struck our children before." A tear spills down her cheek just then, and she wipes it away with her shoulder.

"Frank struck your boy?" My insides churn with an unshakable taste for blood.

She nods, rocking him with greater fervor as his cries penetrate the space around us. "I couldn't stop him. It was like he was possessed. I've never seen him so angry. How could he do this to him? How could he possibly blame David for this? My boy…" She plants a kiss on the top of his head. "It's all right," she whispers into his disheveled hair.

"Blame him for what, Ella? What's going on here?" My impatience grows like a tumor in my gut, and David's sobs are tearing my fucking heart into pieces.

"The baby, she—" Ella chokes, her eyes brimming with a new batch of tears.

"She what?" Never have I wanted to shake her, but the anticipation of her next words is about to twist me into irreparable disfigurement.

"She's gone." Ella plants her lips against David's head and weeps. The sounds commingle, laying waste to my faculties as confusion and disbelief begin driving me mad.

I leap to my feet and rush from the room. Down the hall, I throw the door to Neve's room open and survey it frantically. Not once did I think Ella would ever lie to me, nor use her baby for some sick joke. But I have to see it for myself.

The sight of Neve's empty bed makes me tremble. I brace myself against the doorframe, my stomach sinking into a bottomless pit. Everything is in its proper place, except for a few stuffed animals knocked onto their sides near her pillow. The bedding is pulled back as if she left for only a moment, with every intention of returning to its comforting layers.

I waste little time before checking the room from top to bottom, my search fruitless as I make my way to the large window opposite the door. My heart races as it raises with ease.

It's unlocked.

The night air shoots goose bumps across my perspired skin as I poke my head out the window. One of the roof's dormers, flat on top and making a gradual slope to the edge of the house, butts up against the base of the window ledge. I follow the line of its flat top, my eyes landing on a sliver of lattice poking up past the dormer's sight line. It's the lattice that's affixed to the south side of the house, covered in lush vines and contributing to the house's attractive, European-chic appearance.

The world seems so still—peaceful to unassuming eyes—with the midsummer crickets singing a chorus free of cicadas or even a whispering wind. Reeling with a sense of helplessness I haven't felt since Gabriella herself was taken from me all those years ago, I hurry back to David's bedroom.

"When did you last see her?" I insist, David still cradled in her arms on the floor. His chest heaves now with quieter cries.

She regards me with wide eyes. My abrupt entrance clearly startled her.

"Frank and I tucked her into bed right before we left for the evening. He made plans for our anniversary tonight."

At her words, Gabriella's shimmering blue gown catches my attention. With thin straps and a plunging neckline showing off that ivory skin, torturing me in every conceivable way, she looks absolutely breathtaking.

"He asked David to keep an ear out for her—if she cried or stirred."

"Where is your bambinaia?" I ask, trying everything in my power to mask the fear in my voice.

"She's been sick the last few days. I didn't want to risk getting the baby sick, so I told her to stay home." Her tired eyes drift to the space between us, the irony of the situation plastered upon her sullen face.

I'm not going to lecture her about whether David was old enough to be left watching his sister. He's a responsible kid. There was no reason not to leave him in charge. Besides, it changes nothing now, and the last thing he needs is me or his mother questioning capabilities his father already struck him over.

My gaze falls to David—twelve years of age yet seeming so young and helpless in his mother's arms. I've never seen the boy so terrified. He didn't deserve any of this. He never should've been born from Frank, the man who has taken everything from me and turned the woman and children I love into spoils I must observe from the sidelines.

That boy should've been mine.

I reach for him again and pull him against me with a gentle tug on his arm. He resists at first, reaching for his mother, but I don't allow him to recoil this time. Despite the fact that he's rather tall for his age, David seems like nothing more than a small child in my arms, frightened and shaking through the last of his tears.

"He had no right to do this to you," I say with genuine tenderness, pressing his cheek against my chest. He heaves with a silent sob. Ella covers her mouth, stifling her tears.

"Are you all right?" I whisper to David. He nods against me.

"Look at me, son." I pull David away so I can stare him in the eye. Fury tugs at my insides as I note the swelling and discoloration of his left eye and the broken skin on his cheekbone. Testing my limits, I stay put, despite the need to inflict unspeakable pain on Frank for laying a hand on him.

"Your father is a fucking coward," I confess pragmatically.

"Laz—" Ella cuts in, horrified.

"It was wrong of him to hit you. This wasn't your fault. None of it. You know that, right?"

David's puffy eyes drift elsewhere in the room.

"Answer me, son." My tone is stern, and I rein it in so as not to further frighten the boy.

He nods, but his hesitation tears my heart apart. His tear-stricken face is etched with doubt.

"From now on, you come to me for everything. Understand? He doesn't deserve you, and I'll be damned if I allow him to ever hurt you again."

David meets my gaze, studying me with such intensity that I resist the urge to look away from his tender yet hardened face. Something has changed in the boy, and I fear he may never be the same after tonight. By refusing to look away, I solidify my unspoken vow to *him: to protect him from the man who never deserved him in the first place.*

He sinks into my arms, and I cradle him closely. I've always loved him as if he were my own. In so many ways, he felt like mine despite my chance at fatherhood being taken with Gabriella. But seeing him hurt, damaged, shamed, ignites a newfound purpose in my chest. I may never be able to free Gabriella from Frank's grasp. Not while he's alive. She made it clear that she would never risk her children by disobeying their father.

So I'll take David instead. The wrath of hell engulfed in eternal flames is nothing compared to that of a father detested by his own son. This may be the chance at revenge I've been searching for all this time. And David deserves a father who understands affection is more than the spoken word.

"You're going to be okay," I murmur before leaning in and planting a kiss on the crown of his head. His breathing has leveled out so evenly that I'm sure he's fallen asleep in my arms.

Ella scoots closer to us and places a gentle hand on David's back. Together, the three of us remain in a calm silence as the boy drifts into a deep sleep, his breaths slow and relaxed against my chest. Hypnotized by her beauty, despite her reddened, tear-stricken face, I fall headfirst into this feeling I've not experienced since I held Neve for the first time in the hospital. It was easy, then, to pretend just for a moment that Ella had not brought Frank's daughter into the world, but my own. And now, this feeling of togetherness—family—that Frank's violent outburst has brought me is one I will cherish for the rest of my life. I cradle David—my son—and pray he finds in me the father he needs.

Taking painstaking efforts not to wake the boy, I carry him to his bed and fall to my knees to regard his placidity. Ella climbs onto the bed alongside him and places her other arm around his waist.

I brush my thumb over the bruising under his eye, as if trying to wipe it away from existence. Gabriella reaches for my hand and pulls it away from David to hold it in her own.

Her eyes are riddled with heartache, but behind them is a warmth I don't quite understand despite everything that's torn her apart tonight.

"David's going to be okay," I tell her. "And I'm going to get Neve back. I promise you, I'll find her, Ella. You have my word." Her solemn gaze falls to David's undulating chest, and I've never wished so hard to know what she was thinking. She believes me, right? I would do anything for her and the children who should've been mine.

Giving my hand a gentle squeeze, she locks eyes on me. "You're beautiful," she whispers. "I hope you know that."

The corner of my mouth teases at a smile. But I can't bring myself to allow it, for the aching in my heart far exceeds the reference of affection she's making at this desperate time. "You must be seeing your own reflection in my eyes." I finish the banter with her own words, pulled from a time when she was still mine, and the future lay ahead of us in an ocean's expanse of possibilities.

I lean over David and kiss her. It's a risky move, considering I have no idea if Frank may barge in at any moment. But I don't care. Her lips, softer than the rose petals from which they stole their color, press against mine—possessing a need that matches my own. Our sighs intertwine, filling me with a comfort found nowhere else in this world other than between her parted lips. I inhale her breaths as if they're the elixir of life, our tongues finding each other like reunited lovers.

Before falling too far under Gabriella's spell, from which I may never return, I pull away, lick her taste from my lips, and head for the door.

There's a little matter I need to discuss with Denardo, and the sight of Gabriella pursing her lips as we pull away from our kiss, as if holding on to the sensation of my flesh against hers, is the wrong headspace for me to be in when I confront him.

The living room is vacant, and I find a handful of stragglers who *have moved into the den with Denardo just past the kitchen. They're gathered around the bar at the far side of the room, engaged in a serious discussion.*

"Everybody out," I bark. A response of bewildered faces is all I receive. I move into the den with purpose, tired, heartbroken, terrified for Neve, and thirsty for this fucker's blood.

"I said everybody out. Now. Get the fuck out.*" I point toward the front door, and everyone shifts uncomfortably, looking back at Denardo, who stands behind the bar. He sets his tumbler on the bar top, eyes locked on mine, his silence thick with acrimonious rage.*

With a slight nod, the others obey Frank's command to leave. As the room clears out, leaving me behind with the man I despise most in this world, I see the state of the room for the first time. The couch cushions are in disarray, and a video game console and its controllers lay in a dozen shattered pieces all over the floor.

"Explain yourself," Denardo seethes through gritted teeth as the front door clicks shut from the last of his soldiers.

"I was going to ask the same from you," I say, ready for the challenge.

"Excuse me?" His brow furrows with anger. "You come into my home and start barking orders at my men. *And then presume to ask me to* explain myself? *Have you forgotten who you work for, Moretti? Or do I need to remind you—"*

"You hit the boy," I cut in, jabbing a finger in his direction.

"You're damn right I did." The glass in his tumbler clinks as he swirls it between sips.

The curtness of his response nearly knocks me off my feet. "You had no right—"

"I had every right. I'm his father.*" He slaps his chest. "Me." His eyes narrow as if trying to peek into my fucking soul. "It seems there are a few things you need reminding of these days."*

He's baiting me.

And it's working. Anger overloads my heartrate until it trans-

forms into the hollow drumming of wings, toying with bursting straight from my chest.

"This wasn't David's fault. He's a kid. How could you possibly blame—"

"I gave him one job to do. One. I asked him to keep an eye on his sister. And he was too wrapped up in his stupid video games to notice someone coming into the goddamn house. Because of him, Neve is gone." He slams his tumbler, spilling the last of it onto the countertop.

"Shut the fuck up," I whisper, pointing to the ceiling. I don't want David to hear any of this. "David didn't hear anyone come into the house because they didn't come in on the ground floor."

Frank comes out from around the bar and regards me with skepticism.

"Look." I straighten the couch cushion with disdain, then take a seat. "If David was here the entire evening, there's no way anyone could enter the house without him seeing or at least hearing it." I twist around until I'm facing the kitchen, Denardo once again in my field of view. "See. There's a clear view of the back door in the kitchen and the front door from here. If they came in through the back door, they would have to actually slink past this couch in order to reach the stairs. Anyone coming in through the front door would be in his periphery on his left side. He would have seen something."

"Unless he was too engrossed in his video games to notice. You've seen how he can be with those things. The whole house could come crashing down and he wouldn't notice a fucking thing."

"Or they came in through Neve's window. It was unlocked."

"Unlocked?" Frank's eyes widen as his gaze shoots toward the upstairs.

"Yes. And the lattice on the south side of the house goes all the way up to the dormer outside her window. Did you not check any of this before striking the boy? You came home and found Neve gone and immediately took it out on him? Are you out of your goddamn mind?"

"You're out of line, Moretti. Shut your fucking—"

"Or what?" I slowly make my way around the couch and toward the bar, straightening my shoulders as I approach him. "Why not hit me? Your daughter has been taken. You're feeling outraged, helpless, and hell, probably even guilty. You're thirsty for blood. Well, guess what? So am I. You want blood? Take it. You want to hit someone? Hit me. *Not the boy.*" I open my arms wide, inviting him in with more than just words.

"Nearly twenty years, you've been waiting for this moment, haven't you? You've always been one of my most loyal men. But don't think I don't know the anger you possess toward me for taking Gabriella from you. She isn't yours, Laz. Not anymore. If you wanted her, you should have fought harder for her. But you didn't. Because you're fucking weak."

I lunge at him with the wrath of the devil himself, tackling him to the floor and landing with a sharp thud. Everything fades to nothing more than a desolate wasteland of rage—Gabriella's tears as she's forced to say I do, David's swollen eye, and Neve's empty bed—as I straddle him and land repeated blows to his face. I want to kill him. I've wanted him dead for so long. My mind has fallen just as numb as the rest of me, and as Denardo's punches tear at the flesh of my face and nearly crack bones, I don't feel a single bit of it. There's blood in my mouth, foul and plentiful, which I spit between blows. I land punches on any surface I can find and ignore Frank's screams as I sink my teeth into the arm that attempts to wrap itself around my neck.

Exhausted yet electrified with a pulsating madness that ignites me like a livewire, I punish the piece of shit who took everything from me until I have nothing left to give.

I fall away, panting like a son of a bitch but feeling so alive.

Bruised, battered, and beaten, we sink amid the broken casualties of the tousled room. Aching for air, I wait for Frank to lunge at me again. But instead, he clambers to his knees, his shirt torn to shit and his face bleeding profusely, and bows his head, catching his breath.

Broken wood from the end tables, glass shards from the coffee *table, and throw pillows litter the room. Small cuts dot my arm from rolling around in all of it, but all I can focus on is Denardo as I await his next move.*

"You have a decision to make, Moretti. And you have to make it now," Frank says with heavy breaths, cutting into the dense silence between us. "Help me find my daughter. Continue to work for me." He pauses, catching his breath. "Help me get her back, remember your place, and I'll forget this ever happened."

"I'll never stop looking for Neve," I reply, my words laced with venom. "But I'll do it for Gabriella. For David. I'll never do it for you."

"I could burn you for this, you know?" He wipes at the blood spilling from his cut lip and eyes the destruction throughout the room.

"Then do it." I climb to my feet. "Just know, if you do, you'll be burning the one person who wants to find your daughter more than anyone. Even more than you."

As I turn to leave the room, four little words escape Denardo's mouth in a whisper, stopping me in my tracks. "She'll never be yours."

Part IV

CHAPTER 50
EVIE

SEPTEMBER 2ND — DAY 98

Elizabeth pulls the last button through the satin loop on the back of my dress, cinching the corset closed. It's a snug fit that exposes the top of my breasts, pushing them upward in a way that implies a voluptuousness they don't actually possess. The white sleeveless gown falls to the floor in a small train, which I secure in my hand, swishing it about my legs in awe. It's positively breathtaking. Snowflake embellishments adorn the dress on all sides of the corset and line the bosom. They glisten in the light as I admire the dress from all angles in the multipaned mirror, their prongs creating an irregular edge line as they reach beyond the fabric and onto my chest.

My entire face and body have been covered in a subtle frost-like makeup that shimmers with the splendor of freshly fallen snow. Laz's marks on my body have faded, with only their memory leaving me permanently branded.

The final touch is my mask, which has yet to be unveiled. Upon her arrival, Elizabeth delivered it inside a beautiful black box, sealed with a silver bow. She bore explicit handwritten instructions from "the boss" that it not be opened until I was ready to wear it.

Always the dramatics with Lazaro Moretti.

She stands behind me and locks eyes on my reflection with a warm grin. "*Bellissima.*"

Following her gesture, I take a seat on the sofa in the white room, at which point she hands me the box.

Laz insisted on being surprised by my appearance, so I haven't seen him since breakfast. As a result, I've been with Elizabeth and a small staff of women aimed to doll me up all afternoon. The others have long gone, and now it's just Elizabeth and me in this room too vast for its own good.

The ocean, streaked with gold as the sun dips closer to the horizon, has turned a slate blue in the evening hour. Guests shuffle up the front steps, laughter and conversation carrying up into the second-floor room of the north turret, where Elizabeth and I wait eagerly to see the mask that awaits inside the box.

I slip the bow off and remove the lid. On top is a note written in penmanship I've come to recognize as well as my own.

My darling Neve,
For the woman who, with ethereal
grace and unspeakable beauty,
has truly been kissed by snow.
— L

I'm speechless. But whether it's the elegant mask that resides within or the note of such simple eloquence, I cannot tell.

Elizabeth fusses with my updo as she secures it behind my head, making sure everything is in place. White and silver snowflakes sweep over the eyes and across the mask's brow, rising on one side, creating a beautiful asymmetry that flows into my hairline. The mask glints in sync with my gown and skin, a stunning addition to an already perfect ensemble.

My ebony curls bottom out at the nape of my neck, secured in place with pins that bear solitary diamonds. They create a glistening effect with every movement and catch the light to perfection. I feel like a goddess, truly kissed by snow, and I cannot stop smiling. Butterflies flit about in my stomach as I silently praise Elizabeth's work. I've never seen myself this way. In some cruel, masochistic way, I long for this special night on Eden's Green to never end.

I barely hear the knock on the door when the time comes. Still fixated on my reflection, I'm guided away from the mirrors and toward the door with Elizabeth's gentle hand on my lower back. My usual guard escort, clad in a white tuxedo and a simple white-and-silver checkered Colombina mask, extends his elbow to me upon our greeting.

I glance at Elizabeth over my shoulder, and she gives me a low wave and an endearing smile. I reciprocate before disappearing down the hall.

As we approach the main stairs, orchestral music floods the halls, billowing from the ballroom. The sounds of guests chattering and making merry reach my ears long before I see them. When we turn the corner and transcend the wide hallway, past the picture windows covered by curtains, I catch a glimpse of the decor that awaits in the foyer.

The banister is covered with golden toile, wrapped around the entire S curve in tandem with small twinkle lights of a golden hue. Lit candelabras fill the dark corners with warm light, not to be outmatched by the sconces along the walls. Shadows dance in the twilit space, as if tripling the number of people in attendance. Costumed guests fill the foyer as they filter in through the front double doors, while large billowing skirts take up space and refined masks catch the light.

It's like a fairy tale.

Taking it all in would consume the night, yet I can't seem to peel my eyes away from the gala below.

The guard nudges me gently and gestures to the bottom of the stairs.

Where Laz awaits.

I didn't notice him at first. Not that I could be blamed, really. He's completely clad in Venetian dress, a velvet blazer the color of midnight bearing intricate bronze filigree throughout. Beige ruffles peek out from the blazer's edges, the collar of which is popped up on top of his broad shoulders. The bone-colored mask that covers his face makes me falter. With a sharp nasal bone and contours across the cheeks and brow, it's rather skull-like in appearance. Resembling neither animal nor man, however, its shape is unique— just like Laz. Multipronged antlers of antiqued bronze sweep upward and away from the mask in a dramatic silhouette. Wisps of filigree carvings in the antlers that match his blazer give the mask more fantasy qualities than macabre.

A skull mask is the perfect touch for such a man.

With my train in hand, I make my way down the steps. He watches me closely, a grisly carnality lingering in his gaze that matches that of his costume.

Tonight, I can't say I blame him.

He flicks his tongue over his bottom lip as I descend the final steps, biting it instantly as if catching himself.

"You are, without a doubt, the most beautiful creature I have ever seen," he says as he meets me at the bottom step with an extended hand.

I thank him and allow the blush to sweep my skin.

He kisses my hand, then the exposed part of my cheek. His eyes flit to my lips, but he thinks better of it and extends his elbow for my grasp.

Guests part around us as I'm escorted to the ballroom, admiring the costumes that fill the halls. The large grandfather clock beyond the stairs ticks faithfully as we draw near, the ballroom's double doors just up ahead. They're propped open, with guests passing in and out, revealing a room alive with resplendent laughter and symphonic music.

Once we're inside, my attention immediately shoots upward. Large bolts of white and gold fabric cover the ceiling, scooping upward to a single point in the center like the inside of a circus big top. A large, vibrant chandelier holds the bolts of fabric in place, with narrow braziers situated in the far recesses of the room, casting shadows upon the crowd. The material continues from the ceiling and over the walls, encasing the space in an ethereal cloud of elegance.

A myriad of venetian masks, jewels, feathers, and gaudy fabrics glisten in the chandelier candlelight. No faces, only shapes, and a muted palette of creams, golds, silvers, and whites, enhanced by the gilded glow.

Situated on a stage at the opposite side of the ballroom, a live orchestra sways to the tempo of the lively music it creates. I'm allotted only a moment to miss my cello before a handful of guests approach with wild jubilation. I'm greeted by a swarm of covered faces, to whom Laz introduces me as Neve Denardo, which I do not correct. Unidentifiable figures kiss my cheeks, men raise my knuckles to their lips, and Laz's firm hand never leaves my hip. I smile, curtsey even—only in response to those given—and lose all sense of direction in no time.

Servers clad in white tuxedos and simple white masks, similar to the guard upstairs, offer flutes of champagne and hors d'oeuvres off silver trays, one arm bent behind their backs with necessary aplomb. The room seems to bear its own heartbeat, gowns swishing about as couples dance in a grand soiree of cultivated beauty.

A brief pause in the calamity of praise brings Laz's attention back to me. Raising his mask to lean in closely, he rumbles in my ear, "The next song will be ours."

Confused, I press him for clarification with a slight head tilt.

"For just you and me," he adds.

Before I can protest, he guides me toward the back of the ballroom, where couples sway in opulent splendor, and pulls me close with a firm hand on my lower back.

"Laz, what—"

The music has silenced, the crowd parts before my very eyes, and Laz grips my right hand, poised to dance.

My heart has never beat so loudly.

"I can't," I whisper, a tremble licking up my spine and into my fingertips. If only I could relay my apprehension with an exchanged glance. But those stormy eyes are so recessed behind that mask of his, they're impossible to find.

The violins cue up first, a delicate melody perfect for a romantic dance on this late-summer night. "You can do this," he reassures on a lingering exhale that tickles my ear. "Just like we've practiced. Just let me lead."

I acquiesce with a gentle squeeze of the velvet that covers his broad shoulder.

The first few steps are cumbersome, propelled by anxiety, but I don't look at my feet. And with every ounce of strength I have, I avert my gaze from the crowd that encircles us.

Slowly, deftly, Laz sweeps me around the dance floor. As my steps ease into the music's rhythm, grace overwhelms my trepidation. My shoulders relax as I revel in the brisk, beautiful movements of our joined frames. Laz seems to interpret my grace for comfort, for his grip tightens and his pace quickens, as if possessed by an assertiveness that fears I may stop him mid-dance.

Faces blur when Laz spins me away, my dress trailing behind in a dignified swirl. He pulls me back, and each time, we seamlessly fall back into the sway of the music. Vivacious yet refined, the orchestra steals the night as dozens of bows drag across strings in a final swell of song.

For a moment, the room seems to fade as I home in on his perfect smile. His happiness is palpable tonight, his voice humble and kind. A gentle angel who shows me off to his guests with such pride, I can't help but feel distinguished as I reach for a slice of his mirth for myself.

Laz dips me in a dramatic show as the music fades to a close, holding me tightly as I continue to search for those tempestuous eyes.

An eruption of applause follows a blip of silence.

And that's when I find them. His eyes are crystalline and alive, erupting with a feral hunger. But the roaring crowd fills me with unexpected satisfaction, preventing me from crumbling before his erotic prowess.

Before the cheers wither, he lifts his mask and plants a featherlight kiss on my cheek.

A scuffling sound on the stage behind us catches my attention. The conductor, a masked older gentleman with silver hair, clad in a tuxedo of taupes and creams, situates my cello at the front of the stage.

My cello.

It makes my heart skip a beat.

"Play something for them." The heat of his breath caresses my ear in a whisper.

My blood turns cold. "I couldn't."

"Why not? You play so beautifully—"

"Because," I begin in a panic. "I don't have anything prepared." A pinched exhale slips past my lips as the array of masks seems to triple in my periphery.

"You have a gift, Neve. Play whatever your heart desires." His voice pets my skin like satin as he gives my chin a light squeeze. "They're guaranteed to love you..." In one swift motion, he abandons my chin and reaches for my hand, squeezing it gently. "Once they hear you play."

I'm escorted to the stage, where the conductor stands with my precious instrument, waiting for me to take over. The members of the orchestra sit idly by in their seats as they balance their instruments in their laps.

As the conductor adjusts the microphone to the same level as the bridge of my cello, I take a seat in the single chair poised at the front of the stage and cradle the instrument between my legs.

Conversations cease, and feet go still after the swarm of elaborate disguises, chiffon gowns and ruffled tuxedos, fill the void on the dance floor and consume my field of view.

It isn't long before I decide on a song; it was always Papa's selection when I offered to play for him, so I know it well.

The first drag of my bow makes me gasp, for the acoustics in the ballroom are out of this world. Each note I play reverberates throughout and is absorbed back into my entire being.

Comfort warms my soul as the crowd and I fall into a gentle reverie. Despite the undivided attention my solo concert has awarded me, all apprehension seems to fade. This is where I long to be—behind my cello, listening to the music my hands create.

Laz stands at the front of the crowd below, watching me intently. With his mask firmly in place, he appears ghoulish in the flickering light. His mouth twitches in a little smile at our exchanged glance, making my belly quiver in tandem with the vibrato of my wrist.

An exclamation of intrigue spits high from the crowd as the song crescendos into a whirlwind of rapid finger taps and bow strokes, my body jerking with the rhythm.

When I drag the bow for the final note, a rollicking frenzy of cheers and applause erupts. Holding my cello by its neck, I stand and receive the generous ovation, my curtsey coming naturally this time.

I skim the crowd for Laz.

He's nowhere to be found.

A prick of disappointment attacks my insides in his absence. I'm completely on display up here, and I have no idea what's going on. This was his idea, and now he's vanished when I wish nothing more than to receive his praise.

A figure in the corner of my eye catches my attention as it draws near. Laz has joined me on stage and is eagerly making his way by my side. My belly swoons with relief, and my lips curve into a gracious smile as I pass my cello off to the conductor.

I half expect him to throw his arms around me in a heartfelt embrace. Instead, the hard lines of his body find mine as he presses against me. I capture my lip between my teeth to hide my surprise.

His smile is warm as a single finger finds my lower lip, removing it from its cage. Slowly, he drags it from my lip to my chin. Goose bumps cascade over my body as his finger makes its way down my neck, across the dip, and onto my lifted chest. It loses itself when it hits the fabric over my breasts, but it makes me blush all the same.

Continuing to ignore the onlookers, he raises his mask, reaches for my hand, and cradles it against his handsome cheek. His scars are on full display, and his courage fills me with an odd sense of pride as his eyes bore into mine.

Keeping it there for several heartbeats, he cages my hand with his own, and the moment becomes increasingly intimate with each passing second. A wave of gasps vibrates through the spectators with approval.

Despite its simplicity, it's a powerful display of affection I'm not prepared for.

Without the comfort of my cello, my nerves begin to frazzle from the vulnerability of standing before such a plush audience, and I wonder what exactly Laz's intentions are. Theatrics? The man certainly loves to put on a show. But he doesn't seem to notice the others at all despite the swoon-filled rumblings hanging low in the room.

"They all love you," he says dreamily, running a hooked finger over the exposed part of my scorched cheek. "How could they not?" His eyes are steeped in brazen desire as he brings his hand to the swell of my hip.

At this moment, I realize the magnitude of such a romantic display. Laz has never taken a wife, and I know nothing of his past relationships aside from the only one that seemed to matter. To put on such a show is to announce to the world that we're *together*.

Uneasiness overtakes the carnality of the moment, and I tense beneath his touch. Laz's grin has never been fuller.

I follow his lead as he turns away to address the room.

The glut of onlookers seems to have grown tenfold.

"Ladies and gentlemen. Honored guests." Laz's voice booms as he addresses the sea of faces, and their rumblings fall silent to give full attention to the stage. "My sincerest gratitude for each and every one of you in attendance tonight. Many of you are seasoned guests, coming to my soirees these last ten years. But this year is different. This year, we have far more reason to celebrate." His hand squeezes mine, and my stomach twists in knots. Hundreds of masks, eyeless and macabre, stare back at me. They've taken on an eerie appearance, the firelight casting low, oblique shadows across their contours. I squeeze his hand—just as I have of Papa countless times in my more frightened moments. His reciprocated squeeze is tender but does little to settle my apprehension.

"This year," Laz continues, "someone very dear to me..." He pauses and looks at me. I'm attentive, as required, but want nothing more than to flee from the room and never look back. You could hear a pin drop. "Has come home."

Low, harmonious rumblings of exchanged words flood the room, and I pray my mask is concealing the harsh blush that I'm certain has turned me pink.

"Neve Denardo." He squares his body with mine. I blink nervously, desperate for this to all be over so I can find some corner to hide in for good. "My most beautiful and precious creature." I can't tell if he's still addressing the room. He holds my chin between his thumb and forefinger, another loving gesture in front of this audience of gawkers. Dear God, don't let him kiss my lips. It would be so like him to make *this* moment our first kiss. It's almost a sure-fire way to secure my compliance. Knowing that I would rather fall into a pit of snakes than be up here, in front of all these people— *without* my cello. My discomfort has become a weakness he can exploit in any way he pleases. I would hate to make a scene, and somehow, he knows it.

"I think now is the perfect time..." He pauses again, his eyes bouncing back and forth between mine. My palms are sweating, and my heart hammers with such urgency that I fear I may faint. It would spare me the kiss, certainly, but not the horror of making a scene.

As if waiting for the chandelier to drop at any moment, fear pricks the back of my neck. "To tell our cherished guests the real reason we have asked them here tonight."

What is he talking about?

Laz raises our clasped hands and places a kiss on my knuckles, holding it there far longer than necessary. A chill rakes my spine as a low cough sounds in the distance. Champagne flutes remain still, poised in gloved hands, waiting for a cue to sip. Faces stare lifelessly in the current stagnant state of affairs, despite the way the room brims with ripe anticipation.

"In honor of my beloved's namesake," Laz boasts, "come the first snowfall of winter, beneath a matted, blistery sky that's filled with the warmth of our passion and devotion, Neve Denardo and I..." His vaunting is cemented with a little smirk. "Will be wed."

The crowd is blithe with raucous approval, smiles and cheers tearing through the room as it erupts into a wave of movement; glasses clink, celebratory embraces are had with neighboring guests, masks shift amid the chaos, and the band resumes their music with a newfound frivolity. But it's all mere motions to me, for all I can hear is the agonizing thrumming of my heart as it crescendos in my ears. I fight my tightened throat, each swallow more painful than the last, as Laz guides me off the stage and into the lion's den.

A barrage of people fills the space around us until all hope of breath is lost. As Laz accepts the reverence of his humbled guests, shaking one hand after the other, I recall the nightmare in which I was falling endlessly. Except this time, I'm certain there's no one to catch me. This can't be happening. Countless sets of lips kiss my cheeks with congratulatory affection, skewing my mask every which way. I make no moves to fix it as I make every possible attempt to slink away from the voracious crowd.

Laz wraps a firm, possessive arm around my waist as hands reach for me, taking mine in theirs to admire my "breathtaking ring." For a moment, my mind drifts with avid contemplation, wondering at what point that ring was placed on my finger in the first place. But it's fleeting, outmatched by the panic that's cascading through every inch of my body.

I can't breathe. The lack of air in this godforsaken crowd and the tightness of my dress's bodice make me want to double over. I back away, but the myriad of Colombina and Bauta masks only rush into the gaps I create. As if some rare gem, a prized possession with a thousand onlookers, I'm trapped—*drowning*—in a sea of wicked faces and vulgarly long papier-mâché noses. Gold and silver filigree swirl into a blur as my head spins with apprehension and faintness. Desperate for a calming hand, a pathway through the crowd, or even a single waft of air to cool my perspiring skin, I crane my neck in all directions. Tethered by Laz's unwavering arm around my waist, I throw him a pleading look.

With cordial grace, he escorts me through the crowd and into a private sitting room situated beyond the stage. A cluster of couches and plush chairs decorate the room, moved about in no discernible order by guests who have already come and gone. Heavy curtains and a large, ornate area rug further muffle the deafening music that resounds right outside the door. Within its cage of aged brick, a fire crackles peacefully, enhancing the sophisticated yet pleasant ambiance of the intimate space.

In the corner opposite the door, a man, whose mask rests high upon his head, is burying his face in the neck of a woman still shrouded in venetian mystery. They don't seem to notice us as I hurry to the far corner near the covered windows.

Flush with anger and still fighting for breath, I reel around to face Laz, who is hot on my tail. "What in the hell do you think you're doing?" I ask, seething. "Telling all these people that we're to be married? You must be out of your mind."

Laz lifts his mask to his forehead and eyes the couple in the corner. With a cool demeanor, he awaits my acquiescence. It only infuriates me more.

"I wasn't lying to them," he replies with a stern tongue.

"Like hell," I scoff. "You'll never get me to comply, Laz." Panic forces bile high into my throat, worsened by my welling tears. I rip my mask off and drop it to the floor. "This is so fucked. I never agreed to—"

"You know..." He cuts in as if on the verge of a quip, forcing me to pause. "I've found over the years that I can be *very* persuasive."

I recoil, appalled at the lackadaisical way in which he continues to decide my fate. "You're absolutely crazy if you think you could *ever* persuade—"

"Let me ask you this," he interrupts again with an audacious, velvety rumble. "And I want you to really take a minute and think about your answer before you respond." His breath is hot on my lips, his closeness suffocating. But I'm backed against the drapes and cannot escape. "Not so long ago, you and I were friends. You may deny it now, even doubt its authenticity at the time, but I know in my heart that you cared for me once. We were connected, Neve— symphonically, if you will. A manner unique to us, and understood only by us."

With a hooked finger beneath my chin, he forces my gaze to meet his. Those gloomy eyes make my heart patter acrimoniously with bitter hate and repressed affection.

"What I want to ask is...was there ever a moment, fleeting or otherwise..." He brushes an errant strand of hair off my forehead. "Where you felt in your heart that you could ever love me?"

Patiently awaiting my answer, he softens his expression, and his demeanor changes back to the Laz I once knew: the man who chased away my nightmares as he held me while I slept, my duet partner, the bearer of answers to the questions that eluded me my entire life.

My guardian angel.

I recall the first time I heard him laugh, the lightness in his eyes when he graciously accepted my painting, the velutinous rasp of his singing voice, and his reverence for the darkness that once crippled me with fear. It's the beauty in the deplorable and the salvation in the wicked that muddles my good senses when it comes to Lazaro Moretti. And the memories of our better times—free of mistrust and tattered flesh—remind me of the man I wish he still was. A man I admired with every piece of me.

A man I had grown to love.

It was a love unique only to us...and understood only by us. Laz's words replay in my mind, overlapping with the memory of a requited love that remained unsaid but was undoubtedly borne.

His eyes bounce between mine. Despite the sliver of ardor that still endures within me, my body has only recently healed, and my freedom has never been further from my grasp. It's my inescapable chains—the disregard for my own autonomy—that sway me.

"No." The word is rancid on my tongue despite my courage. *I could never love you.* The lie is there, on the verge of being spoken. But I withhold it for fear of the rage it may spawn in my musical genius of a captor.

He withdraws, pain swirling about in those stormy eyes. A pain I can only assume matches my own.

It doesn't last long.

The whirlwind fades and is replaced with something far more tempestuous instead. "Refute the notion that your heart could ever love me, if you wish. But it won't prevail. And bear in mind, my love, the more you fight it, the harder the next few months will be for you."

Fear skims across the surface of my skin in a myriad of goose bumps.

"Beneath the falling snow," Laz continues, "we will stand together, exchanging vows of respect, loyalty, and undying devotion. Before God himself, you will mean every word, and you will honor them. I don't care how you do it, Neve, but we *will* be wed, and you will find it in yourself to truly love me. Is that understood?"

The brashness of his bold statement brings heat to my neck and cheeks. "How can you ask this of me?" I croak, fighting the urge to cry with every ounce of strength I possess.

His face softens as he sighs, but I fear the worst is yet to come. "I'm not *asking*. Remember that." Bringing the mask down over his face where it belongs, he transforms into a faceless, loveless creature that certainly matches his forsaken soul. "Now, take a minute and pull yourself together. There's a gala of guests out there eager to shower you with adoration. We've been absent far too long already."

He turns away from me, but the anticipation of his absence does little to level my shakiness. I need this night—hell, night*mare* —to end. The tunnels are my only hope of escaping now. If he thinks I'll fall in love with him in only a few months' time and marry him of my own free will, no less, he must be out of his—

"Take comfort in knowing this will all be over soon," he says, turning back to face me before reaching the door. "Time will fly faster than you realize. And when winter comes, you and I will begin a new life together, rife with mutual love and affection." He gestures widely with his arms, a theatrical display of minimizing the situation. But in a sudden change of direction, he closes the gap between us and reaches for me. "And I must say, my love..." He leans in closely and caresses my cheek, making me quiver uneasily beneath his touch. "I do believe the first snowfall will come early this year."

My lungs capsize as he turns away and hurries from the room.

The couple in the far corner are still immersed in each other, seemingly none the wiser that my fate has been forever sealed by the man behind the mask. It makes me want to scream. How can no one hear the way my terrified heart assaults my chest? How can everyone be so blind to the panic on my face, the tears welling in my eyes?

Surrounded by a swarm of people, and yet I've never felt more alone.

I don my mask and exit the sitting room with only one goal: to get the hell away from the sea of faceless guests who rob me of oxygen and hope.

The orchestra's beautiful melodies fill the ballroom as I slip along the perimeter, where the guests are sparse and enmeshed in conversations with haughty, drink-fueled laughter. I don't bother looking for Laz. His whereabouts are not my concern. I just need to get away from the stifling swarm of strangers.

The small train of my dress catches, and I turn in a panic. It's been stepped on, but I tear it away without a word to the nameless guest who glances at me before returning to his champagne and immediate company.

Inside the main hallway that spills from the ballroom entrance, the air is already different. A cool balminess hits me all at once, and I drink it in with abandon. The music deafens the further down the hall I wander, and I'm relieved to see only a few clusters of guests gathered down its expanse. A handful of people amble in and out of adjacent rooms, mostly ripe for sitting and conversing away from the noisy gala. Fortunately, my presence goes unnoticed, and I'm able to compose myself away from the masses.

I run a hand over my chest and discover my skin is covered with perspiration. The mask slips on the bridge of my nose—despite the string that holds it in place—as I brace myself against the wall and run a soothing hand over the front of my corset. Flames flicker in the sconces that sit high upon the walls, casting eerie shadows that dance to the beat of the orchestral musings.

"A drink, miss?" A server dressed in all white appears in my periphery, bearing a tray of full champagne flutes.

"No thanks." I wave him off, ready to double over at the thought of champagne. The night is abuzz as it is. I have no reason to enhance the emotions that hurricane within me.

"Water, then?" he asks.

The mere mention reminds me how parched I've become. "Yes. Thank you."

He hands me a glass of chilled water from one side of his tray and then leaves me to my solitary misery.

I consume the water in only a handful of sips. It's the most refreshing thing I've ever tasted, practically euphoric as it cools my palate and fiery skin. But as I bring the cup to my lips for the last available sip, something on the underside of the glass catches my eye. A surge of adrenaline shakes me as I tilt it to examine it further. Affixed to the bottom is a small piece of folded paper.

It comes off with ease despite my shaky fingers, and I set the cup down on a console table adorned with flowers nearby. I skim the hallway for wandering eyes. Everyone seems to be in their own little worlds. So it's best I find one of my own.

Slithering further down the hallway, I'm stopped twice by guests who show congratulatory affection before allowing me the pleasure to continue on.

I pass the large grandfather clock that faces the foyer, then pass the second junction that veers off to the left toward the back of the manor, where the rear terrace awaits. With my shoulder against the wall, I pause where the guests are few, finding comfort in the quietness.

The paper is folded on itself only twice.

As if typed on an old typewriter, there lies a single phrase:

```
"And down the rabbit hole you go..."
```

My mind races with confusion. Is this another one of Laz's notes? He always signs them *L* or *GA*, but this time, nothing. It's clearly a reference to *Alice's Adventures in Wonderland*, but beyond that, the message is lost on me. Perhaps it was meant for someone else? I wouldn't put it past some of the more salacious guests to use this soiree of faceless flirtation as an excuse to pass notes to one another. For a moment, I debate crumpling the note and tossing it away. My hand encloses around it, and the paper begins to crinkle when a figure at the far end of the hall, where people are absent and the shadows are broad, catches my eye.

A faceless form, standing straight as a pin, with a svelte body covered only by a champagne satin gown, is staring at me. A beautiful head of yellow hair cascades down her back.

She doesn't move. It's the only thing about her that frightens me. It's as if she isn't real.

But what really makes my legs quake is her mask. Matching the color of her dress, with an elegant, golden hue, it bears two ears that aspire to the heavens as they project from outside both of her brows. Her nose is hidden by the mask, which covers the top half of her face.

A bunny nose sits in its place.

She's the only person I've seen tonight wearing a bunny mask. Elegant in its own way with small cracked details, it's as if it's made of porcelain, providing dimension and texture to an otherwise simple face covering.

And she's the only person in the hall who's staring at me.

I don't recognize her, despite how long I return her stare. Neither of us move. This note—

Shit, the note.

I release the paper from the prison of my grasp and peer at it apologetically. It's a mess but still legible. I flatten it between my hands the best I can.

When I look up, she's gone.

No.

I hurry down the hall toward the last place she stood, in search of the champagne beauty.

The only room left at the far end of the hall is the art gallery. I enter, craning my neck all around, searching for her. There are a handful of guests, flutes in hand, admiring the expanse of art. "*All reprints. Nothing original,*" Laz explained to me one afternoon during a long-overdue tour of his estate. "*The originals should be in museums, where everyone has the chance to enjoy them.*"

The woman—my very own white rabbit—stands before Nicolas Lancret's *La Camargo Dancing* painting, in all its gilded-frame glory.

Replete with apprehension and avid curiosity, I join her side. Her gaze remains fixed on the artwork. I debate whether to wait for her to speak first, but soon enough, my patience has ended.

"Who are you?" I ask.

Her stoicism is unsettling as she remains unmoving.

Seconds tick away as centuries before she speaks. "Time is a fickle thing, wouldn't you agree?" Her voice is akin to the satin of her dress. "The way it just seems to pass us by?" She sighs. "I suppose the white rabbit would agree."

My mask shifts as I scrunch my face in confusion.

"It's almost as if it melts right before our eyes."

My palm tingles at her sensual voice, as if spoken by Jenna herself. There's a soothing quality that resides deep within her words, and I'm overcome with the urge to paint myself with its sweet sound.

I wait with bated breath for her to speak again.

But she's silent.

"What does it mean?" I urge in a whisper, desperate for answers. "Who are you?"

She releases another sigh, more dramatically this time, before finally facing me.

A cluster of guests walk past us toward the door. The silence that has befallen the room in their absence is palpable. "Little Alice fell down the hole, bumped her head, and bruised her soul." She finishes with a sly little grin. Before I can inquire further, she slips past me and exits the room.

"Wait," I call after her. "What does it mean?" I race to the door and peer down the hallway.

But she's gone.

This all feels like a dream, as if I'm Alice herself and this party is some weird wonderland of mysterious faces and riddles that cannot be solved. *Why is a raven like a writing desk*? I replay the Mad Hatter's riddle in my mind.

That one didn't have an answer either.

My head is swimming as I amble back into the gallery, wondering with a sickening drop of my gut if there was something in that water I drank.

Drink Me.

I don't seem to have any better sense than Alice.

The woman's words dance in my head as I sink onto a cushioned bench in the middle of the gallery. *"Time is a fickle thing."* What does that even mean? What does she want? Is this Laz's idea of some weird game? If so, it's certainly the wrong time to play it. I'm in no mood to follow his notes to some grand gesture he's bestowed upon me. Unless he's planning on telling me that he's had a change of heart and won't be marrying me after all, I have no desire to see him.

Or follow him down his rabbit hole of tricks.

The room has emptied for the moment, a pause between stragglers that leaves me to my nonsensical thoughts.

Much like the paintings in the dining room at Krelborn Manor, the paintings in this gallery have no rhyme or reason to them. Comprising all different time periods, stylistic eras, and themes, they're arranged erratically, just as Laz wanted. It makes for an unpredictable art-viewing experience, but it's odd, to say the least. Like the way Salvador Dali's *Living on the Moon* painting hangs alongside Bosch's *The Garden of Earthly Delights*.

Wait.

I stand in a flash, my mind racing as I recall my first visit to this gallery. In History of Modern Art class, I recall learning how Salvador Dali created an entire line of illustrations for Lewis Carroll's *Alice's Adventures in Wonderland*. I had only seen them briefly during that day's lecture and never crossed paths with any of those pieces again.

Until I was brought here.

I rush to the far corner of the gallery and scan the assortment of paintings. It was smaller than most in the room, I remember that much.

Ah-ha.

No larger than a standard sheet of paper, deep set in a thick black frame, is Salvador Dali's *A Mad Tea Party*.

A clock melts around the trunk of a vast tree, rife with springtime leaves and colorful butterflies.

Melts.

"*It's almost as if it melts right before your eyes.*" Her words replay on a loop as I examine the painting closely, searching it for answers to a riddle I feel I'm supposed to solve.

"Is everything all right, miss?"

I glance at the door, where a server, identical to the last, enters with an empty tray against his hip. "Mr. Moretti is looking for you."

I shake my head and return my attention to the painting. "Tell him I'm in the gallery and wish to be left alone."

The man shifts his weight uncomfortably. "He seems rather persistent."

I sigh, conceding to the fact that perhaps a compromise is in order. "Tell him that I need a few more minutes, but I'll rejoin the party shortly."

The man hesitates, but I don't give him the chance to reply. "Or I won't rejoin at all. Be sure to emphasize that last part. It's up to him."

He leaves with a stunted bow, and I promptly return my focus to the painting.

There's nothing in it that indicates a clue. How am I supposed to solve a riddle I was never given? And I don't even know the reward?

With great mourning, I recall the escape room at Krelborn. The way the paintings were laid out is not too dissimilar from these. However, in the escape room, I was given a clue beforehand and used it to guess the painting. This time, the painting *is* the clue, and I can't make heads or tails of it.

Then I recall the mirror and how the answer was hidden in the frame itself.

It's at least worth a shot.

I glance around the room one last time, ensuring I'm alone, before running my hand over the frame. Leaning in, I examine it closely. Unlike the mirror in the escape room, I don't see any letters carved within this frame. So I search it for buttons instead. Gliding my hand along the edge of the frame, I grow weary the longer my search proves fruitless. But just as I feel along the bottom, the frame pops away from the wall, and a scroll of parchment falls to my feet.

It's tied closed with a single red ribbon.

Is this some kind of sick joke? David helped design the games on game night, including the escape room. It's possible he informed Laz of the details from that night, and he's replicating it to...what? I have no idea. The whole thing makes me sick as memories of James come flooding back.

Returning to my seat on the bench is the only thing that keeps my knees from buckling.

I slip the ribbon off and open the paper. Inside lies a poem I recognize immediately:

TAKE THIS KISS UPON THE BROW!
AND, IN PARTING FROM YOU NOW,
THUS MUCH LET ME AVOW—
YOU ARE NOT WRONG, WHO DEEM
THAT MY DAYS HAVE BEEN A DREAM;

YET IF HOPE HAS FLOWN AWAY
IN A **NIGHT**, OR IN A DAY,
IN A VISION, OR IN NONE,
IS IT THEREFORE THE LESS GONE?
ALL THAT WE SEE OR SEEM
IS BUT A DREAM WITHIN A DREAM.

It's the first stanza of Edgar Allan Poe's poem "A Dream within a Dream." I know it well.

But Laz doesn't know that.

Does he?

Perplexed, I read it over again, despite knowing it by heart. The word *night*, as well as a variety of additional letters, are in bold, which has me guessing. But without something to write with, I can't lay them all out side-by-side to figure it out with ease.

I pore over the remaining bold letters, which don't seem to mean anything in their written order:

CYESPHDIM

Working with what I have—which is very little—I rearrange the letters in my mind to solve what I can only deduce is an anagram.

DIM

DIME

DYE

YES

SIDE

CHIDE

MID

PSYCH

None of the words make sense contextually, especially in conjunction with another to complete the puzzle.

Focusing on the word *night*, I replay the words I've listed in my head and pause on the letters *d-i-m*.

Perhaps they're meant to be tacked on to "night"?

Dim night?

Wait. Scratch that. **M-i-d.**

MIDNIGHT?

Trudging forward under this assumption, I reexamine the remaining letters:

CYESPH

I rearrange them, landing on only a single word:

PSYCHE

Psyche? As in "Cupid and Psyche"? I know the mythology well enough, but I'm at a loss as to what it means in this context.

All I know is, together, the anagram spells:

PSYCHE

MIDNIGHT

I stare at the poem, having no idea what I'm supposed to do with this information.

Laz can be a romantic when the mood strikes, but why on earth would he send someone to fetch me if there were riddles to solve? I rack my brain, trying to come up with an imagery of Psyche I may have come across during my time here. There are paintings all over the place, which doesn't help, and there are certainly ones I don't recognize. But, overall, I have a pretty solid understanding of Greek and Italian art, especially ones depicting mythological creatures, and I don't recall seeing any paintings that—

Hold on. Unless it isn't a painting at all.

The statuary.

Yes. Of course. The statuary beyond the gardens is full of Greek statues. Now that I think about it, I'm certain I remember seeing a statue of Cupid kissing Psyche as he embraces her from above, his wings creating an amorous V silhouette in its little corner of the hedgerows.

Surely it's nearly midnight, if not already. What exactly is Laz up to?

I hurry down the hall, toward the large grandfather clock, its monotonous ticking inaudible against the ballroom music beyond. I come to a dead stop in front of it.

It's only seven minutes to midnight.

With brisk strides, I rush past several groups of guests dotting the halls, throwing their heads back in their social gaiety. I make it all the way to the French doors that lead to the terrace, open wide for guests to filter in and out at their leisure, before I come to a terrified halt.

What if Laz is waiting for me in the statuary to marry me right then and there? Why else would this all be so secretive? Perhaps the guests have funneled out of the ballroom while I was distracted in the gallery, and they're all waiting for me? What if the promise of the first snowfall was all a ruse?

My feet turn to lead, and I swallow hard. Everything in me is telling me to turn away, to run straight for my room, scream through my teeth as I lock the door behind me, and see how far I can make it through the tunnels.

Hesitating in the doorway, I catch the attention of a cluster of guests. Three of them are seemingly men, bearing their own Bauta masks with exaggerated noses, twisted antlers that reach toward the sky, and ruffled white plackets. The two women hold masks to their faces, one feathered and the other checkered in gold and silver, their dresses billowing wide thanks to the multiple layers of underskirts befitting of a venetian gala. The women rush over to me, congratulate me with swooning grace, and regale me with lavish words of how romantic a winter wedding will be.

"Such a lucky woman," I hear more than once. But all that sticks are their words about a winter wedding, and my preemptive fears about an ambush in the statuary begin to fade.

"I'm so sorry," I say with as much cordiality as I can muster. "I just need a moment alone. For some air." I fan myself to drive the point home, and they oblige with hearty laughs and a caress of my shoulders. "You poor thing. Such a big night for you. No wonder you're so flush."

I smile and hurry past them, toward the stone steps that run along the perimeter of the tiered grass. With the train of my dress raised in hand, I hurry past the yard and through the stone arch leading to the gardens. Crimson roses, muted by the night, line the hedge isles, filling the air with their intoxicatingly sweet scent. Without a glance over my shoulder, and only the waning moon to light my way, I'm soon enshrouded in darkness as I emerge into the statuary beyond.

Its hidden nooks and crannies are oddly reminiscent of the hedge maze at Krelborn. However, the hedgerows are not nearly as high, and the air flows more freely in here. A blanket of stars overhead peek at me as I run about in no discernible order in search of the Psyche statue. I have no idea where it is, so one direction is just as good as another as I follow the stone path to all its dead ends. Each leads to a unique statue, spotlit with garden lights that cast shadows along every curve and crevice. It's eerie yet breathtaking, and a part of me yearns to stop and enjoy their splendor each time I stumble upon them.

At the end of the path that cuts longways through the statuary toward the cliffs beyond, I'm overcome with a sense of defeat when I realize there are few other places the statue could be.

And I wonder if I got the clue wrong.

I turn right at the next junction and emerge into a dead end bearing another spotlit statue. The wings catch my attention first, shooting straight for the stars in a stark V.

Cupid's V.

It reminds me of the Cupid clue from the escape room.

In an instant, I hate this. Despite the beauty of such art, I despise all the ways this little *game* brings James to mind. It's a pain I still cannot bear, and I can't wait to hear Laz's explanation for all the ways he's elected to torture me tonight.

With a hearty sigh, I sit at Cupid's feet, feeling nothing but foolish. I let the paper bearing tonight's cryptic messages drift to the pebbles at my feet, then doff my mask in defeat. There's no one here, and I've wandered so far from the party that I no longer hear the remnants of the joie de vivre from within.

I run a tender hand over my aching feet. These stones are unkind to my heels, and even less kind to the feet that wear them. Thankfully, the humidity has shown uncommon kindness the last few nights, giving cooler, more temperate conditions despite how deep into summer we've fallen.

Surely it's past midnight by now. My shoulders slump as I concede to the fact that my white rabbit has eluded me after all.

Defeated, I stand and brush myself off. My dress still looks decent, although I can't speak for my hair. I admire Cupid and

Psyche in the dazzling moonlight; weathered and spotted with earthy moss, they possess an aged beauty from another era. I imagine their thoughts during their tender yet passionate reunion. Such a display of seduction, romance, and unending—

"*A fervent kiss upon my lips...*" A deep, sultry voice sounds behind me, and my heart trips with confused agony. Without any semblance of time or understanding, my entire body is shaking like a brittle leaf.

"*And a night of carnal sighs...*"

I'm numb. Any sense or wherewithal flees from my consciousness, leaving me a quivering shell of bitter disbelief.

"*A promise made within a whisper...*"

I don't know what's real anymore.

"*Of no more sad goodbyes.*"

But I know this voice. I dream of this voice every night.

I love this voice.

But it's not possible.

Footsteps approach from behind, crunching the pebbles as they draw near. But no matter how much my heart screams for me to turn around, I'm anchored in place, despondent that this is even real.

With trembling shoulders, I bury my face in my hands and pray this isn't another dream.

"Wats," the gentle voice calls out to me.

It can't be.

With an ardent passion reborn at the sound of my nickname only ever spoken by James, I whip around to face him.

Clad in a white tuxedo and a simple white mask that rests over his eyes, he's identical to the servers who have been speckled throughout the party all night long. In a casual motion, as if proving to me that he's real, he removes the mask and lets it fall to the ground.

James. I don't know how, but he's here. Right now. With me.

And he's alive.

It's the closest we've been in months, yet the few paces that separate us feel like miles as we run to each other. Tear-stricken and reeling from the disbelief that threatens to cripple me, I throw my arms around him as he catches me in a deep embrace. Sobs escape freely, muffled against his chest as he holds me close and kisses my hair.

I pull away to admire his face again. It's perfect. *He's* perfect. And I fear being awoken from this unprecedented dream. His face blurs from my tears as he pulls me in and kisses my lips harder than he ever has before. Our tongues fight with abandon, my body aches with need, and my lips cling to his as if for survival.

The warmth of his body against mine.

That euphoric taste.

And the redolence that makes my head swim.

It's as real as my thrashing heart, nearly crippled by the explosion in my chest that was detonated by the sound of his voice.

He's alive.

"James," I say on an exhale, my voice laced with desire. He pulls away long enough for me to admire him. "I don't understand. How are you here?" My neck prickles from the disbelief that still courses through my veins. "He told me you were dead." I choke on the words that have haunted me since the day Laz told me about his fate.

He brushes his thumb through my fallen tears. "I'm sure he thinks so, and I intend to keep it that way. But I'm very much alive, baby girl." He kisses the tip of my nose. "And I've come to take you home."

Home.

I don't even know where that is anymore. But what does it matter? James is alive. He's here. Living and breathing with flesh as warm as my burning cheeks.

"You found me," I whisper against his lips.

"I always said I would." Pulling me in for another kiss, he doesn't wait for a response. His lips, never gentle and always rife with hunger, take mine prisoner in a fell swoop of passion. Even as he trails his aggressive kisses down my neck, I still can't find the breath to speak.

"We need to go," he says, interrupting the eroticism that has my apex pulsating. "There's a boat on the west bank." He grabs my hand. "We need to hurry."

But I can't shake the sickening defeat that tugs at my insides. "Wait." I pull against him, and he turns back to me. "The west bank?" I shake my head. "We'll never make it there on foot before he finds us. Before he finds *you*."

"If we hurry—"

"He likely has men searching for me already. I've been gone too long as it is. And once he realizes something is amiss, he'll have this island surrounded in no time."

A crease forms between his brows. "What are you saying?"

I sigh heavily as my throat is slashed by a thousand razors, inhibiting my ability to swallow. The words have already killed me before they even brush past my lips. "I-I can't go with you."

His eyes widen in horror. "*Are you crazy*? I'm not leaving you here, Evie." He pulls my hand, but I don't budge. "Enough of this. We have to leave. *Now*."

"If he finds us, there's no way he's going to make the mistake of letting you get away a second time. He will *kill* you, James. And he'll make sure of it this time. Do you really think that's a risk I'm willing to take?"

His jaw drops. He's clearly as shaken as I am. "Do you really think I fear death?"

"Do you really think I don't fear yours?" I say.

"This is beyond insane. I won't even consider it," he replies. But I don't shrink under his glower. I don't blame him for being upset, and I hate this as much as he does.

I stand firm, my body shaking at what this may mean for me. But I have to save him. There's no other option in my mind but to ensure I never have to hear the words *James is dead* again.

With a gruffness in his voice, he regards me sternly. "I've been here all night, masquerading as a server, trying to leave you clues in order to get you alone." He plants his hands on his hips. "I was there during his announcement, Evie. I heard what he said." A sharp exhale escapes him as he chokes on the words that follow. "He means to marry you."

It cuts straight through me just as it did the very first time I heard it.

"I know," I whisper, looking away.

"Well..." He straightens his posture and tilts his head, beckoning me to look at him. "Is that what you want?" There's a sadness in his voice that almost drops me to my knees.

"No." My breath hitches. "That isn't what I want at all."

The sadness in his eyes departs as he squints with irritation. "Is that supposed to make it easier for me to leave you here? Knowing you'll be marrying that man against your will?"

I press my palm to my forehead, flabbergasted and unsure how to proceed. It's damp with perspiration. Or perhaps it's my palm? I don't care. I just need James to listen.

But he doesn't give me the chance to speak.

"Do you really think this is the solution? To marry someone just to ensure my safety?" He's shouting now, and I fear his voice may carry where it should never reach. "Because it isn't, Evie. No fucking way. There's only one man in this world you're meant to marry, and it sure as hell isn't *him*." He points toward the manor.

The weight of his words fills our little corner of the statuary as my lungs struggle to catch air.

What?

A long, arduous pause exists before I find the words to speak.

"Is...is that a proposal?" I regret asking as soon as the words leave my lips, but I have to know what he meant.

His shoulders relax a bit, but his hands remain on his hips. "What if it was?" he coos.

I bite my lip as my stomach trembles with apprehension and desire. "Well, I..." Ten minutes ago, I thought James was lost forever. The mere mention of his name was mentally ruinous, but the memories I bore, despite their scarcity, were my greatest treasure.

Amid my grief, I would have married him in a second.

Now he's here. He's flesh and blood and a beating heart. The future I once craved is again within my grasp.

My fate is no longer sealed.

"We've only known each other for a few months. Many of which we spent apart." It isn't a question, but I hope he catches my meaning all the same. I can't believe I'm even attempting logic at a time like this. It's all that's keeping me from fleeing the island this very second.

"That sounds about right for us, considering our timeline with everything else. Don't you think?" His lips upturn into that beautiful smile I adore so much. He approaches me and cups my cheek with a tender touch. "Don't worry, Wats," he whispers. "When the day comes that I propose to you, I promise...you'll know it."

My stomach flips dizzily as he captures my lips in another kiss, which I return with feverish want. When he pulls away, he takes me by the hand and pulls me further from Psyche. But I don't allow us to travel more than a few steps before I stop him. "The first morning we spent together at Krelborn...Did you mean it when you told me you loved me?"

He reels back around to face me, confused. "Why are you asking me that?"

Calmly, I reply, "I need to know, James. Did you mean it?"

That incredible Adam's apple bobs as he swallows deeply. "Of course I did." He squints. "Didn't you?"

I hesitate. "I...I wasn't lying, I know that much. But since that day, I've wondered if I was guilty of being caught up in the whirlwind game night created. There were moments that truly terrified me that night, but honestly, it was one of the greatest nights of my life. And I was afraid that, when all was said and done, perhaps I mistook passion and vulnerability for love."

He releases my hand and steps away. "You're the one who put it out there first," he replies, a hint of defensiveness in his voice. "I'm not sure—"

"I wasn't lying, James," I reiterate. "And I'm not asking if you ever questioned it either." I cross my arms despite the lack of chill in the stagnant air. "The only reason I'm telling you any of this is because, yes, I've wondered whether I spoke too soon when it came to the *L* word. But..." Tears well up, and I don't fight them.

The pained look on James's face doesn't make what I'm about to say any easier.

"When Laz told me what happened in that cave. That you'd been shot..." I choke on the words, each one more painful than the last. "I had no idea you were here on this island that whole time... with me." Tears spill down both cheeks before I say anything further. "I didn't know if you were waiting for me on the mainland, or if you were moving forward with a life that didn't have me in it..."

"Eves, I—"

"Please. I need to say this." I brush a hand over my cheek. "When I learned you were dead, it was one of the hardest things I've ever had to process. It was like my entire future folded in on itself, and whatever doubt I had in my mind as to whether I spoke the word *love* too soon vanished in an instant. Because learning that you were gone forever only made my love for you a certainty. I chastised myself for ever doubting it. And I knew I would never stop mourning you."

He holds me against him as I sob uncontrollably.

"I felt it too..." he whispers after several beats of my racing heart. I crane my neck to meet his gaze, which is contorted with consternation. "That moment of certainty, where I realized the *L* word was undoubtedly real for me."

I urge him to continue with a desperate look.

"Tonight. When the man with the scars announced that you two were to marry..." He looks away, silence filling in all the gaps that remain. But there's nothing he can say that would make me further understand.

His meaning is crystal clear.

"I need you to come with me," James pleads as he studies my face.

This is the universe taunting me with a second chance I cannot take, because there's one undeniable truth that keeps me from running into those woods with my hand in his: *I can't lose him again.*

"I can't," I say, with the same excruciating effort it would take to swallow daggers. "I can't lose you again."

He opens his mouth to protest. "I can't just leave you here—"

"Yes you can." I melt against him again, taking in the sound of his thrumming heart one last time before stepping away.

"I will find you, James."

"Evie, no—"

"You always said you'd find me. And you've kept your word every time. But now it's my turn. Let *me* find *you* this time. Please. I need you to trust that I'll make it off this island, and I'll do so when it's safe and there's no chance of you being harmed."

"I'm begging you, please don't do this."

"I will find my way back to you. I swear." I caress his cheek, trying to ease his pain. "I love you so much." Those creases on the outside of his eyes that I normally love so much deepen, a concernedness that may be etched on his face permanently.

I taste his lips and fall sway to the hypnosis in which they pull me under. I love him. I *need* him.

And I will do whatever it takes to protect him.

Even if it means staying behind.

"I must go," I say on a sharp, erotic exhale as I pull away from his kiss and brush an errant tear from my cheek. "They'll be looking for me." I kiss him one last time, then lovingly wipe my smudged lipstick from his lip. "Goodbye, Sherlock."

It takes every ounce of courage I have to flee down the main path, leaving him behind.

"Evie, wait."

I don't turn back.

"*Evie*." Footsteps crunch the pebbles behind me, and I quicken my pace to dissuade them. This is hard enough without having to hear his pleas.

The footsteps cease, and it stings my tortured chest. As much as I couldn't handle the thought of another goodbye, leaving him only spirals me into a sense of mourning all over again.

With my train in hand, I run away from the man I love and back toward my gilded cage nestled by the sea.

"We will find each other again, Wats." Faint yet discernible, his voice calls out in the distance. I pause but dare not look back, my chest rising and falling rapidly. "Don't you ever doubt that."

Going against my better judgment, I turn to him. He's nearly swallowed in darkness at the far end of the statuary's main path—no more than a silhouette of the man I love, but one that's very much *alive*.

"I love you," he calls out, his outline unwavering. I fight for breath to speak it back, but he turns away and disappears toward the opposite end of the statuary, lost in the woods beyond.

CHAPTER 51
JENNA

"**S**he wouldn't come back with me."

James's words berate my mind on a sickening loop as I drop to my knees in agony. Like the goddamn fool that I am, I agreed to stay behind on the boat, anchored a mile offshore from the west dock on Eden's Green. Me going onto the island was never part of "the plan," and I conceded with little options to the contrary. It's a decision I regret with every fiber of my being.

"You should have made her come back," I scream at him as the island fades further in the distance, taking my heart with it. "How could you let her stay?" I shove him away despite his constant attempts to advance on me. "You're a fucking liar," I wail. "I never should have trusted you."

Does he not realize that I can't take much more of this? *I need her, James. I wish I could tell you just how much, but I can't. This has gone on for far too long. She isn't safe. Don't you get it yet? Every day she spends under Moretti's roof, there's no telling what may happen.*

Those photographs come to mind, and I dry heave over the railing. Deep, grotesque bruises, rough indentations on her perfect skin...

How could he come back without her?

My mind whirls on everything I wish to scream into the night wind as the boat races back to the Cape without Evie in tow.

James holds me against him. Despite the fact that I want to pummel him until his agony matches mine, I allow his arm to remain around me.

When we arrive back at the docks, James opens my car door for me, then hops into the driver's seat. His face is blanched, the stoicism from the boat ride giving way to misery.

"That fucking bitch," I mumble under my breath as he puts the car in drive. I've never been more upset with her. If she were here now, I'd give her hell. I'd chastise her for scaring me like this, for leaving me to pick up my broken pieces. Then I'd kiss her all over and beg for forgiveness.

He throws the car back into park and stares straight ahead as if in a daze. I'm sure he doesn't approve of my choice of words, but I don't give a flying rat's ass.

Bouncing back and forth between regret and conviction by the words I just spoke, I wait for his imminent response.

"She did it for me, Jen," he whispers. "I'm sor—"

"I don't care." I stare out the side window, wanting nothing more than to wake from this nightmare. My gaze settles on the gentle sway of the boats docked at the marina, hidden in shadow from the lights that line the parking lot.

"She promised she'd come back to us." He releases a heavy sigh and rubs the back of his neck.

I swallow a gulp that goes down like knives. "Do you believe her?"

A painful silence passes before he speaks again. "You've known her a hell of a lot longer than I have. Let me ask you something: when Evie says she's going to do something..." He trails off, waiting for me to complete his train of thought.

I already know the answer to this. If there's one thing I know about Evie...

"She does it," I reply, meeting his gaze. "Or she dies trying."

His shoulders relax a bit. "Can't say I'm a fan of that last part," he says with another sigh. "But I'll take it all the same."

Together, we fall silent as we watch the boats sway in their birth. This is the longest night of my life, but I can't stomach the thought of it coming to an end. Because tomorrow, I know I will be achy and hoarse, having cried the whole night through while tearing at my hair with no clue as to how to proceed. Come morning, the sun will rise anew. But it will be the start of yet another day without her.

James pulls me from my wandering thoughts and throws the car in drive. "That fucking bitch," he says, flicking me a weary smile. I never realized how much I missed that smile until now.

"That fucking bitch," I repeat, matching his grin. It's the first time my heart has been given a bit of reprieve since all of this began. And as we head back to the Cape house to deal with the incoming dawn together, I know deep in my heart that I have James to thank for it.

THE PALE MOONLIGHT SLIPS ITS WAY PAST MY OPEN curtains, illuminating my bedroom in a silvery hue. Naked, I stand before the bare window and bathe in the primitive glow. My bedroom window faces east, and as I look out at the Atlantic water—as black as ink and eerily calm—I pretend I can see Eden's Green from here. Pressing my hand to the pane, I imagine her lying in the same light, her perfect, naked figure waiting for me to tame its feral urges. She stayed behind despite our wishes, but I can't bring myself to punish her. Instead, I will seduce her, bring her to the climax she never expected at the hands of a woman, and make her wish she'd have returned to me.

I press my forehead to the glass, drop my hand to the peak between my legs, and part my feminine lips. Each breath fogs the view as I caress myself, imagining it's Evie's hand instead of mine.

She kisses me, her lips so supple and warm that it leaves a tingling sensation in their wake. They fall from my lips and move down, past the curve of my neck and landing on my breasts, which she takes into her mouth like a woman discovering a new world of passion play. A small cry escapes me, blasting a quick streak of condensation over the window.

The small town of Chatham is asleep at this late hour, but there will be no sleep for me tonight. Evie stayed behind like the bad girl she is...

And she needs to make it up to me.

Her lips could not be more perfect for the job.

"Evie," I moan against the glass, my knees buckling under the weight of my pleasure. My fingers are slick with my wetness, and my clit is engorged to the max. Everything goes out of focus before the entire world succumbs to darkness as I close my eyes in ecstasy. I gasp as my feminine twitching teases at a rising orgasm. I penetrate myself with my finger and spasm against it, then drag the slickness over my clit. Over and over, I torture myself this way, with a pain that's outmatched by pleasure.

"Oh God, *Evie*," I moan again. I pinch my nipple, then return my fingers to the place that needs it most. I want to look out onto the ocean as I come. I want to know Evie is there, just past the horizon, as I silently scream her name. It's the only time I wish James wasn't here, right down the hall. If only I could scream...

I collapse to the floor, fall onto my back, and writhe in the beam of moonlight. "Evie," I sigh, seizing my breast with all the anger behind it that I feel for her reckless decision to stay behind. Every second I think of her telling James she won't be coming back, I squeeze my breast harder. It hurts in all the right ways and reminds me—for the first time since she disappeared—that I'm still breathing. I don't stop, despite knowing it's liable to be bruised by morning. Oh, how she tortures me with her foolhardiness, her naive, careless ways. "Goddamn you, Evie," I say in a stymied outcry of pleasure. Her name slides easily over my tongue as I fondle my clit, desperate for her real touch in place of my own.

It all comes crashing down like an explosion of devotion, pleasure, indescribable pain, and hatred for the woman who has unknowingly broken my heart in so many ways. Rougher than the hand that assaulted my breasts, my orgasm tears right through me. I scream into the palm of my hand, my entire figure jerking in the pale light as the pulsation reaches every single inch of me.

My wetness lingers everywhere; my breasts and the inside of my thighs have never felt this slick. I pretend it's Evie's as I coat it across each nipple, erotically charging my body for another round. This is going to be one hell of a night. It's either caress myself angrily to thoughts of Evie or spend the rest of the night sobbing into my pillow. Either way, she's here with me, inflicting pleasure and pain in a way I shall never forget.

When my body is ready, I bend my knees, then let them fall apart in a wide V. I drag my fingers back down to my clit, which is so sensitive that merely getting close makes my body jerk. My abdomen bears multiple trails of slickness, and the inside of my thighs are soiled and ready.

This time, I'll have Evie exactly where I want her: with her face between my legs. She confessed to me that James likes to call her a good girl. Well, Evie, you've been so incredibly bad that there's no way you're a good girl in my eyes.

But she's a hell of a good listener, and she laps up my wetness with a greedy tongue, eager to prove me wrong.

"It won't work, Evie," I moan, my neck arched as I cry out toward the ceiling. "You'll always be a bad girl…" I grip my hair by the root as I coat my palm in my wetness. My clit is far too sensitive for direct stimulation, so I reach inside and fondle my G-spot with a hooked finger.

"Oh God, *yes*."

My scalp screams as I clench my fist tighter, my moans gaining momentum to match my finger. Evie has some making up to do, and I'll be damned if I deny her the opportunity. I release my hair and stroke my breasts, electing to be a bit kinder this time around. I need her mouth on them—her suckling lips. I need *her*.

That pouty mouth of cherry red. "Fuck," I choke.

Those piercing eyes. "Evie."

My G-spot revs up with the power of a live wire, teasing at an orgasm deeper than the last. I'm at the mercy of my own grueling fingers, and it's everything.

Everything.

My G-spot undulates with punishing desire, pushing me over the edge. With a pressure that manifests from deep within, my orgasm devours everything in its path until my toes have curled, my back is arched to the max, and I can no longer control the cries from escaping my parted lips.

"Fuck you, Evie," I bellow into the crook of my elbow as I fuck my G-spot raw. My vagina pumps wildly as my orgasm peaks, forcing me to scream her name one final time, as if willing her into existence between my legs.

If I can't have her here, then I'll be punished by my imagination until I can no longer stand it. My sassy mouth won't get me what I want this time, so I need my fingers to do all the talking.

Exhausted, swollen, and impassioned by a sinful brew of anger and lust, I fall into a trance as the ceiling blurs before my eyes. In the morning, Evie won't be here. It's a betrayal of which I can't make sense. I know, in time, I won't be able to handle it, and tears will overtake me. But for now, I hold on to the hope that Evie stays true to her word and finds her way back to me.

To *us*.

Just as sadness stabs at my throat, my hand wanders slyly to take another pass between my legs. Evie's fingers will just have to do all the talking until I'm ready to face another day without her.

CHAPTER 52
EVIE

James is alive.

The certainty of it all is still so surreal. As if some dream has pulled me in and seduced me beyond any chance of awakening.

I fought to keep him close every day since we parted, yearning for his tender caresses and soothing voice. His loss tore me to pieces. But upon seeing him again, our flesh connected at every possible point, falling back into his arms was the easiest thing I've ever done. The warmth of his touch could never be outmatched, not even by the pelting hot water and cycloning steam of the shower in which I've succumbed to thoughts of the man I thought I lost forever.

Leaving him in the statuary was like leaving behind a piece of me: a severed limb, my body destined to never truly be whole again. But despite Laz announcing plans to force my hand in marriage, my heart is surprisingly at ease knowing James is safe.

"I will always find you. Don't ever doubt me." His words echo in my mind.

But this time, they're meant for him.

Whatever it takes, before the first snowfall of winter, I'll be back in his arms, never to be apart again.

Home.

But the phantom memories of Laz's hand around my waist,

gripping me with a protective yet gentle touch as he spun me around the ballroom during our first dance, tugs at me as if tethered to my very soul. For a moment, I had lost all sense of time, direction, and purpose beyond the swelling music and his intoxicating scent. His complete inability or unwillingness to look anywhere else but at me. It was a feeling all too familiar as it mirrored my dance with James at Jenna's wedding reception.

The light in Laz's eyes bounced with the vivacity of an electrical storm, imprisoning me in more ways than I ever imagined. And for a moment, I felt safe.

In his eyes.

With my heart pulled in so many directions that I'm sure it may never find its true shape again, I shut off the water and step around the half wall.

I reach for my towel on its hook, my hand sliding across the wall as I'm blinded by the impenetrable steam.

The towel isn't there.

I wave the steam aside, but it does little to alleviate the obscurity. It anchors me even deeper into that dreamlike state that consumed me as I bathed, ethereal and weightless as it swirls with each of my exhaled breaths.

My heart skips a beat when a second swirl of steam forms nearby. All semblance of that comforting warmth of the water—and James's touch—has left me with nothing but a bone-deep chill as the steam parts and reveals Laz leaning against the sink counter.

Watching me.

I gasp and cover up my most private areas the best I can. "*What are you doing here?*" I cry out. "Where's my towel?" The steam swirls around my exhaled words, revealing more of Laz, who is perched against the sink counter with pretentious nonchalance. A red apple bearing a single bite mark is held lazily in one of his hands, and my towel is in the other.

"Give it to me," I demand, nodding toward the towel. He makes no effort to hand it over, nor to avert his salacious gaze.

"Quid pro quo," he rumbles.

"I'm not playing games with you, Laz. Give me my towel." I debate exposing my breasts in the interest of extending a demanding hand. But I don't want to reveal any more of myself than I already have, so I keep them covered. He eyes me up and down as moisture drips down my figure.

"I'm not sure why it bothers you so much," he finally says, pushing away from the counter. "It's not like I haven't seen every square inch of your body already."

Fucking asshole. "Not with my consent," I bite, yanking the towel from his grip and wrapping it around myself.

He tosses the apple on the counter and holds his hands up in surrender. "Fair enough."

"What do you want?" I huff. "Why are you here?" The steam has since dissipated, making the air a bit more breathable, but it takes the warmth with it.

"You disappeared on me tonight." His tone is rough and unsettling.

I wrap my arms around myself, still feeling exposed despite the towel that covers me. "What are you talking about?"

"You disappeared on me. I told you to take a moment to collect yourself, but you vanished. Do you realize I had my men looking all over for you?" He readjusts his position and leans against the counter again, crossing his arms as if emphasizing his point. "Explain yourself."

His brash impudence is enough to make me want to tear his eyes out. "I didn't *disappear* on you. I needed to be alone. So I went out to the terrace—"

"My men searched the terrace—"

"I went out to the terrace," I cut back in. "But it was so full of people that I went down to the statuary instead. It was the only place I could be alone."

"Do you have any idea how long you were gone?" His scars are twisted in a simmering rage, and it sends another chill down my spine. "Almost an hour. You were the guest of honor, and no one had any idea where you were. What in God's name were you thinking?"

I exhale an exaggerated huff. "What was *I* thinking? Are you serious right now? You just announced to an entire room full of strangers that we're getting married in a few months—against my will—and you can't understand why I might have wanted to be alone?" I shake my head at his arrogance. "I didn't know any of those people. I wanted nothing to do with that party, and I sure as hell have no intention of marrying you. *Ever.*" My heart is racing so fast that I suddenly feel out of breath.

His eyes are wide with fury, his chest heaving. But I stand my ground. James told me once that I'm worth fighting for. But he isn't here, and I can't take back my decision to stay behind.

So I'll just have to fight for myself.

"You try my patience, Neve. Your obstinance is completely out of hand and is clouding your better judgment. Evident by the fact that you were clearly down in the gardens with *someone* and didn't even have the decency to hide it when you returned to the party."

I flinch at his words. Fuck. Terror—unadulterated and painfully acidic—eats away at my insides. "What are you talking about?" Every ounce of energy is reserved for maintaining my composure.

"Your lipstick," he says, his eyes flitting to my lips. My mind races to get ahead of what he's about to say next, but I come up with nothing. "When you rejoined the party, your lipstick was in disarray. When I had last seen you, it was perfect." He shifts his weight against the counter, his eyes locked on me. "Who is he? Is it one of my men? A guard? If it is, know that it means nothing to me to command him to his knees and put a bullet right between his eyes.

My loyalties lie only with your mother, David, and with you. If any one of them so much as touched you—"

"Jesus Christ, Laz. Are you insane?" My mind swims from the bullet I just dodged—he doesn't suspect James—but also from the maelstrom of implications this situation has now created. "There are a plethora of reasons why my makeup may have been messed up."

"Enlighten me," he challenges.

"Crying."

"You were crying in the sitting room. You still looked perfect. What other lies would you like to throw my way?"

"Eating, for one thing. Drinking the champagne—"

"You didn't touch a bite of food all night, and you barely took two sips of your champagne. Try again." His words burn with an ardent intensity that matches those eyes that seem to look right through me.

"I'm not lying—"

"Then prove it."

My eyes widen. "What?"

"If you ruined your lipstick from, say, drinking champagne, then your flute would still be in the statuary, right? When I left you, you didn't have a champagne glass with you. When you returned, you also didn't have one with you. That means, if your story is true, you must have acquired one during the hour you were gone. Since you drank enough of it to soil your makeup, then you obviously took it with you to the statuary. So you and I will go down there together, and if there's a champagne flute lying around with lipstick on it, then I'll believe you, and we can put all of this to rest."

My stomach plummets into a bottomless pit. "This is crazy. There's nothing going on between me and one of the guards. I left to get some air, and to be perfectly honest, I didn't really care about maintaining my done-up face. I just had to get out of there—"

"Then there's nothing for you to worry about. A champagne

glass will be out there waiting for us, just as you said." He grabs my arm, but I fight against it.

"What? Now? It's the middle of the night. And I'm in nothing but a towel—"

"So it's a safe bet that you won't run again." He grabs my forearm more tightly this time.

"I'm not going." I dig my heels in, but they slip on the damp floor. As I wrench my arm, captive in his relentless grip, my towel loosens. Fueled by sheer desperation, I hold on to it with my free hand, but Laz yanks it off in one swift motion, leaving me gasping and naked as I'm caught in his grasp.

A cry barely escapes my lips before he pulls me onto the countertop, the marble cold against my bare bottom as I'm forced to face him. I cover my breasts with one arm and raise my closed knees to hide my most vulnerable parts, maintaining what little dignity I have left. But he shoves a hand between my knees, forces them open, and stands between them to keep them parted.

"Tell me who it was, little one, and we'll forget all about this." The sibilance in his voice as he whispers in my ear makes me tremble uncontrollably. He runs a seductive hand through my hair, tucking a strand behind my ear as he runs his nose over my cheek. His breath, despite its hellish warmth, only enhances my trembling.

"There was no one, Laz. I swear." My voice shakes as my lip quivers, tears brimming. I place a modest hand over my exposed entrance as subtly as possible.

"I don't believe you," he snaps. "This is what happens when you don't have trust." He plants a rough kiss against my neck, trails his nose across my flesh, and then leaves another in its wake. "I can't believe a word you say."

I blink free the first batch of tears, and they spill down my cheeks, tickling my skin the whole way down. I push against his chest, but it does nothing to impede his unwanted advances.

"But there's a way you can make this right," he breathes against my neck before planting another kiss. "A way we can put this all behind us..."

I shudder to imagine what he has in mind, and before he can answer, my eyes are darting every which way, looking for something I can use to escape.

He grabs my wrist and attempts to pull my arm away from my breasts. I fight it, wrenching from his grip and shoving him away to little avail. In response, he grabs my face, forcing me still as he digs his fingers into my cheeks and leers at me from above. Before me stands only a monster—the devil, as he may very well be. Either way, he isn't the Laz I once knew—the man I thought would protect me from sinister hands no different from his own.

"Do you know what I want?" His thumb glides over my quivering bottom lip as a new batch of tears turns him into a blur. He leans in so close, I can barely make out his face.

"A k-kiss?" I strain, praying this is the answer but knowing deep in my gut that I could never be so lucky.

A vile laugh escapes his throat as he presses his tented slacks against the hand that protects my entrance. My stomach churns with such agony that it nearly makes me sick.

"That's not what I want at the moment," he purrs. He sinks low and takes my breast in his mouth, suckling so hard that I wince between sobs. As he puts all his weight into it, I teeter on my tailbone, my knees pinching his hips for balance. He bites. He takes. He *feeds* on my delicate flesh. Sharp stings set the area aflame, raw, animalistic, and excruciating with each pass of his suckling teeth.

"Stop," I cry out. My pleas, however, go unacknowledged as the tears flow harder than ever. I pull at his hair, shove him, and claw at his scalp, but he only digs in deeper. Finally, he pulls away to look at me. "This is how men claim you, right? I don't make the rules." Aimed for the other breast, he sinks low again, and panic hits me broadside. Just before he reaches me, I bring my elbow square with his nose and jab it hard. He withdraws with a pained cry, holding his nose as he eyes me with a fury reborn. His hands are on my throat in a flash. As his grip tightens, robbing me of breath, I bring my nails to his cheek and tear at his flesh, determined to draw blood. Which I do. Four long, bloody scratches, spanning from his ear to his lips, now ruin the handsome side of his face.

"Fuck," he spits, cradling his tattered cheek. I leap from the counter and hurry for the door. But in only a few steps, he has me by the arm and yanks me back toward the counter. I jerk away, desperate to free myself, but he's far too strong, and now *he's* out for blood.

My breasts and cheek bear the brunt of his anger as he slams me face down onto the counter, pinning me in place by pressing himself against my bare bottom. As my insides turn to ice, chills electrify the nape of my neck. I can't move.

He presses his palm to the side of my face, trapping me against the counter with unrelenting strength. I flail my arms in a desperate attempt to wriggle free, screaming my lungs out. With only one free hand, he struggles to subdue me. Tears stream freely, pooling onto the counter below.

For the first time in my life, I despise my own naked form. I curse every line, every curve...every single inch of me that has ever enticed the man who stands to destroy me from this moment forward. I curse my mother for bringing this man into my life; I curse James for not being here to save me. I curse myself for allowing him to leave.

I await the purring sound of his zipper. But between my relentless screams and my thrashing arms knocking things over somewhere near my head, I'm convinced I may have missed the sound altogether. Which means only one thing: any second now, he will greedily press himself against my entrance, and everything will be lost. I can't bear the thought. Nearly crippled with fear, I claw at the counter, reaching for anything to fight back with. Time is fleeting, and I'm unable to see beyond the limited scope of my pinned vision.

Any second, the sensation of his erect flesh against my most intimate parts will come, and more than anything, I fear it may paralyze me, stripping me of any hope of fighting back.

Of finally ending this.

Forget the wardrobe. Forget Papa and his illusive *monsters*. Forget the fear of being forgotten, all of those moments of hunger and unquenchable thirst, or Papa's screams in the distance as he took his last breaths.

This. This moment, here and now, is the most terrified I have ever felt.

Naked, pinned, overpowered, and so utterly alone—at the mercy of the man with unrequited cravings, who now stands poised to take from me whatever he pleases.

I never want to feel so powerless again. And I won't. Ever. With a silent, solemn vow, I tell myself that, whatever happens, this is the last time anyone will ever treat me and my body as if it belongs to them.

"Neve, stop," Laz says as he finally manages to capture one of my arms. "I'm not going to—"

Screams continue to rush from my lungs with unshakable urgency, fueled by adrenaline and utter terror, drowning out his voice. I blink past the tears, desperate for some miracle to free me from this hell. But this isn't a nightmare James can simply shake me awake from, soothing me while I wait for the numbness to pass. Never before have my nightmares seemed as...insignificant as they do right now. What a fool I was to think my past was all the trauma I would endure in this life. How silly to think that, if only I could put to rest the mystery of Papa's death and the illness that plagued him, I may stand a fighting chance against my demons and live a normal life.

I beseech my nightmares now, and for the clicking sound of engaging locks, enough to fill the room in synchronized horror. For the first time in my life, I pray for those awful red shoes to appear at the edge of my line of sight. How paltry it all seems now as I lie help-less, awaiting my mental and emotional demise at the hands of the man with the marred face.

I wrench my free arm upward, tweaking my shoulder to reach above my head into spaces not yet ventured in my frantic search. My cosmetic pouch grazes my fingers as my shoulder shrieks in pain. Its contents clink beyond my line of sight as they spill all over the counter when I yank it closer. Laz's breath is hot on my soaked hair as it clings to my neck. His free hand comes into view when he plants it on the counter near my face, bracing himself against me as he leans in closer.

"It's all right," he exhales as he squeezes my pinned wrist, almost reassuringly.

Nothing about this is all right.

As my hand feels around the contents overhead, it lands upon something chalky. It's glass, based on the way it clinks against the countertop when I drop it with shaky fingers. But it's covered in something chalky and is rough on both sides.

My nail file.

Laz brushes my hair away from my neck, exposing the skin for the kiss he plants against it. I'm trembling so badly, I doubt my own ability to persevere, to maintain focus and diligence, and not concede to his unwanted advances.

Just as his lips meet my damp skin, a low moan resonates from his throat and into my being. I eye his hand, only inches from my face.

Shaky but determined, I grip the nail file with purpose and drive the pointed end directly into the back of his hand.

He backs away, crying out in agony and cursing my name. The blood comes in an instant, for I catch a flash of it just as I push myself away from the counter and beeline for the door.

My bedroom door is wide open—clearly Laz's ingress point. I'm tempted to flee through it and run until my legs can no longer carry me. But with the guards at every entrance, I can't be sure I'd make it far.

With my frenetic heart nearly bursting from my chest, I snatch my oversized sleep shirt from the bed where I had tossed it this morning, pull it over my head, grab the flashlight from the night-stand, and bank left toward the secret passage.

The frigid air pricks at my skin as I close the secret door behind me and bound into the tunnel.

The light bounces erratically, and adrenaline staves off the bitter cold as I descend into the belly of the manor.

The spiral steps bottom out into the main passage under-ground, the air colder than ever, and I run as fast as my legs can carry me.

I turn right at the first T junction, following my yellow arrow toward the first iron ladder that leads to a locked grate above. My lungs ache as I pass by it, darting right and into the offset tunnel that connects alongside it.

The next stretch is long, but I know it well. Like some echo chamber, every breath, slap of my bare feet, and grunt of panic reverberates between the walls.

The second tunnel that connects to the right, marked with a yellow arrow and *L* for lighthouse, appears in my periphery. I ignore it and continue straight.

The flashlight flickers, and I stop dead in my tracks. I slap it, and it flickers again before losing its luminescence entirely and swallowing me in darkness.

Amid my slaps that merely result in a quick flicker and nothing more, a faint clinking noise sounds somewhere behind me.

I pause.

It's a familiar sound but is unbefitting of the passage. The plinking of water drops or the faint scurry of a mouse are sounds to which I've grown accustomed down here. But not the clink of the flap of a lighter opening and closing repeatedly.

It grows louder by the second but maintains its rhythm. *Clink-shink-clink-shink.*

The floor gives way beneath me as the sounds come closer.

And then, silence.

Only my shaky voice fills the void, and I'm nearly paralyzed by the sudden cold that overwhelms my body.

I never heard a second set of footsteps or breathing other than my own.

And yet, any second, I expect hands to grab me.

The silence is worse than the clinking noise, leaving me with nothing but a tomb of blackness in which I'm forced to await the worst.

At this point, I would rather be snatched by a pair of hands that mean to force me into submission than await their frightening touch a second longer.

The impasse between us runs stale, and I consider making a run for it in the pitch dark. I wouldn't make it far, but at least it would silence the blood pumping in my ears.

A gentle thumping cuts through the stillness. Almost inaudible yet distinct—the sound of something rolling on the floor.

I have no idea what to make of it. I can't see a thing.

When it bumps my bare toes, I release a startled shriek, all thumping noises coming to an abrupt halt.

I smack the flashlight again, but it no longer flickers alive.

Curiosity sways my hand as I crouch for the item. Feeling along the concrete floor, I find it in seconds and bring it close. With all sight lost, I feel its contours, the defective mark on one side, and realize what it is.

Laz's apple.

It appears before me in a sudden flash of light when Laz ignites his lighter mere inches from my face. I never heard him approach, never felt his breath. But he's close enough to me that I should have felt his warmth, heard his soft exhales.

His face illuminates in a grotesque array of oblique shadows that enhance every line of his mangled scars and the fresh blood that's now caked on the once handsome side of his face.

As if pulling me from a nightmare, the single flame dances erratically as a sinister grin spreads wide across his face.

"Run."

His command is hoarse and vile, as if on the brink of a deep chuckle.

Panicked, I drop the forbidden fruit—forever changed from his cruel bite—and run as fast as my legs can carry me.

In an instant, I forget all sense of where I am. The passageway junctions I've come to know by heart have tangled with themselves, and I no longer have any direction of where I've been or where I'm going.

I just run.

With no light, I stumble about, reaching for the walls as guidance, their moisture ripe and their frigidity numbing.

This is it. These tunnels, once my only hope for escape, are where I will lose absolutely everything.

Rapid footsteps sound behind me only a split second before a pair of rough hands grab me from behind. They slam me against the stone wall, scraping my cheek in the process.

"How long have you known?" Laz shrieks in my ear. "How long have you known about the secret passage in your room?"

I struggle to move as he keeps me pinned against the wall, suffocating me in the closeness of the tunnel's air. "N-Nearly since the b-beginning," I stammer.

His sharp exhale tickles the back of my neck. "All this time... you've known about these other tunnels, and you never said a word. These arrows and other markings on the walls...you did these?"

My silence is answer enough. I can barely fucking breathe.

"After everything I've done for you, the sacrifices I've made..." His shouts ring in my ear, rattling my entire core. "I've given you answers, protection from those who hunt you...my fucking *heart*. And this is how you repay me? By finding comfort and solace in my arms one minute, and plotting your grand escape the next? What exactly was your plan? Did you really think I would ever stop searching for you if you up and disappeared on me?"

I try to ease the pressure off my cheek against the stone, but I'm afforded no wiggle room in his relentless grip.

"How could you betray me like this?" he screams. Several frantic beats of silence pass in which I'm too terrified to speak. "*Answer me.*"

Each swallow is more laborious than the last. "I..." What on earth could I possibly say to forestall whatever vengeance awaits me? It's all over. All chance of escape has been thwarted. He will never allow me to be unmonitored again, and whatever liberties I was granted will be no more.

So I don't try to salvage any of it.

"I don't belong to you," I say with as much conviction as I can muster.

"You *do* belong to me—"

"*No.*" I jerk against him, but he only tightens his grasp. "Not you..." I fail to control the quivering in my voice. "My body, my life, my freedom...none of it belongs to you. Not James. Not Papa. Not anyone."

Laz falls silent, his body unmoving. My heartbeat thrashes against my eardrums as I wait for him to say something. "You say that only because you're frightened of me." He exhales softly, his tone more even than before. "But fear *can* turn to love, Neve. You can rest assured of that." He nuzzles his nose in my damp hair, his inhale discernible in the silent passage.

"Say you'll stay with me," he begins, his voice transforming into a soft purr. "That you'll revel in the darkness that binds us as one, and I promise..." He plants a soft kiss on my shoulder. "You'll never have reason to feel frightened again." He doesn't pull his lips away from my flesh. "You'll learn to love me with as much ardor and passion as I've come to love you, little one." He trails his fingers up my long shirt, lifts it high, and hooks it over my shoulder, exposing my bare back. He then plants his hand on the naked swell of my hip.

"All we have is one another," he coos. "Say you'll stay…"

The thumb of his other hand brushes along the scar on the back of my shoulder, a gift from James, as if he's trying to memorize every line.

Tears brim just as my words catch in my throat. "I-I can't. I don't…belong here. Please, just…" Weeping, I struggle to find the courage to continue. Defeat delivers its wicked poison through my body, coursing through every vein as I mentally prepare for my naked flesh to endure whatever awaits it.

"Then I shall just have to clip your wings."

A stab of white-hot pain rakes the back of my shoulder as he sinks his teeth into it, reopening my scar. Unlike James's *kiss* that claimed me in the pouring rain, this bite is raw, deep, and the most extreme physical pain I've ever endured. My violent screams abound through every square inch of the tunnel, shaking my already-rattled core. But the more I scream, the harder he sinks his teeth into me, until my legs fail to keep me upright and they buckle beneath me. With a tightening grip around my waist, he presses me even harder against the tunnel wall. It forces me upright as my cheek scrapes against the rough stone.

The darkness of the tunnel—as black as a nevermore raven and equally as cruel—pulls me under into a horrific déjà vu where I pray for Papa and wish for death.

"Papa, please," I scream, tears spilling freely down my face as the stabbing sensation intensifies.

He sinks his teeth even deeper, as if to take a bite out of me entirely. Blood teases at spilling down my back, but it barely escapes before his tongue laps it up with unhurried motions. Every thrash I make against the wall is met with sharp pain as my flesh remains hooked in his mouth. Each movement only draws more blood, which he licks with abandon. The very idea would turn my stomach if it wasn't for the agony that consumes the entire right side of my body.

Thoughts of James marking my flesh tease my mind. But the memories never come to full fruition as I plead for my captor to free me—to cease this torment.

But my pleas go unacknowledged.

"Please, Papa. Please..." My wailing bombards the tight space, sending my heart racing so fast, I fear it may give out. The piercing sensation overpowers the numbness that has overtaken the rest of my arm. In a matter of seconds, all I can feel is my flesh being torn, my cheek scraping against frigid stone, tears streaming freely down my cheeks, his suffocating grip around my abdomen, and my lungs aching as one scream after another escapes me.

After centuries that dwell within seconds, my hoarse throat can barely pass a single sound. Silently, I plea for this torture to end. I can't endure it any longer.

I await the sensation of James's hands shaking me awake from this nightmare. Through tightened eyes, I see him pulling me close and holding me until it ceases—lulled into serenity as his soft, sultry voice assures me that none of this is real; that I'm here, with him, and nothing will ever find or harm me again.

But my visions of James disappear in a flash as Laz finally frees my flesh from his teeth. The area aches with such ferocity that I feel little reprieve from its newfound freedom, and fresh tears spill unabashedly.

The pitch blackness of the tunnel is nearly as impenetrable as the silence that now hangs heavy between us. But that breath—that hot, sinister breath—caresses my ear as he leans in low and whispers, "Forgive me."

His commanding voice sends a new wave of chills cascading

through every inch of my body. "W-What?" I ask in a tremble, my voice shaky and hoarse.

"Say you forgive me."

This isn't an apology, and he isn't asking for my forgiveness. Once again, he's demanding.

A slight tickle sends goose bumps rampaging my flesh as blood trickles from my open wound, my shoulder screaming in pain as I silently weep against the hollowed bowels beneath the manor.

Visions of Papa pull at my memory, teasing me not with the hope of freedom but with the paralytic fear of being trapped inside my own despair. The icy wall slowly transforms beneath my touch and is replaced by the smooth wooden grain of the wardrobe. In an instant, I am scrabbling for air.

I cannot fight it any longer: the darkness, the frigidity, the hopelessness that stacks itself heavily on my chest.

Plunging me deeper into the iron cage of my own mind.

LAZARO

The metallic aftertaste of her blood lingers on my tongue, and I can't help but revel in its bitter taste. Because it means I've claimed her, just as her midnight lover had.

And now she belongs to me.

Her body is rigid in my arms as she claws at the wall in anguish. She's obscured from me in the darkness, despite our closeness, but I can feel her terror all the same. It's a fear I've never witnessed before, not even in the men who died by my own hands. Her misery pains me. But we are well past the point of no return, and she is so close to opening herself up to me in all the ways I require.

Pressing my palm against the wall alongside hers, I lean in close, my lips grazing her ear. "Say you forgive me," I repeat, my command as brutal as my bite. I'm not fucking around anymore. The lies, the attempts to escape the life I've tried tirelessly to give her. She will surrender herself to me, or we will perish in bitter wretchedness together.

"Fuck you," she ekes out in a sharp whisper, her voice pinched by her sobs.

"Say you forgive me." I refuse to placate her sorrows any longer. She doesn't need someone to wipe her tears away; she needs someone to snuff out the cause of them for good.

My Neve is quite the lucky woman. There's no better killer in this world than me.

"Go to hell." Her tone bites harder now, her disobedience rising to the full occasion as her cries diminish.

"Am I not as worthy of your forgiveness as your papa was?" I spew in her ear. "He was cruel to you, no? Locking you in a wooden cage. And you forgave him countless times. And your midnight lover, who left you permanently scarred? Is my malice not also worthy of forgiveness?"

She pushes against the wall as she scoffs with anger. But despite her antics, I have her caged against me, my chest pressing against her back and my arm wrapped around her waist with a protective grip.

"Don't you ever speak that way about my father. He was warm and gentle. You only wish you—"

"Except when he wasn't," I snap, disrupting the insult that balances on her tongue. "Right? Except when he was unspeakably cruel?"

"Papa was never cruel," she replies, panting.

"*Lies*," I sneer against her cheek, angling her face toward mine with a firm grip on her chin. Our faces are so close, her stunted breath is nearly the kiss I've been dreaming of since the day she awoke in a ratty bridesmaid dress, tear-stricken and rife with displeasure. If only I could see those piercing eyes.

"What did he do to you? I will keep us in this lightless hell for the rest of our lives if I must."

She struggles against me with more tenacity than before, wriggling from my grasp with a new sense of irritation and purpose. But a baby bird with a broken wing is no match for the coyote that hunts it.

After several exhausting moments in which I fight to keep her pinned, she concedes to the capture and collapses against the wall in defeat.

I wait for her to catch her breath and answer my goddamn questions.

The silence nearly drives me mad. And I curse the entombing darkness for robbing me of the ability to see her face, to read those eyes of creamy jade and seek out the truths buried deep within them.

With a delicate hand, I trace her open wound in search of fresh blood, and she flinches when I find it. It continues to expel down her back as I paint her skin with the fruits of my hellish desires. She makes no move to stop me but winces each time my fingers brush her tattered flesh. Before long, my palm is clammy and coated in her blood.

She's shaking now, perhaps on the verge of tears once again. I press my lips to the bare skin between her shoulder blades. A tremble overpowers her, and I relish in the way it forces her to sink against me.

"I've got you," I whisper, my lips grazing her ear as I lean in even closer. "You're all right."

A single yet distinct sob catches in her throat.

"What did he do?" I ask again.

Her trembling escalates, but she adjusts in my arms to brace herself against the wall and find her proper footing. "He locked me in a wardrobe, like I told you," she sniffles, her voice shaky. "But he did it for my own protection, to keep me safe. Because he loved me—"

"And I don't?" My grip tightens around her stomach, and she gasps. "Is that not the same reason I brought you here? To keep you safe? You think I don't also love you?"

"Stop. You're hurting—"

"And yet you worship him but villainize me?" I lash out.

"He was sick," she barks, her stubbornness rising once again. "He didn't know what he was doing. He tried so hard…But, in the end, he couldn't protect me from his monsters any more than you can protect me from yourself."

That last part nearly knocks the wind out of me.

I'm not the fucking villain here, and these monsters can't possibly have been more than a grown man's attempt to manipulate a little girl.

"There were no monsters." I nearly bite off my tongue to keep from chastising her as if she were a child. "There never were."

"Yes there were." Her voice cuts through the darkness like a freshly forged blade, her trembling subsiding as she stiffens against me. "He saw them." She speaks with such conviction that, for merely an instant and not a moment more, I almost believe her.

"The monsters were a lie. You would know this if you stopped idolizing your dead papa for a moment and just think." I force my growl against her ear. "What brought on his episodes?"

She tries to twist away, but my tightened grip commands her to answer me without uttering a single word.

"I have no idea," she states, a weightiness to her voice I can only presume is bravery. "I never saw the episodes coming. He was sick, just like I said—"

"That's not true. *Something* triggered them. Something must have happened to him, to you. Did something change? People don't just go mad, Neve. Think."

"I-I don't know."

"Think. No more bullshit. No more lies. Enough of these excuses and existing in blatant ignorance."

The sudden silence is rich, and the thudding of my eardrums stirs a restlessness in me that makes me want to scream. I can't bear it much longer. So I break it out of sheer desperation, and ask, "There was more, wasn't there? You said it yourself. You said your body belongs only to you. Not me, not James. *Not Papa*. What did you mean?"

Her stillness is as maddening as her silence.

"*Talk to me*," I bark.

She winces so subtly, I would have missed it were it not for all the ways our bodies are connected.

"I..." she begins, and my heart skips with anticipation. "I never meant to hurt him."

EVIE

The aroma of freshly popped popcorn still hangs heavy in the air as I blink away the sleep from my impromptu nap. The movie's over; I missed the entire ending. I squint against the illumination of the television, casting a flicker of light upon Papa and me from the static on the screen. It competes with the multicolored glow from the small Christmas tree in the corner, each handmade ornament hung with care by the both of us over a month ago. Gentle snores vibrate from Papa's lips, and I just know his head is craned back on the couch, mouth agape in his deep slumber. My head rests on a throw pillow in Papa's lap, and I'm clad in one of his favorite band T-shirts. Simon and Garfunkel this time.

Lazing around in Papa's T-shirts is nothing new. I've been using them as sleep shirts my entire life despite my recent growth spurt having done me no favors. But even though they don't accom-

modate my newfound height all too well, I never gave it much thought.

Lying still so as not to wake him, I fall headfirst into the wishful thinking of a child who possesses so little. The cello Papa is renting for me sits propped in its neck stand near the tree, looking as dashing as ever in the colorful hues of the season that has since passed. Christmas of '00 has come and gone, neither of us having the heart to take the tree down just yet. My only wish was to have a cello of my very own. I imagined a beautiful red bow wrapped around its neck, a fresh block of resin for the bow, and a new book of sheet music to dip my musical toes into. It didn't happen this year, unfortunately, but I never made my disappointment known. I would never do that to Papa. Regardless, I nearly drift back to sleep in his lap, wishing for it to come true for my birthday instead. But a sudden sensation on my upper leg jolts me awake, pulling me back to reality.

In my drowsy state, I realize my—Papa's—shirt has hiked up rather high.

And Papa's hand is resting on my bare thigh.

The lump in my throat is altogether new. In an unprecedented moment, I become frozen with fear, confusion, and gut-wrenching embarrassment. Surely, he's unaware. We've cuddled more than a thousand times. Being in Papa's arms is my favorite place in the world. But for some reason, my stomach now twists into knots knowing his hands are in a space I would, for the first time, consider wrong.

I don't know what happened. I don't understand it. All I know is, I don't want his hand there, but I have no idea how to move it without waking him. And if he realizes it for himself, he may end up more embarrassed than I am. That would kill me.

As slowly as I can manage, I reach for the bottom hem of my shirt and try to pull it down. But there isn't much space for it to go before reaching Papa's hand, which I bump unintentionally.

He snorts, low in his throat, and I jump out of my skin. Thankfully, his snores resume, and my jumpiness didn't wake him. The only other move I can think to make is to slide his hand away enough that I can slip out from underneath his draped arm. So I reach for it with delicate intent.

In less than a single breath, his hand begins to twitch. He's in a very deep sleep now. Papa often twitches when he's dreaming, his fingers flexing in quick spasms that always left me wondering what could possibly be dancing through his head. This time, however, his twitching fingers are on my bare upper thigh, so close to the hem of my heart-covered underwear that I nearly choke back a cry.

I can't stand it any longer. Each time his fingers twitch, digging into a space on my body never touched by another, I can't wait out the storm of Papa's sleep-induced antics any longer. I leap from the couch and run for my room, Papa coughing awake, bewildered.

It's the first time I've ever wished to escape Papa's embrace.

"WHAT DO YOU MEAN YOU NEVER MEANT TO HURT HIM? What happened?" Laz demands.

I don't know what he wants from me, and I'm desperate for a break from his violent remarks. If it's answers he's searching for, I don't have them. But when he asked if something had changed between Papa and me, a memory of falling asleep in his lap one late night in the middle of winter came racing back into my mind. I haven't thought about it in so long. It's a memory that fills me with so much shame, I'd just as soon forget all about it. And for the last twenty years, I did.

Until now.

"Something *did* change," I whisper as it twists my insides.

I tell him about falling asleep in Papa's lap, how I awoke to his hand on my bare thigh, and how his fingers twitched against my skin as he slept. How I fled from the room, embarrassed, afraid... mostly ashamed. And how, when Papa leaned in to kiss me good-night the following night, I turned my head, forcing the kiss to land on my cheek instead of my lips, their usual spot. The look in Papa's eyes, however—the glint of sadness as he looked at me, downturned and more morose than I'd ever seen them—I keep entirely to myself. To speak it aloud would be an egregious betrayal of Papa's memory. And there's already enough of that going on. It pains me more than that wardrobe ever did. I'd endure it endlessly if it meant seeing him again.

"How long after this happened did your papa claim he saw monsters?"

I mull it over, but it only takes a few seconds for it all to come racing back. "Only a few weeks." I shudder.

A heavy sigh resounds behind me, and I hope it means Laz is just as exhausted from all of this as I am and will leave it alone. Instead, with a calm, cool tone, he asks, "When your papa would hug you, lean in to kiss your head, reach for you in any way...did you recoil? Flinch? Make your discomfort known?"

Like some sort of montage hell-bent on poisoning my memo-ries, I recall Papa's attempts at kindness after that night. My love for Papa never waned. Not once. Even well after he became sick and tortured me with that godforsaken wardrobe. But I didn't return his warm advances after that nap. Certainly not like I used to. Every time he reached for me, I would hesitate, those twitching fingers so close to my bottom haunting me with malicious intent. Despite my attempts to conceal my discomfort, I realize now how attuned Papa must have been to my body language in those moments—how stiff my body would become as he hugged me, and the excuses I would concoct to avoid cuddling.

A violent tremble shakes me. I feel so ashamed. What I wouldn't give to take it all back. To let Papa shower me with kisses and fall asleep in his arms all over again.

"Yes" is all I can muster in response, a single word that bears enough power to sicken me with regret.

"And after he locked you in the wardrobe the first time," Laz says before pausing. If he's preparing me for some sort of emotional blow by stirring up the worst moments from my past, he's far too late. "What came next? Did you hide from him? Throw things? Scream and curse his name?"

No. I never did any of that. Being locked inside that wardrobe made everything preceding it seem so trivial. All I wanted was to be freed, and Papa was the only one who could grant me that freedom. Twitching fingers on my skin seemed so insignificant compared to those wooden walls and the suffocation I endured inside that cramped space.

All I wanted was Papa.

"No," I choke out, the onslaught of tears tightening my throat.

"You ran to him, didn't you? You fell into his arms and let him hold you for as long as it pleased him. And by doing so, you gave him exactly what he wanted—what you'd taken away from him after that night that changed everything. Your love."

But I never stopped loving Papa. Surely, he knew that.

A rush of panic sends shockwaves through every inch of my body at the very notion that Papa died with even a sliver of doubt that my love for him held true.

"No," I exclaim. "He was sick. He saw things...terrible things. The monsters—"

"Weren't real," Laz interrupts with a slashing tongue. "Don't you get it? You were growing up. The closeness you two shared was changing, but you didn't know how to explain it. So you pulled away as a result. Don't you understand what that wardrobe was for him? Why he chose to lock you inside?"

This can't be happening. And I can't stand to hear one more word of this psychobabble. I wrench myself from his grasp, escaping through the gap he creates when he takes a small step backward.

And then I run.

With no flashlight, I've lost all sense of direction, but I only care about getting away from his venomous words. The echoing of our footsteps thrums in my ear, matching my quick, staccato breaths. There's no air in this horrible tunnel, and I fear it will transform into a tomb from which I can never escape.

I gasp as Laz whips me around to face him with an unexpected pull on my arm. I can't see him, but his rapid breaths are close, and I can nearly taste the rage from his iron grip.

"There's nowhere for you to go, Neve. You will stand there, and you will face me. Just as you'll finally face the truth about your papa lest you and I stay down here forever."

Wriggling in his grasp, I spit, "You're a filthy fucking liar. They were real—"

"That wardrobe was never meant to protect you." He persists with the strictness of a father scolding his child, shaking me to punctuate each vile word. "There was nothing to protect you from. For God's sake. He was *grooming* you. Don't you see that? Not for sex. Not for anything of the sort..."

He sighs, low and deep, and stops shaking me. "But for your affection."

The sobs express freely from my tortured throat, and I do nothing to stop them.

Despite my aggrieved sensibilities and the ongoing tarnishing of Papa's memory, Laz continues his diatribe. "Locking you inside that wardrobe was the only way to bring you back into his arms. And every time you started to pull away, he'd lock you right back inside, didn't he? Over time, it became more frequent, and your time inside would last longer. Because it would always bring you back to him, seeking his comfort and love, which he was all too eager to give." He brushes his thumb over a spilling tear, and I wonder how he even knew it was there.

"B-But...I heard them," I plea, desperate for the reveal that this is all some sick joke. If what he says is true, then all of it—every single last bit—is my fault. And it's a truth I cannot bear.

"You heard Frank's men in your house that night. You heard your papa's final moments." Laz leans in close enough that his breath grazes my cheek. "And you justified all of it by convincing yourself that these were the monsters he always spoke of. It makes sense in the mind of a child."

My legs buckle beneath me, and I slink toward the floor, the weight of everything far too great a burden to withstand. But he scoops me into his arms before I fall and holds me against him. The warmth of his body thaws my frozen flesh as he brushes his hand through my damp hair. But none of it dispels the sadness enough to quell the tears.

I did this. It's all my fault. In shying away from Papa, all because of an incident I didn't fully comprehend at such a tender age, I pushed him to his own maddening decision to lock me away. Over and over again.

As if reading my mind, Laz declares, "None of this was your fault, Neve. None of it. Gino was a good man, and I've no doubt that he loved you very much. He just couldn't bear the thought of losing you, and he went to such extreme—albeit insane—lengths to keep you close." His nose touches my hair, and he inhales long and deep. "Not that I can really blame him."

My sobs go down like glass. "I...I just..."

He continues petting my hair as I scrabble for words.

"I can't bear the thought that he died thinking I didn't love him." I swallow another shard. "I just...have to know." My throat tightens. "But I never will."

Laz cups my cheek and addresses me with a stern voice. I don't need to see him to know those stormy eyes would have captured mine. "I have no doubt that your papa died knowing you loved him. Why else would he have sent me to you? To keep you safe when he no longer can?"

I reply on a soft exhale. "Sent you? You don't mean—"

But he presses a finger to my lips, silencing me. "Little one," he coos. Papa's voice reaches out from Laz's lips, bringing a warmth to my belly that I haven't felt in so long.

He removes his finger and grips my chin, as if staring me down despite the darkness.

"Have you forgotten me so quickly?" Papa purrs. "Your angel?"

A boulder lodges in my throat. "N-No," I reply, inhaling his words like I need them to survive.

He kisses my forehead, leaving his lips planted for so long that a series of amorous shudders ripple through my core. When he finally frees me from his kiss, he holds my face with both hands. I want to see him. I need to know if those unpredictable eyes are as conniving as I fear, or as genuine as I pray.

"You're safe here. Safer with me than with any other creature in this world. Your father saw to that when he sent me. It was his final wish..." His words echo low in the vast tunnel, in synchronicity with my shallow breaths and the plinking of water droplets somewhere in the distance.

"I need you, little one." Papa's voice emanates from his ardent plea, stirring in me a near-crippling homesickness. He then plants a kiss on my cheek and wipes errant tears away with his thumb. "Say you'll stay."

Such longing in those whispered words, stirring Papa's spirit and my heart in turn. But those words, like the forbidden fruit in the utopic garden, may seem a mere solicitation for companionship, while secretly thieving for my soul. My trust in them remains uncertain, and it leaves me speechless for this angel—fallen or otherwise —who has scooped me off the ground and is now cradling me in his arms. The fact that I no longer fight his embrace and have made no further attempts to run seems to be all the confirmation he needs.

He carries me through the tunnels in silence as I rest my head in the crook of his neck. Before long, I drift into a ragged sleep, clinging to the hope that Papa's hearty laughter will dispel the tears that have been flowing far longer than I can bear.

CHAPTER 53
LAZARO

We pass through the painting and emerge into her room, which is now illuminated with the warm hue of the early rays of dawn. A soft sigh escapes her lips as I lay her in her bed and settle in beside her. I nestle her against me and hold her long after her breathing has turned languid and peaceful. I caress her hair, inhale her scent, and allow my fingertips to worship her dove-like skin.

I received no reassurance from her, as she never replied to my final pleas for her to stay. I can't help but wonder if she has yet to truly revere me as her angel. I sigh heavily, rife with defeat but unwilling to surrender to it.

Ever.

How amiable our lives would be if she would just accept me as her ethereal guardian—if she would just love me in return.

But I fear her silence speaks louder than any words of acquiescence.

I can't lose her.

Which leaves me with only one choice.

I slip away, taking great care not to wake her, and leave her room with silent steps.

Once in my office, I scroll through my phone until I find Elizabeth's number.

She answers after only one ring. "Mr. Moretti," she says, her voice sounding surprised to hear from me. "It's so early. Is everything all right?" she asks, only speaking in her native Italian tongue.

"Everything is fine, Elizabeth. I apologize for calling so early. But what I need from you is urgent, and it cannot wait." I pause, waiting for her to inquire further.

"What can I do for you, sir?"

I take a seat in the wingback chair situated behind my desk. "That dress you've been working on for Miss Denardo these past few weeks."

"The wedding dress?" she asks.

"Yes, precisely. Well, there's been a change of plan, and I'll be needing it much sooner than I originally stated."

Elizabeth is silent, perhaps trying her best to disguise any trepidation that may spill from her voice. "How much sooner were you thinking, Mr. Moretti?"

I lean back and run a smug hand through my hair.

"Six days. I'm moving the wedding up to this weekend. And I'll need the dress ready by then. I don't care about the cost—"

"Mr. Moretti, I—"

"You can save your protests, Elizabeth. I won't hear them." I stand and pace along the window. "You have six days. Have it ready by then." I hang up the phone and toss it onto the desk.

Linear rays project off the horizon, creating blinding ripples across the ocean's surface. Neve will be mine, 'til death do us part. It's a picturesque sight indeed, and I can't imagine a more perfect moment to admire the view and bask in the glow of the morning light.

CHAPTER 54

JENNA

SEPTEMBER 5TH — DAY 101

A pair of hands wakes me with urgency.

"Jen. *Jen.* Wake up." James hovers over me with a firm grip on my shoulders. I open my eyes in a panic, waiting for them to focus against the garish late-morning light.

"Jen. I need you to get up. It's urgent." He reaches for my covers and tries to pull them down, but I resist and hold them right where they are.

"I'm serious. We need to go." James's eyes are plagued with concern, and it makes my stomach drop.

Yet I fight to keep the blanket high on my chest. "I know. Just stop tugging on the blanket—"

"We don't have time—"

"James. I sleep naked." My voice is an unfamiliar groggy squeal. His eyes widen to the max, horrified, just before he leaps from the edge of the bed and turns away from me. "Oh my God, Jen. I'm so sorry—"

"It's fine, really—"

"I-I didn't see anything. I swear." He covers his eyes despite how he's facing away from me. Clad in nothing but baggy pajama pants, the ripples of his muscular back look even more defined in the morning light. And yet, his horrified demeanor makes him seem almost childlike. I can't help but laugh.

"It's okay," I say amid my laughing fit, holding the blanket firmly against my chest. "I'm covered up." Dear God, I actually snort, which only makes me laugh harder. "You can turn around."

So slowly it's downright painful, he turns back around to face me. I never thought the sight of my breasts could be so terrifying to another person. When he realizes they're not on display, his shoulders relax.

He doesn't wait for me to stop laughing before dropping back onto the bed. "Jen, we have to go. Now. It's Evie."

All laughter vacates my being in a single instant, replaced with a sickness that nearly makes me drop the blanket. "Evie?" I shift, sitting more upright. "What is it? What's wrong?"

"Frank called. He wants us to meet him now. It's about Evie. He says it's urgent."

I throw the blanket aside in a complete panic, poised to leap out of bed.

"*Gah*. Jen," he exclaims, standing up and covering his eyes again.

"I'm sorry, but we don't have time to fuck around." I race for my closet and throw on the first pair of pants I find. "Did he say what it was about?" I ask as I zip up my jeans.

"No. He just said to 'get here quick.'" James's back is still to me. As I scramble to find my shoes, I curse him for not giving me any semblance of reassurance or even allowing me to search his face for something that will tell me everything is okay.

"Meet me downstairs in five," he says as he leaves the room.

Goddammit, James. Doesn't he realize I'm freaking out enough as it is? Not a word. Not one single word from him that may stave off this nausea that's killing me from the inside out.

Fuck his five minutes.

I toss on a shirt, race down the stairs, and holler for him from the entryway. "Move your ass, Pierce."

He appears at the top of the stairs in seconds, dressed simply in a white T-shirt and jeans. His hair is as messy as mine as he hurries to meet me. "I'm driving," he orders, snatching the keys from my hand.

I don't have it in me to argue.

We sit in silence as the sleepy streets of Chatham pass us by. It isn't until the car pulls out onto Route 2 that I realize we aren't headed for the tavern.

"Where are we going?" I ask, peering out the window.

"He asked us to meet him at his house."

I whip around to face him. "Are you out of your mind? His *house*? James, do you have any idea how dangerous that is?"

"You have a better idea?" His brow is furrowed. I don't think I've ever seen him look so serious. Angry, even. Oddly enough, it doesn't frighten me. I merely accept it as a challenge.

James can be a tough nut to crack at times.

And I'm the queen of cracking nuts.

"Yeah. We tell him to meet us at the tavern."

"He specifically said his house," James scoffs.

"After what happened with Ashton, and you coming back from that island empty-handed, do you really think there's even the slightest chance this isn't a trap?" The pitch of my voice means business.

He doesn't respond. Instead, he shifts into a higher gear and floors it.

I swallow a deep breath before proceeding. James is not in a good headspace right now. "James," I begin calmly. He doesn't take his eyes off the road. "Men like Frank Denardo are dangerous. You got too close. Earned his trust. And then you disobeyed his orders. Don't you get it? You're a loose thread now. This isn't safe for either one of us. How do we know he isn't using Evie to lure you back there to—"

He whips the car onto the shoulder of the highway, brings it to a crushing stop, and throws it into park. I brace myself against the dashboard, struggling to catch my breath and yank my heart out of my fucking throat.

"What the—"

The leather seat squeaks as he turns to face me. It's the first time he's looked at me since we left the Cape house. "Listen to me. *Really* listen, okay?" A deep line forms between his brows. "David lied to me for years. I've gone over everything a thousand times in my head. I've been so..." He looks away. "Desperate for any signs I may have missed all this time. Yet I can't come up with a single thing. But it wasn't only me he lied to. He lied to us both." The Benz shakes as cars intermittently zoom past us. "You got caught up in all of this just as I did, and neither of us deserved it."

My breathing evens out from the shock of our sudden stop. But mentioning David seems so out of left field, and I have no idea where he's going with this. I regard him with wide eyes and a fear for the words that spill from his lips. David is my husband. But he's more of a stranger today than the day I met him. Despite the lies I've endured since we met, it pales in comparison to the lies James has experienced the last *twenty* years.

"What I'm trying to say is, David is not the man he said he was." With a slow turn of his head, he meets my gaze and locks eyes on me. "But *I* am. I will always protect you, Jen." He reaches for my hand, and my pulse skyrockets with a newfangled sense of adoration for the man who fell for my girl. "You mean the world to me, and I will always keep you safe in every way I possibly can," he continues. "So I implore you. Please. Don't ever doubt me." The grievous nature of his expression and tone imprint onto my being.

I don't know what to say. For the first time in my life, words have escaped me. For every bit of his declaration...I believe him. Jesus, do I ever. In an instant, I've come to see the man Evie fell so hard for in such a short while. It seemed ridiculous at first, despite my unending support, to hear that Evie, of all people, could fall so hard, so quickly, for a man she just met. But if he spoke this way to her that night, I can honestly say I don't blame her for falling straight into the arms of James Pierce. His nerdy yet GQ exterior only takes him so far, at least in my eyes. It's the certainty—the assuredness—and the unending devotion that now makes me weak in the knees from his words alone. It's what I need, now more than ever.

I don't love him. At least not in that way. But I get it now. I would follow James into the pits of hell if he told me he'd be there to save me from its ferocious flames.

I get it, Eves.

His eyes bounce between mine as if searching them for doubt.

But he will never find it in me.

"I won't," I whisper, finding comfort in his gaze. He squeezes my hand before releasing it, a twinge of sadness poking my belly at my hand's sudden freedom.

He peels away from the shoulder and back onto the road.

The rest of the journey is silent, but I can't stop looking at him out of the corner of my eye. It's as if I'm seeing him for the first time, and the resulting butterflies frighten me as much as they tease at forcing me into a more amorous disposition.

I don't even realize that we've pulled up to the Denardo estate until James has rolled the window down and is talking into the speaker at the front gate. The iron gates roll apart at a dramatic pace, granting us access to the long cobblestone drive that lies ahead.

The entire house—a sprawling wooden monstrosity I haven't seen the likes of since my winters skiing in Aspen—is aglow with warm incandescent light. It's as if every light in the house is on, despite my inkling that only Frank and perhaps a few others are home right now.

James parks before a grand set of stairs leading to the front porch. I've barely set two feet on the ground before he takes me by the hand and ushers me inside. He doesn't even knock. The comfort he feels just walking into Denardo's house freaks me out. It's so dangerous. All of this. It makes me sick knowing how necessary it all felt to him, to get Evie back. It isn't right.

At the same time, I don't entirely blame him. I'd do anything for her.

He pulls me toward the kitchen, from which the only sounds of life are emanating.

Frank stands before the island, a giant marble slab that's mostly covered with enormous maps and other papers. Clearly, the brainstorming has moved from the tavern to the outskirts of Boston.

"What's going on with Evie?" James asks as he hurries toward the island. Frank's attention remains focused on the sprawling map laid out before him. After several painful beats of silence, he says with a heavy sigh, "We have a problem."

"What?" James snaps.

Frank finally looks up. "An informant of mine just told me that Moretti has moved up the wedding."

A sudden dread makes my legs quake, and I fear they will no longer keep me upright. I scan the room for a chair and land on one tucked underneath the kitchen table at the opposite end of the room. But I realize I'm paralyzed by Frank's news and couldn't make it over there if I tried.

"And since you failed to bring her back," he leers at James before returning his attention to the maps. "We need a new plan."

"He moved up the wedding to when?" he seethes as he ignores Frank's cruel remarks.

"Why don't you have a seat—"

"To when?" James yells.

Frank regards him with pitiful eyes. "This weekend."

He pushes away from the island, shaking his head. "No. No *fucking* way. We can't let this happen." He brushes an irate hand through his tousled hair, turning away from the island and then back again. "We have to stop it. You have to get me back to that island *now*."

Frank holds up his hand to stop him. "I've come up with something, son. Just take a breath."

Based on the way James is looking at Denardo, hands on hips, I fear he may leap over the island and punch him square in the face.

"Let's end the suspense," James retorts. "Out with it."

Frank points to the large map that takes up most of the island. I recognize it. It's the map of Eden's Green. There are black and red markings all over it: Sharpie marks denoting what I assume are the different docks, the paved roads, and what I'm guessing may be trails that cut through the woods. There are also a plethora of hand-written notes along the perimeter of the paper.

Sticking out from underneath it is the blueprint of Moretti's house, also bearing an assortment of handmade markings.

Frank goes over his new plan with James, not once looking at me as he speaks. James seems intrigued—hopeful, even—which ordinarily would set my buzzing mind at ease.

But the more they discuss the plan, the more I can't help but notice that my name, once again, has not been mentioned.

"We're going to need a second boat here." Frank points to a row of docks at the north end of the island. "I doubt we'll be able to leave the island the same way we entered. Moretti's a smart man. I'm certain he'll barricade this dock here." He points to the larger one at the southwest corner. "But it's our only way onto the island with that many men—"

"And me," I say, my patience now razor thin. They both pause to look at me. "I'm going too."

James sighs, and I loathe how patronizing it feels. I can sense the argument before it has even begun.

"Jen," he cautions. "It's way too dangerous for you to go to that island. Even more so this time than the last. I can't risk—"

"I'm not asking your permission," I bark. "I'm coming with you, and that's final."

Frank laughs, and I want to rip a knife from the butcher block behind him and cut him to shreds.

Tears of frustration tighten my throat until I can barely breathe.

James steps toward me. "I'm sorry, Jen. I can't allow—"

"Go fuck yourself," I sneer before hightailing it out of the kitchen and emerging into the living room.

These animal skin rugs are fucking hideous.

Rage sends my stomach into a violent boil. I can't believe him. I can't believe he's actually going to leave me behind. Especially after the last time he had his chance to bring Evie back and fucked it up. Who the fuck does he think—

"Please don't be upset," James says somewhere behind me.

I reel around to face him, ready to pounce.

"Don't you dare tell me not to be fucking upset." My vision blurs with tears. I pace back and forth behind a large leather couch facing a gaudy stone fireplace, arms crossed. It doesn't help much.

James approaches and grabs my arms, forcing me to stop my aimless movements. "I don't want you getting hurt."

I push him back, desperate to free myself from his piercing gaze. But he holds me tight, and I can't seem to pry away no matter how hard I try.

"I need you to understand..." His voice is calm but stern as he tucks my hair behind my ear. "I can't lose you too."

Tears spill down my cheeks as I realize the gravity of James's words. All this time, I've been thinking about Evie. She's my entire world, the love of my life, and I need James to help me get her back. But James is more than a means to an end for me. He's a dear friend, a confidant, and a man who's walking a dangerous line of setting my heart aflame.

But there's so much he doesn't know; if secrets were a tempestuous ocean, mine would run miles deep.

"James, I have to tell you something."

His expression goes crestfallen, and it stabs me with guilt.

"This…" I back away. "Everything…" With a swipe of the back of my hand, I catch my falling tears. My words force their way through my pinched throat. "It's all my fault." I slide down the back of the couch and onto the floor, drawing my knees to my chest.

"What are you talking about?" he asks, towering over me.

"Evie's gone because of *me*." I nearly scream the words. I certainly want to. Hell, it may even make me feel better. But instead, I rest my elbows on my knees and grip my hair by its roots.

He drops to his knees beside me, holding on to the back of the couch for support. "Jen, look at me."

I can't. No way in hell. This guilt has eaten at me since the wedding reception, and I'll be damned if I allow James to see it stretched all over my puffy face. Instead, I bury my face in my hands.

He grips my chin and forces me to face him. "Look at me," he commands. "What are you saying?" His face is so close to mine that I debate kissing him as a way of putting an end to this line of questioning, which I started in the first place.

But I refrain.

Tears tickle as they approach my chin, but I make no move to brush them away. "At the reception…" I sniffle. "When David spilled champagne on my dress…I didn't care in the slightest. The night was nearly over, and it's a dress I'll never wear again. He urged me to grab Evie and have her help me clean it up. I know now why he was so insistent, but at the time, I had refused his pleas for me to go find Evie." A deep swallow jabs my tightened throat. "But then…"

He shifts, sinking to the ground beside me as my story continues.

"I heard it."

"What did you hear?" he whispers.

"The song 'In Your Eyes.'" I meet his gaze, and he seems taken aback. "I didn't add it to my playlist, so I knew a request must have been made. When I heard it, I scoured the room for Evie, and that's when I saw the two of you dancing..."

He runs a hand over his jaw, his shoulder brushing mine. "I don't understand. We'd been dancing all night. What was so different—"

"Everything changed then," I interrupt, wishing he'd just *get it* so I could stop this torture. "Seeing her in your arms, her head on your shoulder, her favorite song filling the reception tent. I just knew at that moment..." I clear my throat, hating the words before I even speak them. "That I'd lost her forever."

"I don't understand. How did you lose her?"

"Evie has always just been there, you know? And I've always wanted nothing but happiness for her. But there was something about seeing the two of you together. I felt it. That you were perfect for each other. And it scared the living shit out of me." I fuss with my hair, tucking it behind my ears and wiping away the newest batch of tears with my palm.

"I wasn't even thinking, really. I just knew I couldn't bear another second seeing you two so entwined. So in love..." I release a gentle sigh. "So I raced over to her, ripped her from your arms, and demanded that she help me clean my dress." My eyes are so heavy. I can't bear the weight of any of this anymore. "So you see...if it wasn't for me and my selfish bullshit, she never would have been in that bathroom in the first place."

I don't have the energy to tell the rest. With a belly filled with regret and disdain, I avoid James in my periphery as long as possible. If only he would scream at me, tell me what a fucking idiot I am, and remind me how this is all my fault, I may be able to berate myself out of this endless cycle of self-hatred.

But he doesn't say a word.

I can't bear it another second.

Climbing to my feet, I aim to put as much distance between us as possible. I have to get out of here.

He doesn't move.

As I reach the front door, he calls out behind me in a gentle voice. "How long?"

Confused, I spin around.

He's standing now, facing me. An eerie calmness stills him, his face placid, and I have no idea how to respond to that.

"How long have you been in love with her?" he whispers.

All the air in my lungs vacates in a flash, as if tied closed with a rubber band. "What do you mean, how long—"

"It's okay, Jen." He reaches me in only a few steps and cups my cheek before I can back away. "You never have to lie to me."

"I don't know what you're talking about." My face scorches with panic.

"I don't blame you," he says, ignoring my lies. "You want what's best for her, even if that means you might lose her. You're a much better friend than you give yourself credit for."

Tears brew all over again. "I'm not." I shake my head. "It's all my fault—"

"Stop," he scolds. "It isn't. And I won't let you blame yourself another second."

"Or what?"

With a soft tug, he pulls me to his chest. His heart is racing as rapidly as mine, which I find oddly comforting.

"Or nothing. I'll just have to keep reminding you over and over until you either believe it, or I've driven you completely mad."

My shoulders relax. "Well, that would be an easy accomplishment. You're annoying as fuck."

We share a brief laugh before his face falls somber again and he asks me the one thing that I truly wish he hadn't. "Does she know?"

All I can do is nod. It's an honest answer devoid of the words I would rather choke on than speak aloud. Yes, Evie knows that I love her. I kissed her and made a complete ass of myself in the process. Fortunately, her heart is so golden that we moved past it as if it were nothing, and she never put me in a position where I had to explain myself—or my feelings—ever again.

Fuck, I fell so much harder *after* the kiss for that very reason.

Thankfully, James does not press the matter further. My silence seems to speak volumes, because he regards me with a look of morose understanding. If Evie knows that I love her, then surely James realizes that my love is unrequited, thus why we were merely friends when he entered our lives.

He pulls me into his arms, and I fall into the lullaby of his heartbeat. With a grasp as warm as my blushing cheeks, I find security and comfort in the arms of the man who now knows my most intimate secret. It's freeing in a way, and the albatross around my neck feels a bit lighter.

I just wish James—a man I've come to truly adore—wasn't the one to take her from me.

Or perhaps that's the best thing that could've happened? It's why I set them up to begin with. I knew he'd take care of her in ways I always dreamed.

Deep down, I knew this time would come: Evie sailing off into the sunset with someone else, and I would be there for the occasional drink and phone call. James is undoubtedly the right man for her. For all my reverence I have for him, however, I can't help but also hate him for it.

He plants a kiss on the crown of my head and runs his fingers through my hair. "Come on," he says, pulling away to face me. "Let's go figure out a way to get the woman we love back, safe and sound." His lips curve into a handsome smile. "Together."

CHAPTER 55

JENNA

SEPTEMBER 7ᵀᴴ — DAY 103

Frank Denardo is a prick. Plain and simple. He has no intention of letting me be part of the plan to get Evie back, which he made clear by only addressing James as they discussed the plan in great detail while the day withered away.

But I was listening adamantly, and he mentioned needing a second boat to wait at the north end of the island and wasn't sure how to secure one on such short notice. So fuck him. I'm going to be part of this plan whether he wants me to be or not.

The docks are alive with visitors today, despite it being the middle of the week. It's a beautiful September day on the Cape, and it's buzzing with people who aim to stave off the heat with a day on the water. Propped against the side of the marina's little fish market, I peer across the parking lot and watch the morning unfold. Families load coolers onto catamarans, fishermen hose off boat decks, and a young couple launches kayaks from the slipway off to the left. Cars come and go, customers bustle in and out of the storefront, a small child squirms miserably as her dad tries to fasten her life jacket around her tiny frame.

I'm not on the lookout for anyone in particular. I just need someone with a boat who can help me.

The sun shifts as the morning inches on, and I shift with it to stay within the shade that stretches along the back of the building. Within the hour, the shadow dissipates entirely as it approaches midday, and the beating sun pushes me to the precipice of forfeiture.

Most of the people have gone from the marina, and I'm left with only the gentle sound of ocean ripples lapping against mooring poles and the hulls of the remaining boats, and the clinking of closed sails against their masts. With the marina practically vacant, my attention shifts solely to a man pushing a broom across the deck of a weathered fishing boat. The muscles in his arms, sleeved in tattoos I can't make out from here, are corded and tight as they flex with each push of the broom. It's a rather large fishing vessel for one man to be working alone, so I wait for others to make an appearance.

He stands and arches his back in a deep stretch before bracing himself against the broom handle. His gaze then sweeps the marina as he removes his baseball cap and runs his forearm over his sweaty brow.

I catch a glimpse of his handsome face, and my belly flits without permission. As he replaces his cap where it belongs, his eyes land on me. Sweat beads along the back of my neck, dampening my hair along the nape. My long, fiery hair is on full display in the blistering sun. Despite the temptation to put it up to ward off this heat, it's my crown jewel, and I need it right now.

Our eyes remain locked for several beats of my steady heart, my confidence rising. This man won't shake me any more than the others. There's nothing special about him. He's handsome, sure, but he's a means to an end.

And I'm no novice when it comes to convincing men to do my bidding.

When he turns away and disappears into the wheelhouse, I fear I haven't made enough of an impression. I pull the scoop neck of my tank top further down, exposing the top of my breasts and the deep cleft my push-up bra creates. Much to my relief, he appears once again, climbs down the ladder to the lower deck, then stalks to the bow.

His eyes lock on me again. I have his full attention.

Gotcha.

I fold my arms over my chest, a silent gesture that indicates I'm not leaving and can play this staring game all day if necessary. He mirrors my actions, folding his arms and leaning casually against the deck's handrails without taking his eyes off me. I wish I was close enough to see the nuances of his expression. From here, he appears completely stoic.

Somehow, this turned into some sort of standoff, and I have no intention of losing. I will, however, make it a bit more interesting. The parking lot gravel protests beneath my feet as I stroll toward the docks, making no effort to arrive promptly. My fingers graze the rope rails with a flirtatious touch as I near the finger dock that butts against his boat.

He remains unmoving as I pause at the bow. He's close enough now that I can confirm the stoicism of his face and make out the nautical nature of some of his tattoos.

"Permission to come aboard?" I ask in a kittenish fashion.

His lips twitch in a little smirk. "Not so fast."

He crosses the passerelle onto the dock, approaching me with as much nonchalance as I showed him. "Is there something I can help you with?"

"Maybe," I reply coquettishly.

"Shall we end the suspense?" he asks, shifting the bill of his ball cap as his eyes scour my body.

Oh brother. I nearly roll my eyes at how easily this fish took the bait.

"Well, you see, the thing is..." I run a finger over his bicep, tracing a tattoo of a ship's wheel, the far edges of which circle around, out of sight. He makes no effort to stop me. "I need your help."

He releases a hoarse, stifled laugh as he leans in closer. "Is that right?"

I nod despite my hesitation. "You're a fisherman?" I ask, flitting my gaze from his bicep to him.

"Yeah." Much to my relief, his stoicism has faded to one of subtle intrigue.

I continue tracing my finger along his arm, trailing it down to his forearm, masquerading under the guise of being completely riveted by his ink. "Where would you say you do most of your fishing in these parts?" I tease another glance his way.

"Depends on what I'm fishing for." His eyes—a beautiful blue that makes the Cape's horizon seem trivial—flare with an intensity that holds me captive.

"Do you have a favorite?" I flirt, bringing my finger back up and toward his shoulder.

"Whatever bites," he replies with a sly squint. "But I will say, I've always favored red fish, personally."

"Is that right?" I ask, looking directly at him.

"The redder, the better," he jests, darting a look at my blazing hair. I smile with a genuineness that cuts me with shame. "But something tells me you didn't come over here to talk about fish."

"Not exactly." I withdraw my tactile hand and secure it in the rear pocket of my jeans. "Like I said. I need your help."

He runs a hand over his chiseled jaw and tilts his head. It's clear he's waiting for me to continue.

"I need a ride."

With limited grace, he reaches for a railing post to brace himself as he leans in even closer. "Is that right?" His voice is a soft rumble that runs the risk of working its magic on me. But I don't bite.

"Yes." I nod toward his boat. "I need a ride to an island offshore."

He jolts back in surprise as our salacious metaphors come to a halt. "Oh."

"A few days from now, I'll need someone with a boat big enough to make it to Eden's Green and back to give me a ride."

His face scrunches, and all signs of flirtation have vanished. "What do you want with Eden's Green?" he gruffs.

"You know it?"

"Of course I know it. Everyone around these parts knows it. But you didn't answer my question. What business do you have on Eden's Green?" The sting in his voice jolts me.

"I—" A flock of seagulls squawks overhead, as if warning me of the dangers of proceeding with this line of questioning. This is a treacherous slope, and I'm not sure how far down I dare venture. This stranger knows nothing about Evie, and it's pertinent that I tread carefully here.

"I just need your help getting there and back. Is that something you would be able to do?" I throw him a teasing glance, but all hope of using flirtation to get my way seems to have flown off with the raucous birds.

"Sorry. Can't help you." He turns away and heads for the passerelle.

"Wait." I run after him. "Please." I tug on his forearm, hoping he'll face me. "I wouldn't ask if I had any other option. I'm begging you."

He reels around angrily. "Lady, do you even know the first thing about Eden's Green? Do you have *any idea* what you're asking me right now?"

"Yes," I reply with a callous bite, standing my ground. "That's why I need your help."

"No way." He reaches the gangplank and crosses onto his boat. I'm hot on his tail.

"You can't be on here," he says, shooing me off his boat.

"I'm not leaving until you agree to help me." I cross my arms and plant my feet.

In a handful of strides, he's on me, lowering his handsome face until it's inches from mine. It doesn't intimidate me, and I maintain my firm stance to spite him. The scent of fish and diluted soap trickles through the air aboard his damp fishing vessel as the silence continues at a crawl.

"Go," he growls, low and cruel. "Now." Without another word, he scales the ladder to the wheelhouse on the upper deck, leaving me reeling in the company of my failures as I trudge back onto the dock.

The several blocks from the marina toward the shops downtown is an arduous walk at best. My mind races with bashful regret, embarrassed by my ill attempts to convince a stranger to do my bidding. Everything I wish I had said bombards me like a maelstrom of ridicule. I'm not easily flustered, and I wasn't even with him.

But I'm feeling it now.

Killing me softly from the inside out, self-ridicule takes root.

I plop down on a bench at the edge of a sprawling, luscious park, situated across the street from a line of boutiques and local cafés. Whipping my hair off my shoulders and into a high ponytail, I force myself to think of a plan B.

But I don't have one. There's just no time.

All I know is, I can't go back to James empty-handed, and I sure as hell can't let our last attempt to bring Evie back fail.

The blushing in my belly quells as I find courage in my endeavor once again. With only a few days left, the fisherman is the only plan remaining. I'm just going to have to make him agree to help me.

There's nothing in this world I won't offer him

If there's one thing I've learned growing up with money, it's that everyone has a price.

A heavy truck door slams across the street. It barely captures my attention as the driver climbs out of the vehicle and saunters toward a café with an artsy, painted sign.

The fisherman.

My heart skips with a new sense of purpose as I hurry toward the café.

Ignoring the din of hissing milk steamers and coffee mugs clinking on tabletops, I scan the room for the fisherman.

It takes only a second to find him as he takes a seat at a small table by the front window. Engrossed in his phone and sipping from a squat yellow mug, he doesn't see me coming.

Which would explain why I'm greeted with crooked eyebrows when I pull the opposite chair out and plant myself across from him.

"What do you want?" he huffs, tossing his phone aside. I lean forward, elbows on the table, and steeple my fingers beneath my chin.

"I want your help. And I'm not leaving until I get it."

"Look, lady, I—"

"Jenna."

He pauses. "What?"

"My name's Jenna. Not 'lady.'"

He shifts awkwardly in his seat. "Okay, Jenna." A heavy, irritated sigh passes his lips. "Are you some sort of head case? Is that what's going on here? Because I already told you I'm not interested."

I lean forward and allow my lips to curl into a smirk. He can call me all the names he wants. Paint me as a lunatic if it pleases him. I don't shy away so easily. In fact, it only makes me want to bite down harder.

"If labeling a woman as crazy makes it easier to leave her hanging, then I certainly feel sorry for the women in your past."

He recoils sharply, his eyes widening in shock as he opens his mouth to speak.

But I don't give him the chance. "Or men," I continue. "Let's be frank, I don't really know what team you play for…"

"You don't know me at all," he exclaims, horrified at my brash assumptions. As he shifts, poised to push his chair away, his phone buzzes on the table. A small string of grumblings spill from his mouth as he reads whatever's on his phone and begins typing. Without thinking, I snatch it from his hands.

Unlocked.

Yes.

"Hey, what the hell?" he protests. A handful of patrons turn their attention toward us, but I ignore them. Before he can snatch it back, I push my chair away from the table, open up his list of contacts, save my number in his phone, and then send myself a text message from it. My nimble fingers are quick as hell, and I've always been a speedy texter.

He never stood a chance.

"Here you go," I say in a blasé tone, tossing the phone onto the table in front of him.

"What's wrong with you?" he barks, snatching his phone back and securing it in his pocket.

"There. Now you have my phone number for when you change your mind." I cock my head and flick my eyebrows. "And now I have yours."

Crossing my arms over my chest, I slouch a bit, making myself comfortable to show I'm not the least bit intimidated by whatever he may say next. One more added touch should do the trick. "Sure, you can always block it." I wave away the notion and shrug. "But I know the name of your boat, and I know your marina slip. If I don't hear from you, just remember, there are other ways of finding you."

He slumps back in his seat, studying me fiercely. If I didn't know any better, I'd almost say he looked impressed. After several moments of another stare down between us, he says, "Well, you're certainly tenacious. I'll give you that."

"I've heard that before." I'm flattered, but I refuse to make it known, so I hold my flat expression.

With a small sigh, he leans forward and rubs his hand over the back of his neck. "Look. I really wish I could help you. But that island is heavily restricted. You can't just come and go as you please. You need proper permissions. You have to be granted special access."

"I know." I choke on my words as I struggle to maintain composure. "That's why I need your help. There's someone on that island who's trapped—" The words catch as I stop myself, but I fear I've said too much already. Cupping my cheeks, I curse under my breath, frustrated with how my big mouth is always fucking things up.

This was a mistake. How can I possibly earn someone's trust well enough for them to help me but keep them in the dark about everything? It's an impossible task. Once again, I feel Evie slipping through my fingers.

It takes everything in me not to run from the café in self-contempt. Despite my assertive nature, I often envy the vulnerability of others and their ability to fold their cards and move on before things irreparably worsen. But nothing is working in my favor lately, and playing the hand I'm dealt is all I have left. So I trudge through the muck and force myself to look the fisherman in the eye once again.

With secret exultation, I find his features have softened, and he seems to be waiting patiently for me to return to the present. I don't have the words to make this right, so I sit in agonizing silence and wait for him to speak. Perhaps he'll be the one to up and leave? Which begs the question: if he does, will I follow him and pursue this useless venture further?

He searches me with an intensity that puts me on edge as he casually rubs his stubbled chin with a hooked forefinger. His sandy-brown hair is matted on one side, courtesy of the baseball cap that now hangs off the back of his chair. I feel a nearly uncontrollable urge to reach across the table and fix it.

"You're looking for the woman," he states, his head drawn back to enhance his judgmental squint. The next words are spoken with a delicateness that sends goose bumps cascading across my entire body. "The one the boss calls Neve Denardo."

All composure is lost as my jaw falls slack. "How did you... what?" I shake my head, confused. "How do you know about her?" Words and proper breath are failing me as I realize who this man might be. Before he can answer, I reach across the table and pull his arm toward me. He doesn't resist, but he crinkles his brow as if appalled as I turn his forearm over.

Just as I expected: a tattoo of a military helmet atop a rifle, with a pair of boots at the bottom. A fallen soldier tattoo, just as James had described it when he told me about the man who saved him on Eden's Green.

"*Emerson*," I whisper, drinking in the entirety of the tattoo. But he reclaims his arm before I'm ready. "Emerson Shaw, right?" I meet his gaze, the tattoo already forgotten. "James told me all about you—"

He holds a hand up, then sits forward. "Wait. Did you say 'James'? As in 'James Pierce'?"

"Yes." My spine tingles with elation. "He said you helped him after he was—"

"Stop." He runs a frustrated hand through his hair and stares out the window as if in a daze.

The din of the coffee shop bombards my eardrums as my heart thrashes in my chest. I want to scream for everyone to shut up lest he finally speaks and I miss what he says. He doesn't seem like the type who cares to repeat himself.

"Look," he begins, standing from the table and snatching his hat. "I already did what I could for him, as a favor to a fellow man in arms. I don't owe him anything else. Now, I'm telling you for the last time, I can't help you. I wish you well, but please leave me alone." Despite his orotund tone, I refuse to waver.

"I'll pay you," I say, trying to disguise the desperation in my voice. "I have money. Lots of it. Name your price, truly. Money is no object—"

"Not interested," he balks, donning his hat and pushing his chair in. It squeaks against the concrete floor, making me shudder from the impending repeat failure. As he passes me, the door not too far behind where I sit, I grab his arm and blurt out the first thing that comes to my frantic mind. "I'll blow you."

He totters before perceiving me with utter repulsion. "What in the hell kind of man do you take me for?" Several customers eye us over the tops of tilted coffee mugs as he wrenches his arm away.

"You don't seem to get it, do you?" I've never been so over-whelmed with exhaustion and determination all at once. It's a polar-izing juxtaposition that may very well tear me in two. "I will do literally anything."

Peering up at him as he towers over me, I've never felt so small in all my life. I would kill for Evie. Die for her without thinking twice. Money, blow jobs...shit, those things mean nothing to me in the grand scheme of things. I just need to bring her home.

"You just don't know when to quit, do you?"

I silently beg him to take pity on me. "No," I whisper, craning my neck to lock eyes on him. "I don't." I study him, just as he seems to be studying me, and neither of us speak as the awkward silence unfolds.

"Let me ask you something," I begin. "Have you ever wished upon a shooting star?"

His brow nearly splits from the confusion that contorts his face. It's all the answer I need, so I don't wait for him to retort. "Have you ever tossed a penny into a fountain, or perhaps wished on birthday candles as they were being blown out? Or heck, have you ever held a dandelion to your lips and made a wish as you blew the seeds into the wind?"

He shifts his weight and shakes his head. It's clear he's eager to know where in the world this is going.

"Neither have I," I reply as I climb to my feet. Leaning in close, I detect a change in his scent since the boat. The briny sea water and soap no longer linger on his form. Instead, a musty aroma laced with spice catches my attention, and I long to rut around in it like a cat in heat. It's positively intoxicating.

His chest hitches with a quick breath as I stand close enough to feel the warmth of his skin on mine. When I place a hand on his chest, he doesn't refuse my touch, permitting me to learn firsthand that his heart is racing as fast as mine.

A pair of people shove past us into the café, but neither of us acknowledges that we're in the way. With eyes boring into mine as I trace a finger down the ravine between his pectorals, it's the only world I exist in right now.

Slowly rising onto tiptoes, I bring our mouths even closer. His breath bears the scent of coffee, which I long to taste. He hooks a finger into the front of my jeans, pulling our bodies together until they're touching, a sly little move that makes me quiver. Tickling my fingers up along the back of his neck, I bring myself so close that our mouths nearly touch. But I bypass his lips and lean into his ear instead, just as his thumb peeks beneath the back of my tank top.

"Do you want to know why I've never wished for anything?" I coo into his ear, waiting for his little tremble to subside. "Because it's all bullshit."

I wind back around to look him in the eye. "Wishes are for people who refuse to take matters into their own hands. I say fuck that. You want something done, you better get off your ass and make it happen. So here I am, trying to save a dear friend of mine, and I'm asking you to help me, just this once, and I'll be out of your life for good. I swear."

Disappointment stretches across his face, and I speculate over which part he's feeling it most: the kiss I teased but did not deliver, me being out of his life for good, or the fact that I've asked him yet again for a favor he's already refused more times than the average person would tolerate.

He bumps the underside of my chin with a finger. "You're one hell of a firecracker, you know that?"

I melt under the weight of his handsome smile.

"And I wish you well." He nods farewell before trudging past me and walking out the door without so much as a verbal goodbye.

All sense of hope vacates the premises right along with him. I failed. So many times, I've been able to talk my way out of things. Referred to as a master manipulator more than once by my mother, I always perceived it as a gift. I'd be an idiot to say it was a surefire skill, and this fisherman only served to spotlight my shortcomings in that department.

Shielding my eyes against the sun, I meander down the sidewalk, past the groupings of tourists who brush past me in their own world, until grief makes me slink along the outside wall of some boutique nearby.

I don't make it far before my legs fail me. Bending and bracing myself against my knees, I try to catch my breath. It's scorching out, and I curse the Cape for not giving us more breeze today when I need it most.

"Evelyn Rae," a woman calls from up ahead. "You come here, now."

Evelyn.

My self-beratement comes to a pause as I catch sight of a young girl wearing a sunflower dress, with her golden curls styled in an updo. As if mocking me, she holds a dandelion weed to her lips, likely plucked from the array that sprouts from the grass in the cracked sidewalk up ahead. One side of the puff scatters about from her innocent exhale, and she squeals with delight at the prospect of the wish I'm sure dangled from her lips.

At the sound of her mother's command, she drops the stem and hurries to catch up.

Superstitions were always lost on me. I focus on what I can control and say to hell with everything else. But *this*...this can't be a coincidence. Can it? If there's anything these past few months have shown me, it's that nothing is as it seems, and everything I hold dear can be lost to the wind in an instant if I'm not careful.

Like the seeds of a dandelion at a child's lips.

I inch toward the strip of grass as if approaching the rim of a sputtering volcano. If everything I hold dear can be lost to the wind so suddenly, perhaps the wind is the only thing that can bring it back? It's illogical, sure, but what other choice do I have?

I pluck a dandelion weed from the ground and spin it between my fingers, admiring it from all sides. This little weed—a dead, discarded shell of a flower no one ever wants in the first place—may be the leap of faith the universe is telling me I need.

Closing my eyes and drinking in the golden sun, I wish for Evie's safe return, pucker my lips, and blow the puff of seeds from its stem. Twirling in the summer air, they fall to the grass below with featherlike grace, taking my wish with them.

A sense of foolishness ripples through me as I stare at the discarded stem in wonder. I debate plucking another and making the wish again, just to be sure, before thinking better of it and turning away from the strip of grass.

I walk back the way I came, the café's sidewalk sign coming closer into view, when I sense someone watching me out of my periphery. Emerson is leaning against the front of his truck, arms folded, watching me with a little smirk, not so unlike his stance during our little stare down at the docks. But this time, my stomach sinks at the prospect that he's been watching me this entire time.

I don't want to see him, and I certainly am not in the mood for any mockery that may follow my little wishful moment. Much to my relief, he pushes away from his truck, climbs into the driver's seat, and pulls away before I'm forced to turn and head in the opposite direction.

My phone buzzes in my rear pocket. Fearing it may be James with more bad news, I reach for it immediately.

It isn't James.

It's a text message from an unknown number, but it has come in just below the message I sent to myself less than twenty minutes ago that simply says, "This is the fisherman's number."

The new message, sent from Emerson himself this time, consists of six simple, heart-stopping words:

UNKNOWN

Wish granted, Dandelion. I'll do it.

PART V

CHAPTER 56
EVIE

SEPTEMBER 9TH — DAY 105

I never imagined my wedding day would be like this—with fear in my heart, guards lining the entire premises, and a groom that was not of my choosing.

This is the first time I've been alone since Laz found me in the tunnels. Elizabeth helped me with my dress, said something to me in Italian, and then left me in the white room, alone.

I've been under strict surveillance by his guards this past week, with at least two stationed outside my room, rotating shifts, with explicit instructions that I not go anywhere unescorted. Laz had the passageway door sealed shut, and I've been a prisoner in my bedroom ever since.

The white room is a welcome change.

The wedding dress is truly spectacular, though it never would've been my first choice. It's far too elegant, and it's unworthy of a woman who wants nothing to do with this entire affair. Bearing an off-the-shoulder cut that falls into a small V, exposing my beautiful collarbones, and long lace sleeves, it fits my form perfectly. Hugging my waist in a satin sheath silhouette, then spilling over my hips to the floor with a lace overlay, it's traditional with hints of modern flourishes.

It makes me nauseous.

My hair, a mess of loose waves that are pulled away from my face in a half updo, is secured in place with a diamond-studded snowflake hair vine. Hints of red have attacked my cheeks as I wait, stomach in knots, looking at my nervous expression in the mirror.

I'm too late.

I should have gone with James.

No.

I couldn't risk his safety.

I thought I lost him once. And I'd do anything to ensure I never have to receive news of his death again.

Even if that means marrying another to keep him safe.

My promise to find my way back to him rattles incessantly in my mind. Tears swell in my chest as my breath hitches. He may never forgive me. And I may forever shoulder the blame for this since I didn't come back with him when I had the chance. I just pray he comes to understand why I couldn't.

If only he knew what it was like to be informed of his death.

I wouldn't wish that feeling on anyone. Not even Lazaro Moretti.

The sound of someone clearing their throat cuts into my wandering thoughts. Through the mirror, I see Laz standing in the doorway, leaning against the frame in a black three-piece tuxedo, staring at me. His hair is styled away from his freshly shaven face.

I refuse to turn to him, and I dispense with the need to remind him that it's bad luck to see me before the wedding. We're well beyond that.

His reflection approaches me, slinking at a pace befitting of the snake that he is. In seconds, the hard lines of his body press against my backside, and his warmth melds into mine.

"Just when I thought you couldn't possibly look more beautiful..." His voice is sensuous as he leans in, wraps an arm around my waist, and kisses the wounded flesh on the back of my shoulder.

Were this a wedding day I wanted, it would kill me to wear a dress that exposed even a sliver of the horrendous bite mark. Despite the team of makeup artists who made me look like a goddess this morning, Laz gave strict orders that the mark on my shoulder not be covered.

One more way to show off to the world that I've been "reclaimed."

"Angel?" I whisper, watching his reflection as my shoulders quiver. "Or Papa? Or the devil with a serpentine tongue?" My chest is heavy with the swell of tears. "Who are you? Who are you *really*?"

He regards me in the mirror, his lips twitching in a smile as they hover above my shoulder. "I'm whichever you need me to be, little one. Isn't it possible that I'm all three?" His words caress my wound. "Consider yourself lucky," he says before placing another kiss upon it. "Most people never get to marry their guardian angels."

"Don't." I shy away from his kiss.

He tightens his grip around my waist. "My darling Rhiannon," he purrs against my neck, the heat from his breath making me uneasy. "My goddess of winter and moonlight." His lips skim the delicate flesh behind my ear. "So stubborn, this muse of mine..."

Fear rapes my flesh with a barrage of goose bumps. How could Papa send this man to me? A man who regards my freedom with a wicked smirk and tears me away from everyone I hold dear? Papa would never play such sick games—

He steps away, that indecent look in his eyes fading in his reflection. "I promise you," he continues with a softened tone, "things will get better after today. You'll see."

Taking me by the hand, he turns me to face him, and I take comfort in the sudden calmer shift in the air. "Here. I have something for you." The folded paper he pulls from his back pocket catches my eye before he offers it to me. I accept it, unfold it slowly, and survey its contents, confused by what I find.

"What is this?"

"It was delivered this morning," Laz begins. "I had one of my men pull Gino's medical history after our...conversation in the tunnels."

I wince at his nonchalance.

"At least the history he had while still living in Boston. Anything after that would be near impossible to track down, especially since he changed his name."

I scour the words on the page. "I don't understand—"

"You see here...?" He points to the document. "Risperidone. He'd been taking it for years." His attention averts to me. "It's used to treat many things; bipolar disorder, irritability, paranoia..." He pauses, the silence brimming with apprehension. "And schizophrenia."

A small exhale escapes him as he regards me with soft eyes. "I don't think your mother knew, and I don't think it was ever an issue until after he left with you..."

Tears prick at my eyes as my head swims, trying to make sense of it all. "Why? He was so perfect. So...healthy. Until one day, he just... wasn't."

His shoulders slouch, as if consumed by my sadness. "If he was unable to get the treatment he needed once he went to Seattle. Changing his name, staying under the radar...Doctors ask questions, Neve."

My heart aches for Papa, wishing I'd known the struggles he endured.

"But..." I choke back a sob. "How do I know...for sure? What if he wasn't sick at all and was grooming me, as you said before? What if this really is all my fault—"

"We may never know why he started seeing monsters," Laz cuts in, shaking his head. "If his delusions were real, or if it was merely a father's desperate ploy to keep his only daughter in his arms. Regardless, I wanted you to see this"—he nods toward the paper—"in the hopes that you may find comfort in knowing there's a possibility that he really was sick. Perhaps you can start to realize that your self-blame is misplaced."

I don't know what to say. I've always believed Papa suffered from some affliction that was beyond my control or understanding. But what drove him to the choices he made during his darkest moments was something I was never able to reconcile.

Until now.

For the first time, a sense of peace fills my chest. If Papa was ill, then there was nothing that could be done. If he wasn't, and he took desperate—albeit horrific—measures to keep me close, then my only hope is that he died knowing how much I loved him, despite my timidness in his final years. The shame I feel would destroy him if he knew, and I don't want to be the one who hurts him.

Not anymore.

"Thank you," I whisper, a single tear breaking free past my lashes.

Laz wipes it away.

"I can't make any promises, but I want you to know that I will do everything I can to find the answers you seek. You're everything to me, and I hope you accept this gesture as my sincere apology for how I treated you in the tunnels." He pauses, his eyes bouncing between mine. If he's searching them for forgiveness, he'll be hard-pressed to find it.

"In the meantime," he continues, as if weary of my silence. "Just cherish his memory, and let the rest fall to ash."

He's right. The guilt will not bring Papa back, and he would never want me to carry this for the rest of my days.

God, how I miss him, though.

How I long to have him here with me, to walk me down the aisle, arm-in-arm, like I always dreamed. To give me away with a light, affirming kiss on the cheek.

This wedding day is all wrong.

"How did we get to this place, Laz?" I whisper as my throat tightens from thoughts of Papa's absence. "Why are you making me do this?"

"You need me, Neve," he says on a pensive exhale, tucking the paper back into his pocket. "In ways you may not yet realize. You need me by your side, dispelling your darkness until you've learned to rule it."

"But what about the first snowfall? You said I'd have time to—"

"To what? Fall in love with me?" A subtle grin follows his response as his eyes narrow. "Believe me, you will."

Just when I thought this nightmare couldn't possibly worsen, I peer down at my wedding dress, a glaring reminder of the fact that I'm being forced to marry my captor.

My angel.

The incoming crowd of guests rumbles from outside. Certainly the setup beyond the rear terrace is complete by now. From the window, I snuck a peek earlier at the arch adorned with crimson roses. Hundreds of white chairs sat in empty rows upon the grass. A perfect ocean view serving as a backdrop on this cloudless afternoon.

A dream wedding for any willing participant.

I beg him to reconsider with a desperate look. But his tenderness from mere moments ago has hardened, serving as a rough reminder of how Laz can change on a dime. "How can you be so heartless?" The words flee from my tongue before I can stop them. "No angel would give so little consideration to the plight of others."

His eyes flit between mine. "If I'm heartless, it's only because I gave it to you long ago. If only you'd give me yours in return, then perhaps I'd be more capable of compassion. We are past the point of no return, Neve. You're mine. Understand? I suggest you find some way to make peace with—"

A loud *pop* echoes from somewhere outside, sending a sharp shiver down my spine as Laz jerks his attention toward the window.

I shuffle my feet to join him, but he shouts at me. "Get away from the window." He yanks me back.

Three more pops sound outside before a brief pause. Then a rapid series that I cannot properly count nor place, which sounds so close, I wonder if they're coming from inside the house.

"Stay here," Laz commands as he hurries to the door. Inching it open, he peeks into the hallway, looking in both directions.

"What's going on?" I ask, biting my lower lip to keep it from quivering.

He ignores my question, approaches me with rapid steps, and then pulls me back toward the door. I'm too frightened to fight him, and I struggle to keep up in my heels as we race down the hallway to the opposite wing of the manor.

When we approach the main stairwell, he pauses and peeks around the corner. At least a dozen pops sound from downstairs, followed by grunts and screams that are quickly silenced. I cup a hand over my mouth to abate my own screams as my heart races violently. The coast must be clear, for Laz forces me past the stairwell toward the south wing. I catch a glimpse of the foyer below and the guards that litter the floor. I'll never forget the sight. Rosey pools upon ivory tile. I doubt my own eyes. But as the gunshots grow louder and the screams more apparent, I know this is nothing I can chalk up to my subconscious playing nasty tricks. This is real. Something is very wrong here.

And I've never clung harder to Laz's side.

The dome-shaped skylights that line the south-wing hallway cast stout beams of sunlight upon the ornate runner that spans the length of the hall. It muffles the click of my heels as we hurry toward the atrium at the far end. Laz's grip tightens around my hand as he pulls me onward. When a series of pops echo from down the hall, small flashes of light accompanying each one, he pulls me to the nearest doorframe, ducking out of sight. For several beats of my panicked heart, we wait.

No more pops.

Laz peeks down the hall, then whispers, "Come on." Confusion overtakes my terror for a split second when he pulls me back the way we came. Except this time, we don't turn back toward the main hallway. Instead, we continue straight.

Where the looming red door of my art studio awaits.

The room still smells like burnt canvas, and a charred stain remains on the floor. It makes my stomach churn with regret as Laz peers out the windows.

"Who's doing this?" I ask, but he doesn't acknowledge me.

With a bewildered look, he merely mutters, "No cars."

"Just tell me what's going on," I press as my anxiety climbs to new levels.

He grabs me by the arm, which is now raw from his forceful grip, and pulls me toward the fireplace. The wooden clock on the mantel—which ticked away the hours countless times as I became mesmerized by my own brushstrokes—sits in its usual place. But there's apparently nothing usual about it. Laz opens the glass face and presses a button in the center where the minute and second hands meet. A groan emanates from the fireplace, and it shifts heavily, swinging away from a central pivot point.

"Oh my God," I say on a breathy exhale.

The passage is wickedly dark. Much to my surprise, I don't fear what lies within. The dangers outside the passage far exceed whatever may wait inside, and I follow Laz freely and with blatant disregard for my own phobias. Within a handful of feet, we approach a spiral staircase of cold stone, and I realize it's the same one I've descended all this time. But we don't take it all the way to the bottom. Instead, we exit at a hallway that spills out on the right as we make our descent. Based on how far down we ventured, it should be in line with the manor's first floor. I've never explored this passageway before, but I trust Laz knows them best, so I cling to him with every ounce of strength I have.

My heels clack loudly against the stone floor as we run toward the back of the manor, the light on Laz's phone guiding us, until we arrive at a metal lever, same as the others. He forces it vertical, and a door pops open, filtering a cone of light inside the passage. For a second, I wonder if we've ended up outside. But when a black marble pillar comes into view, I realize we've emerged on the perimeter of the atrium.

No popping sounds. No footsteps.

Yet I don't believe the worst is over.

We emerge from the secret door disguised within the accent moldings in the wall, my hand in his. Filled with a golden hue, the atrium is almost too bright to properly enjoy and is far too warm for comfort. I wish I knew what the plan was. All I can deduce is that Laz is aiming for the door that leads to the side of the house, where I know his Bentley is parked.

And the shortest route to the door is straight through the atrium.

Our footsteps are shallow, barely audible as we head into the sunny cavaedium.

His grip tightens around my hand to the point of excruciating pain just as a rain of clicks resounds around us. Countless faces appear on both levels of the catwalks above, surrounding us, each one aiming a gun in our direction.

Air evacuates my lungs as I'm nearly crippled with fear.

"It's over," a man I don't recognize hollers from the highest catwalk. "Let her go."

Laz wrenches me closer, his face twisted in anger.

"You've lost, Moretti," the man warns as he leans over the stone railing.

Laz shifts beside me. "Like hell, I have," he seethes through gritted teeth. I barely catch him in my periphery before hard steel presses against my temple.

"*No*," I gasp. My stomach lurches as Laz holds me firmly around the waist and presses his gun even harder into my flesh. Suddenly, everything I thought I knew about Lazaro Moretti falls apart. Every word he's ever spoken about searching for me my whole life, the lengths he claims to have endured to keep me safe...

Denial keeps me from thinking any of this is real.

It's also what keeps me upright.

Laz would never pull that trigger. Not the man who proclaimed me as his queen, his muse, and the one he swore to protect at all costs.

Would he?

There's only one man in this world for whom Lazaro would ever risk everything to claim victory. His only self-proclaimed nemesis.

Frank Denardo.

My father.

Could that really be him? We look nothing alike. But goddamn, he and David sure do. That has to be him. The man who's been searching for me my whole life, same as Laz.

As if the ground has opened beneath my feet and I'm suddenly plummeting into a black abyss, my stomach leaps into my throat when a realization hits me: I have no idea what Laz is capable of now that Frank is here.

"Hold your fire," someone screams from somewhere out of sight. "Goddammit, lower your weapons." James appears beside Frank on the top level, thrusting himself against the railing in a panic.

"James." The word flows from my tongue with a rush of hope.

He came back for me.

But it's short-lived when I realize the danger he's in all over again.

I asked him not to come back. There's no way I can ever lose him again. Sick with trepidation, I purse my lips to keep them steady.

James motions to the men surrounding us. "I said lower your goddamn weapons." His voice booms across the atrium.

One after the other, firearms disappear from sight, leaving only a perimeter of faces dressed in dark suits.

But Laz does not lower his.

"Let her go," James pleads.

Laz takes several slow steps backward, taking me with him. James motions for him to stop, his eyes wide with horror. "I said *let her go.*"

With a quick jerk that makes me squeal, he pulls me back to the edge of the atrium, to the hidden doorway from whence we came. He releases the gun from my temple, presses on the door until it clicks and pops outward, then shoves me inside. He locks it behind us with a turn of the lever, which groans until it's securely in place.

All words of protestation are lost from my lips as I'm pulled away. With his revolver in one hand and my hand in the other, we scale the stone steps in a rush. I'm too terrified to consider my breathlessness, filled with the anticipation of knowing James is here, but so petrified by the dangers that lie ahead for us both.

I honestly have no idea how many steps we've climbed. My feet ache and my lungs burn as I'm forced to keep up. We reach the top of the stairs and race down the passage hallway, guided by the small cone of light from his phone.

Small ripping noises accompany my heavy breathing as I step on the train of my dress more than once.

Another lever. This time, however, when he pushes inward, the door swivels open on a pivot point just like in the art room.

Bookshelves catch my eye first, a sense of familiarity soothing my racing heart.

We emerge in Laz's office via the fireplace, which slowly rotates back into place behind us. He hurries over to his desk, punches in some sort of code that beeps with each keystroke, and rifles through the contents of the drawer that pops open. He removes a document and slaps it onto the desk before racing back over to me. With a violent tug of my arm, he pulls me over to the desk. "Come—"

"Stop." James pops up from behind the plush leather chair at the far end of the fireplace, and I gasp sharply. His pistol is aimed straight at Laz, cradled with two steady hands. "It's over, Moretti. Enough—"

Laz yanks me against him and presses the revolver to my temple, forcing a scream from my lungs. "Laz, don't—"

"Let her go," James bites, his face flush with rage as he moves to the middle of the room, free from occlusions.

"Put the gun down," Laz demands.

"Let her go—"

"Put the fucking gun down." His gun digs harder into my temple, and I wince against it. "*Now.*"

James's hand goes slack around the pistol, which dangles from his digits as he surrenders.

"Toss it," Laz orders.

He tosses the gun, and it lands somewhere near the desk.

"On your knees," Laz says with ophidian flair.

James sinks to his knees, his hands held out in an act of continued compliance.

"Laz, no—" I shriek.

He shoves me away savagely, then turns his revolver on James. I stumble against the back of the couch, bracing myself for what may come next.

"Please don't hurt her. Just let her go—"

A strange chuckle billows low in Laz's throat. One I've never heard until now.

"Do you really think I would ever harm her?" Laz asks, his lips upturned in a cruel smile. His gun remains fixed on James, but he averts his gaze to me. It's the first time he's looked at me since the white room.

The tightness in my throat is impossible to swallow away as tears brim and my hands shake.

"It's time," Laz says to me.

No.

"It's time for you to make a choice."

No. No. No…

"If you wish for your midnight lover to walk away unharmed…" His voice is gruff and painfully cruel. "Then sign it."

I glance over at the document on the desk. I can't read it from here, but I know in my gut what it is.

The marriage certificate.

Deep down, I know this all ends with me signing my life away to the man with the scarred face. I'd never allow anything to happen to James.

This is all my fault.

Tears catch in my lashes, then spill freely as all the ways I've failed whirl around in my mind. What pity I once felt for this evil creature of a man—what longing I once endured to absolve his anguish. There was a time when a smile gracing his lips was worth a day of freedom, and I would've moved mountains to bring about another.

What a goddamn fool I've been; I'm such a fucking child. How I've let my fears keep me prisoner by both madness and man, dictating where and with whom I seek comfort.

"Don't do it," James pleads. His voice is stunted by his nervous breathing. Seeing James worked up hits me with a ruthless blow. He's always been the one to make things right, to remain calm when my anxiety is soaring. He's a soldier, for Christ's sake. But the perspiration on his brow and the creases that line his forehead spotlight his anxiety.

It scares the shit out of me.

"Shut up," Laz growls.

"Evie, look at me."

I meet James's pleading gaze, blurred through my tears.

"It's okay," he coos. "Don't let this man decide your fate. You deserve the world...to be free of this place."

I step toward James, desperate to throw my arms around him and breathe in his scent. To tell him how sorry I am—

"*No,*" Laz roars as he approaches me. His hand encloses my arm before he pulls me away and shoves me with brutal aggression to the floor. A muffled squeak rushes past my lips as I land square on my hip. Too enraged to face him, I bury my face in my hands, my mind reeling with all the things I wish to scream. But the hammer of his revolver cocks back with a sickening *click*, silencing my thoughts.

"Enough of this," Laz exclaims, his tone stiff and surly as he keeps the gun on James. "Sign the paper...or say goodbye to the man who makes such gallant displays of love despite only knowing you for a week before you returned to me."

James turns his attention to Laz. His breathing is steady now and his words articulate.

"To know Evie *is* to love her," James begins, leering from below. "And I feel as if I've known her my entire life."

My heart pitters with affection as a new batch of tears stripes my cheeks.

These past few months have shown me the true meaning of sacrifice. Jenna's lips graze my palm with painful concession, an unspoken acceptance of a love she deemed one-sided; James, on his knees with his hands cradled behind his head, all fight lost in his eyes.

Laz's marred face, the fruits of his sacrifice on grotesque display for the rest of his life.

But I *am* worthy of such sacrifices—I know that now. I always have been.

And so are they.

Sunlight creeps into the room in small slivers beyond the edges of the closed curtains. The illuminated dust particles dance in midair, and all the strength I thought was lost the moment I awoke in the white room over three months ago returns to me in a newfound wave of valor.

I've fought my entire life to escape my mental prison—to embrace my demons and find peace within the darkness. But the shadows are no place for me.

They never were.

I inhale deeply, all tears regressed and replaced with a courage worthy of those I love.

"I see you," I say to Laz in dulcet tones that I'm certain have made him quake.

"What are you talking about?" he murmurs, his eyes still locked on James.

"I see you," I repeat, shifting upright and climbing to my feet. My disheveled dress falls where it may as I take slow steps toward Laz and brush the tears from my cheeks. "I see you...through *her* eyes, Laz."

The gun shakes in his hand in my periphery, but he has my complete attention. "I once mistook you for an angel—*my* angel— of song and firelight. My guardian who could create symphonies with his fingertips and conquer the very darkness that crippled me."

I'm beside him now, craning my neck to speak softly into his ear. This is only for him, and I need him to understand the truth behind every single word. "You bring Papa's warmth to life...But you are no angel," I whisper. "And you are certainly no monster."

He looks at me then, his eyes glistening despite the furrow in his brow. He appears shaken as I bring my lips to his ear. "There are no monsters in this world, Laz." I cup his cheek. "Nor angels." His gaze locks on mine. "There is only you..." I trace a finger along his uneven, mangled flesh, from temple to lips. "And me."

I capture his mouth with mine in a deep, impassioned kiss. He tenses initially, then falls into the graceful dance of our lips becoming one. Everything all at once fades around us as his hand finds my lower back, pulling me closer, and my core ignites in a barrage of hot cinders as our lips part and our tongues connect. I dart mine across his lip as I consume his taste: an amber ripple of whiskey warmth compromising my faculties as if it were the real thing.

His kiss makes me dream of winter when I used to wish for spring—the snowfall of my namesake falling hand-in-hand with the affection I possess for Lazaro Moretti.

My fingers imprison his hair, and his hands worship the swell of my hips as our bodies fuse together in liquid passion. Small moans trickle from his throat—or are they mine?—as I drown in the forbidden desires elicited from his touch.

I pull away and kiss his tear-streaked scars—love, devotion, and unquestionable sacrifice etched in their twisted lines.

Sigh. Those beautiful lines.

My fingers find his fallen tears as I caress his handsome cheek and shower the other with kisses.

We fall into a tight embrace as he sobs into the crook of my neck. Holding him against me, I absorb his strength as his walls come tumbling down. I kiss his hair, then his ear, and pet him as he falls apart.

When he finally straightens, trembling all the while, and I see his red, swollen eyes, I lean in and kiss what's left of his fallen tears. Their taste harkens back to better days by the sea with Papa by my side.

"My mother was never given a choice," I say softly as I trail my fingers through his hair and behind his ear. "Please don't do to me what my father did to her."

His jaw slacks, but he doesn't say a word.

"You can still give me the choice she never had."

The hard line of his body quivers against me as I lean in, place a single kiss upon his scars, and whisper, "I command it."

A hoarse inhale pushes past his parted lips. I rest my palm

against his chest, and his heart is racing so fast, concern soon overwhelms my senses. But I force myself to push it aside.

I can't waver. Not now.

Never again.

For a moment, I fear I've failed. His tears have ceased and he's gone oddly stiff. But he's visibly crestfallen, forcing my nimble heart to ache for him.

In many ways, it always will.

His gun drops to the floor, and my attention follows. When he makes no move for it, hope washes over me as I realize he's surrendered.

Replete with compassion, he holds my face in his hands. "As my queen commands." Tender lips press against the tip of my nose before I sink against his chest, enveloped in his arms.

A torrent of footsteps echo in the hall.

"We don't have much time," he says, stepping away. He turns to James, who still waits on his knees. "You have to get her out of here."

James hurries over to me and pulls me into him, kissing the crown of my head.

"I never meant to hurt her," Laz says, his voice laced with panic.

Based on the silence that follows, James does not seem too forgiving.

"Just promise me one thing," Laz continues. James shifts against me but does not respond. "Promise me that, no matter what, you won't let her fall into her father's hands."

I step away to survey his face. James appears cool and collected. Almost irritated.

"I don't work for Denardo. And I sure as hell didn't come here to help him get his hands on her. I'm here to bring Evie home—with *me*—and I needed his help to get here. End of story. As far as I'm concerned, this whole fucking island can burn straight to the ground...with all of you on it."

"James," I almost say in an attempt to barter peace between them but then think better of it.

"Fair enough," Laz replies. "Follow me." He snatches his gun from the floor and hurries over to the fireplace. A cluster of fire pokers sits in their holder alongside it, unremarkable yet drawing his attention all the same. He pulls the silver one to the right until it clinks, then waits as the fireplace swivels open. "Come on." He waves us on but does not wait before bending low and disappearing into the passageway.

James retrieves his firearm, tucks it into his waistband, then takes me by the hand and follows Laz into the tunnel. When the fireplace closes softly behind us, we are enshrouded in darkness, save for the single cone of light from Laz's phone. These passages are narrower than the ones below the manor. But it widens just as we hit a junction where our options are to continue straight or turn left. We follow Laz left, my heels clicking loudly as I struggle to maintain their pace as we approach a set of spiral stairs.

We do not climb or descend. Instead, Laz stops at a lever in the wall of the landing just as goose bumps overtake me. I long to be free of these frigid tunnels for good. But without knowing what threat lies beyond, I find a certain comfort within their narrow confines.

The heavy groan of the lever is a familiar one by now. Laz pushes it open, and the wall pops outward, revealing a space I know I've seen before.

The large bed with navy-blue bedding comes into view first. Then the nightstands, and the dresser...

I've become so turned around, I didn't recognize that I've been through this secret door before.

It's Laz's bedroom.

And we've emerged from the large mirror that hangs in the corner opposite the door.

Laz motions for us to stay put inside the passage and holds a single finger to his lips to silence us.

I peek around the corner and into the room as he creeps inside. *What are we doing here?*

After scanning the room, he motions for us to follow. The bedroom door stands wide open, and I dread the sound of footsteps coming at any moment.

It's quiet. Too quiet. As my pulse bombards my eardrums, I fear I may double over.

It isn't safe here.

We need to go. Now.

I shift closer to the bed and lean against one of the posters, watching Laz remove the large framed photograph of my mother off the wall over the mantel and lean it against the fireplace. Behind it, a large safe awaits, embedded in the wall. It pops open easily for Laz upon a code entry, at which time he removes a black lock box and sets it on the bed.

"James," Laz says. "Get the door." His eyes never leave the box.

James steps away just as a gravelly voice calls out, "Allow me." The door slams shut with violent force by a man who emerges from the hallway, his pistol drawn.

He locks it before returning his attention to us with a suave adjustment of his blazer.

It's the man from the atrium.

Frank Denardo.

My blood curdles—not from the sound of the lock engaging but from the sight of the man I've been warned about since I was brought here.

Who stands with his gun pointed directly at Laz.

"Neve," the man says. "It's so good to see you." He takes a step in my direction, but Laz darts between us, his revolver drawn on the man. James pulls me away to the far side of the room, nearest the windows, forcing me behind him.

Frank's gaze follows me. "You're every bit as beautiful as I imagined."

"*You son of a bitch*," Laz sneers. "What are you doing here?"

"I'm here to take back what's mine," Frank replies, his lips upturned in a grin. "If you'll kindly hand her over, and the contents of that box, I'll be on my way—"

"Not a chance," Laz replies.

"You don't seem to understand," Frank continues. "It's over, Moretti. You've lost. Your place is surrounded, your guards are dead, and I'm not leaving without my things." His voice has hardened, sending a fresh batch of terror coursing through my veins.

"Now," Frank warns. "I won't ask again—"

"She isn't *things*," James sneers, racking the slide of his pistol and aiming it at Frank. "And there's no way in hell she's going with you."

Frank flits an irate look at James. "What in the fuck do you think you're doing?" His face contorts in anger. "We had a deal, goddammit. I agreed to help get you here if you helped me bring her back—"

"I lied." James twists his gun in a little shrug.

"You stupid son of a bitch." Frank froths with rage, straightening his shoulders and his gun.

A shot rings out, piercing my eardrums. My knees buckle with shock just as a second one cuts through the room. I scream into my hands as my hip collides with the windowsill behind me.

When I peek through my fingers, I realize the only other person still standing is James.

And I can't seem to stop screaming.

Low grunts resonate from the floor as I round the corner of the bed. Laz is on his back, the gore of his wound apparent as he cradles his belly, his face contorted in agony.

James hurries to Frank and kicks his gun away, keeping his own drawn and aimed at my father.

It isn't until I fall to my knees beside Laz that I can see Frank, who is lying on his side, cradling his left shoulder, moaning in anguish. "You're one dumb motherfucker, you know that?" Frank spits, his gaze narrowed on James. "You just signed your death certificate, son—"

"*Son...*" A strange cackle penetrates the room from somewhere nearby. I follow it toward the bathroom, where the door stands wide open at the opposite side of the room. A man in a black suit emerges, with dark hair the color of mine and a scruff of a beard to match. His face is stoic, almost amused, as he casually enters the room.

David.

"I suppose it shouldn't come as a surprise that you would take James under your wing and go so far as to refer to him as your 'son.'" He inches toward his father, who stops writhing on the floor to survey him from below. "How nice that something so romantic as a wedding could bring us all together."

He steps around Frank and moves to our side of the room to face him head-on. "You're one gutless asshole, you know that?" he says to his father with a mocking tone.

Laz winces as I cover the wound in his belly, our hands intertwined in a desperate attempt to quell the bleeding. His brow is covered with perspiration as I brush the hair off his forehead and whisper reassurances I'm not entirely sure I believe.

David steps around the foot of the bed and eyes Laz upon the floor, his face falling sullen as he sees me tending to him helplessly. He snatches a pillow from the bed, removes the case, and hands it to me before placing the pillow under his head. Laz flinches, sucking in a sharp breath through clenched teeth when I press the pillowcase to his injury, blood soaking through the material in seconds.

Teeming with worry, David adjusts the pillow to bring Laz's head more upright. "You're going to be all right," he reassures him. His voice is as calm as I need it to be, but my doubts are unwavering.

He places a hand on Laz's chest and pauses for several beats, studying him. I pore over what he must be thinking and bite my tongue to keep it from spilling questions that are not my business.

David stiffens, drawing his shoulders back. "He only ever meant to keep you safe," he fumes, his focus cemented on Laz. I know it's meant for me, and it strikes me with blunt force.

"David," Laz wheezes.

"He and my mother both," he continues, ignoring Laz's weak pleas. "You weren't taken. She arranged to have you sent away. Did you know that?" He peels his gaze upward to look at me, his eyes glistening with a sinister resentment.

Laz raises a shaky arm to stop him, but David stands and moves outside of his reach.

"I know," I whisper, craning my neck to see him.

"Did *you*?" David sneers, turning his attention to Frank and taking large strides to reach him. He grabs Frank by the collar, who raises a bloody hand in surrender as David yells in his face. "Laz told me my mother arranged everything to get Neve away from you. Why? What did you do? You sick son of a bitch..." Sharp groans pierce the room as David's fist pummels our father's face. I bury myself in the crook of Laz's neck, unable to watch.

"Enough," James hollers. Scuffling and muffled grunts follow. I don't look until they've stopped.

"Did you know?" David screams at his father again. "Did you know that Neve wasn't kidnapped? That my mother was desperate to keep her away from you?"

Frank shifts awkwardly to his knees, his breathing heavy. "Yes," he replies, wiping the back of his hand over his bleeding nose.

David stumbles away as if the wind has been knocked out of him.

"She confessed it to me one night," Frank continues, leering at David with a tone of pure malevolence. "Believe me." Frank's eyes narrow. "It's the last thing she ever did."

David cradles his midsection with a protective arm. He backs into one of the bed posters as if in a daze. "You covered it up," he mumbles under his breath, as if to himself.

A sharp cough spews past Laz's lips, and I return my attention to him, a small spray of blood finding the placket of his shirt as it coats his lips. I press harder on his wound. "We have to get you to a hospital," I whisper, tears falling past my chin and onto my gore-covered hands. He shakes his head, each breath more labored than the last.

"What did you do?" David jeers, snapping out of his stupor and transcending into something far more vengeful.

He pushes away from the bed poster and leaps at Frank, landing blows that seem to crack bones. "You killed her, didn't you?" he screams as James tries to pull him off. "What did you do, huh?" He lunges for his father again, but James's grip around him holds firm. "What did you do?" Shrugging James off, he advances on Frank but doesn't strike another blow. Instead, he elects to spew hate from his lips. "Did you pay the pathologist to lie on the death certificate? Make up some bullshit about her swallowing pills?" He towers over Frank, who remains on his knees, James hanging close by, ready to pounce in an instant. "*Answer me.*"

Frank watches his son's antics in silence, one that speaks more than a thousand words, and my blood goes cold as I realize David's accusations are true.

"How did you do it?" he asks through clenched teeth. "You couldn't risk doing anything that would have conflicted with your bullshit story. Did you smother her? Choke the life out of her so no one would find out about who you *really* are?"

James reaches for him, and they slink to the floor in tandem as David's knees begin to buckle. He keeps his friend at bay while offering what little comfort he can.

David grips his hair by the root, his face flush with anger. "I knew it," he mutters. "I fucking knew it. I always knew you had something to do with her death." He pulls away from James to sneer at his father. "Do you have any idea what this has done to me?" His eyes are red-rimmed and glistening profusely as he shouts. "You knew I bore that, blaming myself for so long...thinking it was my fault that Neve disappeared." He covers his eyes. "She knew you were dangerous. And you murdered her." Sadness assaults him, and his voice cracks beneath the heartache. "How could you do it?" His voice devolves into a whimper, tearing my fucking heart into pieces.

"Murdered?" I whisper, wishing my ears deceived me. I look at Laz in horror. "Did you know?"

Several labored breaths pass in silence, his eyes fluttering heavily. "I always...suspected." The weakness of his voice suffocates me with impending tears. I can't believe he never told me this.

"Here." He removes the key hanging from around his neck with great pains and hands it to me. It's the closest I've ever been to the old antique key. Its intricate scroll patterns enhance its mystery as I admire it in my bloodstained palm.

With a shaky finger, he points to the box on the bed.

I hand the key to James, refusing to leave his side.

Caressing Laz's scars, I watch James slide it into the keyhole, twist it once, and pop the lid open.

For a moment, nobody moves. David watches from his knees; Frank cradles his nose with his palm, blood dripping onto his white button-up shirt.

Laz's eyes are on me.

I'm only afforded a partial view, blocked mostly by James's frame as he removes the contents from the box and lays them on the bed. From what I can see, it's mostly papers.

"What is it?" I ask, my cheeks itching from the tears that have begun to dry.

James scrutinizes the papers, flipping through them one at a time. When he slumps against the edge of the bed in dismay, I know something's wrong.

"James," I press.

"Is this real?" he mutters, flitting a look over to Laz with widened eyes.

A weak nod is his response.

"Those don't belong to you," Frank rasps with a wicked tongue.

"What is it?" I ask, terrified by what I might find.

James shows me one of the pages. It's a ledger bearing a long list of names in the far left column, a list of dates, city names, and dollar amounts in others, with a seemingly random four-digit number in the far right column. "I don't understand," I reply, looking up at James.

"The names," he begins, addressing Laz. "There's only one word. These are all last names?"

Laz nods.

"What are these dates?" James asks, pointing to the sheet.

"None of your fucking concern," Frank harangues. David leaps to his feet, grabs Frank's pistol off the floor from the corner nearest us, and points it at him. "We're *making it* our concern." He presses his index finger against his father's forehead, making him waver. "You blamed me for Neve's disappearance. Treated me like a complete fuckup my entire life because of it. Now's your chance to tell me—to tell *us*—why my mother gave up her only daughter to keep her away from you."

The silence is palpable as James brings one of the papers over to David and angles it at him.

"No need." David brushes it off. "I've seen them."

"What?" James asks, his mouth agape.

"I'm the one who stole them from my father's office years ago."

Frank's face curves into a snarl. "You traitorous little shit—"

"Not that I knew what in the hell they were. I was just following orders. But now's your chance to explain yourself." He presses the pistol to Frank's forehead. "I insist."

But Frank doesn't say a word.

David steps away, pacing with frustration, and I sit on pins and needles, waiting for him to explode.

"Birth...dates," Laz wheezes. James turns his attention to us and falls to his knees next to Laz.

"These—" James trails his finger down one of the columns. "These are birth dates?"

Laz gives a slight nod. I caress his hair, caring so little about anything other than getting him help. If what Frank says is true about the house being surrounded, I fear the worst. But I push it aside, refusing to cower to my trepidations when Laz needs me to be strong right now.

"And these?"

Laz winces in pain.

"Shhh...it's all right," I try to soothe him, pressing kisses to his damp forehead.

James flips through the other pages of the ledger again, trying to make sense of it all. "There are hundreds of names. Each with a date of birth. And cities that span the world. Like here"—he shows me the paper again and points—"is some name Genoa, date of birth October 7th, 2003. Then there's another date, July 11th, 2006, 3.1 million dollars, the city of Istanbul, 3409." He flips to another page. "And the list goes on and on..."

I'm barely afforded a moment to process it all before the pages sail nearby. James has dropped them, his body stiffening as he stares at the single page remaining in his hands. "*My God...*"

David hurries over to him and peers at the paper.

"What is it?" I ask, skin clammy.

"It's..." James remains motionless, and it takes everything in my power not to leap to my feet and shake him. "A name." He lowers the paper to look at me, his downturned eyes filling me with dread. "Denardo." He wipes the back of his hand over his mouth before continuing. "Date of birth, January 9th, 1992. Followed by another date: January 9th, 1997. 27.9 million dollars. Zurich. 8108."

"What?" I say on a pinched exhale as I turn to Laz for answers. Tears well up the longer I wait.

Frail and pallid, he peers at me. A softness in his gaze pulls me in, and I would kiss him were it not for the uneasiness that holds me captive upon hearing my real last name and date of birth on this mysterious document.

"Date..." Laz swallows deeply. "Of purchase."

My entire body turns to ice.

James consumes an audible gasp, then scoops the other papers off the floor, studying them intently. "A purchase date," he repeats, bewildered. "Which falls on your fifth birthday."

David shifts his weight, and his head falls back, as if a wave of understanding has washed over him. "She knew." It's more a statement of realization than a question, directed at no one in particular.

He turns toward his father. "She knew, didn't she? She found these papers. Saw her own daughter's name on them." David crumples the paper, infected with rage. "You already had a buyer all lined up, didn't you? You fucking asshole. You were going to *sell her*."

"You'll all burn for this," Frank threatens.

James drops next to me and shows me the names on some of the other pages, then whispers, "They're all children."

I shake my head in disbelief.

"Look at their dates of birth compared to their purchase dates." He looks at Laz, whose eyes are heavier than ever. "He was trafficking children."

Laz nods slowly.

"How long have you known?" I ask him.

He takes a deep breath and shudders on the exhale. "Your mother told me...after I was... given these." He points weakly to his scars. "Shortly...before...her death."

With a blood-soaked hand, he reaches for my cheek. I lean in to meet him halfway, embracing the gore, for it's so insignificant, and I welcome any form of tenderness that might shake my numbness.

"You must know..." His voice is raspy and laborious. "There's still...an active price...for her. Frank..." His eyelids tease at closing. "Still needs her..."

David fists his hair and screams, the gun still in hand. Raw, chilling screams that still my heart. As if his entire world has come crashing down, and he's searching for air amid the rubble.

Without another moment's thought, I leave Laz's side, cross the room to David, and throw my arms around him. His frame presses against mine as he sinks into our embrace, sobbing into my shoulder. I don't fight my own tears—impossible in the presence of his—as the world goes still and my brother fights for strength. "It's okay," I whisper soothingly. "You aren't alone in this anymore. None of this was your fault. None of it."

I brush the tears from his cheeks.

A low murmur sounds behind us. "He still...needs her..." Laz repeats.

The softness in David's face twists into something violent before he steps away from me. "Not anymore." In a motion too quick for me to process until it's too late, David points the gun at Frank and fires until the only sound remaining is the clicking of an empty clip.

Frank slumps to the floor, blood pooling around his head and seeping toward the baseboard.

I squeal into my hand as David tosses his gun to the floor with an air of satisfaction that terrifies me.

Footsteps close in on us from the hallway.

"We have to go," James says.

I fall beside Laz and grab his hand. "We need to get you to a hospital." My chest hardens as tears brew from within, knowing Laz will likely refuse.

His expression is so peaceful that it angers me. He's given up, and I won't stand for it.

"*Please,* Laz," I beg as my vision blurs all over again.

"You…" He reaches for my hair and tucks it behind my ear. "Look so much like her…"

I know all of this. Please. Just let me help you.

"But you are…so different…in so many ways." His eyelids droop heavily, all color gone from his face. "It's in your…differences…that I've…come to…love you."

I choke on a sob as his words escape in a whisper.

"Evelyn Foster."

The sound of my real name on his lips consumes me, heart and soul, as sobs rack my entire body. I kiss his scars—those perfectly imperfect lines that have saved my life in so many ways. I shower them with the adoration they deserve as a low rattle emanates from his chest. It gives me pause.

Pressing my forehead to his temple, teardrops trickle from the tip of my nose and onto his marred cheek. "I love you," I whisper as I caress his face, all the warmth faded from his skin.

When I pull away, his eyes are vacant and his chest static.

He's gone.

CHAPTER 57
EVIE

A barrage of gunfire penetrates the bedroom door just as David, James, and I escape through the mirror, into the passageway. It closes softly behind us as I squint into the darkness.

"Where the fuck are we?" David asks, aiming the flashlight on his phone along the stone walls. The papers he gathered from the room are tucked neatly under his arm.

James's hand finds mine and grips it tight. "I have no idea."

"This whole place is surrounded by Frank's foot soldiers," David continues. "How did you all get here, anyway?"

James waits, as if mulling over his answer. "We hijacked the ferry that was meant for the wedding guests." He cranes his neck, surveying the arched ceiling. "They're still ashore."

David almost seems impressed. "There's no way the west dock hasn't been locked down by now. Laz always has men patrolling the western bank."

The sound of splintering wood in the bedroom beyond ignites a sense of urgency in all of us. James ejects the magazine from his firearm, the cartridges within catching the light, before he snaps it back into place, racks the slide, and tucks it back into his waistband.

"That's why Frank arranged for a boat to be waiting at the

north docks," James replies. "In case the other one was surrounded. We just have to find a way to get there."

"We're so fucked," David says with a heavy exhale as he examines our surroundings.

"No," I say. "These passageways lead to tunnels underneath the manor. There's an entire system that goes all over the island."

My eyes have adjusted enough that I can see the look of surprise on James's face. "How do you know that?"

David cuts in before I can respond. "A maze of tunnels?" Defeat is ripe on his tongue. "I mean, that's great and all, but how are we supposed to navigate them and get the hell out of here?"

I sigh and brush the back of my hand over my cheek. It's horribly tacky, and I can't tell if it's from the tear shed or the blood that's since dried and left my hands a crimson mess. "Follow me." I drop James's hand and lead the way to the spiral staircase that awaits up ahead.

Our descent into the underbelly is quick, the slope in the floor unkind to a woman in heels. David fires questions as we go, some filled with uncertainty, others with irritation that Laz never told him about any of this.

I ignore them all.

We pass the first iron ladder, into the second passage that cuts off to the right. "What about—" James begins, pointing to the ladder that leads to the middle of the woods somewhere due west of the manor. "No," I reply without a glance over my shoulder. "It's locked. This way."

My heels click loudly as we pick up speed down the long stretch of tunnel. It'll be several minutes before the next junction.

The yellow *L* above an arrow appears briefly in the bouncing beam of light as we approach another junction.

"Now what?" David asks between pants.

I don't hesitate. "This way." I wave them to continue straight. There's a brief pause before their footsteps echo behind me.

"How do you know where you're going?" James calls out.

"Because." I stop and wait for them to catch up. "I've been mapping out these tunnels for months." James reaches me first. "It's how I was planning on finding my way back to you."

A brazen flare flickers in his eyes as he stops to face me. Without a moment wasted, he brings his parted lips to mine, as if drinking me in with an unprecedented need. It's only been a week since our clandestine meeting in the statuary, yet it sets my heart aflame as if I'm tasting him for the first time. He finds my hips, caressing the wedding dress that was meant to be touched by another.

Thoughts of Laz take root at the forefront of my mind, where I suspect they'll be for a very long time. My throat tightens when I imagine the way he looked when I touched his cheek for the last time. I ache for the vision of his face as it was when it was full of life —brooding but impassioned, stoic but often on the brink of laughter.

"We don't have time for this," David growls as he shuffles past us.

We continue the rest of the way in silence, the two of them following close behind me. When the sound of water plinking into small pools becomes more apparent, I know another junction is close. The main tunnel continues straight, but another branches off to the right at a slight angle.

I can't remember which way to the north end. There are no letters or arrows indicating the proper way; I had lost the grease pencil in the rainstorm, and I was so discombobulated on the way back.

Before either of them can say anything, I motion for them to follow me down the tunnel that continues straight, hoping I'm not leading them on a wild goose chase. There are tunnels I never had the chance to explore, and a wrong turn may keep us down here far longer than we're prepared to face.

We pass a ladder of metal rebar in the center of the tunnel, small cylinders of sunlight shining down from the holes in the grate above.

"Here?" David asks, grabbing one of the ladder rungs.

"No," I reply. "Further."

I don't recall this central ladder, and I fear I've taken us the wrong way. Fueled with the hope that this tunnel will lead us somewhere at the north end of the island, I trudge onward. The walls have grown damp, the scent of briny must and wet soil hanging heavily in the air. Fallen leaves that found their way past the grates stick to the bottom of my heels.

A full beam of light shines from above at the far end of the hall. Picking up speed, I run for it, filled with adrenaline as it all starts to feel familiar. The walls widen into a circular dead end, a metal ladder in the center with a puddle at the base.

A small object catches my eye on the floor against the wall.

David has already scaled the first few rungs, the papers held in his teeth, by the time I pick the item up. It's my grease chalk. It's filthy, but it tells me everything I need to know.

We're in the right spot.

"This is it," I say.

David climbs to the top as James pulls me in for another kiss. For a moment, I debate letting David figure out the next steps on his own while I relish James's touch.

A sharp whistle steals my attention. "Come on," David says from outside the tunnel, a mere silhouette against the sunlight.

James ushers me up first and follows quickly behind.

The daylight is stark, and I shield my eyes against it. It's a beautiful, cloudless day, and there's not a soul in sight.

A handful of small houses with shaker siding dot the roadside where we've emerged. No cars to be seen or heard, no voices, only the gentle call of birds that flit across the sky and the lapping of water against the boathouses.

A light breeze rustles the leaves as James joins me by my side.

"Where is everyone?" he asks.

I look both ways, searching for any signs of life. "I have no idea," I whisper. "Maybe Laz had the island cleared out for the wedding?"

A pained look furrows James's face, and I instantly regret my words.

"Which dock is it?" I ask, changing the subject.

"Emerson said to look for a blue boathouse with an American flag," James answers.

"Emerson?" I crinkle my face, confused.

With my hand in his, we cross the dirt road to the waterside. James keeps glancing at the hillside to our right as if waiting for a hail of gunfire to rain on us from the forest's edge.

It's making me nervous as hell.

"There," David calls out with a pointed finger, pulling me away from my gruesome thoughts.

An American flag flaps in its mount on the gable of a boathouse the color of the sky.

We shuffle alongside the small Cape Cod house with weathered gray shingles and white trim, past a black moped in the side yard, and onto the dock beyond.

The boathouse door stands ajar. James tilts an ear toward the opening.

"What is it?" I ask. "Is this Emerson person not here?"

"Only one way to find out." David pushes the door open with a loud creak, filling the boathouse with sunlight.

The walls are lined with fishing rods, narrow wooden shelves of tackle boxes, life vests, coolers, and hose attachments. A large fishing boat sits within the structure on the opposite end.

But none of it matters, because my heart is in my fucking throat.

Her wildfire hair catches my attention first, but only a split second before the streaks of mascara that line her cheeks and the terror that plagues her eyes.

Click stands facing the door, his hair slicked back, his arm around the woman I'd gladly die for.

With a gun pressed to her temple.

Blood bombards my neck and ears as I lay waste to the man in all the ways my tormented mind can conceive. When his lips curl into a malicious grin, I've already mentally cut it from his face until he's screaming in agony.

A man I've never seen before, with a distressed baseball cap and simple clothes, is on his knees, his hands held in front of him in surrender.

The déjà vu is almost too much for me to bear.

"Jenna," I exclaim, taking hurried steps toward her.

"Another step, and she dies," Click growls. Jenna winces at the pain as he presses the gun harder to her temple.

"You fucking—" David begins.

"Finish that sentence," Click interjects, tightening his grip around her waist. "By all means."

Bile rises high in my throat as I try to figure out what the fuck to do.

"Hands where I can see 'em," he instructs. We raise our hands in compliance.

"Whatever you want, Click. It's yours. Just please don't hurt her," David begs, his tone softer than I've heard it in ages.

"I want the papers." He nods toward the stack that's now held high in David's raised hand. "And I want her." Click looks at me.

"No fucking way," James seethes, stepping forward aggressively. Jenna yelps in agony as Click jams the gun harder against her temple.

I grab James by the arm to stop him and hold my hand out to Click. "Stop. Please." I bite my lip to impede the quivering.

With a stern look, I direct James to take a step back before returning my attention to Click. "I'll go with you. Just let her go."

Tears cascade down Jenna's face. "Evie, don't."

"Laz and Frank are dead," James huffs. "She's of no value to you—"

"She's of high value to someone. Buyer 8108, to be exact. And with Frank gone, I'll be the one to collect." He flicks his tongue over his lower lip, and it churns my stomach raw.

"But she's an adult now," James says, confused. "You're saying—"

"She's still the daughter of a boss." He tightens his arm around Jenna as she wriggles in his grasp. "As long as his empire is intact, men will be clambering to marry her off to their sons...or take her for themselves. Especially since she hasn't borne anyone else's children."

Faintness washes over me, an unpleasant tingle attacking my legs.

"I'll never let you take her," James barks, inching closer despite my attempts to keep him in place.

"It's not up to you to decide." His smile widens. "So what do you say, baby bird? You for her?"

I cup my mouth to cover the sobs that are becoming increasingly difficult to choke back. I'd die for her. Absolutely. And, as it would seem, I'd even allow myself to be sold for her. But my legs have turned to lead, despite my best efforts to complete the exchange.

"What's the matter?" he taunts. "Your wings still broken? Haven't yet figured out how to fly?"

His laughter cuts me with a thousand knives. But it's nothing compared to the sheer malevolence of Papa's nickname for me on this dastardly man's tongue.

"Where did you hear that name?" I ask, tears burning my eyes.

A chuckle rumbles low in his throat.

"You may have had Laz fooled, but I see you for exactly who you are. You've been working for Frank all this time, haven't you? A goddamn rat?" I scream.

Jenna sniffles, but I don't take my eyes off Click. "You were there that night. *I saw you.* Now tell me where in the hell you heard that name."

The pause has me in a chokehold. I await the sound of a gunshot taking everything from me in a single instant. But a man as cocky as Click, who's taunted me every chance he could get, wouldn't end this little charade so abruptly.

Especially knowing he'd be a dead man when it's all over.

I take a daring step forward. "I'm not going anywhere with you until you admit it."

His brow scrunches as his smile fades, piercing the base of my neck with a wicked chill. The calmness of his demeanor is worse than his haughty laughter.

I brush a hand over my racing heart.

"Fly, baby bird," he says deliberately, savoring my death sentence as each word robs me of breath. "*Fly.*"

My chest quivers, strength eluding me with each passing second as my mind is consumed with a vile, homicidal hatred for the man in the fucking reptile shoes.

"Your father's final words," he continues, his delivery even slower than before. "As he choked out his last breath."

I'm hyperventilating. My breathing has turned to wheezing, my shoulders suddenly solid stone. James reaches for me as my knees threaten to buckle. "Hands where I can see 'em," Click hollers. But it's muffled by the ringing in my ears.

Papa was murdered.

I hold my hand under my nose, stifling the sobs that continue to torment me.

It was true all this time.

He didn't leave me.

"I believe his last words were meant for you," he jeers.

Fly, baby bird. Fly.

Words spoken by a man strung up, clinging to life, with only one thing on his mind as he slowly slipped from this world.

Me.

My capacity to think rationally flees with each word he utters, my vision flooding with redness the shade of my blood-soaked hands.

I shift closer to James, our shoulders touching, but address David. "Give him the papers."

David and I exchange looks behind James. His eyebrow flicks with confusion.

"Give him the papers, David," I repeat, more sternly than before. Except this time, I make a gesture behind James's back where Click can't see it. I start with a closed fist, then raise my arm and open it, splaying my fingers wide.

James's gun sits snugly in the back of his waistband.

It's a Glock, according to the markings on the hand grip.

There's no safety lever. The safety is in the trigger. Which means it's ready to fire so long as there's a round in the chamber.

Laz taught me that.

I brush a finger against the hand grip, making sure James doesn't feel it. David looks at the firearm, then back at me, a silent moment of understanding etched in our exchanged glance.

"You want the papers?" He turns his attention back to Click. "Then you can have 'em." David tosses them upward dramatically, and they sail to the ground in a scattered mess.

Click's gun goes slack as his eyes widen in horror, his attention following the documents that land in the water alongside the dock.

Gabriella's lifeless eyes, my father's panicked voice, Jenna's tear-stricken face, the sound of those clicking shoes haunting me in the night, and James's unshakable convictions are what propel me forward. Devoid of all thoughts except for what comes next, I remove the gun from James's waistband, reach Click with a sense of purpose that pumps life into my veins, and aim the gun at his temple. "Can you fly, you son of a bitch?" Tears spill past my lashes as I scream his nightmarish taunts back at him. "*Can you fly?*"

Blood spatters onto my face as the gunshot shakes the boathouse.

There's screaming—lots of screaming.

And shuffling feet.

Hands grip me by the shoulders as if expecting me to drop. But I've never felt more surefooted.

Click's lifeless body is splayed across the dock.

For several seconds, it doesn't seem real. As if my mind has left my body.

But it *is* real.

It's over.

The gun is no longer in my hand. I'm not sure who removed it.

"Evie," a faint voice calls out.

Blood seeps between the boards, pulling me into some sort of daze.

"Evie," the voice calls out again, louder this time.

"Jen," I whisper, peeling my gaze away from Click.

Like a light switch snapping me back to reality, I fall to the ground beside her and scoop her into my arms. David sinks to his knees and presses a loving hand to her back, but it's my shoulder on which she sobs.

James kisses my hair as I cradle Jen.

"Is she all right?" Emerson asks, looking at her morosely.

"She's going to be fine," I whisper. I pull her away to lock eyes on her. "You're going to be fine," I tell her before kissing her forehead. Her puffy, tear-soaked face is the most beautiful thing I've ever seen.

"You guys should go," David says, moving away to gather the fallen papers.

Jenna regards him with a worried look.

"You're not coming with us?" I ask.

He scoops the last of the papers from the water and plops them onto the dock.

"I can't. There are things I need to take care of here."

"Wait, what—" James begins.

"The three of you go with him." He nods toward Emerson. "And don't stop until Evie is far away from here."

"I don't understand," I say.

David plants his hands on his hips, his tone sharp. "With Frank and Laz dead, there'll be assholes from all over looking to claim a piece of this ash heap. These documents"—he scoops them up and holds them ostentatiously—"contain information that would make a man rich beyond his wildest dreams through blackmail alone." He releases a heavy sigh and looks away. "And if the wrong people discover Laz and Frank are dead, there's no telling who might come for Evie." He rifles through the papers and pulls one from the pile. "When I was gathering everything from inside Laz's box, I also found this." He hands it to James. I wait with bated breath for him to shed some light as he examines it. "It's a notice of advancement," David continues. "A glorified bill of sale, if you will." He looks at me. "For her."

"My God," James mumbles under his breath.

"Someone paid a pretty penny for her when she was still a baby, the exchange due on her fifth birthday. They will be looking to collect." He pauses as James's eyes widen.

"Unless, of course, I destroy these," David continues. "And everything else..."

James shakes his head in disbelief. "You never looked at any of these documents when you stole them from your father?"

"Nothing more than a cursory glance." He shakes his head. "I was ordered to recover the file. Not to look through it. I would never disobey Laz's orders." A sense of dispiritedness is etched on his face, as if realizing all over again that Laz is gone.

"Now go. We're running out of daylight, and there's still so much to do."

Emerson reaches for Jenna's hand and pulls her to her feet. "Come," he says, waving me toward him as he guides Jenna to his boat.

"You aren't going back to that house?" James warns, looking at David. But it sounds more like a command.

"Yes."

"With all of Frank's men there? They'll kill you—"

"It's a risk I have to take."

"But how? Back through the tunnels?" James's voice is pinched with frustration.

"He can use my moped," Emerson calls out from the other end of the dock. Once Jenna has boarded his boat, he hurries back over, removes his keys from his pocket, and unhooks a single key from the cluster. "Here." He hands it to David. "And after I take them to the mainland, I can come back and pick you up. Just meet me here."

David's expression softens with a sense of reverence. "You're a good man." He slaps Emerson on the arm. "I can't thank you enough."

"This is crazy," James cuts in sharply with a slice of his hands. "I'm coming with you."

"No," I cry out.

David slowly closes the gap between them. "James, I need you to do something far more important right now." He glances at me, and his lips curl in a soft smile. "I need you to take care of my sister."

A rush of warmth floods my insides at the sentiment that seeps from his words.

"I've been a cog in this criminal wheel for far too long." David expels a deep sigh. "It needs to end."

James studies him in silence before replying, "You have my word." He pulls David into an affectionate hug. "Please be careful."

David breaches the doorway when I call out to him. "David. Wait." I hurry back down the dock and throw my arms around him. I could hold him for hours, and it wouldn't be long enough.

He's my brother.

And I can't bear the thought that I may never see him again.

When I pull away, his eyes glisten, same as mine. He gives my chin a playful pinch and says, "Take care of yourself, kiddo."

He kisses his fingers and holds them up to Jenna, as if blowing her a kiss from afar.

I don't turn to see her reaction.

I watch him from the doorway until the moped revs up and he disappears down the road.

As we peel away from the dock, back out into the blistering light, James holds me in his arms as I hold Jenna in mine. The rippling waves lull us into a state of tranquility as the sun chases the western horizon.

In only a handful of minutes, she falls into a restful state in my lap. My eyes flutter, threatening to close, when a plume of smoke from the island catches my attention.

"What is that?" I ask in a panic, sitting upright. Jenna stirs awake, and James stands for a better look.

Fearing the worst, I tell Emerson that I have to see it.

"It's not safe," he replies.

"I have to know where it's coming from." I place a hand over my heart and give him a pleading look. "I need to see it."

He increases the throttle, and we speed back toward the island, the plume growing mightier with each passing minute.

We crest the north end and speed along the eastern shore.

Before long, it comes into view.

Laz's home is engulfed in flames.

"Closer," I cry, my stomach dropping at the sight.

Emerson brings us closer until James orders him to stop. The crackling of burning cinders skims across the water as smoke billows savagely toward the sky. The roof collapses, windows shatter, and everything falls to complete devastation. Ash rains from above, drifting onto the deck of the boat, into my hair, and clinging to my wedding dress.

I peel a flake from my hair and let it fall into my palm. As the fire snaps with abandon in the distance, I recognize everything I hold dear within this speck of ruin: the passions, the sacrifices, the *future* I now get to forge.

A sense of calm washes over me—a stillness perhaps only felt under the gentle wisps of falling snow that dance so slowly, they seem suspended in midair.

As the ash cascades around me in a peacefulness befitting of my namesake, I realize that Laz was right: the first snowfall did come early this year.

Just as he predicted so gruffly in my ear one summer night— words that were frightening then but are now unapologetically riddled with truth—I have come to see, *truly see*, the man behind the scars.

And I am indubitably in love with him.

EPILOGUE
EVIE

SEPTEMBER 16ᵀᴴ — ONE WEEK LATER

Jenna shuffles between her walk-in closet and the bedroom, frantically pulling items from their hangers and tossing them into a pile on the bed. I watch from my spot against the headboard, legs outstretched and crossed at the ankle, debating whether I should stop her.

"You'll need long pants too. Jeans. I have plenty." She runs her fingers over her tousled ponytail. "Is it cold where you're going?" Without waiting for a response, she darts back into the closet, where the sound of rustling soon follows.

"Jen," I call out softly. I've never seen her so scattered, but it oddly comforts me. Usually, I'm the one who can't decide, opting to paint, play my cello, or bury my nose in a book when too many things are thrown at me.

It's nice to be the anchor for once.

Besides, ensuring I have enough things to wear for the foreseeable future seems so...insignificant. But we all handle our stresses in our own ways. Jenna is a control freak, and focusing on others keeps her mind off her own shit.

She emerges from the closet. "Yeah?"

"You don't have to do all of this." I hop off the bed and approach her.

"James will be here any minute to take you God knows where." She brushes the back of her hand over her brow. "There are things you're going to need, Eves." Spinning on her heels, she heads to the dresser.

"It isn't forever, you know," I tell her in barely a whisper.

She pauses, a drawer half out, her shoulders slumped. "I know."

I spin her around and pull her into my arms. Her forehead falls onto my shoulder as she trembles against me.

I inhale her scent, memorizing it for the last time. It never left me while I was on Eden's Green, and I know deep down, it never will. The curves of her face, the softness of her skin, her delicate laugh...these are things I take with me everywhere.

"It's just until we know it's safe to come back."

"Well." She pulls away. "Let's just hope that the FBI can do something with all of those documents David turned over to the police."

A somber shift in the air permeates the room when she meanders over to the suitcase on the bed and starts folding the last of the clothing within.

I wish she could come with me. As much as it tears me apart, it's something I just can't bring myself to ask. After what happened in the boathouse, what I believe she needs now is stability—to go back to the routines that keep her motivated and preoccupied.

A car pulls up outside as Jenna zips up the suitcase and flings it off the bed.

James is up the stairs in seconds, taking the bag and shuffling it to the car.

The air outside is damp and grossly stagnant. Now that it's mid-September, Boston will soon be rid of this awful humidity for good. But the crickets worship the night with their self-made song, adding a pleasantry to the evening air otherwise left unnoticed.

I've been dreading this goodbye since I returned to the mainland. She's part of me—embedded into my soul—and I can't believe I have to leave her again.

Tears have already found her cheeks by the time we reach the car. She throws her arms around me, making no attempts to stop her weeping. "Please be careful," she chokes out.

I can't manage to push out words, so I simply nod.

"Take good care of her," she says to James, all the while brushing my hair back over my shoulder.

"You know I will," he replies before hugging her close. It lasts longer than I would ordinarily expect—long enough for James to brush his nose against her hair and relish her scent.

Just as I did.

It gives me pause. Not because it pricks me with jealousy, and not because it strikes me as odd or inappropriate.

But because it doesn't make me feel any of those things.

There's something strangely befitting of James and Jenna coupled together. In many ways, they'd be perfect for each other. I know they've become close this summer, being there for each other when they needed it the most.

James shuts the car door behind me as I watch her through the window. She remains on the porch of her parents' house, watching as we pull away, dwarfed by the large white pillars that stripe the front facade.

The sight of her shrinking in the side mirror makes me want to scream. It's as if her diminishing silhouette is taking all of the oxygen with it. This is all wrong. Leaving her. Jenna—*my* Jenna. Her breath on my skin as she whispers secrets in my ears, hair as red as the speakeasy firelight, and those sultry fucking lips pressed to the palm of my hand...

Butterflies run rampant in my belly.

I can't do this.

"Stop the car," I protest.

James darts me a worried look.

"Stop the car," I cry out again. "We have to go back."

"Eves—"

"*We have to go back.*"

James throws the car in reverse and brings us back up the drive. It isn't even in park before I fling the door open and race to the porch steps, where Jenna still waits.

She meets me on the bottom step, her eyes wide with confusion. "What's going on—"

No hesitation.

No more wondering *what if?*

I press my mouth to hers in a deep, eager kiss, silencing her protestations and giving those butterflies everything they've been asking for all this time. She stiffens in my grasp but doesn't pull away. I want her mouth to open. I want to taste every bit of that wisecracking tongue.

But it doesn't happen.

"Evie," she says, pulling away and regarding me with complete shock. "What are you doing?" Her tone is soft but far from accusatory, for which I'm grateful. Ordinarily, I'd shy away from such vulnerability—take my feelings and incessant thoughts and squirrel them away to be muddled alone. But something has changed in me. I never really knew what I had until, one morning when I woke up in a stark room, staring at a man with scars on his face, everything and everyone I held dear had been lost.

I'll be damned if my future—my *choices*—are ever out of my hands again.

"You. You're my person, Jen," I say, remembering her words on Eden's Green. "You always have been."

Her eyes glisten in the porch light. "I don't understand."

"I can't leave you. Not again. Please come with me."

She withdraws, but her expression's pensive, which I hope means she's considering it.

"You don't have to do this"—she touches her lip, alluding to our kiss—"to coerce me to go with you. I know you don't feel the same—"

"I'm not..." I sigh. This isn't going how I planned. The humidity is making my hair stick to the back of my neck, and I resist the urge to scratch it. "I just..." How in the hell do I articulate this? How do I explain all the ways I've come to crave her, long for her, *need* her. It's confusing even to me. But she's become infused into my very skin, and the old Evie no longer exists. "I don't think I was allowing myself permission...to recognize what's always been there, deep down." I trap my lower lip in my teeth. "Does that make sense?"

She cocks her head and eyes me questioningly. "I'm not sure."

Fuck it. *Just say what you're thinking, Evie. Enough with the bullshit.*

"I love you, Jenna."

Her jaw slacks, but I don't allow it to give me pause. Instead, I straighten my shoulders to further enhance my conviction. "I love you in a way that some people go their entire lifetime and never find. The kind of love you only read about in books. A soulmate, 'written in the stars,' your-pain-is-also-mine kind of love."

I close the gap between us and reach for her cheek. "Please tell me you still feel the same."

A tear spills past her lashes and collides with my thumb. Her lip quivers, and I resist the urge to bite it still and strip any pain that lies behind it.

"You know I do," she whispers, her eyes locked on mine.

"Then kiss me, you fool." I quirk a smile that matches hers as our lips find each other once again. This time, she melts into me like liquid honey, running her fingers through my hair as I hold her frame to mine. My tongue finds hers easily, and our moans meld into one solitary purr as she presses her hips against me. Sweeter than the strawberry James teased across my lips and twice as sinful, her taste is more than I ever imagined.

The chokehold she has on me tightens as I ache with need down below. To think, if only such desire had been realized when she first kissed me more than a year ago. But it wasn't that kiss that did me in. No. It was the one she planted on my palm one week before I was taken from her. There's no way to rationalize it, but for me, that kiss—which started as a small vibration in my hand—spread its way into parts of me in which there was no coming back from. And it was that tingling palm that served as a reminder of the woman I've always loved, at a time when I never thought I'd see her again.

When we part, I let my eyes remain closed just a bit longer, savoring every moment like it may be my last.

"What about James?" she asks as my eyes flit open and find her peering at me with a touch of despondency.

The Benz is still running in the driveway. James is watching us from alongside the open driver's door, his arms braced against the roof of the car. A twinge of sadness and guilt prods at the butterflies that once took flight with ardor and grace.

"You still love him?" she asks.

My eyes don't leave him. "Very much."

She shifts in my periphery. "So what happens now?"

I wave James over. He shuts the driver's door and hurries to the porch steps.

"James, I..." The melancholy look on his face forces the words back down into my throat. I swallow hard and force myself to continue. "I can't leave her."

His face is too stoic for me to decipher a single thing he might be thinking. It's odd, actually. The James I know is so quick to react. It's a stoicism that harkens back to Laz, a mysterious man with so many tangled layers to unravel.

"I know," James says tenderly, making my heart skip a beat. "And I know she loves you, Eves. More than she may ever admit to you. But…" He turns to Jenna with softness in his eyes. "I can't let you take her from me."

A shimmer finds her eyes again, twisting me up in knots. "I know," she says, shying away in an act of surrender that makes me want to punish her with a slap on the ass.

"That's why you're coming with us," he says.

She shoots him a look of utter surprise.

As do I.

"What?" I ask him, unsure if I heard him right.

"Are you in love with me?" he asks me pointedly.

"Of course I am."

"Are you in love with her?" He nods toward Jenna, who looks just as surprised as I feel.

Deep red splotches have overtaken her neck and chest, and I catch a small tremor that rattles her shoulders. "Yes," I say on a dramatic exhale.

"Evie, look at me."

I tear my eyes away from Jenna and lock them on James.

"I'm not going to make you choose. I've seen what this has put Jenna through, and I care for her immensely. So if there's a chance you reciprocate her feelings, I can't take *this*"—he waves a hand between us—"away from her."

He turns to Jen with a soft smile. "Besides." He brings a delicate hand to her cheek. "I made a promise that I would never leave you behind, remember?" They look at each other for a long time, as if searching for validation in the other's eyes.

In a truly rare occurrence, Jenna seems speechless.

"Just know…" Turning back to me, he takes me by the hand, and my stomach does a drunken flip. "I'd rather share you with another than have no part of you at all." His gaze bounces between Jenna and me. "If you'll both have me."

No sense of jest in his stance, no levity in his tone. This man is seriously asking something of me I've never considered in my life.

We exchange glances for several moments, perhaps waiting for someone else to speak first.

The old Evie would wait until someone else broke the ice. Not anymore.

"I could never ask that of either of you," I say.

"You're not asking, Eves," James replies.

"He's right," Jenna inserts. "I did tell him about my feelings for you. He knows full well what it means for me to hear you say you feel the same way. It's all I've ever wanted..." Her voice trails off, and I silently beg her to continue. "And I adore James, more than I ever expected to."

I'm waiting for the *but.* My heart can't take it.

"I think it's best if you both take some time and really talk about all of this together. It's a big decision, and I don't want to be the reason this all falls apart," she says.

"But, Jen, I—" I begin.

"It's the right thing," she argues, taking a step back. Her attention shifts to James. "Please. Take her somewhere safe." She brushes an errant tear from her face.

"I won't leave you. I can't..." Goddammit. Fuck these fucking tears and the way they make me choke on all the words I want to say.

She steps into me with purpose and cradles my face in her hands. "It won't be forever," she whispers, repeating my words from the bedroom. "When you're both ready to call on me..." She glances at James. "You know where to find me."

She presses her lips to mine in a soft, sensual kiss. No tongue, no moans. Just a kiss rife with the anticipation of endless longing.

A kiss goodbye.

When we pull apart, James leans in, plants a hand on her hip, and kisses her on the cheek, holding it there for a long time. Her eyes flutter closed, absorbing the touch of his lips, just as I have a hundred times.

"Goodbye, Jen," he whispers in her ear.

She touches his cheek, keeping it there until tears brim. "Goodbye, James."

As we pull away in the car once again, and Jenna's silhouette shrinks against the porch light, I find peace in Jenna's words and know, with all my heart, that it won't be forever.

I will see her again.

JAMES

Evie is out on the balcony terrace, one leg bent as she leans against the railing and admires the stretch of sapphire water that kisses the horizon. It's been almost seven months, and she still speaks about the view—the terracotta rooftops that dot the hillsides and the sparkling water that's befitting of a dream—as if she's seeing it for the first time.

But it isn't the view that holds me enraptured. It's the white strapless sundress that flows over her figure and brushes against her bare feet. With skin as fair as the morning light and ebony hair that casually skims her back, the dress only enhances her angelic features in the Grecian sun.

Her cello rests in its neck stand nearby—my gift to her on her real birthday this past January. She's been playing it all morning, filling our little home with goddess-like musings that take my breath away. In fact, it was the sudden silence only a few minutes ago that diverted my attention and brought me out to the balcony to check on her.

I've been standing here admiring her ever since.

She still refuses to treat her real birthday as such and instead insists that it be a day to celebrate her mother. The painting she made that day of her mother's likeness—a woman in a white dress not so different from the one she's wearing now, wading in the surf of a long stretch of empty beach, her face on full display as it basks in the sun—hangs in our entryway. As far as I'm concerned, it's a breathtaking *self*-portrait, and I love it almost as much as I love her.

When I approach her from behind and wrap my arms around her waist, she doesn't stir. It's as if she was expecting me all along. I press my lips to the snowflake tattoo on the back of her shoulder, which now covers the scar I gave her one fateful morning in the pouring rain.

A slight chill rakes her.

So I kiss it again.

She turns to me, light dancing in her seafoam eyes, and kisses me softly on the lips. Her fingers play with my hair as my tongue enters impatiently. It has its fun against hers, pulling moans from deep in my chest as she grips my hair with a touch of violence.

And that's all the invitation I need.

Our kiss still in full swing, I pull the dress down past her breasts and hips and let it fall to the balcony floor. She giggles when I force her panties down and allow gravity to carry them the rest of the way.

But when I lift her up, wrapping her legs around my hips and balancing her on the stone railing, she pulls away. Her eyes darken like a bank of clouds rolling in over the sea.

I know that look.

I've fucked that look right off of her many times.

And today will be no exception.

I lean in to kiss the light back into her eyes, but she turns her head, and my lips land on her cheek. My stomach ripples with the challenge she's presenting me as blood rushes to my groin.

With a hard grip on her chin, I force her to face me, my eyes narrowing to match hers, and bring our mouths together in a punishing kiss. She resists me, going stiff and tightening her legs around my waist.

A small squeal teases past her lips and onto mine when I capture her bottom lip in my teeth.

When I release it, she slaps me. Hard.

I pinch her nipple as payback. She screams in pain and shoves me away, then hops off the railing, crosses her arms, and waits for me to make my next move.

We eye each other for a long time, our power struggle reaching its max. My cock is ready to come out and play, her "fighting" exciting him to the point of sheer pain. I pull my shirt up over my head, but a shuffling noise catches my attention once my vision is obscured. As I toss it aside, I catch her running past me and back into the house.

She squeals as I chase after her, our feet pounding the tile floor as she cuts the corner down the hallway and races into the bedroom. The door slams in my face right as I reach it, but I shove it open with brute force, and it strikes the wall. I lose sight of her briefly as she ducks into the walk-in closet and shoves the door closed.

The lock engages just as I grab the handle. Through her healing, my little minx learned that locks are equally paramount in keeping bad things out as they are in keeping her in, which has helped her control her anxiety around locked doors.

It has only enhanced our "playtime."

The hinges rattle in their mounts as I slam my shoulder against the door. Small bits of laughter sound from inside, fueling my adrenaline to tear down the walls that stand between me and the holes she's hiding from me.

A sharp *crack* sends wood splintering at my feet as the frame splits and the closet door crashes open. I find her sitting on the floor, her knees drawn to her chest, waiting patiently for me to breach the room and take what I want.

I grab her ankle and pull her toward me, a shrill scream filling the small space around us. She kicks. She hits. She screams. But I throw her legs apart like a ragdoll and shove my raging cock inside her nonetheless. Her wetness sends me into a tailspin as I thrust deep, finding her end with ease and forcing a small cry from her lips each time I strike.

"I *always* find you. Remember that, Evie." My proclamation only pumps more blood into my cock, threatening to make me come before I'm ready.

As I plant kisses on her neck, she shoves my face away.

So I pin her arms to the floor above her head.

Yet she still fights me.

It's cute, in a way, to think such a creature could overpower me.

Fuck, I'm gonna come.

"No," she exclaims, then bites my arm. I release it from the grip on her wrists and cry out in agony.

"The fuck?" I groan, shaking the pain out and leering at her from above.

"No," she screams again and pushes against my chest with a free hand.

My cock slips out as she scoots away, still on her back, escaping my clutches and slinking further into the closet.

I'm on her in a second. This time, I'm not fucking around. I flip her onto her belly and mount her, pinning her to the floor. Her breathing is heavy as I find her entrance again with the tip of my cock.

"Stop," she repeats with as much conviction as the last. I push my cock back into her wetness.

"*Milkshake.*"

Everything in me goes stiff at the sound of our safe word on her lips. A surge of adrenaline makes me quiver as I pull out, climb to my feet, and await further instruction.

She stands, her eyes piercing mine, all sense of helplessness long gone from her demeanor. Her shoulders are pulled back, our bodies squared. Not a drop of fear to be found.

"On your knees," she instructs.

I swiftly obey.

She seems so powerful as she stands over me, her breathtaking eyes narrowing on me like a queen would regard her faithful subjects.

Ever since Evie returned from Eden's Green, there are many changes I've noticed in her, revealed over time, bit by bit. So far, there's not a single one that hasn't been a pleasant surprise. She likes to be hunted; that much will likely never change. But there's a side to Evie that I think still surprises her as much as it does me: her will to dominate. We discovered it shortly after arriving in Kardamyli, our safe word becoming what cues the transition of power from one to the other.

This change in her is by far the most arousing, taking me to erotic depths I never thought I'd enjoy. So much so, that even hearing the word *milkshake* these days turns my dick rock-hard.

"Good boy," she coos with a gentle hand beneath my chin. *Please pet my hair. For the love of God, pet my—*

She runs her fingers through my hair as she repeats the words that drive me wild. "Such a good boy." Precum drips from my cock.

Her fingers caress my cheek. *Please, please, please slap me.* My cock pulsates from the mere hope of the commands and tender abuse that's to come.

She slaps me hard and smirks.

Fuck yes.

"You like that, don't you?" she teases. My eyes drift to her shaven slit. I want to taste it, consume every drop of wetness that glistens at her peak.

"Look at me when I'm speaking to you," she barks, gripping me hard by the chin and forcing my gaze to meet hers.

"Apologies," I reply as feebly as I can muster.

"Apologies, what?"

"Apologies, my queen."

"That's better." She smiles. "Now. For being such a good boy, I shall reward you. Would you like that?"

I nod, my cock aching with approval.

"Would you like to taste me?" she asks. "Would that please you?"

Maintaining my composure suddenly feels like an impossible feat. "Yes, my queen."

"Good." Using the closet's clothing rods for balance, she slides both of her legs onto my shoulders and thrusts her slit against my face. My tongue parts her lips, finds her clit easily, and flicks with abandon. Her entire body clenches around me as I tongue fuck my queen, her head thrown back and the clothing rattling on their hangers.

Piercing her pussy with my tongue, I lap up her wetness just as I wanted—the real reward for being so good—and find her other entrance with my finger. She bucks wildly as I penetrate her, pressing my finger deeper and suckling on her clit with as much force as I want.

"Touch yourself," she commands on a sharp, erotic exhale. "But don't you dare come."

I lower her onto the floor and sink back between her legs, stroking my cock to the same rhythm as my lapping tongue.

Wetness pools from her pink, soaking me with her butterscotch sweetness. I shove two fingers inside of it, thrusting hard, then rub it all over my cock.

Her cries escalate.

She's so close.

And so am I.

"I want you to get yourself close," she orders. "But don't you dare come."

Such a tortuous little wretch, this woman of mine. To force me to such depths of pleasure and then prohibit me from the explosion I so desperately crave.

"I'm going to come," I moan loudly against her pussy.

"Me first," she instructs. But I can tell she's fighting it. Her wetness is everywhere, her nipples are as hard as my cock, and her body is writhing so much that my tongue can barely maintain contact. I know when her clit is so sensitive that she's about to burst. And yet she hangs on.

To keep me from being able to come.

I stop stroking my cock in a desperate attempt to quell my impending orgasm.

She jerks away from me suddenly. "I never told you to stop stroking yourself. Did I?"

I sit back on my heels and hang my head low.

"Answer me."

"N-No, my queen."

"On your back," she commands with an angry point of her finger.

I do as I'm told.

My cock stretches her walls and contorts her face with pleasure as she mounts me. "Don't even think about coming until I give you permission." Her hips sway, slowly at first, tormenting a cock that's already endured enough pleasure and is now desperate for release.

She allows me to fondle her breasts as she arches her back and rides me like we may not live to see tomorrow. I grit my teeth as more precum spills, begging it to obey her orders and not release just yet.

It hurts in the best possible way, but I'm seconds away from calling her all the degrading names that I know she loves, just to get her there so I can finally come.

It's a risk, but I ask, "May I call you names, my queen? Just as you like?" I cup her breast and pinch her nipple hard. But she doesn't squeal from the pain this time. She's so close to coming that I'm certain all sensations have melded together, each one enhancing the speeding train of an orgasm.

"Yes," she grunts as she picks up speed.

I sit bolt upright, hook an arm around her back, and force her down onto my cock until she bottoms out with such aggression that she can't seem to stop shaking. "Only a little slut would torment me so," I growl as I grip her hair and bring her closer to the edge. "Now fucking come."

She holds on all the while, biting back her orgasm despite the torture it's clearly causing.

Sweat beads along my back, the muscles in my arms corded as they shove her down onto my cock angrily.

I'm at a loss for what will take my queen over the edge, and I know my cock can't hold out much longer.

"How do you want it?" I pant, leaning in to bite her lower lip. "Shall I fuck you like you're my good girl, Wats. Or like you're my goddamn queen?"

She wraps her arms around my neck, holding me close. "I don't care, Sherlock," she replies, nipping at my earlobe. "Just fuck me like you're mine."

Her salacious words skate across my ear, sending my cock into a throbbing frenzy. I find her hips and buck her rapidly, grinding my pelvis against her where she needs it most.

She screams her orgasm toward the ceiling as her wetness tickles my sensitive parts and her pussy clamps down around me. It's the best and worst thing in the world right now, as her pulsations edge me to a brink I can no longer control.

Her orgasm ebbs, but she doesn't stop riding me, torturing me with every bit of her flesh against mine. I'm still waiting for her fucking permission. But any second now, my cock will be making that decision for us.

"Please, Evie," I beg, my voice catching in my throat. "Can I come?"

She jerks her hips forward, then slams them down hard in a vicious movement that angers my cock further. "Yes," she cries out, repeating the motion over and over but more faster with each pass. I hug her against me, and she bites down on my earlobe just as I spill myself inside her. Sharp, unencumbered, and all the heaven I ever need to know, blood bombards my cock and takes my orgasm to new levels that make all of the torturous waiting worth it. *Goddamn, Evie.*

She places a delicate kiss on the front of my injured shoulder, a battle scar from Eden's Green of my very own. I sigh against her ear and kiss her deeply as I pull her down to the floor, my cock still buried inside her.

Remaining connected to my queen in every possible way.

THE SUN DIPS PAST THE HILLSIDE FINGERS OF THE Peloponnese, turning them to violet silhouettes as the sunset begets the night—"*a little slice of paradise where the Ionian Sea meets the Aegean Sea*," per Evie's words.

We watch from the balcony as I hold her from behind in a warm embrace. "Jenna's plane will be landing soon. We should head out."

She turns to face me, a pensive look on her face. "Are you sure you're okay with this?"

A tendril of hair catches her eye, and I brush it away. "I adore Jenna. And I'm madly in love with you." I sigh and run my thumb over her cheek. "There's a lot to discuss, but I think it's going to be really great."

A smile graces her face as she brings her lips to mine. "Thank you," she whispers as she pulls away, playing with the hair on the nape of my neck.

"I'd do anything for you, Eves," I remind her. "And so would she."

Honestly, I look forward to bringing Jenna into the fold. She's beautiful, full of vigor, and someone I imagine is quite easy to love.

Besides, Evie needs her. And I meant it when I said I would do anything for her.

"Just promise me one thing," I tell her with a hooked finger under her chin. "When the day comes that you're about to take someone's hand in marriage..." I wait for her to cock an impatient eyebrow at me...

There it is.

"It'll be *me* who waits for you at the end of the aisle."

She bites her lip, but it doesn't disguise the smile that emerges. "Is that a proposal?" she teases.

With a softness that mirrors my words, I kiss her.

"Trust me, Wats," I say as I pull away. "When it's a proposal..." My thumb traces over her naked ring finger. "You'll know it."

☙❧

JENNA

Ordinarily, the perpetual hum of a jumbo jet lulls me right to sleep. Today, however, I'm as restless as ever. Excitement has me all in knots as I admire the ocean's expanse from my first-class seat. Evie and James called on me last month, telling me they talked it over at great length and wanted me to join them. It has taken me several weeks to get my affairs in order enough that I can put my life in the States on pause.

My parents are understandably confused; I told them so little about why in the hell I'm flying off to Greece indefinitely. I assured my mother that it would only be for a few months—a statement of which I still doubt the validity. The less she knows, the better. Truth be told, I have no idea what the future holds for the three of us. James and Evie are surviving on work visas, teaching music and science at a local school, which she seems to love. I'd support both of them until the day I die, no questions asked, if they'd allow me.

James is a stubborn man, sure, but my charm rarely fails, and I need them to know that we'll be okay, no matter where the wind might take us.

For a brief moment, my mind flits to Emerson and the passionate kiss we shared on the bow of his boat beneath a starry sky. It was shortly after Evie and James left, and I suppose, looking back, I fell into his arms for the wrong reasons. A surprisingly tender man, Emerson Shaw, despite his calloused hands and gruff exterior. But goddamn, did he know how to kiss. We explored each other's bodies in depth in the cuddy cabin that night. Though we did not have sex, his natural scent remained on my clothes long after, and I couldn't bring myself to wash it away.

It never would've worked out, and I told him as much. I love Evie, and I can't imagine my life without her. I was clear that, if ever she called on me to come to Kardamyli, I would be there in a second. Despite the sadness that made him look away far too often, he insisted he understood. I found myself lost in the void their absence created, especially the uncertainty of whether they would call on me at all. Deep down, I never expected James to share her, and Emerson became exactly the distraction I needed.

The docks where we first met were the last place I ever saw him. Before we parted ways, he leaned in low, close to my ear, and whispered, "Never be afraid to leave things to fate, Dandelion. Stop and make a wish every once in a while." Our mouths found each other for the last time—a deep, wistful kiss sealing the end of our autumn courtship.

The plane shakes in a wisp of turbulence, and I accidentally crinkle the envelope in my hands. I've been holding it nearly the entire flight, dreading its contents, yet it somehow managed to slip my mind as Emerson replaced my apprehensions with something more pleasant. I glean the return address uneasily: *Massachusetts Department of Corrections.*

It's from David.

I've received dozens of letters from David since he turned himself in. Using the stack of documents from Laz's box as leverage, as well as giving his full cooperation to the authorities, he managed to acquire one hell of a plea deal with the feds. Even after confessing to the multiple arsons on Eden's Green and the fatal shooting of Vincent "Click" Forelli.

David's attorneys have been keeping him abreast of any information regarding this network of traffickers, which he's been relaying to me consistently via letters. I've never responded to any of them, but I diligently inform Evie of everything. David's cooperation has aided in a worldwide manhunt, headed by the FBI. Many of the buyers have been identified by their serial numbers as a result.

But not buyer 8108. Not yet.

Until then, James insists they stay away and never speak Evie's birth name aloud.

I'm certain the day will come when we can return to the States in peace. In the end, we have nothing but the future to look forward to, no matter where we are. For now, that's all the peace I need.

I flip the letter over, eyeing the sealed flap. *This* letter, I suspect, is going to be different from the others. It's the first letter I've received from David since I had him served with divorce papers three weeks ago.

Finding it difficult to breathe, I suddenly wonder if the cabin pressure has changed.

You can't put this off forever, Jen.

I gulp down the last sip of my gin and tonic, then slip a shaky finger into the envelope and tear it open.

Swallowing the lump in my throat, I unfold the handwritten letter.

Dear Wife,

I honestly don't know what to say. Months of reaching out to you without a word, and now this? You don't trust me, and I don't blame you. I will always regret the lies I told, the people I've hurt, and the fact that these fucking divorce papers have been filed because of my actions. There isn't a day that goes by that I don't wish I could hold you and tell you how sorry I am. I've been so transparent about everything with you since Evie came home, and I'm doing everything in my power to be the man you deserve.

My attorney still holds firm that I'll be released this summer. I've told the FBI everything I know, and according to the news, they've made dozens of arrests. The search of my father's house sealed the deal when they found coded documents that identified the purchasers based on their ID numbers.

My father's empire is gone. The feds have raided it all. There's nothing left. And I've always known that Laz would never want anything of his left behind that could lead the wrong people back to Evie or me. That's why I burned it all.

So you see? It's all over.

What isn't over is us, Jen. We took vows. For better or worse, remember? And this, babe, is our "worse." I need you. I'll always need you. And I refuse to give up on us.

Please tell my sister that I love her, and I hope she's well. Tell James I'm sorry, and to always take good care of her.

I'll be out of here soon enough, and we're going to figure this out. In the meantime, no, I will not sign these papers. You're going to have to try harder than that to get rid of me, if that's your prerogative.

I love you always, and I will never stop fighting for us.

Sincerely,
Your Husband

PS You've been ignoring me plenty, but you can't hide forever, Jen.
Or should I call you "Dandelion"?

THE END

Acknowledgments

I asked my husband if he wanted me to include him in the acknowledgements section of *Come the First Snowfall*. Here's how the conversation went down:

Me: "Everything's finished! I just need to complete the Acknowledgements section."
Him: "The part where you thank people?"
Me: "Yes."
Him: "Sweet. But this book was all you, babe. Who are you thanking?"
Me: *laughs* "It wasn't all me, though. I'd thank my cover designer, my editors, readers, promoters...*you*."
Him: "Why would you thank *me*? For what?"
Me: "For putting up with me throughout this whole process. All the stress, late nights, emotional meltdowns..."
Him: "Babe, I'm your husband. That's what I'm here for. No thanks necessary."

God I love him.

To my husband, Jeff (yes, I'm still including him because, shit, I'm just as stubborn as he is), who is my rock, my shoulder to cry on, my biggest fan, and the absolute love of my life!

To my cover designer, Cat, who always knocks it out of the freaking park. My covers receive compliments all the time, and I cannot thank you enough.

To my editors, who polished the hell out of both manuscripts and really made them shine. My books would not be the same without you.

To my beta and ARC readers, who took precious time from their daily lives to dive into my stories when they were still in the "working stages."

To my promoters, who were absolutely everything when it came to building a buzz around my books and made the release days a truly magical and memorable experience. You all are absolute rockstars.

To my Washington, DC coworkers, who discovered my pen name behind my back, read my books in secret, scared the piss out of me when they revealed they'd read it, but then showered me with love, support, and adoration for the "smut" I had written. First off, fuck you for being so sneaky. Second, I love you all so much. Thank you for proving me wrong for being hesitant to share my book "babies" with you.

To Andrew Lloyd Webber and Francis Ford Coppola, whose *The Phantom of the Opera* musical and *Bram Stoker's Dracula* film portrayed twisted, macabre love stories in a way that has captivated me since I was a child. It's through these tales that I've discovered my deep, intrinsic love for dark romance. Thank you for such breathtaking sources of inspiration.

To the child version of me: you want to be a published author. Trust me, I know. Stories have been swirling around in your head for as long as you can remember. But your love of forensic science will set you on a path that will delay it for many years, and that's okay, because both paths *are* possible. And I'm here to finally tell you, "We did it, kiddo!"

And last, but certainly not least, to my READERS. You took a chance on an indie author, who works full-time in STEM and has never written and novel in her life, and made her heart soar. This duet is for you!

This process has been one hell of an emotional rollercoaster: overwhelming even on good days, rewarding beyond words, filled with judgement, stress, heartache, and being ignored on the regular…but also brimming with love, encouragement, affection, and admiration, and bestowing upon me a giddiness of which I didn't know I was capable.

And I wouldn't change a damn thing.

Thank you for helping me make my dreams come true.

I fucking love you all!

About the Author

Charlotte Dae is an indie author who loves exploring the darker side of romance. Such taboo topics have a place in literature, and she is clamoring to bring them to light in her own way. When she is not spending her free time writing, she is working full-time as a Forensic Scientist and living her best life with her husband and two puppies.

Feel free to stalk Charlotte at:
www.charlottedae.com
www.instagram.com/charlottedaeauthor
www.tiktok.com/@charlottedaeauthor

www.ingramcontent.com/pod-product-compliance
Lightning Source LLC
Chambersburg PA
CBHW061847310726
48972CB00004B/926